Also by Bridget Wood
Published by Ballantine Books

WOLFKING

THE LOST PRINCE

BRIDGET WOOD

A DEL REY BOOK

BALLANTINE BOOKS • NEW YORK

A Del Rey Book
Published by Ballantine Books

Copyright © 1992, 1993 by Bridget Wood

All rights reserved under International
and Pan-American Copyright Conventions. Published
in the United States by Ballantine Books, a division of Random
House, Inc., New York, and distributed in Canada by
Random House of Canada Limited, Toronto.
Originally published in slightly different form in Great Britain
by Headline Book Publishing PLC in 1992.

This edition published by arrangement with
Headline Book Publishing PLC.

All characters in this publication are fictitious and any resemblance
to real persons, living or dead, is purely coincidental.

Library of Congress Catalog Card Number: 92-97324
ISBN: 0-345-37976-4

Text design by Holly Johnson

Cover design by Judy Herbstman
Cover art by Keith Parkinson

Manufactured in the United States of America

First American Edition: July 1993
10 9 8 7 6 5 4 3 2 1

For G.

AUTHOR'S ACKNOWLEDGMENT

Grateful thanks are due to my agent, Jane Conway-Gordon, for her enthusiastic encouragement and support; also to Caroline Oakley and Sarah Thomson at Headline (UK), and Veronica Chapman and Deborah Hogan at Del Rey, all of whom made valued and valuable contributions.

CHAPTER ONE

THE COURT HAD decided that the only thing to be done was to escape into the future.

"But not too far into the future," said Fergus, whose idea it was. "Not so far that we encounter the Apocalypse."

"No, we must be careful about that."

No one wanted to meet the Apocalypse, who had stalked the world a long way in the future, burned it with his terrible scorchy breath, and left it a smoking ruin. Everyone knew about the Great Devastation that was to smite mankind, thousands of years hence, and nearly destroy humanity. They all knew, because Time Travellers came to Tara now and again, people from worlds not yet born, and these Travellers told the most remarkable stories. There was nothing particularly astonishing about Time Travellers any more; the Court had long since accepted that there were chinks in the fabric of Time; tears, or perhaps flaws, in the warp of Time's structure. People fell through or pushed through or were enticed through them, and it was all very interesting.

Fergus's idea was very interesting as well. Everyone was listening to it carefully, because this was a very important meeting, at which they must decide how they were going to regain Tara for the High Queen. And wasn't it a truly terrible thing for them all to be living out here in exile, instead of inside Tara, the Bright Palace, the beautiful shining seat of the Wolfkings. But Tara was lost to them. It was in the evil hands of the dark sorcerer, Medoc, who had thrown open the Gateways of the fearsome Dark Realm, and ridden out through them, and brought his evil armies down on Ireland, and taken Tara for his own sinister purposes. They had

1

to think of a way to destroy Medoc before he swallowed Ireland up altogether with his evil darkness, and anything that would help them to mount an attack on him and regain Tara for the High Queen had to be given extremely serious consideration.

Fergus was the head of the *Fiana*, the High Queen's mighty army, and therefore a person of considerable power. People listened to him. It was whispered that a great many of the ladies did more than just listen to Fergus as well, but this was not just now the thing to be thinking of. And so everyone looked alert when Fergus strode to the centre of the ruined Stone Palace, where the Court and the Druids had gathered for their Council of War, and a ripple of delight went through the Court, and a feeling of sudden hope. Wouldn't Fergus be sure to find a way out of exile for them, and wouldn't he be able to think of a means to drive out Medoc and the Dark Lords, and restore the light to Tara again and the Wolfqueen to Ireland.

He was carelessly dressed—"He always is," said Dorrainge the Druid, who liked people to be neat. But it did not matter really, and it particularly did not matter to the ladies. Fergus was black-haired and blue-eyed, and always looked at you very directly, so that you might almost imagine he possessed the ancient, almost extinct Mindsong, the Samhailt.

Fergus, standing before the assembled Court, felt the ruffle of interest and anticipation, and smiled rather sadly to himself. He did not possess the Samhailt; he did not think anyone in Ireland did any more, because this was one more ancient enchantment that had somehow been lost. But he was certainly sufficiently intuitive to sense the feelings of others, and he thought that everyone in the Stone Palace would listen to his idea, and that most of them—with the probable exception of Dorrainge—would support him.

"We'll go forward into the Future," he said, looking at them all intently, seeing the mixture of fear and excitement in their faces. "It's the only way. If we can once get to the Future, we can raise the strongest army Ireland has ever seen." He grinned. "And so we'll go into the days when the world had machines and great cities and powerful men and women, and we'll harness all of their power and their knowledge. Don't we know of some of it from the Travellers already?" cried Fergus, and so enthralled were his listeners that no one moved or spoke.

"The world was a great place in the Far Future," said Fergus. "With all of its powers, we could vanquish Medoc and slay the Dark Lords, and drive back the Dark Ireland for ever! We could reclaim Tara for Her Majesty! Well?"

There was a thoughtful silence, and then, "But," said a slightly belligerent voice from the back, "supposing we miscalculate? Supposing that we go into the wrong bit of the Future? Supposing we find ourselves in the days after the Apocalypse burned the world?"

A rather nasty silence fell. Fintan, who was sitting near to the front, and whose family had served the High Kings as far back as the great Cormac of the Wolves, said wasn't this only Lugh of the Longhand pouring gloom and doom on good ideas, and shouldn't he know better, and him a general of the High Queen's *Fiana*. But quite a number of people looked worried.

"The wrong bit of the Future wouldn't be much use," said one of the Druids. "We don't want to be going to the days after the Apocalypse. That's a terrible time."

Fergus said, "But we aren't going to that time," and looked round at them all. "Of course we aren't. Would we want to go into that miserable old world? Wasn't it all wastelands and scorched ruins, and people fighting each other for a bite of bread or a mouthful of water? We'll get it right," said Fergus, "and we'll go to the time just before the day the Apocalypse came riding into the world!" He moved round the circle, fixing his audience with his straight blue stare. "Won't you think of that! The world at its height! The marvels and the inventions and the power! We'd harness it all," said Fergus. "We'd bring it back with us, and we'd mount the greatest attack on Tara ever known. We'd regain the

Palace for Her Majesty and drive out Medoc and the Twelve Dark Lords!" And Fergus, who knew what was due to a High Queen of Ireland quite as well as anyone, turned round very deliberately, and made his bow to the Queen, who was seated at their centre, listening intently to everything.

"But," said Lugh, who was nothing if not dogged, "we need to know that the power will be enough. We know the stories of the Far Future, but we know the might of the Twelve Dark Lords as well," he added, and several people shivered, because wasn't it whispered how the Twelve Lords each represented one of the great wickednesses, and how they could materialise at Medoc's whim. They had names like Decadence, Hatred, Lust, Perversion . . . Nobody wanted to see *those* sort of creatures taking form.

"The attack would be quite strong enough to rout Medoc," said Fergus, and he grinned at them all. "It would be strong enough because we should lie in wait for the Apocalypse."

"Yes?"

Fergus paused, and then, turning his head, looked directly at the slight, dark-haired figure at the head of the table.

"With Your Majesty's permission," he said, "we should chain the Apocalypse, and bring him back with us."

GRAINNE HAD BEEN High Queen for four years, and in exile for three. She had succeeded to the Ancient Throne when her grandmother died, and although it had been very sad, because Grainne's grandmother had been strong and very much loved, everyone had been pleased and interested. They had all looked forward to the new reign, because hadn't they all of them known the Crown Princess since she was born, they said, and wasn't she the mirror image of her beautiful reckless grandmother?

Grainne did not really think she was Dierdriu's image, because Dierdriu had been so dazzling that Kings and Princes had fought for her favours, and waged wars for the privilege of marrying her. She was supposed to have had rather a lot of lovers as well, although nobody had ever actually come out and said this. The ballads written about her and the stories told about her all related how she had had black hair like a silken cloak over her shoulders, and high flaring cheekbones and the slanting golden eyes of all the Wolfline.

Grainne had the black hair as well, and the golden eyes, but she was smaller and rather delicate looking and pale, so that people nearly always looked at her with a special *kindly* look as if they thought she might be fragile and easily hurt.

They had been preparing for her Coronation when Medoc and the Twelve Dark Lords had somehow found a way in from the Dark Ireland, that terrible other-world that existed just out of sight and just beyond hearing and just beyond consciousness. People had afterward blamed the Court sorcerers, because if you could not trust your own sorcerers to keep proper watch on the Gateways between the true Ireland and the dark underworld of Medoc's Ireland, you might as well not bother having sorcerers in the first place. When you remembered what the sorcerers charged, it was little short of disgraceful.

The Court sorcerers had been locked away in the Sorcery Chambers at the time, and they had been trying very hard to summon the *sidh*, who were the most purely magical beings in all Ireland. The *sidh* had not been seen for some years, and it was known that you could not entirely trust them, because their King, the elven Aillen mac Midha, had always had his eye on Tara. But in their way, the *sidh* were loyal to the Wolfline, and it would be a very good thing indeed if the sorcerers could somehow lure them back to Tara, and so no one had dared to interrupt this important proceeding. Nobody actually believed that the *sidh* would answer the summons, but the sorcerers had been working quite hard to call them, because you might as well try to get all the enchanted help you could.

And so what with the sorcerers busy, and the Druids trying to find out what they were up to, and what with the preparations for the Coronation, nobody had been thinking about invasions, and nobody had been thinking at all about Medoc.

And that had been the pity of it, because right at the height of the preparations, Medoc had sent the Twelve Lords to drive them all out; they had swooped down on Tara in a fearsome flurry of ancient dark magic, and evil screeching enchantments, and the Gateway to Medoc's Dark Realm had yawned wide, so that people had glimpsed the terrible crimson lakes and the dark fields and the Black Citadels of the necromancers.

And Medoc had ruled from the Bright Palace ever since; he had quenched the light that had once shone across Ireland's width and breadth, and no one had been able to get within touching distance of Tara ever since. And the Court had lived in exile on Innisfree for three years.

Nobody blamed Grainne for any of it, but Grainne blamed herself. It was impossible to avoid the thought that Dierdriu would not have allowed such a thing to happen. It was one of the things they said of Dierdriu: not only had men gone mad for love of her, they had ridden into battle for her as well.

Grainne would have liked to ride into battle with her hair flowing down her back as Dierdriu had done, perhaps with the icy blue-green *sidh* at her back, but she knew that you had to plan these things. You had to do it with the backing of the armies and the Druids, and the support of the *Fiana*.

The *Fiana*. It was still difficult to sit in a Court Chamber and listen to Fergus and look at him as calmly as if she had never loved him.

Did I love him? Did I really feel for him the pure strong emotion that people write of and sing about and weep over?

Seven years ago she had loved him, certainly. In the mist-shrouded mornings that surrounded Tara, and in the long drowsy afternoons when nothing stirred and no one knew where anyone was. Grainne had been able to steal through the Palace and out into the forest. Seven years . . . An enchanted magical summer it had been. People had begun to talk about the old lost enchantments stirring; they had begun to hear, just very faintly, the *sidh* singing again.

Seven years. And I believe I would sell my soul and go barefoot through Eternity if it could happen again . . .

Grainne took a deep breath, and turned back to the Court.

FINTAN HAD GOT up to speak, and people were listening, because Fintan had sometimes the way of speaking sound good sense.

Fintan thought that Fergus's idea of travelling to the Far Future was fine and altogether great. He was all for new peoples, he said. But there was another idea. Something they might consider—not instead of Fergus's plan, but as well as. He looked round the circle of faces. Had they all of them forgotten Ireland's lost people? said Fintan. Had they forgotten the Cruithin? he demanded, and people sat up and looked alert, because while no one had forgotten the Cruithin, no one had actually remembered them either. They were the original Gael people, the first race ever to inhabit Ireland, and some people said they were the only true Irish race. It was many generations since they had been seen, but everyone knew them to be small dark people, with elfin faces and intelligent eyes. They had always been fiercely loyal to the Wolfkings, and they were full of strong gentle magic. They had disappeared without warning one night towards the end of Dierdriu's reign, and a belief had crept into Ireland's folklore that when the Cruithin had disappeared, Ireland's ancient magic had disappeared as well.

Cermait Honeymouth, who was sitting next to Fintan, said, rather apologetically, that most people believed that the Cruithin had vanished into the dark and terrible Grail Castle, and wouldn't they all remember that no one had ever returned from journeying to the Grail Castle. The Grail Castle, said Cermait Honeymouth, looking unusually solemn, was believed to be bastioned by every dark enchantment ever spun, and you had to be very brave, or extremely foolish, to try to find it.

Fintan said, very firmly, "Even so, I believe we should try to find it, if it will mean finding the Cruithin." He glared at the Court and then said in an extremely loud voice, "And with Her Majesty's permission, I shall journey to the Grail Castle and seek out the Cruithin and form an army!"

He sat down and scowled, and Cermait Honeymouth clapped him on the back and said wasn't it the grandest idea ever, and if Her Majesty would permit, he himself would accompany Fintan, and they'd find the Grail Castle and seek out the Cruithin in no time, and then they'd be back to drive out Medoc.

Fergus, listening, watching, knew Fintan's idea for a good one, even while his mind was recoiling from the thought of the journey that Fintan and Cermait would have to make along the dark and lonely road that sometimes took travellers on to the Grail Castle, and sometimes swallowed them up so that they were never heard of again. Every dark enchantment in Ireland was believed to hide the Grail Castle from the curious. Fergus thought that even he would hesitate at such an undertaking. But Fintan and Cermait were sensible and dogged, and if anyone could brave the castle's ancient magical defences, it was surely those two.

But one thing could truly defeat Medoc, and that was the power and the might of the Far Future.

The Apocalypse.

FINTAN AND CERMAIT were pleased with their plan. They rounded up a bunch of friends and took them off to the Council Chambers at the rear of the Stone Palace to hold their own meeting.

"They're being very noisy about it," said Dorrainge, as Fintan and Cermait stamped out of the Stone Hall, saying things like "Don't forget to bring the lights" and "While we're about it, we'll take the large wine flagon" and "Who knows the spell for calling up the four winds?"

"I hope they don't call up the four winds," said somebody, worried. But Dorrainge said that the only creature who had ever been able to call up the four winds was a sorceress called Spectre, and nobody had heard of her for ages; and everybody relaxed again.

Fintan and Cermait sat their supporters down, and Cermait went round with the wine flagon and then had to send out for another one because it gave out half way round, and everyone drank death to Medoc and lasting destruction to the Twelve Lords. Cermait said they'd be off to find the Grail Castle at first light, to be sure they would.

One of the Druids, whose name was Cathbad and who had unaccountably thrown in his lot with Fintan, said he had heard that the road to the castle was guarded by necromancers.

"And," said Cermait, worried, "Medoc's a necromancer himself. I do think we should remember that."

"*Is* he?" a new voice said from the back of the room.

"Well, he's a sorcerer anyway."

"*Is* he? Are you sure?" said the same voice, and several people turned round rather quickly to see who had spoken, because it was not very nice to hear a sly slimy whisper coming from behind you in the dark.

"It was Custennid the Tusk," Fintan said. "Wasn't it?"

"Certainly not," said a cross voice.

"No, really, wasn't it you, Tusk?"

"If I've got something to say about Medoc," Custennid the Tusk said with dignity, "I shan't whisper it in the dark."

"You know, it is dark," Cermait said.

"Yes, it is. Who's dowsed the lights? Dear me, if I'd known it was going to be this dark, I'd have brought up more torches," Fintan said, and stamped around, until several people's feet had been trodden on and Cathbad had been sat on.

"Light the torches," Cermait said. "Light the torches 'til we see who it is," and as he spoke, every torch flickered wildly, and huge distorted shadows leapt and danced across the stone walls. For a moment, no one spoke or moved, and then a really terrible low bubbling chuckle rang out so that several people moved quickly away from the outer walls.

The outer wall of the Council Chamber was cracked and crumbling, and in places it did not quite meet the ceiling. There was an oblong, about eight feet up, where the stonework had fallen away altogether and where you could see out to the night sky. The low bubbling chuckle filled the room again, followed by a harsh, cawing sound, a dreadful horn-on-bone sound that made your teeth wince. Where the walls stopped being a wall, a huge pair of fishlike, lidless eyes was looking in.

Fintan said in a voice from which most of the breath had been driven, "There's something looking over the wall at us."

"It's one of Medoc's creatures," said Cermait Honeymouth.

"Medoc's creature!" shouted Fintan, snatching up the nearest torch. "After it quickly! It's heard everything we said!"

FERGUS HAD STAYED at the centre of the Stone Palace with the Court. If they were going into the Far Future, they must do so quickly, and they must discuss how they would go about it.

Fergus's plan had by far the most supporters, although the Druids were only there because Grainne was there. Cathbad was not there, because Cathbad had gone off to listen to Fintan and Cermait Honeymouth, but Cathbad was always doing things he should not. The Druids did not really approve of Fergus's idea, and they certainly did not intend to accompany Fergus into the Future, always supposing he could get there.

"I wouldn't mind going," said a mild voice from one of the front rows, and Dorrainge tutted, because this would be Fribble, the Chief Druid, who was getting a bit hard of hearing. It was quite likely that Fribble had not properly heard Fergus's plan anyway.

"Yes, I did," said Fribble. "You're going off into the Far Future, where all the licentiousness and lewdness and greed and self-indulgence reached its height. I'd like to see all that."

"We shan't be—"

"Fergus would have to be sure to bring me back safely."

"Fergus isn't going to be taking—"

"Because we don't want him forgetting and leaving me there," said Fribble. "That would never do. I'm Chief Druid, you know, and it won't do for me to be away from Tara for too long—well, it won't do for me to be away at all, but if the Druids are going to support this scheme, somebody ought to go."

"But—"

"Well, there it is," said Fribble, resettling his robes and beaming. "I feel quite young at the idea. Just a very little trip, mind. I shan't want to stay for more than a week or two. You'd better make sure Fergus knows."

"It's impossible," Dorrainge said crossly.

"I don't see why—" began Fergus, when Grainne said softly, "But how are you going to get into the Future?"

A rather anxious silence fell, and then Fergus, squaring his shoulders, said, "There is only one way."

"Yes?"

"By summoning the Time Chariot of Fael-Inis."

Grainne said, "But that means—" and stopped.

"Yes," Fergus said softly. "There is only one group of people in Ireland who can summon Fael-Inis.

"We must go to the sorcerers."

CHAPTER TWO

CUSTENNID THE TUSK considered that he was being extremely clever. When everyone had gone rushing and scurrying out into the forest to chase down Medoc's spy, Custennid had held back, because if there were any servants of Medoc lurking out there, Custennid was not going to be meeting up with them. But it was necessary to put up some kind of show, and so he waited until everyone else had disappeared, and then walked quite firmly and calmly outside. It would be perfectly possible to just skirt the edges of the forest. He did not need to go into it very deeply at all.

But even on the forest's edges, it was queer how a man's footsteps echoed, even when it was soft bracken he was walking on, and it was queer how the night noises were different to the ones you heard by day. There were rustlings, the scurrying of feet; there was the feeling that the bushes were about to part and show something that crouched there waiting . . . Custennid began to wish that after all he had stayed with the others.

And then he heard it. And as soon as he heard it, he realised that he had been hearing it for quite a long time. *The padding of footsteps* . . .

Custennid stopped and looked about him, trying to penetrate the darkness. Of course it would only be a fox or a weasel or a stoat. It would be more frightened of him than he was of it.

The footsteps were nearer now, and there was something very menacing about them. There was a purposeful air about them, almost as if the creature that was padding through the forest had sensed him, scented him, and was saying, Aha!

Here is something of interest. *Here* is a very tasty morsel indeed!

Custennid wished he had not lit on that word *morsel*. He certainly wished he had not lit on the word *tasty*. It conjured up very nasty visions indeed. And although the Tusks were not people of learning, you could not live in these times without hearing a thing or two. Custennid had heard a thing or two, and he had not liked what he had heard.

Medoc's creatures. Medoc's servants. The Dark Ireland waking. The twilight things, the darkling beings. The Twelve Dark Lords who served Medoc, and who were said to hold sinister revelry every night in Tara. The terrible necromancers of the Dark Citadels . . . The merciless Lad of the Skins who scavenged for human souls, and walked abroad with a dripping sack . . .

There was the rasp of claws on stone now, and there was a terrible low chuckle, and a triumphant harsh cawing sound, and Custennid thought, They are right! All the stories were right! And then he remembered the most terrible story of them all.

As he turned to run, the bushes in front of him parted, and a low bubbling chuckle rang out in the quiet forest.

There was no time to think and there was no time to cry out. All the tales flooded his mind: Medoc's Servants—the Dark Ireland waking—

And then the creature was upon him, and there was a whirling blackness, and the sound and feel of teeth and claws and a great harsh curving beak . . . There was time to remember that this was the creature who ripped out the living hearts of its victims and offered them, dripping and warm, to its Master.

There was a crunching, snapping, *sickening* sound, and Custennid knew it for the breaking of his own bones. The forest swam in a sick dizziness, and the darkness became shot with crimson, because crimson was the colour of pain, and it hurt, it *hurt*, and somebody must do something, because it *hurt* . . . His bones were being crushed and his flesh was being torn away . . . something deep inside him seemed to collapse, and he felt a warm wetness between his legs and knew that bowels and bladder had given way. The creature held him up as if to inspect him before finally tearing out his heart—and there was a stale stench, like bad fish and ancient blood and rotting meat, and it was drawing him into its embrace and there were gristly jointed arms and sinews and clutching talons, and its breath was ancient and dry and evil beyond belief . . . stale eggs and long-dead marrow . . . Custennid felt his stomach lift, and he retched and vomited and screamed for help.

The creature was tearing great gobbets of flesh from bone, and it *hurt* . . . There could not be so much pain in the world . . .

Lumps of his flesh were flying all around now, as the creature tore deeper. Talons slit open his chest, and his ribs burst apart, and if it would only stop, just for a minute, if somebody would help him . . .

And then he felt the great pointed talons reach down into his open chest, and he felt the sudden violent pulsing of his heart as it was exposed, and he felt it ripped from his body and held, dripping and steaming, triumphantly aloft.

CUSTENNID'S SCREAMS HAD almost died away by the time Fintan and Cermait Honeymouth reached the clearing.

"We ran as fast as ever we could," said Fintan afterwards.

They had both run as fast as they could towards the sounds, but the screams were dying away when they reached the clearing, and they both stood for a moment, their minds tumbling, unable to make sense of what they were seeing.

A massacre. A bloodbath. Some poor mutilated creature fallen victim to a predator. Fintan had known a second of relief: *At least it was not human,* and then Cermait said softly, "Yes, it was human," and pointed with a shaking hand.

Hair; eyes; a hand, five-fingered and covered with pale, unmistakably human flesh. The remnants of a cloak.

They moved nearer, feeling the miasma of evil that lingered in the clearing. Fintan, a little ahead, looked down at the thing that lay on the ground and felt his stomach heave.

Ripped open. Clawed and lacerated and torn. Liver and lungs and kidneys, all spilling out, wet and faintly glistening in the silver moonlight. Here and there, the whiteness of bone gleamed where once there had been arms and thighs. A man.

Custennid the Tusk was not quite dead. Incredibly, there was still a flicker of life, his brain was still receiving images, his lips could still move. From where he stood, Fintan could see the bloodless lips trying to speak.

"Help me . . ."

"Yes. Lie still now. There's help on the way," said Fintan, and he cast a hunted look at Cermait, for what help could there be? No one else had come in answer to Custennid's screams; there was no one but their two selves to get Custennid back to the Stone Palace.

Cermait bent down and took Custennid's hand. "Can you tell us what happened, Tusk? What—hurt you?"

There was a short, not quite silent pause, and both Fintan and Cermait recognised the bubble of the death rattle. Blood and saliva trickled from Custennid's lips.

Custennid said in a wet, clogged voice, "Footsteps—in the dark—"

"Something followed you? Tusk, try to tell us."

Custennid the Tusk, blind now, deaf, and almost beyond the agony of his mutilated body, said, "The Conablaiche. The Conablaiche walking in Ireland again."

There was a final choking rattle, and Fintan and Cermait stood up and looked at one another.

THE CONABLAICHE WALKING again . . .

"We ought to have known," said Fergus, rather sickened. "We ought to have realised that Medoc would call up the great evil creatures out of the Dark Ireland."

"Yes, but *that* one—"

Cathbad the Druid, who liked to know everything that was happening, asked to be told about the Conablaiche.

"Well," said Fribble, who was so much concerned at what had happened that he was quite wide awake, "well, that's rather difficult. Dear me, this is all very worrying. Fergus, I'll take a smidgeon of that mulled wine, if you please."

Fergus, who was seated at the table, draining a large chalice of warm spiced wine which some of the younger ones had brewed, and who was looking rather white, dipped a fresh goblet into the silver bowl and passed it to Fribble.

"Isn't it a very old Gael word, Fribble? *Conablaiche?*"

"It means 'mutilate,' " said Cermait, who was white-faced.

" 'Lacerate,' " said Fintan, who was green.

Fribble said, "The Conablaiche is a—rather a terrible creature. Perhaps the most terrible of all the beings that dwell in the Dark Ireland. He is merciless and hungry for blood. He is a creation of the dark necromancers, and he was called into being by their powers many centuries ago—so long ago, that it was before people began to record Time."

"But what is he?" someone asked.

"He is a servant," said Fribble. "He is believed to possess a little of the necromantic powers, and he can appear in several guises. For generations he sleeps in the darkness of the Mountain Halls, but once a sorcerer sufficiently powerful summons him, then he wakes, and then he walks. He has been glimpsed in Ireland several times over the centuries, and in some places," said Fribble, "he is called the Conail, which, as you all know, means 'Plague.' "

A shudder round the Stone Palace. Everyone knew of the terrible scourges that had stalked Ireland.

"The Conablaiche will serve many masters," said Fribble, "but it is whispered that his greatest allegiance is to the monstrous god-idol Crom Croich."

There was a rather horrified silence. Most of the Court, and certainly all of the Druids, knew about the terrible hungry god-idol Crom Croich, the being of pure gold who must suffer Human birth into the world of Men before it might reign, and who had appeared in Ireland's history at various times.

Dorrainge said slowly, "But the worship of Crom Croich is utterly and absolutely forbidden." He looked across at Grainne. "Wasn't it Your Majesty's great-grandfather, Cormac of the Wolves, who stamped it out?"

"Yes. Yes, it was towards the end of his reign when Crom Croich was called into being, and the cult was revived." Grainne looked at Fergus. "They say that the Conablaiche and the Lad of the Skins walked the land then, also."

"The Conablaiche and the Lad are nearly always seen if Crom Croich is awakening," Fergus said. And then, because he knew Ireland's history as well as anyone in the Stone Palace, he said, "They say that when the Conablaiche is awakened, it prowls the countryside by night, seeking the first-born boys of every family, so that it can tear out their living hearts and offer them to the god. A barbaric and pitiless cult," Fergus said.

"And Medoc is reviving it," said Grainne. "Medoc has called the Conablaiche out of its sleep." She looked at Fergus. "There can only be one reason for Medoc to call up the Conablaiche."

"Yes," said Fergus, his eyes never leaving her. "He has heard the legend of the Lost Prince."

A terrible silence fell on the assembled Court.

THE LOST PRINCE ... Ireland's once and future King, who would appear in Ireland and drive out her enemies and defeat the terrible Dark Ireland once and for all. The legendary Wolfprince who would lead his people to prosperity and peace and to a new Golden Age. Every person present knew the legend; every person, to greater or lesser degree, believed it.

And then Fergus said, "If Medoc has in truth heard the legend, he will want to destroy the Prince. He would *have* to destroy him. Medoc will never feel completely safe until he can be sure that the Prince does not pose a threat to him."

"But," said Fintan, "don't they tell of how the Prince was shut away for ever inside the Prison of Hostages? Wasn't that one of the reasons for the Crusade Wars of Cormac's day? To find the Prince and bring him out?"

"I never heard that," said Cermait Honeymouth.

"Well, I wouldn't be sure about it."

"But," said Dorrainge, "if Medoc is to loose the Conablaiche on Ireland again, then it means that—" He stopped, appalled.

"Yes," said Fergus. "It means that the Conablaiche will again prowl the countryside by night, and that every male child will be slaughtered and its heart torn out and its soul flung into the eternal light of the Prison of Hostages."

"And," said Grainne softly, "once inside the Prison of Hostages, there can be no escape."

"To kill the children would be the only way that Medoc could be sure he had destroyed the Prince," said Fergus. "And we dare not let it happen." He looked at Grainne, and said very softly and very gently, "We will not let it happen, ma'am." He turned back to the Court. "There is no time to lose," he said. "Unless we can destroy Medoc and send the Conablaiche and the Lad of the Skins back into the darkness, before many moons have passed, Ireland will be in the grip of a new reign of terror. No male child in the land will be safe."

THEY BURIED CUSTENNID the Tusk at noon the next day. Custennid's family were all there; his grandfather, who was called Rudraige the Tusk, and who was an enormous old gentleman with red hair and a fiery eye, told Fergus it was a terrible thing. "And although I'm sorry to see him go," said Rudraige, "I'm even sorrier at the manner of his going. The Conablaiche walking again . . . Dear me, something will have to be done."

The youngest member of the Tusks, who was called Tybion, was round-eyed at the ceremonies and awed into silence by the proximity of such legendary figures as the great Fergus of the *Fiana* and the High Queen. Hadn't he only glimpsed these glittering beings from afar until now, demanded Tybion of his grandfather, to which Rudraige tartly replied that *when* Tybion had a few more years under his belt, and *when* he had a battle or two to his credit, then he might think himself fit to address such people. Until then, said Rudraige, Tybion had better keep quiet and mind his manners. A remark which was quite unnecessary, because Tybion was extremely well mannered and not a little chivalrous.

FERGUS HAD ATTENDED the burial of Custennid the Tusk, along with the rest of the Court, but his thoughts had been chaotic. If Medoc was in truth preparing for the killing of all the male children of Ireland by the Conablaiche, then they must stop him. And although Fergus did not care very much for the use of spies, it occurred to him that this might be an occasion where a spy, sent into the enemy's camp, might be able to find out a great deal about Medoc's plans.

Medoc's creatures were all over Innisfree. The entire Court knew it. They were for ever prowling outside the walls of the Stone Palace and slinking into the wine shop, trying to overhear people's conversations. There was a furtive slithery look to them. Something about the eyes and the curving of the hands. Surely all that was needed was for a carefully chosen person to go into the wine shop and fall into casual discussion. Spying always worked two ways in any case.

Fergus knew that he could not do it by himself. As head of the Queen's *Fiana* he was known. He would be recognised, and the entire ploy would fail. But he would not be recognised if he went heavily cloaked, perhaps with a companion.

A companion. Yes, that was a good idea. It was an idea that might work very well. Who should the companion be? Fergus let his mind run through the people of the Court, thinking that what was wanted here was a bit of a rebel. Somebody whose loyalty would be strong and safe, but somebody who was just a little at odds with the conventions. Somebody who would not mind employing slightly unconventional tactics. Fintan and Cermait Honeymouth would have done it, but Fintan and Cermait were both, in their own ways, fairly well known.

And then Fergus thought, Of course! Tybion. Tybion the Tusk, the youngest member of the clan, of the fiercely loyal, unfailingly dependable Tusks. And Tybion already, at sixteen or seventeen, wanting to be off with the *Fiana*, quarrelling with his family who thought him too young.

Fergus would have a discreet talk with Tybion.

TYBION THE TUSK walked with Fergus into the little wine shop at the centre of Innisfree and stood for a moment looking about him. It was very crowded and rather smoky, and there was a thick warm scent of wine and newly baked bread on the air. Here and there, groups of people sat at tables, and the serving girls, who wore the scantiest gowns Tybion had ever seen, moved cheerfully in and out of the tables, fetching wine, evading the hands that reached out to them. It was not quite what Tybion was used to, but he summoned up his confidence, and squared his shoulders, and was glad he had put on his best green jerkin and the cambric shirt, and that he had brushed his hair until it shone, although he had not been able to straighten out the cowlick, because he never could. But it was as well to look your best if you were going on an important mission, and Fergus—actually the great Head of the *Fiana* himself—had impressed on Tybion that this was a very important mission indeed. Spying was a rather nasty tool, Fergus had said; it was not something they normally did. But circumstances altered cases.

Tybion had understood; he had listened carefully, and he knew what they had to do. Go into the wine shop, quite casually and ordinarily, and then fall into conversation with Medoc's people. Ply them with wine. And then somehow find out as much as they could about Medoc's plans.

"Wine's a great tongue loosener," Fergus had said, grinning.

But now, threading his way carefully to a table in the wine shop in Fergus's wake, Tybion knew that the brief lightheartedness had fallen from Fergus, and that Fergus was feeling an immense weight, the burden of the Queen's exile and the loss of Tara. For a brief moment, Tybion felt it as well, a terrible, dragging despair, and a deep wrenching pain.

For Tara, the Shining Citadel, is in the hands of the Dark Lords, and Medoc has quenched its light, perhaps for ever . . .

Tybion had known—they had all known—that Fergus loved Ireland and that he would give his life for Ireland if he had to, but it was disconcerting to suddenly feel it like this. It is as if Fergus is no longer whole, thought Tybion.

He would have liked to have told Fergus that he shared the pain and the sense of loss, but it might be presumptuous. And they must be casual and very off-hand with the people here, even though what was ahead might affect the whole history of Ireland. I hope I can do this, thought Tybion. I do hope I can. But the idea of affecting Ireland's history was as stirring as it was terrifying, and Tybion managed to look round the crowded smoky wine shop quite normally.

Fergus had called for a flagon of wine and exchanged grins with one of the serving girls, and now he indicated a small table near the window and led Tybion across to it. Tybion, who had not actually drunk wine very often, sat down and sipped cautiously, looking about him.

And Medoc's creatures were here. Tybion saw and sensed and acknowledged them, and felt his stomach lurch. It brought Medoc abruptly closer to see his creatures drinking wine, laughing, and playing dice. Ireland is becoming over-run with these terrible evil beings, thought Tybion.

Medoc's creatures occupied three of the tables. At the distant window table at least half a dozen of them were engrossed in some kind of game with dice, and three more were leaning on the high table where the great wine casks were stored, laughing with one of the serving girls. Tybion sat quietly watching and listening, absorbing the sights and the scents and the sounds of this place and, little by little, he became aware of narrow sly eyes, and of greedy talonlike hands that were not quite claws, but that were certainly not Human hands, curling and uncurling.

Medoc's creatures were watching them. Medoc's jackals were listening to them. And with that thought came the sudden memory, half-buried, of Ireland's dark history; of the race of rodent creatures created by an evil sorcerer many centuries earlier by mating rats and jackals and weasels with humans, and producing creatures neither quite human nor quite rodent, but a nightmarish blend of the two.

These are descendants of those people, thought Tybion with horror. Descendants of the rodent armies of the Dark Ireland. And he remembered, in the same moment, that other sorcery; the gentle strong Enchantment of the Beastline, spun at the beginning of Ireland's history, that had allowed the Royal Houses of Ireland to lie with the Wolves of Tara, and that had resulted in the beautiful wild Wolfkings and Queens. He remembered that the High Queen herself was a direct descendant of the first Wolfkings, and he saw these slit-eyed mean-mouthed creatures as a terrible travesty of the Royal House.

Fergus had allowed his eyes to rove in leisurely fashion around the room and then come to rest on the single creature at the adjoining table. Like Tybion he saw at once the mixed ancestry, the faint traces of rodent blood, and like Tybion, he knew of the dark evil sorcery that had created that line. There is a slithery deceitful look, thought Fergus, who disliked rats intensely, a sly vicious look. If I obeyed my instincts I should fall on this filth and tear it limb from limb, and purge Ireland of Medoc's tainted armies for ever.

But he smiled offhandedly at the lone wine-drinker, and lifted his glass of wine in vague amity, and saw Tybion do the same, and was pleased with Tybion, who was behaving exactly as he ought; and presently, the creature nodded in return.

"The wine shop is crowded tonight," said Fergus, to Tybion, and Tybion heard that he was slurring his words slightly. "But of course," said Fergus, "people are probably marking the newest victim of the Master."

There was a brief silence, and Tybion, hardly daring to look, saw the narrow eyes of the next table's lone occupant take on a wary gleam. He does not trust us, thought Tybion, and at once felt Fergus's response: *No, not yet . . .*

"Can't you always tell," said Fergus, aloud, "when the Master has notched up another victory against the enemy." He leaned back in his chair, apparently wholly at ease, the fingers of one hand curled negligently around the stem of his wine glass, and fixed the rat creature with a rather vapid smile. Tybion saw the rat creature narrow its eyes again, as if assessing Fergus.

"Another heart for Crom Croich," Fergus said in a cheerful, let's-celebrate voice.

Tybion said carefully, "I suppose we can be sure of that, can we?"

"The Conablaiche would not return empty-handed," Fergus said, and lifted his hand to the serving girl for more wine.

"And a glass for my friend there," he said. "No man should celebrate alone." He looked lazily across to the rat creature. "Join us, sir," he said. And then, without waiting, "Bring him a flask of your best wine, my dear," he said.

Medoc's servant regarded Fergus for a moment, and although his eyes did not quite show red, Tybion thought they nearly did. But he said, "Celebrate?"

Fergus leaned forward, with the overeager mien of the

wine-imbiber. "The Conablaiche," he said, stumbling a little over the word now. "Is it not walking?" He leaned back in his chair again and raised his glass. "To Crom Croich," he said loudly. "To the return of the great god-idol of Ireland."

Tybion held his breath and waited, and after a moment, the rat creature said, "You are generous to a stranger. I shall be glad to take wine with you."

Fergus waited until the wine was brought and then said, "We drink to the Conablaiche, my friend!" He tilted his chair back and raised his glass yet again.

"Indeed?"

Fergus crashed the chair down to the floor and sprawled forward on the table. "Let us be frank. People who are in the service of the Master are not truly strangers. Hey?" He turned to Tybion as if for confirmation, and Tybion said, "My father believed it was a wise army that knew its own people," and was glad to hear that his voice was quite steady.

"There are many loyalties on Innisfree and many armies," said the rat creature, noncommittally, but he took the wine.

"To Medoc," said Fergus, apparently not hearing this. And then, lifting his eyes in an apparent attempt to focus, "Forgive me—Have I misread? I see that I have." He looked at Tybion, as if begging for help, and Tybion said severely, "You have allowed the wine to uncurb your tongue, sir."

"And I have said too much," said Fergus, shaking his head. "Sir, please to pardon me, and my companion and I will bid you farewell." He made as if to get up and stumbled so that Tybion put out a hand. "My tongue betrays me," said Fergus. "It is the fault of the wine, I fear."

"Your tongue is certainly loose," said Medoc's servant, frowning. "And in times of war, it is as well to be careful."

Fergus sat down again and smiled ingenuously. "I am the most careful of all the Master's servants," he said.

"The Master?"

"Medoc," said Fergus, in surprise, as if this ought to have been obvious. He tipped wine into all the glasses with a generous hand, and rested both elbows on the table. Enunciating with extreme care, he said, "I am Medoc's loyallest servant. I know all about Medoc and his plans."

"Indeed?"

"Medoc," said Fergus, in a patronising I-know-more-than-you tone, "has woken the Conablaiche. Did you know that?"

The rat creature said, "Medoc would do well to beware of the Conablaiche," and then glanced over his shoulder as if fearful of being heard.

"Powerful," said Fergus, shaking his head. "A powerful being, the Conablaiche."

"If we all said what we knew about the Conablaiche, Medoc would have terror in his ranks," said the rat creature.

"I have often thought that," said Fergus, and Tybion, feeling that it was time he made a contribution, said, almost at random, "I heard that the Conablaiche had escaped again."

At once a look of pure terror came into the rat creature's eyes. He leaned forward, and Fergus and Tybion both saw the long upper lip and the sloping chin. And I believe, thought Tybion in horrified fascination, that his ears are pointed . . .

"I beg you," he said, "I beg you not to say that aloud."

"But it is true?" said Tybion.

"Well, of course it is true," said the rat creature crossly. "Everyone who is the least bit close to Medoc knows what happened." He eyed them both, rather pityingly, as if he might be thinking, Well, you two are not so very high in Medoc's service after all!

"We all knew how the Conablaiche broke away," said Tybion.

"Oh, everyone knows it now," said the rat creature impatiently. "And for all that Medoc has tried to keep it a secret, most people believe it rode in the Time Chariot of Fael-Inis." He glanced at Fergus, and then leaned forward. "But how many people know what happened then?" he said, and nodded, half to himself.

"People tell so many stories," said Tybion, half apologetically, and at his side, Fergus slumped back in his chair, as if overtaken by the wine.

"Oh, everyone has a different one," agreed the rat creature. "But I was there when it happened, you know."

"Were you really?"

"I was there when it came swaggering back to Medoc," he said. "When it was summoned to Tara, and when it stood before Medoc's Throne in the Sun Chamber and told of how it had tricked Fael-Inis."

"Yes?"

"It rode in Fael-Inis's Chariot," said the rat creature, and Tybion felt the beginnings of a new horror prickle his skin. He waited, but Fergus said, half to himself, "Medoc's Throne in the Sun Chamber," and the rat creature looked sharply at him, and said, "The ancient Throne of the accursed Wolf-kings, friend. *Medoc's* Throne."

"I had forgotten for the moment," said Fergus, quite humbly, but Tybion had heard the flare of anger.

"Perhaps you have not been inside Tara," said the rat creature condescendingly.

"Perhaps not. But you were saying . . ." Fergus tipped the wine flagon up again. "You saw the Conablaiche and Medoc."

"It went into the Far Future," said the rat creature, his eyes suddenly far away. Tybion stealthily tipped in the rest of the wine.

"It went into the Future," said the rat creature. "Although whether it was truly in the Chariot, we do not know."

"And Fael-Inis has never yet been tricked," said Fergus softly. "Go on."

"It walked in the world of the Future," the rat creature said, and reached for the wine again. Fergus and Tybion received the impression that he had forgotten their presence.

"It walked amongst the creatures of the worlds yet to be born," he said, and stopped, and raised his eyes to them, red-glinting and cruel. Tybion felt a bolt of sudden fear from Fergus, but he stayed where he was.

The rat creature lifted the wine again, and the dark red glow cast eerie shadows across his face.

"It was not as the stealer of living hearts it travelled to the Future," he said softly, "but as something different."

"Yes?"

"When it went into the Future, the Conablaiche went in its aspect of Plague," said Medoc's servant, and he smiled at them. "It set in motion the ancient and terrible prophecy.

"It unleashed the First of the Four Horsemen of the Apocalypse on the world."

"WHAT DID HE mean? Fergus, what did he mean?" Tybion stood in the thin moonlight outside the wine shop and faced Fergus, and barely noticed that he had used the *Fiana* Captain's name so abruptly and so fiercely.

Fergus was staring ahead of him, and Tybion thought that Fergus was not really seeing him. And then Fergus said, very softly, "We know of the coming of the Apocalypse. We know a great deal about it, for the stories have come back to us with the Time Travellers. We believe that the people of the Future knew of the Apocalypse's advent long before it came riding into the world, for it is in the literature and the folklore and the predictions of every century."

He stopped, and Tybion said in a voice of extreme horror, "That—Medoc's creature said something about a prophecy."

"Yes. And although," said Fergus, smiling rather bitterly, "the prophecies were ancient when the Apocalypse walked, for us they are still to be written.

"But our descendants knew the prophecies well," said Fergus. "They knew of the harbingers that would precede the Apocalypse. They knew of the auguries and the warnings. They knew of the entities that would come into the world to prepare the way for the Apocalypse." He stopped again, and Tybion, horrified, said in a whisper, "The Four Horsemen. *That* is what that creature meant."

"Yes," said Fergus. "The Four Horsemen of the Apocalypse, sometimes called the Four Heralds." And without in the least altering his voice, he quoted the words that had been ancient when the Apocalypse had entered the world, but which had not yet been written:

"*'And Four Heralds shall come into the world to announce the Beast Apocalypse . . . They shall stalk the earth and lay it waste in their several ways, and after their coming the skies shall darken and the seas shall boil and the world shall burn for fifty days and fifty nights . . . then shall the Apocalypse ride into the world . . .'*"

"Four Heralds," Fergus said. "And we know the names of those Four Heralds, for their legend also has come back to us with the Time Travellers." He looked at Tybion, and Tybion said,

"*'There shall be Four Heralds who shall come into the world, and each shall have a name, and these names shall be War, Plague, Famine, and Death . . .'*" He stopped, and Fergus picked up the words.

"*'And the first of these Heralds shall be Plague . . .'*"

"Plague," said Fergus, his eyes dark in the moonlight. "By allowing Medoc to reign and to awake the Conablaiche, we have been responsible for allowing the creature to spill its filth into the Future." He stared at Tybion, his eyes brilliant now. "When the Conablaiche went into the Future, it took with it the seeds of destruction and death. It set in motion the prophecy of the ages."

War, Plague, Famine, and Death . . . And the first of these shall be Plague . . .

"We have sent the first Herald into the Future, Tybion!" Fergus said, and now the agony blazed from his eyes. "It was not our descendants who burned the world and destroyed civilization.

"It was *us!*"

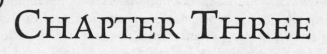

CHAPTER THREE

TRAVELLING TO THE mainland, after the quiet of Innisfree, awoke something in Fergus that he had almost forgotten he possessed. Here was life and vigour and interest. Yes, and hope. As he walked through the teeming streets, confidence poured into him, and his spirits lifted. I am coming alive again. I am regaining strength. I shall succeed.

But I shall hate the means by which I shall succeed . . .

The money lenders. The strange, rather secret people who had come to Ireland from the East, and who lived and worked and studied in Ireland, but who were shunned and rather feared. They possessed immense wealth, and they would bargain with the goldsmiths and the silversmiths for those who sought their help. They were said to be clever and subtle and sometimes cruel, and they were distrusted. But only with the money lenders' help could the exiled Court pay the sorcerers to take them to the Future and turn back the Conablaiche's malevolence.

There is no other way, thought Fergus.

The Street of Money Lenders was narrow and long. The houses were very old. Fergus thought they must have been built during the Golden Age of Cormac's reign, and he thought that something of that Age's prosperity lingered in the tall, rather beautiful buildings.

The houses were high and overhanging, so that you felt as if they might topple over onto you. Signs, elegantly lettered, hung outside some of the buildings, and small, dusky-skinned boys ran everywhere, taking messages, collecting gold, carrying bonds. There were warehouses and gold and silversmiths; shops that sold carved jewellery and amulets and trinkets. Fergus thought the work had an Eastern look, and remembered that the money lenders were thought to be nearly all Tyrian by origin; and he was intrigued, for little was known of the Tyrians who had come to Ireland from the East, bringing with them their secrets and their odd, barbaric religions.

He moved on, seeking one of the smaller houses—thinking he might do better with a less impersonal place, marking out one narrow, several-storied building—"More or less at random," he said afterwards.

There was a sign outside proclaiming the owner's trade, and there were archways over the doors. Fergus pushed open the door and, confronted by twisting stairs, went cautiously up.

THE MAN SEATED at the wide table in the room overlooking the street was very much younger than Fergus had expected. He was dark and thin-faced and sardonic looking. But his eyes were intelligent and his mouth was fastidious and sensitive. He was working at some papers, and he was surrounded by sheaves of documents and by money scales, and what looked like chunks of raw gold, and his room was the untidiest Fergus had ever seen.

But he thought there was a tumbled charm about it; he liked the latticed windows that looked out over the street and caught the sunlight, and he liked the leaping fire in the hearth and the rows of books that studded the walls. All of this he took in, and then he turned to the young man at the table and at once thought, But this is someone I can trust.

The man at the table said, "Yes, I am a Tyrian and my rooms are very untidy, but it does not affect our dealings." He regarded his guest. "Please be seated, Fergus, the chairs are cleaner than they appear."

"You knew my name?" Fergus said.

"The ancient art of the Samhailt is not reserved solely for the Irish," the young man said. "I wish you would sit down. I cannot conduct business with you if you persist in towering over me."

Fergus sat facing the table and looked at the young man. "Do you also know why I am here?"

There was a shrug, the spreading of hands in a slightly foreign gesture. "You are from the exiled Court. And wars fought to regain kingdoms are expensive." He stood up. "Will you drink wine with me? My colleagues will tell you that I cannot conduct business unless I am three parts drunk."

Slightly against his will, Fergus said, "Can you?"

"You shall judge for yourself." The Tyrian brought two brimming chalices of wine to the table, and Fergus sipped it, warily at first, and then with enjoyment.

"Yes, it is very good wine," the young man said. "I buy it by the barrelful from sailors. How much money do you want?"

"You are very direct, sir," said Fergus.

"My name is Taliesin. I am Tyrian by descent and a money lender by trade." He leaned back in his chair, sipping his wine, and regarded Fergus. "I am shrewd and intelligent, and it is my business to make money from you. If you leave money with me, I will invest it and you will become richer. If you take money from me, I will make you pay and I will become richer. You have not yet told me how much you want."

"Twenty thousand royals," Fergus said, and Taliesin's brows went up.

But he only said, "That is a very great sum."

"Beyond your means?"

"No sum is beyond my means. I can find a King's ransom if I have to. Or," Taliesin said thoughtfully, "a Queen's. And they tell me that the sorcerers of Tara are very expensive these days." He grinned suddenly. "My people are outcasts and pariahs and we are reviled and looked on as thieves and robbers." The sudden attractive smile lit his face again. "We care for no man and no man cares for us. You should not trust me, Fergus, for I may betray you."

"I don't think so," said Fergus.

"I don't think so either," Taliesin said. "What security do you offer for this sum? What is the bond, Fergus?"

Fergus said slowly, "All of the wealth of Tara lies deep in its vaults, and once we regain Tara, we shall be able to pay you many times over."

"Once with interest will suffice. You still have not told me of the bond."

"I pledge the *Fiana*," said Fergus, watching the other one.

"I see. And if the bond has to be called in? If you fail to regain all the wealth of Tara's coffers?"

"Then as Head of the *Fiana*, my life must be forfeit," said Fergus, and Taliesin's brows went up again.

"Unusual."

"Unacceptable?"

"No. If I am not paid, then I may take your life to do with what I wish, yes? Yes, I thought that was what you meant. I daresay there have been odder arrangements. Shall we write the bond in your blood, or will ordinary juice of husks suffice? I suppose that since swine root among husks, that will be appropriate."

"Then you can lend me the money?" said Fergus, trying to keep the eagerness out of his voice.

Taliesin said, "I can do it, certainly. But even so, I shall have to go to the Elders of the Council."

"Because it is so large a sum?"

"Because of the bond," said Taliesin. "More wine?"

GRAINNE AND TYBION the Tusk with Fintan and Cermait Honeymouth had set out in the grey light of dawn in search of the Grail Castle. The court had not been very happy for the Queen to be off like this looking for the Cruithin, what with Fergus off to the money lenders and Lugh Longhand to sneak the army onto the mainland to spy on Medoc and Tara. Grainne had listened with her usual gentle courtesy to their various objections. Then she had quietly bade them pack and be ready to leave at dawn, and although she had spoken softly, her eyes had flashed and no one had quite dared say her nay.

And now after a long day in the saddle, they were coming through the shadows to the road that was believed to lead to the Grail Castle. They slowed, and the horses tossed their heads as they moved to the grassy verge. Nobody quite liked to say it, but each was secretly rather afraid of actually setting foot on the road.

Fintan said wasn't it the longest darkest road you had ever seen, and Tybion the Tusk asked what a grail was exactly.

"Well," said Fintan, "it's—well it's a—dear me, it's not easy to explain. See now—"

"It's an object of quest," Grainne said. "Something precious and priceless and lost." And Fintan said hadn't that been the very description he'd been searching his mind for.

"Thank you," said Tybion. "I see."

Cermait said you didn't like the look of the road one bit. "Shadowy," he said. "And would you look how it snakes away from you," and Fintan said it ought to be renamed, because to call it the Castle Road was not warning people properly how dark and nasty-looking it really was.

In fact as they set off again, the road was easily as frightening as they had feared, although none of them could quite have said why.

Grainne was very apprehensive, but she was exhilarated as well. I am fighting for Tara, she was thinking; I am riding out to try to regain what is truly mine. I am out here in the wilds of my land and I am approaching an ancient sinister castle, along a road which most people believe to be haunted by evil dark magic. I am dressed in plain breeches and a leather jerkin, and I have cut off my hair, and nobody knows who I am, and *anything* could happen to me tonight, thought Grainne. And with the thought, something that she had until now been only dimly aware of, stirred, and then woke in her.

A surge of golden strength, a swift current of glinting courage . . .

The wolfblood, the ancient enchantment created long ago, by the first sorcerers of all, so that her ancestors could lie with the wolves, and so that the beautiful, wild Wolfline could rule Ireland.

The power and the light and the strength of the Wolves of Tara . . .

She had the impression that the strength was not really hers, but that it was a loan, a gift from the forebears she had never known, who had lain with the Wolves, and that she had held it in trust. *It is a loan and a pledge, and it is something I must preserve so that I may hand it on to my heirs . . .*

Heirs. The little slant-eyed boy with dark hair and smooth skin, full of light and fire and life . . . He did not exist except in her imagination and in her dreams. It was certainly pointless to still feel the ache that could sometimes cut her from breast to womb. Even so— Oh, Fergus, thought Grainne. I wonder where you are now. I wonder if you will succeed. I wonder if you will return. But riding quietly along like this, it was possible to touch, in her mind, Fergus's parting words, and derive comfort from them.

"Be sure I shall return," he had said. *"Be sure that Ireland will not be lost."* And then with the sweet secret smile she had once traced on his lips with her fingertips in the magical dawn outside Tara, *"Nothing that has once been precious can ever be lost, my love,"* he had said.

It would never be wholly lost to them, thought Grainne, and then, because to think of Fergus was profitless now, she turned her mind back to their quest, and to her companions.

Tybion the Tusk was happier than he had ever been in his life. He had never been so close to the High Queen before, although he had known all the stories about her; how she was lovely and gentle, and how she was like her famous grandmother, the dazzlingly beautiful Dierdriu. But he had not known that she would have eyes the colour of molten gold that you felt might see into your soul, or a skin like buttermilk, or that she would be so delicate and fragile-looking that you would want to go bounding all over Ireland and tear apart every creature who had ever hurt her. She had cut off her rippling black hair, and the court had all been very shocked—Cathbad the Druid was reported to have wept—but Tybion thought she was the most beautiful creature he had ever seen.

When they stopped for a bite of supper, he gathered apples and rich wild blackberries and simmered them carefully over the fire with a drop of Fintan's best mead, which was a recipe that had been in his family for generations.

"It is very good," said Grainne, eating it with enjoyment, and Tybion thought he would gladly have died for her.

He was entranced to be allowed to sit beside her as they ate their supper in the gathering twilight. Fintan had caught several fish earlier in one of the streams, and they grilled these over the fire and found them wholly delicious. Tybion thought that out here, Grainne was closer to the forest creatures and to the wolves whose blood she possessed. He looked at her again and saw, for the first time, the unmistakable traces of wolfishness. This ought to have been faintly sinister but was somehow not. Grainne was beautiful and gentle, and Tybion would have died for her. As they set off again, the long dark road was very quiet.

"It's too quiet," said Fintan.

Even Cermait said he wished they knew what was ahead.

"Something nasty," said Fintan, with gloomy relish.

"Something powerful," said Cermait. "Can't you feel it?"

They could all feel it. A heavy dark menace, as if some immense force was summoning all of its strength. Grainne, who had grown up with the sinister legend of the Grail Castle, and who knew that no creature who had ever set out to find it had ever returned, felt a cold dread. It was along this road that the prowling hungry Conablaiche was sometimes seen, and it was along this road that the Lad of the Skins, who scoured the world for Human souls, walked abroad with a dripping sack . . .

Grainne rode quietly along, between Fintan and Cermait, and thought, But why has no one ever been able to reach the Grail Castle? Why is it surrounded with dark enchantments that unfailingly devour those who try to penetrate it?

What is inside the Grail Castle that is so terrible that no one has ever been allowed to look upon it?

And then they rounded the last curve in the road, and there it was.

The Grail Castle.

IT WAS LIKE nothing any of them had ever seen, and it was like every nightmare and every dark castle they had ever visualised.

"Black," said Fintan, staring.

"Massive," said Cermait.

Tybion, who was a little to the rear, shivered and tried to look away, and Grainne, who was staring at the great grim outline, felt a dreadful heavy coldness.

For inside there is something so nightmarish and so unbearable that it is beyond ordinary comprehension . . .

The castle was set squarely on a massive jutting rock and it was surrounded by a deep, wide ravine. A rock bridge stretched across to the immense portcullis.

"And it is the only way we can get in," said Fintan.

"It's very narrow," said Cermait.

"Yes, we'll have to go singly. Who'll lead the way?"

Tybion said, "I should be happy to go first, ma'am—" but Grainne said, "It is for me to lead you," and they fell back. As Cermait said in a whisper to Fintan, although you now and then forgot Her Majesty's ancestry, she had only to tilt her head in just that way, and you remembered.

"Breeding," said Fintan. And then, "But I don't like the look of this place."

None of them liked the look of it. The Grail Castle, sometimes called Scáthach, the Castle of Shadow, reared up before them, its great bulk black and menacing against the sky.

Closer to, it was silent and secretive. Grainne thought it was easy to imagine that all manner of things walked its halls and lurked in its lonely turrets; it was easy to imagine as well that its dungeons housed ancient grisly secrets.

A wind had got up as they neared the great drawbridge, and Tybion said softly, "Your Majesty—ma'am—see there? Lights burning," and Grainne followed the direction of his pointing finger and saw that on each side of the door were flaming torches, thrust into metal sconces, flickering wildly in the moaning, keening wind, casting eerie shadows on the stone walls.

"Then at least someone is at home," Grainne said quite calmly, and she thought, Well, at least I do not *sound* afraid. And she moved forward, aware of the others falling into line behind her, but not really thinking about them; thinking instead of what lay ahead, on entering the castle, and on what they would find.

The Cruithin? After all, would the Cruithin be here? Were Ireland's lost people for some reason living in hiding in this terrible place? Was *that* the reason for the shrouding spells?

There was a moment—heart-stopping and fearsome— when the wind blew gently on the torches, so that they flared as if a giant's breath had been huffed onto them. And there was another moment when the wind swooped about them, so that each had the impression of beating wings overhead.

They dismounted cautiously and tethered their horses to mounting posts in the courtyard.

"Deserted," said Fintan, as they looked about them. "Wouldn't it be a fine old joke if after all these years, and after all those legends, the Grail Castle was no more than an empty shell?"

Grainne said softly, "I think we are being watched. From somewhere above." She scanned the rows of blank windows for movement, but there was nothing.

"I suppose," said Cermait, "that we're just going to go up to that door and ask them to let us in."

"Yes."

"Ah," said Cermait, and Grainne smiled, and Tybion moved forward, in case there was anything he could do to help.

But there was no need to pull the immense bell rope, and there was no need to ask anyone to let them in. The drawbridge swung upwards of its own accord, and the doors of the great, dark Grail Castle opened up before them.

As if they were expected.

FERGUS STOOD AT the corner of the Street of Money Lenders and waited for Taliesin.

Dusk was creeping down the street, shrouding the tall narrow buildings, and Fergus felt, as always, the heady bewitchment of the Purple Hour. He thought that surely, if there was any magic left in Ireland, this was the hour when it would be waking and walking.

He had been listening and watching for Taliesin, but when Taliesin appeared, he jumped, for the Tyrian had come so quietly that Fergus had neither seen nor heard his approach.

"Are you ready, Fergus?" said Taliesin, and he smiled as if he knew he had disconcerted Fergus.

"Where are we going?"

"To the Elders of my people." He regarded Fergus thoughtfully. "You may be a little surprised at what is ahead."

"What is ahead?" said Fergus.

"I am not permitted to tell you that." He paused in a doorway and took out a flask. "Wine?"

"Thank you." Fergus took the flask. "Is it true that you cannot conduct business unless you are drunk?"

"There are worse things that could be said of a man," said Taliesin. "Through here, Fergus. It is not very far. Thank you, I will take back my flask."

They passed down side streets and courtyards, and through a low stone archway, and Taliesin stopped before a tall house with flaring torches on each side of the door.

"Discreet," said Taliesin, surveying it. "They do not care to draw attention to themselves. I daresay they are right."

"Do people never come here by chance?"

"No." He was standing motionless, looking at the shuttered and darkened windows, and Fergus suddenly received the impression that he was reluctant to go inside. "I *am* reluctant," Taliesin said softly. And then, with a shrug, as if it did not matter after all, he pushed open the door. "And," he said, "we are expected, it seems. Come inside, Fergus."

Inside, the house was clean and cool and austere. Fergus, who knew little of the tastes and fashions of the Eastern lands, rather liked the low, pointed arches and the patterned mosaic floor. The floor was engraved with curious symbols, and he would have liked to inspect them more closely. There were alcoves at intervals, set with strange bronze winged creatures, and beneath each of these was a small flame.

"My people worship strange gods," said Taliesin, and Fergus could not decide if he was being mocked now.

"And you?"

Taliesin tilted the flask to his lips again. "I worship the red river of life which runs through the veins of no man," he said. "Through here. We are going below the city. You are entering into another world, Fergus." The shrewd eyes regarded him. "I believe I have judged you rightly," he said suddenly. "But if I have not, I am sorry."

Fergus started to say, "What—" and Taliesin said, "Hush. We are nearly at the central chamber," and returned to his former disinterested manner. "The stairs are steep. Go warily."

"What of you?" said Fergus, for Taliesin seemed to move effortlessly downwards.

"I am lent wings by the wine. You should have taken more." The stairs opened into a large high-ceilinged hall, and Fergus stared about him. He was not especially afraid, but he was certainly intrigued.

"To outsiders, we are very intriguing," Taliesin said. "It is only when you come to know us—if, that is, we permit you to—that you realise we are in truth thieves and robbers."

"You do not care very much for your own people," said Fergus, looking at him.

"I was born into a world where the making of money is the reason for existence and the bread of life," was the response. "That does not mean that I must care for it."

"You dislike it so much?"

"I find it boring," said Taliesin, and moved away, leaving Fergus at the centre of the hall.

A soft light spilled into the chamber, and Fergus, trying to pierce the dimness, received the impression of shadowy archways and passages that might lead anywhere. At the centre of the chamber was a long dark table, polished to a mirror-bright shine, and carved chairs were ranged around it. Nine, thought Fergus, his eyes going over them. Yes, of course. Always the magical nine.

There was a warm dry scent in the air—something exotic and unfamiliar—and there was a sudden feeling of being watched. Fergus felt the appraisal of the money lenders before he saw them, and he turned at once to see the hooded figures standing in the shadows at the far end.

You are meant to be impressed by their sudden noiseless appearance, Fergus, came Taliesin's mocking thoughts. *Do not be too impressed if you would retain mastery of the situation.* And Fergus, who was a little impressed, but who had long since learned how to hide his feelings, stayed where he was, and looked at the hooded figures, and waited for them to speak.

The money lenders moved forward and seated themselves at the table. As the soft light touched them, Fergus saw that they were younger than he had expected. He thought that in the main they were not a great deal older than Taliesin.

"But we are venerable in ways other than years," said the one nearest, and Fergus jumped. "You seek money, do you, Captain?" he said.

"I do seek it," said Fergus.

"For yourself?"

"For the Court," said Fergus. "But you know this."

"Yes. It is a great sum you ask," said the man. "What do you offer as security? What is the Bond?"

"Myself," said Fergus, holding the man's eyes unwaveringly. "As Head of the Queen's *Fiana*, I pledge myself. Is that sufficient for your purpose, sir?"

"It is unusual," said the Tyrian in his soft voice, and studied Fergus thoughtfully. "You know of the enmity between your people and mine?"

"A very little of it," said Fergus cautiously.

"You know that your people spurned mine, spat upon us, and called us dogs and curs? And yet, despite those courtesies, you still come to us for money?"

"If I had any other choice, I should not do so," said Fergus, rather harshly. "Had we access to the riches that still lie in Tara's halls—"

"Ah," said the Tyrian softly, "but you do not have access to them, Captain. The necromancer Medoc holds Tara, and your armies and your people can not regain what is theirs." He studied Fergus thoughtfully. "I am a practical man, Captain," he said at last. "If I have money, I make it breed. Taliesin will tell you that, although—" A brief smile lifted his lips. "—although Taliesin regards the breeding of money as tedious."

"If studied to the exclusion of all else," said Taliesin, "it is quite stultifyingly tedious." He turned up the collar of his cloak and leaned carelessly back against the ancient stone wall, apparently disassociating himself from the meeting.

"Taliesin is one of the finest usurers in the Street of Money Lenders," said the man, regarding the bored Taliesin with something between exasperation and affection. "But it comes too easily to him, and for that reason it bores him."

Taliesin said, "Money is boring, wealth is tedious, life is an endless series of greedy grasping hands and avid eyes. I see no reason to pretend that I am not bored."

The Tyrian turned back to Fergus. "Your race has long since been at odds with mine," he said. "Many years ago, when my people came to Ireland, they were harshly treated. Why, we cannot tell, for the Irish are a generous and hospitable race. Perhaps it is that we were a little too wealthy and a little too successful. Your people found that uncomfortable." He smiled, and this time it was a truer smile, and Fergus relaxed for the first time. "The Irish are a brilliant but an erratic race," said the Tyrian. "But they are improvident children. They are wild and irresponsible and quarrelsome." Again the smile. "They were envious of us, Fergus, and that is unusual, for the Irish do not, as a rule, possess the taint of envy. But that is how the enmity between us began."

"I understand."

"In the end, we asked your Queen for help," said the Tyrian. "We sought audience with your Queen's grandmother, the Lady Dierdriu, and told her that if she would help us and support us, then she would have our unswerving devotion, and that if ever there was a service we could render to her line, we would do it unhesitatingly." The smile thinned a little and became faintly calculating. "She knew our worth, your High Queen," said the man. "She knew that we have always been clever and learned, and also that we are secretive and tenacious. We look to our own," said the Tyrian, and a murmur of assent went round the chamber. "And we cleave only to our own kind," he said, and by the foot of the stone steps, Taliesin sighed, and produced his wine flask.

"Dierdriu helped us when no one else would," said the Tyrian. "And for her and her descendants there is nothing we will not do." He looked at Fergus. "That is why we will lend you the money," he said. "Not for yourself, but for Grainne, Dierdriu's granddaughter, who commands our allegiance."

"Yes. I am grateful," said Fergus, and he heard Taliesin mutter, "O gratitude, thou burden upon our imperfect souls."

"You will ignore our brother's mockery," said the Tyrian, quite seriously it seemed to Fergus. "He keeps strange company and reads in strange annals."

"Also I am wedded to the daughter of the vine," remarked Taliesin, apparently to nobody in particular.

"Dierdriu rarely gave without ensuring that she would later receive," said the Tyrian, who seemed to be accustomed to Taliesin's methods of speech. "She helped us and we continue to be grateful to her." He glanced at Taliesin as he said this, but Taliesin only smiled and said nothing.

"In return, she asked us to work in secret for her," said the Tyrian. "She summoned us to Tara one night towards the end of her reign, and charged us with a task of such immense importance that we have never been able to lose sight of it."

A sudden stillness fell over the other money lenders, and Fergus thought, They know what is coming, but still they feel apprehension. Why? This is something of such magnitude and such secrecy that these people have brought me to this hidden underground chamber to tell me of it.

The Tyrian appeared to be selecting his next words very carefully, but when he spoke, he only said, "Will you be seated, Fergus?" and indicated the vacant chair at the foot of the table.

Fergus sat, and the Tyrian said, "And—perhaps you will have a goblet of wine? Yes, that is better." He sat back and sipped his own wine, and again appeared to marshal his thoughts.

"Many centuries ago, the Royal line of your country had in keeping an ancient and strong enchantment," he said. "It was known as the Enchantment of the Beastline, and it en-

abled the Royal Houses of Ireland to lie with the beasts of
the forest and produce the beautiful cruel strong High Kings
and Queens." He looked at Fergus, and Fergus said,

"Yes. The Enchantment was created by the sorcerers for
the first High Queen of all, to deflect an ancient curse." He
narrowed his eyes and quoted the ancient curse softly. " *'If
ever Tara should belong to a pure-bred Human, then it will fall
into ruin, and the Bright Palace will be no more, and Ireland
will surely die . . .'* It is a part of our heritage. There is a Panel
of Judges who constantly measure the strength of the Beastline and pronounce when the line must be mated with the
beasts. Then there is what is called the Ceremony of the
Beastline, and the mating takes place. Contrary to what you
would imagine," Fergus said thoughtfully, "it is a rather solemn and ceremonious occasion."

"You have never been present at one of these ceremonies?"

"No."

"Has it never occurred to you that the present Queen
possesses only a thin trickle of the Enchantment?"

Fergus started to speak and then stopped.

"And that being so," said the man, "has it never occurred to you to wonder why the Judges have not ordered
the ceremony? For the Queen?" He looked very intently at
Fergus, and Fergus had the impression that he was seeing
very clearly those warm drowsy afternoons, those mist-
shrouded mornings with Grainne. *And, oh, my love, my dear
love, how could I ever bear it if you had to lie with the wolves,
and accept their seed, and give birth to a Wolfprince . . . Because
the Wolfprince should have been mine!* cried Fergus in silent
agony.

But he allowed none of this to show; he looked back at
the Tyrian calmly and said, "The wolf blood is strong
enough."

"No." The Tyrian returned Fergus's regard rather sadly.
"Your Queen has only a trace of it. For all that she can
sometimes summon what is called the golden strength of the

wolves, she has only a thread of the Enchantment in her."
He leaned forward, his eyes hard and shining in the candle-
glow. "If the Wolfline is to be saved, she *must* be joined with
the wolves. She must give birth to a Wolfprince."

"The Judges have not ordered—"

"The Judges have not ordered it," said the Tyrian, "because the Enchantment has been lost." He looked very
straightly at Fergus. "The ancient and powerful Enchantment, spun by the first sorcerers of all to protect Tara from
the long-ago curse, is dead."

FOR A LONG time Fergus did not speak. He was distantly
aware of the Tyrians watching him, waiting to see what he
would do.

The ancient Enchantment is lost . . .

The strong bewitchment, the spell woven by the sorcerers in the very beginning so that a pure-bred Human should
never occupy Tara's High Throne, was lost.

Fergus knew the words of the ancient curse as well as
and probably better than anyone else in Ireland. He knew
that for the Beastline to die out, for the magical enchanted
wolf blood to fade, would mean the fall of the Bright Palace.

*A Human on the Throne, and the final triumph of the Dark
Ireland.*

He turned back to the Tyrian and found the man was
watching him closely. I must be wary, thought Fergus. I must
be very wary indeed, for these are clever and subtle men.
"Tell me what you know," he said, and the Tyrian seemed
for the first time to relax.

"You did not know of this, Captain?" he said. "Of the
Lost Enchantment?" and there was faint surprise in his voice.

Fergus smiled into the Tyrian's eyes. "Nothing is ever
entirely secret at Court, sir," he said with perfect courtesy.
"But let us say that the little I know is a very little indeed.
And let us say I should be glad to hear your part in it all."

"Our part in it . . ." said the Tyrian. "Yes, we have
played our part, Captain. We shall continue to do so." He

sipped his wine, and Fergus received the impression that he was collecting his thoughts. "Once," he said, sipping his wine reflectively, "there were the six great Royal Houses of Ireland who served the Wolfkings. All of them possessed the enchanted blood, and all were answerable to the Panel of Judges. The Eagles and the Wild Panthers were next in line after the Wolves, and were regarded as Princes of Ireland; after them came the White Swans, who were a very old and very strong noble line, and had intermarried with the Panthers. After them, there were three lesser, but equally noble houses: the Deers and the Lions and the Chariot Horses. It was a strictly ordered, but very well balanced, hierarchy."

"Yes," said Fergus, and waited.

"There were minor Beastlines, as well," said the Tyrian. "Lesser, but important, nobility who were admitted into the Enchantment because of some service rendered to the King, or bravery in battle perhaps. We know of the Beavers and Badgers; Foxes and Hawks. But the blood has thinned and grown weaker in all of these Houses, Fergus, and although you may see traces of it here and there, it has almost disappeared." He leaned forward again, his eyes still bright. "And it must be rediscovered, Fergus. Dierdriu knew that.

"And so she asked us for help. She knew our sorcerers were amongst the finest in the world, and she knew that we could be entrusted with the secret. We have many faults," said the Tyrian, "but we guard well those things which must be guarded. Dierdriu knew that the enchantment must be rediscovered or rewoven. The Princes of Ireland must be able to again lie with the beasts." He paused. "Have you ever seen an enchantment being woven, Fergus?" he said. "It is a truly remarkable experience. The sorcerers use great looms, as the robemakers do, but the sorcerers' looms are of pure soft silver, and the stuff they weave is not velvet and silk, but the dreams of men, and the living colours, and the music of the world made liquid, so that you can pour it between your hands. Beautiful and terrifying." He stopped again, and no one moved.

"Our work has taken us down some strange paths," said the Tyrian. "We have suffered terrible defeats. But we have gone on, because we have never forgotten how Dierdriu helped us when no one else would, and we know that if Ireland—the true Ireland—is not to die, the Enchantment *must* be rewoven. Even so . . ." again the pause, and the faraway stare, "even so," he said, "there have been dreadful travesties. Times when we had thought the Enchantment whole and safe, but when it was neither. Pitiable beings who we believed would found a new Royal Line, but who were little better than monsters. Can you imagine, Fergus, can you visualize the results of a union between animals and humans without the protection of an enchantment? Nightmare creatures." He stopped again, and behind them, Fergus had the impression that Taliesin made a movement of distaste. But the Tyrian at the table seemed not to notice it. After a moment he said, "But since we pledged our help to Dierdriu, then we must also help her descendant. There is no question but that the Enchantment must somehow be found again, so that Medoc can be driven out of the Bright Palace, and there is no question but that you must go into the Future to chain whatever forces you find there and bring them back."

"Yes," said Fergus. "Yes, I see all that." He sat back and looked at them all. "Your loan will pay our own sorcerers," he said. "Only with their help can we hope to travel to the Far Future."

"And then you will return to repay the loan and its interest, will you?" said the Tyrian, rather cynically.

"You have my word," said Fergus in frosty tone.

"And the Head of the *Fiana*'s word should be sufficient?"

"Amongst my own people it would be. And once we have regained Tara, there will be the riches and the wealth of the High Kings. We could repay your loan many times over."

"Once with interest will suffice," said the Tyrian.

"I *will* return," said Fergus seriously, "and if our attack on Medoc fails, then you may claim the Bond, and I believe I should die gladly. But you may believe that I will return."

"We do believe it," said the Tyrian. "But we are a people who believe in bonds, Fergus." He regarded Fergus with the same thoughtful appraisal, and Fergus caught a movement from Taliesin. "And so," said the Tyrian, "we are going to—persuade—you to make a committment to us before you leave for the Future. You are to pay a little of the Bond in advance."

The silence that followed his words was so sudden and so complete that for a second, Fergus thought he had misheard. A myriad of different thoughts churned through his mind, but at length, he said, quite calmly, "Would you explain that, please?" and the money lenders seemed almost to relax.

"I have told you of how our sorcerers are pledged to help your Royal House, and to rediscover, or reweave a new Enchantment of the Beastline."

"Yes."

The Tyrian paused, and then said, "In order to test their work, it is necessary to—make use of Humans." He regarded Fergus. "You understand my meaning, Captain? It is necessary to mate Humans with animals, within the confines of the Enchantment, and study the results of that mating."

He waited. Fergus did not speak.

"And so," said the Tyrian, "we require you to—assist the sorcerers, Fergus.

"Before we release you from this house, and before we agree fully and unreservedly to the loan you ask for, you must lie with a she-wolf."

And then, as Fergus did not speak, "If you agree," said the Tyrian, "we shall view your petition seriously.

"No Human who willingly gives his seed to a wolf is other than deadly serious in purpose." And then, the glint of amusement in his eyes, "Well, Captain?" he said.

CHAPTER FOUR

FERGUS SAT IN the anteroom and eyed Taliesin. "You knew."

"Yes."

"You did not warn me."

"You will accept," said Taliesin, "that it was a little difficult to explain." His expression was bland, but a glint of amusement showed in his eyes. But he said, quite seriously, "It is the only way they will lend you the money, Fergus. Our sorcerers are forever studying the Enchantment and forever making new attempts to reweave it. And although it will be strange and bizarre, they are serious about what they are trying to do." He eyed Fergus. "The Silver Looms have been spinning ceaselessly for many nights now. The sorcerers are ready to—"

"Create another monster?" said Fergus harshly. "Bring into the world another poor mutilation born of a mating between a beast and a Human without the true Enchantment?"

Taliesin regarded Fergus. "You have never seen a spell being woven, Fergus," he said unexpectedly. "They say it is the most marvellous sight you could ever witness. The stuff that dreams are made on." He leaned back. "But to weave the Enchantment properly, the sorcerers require a willing Human . . ."

A willing Human . . .

"And you are going to do it, aren't you," said Taliesin very softly.

"Yes," said Fergus, staring at him. "Yes, I believe I am."

For Grainne. He would do it for Grainne, and he would

49

do it for Ireland, and for the loan that would enable him to travel into the Far Future. For no other reason? said his mind cynically. What of the hidden ancient bewitchments you are certainly about to witness, and what of the secret arts of the sorcerers which you will almost surely be party to? To see a spell being woven, perhaps actually to witness the re-creating of the Lost Enchantment of Tara . . .

And if it should succeed, then my son would be High King of Ireland . . .

"WHERE ARE WE going?" said Fergus, as Taliesin led the way along a narrow stone tunnel that snaked under the ground.

"We are directly under the Street of Money Lenders now. We are going towards the place my people call the Chamber of Looms," said Taliesin, "although I think that is the name given to all such places."

"Yes. At Tara there are many such."

Taliesin was leading them under the low-ceilinged tunnels, where the wall torches threw soft shadows and the walls gleamed with a gentle silver light. Fergus thought the light was some kind of phosphorescence, and then was not sure.

"Escaped spells," said Taliesin, reaching out to touch the glistening rockface. "Fragments of raw bewitchments that have seeped through the sealed walls of the Sorcery Chambers." He glanced at Fergus, and Fergus said, "I am not sure if you are being serious."

"I am rarely serious and seldom sober," said Taliesin at once. "But you have stood in the Street of Money Lenders at dusk, Fergus, and you have felt the enchantments on the air."

As they walked on, Fergus saw that now and then a thread of brilliant colour poured itself across their path, as if a length of iridescent silk had come alive, and he glimpsed vague drifting shapes, and was aware of strong exotic perfumes.

The tunnel opened suddenly into a high-ceilinged cavern. There were more of the pointed arches that Fergus had seen on the upper floors, and he thought that tall shadowy figures, cloaked and hooded, stood waiting. The sorcerers! thought Fergus. The Tyrian sorcerers who have worked ceaselessly for Ireland's Royal House. He looked at them, and remembered the old belief that sorcerers were not quite immortal, but not entirely temporal either. There had to be a vein of the ancient Amaranth blood in them, and it was something they preserved jealously. Were these true Amaranthine creatures?

"Certainly we are, Captain," said the nearest of them. "Although the strain is somewhat diluted in us."

"But then we are Tyrians, you understand," said another. "We are Tyrians, and therefore we are little better than outcasts and vagabonds."

They were all about him now, courteous and approachable, but in the dimness, Fergus thought their eyes glittered and their hands seemed to be reaching for him.

For a willing Human is all that is needed at this stage . . .

But after all, I have agreed to it, thought Fergus, and he allowed them to take him across the echoing cavern through a low pointed door at the far end. He was aware of Taliesin still at his side, and there was unexpected comfort in this.

Beyond the low door was a silk-hung chamber, with gold symbols etched into the floor, and although Fergus had never penetrated to a Chamber of the Looms—he thought no one who had not the Amaranth blood could do so—he had several times been into minor Sorcery Chambers. He knew this at once for such a chamber, and in the carved symbols he thought he could make out the Cauldron of Dagda with the fire god's horned features etched into it, and also the writhing shapes of the *sidh*, who were said to spin the strongest and purest magic in all Ireland. There were other shapes as well; Fergus recognised the Cup of Lyr, and the Nine Hazels of Wisdom, which the Druids used in some of their rituals.

Opposite the door through which they had entered was a second door, a massive silver door, ornate and bearing immense seals, wreathed in symbols even more ancient than those on the floor, and this time carved with what Fergus knew must be the ancient Fertility Tree of Amaranth.

Heat poured outwards from the silver door in great solid gusts, and Fergus flinched. In the same moment, he was conscious of a steady purring note and a continuous spinning palpating. He took a step nearer to the door and gasped as the heat engulfed him.

"The heat from the Looms is the fiercest heat there is," said one of the sorcerers. "And unless you know the protective spells, you should not venture too close." He regarded Fergus. "When the Silver Looms are spinning, the force they harness is more powerful than anything you could comprehend; you would be pulled in to its heart and consumed by it." He paused, and in the silence Fergus could hear the thrumming of the great Looms, and the slow rhythmic pulsating . . .

For the Looms have been spinning ceaselessly, and now all that is required is a willing Human . . . And I am the Human, thought Fergus . . .

The lights were not so dim here as they had been elsewhere in the house, but there was a reddish tinge, and there was the same silvering on the walls of the chamber as there had been in the tunnel. Here and there, a thread of colour showed, as if tiny streams of enchantment were trickling down the walls. There was a warm dry scent, and as Fergus stood waiting, the wall torches seemed to burn with a steady pulsing beat. Like a mind or a heart throbbing, thought Fergus . . .

He thought that the spinning of the Looms had increased—had it quickened?—and then he thought that the lights were deepening in intensity. The nearest of the sorcerers moved to the silver door and began to break the seals. Strong crimson light, shot with gold, poured into the anteroom, and with it curling tongues of flame, so that Fergus and Taliesin both fell back under the furious gust of heat and force and energy. Fergus, shielding his face with his hands, saw, in the belching flames, great shadowy edifices, rearing turrets of power that glinted and whirled in a maelstrom of light and colour. There were immense waterfalls of strong raw colour, as if living rainbows were pouring into the Chamber of the Looms, and Fergus, his eyes dry and burning, his skin prickling with the heat, thought there was a moment when the Looms became alive and reached upwards, almost like silver giants stretching their hands up to heaven to pull down primeval energy.

And then the silver door closed to and the seals snapped into place and the sorcerer was facing Fergus with something between his hands that shimmered and undulated, and Fergus knew it for a newly spun enchantment.

And then he saw the wolf.

She was a golden-eyed, satin-sleek creature, and Fergus, looking down at her, saw that there was intelligence in her eyes. It was impossible not to think, *But this is how Grainne looked at me that summer!* and it was impossible not to remember that Grainne and this lean silky creature were of the same root. Fergus had thought that when he was brought face to face with the reality of taking a wolf, of embedding her with his seed, he would falter, but now, with the steady resonance of the Looms all about them, and with the golden glowing eyes of the wolf, he knew he would not. The steady thrumming from the Looms was invading his brain and descending low down into his body. He thought, *I am to lie with a she-wolf,* and the idea was immensely arousing now.

He thought the sorcerers had moved back a little, and they had certainly begun a low, faintly musical chanting, and he thought that Taliesin was standing by the door, but he did not really notice.

He fell to his knees and held out both his hands, and the wolf approached him cautiously, her head tilted, her eyes alert. Fergus ran his hands over her flanks— Beautiful! he thought. Oh, yes, my dear, we shall surely succumb to the Enchantment, and perhaps together we will make a Wolfprince for Ireland, my lady.

She came closer to him, and as he began to caress her lean underbelly, he felt the nipples harden beneath his fingers.

Heat rushed to his loins at once, and he spread his thighs, and turned the wolf about, still stroking her, his other hand going to the fastening of his breeches.

There was no awkwardness, no fumbling . . . So natural, thought Fergus, his body on fire. How could I have thought I might falter?

He did not falter. He pulled the wolf to him, feeling the strong smooth flanks quiver with delight, and, as he entered her, delight exploded within him, for the creature was tight and clutching, she was soft and smooth, and it was like driving into silk . . . He could feel the warm sable and black fur against his thighs, sensual and arousing. And after all, he thought, after all, the Wolves of Tara were once very nearly sacred . . . It is not so very long since the Royal House lay with them to produce the Kings of Ireland . . . *And perhaps I am now doing the same . . . Perhaps my son will be King of Ireland,* thought Fergus, and the thought was so dazzling and so brilliant that delight exploded in his mind, and for a moment he could have believed that no enchantment was needed to achieve what the sorcerers wanted.

The wolf was panting now, her eyes brilliant in the red glow from the wall sconces, and Fergus could feel her muscles bunch and tense. He was moving faster now, and he could hear the Looms still pounding and spinning, and they were going faster, and he was moving against the wolf frantically, and the lights were whirling all about them, and the Enchantment was surely being reborn . . . The colours of the room were merging and control was beginning to spin away from his grasp, only it did not matter, because this was what they wanted of him . . . a new Beastline . . . a Wolfprince . . .

Fergus gave a low groan and felt the hot seed, the life-making fluid, gush from his body and flood the she-wolf's womb.

THE STREET OF Money Lenders was cold and fresh and there was a clean sharpness in the air. Fergus stood for a moment,

drawing in great lungfuls of air and, at his side, Taliesin
grinned.

"You are purging your soul of magic and the sorcerers'
manipulating?" he said, and Fergus said thoughtfully, "It feels
as if it was just a dream."

"That is all enchantments are," said Taliesin, and then,
"When do we leave?" he said.

Fergus turned round to look at him. " 'We'?"

"My dear Fergus," said Taliesin lazily, "did you really
think the Elders would permit you to go from here alone?
In possession of their great secret? Dear me, how trusting of
you."

"You are coming with me to Innisfree?"

"I am coming with you to the Future," said Taliesin,
and in the thin dawnlight, there was no mistaking the brilliance of his eyes. "I am resigned to it," he said solemnly.
"As the Elders decree, so must I obey."

"It will be extremely dangerous," said Fergus, who
thought he would very much like to have Taliesin with him.

"Will it really? Dear me, how tedious." Taliesin was
walking along the street now, his shoulders hunched against
the cold, raw morning. "Even so, the idea of saving the world
is a stirring one." He sent Fergus a sideways glance.

"Is that the only reason?"

"No. I am bored," said Taliesin. "I am bored with usury.
I have too long endured the greed of the fools who seek me
out, and I have too long dwelled in the dusty purlieus of
money lending. I am at odds with the world that measures
success and contentment by the wealth a man has amassed."
The amusement flickered in his eyes again. "Also," he said,
"I find that I have a wish to be a hero. Shall we save the
world, Fergus?"

"I don't know," said Fergus, who did not.

"Well, even though it is a tedious world, I am still intrigued by the notion of saving it. And it will certainly be a
far better thing than anything I have yet done here. Probably

it will be a far better world than anything I have yet seen here as well, although that remains to be discovered." The mockery was still in his voice, but there was something else there, as well, that made Fergus think he would be unexpectedly strong.

"I am as inconstant as the moon when it comes to bravery," Taliesin said at once, and he grinned at Fergus again, and this time a chink of light from a nearby window made pinpoints of light dance in the depths of his eyes, giving him the look of a devil.

"Oh, I am not a devil," said Taliesin. "If you would meet a devil, Fergus, you should wait until we have found Fael-Inis, for that is the only sure way to cross Time, and Fael-Inis is called, and truly, the rebel angel from the beginning of the world.

"But if we travel in the Time Chariot, you will find that out for yourself. Wine?"

THEY RETURNED TO a depleted Court, since Grainne had already left to find the Grail Castle, and Lugh Longhand had taken most of the army onto the mainland to spy out the land there.

Lugh had, in fact, told a great many people that they were going to be preparing the way for victory, and that a good many people would be very surprised indeed at the outcome of what was ahead.

Dorrainge had gone with them, because he said that somebody should represent the Druids, and Fribble was holding to his absurd idea of going with Fergus into the Far Future. He would take Cathbad with him, said Dorrainge, and Cathbad looked up and said, "Onto the mainland with the army? Oh, dear me, all that *fighting*. Couldn't I stay here?"

But Dorrainge said no, because for one thing, Cathbad could cook, which nobody else in Lugh's party could, and whatever else they did, they were not going to starve.

Fribble said, "Trust the fat fool Dorrainge to think of

his stomach," but Cathbad, who rather prided himself on his skill with the cookpots, brightened up, and began to enumerate the dishes he would prepare for Lugh's men. "And they will *not* be too dainty, because there will be all those *warlike* men."

"They're like sheep," said Fribble, who had been woken up by Lugh's early departure. "I didn't think Her Majesty had so many sheep in our Court. I'm very glad they've all gone."

Fribble was pleased to see Fergus, whom he liked, and explained to him about Lugh and his idea of spying on Medoc, and creating a base for them to mount a final attack on Tara.

"Lugh's taking that fat fool Dorrainge with him," said Fribble. "We're very glad about that. Cathbad's going as well. I don't know about him, he's very odd. Are we leaving now? Oughtn't we to take some wine with us? It won't do to find ourselves utterly wineless in the Future, you know."

Fergus, grinning, said, "Sir, there'll be enough wine in the Far Future to drink the entire Court into oblivion," and Fribble said, "Well, then, I think we ought to take them some as a gift, don't you? It would be polite. Are we ready? I don't want to be kept standing around all day. And if we're taking the tilt cart, I'll have a cushion to sit on."

"We're quite ready, sir," said Fergus. "We're going to the House of Calatin." And Fribble, who had been stowing away a large leather skin of the Court's best woodsorrel mead, turned round and said, "Are you sure that's a good idea? I heard that Calatin and the Sons haven't done very much in the way of decent sorcery for several seasons. And it's quite a long way."

"Well, we thought—"

"Of course, they've only got one eye and one foot each," said Fribble. "It's something to do with relinquishing the Human side of their natures."

"A very old ritual," Taliesin said gravely.

"They've always been very loyal to all the High Kings," Fergus said.

"Yes, but you can't go through life on one foot," said Fribble. "That's very awkward. Does anybody know if the Sons of Calatin hop everywhere, or do they have a walking stick?"

Fergus said, "We none of us know, sir, because none of us has ever met any of the Sons. And we're going to Calatin, because he's the most faithful of Tara's sorcerers."

"Also," Taliesin said in dulcet tones, "he is cheap."

"Rubbish," said Fribble at once. "No sorcerers are cheap. Who's this person? Is he coming with us? We'll probably have to go in the Chariot of Fael-Inis, always supposing Calatin can summon it, and there won't be much room. Does he know that? Fergus, have you told him?"

Taliesin said, "Sir, I am as insubstantial as the pageantry of dreams, and I am as a wraith in the night, and I shall take up no more room than a shadow."

"Wraiths? Wraiths? I hope we aren't having any of *those* with us, nasty chilly things," said Fribble, and he shivered and had to be given a drink from Taliesin's flask.

"Only for warmth," he said. "I don't want to take cold and miss anything. It's very good wine, this. No, I won't have any—well, I daresay another drop won't hurt. Did Fergus say you were a money lender? I've never met a money lender."

"I am a dealer in people's dreams and I am a merchant of souls," said Taliesin.

"I suppose you're a Tyrian," said Fribble. "Yes, I thought you were. Still, you brought your own wine, I have to allow that. Are we starting now? Isn't it a bit early?"

"We don't want to arrive too late," explained Fergus. "We're not sure of our way."

"Nor of our welcome," murmured Taliesin.

NEITHER FERGUS NOR Taliesin was faint-hearted; both, indeed, possessed a strong vein of courage. Taliesin, who had said that he cared for no man and no man cared for him, had, beneath his indifference, a restlessness and a desire to know other worlds and other cultures. He had sat out the dreary years in the Street of the Money Lenders because there was nothing else that a Tyrian in Ireland could do. But for all of that, he had been bored. He had derived cynical amusement from challenging the shibboleths that bound his people, and although he had tried not to think *Is this all there will ever be?* he had thought it many times.

Now, riding through the dark forest with Fergus at his side and Fribble behind them in the cart, Taliesin knew that after all, it had not been all there would ever be. There was more, there would be difficulties, and there would certainly be dangers, but, *I shall be alive,* he thought, and felt a tremendous anticipation. I am coming alive again.

Even so, it takes an unusual degree of courage to ride up to a sorcerer's house by night and demand admittance therein, and as they saw the trees begin to thin and glimpsed the outline of a huge grey house, both Fergus and Taliesin reined in their horses.

"Is that it?"

"I believe so." Fergus sat very still on his horse.

"I do not admit to apprehension, you understand," said Taliesin, "but I could wish, Fergus, that you had chosen another way for us to travel to the Future."

"It is the only way," said Fergus, and he grinned. "Only a sorcerer with Calatin's power could summon Fael-Inis—"

"And only Fael-Inis can take us across Time," said Taliesin. "Yes, of course."

"But," Fergus said, "Fael-Inis has not been glimpsed in Ireland for a century or more. It may be an impossible task."

But as he spoke, Fribble, who had been enjoying his ride in the tilt cart, said, "Dear me, I don't think that's right, you know. I believe Fael-Inis was last heard of in Dierdriu's reign, and that's not so very long ago. Is this the House? It isn't as long a journey as I thought it would be, after all. I expect they'll ask us to supper, will they? I always heard that Calatin and his Sons were extremely hospitable."

Taliesin wanted to know how many Sons they would meet.

"Twenty-seven," said Fribble. "The magical three times nine it is. All the sorcerers go in for that sort of thing. Myself, I can't see that it makes any difference, although they say it strengthens an enchantment to include three times nine somewhere. This is a very bad road, isn't it? I'd better have a drop of wine, to help me over the bumps. Only a thimbleful; I don't want to arrive roaring drunk. It would create the wrong impression, and I might fall asleep and miss everything."

As they drew nearer, there was the faint stirring of wind above them and, with it, a low keening note.

"The wind in the trees," said Taliesin, and he glanced at the other two, and thought, Did they hear that other sound just beyond the sound of the wind? And he listened again and wondered after all whether he had heard anything other than the wind.

The faintest, frailest thread of sound, nothing more . . . Music, thought Taliesin. Did I in truth hear it? Yes, I believe I did. And so soft and so sweet and so achingly sad that it would melt your soul, and you would follow it into hell and beyond if only it would continue . . . He turned back to the others and saw that Fergus was standing very still, staring into the dark forest, and there was a look in his eyes that made Taliesin's skin prickle with fear.

Fergus said, rather uncertainly, "I thought there was something . . ." and stopped, and Taliesin said with all the force he could muster, "Fergus, there is nothing out there."

"Yes . . . music. And—a sound like a child crying—"

Taliesin thought at once, *The Lad of the Skins!* And at once every grisly legend and every nightmarish tale ever told about the soul-stealing Lad of the Skins flooded his mind.

For the Lad, when he comes, always comes with the chill beckoning music, and with the creeping ancient cold, and with the heart-tearing crying of a lost child in the night . . .

Cold horror touched him. If the evil, insidious sounds did indeed herald the Lad's approach, and if Fergus were to fall under his terrible bewitchment, what would happen to them? And in the same moment he knew that if it was the Lad, it would certainly be Fergus he would want, for Fergus was their leader.

Fribble was listening as well, his head on one side. "I can't hear anything," he said. "Although I'm getting a bit hard of hearing now, of course."

Taliesin's mind was tumbling with grisly images. He was cold with dread and he thought they must try to seek safety inside Calatin's house. He took Fergus's arm, and began to lead him along down the path towards the House of Calatin, and despite the urgency of the moment and the need to somehow get away from the creeping, eerily beautiful music, he was conscious of a small bubble of cynical amusement. Am I to take control of this ill-assorted and surely ill-fated venture? But if the Lad of the Skins was spinning his dark evil about Fergus, Fergus would certainly be unable to lead them. He thought that Fergus was still responding to the beckoning music and the faint far-off crying, and there was nothing for it but to get them to Calatin's house and safety. And then he thought, I suppose it *will* be safe in there.

Fribble, who had been scanning the darkness, said, "I can't hear anything, you know, but I do think we shouldn't stand out here in the middle of the forest with night coming on." And Taliesin smiled, and said, "You are entirely right, sir. Let us go up to the house, where at least we can be sure of food and warmth and lights and a little Human companionship."

Fribble looked sharply at Taliesin and said, "Oh dear, you haven't been thinking that Calatin is *Human*, have you?"

"What is he?" said Fergus, and Taliesin knew a rush of relief, for Fergus had spoken in what was very nearly a normal voice. Had the faint haunting music withdrawn its hold? I do not believe in any gods at all, thought Taliesin. But if I did, I should be praying to every one of them that it has withdrawn. Aloud, he said, "Tell us about Calatin, Fribble," and Fribble, who had been gazing at the house, said, "Didn't you know? Calatin and his Sons are giants. Every one of them."

IF IT TAKES courage to approach a sorcerer's house and request admittance, how much more courage does it take when you have learned that the sorcerers are giants, and when your approach is being made at nightfall through an ancient, listening forest?

Taliesin knew that something deep within the forest was still watching them. He knew that it was following them, creeping along the dark forest path behind them, always just out of sight, so that if you whipped round without warning, it would dodge back into the shadows. He was very nearly certain that it was Fergus that the creature wanted, and he thought that if only they could get Fergus inside Calatin's house, they might think themselves safe for the moment.

But I do not know whether the creature is good or evil.

The angel from the bottomless pit ... Was there any possibility of that? Was there any chance that it was the wild beautiful untamable Fael-Inis? The creature they would have to summon to travel across Time? The rebel angel who rode the Time Chariot and consorted with the fire creatures?

He did not think it was Fael-Inis, for Fael-Inis, when he came to the world of Men, never came furtively and creepingly, with icy evil music, but warmly and glowingly, and with the heat and the fire of the Time Chariot all about him.

It was something darker that was stealing through the forest. Something infinitely sinister. Something hungry that insinuated itself into men's houses and took their souls ...

Probably I am imagining it, thought Taliesin. But he knew that he was not, for he possessed traces of the ancient, almost-extinct Samhailt, the strange elusive power to hear and understand the thoughts of others, and to hear and be aware of the unseen creatures who prowled the world, just out of hearing and just beyond consciousness. But despite all the dangers, he knew that he was alive and alight again.

When Fergus, helping Fribble over the last rough piece

of ground, said, "Do you feel at all afraid?" Taliesin smiled in the old mocking way, and said, "I am terror itself, Fergus," and knew that Fergus knew this was not true.

As they neared the house, they saw that it was much larger than it had first seemed. Taliesin thought it had a lowering appearance. It was built of some kind of dark roughish stone, and there was a steep overhanging roof, and row upon row of narrow windows. But the windows had a blank look to them, as if the rooms behind had been closed up and forgotten. An immense flight of stone steps led up to the house.

"Difficult to climb," muttered Fribble. "Deep. Well, of course, they're giant steps." He sat down and hitched up his robes. "It won't do to be tripping up," he said.

They climbed the stone steps carefully. "Each step was at least four feet deep," said Fribble, dusting himself down as they reached the top. "I wonder how big the giants are." He examined the massive iron-studded door. "Do you suppose anyone's at home? I think we ought to ring the bell. Can you reach it? Dear me, it's rather a long way up. Of course, they'd only be used to other giants as guests. Did somebody say it was supper time? I'm very hungry, aren't you?"

Taliesin grasped the bell rope and pulled it, and deep within the House of the Giants, a clanging, sonorous bell sounded. It was followed by a moment of most-profound silence and then, from somewhere deep within the great house, they became aware of a slow measured tread approaching.

"Not hopping," muttered Fribble. "So it won't be a giant."

"Is that meant to make us feel better?" said Fergus, and Taliesin, listening, thought that Fergus was sounding more ordinary with every minute. He glanced back into the forest, and thought he caught a scuttling movement deep within the trees, and then was not sure.

The footsteps were on the other side of the door now,

and there was a snuffling, as if some huge creature was trying to find the door handle. Taliesin caught the sound of claws ringing out on the floor, and his heart began to pound.

Slowly, inch by inch, the door swung open, and Fergus, who was a little ahead, said very loudly, "We bid you good evening, and have come from the Court of the High Queen of Ireland. We ask for discourse with Calatin and his Sons—"

"And beg for shelter and hospitality," said Fribble, and then in an aside, "They usually like you to say that."

There was a pause, as if the creature in the shadows was considering them. Taliesin caught again the sound of claws.

And then a deep, echoing voice said, "Come inside, travellers," and the door swung open to admit them.

"You are expected," said the voice, and the three travellers stepped over the threshold, into the House of the Giant Sorcerers.

CHAPTER FIVE

THE MINUTE THAT Grainne and Fintan and Cermait with Tybion stepped inside the Grail Castle, they were conscious of a feeling of great desolation. A shutting out of the light, and a cutting off of hope and warmth and ordinary companionship. It was like waking in the dark of the night— *'In the terrible loneliness of the night watches, when all sleeps and the world spins on silently and the soul knows the infinite isolation . . .'*

I have never heard those words, thought Grainne, but I know them.

Ahead of them was a stone archway and a flight of steps leading down to a sunken hall. There was firelight and shadowy figures, and there was the sudden hush that falls on a roomful of people when a stranger enters.

Grainne moved towards the archway and stood framed there, looking down at the firelit hall. The light flickered wildly, throwing huge, distorted shadows across the walls, and sending grotesque phantoms and phantasms dancing on the ceiling, and Grainne stood transfixed.

There was a moment—unwished for and never to be forgotten—when shock and horror rose up in her throat, and a terrible sickness threatened to overwhelm her. She fought for control, and the sickness receded, and presently she was able to look without flinching on what was below in the stone hall.

People seated at a long table. No, not people. Creatures. Travesties. Half-Humans. Terrible, pitiable beings. Grainne took another step forward.

Creatures neither quite animal nor quite Human. Fur

and claws and hoofs and snouts. Cloven and webbed and pointed-eared and triangular-featured. Whiskers and skin and hide. Flesh and fur. Parodies. Dreadful, grotesque creatures.

As Grainne stood and looked, unable to speak or move, a pity so immense welled up inside her that she wanted to run down into the red glow of the hall and hold out her hands to the poor pitiful things, gather them to her.

For there was intelligence in the eyes that watched her, and there was understanding and tolerance; a patient acceptance of the cruel fate that had shaped and misshaped and caused these beings to be shut away.

They know what they are.

Grainne turned back to where Tybion and Fintan and Cermait waited by the door, and looked at them very steadily. "Wait here for me." She thought that for a moment Fintan and Cermait made as if to protest, and Tybion certainly moved, but her voice brooked no argument.

Grainne said in a different, gentler voice, "It is all right. Truly. They will not harm me." And knew they would not.

Even so, it was harder than she had expected to walk calmly down into the sunken hall with the deep stone hearth and the flagged floor and the flickering wall sconces. Their eyes watched her, and they were the eyes of animals, bright and dark and slanting. Unblinking cats' eyes, and slitted reptilian eyes, and here and there small birdlike eyes.

And claws and fur, and talons and teeth . . . Yes, it was all here. Catmasks and eagle eyes and pointed muzzles . . . Don't think about it, thought Grainne. Don't notice it.

She walked in silence to the head of the table and stood looking, and now that she was closer, she could see the evidence of beast and Human more clearly. She could see where men or women had been matched with foxes and with eagles and with panthers, and with prowling, growling things, who might sometimes walk on all fours, and sometimes upright like Men . . .

At the head of the table sat a golden-eyed creature, with the strong features of an eagle or a hawk. He had arms which were nearly but not quite wings, and skin that was nearly but not quite feathered, and there was a hard unblinking look in his eyes as he watched her.

The others had flinched from her gaze, as if they could not endure to be looked on, although the eagle creature sat calmly watching her.

At length, she said softly, "Will you permit me to join you?" and felt a stir of unease go through them.

"I mean you no harm," Grainne said. And she waited.

The eagle man said, "You honor us, Your Majesty," and a murmur went round the table.

"You recognise me?"

"The Wolfqueen. Yes, how would we not recognise you?" He gestured to a place at his side. "You are welcome at our table," he said, "and your companions, also." And although there was courtesy in his tone, there was no sub-servience.

She took the seat indicated and sat quietly watching them, waiting, not moving, as deliberately still as she would have been if she was reassuring a nervous horse or dog, and after a time she felt a wary acceptance from them.

The eagle man said, "Will you drink a glass of wine with us, ma'am?" and Grainne saw a small badgerlike girl with a furry snout and soft dark eyes step forward and pour wine.

The wine, when she drank it, was very good, and she sipped it gratefully, feeling it set up a little core of warmth. And slowly, little by little, so gradually that she was hardly aware of it happening, she began to feel a kin with these creatures, and a sense of closeness. At her side, the eagle crea-ture said, very softly, "Do you not know yet who we are, ma'am?" and Grainne turned to look at him and said, "Tell me."

There was a pause; then, "We are the Royal Houses of Ireland," he said, and understanding flooded Grainne's mind.

These were the results of Humans mating with Beasts without the protection of the ancient Enchantment.

————

"THE ENCHANTMENT WAS lost," said the eagle man, who was called Raynor. "It was lost in the reign of your grandmother."

"Nobody knows how or why," said the badger girl who had served the wine.

"But enchantments do die," said a man with leather-pad paws and the features of a fox.

"But for the Beastline to die out," said Raynor, his eyes on her, "has been the most dangerous and the most terrible threat ever to touch Ireland. For without the Beastline to rule, Ireland will fall," he said, and Grainne remembered the old, old prophecy that if Tara should ever be possessed by the Humans, then the curse once directed at the first High Queen of all would revive, and the Bright Palace would crumble.

'And all Ireland will seethe with evil, and the skies will be crimson, and the doors will open to the terrible Forces of the Dark Ireland that forever waits . . .'

"Forgive me," said Grainne. "I did not know."

"Your grandmother kept the knowledge from all but the most trusted of her sorcerers," said Raynor, and now his eyes held compassion. Grainne remembered how she had marked the lack of subservience, and thought, But of course they are not subservient. They are the Ancient Bloodline, the Beastline that was once the nobility of Ireland. They are the Royal Enchanted Houses of Ireland, but with the enchantment revoked.

The rough magic abjured and the spell wound up . . . and all your darknesses and all your nightmares dragged protesting into the light . . .

"Dierdriu charged a particular group of sorcerers to work in secret to rediscover, or reweave, the lost spell," said Raynor. "We believe they are Tyrians, although we are not sure." He looked down the table. "But since then, those sorcerers have worked ceaselessly. We do not know if they have succeeded, and we do not know if they will ever succeed." A pause. "We are the results of their attempts, you see."

"We are the failures," said the fox man.

"We are failed spells," said the badger girl sadly, and Grainne stretched out a hand, because there was the dreadful animal tolerance and the patience again, and so wretched was it that she could hardly bear it.

"We are of the same blood as you," Raynor said steadily.

But you are whole and beautiful, and we are ugly and deformed . . . The words lay unspoken on the air, but Grainne thought that every person present in the sunken firelit hall heard them clearly.

Grainne said, "How long have you been here?"

"All our lives. We are brought here from the Sorcerers' Chambers immediately we are born."

"While we are helpless and blind," said the badger girl.

"And—looked after?" It was very nearly unbearable to think about the poor pitiful newborn creatures, defenceless and vulnerable, carried here by night, thrown into the dark fastness of this great castle.

"Yes," said the badger girl softly, "yes, we are well looked after, although it is not part of our beliefs that one person should work for another." The dark eyes surveyed Grainne. "The Cruithin look after us," she said. "It is the Cruithin who keep watch on the sorcerers' attempts to reweave the Lost Enchantment. It is the Cruithin who carry away the sorcerers' failures."

"Dierdriu knew that the Cruithin were the only people other than the Tyrians whom she could trust," said Raynor.

"That is why the Cruithin vanished. That is why they have never been seen in Ireland since Dierdriu's reign."

THE CRUITHIN AND the rescinded Bloodline. The proud loyal Cruithin, serving Ireland's noble houses, staunchly and in secret. Protecting them. Using their gentle pure magic to surround the Grail Castle so that no one could reach it.

But I reached it, thought Grainne. I reached it.

Because you were allowed to. Because you are the Wolfqueen, the last of your line, and for you the Cruithin withdrew the spells they had spun around these creatures.

These creatures ... There was an image, terrible, soul-searing, of the Cruithin, small-boned and fiercely loyal, carrying the poor unwanted things created by the sorcerers away from the prying eyes of the world. Hiding them and serving them, and summoning their own woodland spells to bind the Grail Castle with legend and myth, so that no one should ever discover its secret.

Grainne looked around and thought, These are my people as much as any creature in Ireland. They are *mine*, she thought fiercely, and I shall fight for them.

And when we drive out Medoc and the Dark Ireland, they must be with me.

IT WAS A strange meal they took together that night, Grainne and Tybion and Fintan and Cermait, along with the creatures of the Grail Castle.

"Like something from another world," said Fintan afterwards, but Cermait said it was as if they had been made free of a world that should not have been born. An unborn world, peopled with the creatures of a sorcerer's nightmare ...

They were made courteously welcome by the Beastline. "What we have is yours," the badger girl said, and the others nodded and brought chairs to the table and poured wine. The man with a fox's slanting mask and red-brown eyes brought in extra dishes of the food they had been eating: fresh lake fish with sorrel and wood parsley, and great platters of firm, crisp vegetables in some kind of sauce. There were wedges of warm fresh bread with the butter melting into them, and the honey cakes that Grainne remembered eating as a child. She smiled and ate everything they offered and watched carefully to see how they ate their own food, so that she might match them, for it was not to be thought of that the poor creatures should be made to feel themselves rough or uncouth.

But their manners were the ones that Grainne herself had

been taught as a child, and their attitudes were of wary consideration for the strangers in their midst.

Grainne knew a deep gratitude to Tybion, and to Fintan and Cermait, who had accepted the inhabitants of the castle naturally and tranquilly. Tybion had helped to hand round the plates for the fish, and Cermait had wanted to know about the wine they were drinking and asked was it their own brew, because it was one that he had not come across before. Fintan, who would have found something to say even had he been cast amongst thieves and murderers and child-eaters, fell into a discussion with a small stunted creature with the jaws of a hound about the precise route they had taken to get here.

At Grainne's side, Raynor said softly, "You perceive that we are a cultured breed, ma'am," and Grainne looked up sharply, because he had guessed her thoughts so exactly that for a moment she believed him to possess the Samhailt.

"I do not possess it," Raynor said. "The ancient gift of the first High Kings is not for such as we are."

"But—forgive me—you do not seem in the least bitter," said Grainne, and Raynor said at once, "We are very bitter, Your Majesty. But we have striven for . . ."

"Contentment?"

"Acceptance," said Raynor, and he smiled at her, a pure winged smile, and Grainne stared at him and was aware, all over again, of a strength and control within him. She thought, There is a fire that has been fiercely banked down inside him. Is it passion? Or hatred? Or something entirely different?

"I have achieved acceptance, Your Majesty," said Raynor, and turned to refill her glass.

Grainne sat sipping the wine, listening to the quiet conversation, and felt her mind tumbling and her pulses racing.

He is neither animal nor Human. He is a creature of the skies. And he is the malformed result of a sorcerer's search for an ancient, lost Enchantment. He has spent his life shut away in this dark castle.

And he has the face of a gentle hawk and his arms would be stronger than any Human arms, and he would have the sinews of a bird of prey, and once in his power it would be impossible to escape, only that you would not want to escape, because he would be powerful and strong and exciting . . .

And, thought Grainne, seated next to this strange disturbing creature, and I should like to feel about me those arms which are not quite arms and not quite wings, and I should like to feel myself sink against the skin that is not quite skin, and I should like to feel the hard narrow thighs pressing against me . . . Oh, Fergus, my one and only love, forgive me . . .

It did not then occur to her that the thin trickle of wolf blood had woken in her more strongly than it had ever done before, and that for her to be physically drawn towards another creature with half-Human–half-beast blood was no more than her inheritance. Her ancestors had been wild and amoral; they had lain with the Wolves, so that their issue should have the mixed magical blood . . .

If Raynor sensed Grainne's thoughts, he gave no sign. He continued to talk to her, quietly and courteously; telling her a little of the history of the Grail Castle, listening with deep interest to her own tales of Tara, the Shining Palace, which he might so easily have shared. He was gentle and attentive and rather remote.

When they rose from the table, he stood before her and said, "And will you come with us now, ma'am?"

"To the Cruithin?"

"Yes."

It was a strange experience to be taken in procession through the dark halls of the old castle to meet the people who some said were the first and only Irish race.

The Cruithin. The ancient kindred, who had once ruled Ireland, who had all of the gentle pure magic and the woodlore and the knowledge of the Old Ireland. They had been driven out and driven back many centuries ago; they had been sent underground by the greedy, land-hungry traders from the east who had coveted the blue and green misty Isle of the Northern Seas, and who had fought to possess it.

But they had returned with the first ascent of the Wolf-line. "To serve," they had said. "For it is the Wolfkings who will make Ireland truly great. It is the enchanted Wolfline that will bring our country to a Golden Age."

And when the Golden Age became threatened, when the Enchantment dimmed, they had again vanished, still serving but doing so quietly and unobtrusively now, going by night into the darkness of the Grail Castle, protecting the travesties created by the sorcerers in their attempts to reweave the lost spell.

Unswervingly loyal to the Wolfline still. Grainne felt her throat closing with emotion, and when Raynor said, "Are you ready, ma'am?" it was a moment before she could speak.

Without Fintan and Cermait and Tybion, she would have been uneasy walking openly through the castle. It was not that the passages were long and draughty—although they were. And it was not that the torches they carried flickered wildly and cast huge fantastical shadows everywhere—although they did. It was certainly not the presence of Raynor and the others.

There are pockets, thought Grainne, staring about her, deep and unexpected pockets of despair, and of sadness and pain. She thought that all manner of creatures had dwelled here, and she wanted to know about them, and in the same breathspace wanted to know nothing of them.

"But there is no evil here," Raynor said softly, and Grainne looked up. "Your heart flinched for a moment, ma'am," he said, and smiled, and Grainne stared, and knew a great wish to hear her name on his lips instead of her ti-tle . . . No. Oh, no, for it would be pain and torment and delight, and I must quench the thought. He is not for me, nor I for him, and that way surely lies heartache.

But when Raynor touched her arm to steer her across an especially uneven section of floor, delight ran all over her. Oh, no—quench the thought and douse the longing, for a thought, once formed, has too much reality, and a longing, once admitted to, has too much power.

The Cruithin were waiting in a small low-ceilinged chamber—Grainne thought it might be some kind of communal room where they might forgather and spend their evenings, and drink and talk and smoke their pipes. There was firelight here, also, but a different, stronger glow that cast shadows on the faces of the Cruithin. There was the warm woodsy scent of clay pipes, properly seasoned, and of clean wool, and apples roasting before the fire in autumn. An immense longing for the Old Ireland, the True Ireland, the Ireland of the Ancient Kindred and the Lost Enchantment of the Beastline, filled Grainne, and she wanted to fling wide her arms and embrace the lost land of her ancestors, and she wanted to summon every ounce of strength to conjure up and bring back all of the marvellous wild magic. For a moment, it was with her, that ancient misty land, where men had lain with beasts, and where beasts had sometimes walked upright like men. Where the magical eerie *sidh* and their King, the elven Aillen mac Midha, had served the Royal House, and where the courtiers of Tara had possessed three-cornered slant-eyed smiles that you would never quite trust.

And the Enchantment, the precious ancient Enchantment that had created and kept alive the mystical Beastline, was lost. If the sorcerers did not succeed, then the land of the Wolves would die, and the Dark Ireland would come flooding in, and Ireland, the real Ireland, would be lost.

She would not let it happen. Somehow, in some way, she would find the spell again, she would discover the lost magic and restore it to her people.

It had to be done. Standing at the centre of the grim terrible Grail Castle, with the secrets of countless ages, and with the sufferings of numberless exiles weighing on her heart, with these strange pitiful half humans, and with the Cruithin, Grainne knew it had to be done.

For Ireland.

And for Dierdriu, and for all the long-ago Wolfkings and Queens.

For Fergus, and for the Lost Prince, for Tara's heir, who had never existed, and who might never exist.

A slow sweet smile spread across her face as she looked at the Cruithin waiting for her and sensed, at her back, Fintan and Cermait and Tybion, with Raynor and the others close by.

These are my people.

Grainne held out her hands, and the Wolflight, muted and glowing and luminescent, and infinitely loving, shone from her eyes.

CHAPTER SIX

As FERGUS AND Taliesin and Fribble stepped across the threshold of the House of Calatin, the shadows receded.

"Empty," said Fribble, looking round. "That's interesting. Do you suppose we imagined that voice and those sounds?"

They looked about them. The light was draining, so that purple and grey shadows were stealing across the floor, and Taliesin thought he caught the faintest of movements, so that for a moment he could have believed that something *did* lurk there, something that was misshapen and shuffling, but that could melt and dissolve and change into something huge and rearing, with claws and talons and teeth . . .

"We should search the house before anything else," said Fergus, standing in the centre of the empty hall, and Taliesin heard with relief the incisive voice of the *Fiana*'s leader again. He's himself again, thought Taliesin. I think it will be all right. But he found that he was still listening for the cold beckoning music that might herald the Lad of the Skins . . .

Fergus had already started in the direction of the stair, and Taliesin and Fribble followed more slowly.

"The house is empty," said Fergus, but he sounded uncertain, and Taliesin, following more slowly, thought that the house was not empty at all; there was no one here, and yet they all knew there was someone here. They could feel it. Something very terrible has happened here, thought Taliesin. Do the others feel it? I believe Fergus does, just a little.

The corridors on the upper floors were long and winding, and there were unexpected mirrors set at odd angles, so that you rounded a corner and caught sight of yourself and jumped. And there were huge ornate bedchambers, richly furnished.

"Sorcery is a profitable business," observed Taliesin. "Almost as profitable as money lending."

"I thought you were all beggars and paupers," rejoined Fergus, and Taliesin eyed him, and thought, The sense of humour is back as well now. I believe we have somehow driven back whatever it was that was shadowing us through the forest. I believe that Fergus is safe. Aloud he said, "Money lending is only profitable because there has to be a reward for the way in which we are mocked and scorned, my friend. We make money purely as a revenge, I assure you.

"And that carpet is rather frayed, and if you do not watch your footing, you will fall down the stairway."

Fergus, leading them through the great shadowy house, thought that for all his assurances, they were certainly not alone. There was something here, watching them, perhaps grinning, rubbing its hands together, licking its lips . . .

Someone who served Crom Croich and Medoc, and who walked abroad with a dripping sack? Someone who prowled the world by night, and peered through latches and chinks in curtains, and stole away the first-born sons to offer up to its terrible Master . . .

Were the Conablaiche and the Lad of the Skins walking tonight?

Fergus found himself constantly looking over his shoulder, searching the shadows, listening for a soft footfall. At his side, Fribble said softly, "I believe we are approaching the heart of the house now."

"Yes," said Fergus. "Yes, I know." And looked at the other two. "The Chamber of the Looms," he said, and Taliesin looked back and saw, reflected in Fergus's eyes, the shared memory.

"I can hear the Looms now," Fergus said softly, his head tilted, his eyes brilliant. "Listen . . ." As they stood silently, each of them was aware of a low-pitched resonance, a steady thrumming. And then Fergus moved on again, and they rounded a gallery where several staircases ended, and there, ahead of them—

"The silver door," said Taliesin softly.

"The Chamber of the Looms," said Fergus, staring.

"And it's solid silver," added Fribble. "My word, that will have cost somebody a pretty penny."

Fergus approached the silver door cautiously and reached out to trace the carvings. The Tree of Amaranth, and the Nine Hazels of Wisdom. Writhing *sidh* creatures, and here and there the wolf emblem. Yes, almost exactly as those in the Tyrian sorcerers' house. It brought back sharply the strange exotic house and the bizarre pact he had made with Taliesin's people.

Taliesin said, "The Looms are not spinning now, I think?"

"I don't think they can be," said Fribble. "We should never stand it if they were," and Fergus and Taliesin both remembered how they had fallen back under the great gusts of solid heat below the Street of Money Lenders.

"It's all very interesting, isn't it?" said Fribble. He stepped forward and laid his hand against the massive silver door, and when he brought it away, the flesh was scarlet as if it had been dipped in boiling water. "*Very* interesting," he said. "I *am* glad I came." He eyed the door again. "I'd like to go in there," he said. "Wouldn't it make Dorrainge angry if I told him I'd seen a spell being spun? He wouldn't speak for a week, the fat fool."

Fergus said hesitantly, "They say there are ways of protecting oneself from the heat—" and Fribble turned round and said at once, "Oh, yes, I believe there are. But I've never seen it done, and it's quite dreadfully risky. I think we ought to finish our search, don't you? I'd like to see a spell being spun—well, who wouldn't—but they say that the power is so tremendous that it would burn out your eyes."

"A fate I think we ought to avoid," said Taliesin.

"Quite right," said Fribble. "For a Tyrian you show common sense. I told Fergus not to bring you," he said, as they retraced their steps, "but I'm glad you came now. I'm very glad you brought the wine as well."

"Will you have a drop more, sir?"

"That's very kind," said Fribble.

They continued to search the house, and now, in every room they looked into, a fire burned merrily in the hearth.

"The stoves are warm," said Fergus as they stood in the scullery. "And look at this."

"What is it?"

"The kettle is singing on the hob," said Fergus.

An empty house, where fires burned and stoves were warm, and where kettles hissed . . . In silence, they retraced their steps and passed beneath a great stone archway.

"The banqueting hall," said Fergus. "The only place we have not yet searched." But Taliesin thought that Fergus hesitated, and he certainly caught a ripple of uncertainty from him. Because Fergus sensed that there was something ahead of them that was waiting for Fergus alone? I am probably being absurd, thought Taliesin, but still the feeling that Fergus was listening and waiting for something persisted, and the fear that some kind of darkness had been cast over Fergus became more firmly entrenched.

The shadows clustered more thickly in the ancient banqueting hall, and the quiet was in some way different here. Hushed. Dead. A place outside of Time.

The long oak table was laid as if for a meal. There were great platters of fruit and cheese; a steaming tureen of some savoury soup; crocks of butter and wedges of newly baked bread, warm from the oven. In the huge silver tureen, the soup was steaming, as if it had just been taken off the stove . . .

As if, at any minute, the occupants of the house would return, or as if, at any minute, the figure at the far end would open its eye and sit up and start eating . . .

At the far end of the table, still and silent and unseeing, slept a massive figure.

As Fergus and Taliesin stood motionless, Fribble said, "Calatin, the Sorcerer."

"Is he—dead?" said Fergus.

"No," said Fribble, moving forward carefully. "No, he is not dead." He stood looking at the slumped silent shape, and something crept into his expression that sent fingers of ice down Fergus and Taliesin's spines.

"But I believe his soul is in pawn," said Fribble softly, and then, looking at them very straightly. "The Lad of the Skins was here before us.

"And he has stolen Calatin's soul and thrown it into the Prison of Hostages," said Fribble.

HE WAS IMMOVEABLE and cold and terrible and pitiable. The soulless one. The sleeping giant. Calatin, the sorcerer who had served the High Kings. His body slept and his soul was in pawn; he was unseeing and unhearing, and he slept the terrible sleep of all who lose their souls to the Lad of the Skins. As they moved cautiously closer, they could see that his skin had a cold, stony look to it, and that spiders had begun to spin webs between his fingers.

"And over his eye," said Fergus, shuddering.

Taliesin said, "The plates and bowls and cups are covered with dust, but it is a very thin sprinkling." He looked at them. "I do not think he can have lain like this for long."

Fribble said, "Dear me, this is very upsetting. It's something I never thought I'd see. A soulless giant. An undead sorcerer. He's very nearly a legend, you know. They're a very highly respected branch of the Amaranthines, Calatin and his Sons. He's been going for a good long time, even for a sorcerer. Since well before the present Queen. As far back as Dierdriu, so I believe. I suppose it would be discourteous if we sat down at the table, would it? Yes, I thought it might be. That's not to say we'd have any appetite if we did. Is there a drain of wine left? Do you know, it's made me feel quite ill to see the old boy like this, never mind making it difficult for you two, because offhand I can't think of another sorcerer who could summon Fael-Inis, can you, Fergus?"

Taliesin produced his flask and said cautiously, "Is he sleeping or—"

"Or dead? No, he isn't dead precisely," said Fribble, drinking the wine gratefully. "I don't know what you call it, only that it's a perpetual sleep, and he can't be woken."

"Only by the forfeiting of another soul in exchange," said Fergus in a rather odd voice, and Taliesin looked at him sharply. But Fergus only said, "I wonder what happened?"

"Well, the Lad of the Skins got into the house," said Fribble. "I do think we can be sure about that. And of course, once you've let *him* into your house, it's very nearly a foregone conclusion. You lose your soul and your body goes into what they call a petrified state. Like trees. And I believe," said Fribble, thoughtfully, "I believe you have to be very careful over the body, as well, because the soul can still feel pain. You can't spill hot soup on it or tread on one of its toes, or drop anything heavy on it, because the soul would feel it. Dear me, and Calatin was one of Dierdriu's favourite sorcerers. Very able. They say he taught everything he knew to his Sons, but they aren't thought much of, so I understand."

Fergus said, "I wonder where the Sons are? Because the fires were all burning, and there was a kettle on the hob." He indicated the twenty-seven chairs pulled up to the table.

"You'd think they couldn't be far, wouldn't you?" agreed Fribble. "But they aren't in the house, because we've searched everywhere. And you couldn't exactly lose twenty-seven giants, not even if they were smallish ones."

"We ought to try to find them," said Taliesin. "Because even if they aren't thought much of—"

"Yes, you've got to call up Fael-Inis's Chariot somehow," said Fribble. "And the Sons *might* be able to help, of course."

Fergus said, "There is one place we have not looked."

"Yes?"

"The Chamber of the Looms," said Fergus.

THE CHAMBER OF the Looms. The sorcerers' workroom. The great dark room that lay at the heart of this ancient mansion, where Silver Looms hummed and spun, and where the enchantments and the spells and the curses and the bewitchments of the world were harnessed. They would have to go into that chamber where the heat would be so fierce it could burn out their eyes and shrivel their skin, and where the power would be so tremendous that it would scald their minds. Fergus and Taliesin, who had glimpsed the power and the relentless force of the Silver Looms with the Tyrian sorcerers, stared at one another.

"But we have to find the Sons," said Fergus doggedly. "Somehow, we have to summon Fael-Inis and the Time Chariot."

Somehow we have to travel to the Far Future and turn back the Four Heralds ... No one said the words, but a sudden silence fell on them.

They retraced their steps, to the great galleried landing at the centre of the house, and stood looking at the massive carved silver door.

Fergus said, "Fribble—you said there were ways—"

"Yes, there are ways to protect yourself," said Fribble thoughtfully. "But I've never seen any of them actually working, you understand." He went on studying the silver door, and then, with the air of one who has made up his mind, said in a matter-of-fact way, "It's probably all a myth, but I suppose we could try the Ice Cauldron.

"Didn't you know about all that?" he said. "Dear me, didn't you? I don't know what they teach people nowadays. Of course, it isn't very widely known. That would account for it. I don't know if it would work, either."

Fergus said, "But what is the Ice Cauldron?" and Fribble, who had been examining the silver door and tracing the carvings with one hand, turned round and said, "Well, it's rather difficult to explain. And we haven't much time."

"Try us," said Taliesin.

"But don't take too long about it," said Fergus.

Fribble sat down on the floor. He looked oddly comfortable and entirely composed, and both Taliesin and Fergus remembered, with guilty surprise, that Fribble, after all, was Chief Druid of all Ireland.

"There's a group of people somewhere in the east with some very curious beliefs. It's no good asking me where they're from, because I've forgotten, if I ever knew, which I probably didn't. But they're quite learned. They have begun to follow a belief and a teaching that they call Dualism. Two worlds, you see. Light and darkness. Good and evil. Quite sensible if you think about it," said Fribble. "If you pursue the belief a little further, you have to admit that for every good act there is a corresponding evil one; for every sliver of light in the world, there is a sliver of darkness. We know that night follows day, or perhaps it's the other way around, I forget.

"If you accept that every single thing has its opposite, you begin to accept the belief that a thing cannot have an existence without that opposite. Good cannot exist unless there is evil, and evil cannot be defeated unless there is good. You can't ever rout evil, of course," said Fribble seriously, "because so far as we know, good and evil are both pretty much equal. That's another story. You don't want me to start telling you about the two Great Masters, one on the side of darkness, the other on the side of light, fighting their eternal battle. No, I thought you didn't. But it is there. Disbelief in something does not kill its existence.

"Hunger and thirst have their counterparts and their vanquishers. By eating, we can defeat hunger for a time, and by drinking we can defeat thirst. But the one must be dependent on the other. You see? It's all quite simple and sensible and easy to understand.

"By applying cold water or ice to a fire, we defeat the fire. If we could walk into the heat and the power of that room behind the silver door, somehow protected by cold water or ice, I don't suppose the heat would hurt us at all."

Taliesin said slowly, "But the heat is not a tangible heat, Fribble. It is invisible."

"Yes, that's the point," said Fribble, getting up and dusting his robes down. He looked at them. "You defeat an invisible force with another invisible force," said Fribble. "You fight the heat with something of your own. You *imagine* the ice," said Fribble, and he beamed at them . . .

IMAGINE THE ICE. The three of them sat together—"Cross-legged," said Fribble, "because it distributes the body's weight evenly. That's important, because it frees your mind."

They linked hands. "For strength," said Fribble.

And they closed their eyes. "Uncomfortable," said Fergus, who was wary of sitting in a great dark mansion with evil all around and his eyes closed against it.

"You must do it," said Fribble severely. "And now you must conjure up the Ice Cauldron in your minds. Think of it so hard that it appears to you. A great, ice-cold cauldron. Steamy with cold and white with frostiness. Great ice lumps floating on the surface. Fathom upon fathom of cold, cold water, blue and silver and glacial. Everything you can think of that is icy cold. Frozen mountainsides and iced-over lakes. Snow and frost. White on white."

Slowly, almost imperceptibly, a chill crept over the three travellers. Fergus thought, and then was sure, that Taliesin's hand on his left and Fribble's on his right had grown noticeably cooler.

The Ice Cauldron. Think of it. See it. Feel it. Feel the coldness burn your skin, and remember that there is nothing to be compared with the pain of an ice burn. He drew in a great breath and felt it tear his lungs.

Yes. Cold on cold. Ice mountains and glaciers and the dark frozen wastes of the Northern Seas.

At his side, Fribble stood up slowly and carefully, and

Fergus felt Taliesin follow suit. There was a moment of panic—*I am not ready!*—and then he was following them to the silver door, and the door was swinging open at Fribble's touch, and the Chamber of the Sorcerers stood before them.

THE HEAT WAS like a solid wall. They flinched, and then—*the Ice Cauldron!* said Taliesin silently, and they picked up his thought and took strength. Ice on ice. Every cold thing you have ever known, every freezing dawn you have ever woken to.

The chamber was dark and immense. It was the most gigantic room any of them had ever seen. The ceiling stretched far above them and the floor seemed to fall away. The air was thick and heavy with heat and the smell of warmth, and there was a sizzling feel to the air, and a dryness. Ice on ice, thought Fergus, striving for calmness. Glaciers and frozen wastes.

For a moment, he could almost see the Ice Cauldron—huge and black, but rimmed with the heavy hoar frost that you would see on the skeletons of trees in the depths of winter. Solid lakes that you could walk across. Confidence surged up in him, and he thought, We can do it! Of course we can!

The silver door had opened halfway up the wall of the chamber, and they were standing on some kind of platform with steps that led down.

"And down and down," thought Taliesin, staring, and remembered, and wished not to remember, the echoes.

Down, down to Hell and say I sent thee thither . . . for there awaits the fiery gulf . . .

Down into the bowels of hell . . .

The fiery gulf. The gaping chasm of fire and the huge furnaces of flames belching out heat, so that your eyes will burn and your skin will shrivel, and the blood will boil and burst your veins . . .

But remember the Ice Cauldron . . .

Fergus, his mind tumbling, his skin already flinching from the heat of the Looms, thought it was like every nightmare he had ever experienced.

Heat and darkness, and a great heavy stifling weight all about them. There was the dull thrumming of vast machinery all about, and there was the red glow of heat everywhere.

But remember the Ice Cauldron, and remember the frozen dawn of every winter morning . . .

Stretching away before them were the great silver Looms, the spinners of spells, the weavers of enchantments. The power and the force and the might of the sorcerers.

Great rearing edifices towered above them, and had their feet in the depths of the earth. Immense and powerful and awe-inspiring. Ceaselessly weaving and eternally spinning. Forever alive with the power they harnessed for the sorcerers.

There were roads between the Looms, little pathways, and at intervals, there were shelves full of ancient vellum books.

"The sorcerers' library," whispered Fribble, and Taliesin and Fergus nodded.

As they moved nearer to the Looms, they could see great tumbles and piles of raw spells heaped about the Looms' feet.

"Raw bewitchments," whispered Fribble. "We are seeing something that very few Humans ever see."

The nascent magic of the sorcerers. Unborn spells and formless bewitchments. Living colours and breathing scents and great rainbow swathes of shifting light.

The raw spells were lying in silken heaps, as if they had been taken from cartons like bales of material, and flung down by the nearest Loom until they should be wanted. There were huge spindle-like shapes as well, wound with skeins of glinting iridescence that caught the light and sent rainbow colours cascading everywhere. Fergus put up his hand again, but the other two knew that this time it was to shield his eyes from the pure brilliance of the unborn spells. Taliesin, who had seen the bazaars of the Tyrian silksmiths and the robemakers in the Eastern quarter where the money lenders lived, thought that the substances resembled rich, unfashioned garments, and then that they were more like unhewn gems.

"But there are visions within them," said Fergus very softly at his side, and Taliesin looked sharply at Fergus, and saw that Fergus was staring into the depths of the formless matter that were embryonic spells, and that his eyes had an unfocussed far-away look, rather as a cat will look when staring into the leaping flames of a fire. "There are worlds within them," said Fergus, and Taliesin, who had also glimpsed the worlds, and who had seen great rivers of flame and pouring cascades of molten colour, and felt his eyes becoming dry and harsh, took Fergus's hand and felt it growing hot.

"Fergus, remember the Ice Cauldron," he said, and summoned up every shred of the ancient powerful Samhailt, and closed his eyes, and concentrated on throwing about Fergus the carapace of coldness and hard-packed ice. On Fergus's other side, he was aware of Fribble taking Fergus's arm, and saying calmly, "Ice on ice . . . frozen dawns . . . snow and sleet and solid lakes and rivers . . ." And then Fergus's skin grew cooler and Taliesin withdrew the images and saw Fergus grin, rather waveringly.

They moved warily on, searching the shadows, and Taliesin thought that every one of them could feel the Ice Cauldron all about them now, like solid armour. Fergus said, in quite an ordinary voice, "I suppose we *do* want to find the Sons, do we?"

"Beard the sorcerers in their lair?" said Taliesin with a lightness he was not feeling. "I admit, Fergus, that it takes extraordinary courage to do that. And when the sorcerers are also giants, and when there are twenty-seven of them . . ."

He stopped, and felt Fergus's hand come down on his arm, and saw Fribble pause.

Sounds. Dreadful sounds. The sounds of a creature feeding. Sucking, guzzling, chewing . . . a beast, a monster taking in sustenance . . .

As they rounded a corner, they all heard the terrible low chuckling that Taliesin had heard earlier, and there was a sudden movement in the shadows ahead of them, and then the sound of huge leathery wings beating on the air. For a moment, the chamber darkened, and they thought that something reared up and flew over their heads.

There was a harsh, cawing sound, and there was a stench of rotting meat and bad fish and old blood.

Fribble said loudly, "All join hands. *And whatever you do, remember the Ice Cauldron.*"

But in each of their minds now, was the thought, Have we been lured here to be killed? Are we about to meet the Conablaiche and the Lad of the Skins?

And then the path widened, and they caught again the stench of blood and rotting flesh, and saw what lay ahead.

Neatly laid out, every one of them. Sightless eyes turned upwards, skin cold and waxen.

Every single one had been ripped open, so that their entrails spilled out, glistening wetly in the light. There were glimpses of lungs and liver; here and there the purple-veined sacs of stomach and bladder; the red stringiness of muscle . . . giants' blood, giants' marrow, and viscera . . . kidneys and bowels and skin.

The twenty-seven Sons of Calatin, butchered by the Conablaiche and their beating hearts torn from their bodies.

Giants' hearts for Crom Croich . . .

The stench of blood was in their nostrils, and there could not be the smallest doubt that it had been the Conablaiche who had torn open the Sons of Calatin and left their ruptured bodies lying on the floor, like badly cured meat . . .

There was nothing they could do for the Sons. "But we can cover them," said Fribble, who took death calmly, and they found some pieces of sacking and threw them over the bodies. Fergus and Taliesin hoped they would be able to forget the slimy trails of blood that ran from beneath the sacking, and they would certainly be able to forget the sight of the not-quite-colourless liquid that stained the sacking.

Taliesin stood up and wondered whether he would ever be able to get the taste and the smell out of his mouth, and as he did so, Fergus took his arm in a sudden grip, and said, "Look."

"Where?" Taliesin, his mind still raw from the sight of the Sons' bodies, took a deep breath and prepared to meet whatever else might be in store for them. "What is it?" Fergus was standing very still, pointing at something that lay very close to the Sons' bodies.

Something that was nearly, but not quite, formed into the outline of soaring wings, and that was fashioned from some substance that was nearly, but not quite, gold.

Something that was molten gold and incandescent flame, that held within its depths slanting wildfire eyes and the whirling brilliance of a creature who could travel at immense speed . . .

"What is it?" said Taliesin again, and Fribble, who was staring intently at the half-formed shape, said, "Bless my soul, I believe it's the spell to summon Fael-Inis."

"Can we touch it?" said Taliesin, and Fribble started to say, "I don't think—" when Fergus bent down and scooped up the beautiful strange thing that was the incomplete spell.

Iridescence whirled, and there was the blinding flash of skeins of colour fusing into a dazzling kaleidoscopic mesh.

The rushing sound of chariot wheels mingled with music poured through the house.

Fael-Inis.

FERGUS AND TALIESIN were never afterwards aware of having moved out of the Chamber of Looms. Fergus had the impression of the immense Silver Door swinging open before them, and of the fierce heat suddenly fading, and Taliesin was aware of moving between the other two. And I believe that Fergus has laid down the spell, he thought vaguely.

The sounds of the Chariot drew them irresistibly down to the great square hall, and they could see that the shadows had crept back into the corners, as if they were being forced there by strong pure light.

Strong pure light ... And it is coming towards us, thought Fergus. It is coming through the forest towards us.

Fael-Inis, the rebel angel, the nearly immortal being who could travel through and across and beyond Time, was answering the summons.

There was a moment, terrible, never to be forgotten, when they waited, fearing the Chariot would not stop. Fergus thought that if that happened, they would not know how to bear it, for he knew that all the stories told of how Fael-Inis was a wild, elusive, fly-by-night creature. The spell, half-formed as it had been, might not be strong enough, and if it failed, there would be no second chance.

The music was coming steadily nearer, it was reaching out to them, and so sweet was it, so brimful of a beckoning and a potency, that they stood still and let it wash over them, and in each, a deep inner chord was touched.

For Fribble, it was a simple matter of peace and tranquillity, and the freedom to return to the Tara of the Wolf-line, and to read and study and teach.

For Taliesin it was freedom also, but a very different and a much more complex freedom. He felt the music engulf him, and he felt the boredoms and the dissatisfactions slough away, and he saw, more clearly than he had ever seen before, that all that was needed to break from the narrow Tyrian world of money that must earn more money, and of clients that must be appeased, was the courage to do it. As simple as that. And I was already branded by the Elders as a rebel. He stayed quietly where he was, but he could still feel the strong beautiful music coursing through him, and he could feel the courage and the strength and the awakening. *And after all this, how could I ever return to the Street of Money Lenders?*

As for Fergus, he felt his heartbeats slow to a warm sensuous joy, and desire stirred within his mind, so that the dark hall blurred. Six years dissolved, and he was back in that misty dawn in the woodlands surrounding Tara, and Grainne was running to meet him, her eyes on fire with love and longing, her hands outstretched towards him. He thought, Oh, yes, my lady, my love, this is all of it for you, all I am doing and all I am about to do, it is all of it for you, and there will never be another.

She is not for me, nor I for her. But I can give her back her kingdom. I can give her back Ireland.

The Chariot was coming directly towards the house now, and they could see the golden glow and the tongues of flame.

And the creatures drawing the Chariot, thought Fergus, staring through the deep windows that framed the door, his eyes adjusting to the darkness. Six—or is it eight? Or more? He narrowed his eyes, and thought he could just discern the beasts' shapes now. Strange, half-formed creatures, with arched necks, and patrician faces and glossy flanks. Like light made liquid. Like melting rainbows. He had the fancy that if he reached out to touch them, his hand would sink through them. For they have no substance, and no reality; they are like the unfashioned spells, they are creatures of dreams and legends . . . . He remembered the legends of the Fire Mountains, and of the beasts of fire and light and speed, who possessed the ability to travel at such immense speeds that Time ceased to matter.

For if you have the power and the light, you can cheat Time . . .

The Chariot was outside the house now, and there was a warm sweet fragrance and a sensual stirring. Fergus and Taliesin both thought that the trees sighed and murmured, and the grass whispered, and all about them was an awareness, a feeling that something tremendous was about to happen.

And then the door opened, softly and easily, and he was there, framed against the dark forest, golden and glowing, bathed in radiance, more beautiful than anything they had ever seen, more alien than anything they had ever encountered.

Fael-Inis—the rebel angel—the strange, wild, defiant creature who had turned his back on the grim and terrible battle at the beginning of the world, when the heavens had been rent asunder and a brilliant overreaching angel had mutinied and been cast out . . . Lucifer, Son of the Morning, summoning his followers and leading the First Great Rebellion of Heaven, but failing to gain his victory, certainly failing to master Fael-Inis, the creature of fire and speed.

He was smaller than they had expected, and slender and fine-boned. But there was an immense power and a great strength, and there was an arrogance as well. Taliesin, his eyes never leaving Fael-Inis's face, thought, A prince among princes. He is imperious and mischievous and exotic. I believe he has defied everything there is to defy, thought Taliesin. He saw the Beginning, the Creation, and he is the one who declined to play a part in Lucifer's Fall. Dare we trust him? thought Taliesin.

Fael-Inis was studying them, wholly at ease, leaning against the door post, arms folded, head on one side. His skin was translucent and golden, and his hair was red-gold, tumbling about his narrow skull like silk. But his eyes— Oh, yes, it is in his eyes, thought Taliesin.

The eyes had it. Slanting and molten and all-seeing. Impossible ever to think him Human once you had seen his eyes.

Fael-Inis said, "Well, Mortals?" and his voice was as soft and as golden as the rest of him. "You called to me. I am here." He moved nearer, and studied them, and a smile lifted his face, and it was a smile that said, And now let us take the world by the ears and turn it upside down. Let us challenge the gods, and take what we will. The rebel angel . . .

Taliesin said warily, "We welcome you," and the grin widened. "Can you help us?"

At once Fael-Inis replied, "Yes, I can help you. But there will be a price, you know." He looked at them thoughtfully. "It is always as well to know the price." The smile slid out again, tip-tilted and beckoning. "But I can help you, Mortals. I can take you on the fire tongues of Time into the Far Future, and there we will defy the Apocalypse and turn back the Four Horsemen." He grinned, and Fergus thought, He is enjoying this, and Fael-Inis looked at Fergus, and said, "But of course I am enjoying it." He smiled gently, and said, "You will have to trust me, of course," and moved closer. "Will you do it, Mortals? Will you risk your lives and your minds and your souls to ride with me in the Time Chariot? You will have to pledge to me your sanity, and perhaps your lives to come. Will you do that, Mortals, for it is certain that you have other lives still to live?"

The quality of his smile changed, and he held out his hands to them, and suddenly the mischief was gone, and he seemed younger and more honest and very strong. "I will take you," he said, "for there is a mission to fulfill. But first we will talk together, and before that we will eat."

He led the way to the sculleries as naturally and as familiarly as if he had been doing such things for years. "For I am substantial and I can feel hunger and pain and passion and anguish," he said. "And I am extraordinarily hungry tonight." He moved about the stone-flagged scullery, peering into cupboards and pantries, selecting plates and cups. "I am the rebel from the seraphic hierarchy," he said, looking at them from the corners of his eyes, "but I am sometimes very Human indeed. We shall eat a huge supper together, and certainly we shall drink wine, for without wine there is no feast."

Fribble, who had been investigating the contents of an immense bread bin, turned round at this and beamed, and said, "I am very glad to hear you say that, sir," and Fael-Inis smiled at Fribble, and said, "But wine is the water of life. Wine and music are as necessary to life as food and water. In some cultures, I am known as a god of music and wine and love."

He looked at them, his head tilted, and Taliesin said softly, "Pan. The shepherd god," and Fael-Inis turned rather sharply and something very different crept into his eyes. But he only said, "I have many names, and many guises."

"Can we trust you?" said Taliesin, and Fael-Inis said, "Yes, for today you can trust me."

"You know what is ahead," said Taliesin.

"Yes, I know. 'Plague, War, Famine, and Death . . . they shall stalk the earth, and after their coming, the Beast Apocalypse shall ride into the world . . .' Perhaps we can turn them back, and perhaps we can not. But we will try." He studied them. "Your descendants will burn the world and destroy civilization unless we can stop them," he said, and then his face softened. "But they should not be wholly blamed," he said, and standing in the cold scullery, he said a curious thing.

"They should not be blamed, for it is the sins of their fathers that are visited on them."

A sudden coldness washed over the three travellers, and Fael-Inis, watching them, said softly, "You see? Each of us is responsible in some measure for events. Your sins will echo down the corridors of Time, and it may be that your descendants will be destroyed as a result. It is not fair," he said gently. "But who said that life was intended to be fair?"

Fergus said slowly, "But surely we did all we could . . ."

"There is always a little more that each of us can give," said Fael-Inis. "We can always take ourselves a little further than we realise."

"That is sometimes very hard," said Taliesin.

"Who told you that life was intended to be easy?" said Fael-Inis, and smiled suddenly, and returned to his task of slicing the beef. "The first Herald is already in the Far Future," he said. "Plague. The people go in constant fear and try to protect themselves by having little contact with one another." He reached for another knife and tested its sharpness thoughtfully. "In some measure they are to blame," he said, "for the Conablaiche, in its guise of the Conail, could not have sowed such evil if the soil had not been fertile." He raised his eyes. "Medoc has let it be thought that the Conablaiche rode the Time Chariot, and escaped into the Future at my hands," said Fael-Inis, and grinned suddenly. "Medoc will pay heavily for that one," he said, and the three travellers instantly felt a deep trust and an immense confidence. It will be all right. We shall succeed.

Fergus said carefully, "Do you know anything of the Far Future?" and Fael-Inis regarded him.

"The world of the Future, the world we shall travel to, has seen the greatest and the most remarkable sexual freedom ever known," he said. "Your descendants observed no restraints. They took their pleasure where they would and with whom they wished. Men with men, frequently. Women with women. The gratification of their lusts has become the meaning of their existence." The eyes became mischievous. "The gratification of the senses is a thing of delight," said the rebel angel. "But the people of the Far Future took it far beyond that. Now they dare not lie with anyone lest they contract a terrible and incurable disease."

"That is the Plague?" said Fergus hesitantly.

"They do not call it Plague. They have another name for it. But it *is* Plague all the same. And it is deadly."

Taliesin said, "What of the Second Herald? Famine?"

"Famine is nearly there, even as we speak. The world we shall go to is overcrowded. There is no longer sufficient food." He looked at them. "The poorer countries suffer terrible privations. Children die for want of a sip of water, or a mouthful of bread." He turned back to the supper they were preparing. "To the children of the Future, this would be a feast beyond their wildest imaginings," he said. And then his mood shifted yet again, and the golden light danced in his eyes. "Did we find the wine?" said the rebel angel. "Oh, good. Shall we go up to the banqueting hall? The chairs will be a bit large, but we shall be able to make ourselves reasonably comfortable."

CHAPTER SEVEN

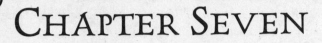

THEY ATE IN the banqueting hall at the farthest end of the table from the motionless Calatin.

"He cannot hear us, of course," said Fael-Inis. "His body sleeps the sleep of all whose souls are held captive inside the Prison of Hostages."

Fergus said, "Has anyone ever returned from the Prison of Hostages?" and Fael-Inis regarded him thoughtfully.

"It can be done," he said evasively. "But a very high price has to be paid."

"A soul for a soul," said Taliesin softly, and Fael-Inis turned his strange inhuman eyes onto him.

"You have understanding," he said at length. "Yes, that is the immutable law. Measure for measure. Have we honey in that dish? Thank you."

Fergus said, "But—would anyone offer his own soul to free another?"

"Would you?" said Fael-Inis with one of his direct looks, and Fergus, thinking of the terrible finality of the Prison of Hostages, said, "No. No I suppose I would not."

"You have to love someone very greatly and very selflessly to make such a sacrifice," said Fael-Inis, and Taliesin looked up, because there had been something unexpectedly gentle in Fael-Inis's tone. But Fael-Inis was concentrating on spreading honey onto a wedge of bread, and seemed not to notice.

"What must we do to travel with you?" asked Taliesin, and for a moment Fael-Inis did not reply: Then, "I cannot take you with me without the sorcerers' help," he said.

"But—"

"I cannot," he said. "You are Mortal, and you would die in the Time Fire. It is white hot. It is so fiery that you would shrivel instantly. The heat you encountered inside the Chamber of Looms is as nothing compared to the heat of the Time Fire."

"Then—"

"You must be given the sorcerers' protection," he said. "It is a spell which Calatin will know."

"But Calatin is lost to us," said Fergus.

"Is he?"

"Well, his soul is in pawn."

"That is rather different."

"And the Sons are all dead."

"Yes."

"Butchered by the Conablaiche."

"The Conablaiche takes what it will. It will have offered their hearts to Crom Croich, and Crom Croich will be surfeited. For the moment, that is," said Fael-Inis, "for he is a greedy god, Crom Croich, and he will soon require more."

"The slaughter of the first-born boys," said Fergus slowly.

"Yes," said Fael-Inis, eyeing Fergus again. "Medoc will revive that, for it fits well with his fear of the Wolfprince, whose birth has been prophesied. He will send the Conablaiche to kill every male child in Ireland," said Fael-Inis, "for he believes that in that way, he will kill the child who will one day rise up to challenge him."

"But," said Fergus, leaning forward, his eyes absorbed, "surely that is just a legend?"

"Is it?" said Fael-Inis.

"Well, it's a very old story at any rate," said Fergus.

"*Is* it?" said Fael-Inis, the golden eyes glowing and piercing, so that Fergus felt as if Fael-Inis was seeing into his mind.

Fribble, who had been eating his supper with industrious pleasure, said, "I never heard that story until lately, you know. The lost Wolfprince—dear me, there's a very evocative ring to it, don't you think? And, of course, Medoc would be sure to know if there was such a child in Ireland. He has his sources," said Fribble. "Well, don't we all. But Medoc's servants are nasty creatures. I daresay he's used the Guardians more than once," he added, eating cheese with composure.

Taliesin said, "But no such child has been born—" and Fael-Inis grinned at him.

"For all your surface cynicism, you are very innocent," he said. "Have you never heard of bastard lines? Of children born and hidden away? Medoc believes that a child exists somewhere in secrecy, and that it possesses the ancient wolf-blood."

Fribble, still eating his cheese, said, "And the legend has never said a *legitimate* child."

"I should like to believe the legend," said Fergus slowly. "But I don't think I can, you know."

"No?" said Fael-Inis. "And yet six years ago the music of the *sidh* was heard in Ireland again, Fergus."

The *sidh*, the strange, cold, faery race, who would steal up to the gates of Tara and sing the Wolfline into the world . . .

"But," said Fael-Inis, "for the moment we are concerned with the Conablaiche, and with turning back the First Herald. Plague . . . Calatin will be able to weave the spell that will protect you from the fire of the Time Chariot."

"You are saying we must wake Calatin?" said Taliesin.

"Yes." Fael-Inis continued to eat his supper. "He is not dead," he said and smiled at them.

"But to wake Calatin," said Fergus, "then a soul must be given in return."

"Yes," said Fael-Inis, and it seemed to Taliesin that he watched Fergus very intently now. "The supreme sacrifice," he said softly. "One of you must be prepared to lose his soul in exchange for that of Calatin.

"And since the only one who can cage a Mortal soul and carry it to the Prison of Hostages is the Lad of the Skins, we must call him up." He stood up and light streamed from him.

Taliesin had not thought it would be possible for the

darkness surrounding the House to deepen, but it deepened in those minutes after Fael-Inis made his pronouncement. He knew that the darkness had not really changed, that it was because of the strength of the light within, and that it was because of Fael-Inis's radiance.

The brightest of all the angels before the Fall ... Son of the Morning ... But no, that had been that other one, the wicked, overreaching Lucifer. Yes, but this creature would have known him, this one had been there, he had seen the Creation and the Fall ... Do I believe any of this? wondered Taliesin. How does any of this square with the teachings of my own people? And he thought that it did square, that there was a common root, a matrix of beliefs. Even so—are we being manipulated? he thought. And then, *Are we being bewitched?*

Fael-Inis caught the thought at once, of course, and the slanting eyes rested on Taliesin with amusement. "You have an enquiring mind, Mortal," he said. "But you may be at ease. I *was* there, and I *did* see, and were I to tell you, your Mortal mind could not comprehend." Suddenly he looked remote, and there was an aching sadness about him. "It was all lost to us," he said, half to himself. "All of the beauty and all of the love. We might have had it all, had it not been for that One."

That One ... the Shining One ... the Son of Aurora ... Lucifer the Light-Bringer ...

"He is destruction and decay and despair," said Fael-Inis. "He is corrupt and evil beyond belief. He has many servants in the world, and the Dark Lord Medoc is one of them." He looked at them. "But you knew that," he said.

"I saw the Fall," said Fael-Inis, his eyes distant. "But I did not declare for the Light-Bringer, and I have never done so since. You may trust me, Mortals."

I am what I am ...

"And if you are being bewitched," said Fael-Inis, "and if you are being manipulated, then it is only so that we may save the world."

*For the Four Horsemen are waiting, and already the First
has gone into the Future . . . There is no time to lose . . .*

Fribble, whose eyes were bright and whose whole bearing was alert, wanted to know what they had to do. "It's all
very interesting," he confessed. "I've never seen the Lad of
the Skins . . . well, I never wanted to. I don't suppose anyone
really wants to see him, do they? Will he come? I expect I
ought to take notes, because the other Druids will like to
know all this. The fat fool will never get over it. I'm very
glad I came," said Fribble, and accepted a glass of the wine
that Taliesin poured. "And I'll say this for you," he said, "I
didn't want to bring you. I knew how it would be. A Tyrian,
I said. Dear me, *that's* not such a good idea. But it's turning
out remarkably well." He beamed and drank his wine.

Taliesin said almost automatically, "Wine is as the breath
of life, Fribble," and raised his own glass in salutation. And
then, looking at Fael-Inis, "Will the Lad come?" he said, and
Fael-Inis said, "Oh yes. Oh yes, he will come. He fears me
a little, but neither can he resist me, and he will certainly
come when I call. We have had many battles, he and I, and
many confrontations. We are old enemies. But I have always
defeated him. That is why he will come."

"To try for victory?" said Fergus, and Fael-Inis said,
"Yes, of course. He believes that one day he will prove to
be the stronger, and for that reason, if for no other, he will
never resist when I call to him. He will come," said Fael-
Inis, looking round the table. "But when he does, you must
be ready for what will happen."

"What will happen?" asked Taliesin.

"That is up to you," said Fael-Inis, and without warning
his eyes grew remote and fiery; they became inward-looking,
and slanted more strongly than before. Light streamed from
him, and his hair became a golden aureole about his narrow
skull.

They saw that between his fingers he held a slender, intricately carved set of silver pipes and, as they waited, he
lifted the silver pipes to his lips and began to play.

IN ALL OF the stories of enchantment and in all of the legends of bewitchment, there is one that stands above the rest. A persistent, recurrent theme; a single strand of ancient lore in the weave.

The beckoning of enchanted music. The allure of pipes, of a lute, of a lyre, a flute. Pan, seated on his grassy bank, leading the naiads and the dryads where he will. Orpheus, using a lyre to charm the denizens of hell into giving him back his lady.

And others. Sinister stories. The Black Man of Saxony, playing grisly tunes so that the children would follow him to his terrible mountain lair, there to be given up to the Man of the Mountains. Ireland's own counterpart: the Old Woman of the Mountains, who lures children into her warm firelit cave to weave their skin and flesh and hair and nails into her dreadful cloth.

The Macaber, the hooded, skeletal apparition, coming down from the Black Tower to dance amongst the plague-ridden townships of the Middle Ages, leading them in the dread *danse macabre*, forcing them to dance with him until they dropped . . . Shoes that must obey the call of the music and dance on and on until their wearer fell from exhaustion.

And perhaps the best-known of them all: the apparently harmless street musician who came to a little township called Hamelin, and agreed to rid the town of rats by means of his music . . .

The travellers knew some of the stories, for Tara had met many Time Travellers, and the tales had echoed back. What they did not know, they could imagine. The music of allure. Enchanted music. Cold and inexorable and wholly irresistible. As Fael-Inis began to play, each of them drew a deep breath and surrendered, and each of them experienced the deepest contentment at hearing the silver pipes of enchantment.

Fael-Inis was seated against the window, his whole outline bathed in light, his hair liquid gold, his eyes burning slits of topaz. His fingers closed about the pipes and they were translucent, as if the substance that ran in his veins might be light instead of blood.

The music was like a gentle bewitchment; it spun tiny filaments of delight, brittle and cold and cobweb fine. You could not be afraid of it, you could not possibly fear something so delicate and so insubstantial.

They could not have told when the music tightened its hold and began its pull, but to Taliesin, afterwards, it was as if there was a moment when he knew that he was able to resist, and then another moment when he had surrendered completely.

Taliesin thought there were voices inside the music now . . . *Follow me, for I can give you beauty and I can give you joy, and all the delights and all the pleasures of the world . . . Follow me, for I am the core and the centre, and there is nothing now but the music . . .*

There was a moment when Taliesin was able to stand back and think, We are being bewitched. And then he felt the music's pull again, and thought that hadn't they summoned Fael-Inis to help them, and wasn't it sensible to obey him? And a man might die and count himself honoured for music so sweet . . . Any man, any creature, might be pardoned for answering the music's lure . . .

Any creature . . .

Through the dark forest, along the narrow woodland path, came the sound of slow, dragging footsteps, and on the chill night air came the sound of crying.

The Lad of the Skins, walking abroad, scouring the night for victims . . .

"Let me in, for I am cold and desolate and hungry."

Into the drugged minds of the travellers crept a warning note. Something out there asking to come in? Danger! But it is so cold, they thought. And the creature is surely little more than a child.

"Let me in, for I am lost and alone and frightened. I have no one and nothing in the world."

Careful! thought the travellers, struggling to remember. Careful now. There is something here we have to be very wary of.

"*Take me in by your fire, for I am shivering with cold and I am lost in the forest . . . oh, be merciful and let me share your fire and give me a cup of milk to sup and a mouthful of bread . . .*"

There was doubt and anguish in the faces of the three travellers now. Even so, thought Taliesin, struggling against the Enchantment, even so, there is something—if only I could remember—we have to be very wary of the crying in the night outside . . .

Fael-Inis continued to play without ceasing, and the music spun and shivered and soothed, and across the slanting features there was a look of the utmost concentration now, for it is only at the invitation of a Mortal that the Lad of the Skins can enter a house and do his terrible work. For Calatin's soul to be rescued, one of the three travellers *must* lose his soul in return, and for the Lad to take the soul, it must be one of the Mortals who invited him in.

"*I have not eaten and I am in rags and all I ask is a share of your fire before I am turned out into the cold night again . . .*"

There was a long sigh and then a sobbing, and so desolate and so hopeless was the sound that the three listening minds were splintered with anguish.

"*Let me in, of your charity . . . I shall be no trouble, all I ask is a quiet corner of your warm room . . .*"

There was the sound of footsteps outside, hesitant, light, submissive . . . Sure there was nothing here that could threaten.

"*All I ask is a corner to warm my cold hands and a sip of milk . . . oh, let me in . . .*"

There was a tapping at the window now, light fingers, child's fingers, poor weak fingers numb with cold and tired and trembling with hunger.

Fael-Inis spun the music fractionally quicker, and in that fraction of a moment Fergus stood up and moved to open the door.

At first he thought it was a bundle of old clothes left on the step. "I gathered it up," he was to say, "I actually scooped up the evil hungering thing in my arms and carried it into the house and laid it down by the fire."

It felt light in his arms; a child starved of love and food and warmth: "And although a part of me, deep buried, hidden away, *knew*," he said, "still I wanted to weep for the pity of it."

But yet the pity of it, O the pity of it . . .

He laid the thin little thing down close to the blazing fire, and he moved to the table and poured milk and wine into a cup, and sliced bread and meat.

The creature that Fergus had carried in was sipping the milk, crouched, shivering, near to the fire. Lapping it up like a weak kitten, thought Fergus.

And all the while, while he was handing him the plate of meat and bread, and while he was holding the cup to the trembling lips, a little silvery voice was beating inside Fergus's head: This is all wrong. I know it is wrong. I cannot remember why it is wrong, but it is something to do with the music, and it is something to do with Calatin . . .

And then the music stopped and Fael-Inis laid down the pipes and turned his golden gaze on Fergus, and the spell faded, and a cold awareness flooded Fergus's mind.

The Lad of the Skins! The hunter of souls! And I have asked him in and I have fed him and given him milk and wine and a share of the fire!

The Lad of the Skins. The hungry soulless being who served Crom Croich and walked abroad crying to be let in, and who carried on his back a dripping sack . . . He was sitting up now, regarding Fergus with a sly glittering smile, and there was a terrible knowledge in his eyes, and there was a knowing look.

For you know what is in store for you . . .

He was slender and pale and dark-haired, and his hair fell raggedly about his ears and his eyes were huge and dark-rimmed.

And there are some eyes that can eat you, Mortal . . .

Fergus stood, unable to speak or move, and the Lad smiled, and Fergus shuddered, for although the Lad was young and firm-fleshed, the smile revealed the evil beneath. His lips were red and full and soft, like an overripe fruit with the juices bursting through the skin—a fruit turned, and just beyond its best, so that while the outer layers remained fresh and moist, just beneath would be the beginning of soft over-sweetness. Decay and corruption. Putrefaction. And greed. Above all, the most overwhelming greed . . .

There are some eyes that will eat your soul . . .

The Lad moved then, grinning, his hands reaching out. Terrible hands, claws with the nails curved and nearly but not quite rotten and ready to fall out, the fingertips swollen and ripe and splitting and spilling pus in little dribbles. And there was a stench now; rotting flesh, warm cooking meat, corpses oozing decay and filth and dissolving into putres-cence.

Fergus was back against the table, one hand held up to ward the Lad off, and Taliesin and Fribble had sprung to their feet, both free now of the insidious music of Fael-Inis's pipes.

But the Lad had his eyes fixed on Fergus. And Fergus will never escape him, thought Taliesin, and caught an an-swering thought from Fael-Inis. *But Fergus does not want to escape him.*

This is what Fael-Inis wanted, thought Taliesin, and knew, even as the thought formed, that Fael-Inis had not wanted it, but that it had been necessary.

For Tara, and for Ireland, and for the world of the Future, and perhaps also for the legendary Lost Prince who will one day rise up and defeat Medoc . . .

A soul for a soul. Fergus in exchange for Calatin, for only Calatin could weave the Enchantment which would al-low them to ride in the Time Chariot.

It has to be done, thought Taliesin, torn between agony for Fergus and the knowledge of what they must do.

A soul for a soul . . . Because already the First Horseman
is in the world of the Future. Plague. Plague already stalking
the world, scattered by the Conablaiche. Famine beginning.
"And then shall the Beast Apocalypse ride into the world . . ."

Weighed against all that, what did one soul matter?

But it is Fergus! cried Taliesin silently.

The Lad was coming onwards, his eyes glittering, his
hands outstretched, the nails curved and predatory. Saliva
dripped from his parted lips and ran down over his chin, and
Taliesin and Fribble both shuddered, for the Lad would savour Fergus; he was licking his lips and salivating over him.

*I shall tear out your soul, and carry it away to the Prison
of Hostages, and then perhaps the Conablaiche will come to tear
out your heart, for there is nothing my Master likes so well as a
warm heart, a Mortal heart, still beating, fresh and running
with blood and juices . . .*

Fergus had fallen back across the table and Taliesin and
Fribble both moved to stand between him and the Lad. "We
would have done anything to prevent the Lad getting to Fergus," said Taliesin later. "There was nothing we would not
have done."

And then Fael-Inis stood up, and the Lad stopped and
looked round, and his eyes fell on Fael-Inis, and Taliesin
thought he had never seen such fear and such undiluted hatred in any living creature's eyes.

Fael-Inis regarded the Lad quite coolly, and at length he
said in an amused voice, "So, jackal, we face one another
again, and fight for a soul," and the Lad drew back with a
snarl, his eyes showing red. He stood looking at Fael-Inis
from the corners of his eyes, like a trapped hare.

"You cannot escape me," said Fael-Inis. "Your mind is
subservient to mine. You have owned me to be your superior
before, and you will do so now." He began to move round
the Lad, and Taliesin, who was watching closely, thought
that Fael-Inis was creating an invisible circle. For a moment
he thought that a sprinkling of light fell wherever Fael-Inis
walked, but as it touched the floor it vanished, and he could

not be sure that he had seen it at all. But he thought that it was as if Fael-Inis had somehow taken a shard of pure light and splintered it, and then scattered it about them.

Fael-Inis was perched on the edge of a chair now, his eyes never leaving the dark-eyed figure of the Lad. After a moment he said, "Come now, a bargain. We both know what is wanted." He looked to where Fergus stood, and the Lad snarled again and wiped his mouth with the back of his hand.

"Let the old man go," said Fael-Inis softly. "You have had your fill of him. Take this one instead. You know who he is?" He paused and the Lad nodded. "I will allow you to take his soul," said Fael-Inis again, "but I must have your promise that you will not give his body to the Conablaiche. Well?" And then, as the Lad hesitated, "You know I always keep my word," said Fael-Inis. "You know that I am a prince of a very high order, and you know I obey the Ancient Code of Honour." He looked at the Lad and Taliesin thought the Lad nodded very slightly. Fael-Inis seemed to withdraw his gaze fractionally. "Very well," said Fael-Inis, as if something had been settled. "Very well, I will let you take Fergus in exchange for Calatin. Do what you must." In that instant, the Lad leapt on Fergus.

There was nothing any of them could do.

"It was over before we knew it," said Taliesin later, "and even if it had not been, I do not think we could have got near to the Lad."

"It was the Light," said Fribble. "The Knife of Light, Fael-Inis called it. White and dazzling."

Fergus had been knocked backward by the Lad's spring; he was lying on his back on the littered table, and the Lad was crouching over him, his eyes enormous, his face intent. His ragged hair fell across his brow, and his hands slid under Fergus's skin.

The Knife of Light was hard and brilliant. It seemed to slither across Fergus's skin, and they thought that he cried out. And then the Knife flashed again, describing an arc in the dark room that stayed in the watchers' vision for a long time. Fergus gave a truly terrible cry, and for a moment it seemed as if a sudden coldness had descended. Something has gone from here, thought Taliesin. Something that was warm and alive and filled with hope and joy and fear and laughter, and all the living things, has suddenly gone from the room.

And then the Lad held up something that shimmered and rippled before their eyes, and that was beautiful and terrifying and— Powerful, thought Taliesin. So strong and so powerful and so vulnerable. Whatever it is, it is a force field, a magnet. It will attract every good influence in the world, and every evil one as well, and it will reject or accept, as it wishes. Wonderful and fearful and filled both with great weakness and immense strength. But he never spoke of the pitiful way in which the soul bowed its head humbly and submissively before the Lad. He thought later—"When I could think," he said—that it was as if the soul knew that it must surrender itself into the Lad's hands, to do with as he wished. There was a terrible resignation about it and a patience, and the pity of it slammed Taliesin at the base of his throat.

The Lad stood for a moment, his hands caressing the formless thing. As he did so, Fribble and Taliesin caught a flicker of movement from Calatin.

Then the Lad darted across the room like a fleeing hare, and vanished, and Calatin opened his eyes and looked right at them.

FAEL-INIS SAID very softly, "There was no other choice," and his hand came out to rest on Taliesin's arm for a moment. "I am strength and power and light and speed, Taliesin," he said, "but even I cannot protect you from the Time Fire. Only Calatin can do that."

Fribble said, "He's awake, you know," and they turned to look to where Calatin was sitting in his chair, his single eye open, searching the room with a look of bewilderment.

"Bless my soul," said Calatin in a deep rumbling voice,

"bless my soul, I believe I dropped off for a while. Where's that pesky creature that was footling about outside? Did he get in? The boys said it was the Lad of the Skins, although I don't suppose it was any such thing. Still, you can't be too careful. And the boys would let in anyone who asked politely, of course." He rubbed his single eye and beamed. "And we have guests," said Calatin. "Dear me, not the thing to fall asleep when there are guests. You'll forgive the discourtesy, sirs? Well, I daresay you'd know I wouldn't nod off in the normal way. Have we finished supper? Dear me, here's a littered table. And dust! My word, I shall have to speak to the boys about this. Of course, you get a lot of dust in from the forest. But they might have run round with the mop and a bit of beeswax. I don't know what they do all day, I don't really."

Fael-Inis said, "You have been sleeping the sleep of the soulless, sir," and Calatin turned a look of great astonishment on him.

"*Have* I? Well, do you know, that's a very curious thing. Inside the Prison of Hostages, was I? Well, now *there's* a place not many escape from ... well, there isn't anyone that has that I can think of offhand. Now I come to think about it, that pesky Lad was dancing about somewhere outside. Did he get in? Did he? I suppose he told a good tale and the boys let him in. Kind hearts every one of them, but no brains. Just like their mother. Dear me, she'd have been sad to see this day." He drew out an enormous red spotted handkerchief from a capacious pocket somewhere and mopped his eye.

"Of course, the Lad can be very clever," he said, having blown his nose vigorously. "And the boys would never see they were being fooled." He moved one arm cautiously. "Yes, I am a bit stiff," he said. "Dear me, I must have been asleep for ... No, I'd better not be told, because I should only begin counting up all the things I'd missed, and you're better off not knowing what you've missed."

"Indeed you are, sir," said Fribble, fascinated.

"Well, if the boys let the Lad in, it's their lookout," said Calatin. "Time and again I've warned them, but they think they know best. They like things to be loud and dramatic, and if there's one thing you can't have in good sorcery, it's loud noises and drama. Bless my soul, it's all down in the Amaranth Chronicles. Get the spell right, I tell them. Keep the Looms well oiled and follow the Chronicles, I tell them, but they don't listen to a word I say. You'll forgive me, sirs, but I've forgotten your names for the moment. My memory isn't what it was, although I daresay your names would come back to me if we waited a bit." He tapped his forehead. "Old age," he said. "Dear me, it's a sad trial at times. A very sad trial." And looked at them expectantly.

Fael-Inis said, "We are merely travellers, Calatin. But seeking your assistance," and Calatin sat up straighter and looked pleased.

"I'm often sought out," he said. "All kinds of people come to ask my advice, you wouldn't believe. Well, we had to make a better road through the forest, although I see through the window that it's grown up a bit. And of course, the boys don't tell me things these days. They'd like me to retire if the truth was told, but what I say is, why retire when you don't want to?" He beamed amiably at Fribble, who at once said, "Quite right. Dear me, sir, you possess good sense, I see," and Calatin looked pleased, and slapped Fribble on the back, which, as Fribble later pointed out, was rather alarming, because—"Although he's quite a small giant as giants go"—Calatin was still twelve feet tall and his hands were like York hams.

"I was bruised for days afterwards," said Fribble, "but I didn't say anything, because it wouldn't have been courteous. And he's very amiable. It's all very interesting, isn't it?"

Calatin was very amiable indeed. He insisted on them taking supper with him, and would not hear of a refusal.

"We've eaten supper," began Taliesin.

"But we can always manage another one," put in Fribble. "And the Tyrian has some rather good wine."

"Oh, so you're a Tyrian, are you?" said Calatin, inspecting Taliesin with interest. "My word, *our* ancestors had some rare old times together, didn't they? Haven't you heard of the sorcery wars between the Amaranths and the Tyrians? *Haven't* you? Well, it makes a very good tale, only I don't know if I could remember any of it—" He beamed on Taliesin, and then said in an aside to Fribble that he had never yet heard of a Tyrian who didn't judge his wine remarkably well.

Taliesin, hearing this, at once uncorked the wine flask and offered it to Calatin, who accepted it, said he took it very kindly of Taliesin, and drained the flask in two gulps.

"Very good," he nodded, mopping his mouth. "I never thought to see a Tyrian at my table, but you're very welcome, sir."

Taliesin said, "I will dine with any man who will serve wine, and I will talk with any race who will provide interesting discourse." He raised his glass to Calatin. "You are providing both, sir," he said, and Calatin said, "Am I really? My word, that's very true," and turned with relief to Fribble, who was trying to explain about their journey and about Medoc having taken Tara.

"Ah, you're from the Court, are you?" said Calatin. "Well, that *is* interesting. I daresay I shall be a bit of out of touch, of course. But the boys will tell me everything." He took another sup of wine reflectively. "Dear me, Medoc's got Tara, has he?" he said. "I never cared for Medoc. My word, it's a bad business and no mistake. Dear me, I don't like to think what the end might be. He's arrogant," said Calatin, nodding and tapping the side of his nose with a forefinger. "Very arrogant, that Medoc. One of the Northern lot, you can always tell. They think they can rule the world, well, to be fair, they probably could, only it's as well if you don't let them know it. And it's always a good idea to let them think you've got better enchantments in your armoury than you actually have, if you take my meaning, even if you haven't got any enchantments at all. But that's

for you to worry about. I'm only a plain sorcerer. An arti-
san. It's all quite easy. So long as you keep the Looms properly oiled and follow the rules, you can't really go far wrong.
No need to pretend otherwise, although I could tell you some
stories . . . But I mustn't breach trade secrets. I'm going to
write my memoirs one day," he said confidingly. "That'll
make a few people sit up. I'm looking forward to that. But
I don't gossip," he said again. "I'm quite safe. You can tell
me anything you like. The boys are a bit over-chatty sometimes. I wouldn't like to tell them anything that oughtn't to
be widely known. They go to all these get-togethers. Sorcerers and wizards, and a few necromancers as well, I shouldn't
be surprised. One of them had the effrontery to bring a
wraith back once. Over my dead body, I said. You take that
hussy out of here, or you go through that door and don't
come back. Well, we couldn't be having that sort of person
in here. I don't know what his poor mother would have said.
But they're good boys. They work very hard." He nodded
portentously, and Taliesin said in an undertone to Fael-Inis,
"This is terrible. We'll have to tell him."

"In good time," said Fael-Inis gently.

"I won't ask too much about why you're here," said
Calatin, looking hopeful all the same. "Unless there's a plot
against the Throne. Now that *is* something I won't have
anything to do with. I'm very loyal." He looked quite fierce
as he said this, and Taliesin and Fribble both backed away,
because when a giant—even a small one—looks at you
fiercely, it is not easy to stand your ground. Fribble poured
himself another measure of wine. "For courage," he explained.

Taliesin said, "You may be sure, sir, that we are the
Queen's men through and through," and Calatin said he was
very glad to hear it.

"If you're fighting for Her Majesty, you have my support," he said, rather emotionally. "And you'll forgive me
for making the point, but you do get the odd rebel, of
course."

He nodded, and finished his supper with enjoyment. "Because," he said, mopping his plate industriously with a piece of bread, "when you've been asleep for a bit, you're bound to feel a bit peckish when you wake up." He ate a gargantuan meal, starting with some plovers' eggs they had overlooked earlier, working on through a few roast geese with a brace or so of ducklings on the side, and ending with one half of a cheese and a couple of bowls of fruit.

"And now," he said, having mopped up the last crumb, "now, what is it I can do for you? I should mention the— dear me—the *fee*," he added, lowering his voice to a whisper, as if this was rather an impolite word.

Taliesin said, "We have not the riches of the East, nor the wealth of the world, sir. But I believe we can meet your fee."

"I have to be expensive," explained Calatin, sounding apologetic. "For one thing there's this house—you wouldn't believe the way it gets through money. If it isn't the dry rot in the roof, it's insects chewing the timbers. And the boys aren't cheap," he said. "They like their little get-togethers with other sorcerers—and why not, I say. But they will belong to the Sorcerers' Fellowship, and then there's the Old Boys' Academy of Wizardry—mind you, I like to go along to that myself. And they're all Comrades of the Loom, which of course is *very* useful. Secret handshakes and rituals," he said, lowering his voice impressively which, as Fribble said, could still have been heard on the other side of the forest.

"And it all costs money," said Calatin, shaking his head and refilling everyone's glass.

"I oughtn't to have any," said Fribble. "Just a half glass perhaps. Well, if you insist—your good health, sir!"

"Yes, it's all very costly," said Calatin. "Subscriptions to this and that, and then suppers at people's houses, and of course you have to return the hospitality. And my family weren't what you'd term *rich*," he added in another of his vast whispers. "Everyone thinks the Amaranth line was enormously wealthy, but so much of it went in the Sorcery

Wars—dear me, I intended no discourtesy, sir. But sorcery itself isn't a well-paid profession, you know. We get what we can. But it's as well to make these things clear."

Taliesin murmured something that sounded like, "All the riches of the world we shall lay at thy feet," and Fribble, who felt that a note of practicality was called for, said, "Be assured that we can pay your fee," and Calatin looked pleased.

"And you know, you haven't yet told me what it is that you want," he said, and sat back, and eyed them expectantly, first one and then another, which Fribble found disconcerting.

"If he had two eyes like any one else," said Fribble, "I could stand it. It's this single unblinking stare I can't cope with."

But no giant single-eyed stare could prevail against Fael-Inis. He leaned forward and looked directly at Calatin.

"Well?" said Calatin, who was, truth to tell, becoming just the smallest bit afraid of this strange, golden-eyed creature, but who would not have dreamed of showing it, because you did not show discourtesy to guests, not if you wanted business from them. And so he waited for these really rather unexpected people to explain what they required, and hoped he would be able to do whatever it was.

And so when Fael-Inis looked at him and said, "It is something that is easily within your capabilities, good Calatin," Calatin was very pleased, and said at once that he'd do his best.

Fael-Inis said softly, "Protect these men from the Time Fire."

Calatin sat back in his chair and stared at the three strangers in his house and said, "Oh *dear*, you're not going into the Far Future?"

"I'LL DO IT," said Calatin at last. "I don't like it, but I'll do it."

"Is there a difficulty?" asked Taliesin.

"Well, there is and there isn't," said Calatin, frowning, which made him look rather odd.

"A one-eyed frown," murmured Fribble. "Dear me, I never thought to see such a peculiar thing."

"The spell can be spun very easily," said Calatin. "My word, it's basic stuff, that. I can do it standing on my head, although I won't. And fresh off the Loom it will be. And there's the thing." He leaned forward. "It's a spell that has to be very fresh indeed for it to work," he said. "You'll have to be inside the spell and out of here into the Time Chariot so fast you couldn't say 'caterpillar's boots,' always supposing you wanted to say such a ridiculous thing, which I don't suppose you do.

"But then you'll want to come back," said Calatin, "because it stands to reason that you won't want to stay in the Future—well, no one would. A nasty place, the Future," he said, with a shudder which rocked the table and made Fribble spill his wine.

"You'll want to come back," said Calatin, "and there's the problem. You'll have the spell with you," he said, "but will it stay potent? And if it doesn't, what will you do? I don't know a great deal about the sorcerers of the Future," said Calatin, who actually knew nothing at all about them, but thought it would sound unprofessional to admit this, "but I don't think we should rely on them. For one thing we don't know what they'd charge, and for another they might not understand about the Time Fire. It's a bit risky. Are you *sure* you want to go? Yes, I can see you do." He looked at them. "Shall we say noon today?" he said. "But you'll have to remember that under no circumstances at all can you expect the spell to last longer than seven days.

"If you stay in the Future for longer than that, the spell will certainly be dead. You would never be able to come back."

IF THE GALLERY outside the silver door had hummed and quivered and thrown out heat before, now the sensations were magnified and multiplied a hundred times as Calatin set the Silver Looms to harness the power of the sorcerer.

"He's a very able sorcerer," said Fribble, as they sat together in the banqueting hall. "He might seem a bit bumbling, but he's very good."

Taliesin said, "The bodies of the Sons . . . ," and Fael-Inis said, "He will not see them."

"The Cloak of Invisibility in addition to all else?" said Taliesin lightly, and Fael-Inis said, "Exactly," and Taliesin looked up sharply, because although he had not been entirely flippant, neither had he been altogether serious.

Fael-Inis said tranquilly, "Calatin will not see the bodies until he has woven the spell we need."

"Have you any of the higher feelings?" said Taliesin, and Fael-Inis looked amused.

"I have deeper feelings than ever you could comprehend," he said. "When I walked away from the Great Rebellion, my heart bled with the pity and the waste and the anguish of it. When the doors closed on the place in which I had dwelled, and I found myself alone in the world of Men, I was in more agony than you could dream exists. There has never been a day, nor yet an hour, when I have not ached for the loss of that which existed before Lucifer led his followers against the gods. He suffered defeat and banishment, but there were others who had to suffer it with him. And though I cannot return until it pleases the gods to end the world, I have never ceased to long for it." He looked at Taliesin. "I have many of the higher feelings," said the rebel angel softly, "just as you have, Mortal."

Taliesin said lightly, "I am uncaring and careless. I have no feelings for anyone." He reached for the replenished wine chalice at his elbow, and lifted it rather challengingly.

Fael-Inis smiled. "You have imagination and sensitivity, and you care a very great deal," he said. "You care for the future of mankind, and you care for the future of Ireland as well. That is why you accompanied Fergus and Fribble."

"I cared only to escape from a life that was irksome and narrow," said Taliesin, drinking his wine and reclining in the chair rather negligently.

"Rubbish," said Fribble unexpectedly. "Guts and imagination, that's what you've got. Unusual to find both together, you know. Especially unusual to find them in a Tyrian, because as a rule Tyrians only care about making money. That's all very well in its way," said Fribble, beaming, "but there're other things to life as well as making money."

"Other things in life—" Taliesin grinned at them both, and lifted the wine to his lips.

"Fribble is right," said Fael-Inis, sending Fribble his sudden smile, and Fribble said at once, "Of course I am. People think I'm silly, but I'm not nearly as silly as I appear. It's quite useful to let people think you're silly sometimes. You get away with a good deal," he said, looking at Taliesin thoughtfully. "It's nearly as clever to let people think you don't care as it is to let them think you're silly. For a Tyrian you're quite an interesting person."

Taliesin laughed, and Fael-Inis said, "Why did you accompany Fergus and Fribble?" and Taliesin glanced involuntarily to where Fergus's body lay on the velvet-covered couch beneath the window that looked out on to the forest.

"To save the world," said Taliesin in a mocking tone. "What else?" and Fael-Inis smiled.

"Is that also the reason you will assume Fergus's mantle and go into the Far Future to bind the Apocalypse and turn back the Four Horsemen?"

"Must I do so?"

"Don't you think you must?"

There was a silence, and Taliesin felt Fael-Inis's eyes boring into his mind again, and thought, Of course he knows what I am thinking, and of course he knows what I am feeling. Does he? Do I know myself? Despite himself, he heard again Fael-Inis's words earlier: *Who told you that life was in-*

tended to be easy, Mortal? Aloud he said, "Is Fergus completely lost to us?" and for the first time saw the golden-eyed creature hesitate.

But Fael-Inis only said, "We have certainly saved his body from the Conablaiche, for the Lad will not dare to break his promise to me."

"Can we be sure of that?" Fribble wanted to know.

"Assuredly we can. The Lad will not invoke my wrath," said Fael-Inis, and his eyes glittered rather frighteningly. "Did I not say we were old enemies, he and I? Fergus's body will stay as it is."

"And," said Taliesin, "his soul?"

"That is rather different," said Fael-Inis. "For there are other powers, and other laws that govern the soul." He looked at them very gently. "But it is possible that Fergus's soul will never return," he said.

"Are you using Fergus's sacrifice to compel me to take his place?" said Taliesin suddenly.

"No. Are you?"

"I thought I was not," said Taliesin slowly.

"But you are thinking that it would be a dreadful irony if Fergus had given his soul into the captivity of the Prison of Hostages, only to have his quest abandoned?"

Taliesin stood up and regarded Fael-Inis steadily. "Well?" he said. "Wouldn't it?"

"You will do it?"

"Save the world?" said Taliesin, and all of the old careless mockery was there. "How could I do otherwise?"

And then Fribble said, "The Looms have stopped."

"I THINK IT will work," said Calatin. "It's being finished. It's cooling, you might say. You'll have to treat it carefully, because it's a fragile sort of spell. Don't let it get torn or worn." He eyed them severely. "Are you ready to leave?"

"The Chariot will be here at dawn, good Calatin," said Fael-Inis, and Calatin at once said that this was a very good time for a journey.

"Dawn, there's the thing. My word, you can't beat a dawn journey," he said, pleased. "I'll bring the spells down to you, and then you'll be off and away. Dear me, what an excitement. I've made one for each of you, of course."

It was then that Fribble said, "I'm not going."

He was very definite about it. "I should be in the way," he said firmly. "Dorrainge was quite right, only I wanted to argue against him, fat fool. It doesn't do any good to let him think he can overrule me either—well, he can't really, because I'm Chief Druid after all. But he needs to be reminded now and again. I was reminding him when I said I'd come with you. And I've enjoyed it all very much," said Fribble, quite seriously. "It's all been very interesting and I've learned quite a lot of things I didn't know before. But I should be in the way from here on. Taliesin will do very well on his own."

Taliesin, rather appalled at the "on his own" part of this speech, said, "But we might need you for all kinds of things, Fribble. We might need your knowledge. You know things that I don't. You certainly wouldn't be in the way."

"Yes, I should," said Fribble. "It's polite of you to say that, but it's a young man's venture this—well, that's not to call Fael-Inis a *man* precisely, and that's meaning no disrespect either," he added to Fael-Inis, who replied with grave courtesy, "None in the world."

"You will be in my thoughts, of course," said Fribble in a down-to-earth tone. "Well, you'll know that. And there's a lot of strength in properly ordered thoughts, you know. People don't think of it, but there is. I shall set aside a part of each day to think about you." He regarded them quite severely.

"What will you do?" said Taliesin.

"Well," said Fribble, "Calatin here has been so kind as to invite me to stay for a while." He glanced over his shoulder to where Calatin was trumpeting into a red spotted handkerchief. "It's hit him very hard, you know," said Fribble. "About the Sons and the Conablaiche. Fael-Inis told him very gently and very nicely, but you can't expect him to be other than quite dreadfully upset, can you?

"So I thought I'd stay with him," said Fribble. "We shall have a good deal to discuss, you know. I shouldn't be bored. We're going to write his memoirs, well, we're going to *start* writing them, and that will be extremely interesting. And then we're going to edit the Chronicles of Amaranth, and after *that*," said Fribble, "after *that*, we're going to embark on a history of the Sorcery Wars between the Amaranthines and the Tyrians. Of course, that will take a very long time indeed. But I expect I shall learn quite a lot. Also," said Fribble, glancing to the velvet couch beneath the forest window, "also I do think that one of us ought to stay with Fergus."

"Yes of course," said Taliesin, his eyes going also to the motionless figure, because it was certainly unthinkable that they should leave Fergus like this, in the middle of a dark old mansion at the heart of an ancient forest.

Fribble beamed. "Do you know, you're improving by the hour," he said. "You'll be quite a good sort of person by the time you return from the Future, supposing you do return, of course, because I didn't like the sound of that spell, did you? Seven days only, that's not long. I should miss you," said Fribble seriously. "Dear me, yes, I should."

"That is extremely ki—"

"Well, I should miss your wine," said Fribble, "because it's really very good. No, I wasn't hinting—well, perhaps we ought to speed you on your way. My word, that's a large helping you're pouring me."

DAWN. BIRDSONG AND rebirth and the sheer undiluted delight of living creatures awaking to face another day. Tongues of colour washing over the old grey mansion. The vibrant hues of coral, and the rose and gold of dawnlight. The shimmering dusky pink of a poppy field under a dawn sky.

Fergus should have been standing here, thought Taliesin, and there was a pain and an aching void at the knowledge, for this had been Fergus's quest and his covenant. Standing

in the dawnlit hall of Calatin's house, Taliesin knew that for
Fergus this had been not just a venture, a battle for the *Fiana*,
but something much deeper. The restoration of the
Wolfqueen . . . And Fergus had made that final, overwhelming sacrifice so that Ireland should be safe, and so that the
Wolfqueen should regain Tara. He should be here, thought
Taliesin again, but since he is not, since he is forever inside
the Prison of Hostages, then I must carry out the quest for
him.

The morning light was piercing the old house now, sending shafts of pure colour sliding across the floor, making the
dust motes dance in and out of the rays. With the light came
the music. "The Beckoning," said Fael-Inis.

Taliesin could never tell afterwards where the light ended
and the music began. "The light ran into the music," he said,
"and the music into the light. I was dazzled and bewitched."

Even so, he was able to look at the fireglow of the Chariot, and he was able to look into the light and see the salamanders with their wise faces and their eyes filled with ancient
knowledge. He felt the cool silky spell woven by Calatin brush
his skin like a thin liquid cloak, and he remembered that there
were only seven days for Fergus's task to be performed.

There was a strong sweet scent: sandalwood and patchouli
and freshly cut grass on a summer morning. Applewood burning on an autumn night. Everything that makes up Ireland, he
thought. I wonder if I am afraid? And he knew he was not the
least afraid, he was only afraid of failing Fergus, who had surrendered his soul that the Wolfqueen might rule again.

And then the music was drawing him into the fire and
the light, and he could see the massive shape of the Chariot
limned against the forest now, bathed in its own radiance,
hung with silk, lined with satin . . .

The echoes were all about him now, and the beautiful
fragile images created by the people of the worlds not yet
born . . . *A Chariot of the Sun is being given to you . . . And
the light is a garment . . . A flying chariot through the fields of
air . . .*

And time and the world are ever in flight
And love is less kind than the grey twilight
And hope is less clear than the dew of the morn.

And I am going into the light and I am going into time, and if I am to save the world, then I shall have served the world, and if I do not save the world, then at least I shall have tried.

Because nobody ever said life was meant to be easy anyway...

He caught the glint of a smile from Fael-Inis at that, and felt a sudden delight, because the fire was surging up all about them, and Fael-Inis had taken up a stance at the fore of the Chariot, and he was gathering up silken reins between his hands, only the reins were of living colour and shifting light, and there were certainly spells within them as there had certainly been spells in the Chamber of the Looms . . .

There was the sweet warm fragrance of gentle heat and of silken bodies, and the salamanders tossed their manes, and sparks of light cascaded across Taliesin's vision.

And then Fael-Inis lifted the silver pipes to his lips, and there was a final burst of music, and the forest and the house and the Ireland of Tara's Court vanished, and they were pulled into the Far Future.

CHAPTER EIGHT

LUGH OF THE Longhand thought things were going rather well. It was not everyone who could lead a party of men from Innisfree on to the mainland without being spotted. Lugh was certain that there had been nothing in the least bit noticeable about their journey. There had been a certain amount of bustle about it, but you could hardly have a journey—any journey—without a bit of bustle. You certainly could not lead upwards of twenty men, never mind a pair of Druids, on to Ireland's mainland without being a bit noisy.

But nobody would think anything of it. As for Dorrainge's idea of travelling by night, stealthily and furtively, Lugh had never heard anything like it. They would go openly and honestly by day, he said, and pretended not to hear when Dorrainge said they were inviting all kinds of trouble.

What Dorrainge did not realise was that Lugh was being subtle. It would pay off, they would all see. Lugh was going to be playing a decisive part in this victory. Dorrainge was in for a very big shock.

The setting up of the secret camp and the training of the men was a blind and a cover to fool Medoc, and people who said lugubriously that Medoc could not be fooled did not know what they were talking about. Lugh was going to fool Medoc very neatly, and they would all eat their words. While the men were training and getting their eye back for archery and broadsword fighting, Lugh would be creeping up on Tara, studying the Bright Palace to find out its weaknesses; he would be charting the movements of the guards and sentries, and counting up the number of people on watch at the Western Gate.

He knew that there was a whisper among the men that they ought to have had Fergus with them, but Lugh knew that Fergus was no great loss. It was plain to Lugh, as it should have been to everyone else, that Fergus—and whoever he took with him—was going to get into severe difficulties in the Far Future. Lugh had never thought it a good idea, and he had said so at the time, only nobody had listened. The Queen had agreed to it because the Queen would agree to anything Fergus wanted; everyone knew that.

Lugh had heard a few extremely surprising tales about Her Majesty and Fergus, but he had not gossiped, because Longhands did not gossip. You could not call what Lugh had done gossip, because he had done it for their own good. And he had done it tactfully as well, just mentioning to one or two people who had Dierdriu's ear that Grainne and Fergus were sometimes seen together in rather questionable circumstances. Tact and discretion he had used, and he dared say that Dierdriu had been told who had been at the back of it. She would have thought the better of him for it as well, Lugh knew he could be sure of that. He had not liked doing it, but he had known his duty. Anyway, it had been a very long time ago, goodness gracious, it had been at least six years. It might even have been seven.

Fribble was not really very much of a loss to this expedition, because he would only have got in the way, falling asleep at important meetings (Lugh liked meetings), and eating all of their supplies. Lugh was being very fair about distribution of supplies.

"It's to be fair shares for all," he had said to Cathbad, and Cathbad had at once said, "Oh, dear me, yes, of course. I *don't* know how else we should do it," and had gone off to prepare their evening meal. And it had been extremely unkind, not to say ill-bred, of several of the younger ones to remark on Lugh's own plateful of stew and to compare it unfavourably with their own portions. Everyone knew that the leader of the party had to be given larger helpings than anyone else.

But Lugh would rise above it all, and would not bother to listen to complaints about who was getting larger helpings of stew, or who was having the most comfortable sleeping quarters, or even who was getting up a bit later than everyone else. Leaders needed their sleep more than the people they led.

Lugh was not sure, now, if it had been a good idea to bring Dorrainge. He ought to have known that Dorrainge would meddle, well, he had known it, but it had actually been rather difficult to leave him behind.

"He's Second Druid," said Cathbad. "You can't leave him behind." And he had gone off to brew up a kettle of some herbal concoction, which he had said would do wonders for the men's aching joints after the long march. "Legs and knees," said Cathbad busily. "Legs and knees, and probably thighs as well. My word, thighs have to be looked after, don't they? You can't march an army unless your legs are in order. I'll just give them all a little bit of a massage, shall I?"

Dorrainge was turning out to be very meddlesome. He poked his nose into things that ought not to have concerned him. "*How* much dried bear meat have we?" he asked. "Dear me, is that all?" And, "Are you sure we ought to make camp here?" he said. "Don't you think we can be seen too easily? We're in a direct line from Tara for Medoc's spies. Of course, it's nothing to do with me."

It was nothing to do with Dorrainge at all; Lugh would make the decisions about where they pitched camp and how much bear meat they brought. They would probably not bring very much bear meat at all, because Lugh was not especially partial to bear meat, but it would have looked odd to say this.

Lugh would address all the meetings as well, and Dorrainge would not get a look in. Lugh always showed well at meetings, and he was good at speeches. It was not many who could make a speech like Lugh.

"It's not many who'd want to," said Cathbad, distracted by the necessity of having to provide supper early on one of Lugh's meeting nights. "There's me with thirty-five men to feed, and not a *morsel* in my larder tent!"

Cathbad did not contribute very much to the meetings, and so Lugh did not pay him very much attention. As for Dorrainge's complaints, the camp site they had chosen was very good. It was unkind of Dorrainge to criticise and say that Medoc would be able to see them, and that Medoc would be able to tell everything they did. Medoc would not be able to see them, not when Lugh had finished his cunning arrangement of branches and twigs and leaves. Ah, the Longhands knew how to conceal things.

"But it'll take you the best part of two days to *provide* the concealment," said Dorrainge, surveying Lugh's neatly drawn plans and watching the men sawing off branches and raking up leaves from the forest floor. "What do you suppose is happening all the time we're making the cover?"

Lugh said it would not take two days and it would not even take all night. Medoc would not see them.

"It's too close," said Dorrainge. "I said it was and now I see I'm right. We'll be seen. We've probably been seen already."

Lugh kept his temper extremely well and pointed out all the advantages of the site. He was logical and courteous, so that it was unnecessary for Dorrainge to say that he supposed a Longhand had nearly always featured in Ireland's greatest defeats, and Lugh was only following tradition. "We'll be seen," he said again. "You mark my words."

Lugh did not enter into an argument. He walked away with dignity and went off to tell Cathbad to make several small fires instead of one big one that night, just in case their usual large fire was large enough to attract unwelcome attention.

"Little groups of us," said Cathbad, nodding. *"Cosy."*

Cathbad thought it was a good site. "Plenty of nice dry wood for the cooking," he said, "and I'll just collect some of those wild mushrooms, shall I? There's nothing to beat a handful of mushrooms in with a rabbit stew. And look at the wild sorrel! Sorrel with fish. I must gather some."

Dorrainge said that at any minute Cathbad would start talking about holding a pig-sticking party, and Cathbad, who was plunging about happily in the wild sorrel, said, "And if we could only hold a pig-sticking party . . ." Several of the younger soldiers hooted with laughter, and Cathbad looked hurt and had to be brought out of the sorrel and soothed.

"*And* I've been stung by nettles," he said, injured, and pretended not to hear Dorrainge, who said it was a mistake to pamper nettle stings, and they hadn't the time to soothe people's silly imagined injuries.

The soldiers liked being close to the Bright Palace, and they thought that Medoc would probably not be able to see them. Medoc was not that powerful, surely he was not, they said.

"Yes, he is," said Dorrainge. "I've *told* you."

But the soldiers thought it was great altogether to be near to Tara, and began to talk about getting up a party to go along and take a look, because wouldn't it be the finest old inspiration a man could have to see the Bright Palace again.

"It's not bright any longer," said Dorrainge, and the soldiers looked as disappointed as children. Cathbad clicked his tongue, because this was not the sort of thing you should say to soldiers, who were easily cast down and sent into gloom and doom, something you should certainly avoid before going into battle.

Somebody asked why the Bright Palace was no longer bright, and Dorrainge said, "Because of Medoc's dark enchantments of course," and looked at the soldier as though he thought him a complete fool. "Which," said the soldier afterwards, "I am not. I only asked a polite question."

"To be sure you did," said his colleagues, "and isn't that the way of Druids to be so squashing."

"I wouldn't have come," said the soldier, who would not have missed it for worlds, "I wouldn't have come if I'd known there would be Druids squashing and glooming. Because if it isn't Dorrainge telling you how we'll be defeated, it's Lugh Longhand making speeches half the night."

Several people said it was, to be sure it was, and didn't it make a plain man flinch.

"And if it isn't that," said the soldier, who was a man of fixed purpose, "if it isn't that, it's that Cathbad forever trying to get his hands on your—"

"But Lugh makes quite rousing speeches," put in another soldier, rather hastily. "And it's all quite friendly."

"It isn't so friendly out here," said the first soldier with a shiver. "It's downright sinister. We're far too close to a lot of nasty things."

"What sort of nasty things?"

"Medoc's sentries. Medoc's spies. The Twelve Dark Lords."

"Oh, these woods have seen far worse than Medoc and the Twelve Lords," said Lugh airily, who happened to be listening to this. "Much worse," he said wisely, but Cathbad said that nothing could be worse than Medoc.

"Medoc comes from the most ancient line of necromancers," said the soldier who had asked why Tara's brightness had been quenched. "The ancient unbroken line; the evil sorcerers who command the Dark Ireland."

Somebody asked, a bit hesitantly, how you would define the Dark Ireland, and Dorrainge, who felt he had been left out of this conversation for too long, said it was rather difficult. "Because nobody has ever seen the Dark Ireland, and nobody has ever visited it," he said. "But it's believed to be a kind of dark mirror-image of this world. The creatures who inhabit it are cold and greedy and evil and corrupt. Perhaps they are distorted and warped. Certainly they are forever trying to find a chink between their world and this. They would devour us if they could, and rule the land until the skies were dark with blood and the river ran with gore.

"The Dark Ireland is ruled by the powerful wicked enchanters of the North," said Dorrainge. "Beings such as Medoc and the old Erl-King, although the Erl-King was vanquished by Cormac in the last century."

The first soldier remembered that Medoc had always been called the dark, evil, beautiful one, and Dorrainge said, "Oh, yes, he is all of that," and several people looked thoughtful.

One of the soldiers wanted to know if it was true that Medoc was preparing for the birth into the world of the monster god-idol Crom Croich, and an argument sprang up as to whether Medoc and Crom Croich were the most evil and most powerful forces ever to come out of the Dark Ireland, or whether the Erl-King had been worse.

"The Erl-King ate the children," remembered one of the soldiers softly, and Cathbad shuddered, and wished people would not remember this sort of thing.

"But if Medoc does summon Crom Croich," said another soldier, "he'll send out the Conablaiche to tear people's hearts from their bodies, and that's just as bad as the Erl-King."

"But the Erl-King didn't—"

"And then he'll offer the hearts to Crom Croich."

"I still don't think—"

"On a silver platter," said the soldier obstinately.

Several people said you could not get anything nastier than a warm and dripping heart on a silver platter.

"And then Crom Croich eats the hearts," said the soldier, and Cathbad, who had been very busy all afternoon supervising the skinning and jointing of an ox and had been planning to serve braised ox heart for tomorrow's midday meal, turned quite green and tried to remember if they had any salted pig left.

Lugh said with amused tolerance that these were all fairy tales, but some of the soldiers said, *were* they indeed. Didn't they all know about the terrible appearance of the Conablaiche last time, and how it had prowled the country, snatching sleeping children from their beds and tearing out their hearts for its Dark Master.

"And they say that after the Conablaiche would come

the Lad of the Skins," said the soldier, and a sudden silence fell, because everyone knew about the Lad of the Skins and the Knife of Light, and how, if you fell into the Lad's clutches, he would take your soul and you would be thrown for ever into the Prison of Hostages.

"They do say," said Cathbad, "that if you ever found your way to the Prison of Hostages, you would find all the children whose hearts were given to the Conablaiche during that time, and whose souls were taken by the Lad. The Lost Children, they call them."

Several people said wasn't that the most heart-rending story you'd ever hear, and had they finished all of the mead yet? The mead was passed, and the mugs were refilled, and the fires burned a bit lower.

Lugh, who had listened to all this with tolerance (because of being a good leader), thought that now was probably as good a time as any to slip away and take a real look at Tara. It was not everyone who would have relished going off into the dark forest; Lugh did not relish it at all, in fact. But he would be quite safe because he would keep a sharp look-out for anything and everything, and he would not be captured because no Longhand ever had been captured.

He moved warily through the forest, making very little sound. He was not really so very far from the camp either. He could hear the men beginning the old bawdy "Thousand and One Nights of the Wolfking," which had been written about Cormac, and which Lugh did not care for overmuch, because even if you discounted half the things it said, you were still left with a patently exaggerated tale.

The trees were thinning now, and he was drawing farther away from the camp. Moonlight was pouring over the valley, black and silver, and presently Lugh was standing at the edge of the forest, looking down into the shallow dip that sheltered the great Manor of Tara.

Tara. The Shining Palace, the bright centre of all Ireland. The heart and the core and the living, breathing pulse. The place that the High Kings and Queens had called *Medchuarta*.

Seen like this, across the valley, seen by thin moonlight and mists, it was a place of shadows; it was a dark, rather forbidding fortress of night enchantments and of black sorcery. Lugh knew, as they all knew, that Tara's light had been quenched by Medoc, because Medoc was a necromancer, a dark enchanter of such power that no light could live in his vicinity. If Tara's brilliance, if the radiance that had once shone for Ireland's High Kings was ever to be kindled again, Medoc must be driven out and destroyed. Lugh was the man to do this, of course.

He stood, fascinated, watching Tara. He was not a fanciful man (the Longhands did not believe in fancies), but he felt as if it was a miasma rising from a swamp, a sickness and a corruption.

Because the Dark Ireland is waking . . .

He thought he could hear voices now; silvery, gentle voices, *dark* voices, that made you think you might be being watched. He remembered the ancient legends of the Guardians, the Brotherhood of Sorcerers who would serve any master if they were paid enough, and who would guard anything in the world if someone would employ them sufficiently profitably; he remembered as well that the Conablaiche and the Lad of the Skins were abroad in the world again.

What might be watching him from the shadows?

The thin light was casting curious shadows everywhere now, and Lugh blinked and rubbed his eyes, because just for a moment it had seemed that figures were appearing through the mists ahead of him. The swirling greyness shifted again, and the shadows flooded nearer, but after all there was nothing to see. Or was there? Had that been a silent watching figure just over there? Something dark and anonymous? Something that wore black armour and had a visored face, and who would not materialise unless a dark and terrible enchantment was spun . . . *Were the Twelve Dark Lords close by?*

And then the shadows moved again, and Lugh could see that there was nothing there at all, and that he was nearer now to Tara than he had thought, and after all it had only been a trick of the light.

He remembered that he was being extremely clever and extraordinarily subtle about all of this, and that it would be subtlety that would win this war. Ah, they would all of them be astonished at how well Lugh of the Longhand had done tonight. He would go very quietly now, and he would go very stealthily, and he would slink inside Tara, and he would find out quite a lot about Medoc.

And there was nothing at all to be afraid of.

CHAPTER NINE

FERGUS HAD NOT been aware of the precise moment when the Lad of the Skins drew his soul from his body with the Knife of Light, but he had known a great coldness, and a sense of desolation, and an abandonment so complete that it had overwhelmed him, and for a time he had scarcely been aware of what was happening.

He had wanted to wrap his arms about his body for warmth, but he had not been able to move, and his vision had been blurred. He had tried to cry out, but something had smothered his cries, and he had wanted to reach out and clutch on to everything that was dear and familiar and real and safe.

But Calatin's banqueting hall and the house in the forest had wavered and grown dim—As if I am seeing it through water, thought Fergus—and there had been a great heaviness within him so that it was difficult to breathe. He thought he was dying, and panic seized him. And then he remembered the piercing coldness of the Knife of Light slicing deep into his body, and the Lad's evil greedy eyes and grinning mouth, and he knew that he was not dying, that this could be worse than death, for he was to suffer the soulless existence of all who become victims of the Knife of Light.

I shall never die and I shall never be released, and henceforth I shall wander alone in the eternal light . . .

Black despair engulfed him, and a loneliness so absolute closed over his head that he felt himself drowning in it. Forever alone . . . From now on, I shall be forever alone . . .

The cold was within his heart now, and he knew it for

133

the heartcold of the truly bereft. I shall never see my own world again, he thought. I shall never see Grainne.

The house was becoming smaller now and distant, and he had the impression that he was being drawn away from it, and drawn away from the living warm world he had known. For a breathspace he saw his own body; he thought that Taliesin and Fribble had carried it to a settle beneath a window, and he wanted to grasp at them, for they had been dear, good friends, and the knowledge that he would never see them again was scarcely to be borne. But the pull on his soulless mind was too strong now, and he felt himself being drawn up and up into a vast emptiness, and into the endless skies of infinity. He knew that he was being sucked into the Prison of Hostages, for it is to that great and aweful dwelling that is not quite in the world of Men but not quite out of it that all soulless ones must go. Panic threatened to engulf him again, and the terrible desolate coldness was like an icy vise about his heart, and he knew he had never been so completely alone.

There was the sensation of immense speed now; he thought the skies were rushing past him, and there was a whirling, dizzying feeling, as if he might be at the centre of a maelstrom. He remembered how the travellers and the seafarers who came to Tara had always told that at the centre of every whirlpool, at the heart of every tempest, is a great tranquillity, and he caught and held on to this thought.

He glimpsed the Gates then— Ornate and tipped with something that catches the light and gleams, he thought. And saw, within the Gates, glinting points of colour . . . *the Gates of Paradise, studded with chalcedony and jasper, inlaid with firestones and cedarwood, rimmed with turquoise and moonstones* . . . But these are not those Gates, thought Fergus, these are the Gates of a place reserved for those who are denied admittance to Paradise.

But the Gates were opening, and he could see that they were more beautiful and more majestic than anything he had ever seen or dreamed.

Sea-washed, sunset Gates ... the Gates of Light, unbarred and ajar ...

And then he was passing beneath the huge, towering Gates, and he saw how they stretched above him into infinity, and he felt the timelessness of the great Prison descend on him like a huge, unseen weight.

The ceaseless light closed all about him.

FOREVER IN THE light. Forever open and vulnerable to the never-ending light of the skies.

There had been some kind of vast domed hall as he passed through the Gates; he thought there had been colours within the light then, and he had received a dim impression of a far-off vaulted ceiling. From somewhere deep within his mind, he remembered the whispers of the great and terrible Hall of Light, through which the soulless one must journey before being allotted a resting place here. But the Hall of Light faded, and the impression of great elegance and immense silence and a drifting unfamiliar scent faded, and he was falling forward and there was some kind of cell waiting for him, and this was surely the end of everything, and this was surely all he could ever expect anywhere in the entire world ...

He thought that he lost his hold on sanity for a time then; he knew, later, that the black despair and the agony of loneliness had closed about him fully, and for an unmeasurable time while his reason spun wildly out of control.

But the training that had been such a part of his life, the long hours of studying the Twelve Books of Honour for entry into the *Fiana* at the age of eleven, the days and the weeks spent schooling his mind so that all situations could be calmly appraised, came to his aid and, at length, exhausted and drained, Fergus began to look about him and assess this strange, out-of-the-world fortress.

He had thought, insofar as he had thought about it at all, that all prisons must be akin; that there must be stone cells, barred windows, grilles, gaolers, other prisoners close by.

But although he could see areas of hewn stonework that seemed to close him in, and although he could certainly see barred windows through which light streamed, there were no gaolers, and there were no other prisoners. There was only himself and the vast, endless mansion of the skies, and Fergus, used all of his life to human companionship, thought that this solitude would be more than he could bear. And then he remembered that it had to be borne, that there was no other choice, and that there would be no escape from this place.

Would there? Fergus knew the stories; he knew how it was whispered that once inside the Prison of Hostages no one ever returned to the world of Men, but to Fergus, who had led the *Fiana* from the age of eighteen, and who knew the secrets and the devices and the weaknesses of half the ancient fortresses in Ireland, no prison was ever sealed so utterly and so completely that there was not a way out of it.

He began to study this idea, and he was to think later ("When I could think sanely again," he said) that this was one of the things that saved his reason.

There is no prison from which an initiate of the Fiana *cannot escape.*

It was not quite one of the codes of the *Fiana*, but it was very nearly so. Fergus, who had stormed castles and laid siege to fortresses and who knew the arts of infiltration as well as he knew the Twelve Books of Honour, found himself summoning every shred and every tag-end of legend and myth and lore ever whispered or recounted or imagined about the Prison.

For if there is the smallest hope of escape . . . if there is the merest chance that I could return to the world and to Grainne, I would tear this place down stone by stone.

He knew that escape would not be made by force, but, even so, his mind returned again and again to the grains and snippets of stories that had somehow (how?) permeated into the world of Men.

The Great Hall of Light through which the soulless one must first pass—yes, I came through that, thought Fergus. Great pouring swathes of golden light, and the far-off glint of blue and silver, as if there might after all be something solid and man-made within the Prison. And some kind of early judgment had there been? Yes! thought Fergus. Yes, as if I was being assessed for a place, a level, a *grading* here. This was unexpectedly encouraging, because it was familiar. Within every structured society, certainly at Tara and very definitely within the *Fiana*, there were strata, tiers, sections and subsections. So there's a structured society here, is there? thought Fergus, and felt at once warmer and less alone.

And then, because it was inherent in his nature to question and appraise and assess, he continued his exploration of the threads of knowledge he possessed about the Prison.

The Twelve Chambers of the Blameless and the Praiseless—which is to say fools and idiots, thought Fergus caustically. Yes, that certainly comes next. I suppose that is where I am.

And there were others, places with exotic, sometimes meaningless names ... the Vale of Mists ... the Hall of Golden Columns ... Yes, I know these, I have heard them. He was concentrating furiously now, for, he thought, if I know of these places, then surely it must be because people have been able to talk of them. It must be because people have come out.

People have come out.

The knowledge gave him renewed confidence, and now the strange bizarre names came to him more easily. The Cage of Stars, the Lake of Darkness. The River of Souls which flowed nine times round the Prison. Was there a way out there? If I could find the River, I could ford it somehow, thought Fergus, his mind tumbling now with ideas and plans, and with half-forgotten memories. And there was the Star of the Poets, and surely there was—

Oh yes, thought Fergus, how could I have forgotten?

The Stone Hall of Judgment.

It was that through which he must pass next. But he did not know how long he would have to wait to do so.

It was this last that gave him pause, for, he was to say, "Although I had no knowledge of it—that place where the Twelve Judges sit—I believed that I had long since dreamed it, and I knew it for a place of great finality and immense power. Once inside the Stone Hall of Judgement, once subjected to the decision of the Twelve Stone Judges who pronounce on all Mortal creatures, I believed I should be beyond all hope of escape."

And once that happened, Ireland was lost to him, for although he supposed Taliesin and Fael-Inis would continue the fight, he would never know its outcome. He would never see the world again. Far beyond and far above that, Grainne was lost to him. A bitter smile touched his lips at that, for hadn't Grainne long since been lost? Hadn't she been lost seven years ago, in the misty dawns and the drowsy afternoons? Hadn't she been lost to him before even he had seen her.

Seven years. He had been the newly appointed Head of the *Fiana*, eighteen years old, heady with the power of it.

He had been the youngest ever to head the ancient, honourable *Fiana*; there had been seven years within its ranks only, and he had been intoxicated with the knowledge. Perhaps he had been arrogant, and certainly he had been imperious. But after all, he thought, after all, I was very young.

He could remember how his father had said that he need bow his head to no man in Ireland, save the High Queen, and he could remember how he had laughed, and said to be sure he would call no man master, and certainly no woman either. He had been wildly ambitious and intensely purposeful; he had been sure of his own worth, and determined to succeed.

It had been the confidence of ignorance, of course, but he had not known it then, for who at eighteen recognises such a thing? He had been ready to defy the conventions and take on the world—and win! he thought. Yes, I was ready to fight the world and win. If you intend to climb a mountain, you do not look at the foothills and worry; you keep your eyes fixed on the summit, and that way, if you are very lucky and very determined, you may achieve it.

The summit. He had achieved it more easily and more quickly than ever he had expected.

"Charm," had said the tolerant, smiling on the young Fergus, prepared to accept him for what he was, but, "Arrogant," said the older, more cynical courtiers. And, "Favouritism," said yet others, who remembered how the High Queen Dierdriu had ever an eye to dark-haired, blue-eyed young men who smiled with charm and impudence, and who could woo birds from trees and noble ladies into bed.

It had not been charm alone, and it certainly had not been favouritism that had taken Fergus on his upward journey.

Dierdriu had been kind, certainly. She had smiled on the new young courtier, and she had helped him, and he had been fascinated by her, for although she was ageing, there were still easily discernible traces of the famous beauty who had led armies into battle and lovers into bed; who had brought Ireland to the brink of something so truly great that its fame would echo down the centuries.

Dierdriu had maintained the legend begun by the first Wolfkings, but her granddaughter would create a new legend altogether.

Grainne. Barely eighteen, wide-eyed and a little awestruck by the Court; receptive and responsive.

The Crown Princess, the future High Queen, beautiful and untried, and more desirable than any woman Fergus had ever seen before or since.

But she is not for me nor I for her.

He thought she had not known of his feelings, until the night of the receiving of new candidates into the *Fiana*, at which Fergus, as its head, must preside.

It was an ancient and rather solemn ritual, the admitting

of young men of good family into Ireland's small and carefully chosen band of warriors. The *Fianaigheacht* said, "Only the very highest in the land may enter."

Fergus had questioned this, because his own father had been an ordinary townsman, one of the small landowners near to Tara. Well-to-do in an unassuming way; certainly respected. "But of the people," Fergus was to say with unconscious arrogance. "Not of Ireland's nobility." Why then had his father made that curious statement: "You need bow your head to no man in Ireland save the High King or Queen."?

The candidates had strength and stamina and charm, and Fergus, presiding over the banquet, watching them perform feats of skill and endurance and strength, smiled. He would accept all of them; presently he would cross the floor to where they would stand, and he would bestow acceptance on them.

He had started to move across the Sun Chamber, and a hush had fallen, for at such a ceremony, as the *Fiana*'s head, Fergus commanded absolute obeisance. And then he had turned his head and seen that Grainne was watching him, and a sudden, surprised joy unfolded within his heart, for there was such desire in her eyes that lights exploded inside his head, and he wanted to stand still and savour the moment. He wanted to drink it and touch it and explore it, for, he thought, surely there can be nothing so magical as the moment when you know, beyond all question, that the woman you desire desires you in return.

He had turned it aside, of course, for the Court was waiting. But the knowledge had lain beneath his thoughts, a warm, secret spring of joy. If I beckon, she will come!

Performing the ritualistic Acceptance almost without thinking about it, he had seen, quite clearly, the two paths down which he could travel. He thought, We are still safe, she and I. I have not yet taken the step. I have not yet beckoned to her so that she will come running to me, so that I shall lie with her today and tonight and tomorrow, and for a great many tomorrows. He was aware of the immense arrogance of this, but he knew he had not mistaken that long, steady look. *If I beckon, she will certainly come to me!* he thought, and his mind whirled, so that for a moment he barely saw the waiting Fiana candidates and the glittering Sun Chamber.

Or should he turn desire aside and pretend that there had never been that brief, blinding flare of longing between them? Should he take the honourable path, the virtuous path? Should he bank down desire and quench the longing, so that in the end desire would die and longing would shrivel and life would go on very much as before . . .

He had waited for her in the forests that fringed Tara, his mind filled with light and hope, his body more fiercely aware than ever it had been in his entire life. He felt as if he was about to take his first woman, and as he stood beneath the trees, watching her running towards him, Fergus felt himself trembling. He could not move, and he thought he probably could not speak either. He thought, I believe that *this* is how I shall remember her when it is over, as over it will surely be sooner or later. This is the image, the picture, the memory I shall fold away, so that somewhere in the future, somewhere on the other side of the pain I know awaits, I shall be able to unfold the memory and I shall never quite lose her.

If I can lie with her once, thought Fergus, if I can taste the sweetness, if I can *possess* her just once, she will be forever mine . . .

He had caught her in his arms, and there had been a soaring delight, an exchange of joy, wordless, mindless, stronger and infinitely sweeter than anything he had ever known. She clung to him, and his mouth found hers, and she tasted as fresh and as new as the morning, and desire had exploded within him, and he thought that after all he had been wrong: once would never be sufficient, he wanted her for always, he wanted to be with her, to share everything with her.

Share Tara? said a small treacherous voice he had not known he possessed. Would you share Tara if it was offered?

The thought slid serpent-like into his mind, and he thought, To share Tara. Oh, yes, to be with her and be at her side. Oh, yes, I could do that.

And my son would rule Ireland.

For a moment he had seen it clearly; himself and Grainne in the Sun Chamber; he had seen as well the child, the dark-haired creature of life and light and mischief ... Grainne's son and mine ... A sweet, deep pain closed about his man-hood, and it was then that desire rocketed out of control, and he felt himself become as hard and as high as the beech trees that stood sentinel to Tara's western avenue ...

Grainne arched her back like a cat, and Fergus began to peel the thin robe from her shoulders, kissing her bare skin, feeling her response, feeling the swing of her hair against his shoulders and chest, and exulting in it, for there is something so intimate and so wholly precious about the feel of a loved one's hair against your skin ...

There had been a moment when he sat back and looked at her, naked and submissive in the grass, and his heart started to sing and his mind spun into a dazzling vision of what might be ... because we can only ever be a might-have-been, my dear love ... that little boy with dark mischievous eyes, slender and supple, and Ireland's future Prince ...

Fergus had been so intensely aware of every separate part of her that it had been a pain and a torment. He had wanted to take each part—eyes, skin, hair, bones—and he had wanted to scoop her up and hold her between his hands and never release her again.

Passion had swept in then, and he had entered her, un-able to help himself, clinging to her as she had earlier clung to him, and although he had been gentler than he had ever been with any other woman, she had cried out, and her face had twisted with pain, and Fergus had felt blood on his thighs.

And although I was sharing the pain with her, still I was

exulting, because I had made her mine, and what I had had and what I had taken, no man ever in the world could have of her.

White-hot heat coursed through him, and with it came the rare, precious fusing of mind and body, so that her thoughts and her emotions flowed out to him, and his to her . . . we were truly one on that morning, thought Fergus. We were swept into the bitter-sweet dream, and there would be no going back, but on that morning we were truly one.

THE DREAM HAD turned sooner than he had thought. Alone, in the eternal light of his timeless Prison, Fergus winced away from the memories, and then, with sudden resolve, turned about and faced them. *For memories are the only things I can ever have of you now, my sweet, lovely girl . . .*

He remembered every single one of the stolen meetings; how he had gone to her bedchamber by night, how she had come into the warm drowsy afternoons to find him, when everyone was busy about something and no one knew where anyone was and she would not be missed. He had been lost to all sense of preservation, both for himself and for Grainne.

The summons had come within a week. "The High Queen will receive you in the Sun Chamber," and Fergus had known at once what was ahead.

But he had been unafraid, although a tremor had gone through him as he entered the great Sun Chamber and found Dierdriu alone and waiting for him. He paused in the doorway, because it was rare to see the High Queen without at least a dozen courtiers; certainly he had never seen the Sun Chamber like this, bathed in the glow from the dying day, alive with the strong, pure magic of the Purple Hour, the huge crystal windows that looked out over all Ireland ablaze with light. He thought that Dierdriu was outwardly calm, but that, in reality, she was not, as he was not. She turned and regarded him, and after a moment walked slowly and deliberately to the Ancient Throne of Niall of the Nine Hostages and seated herself on it. In the fading light, her eyes were yellow-gold and gleaming, and Fergus thought, Wolf-eyes! and saw Dierdriu smile, for she had picked that one up with ease. Of course she did, thought Fergus. Was not the Samhailt, the ancient art of hearing the thoughts of others, bestowed on the Royal line long ago?

But Dierdriu only smiled at him, and Fergus saw that it was the cruel, charming smile of her ancestors, who had lain with the wolves. She said, "Do you find it strange to see the Sun Chamber so empty, Captain?" and Fergus thought, Oho! she is calling me Captain. Then we are to be formal, are we!

He said mildly, "I am accustomed to seeing it filled with people, ma'am." And waited for her to make the next move.

But she only said, "I am often here alone at this hour."

"Why have you sent for me, ma'am?"

Dierdriu regarded him thoughtfully. "We shall not play games," she said. "You have transgressed the law."

"Yes?" Fergus put up his chin. "We all of us do that at some time or other." *You* do, said his tone.

The smile deepened. "Oh, Fergus," said Dierdriu softly, "you will have to curb that rebellious arrogance if ever you are truly to serve Ireland."

Fergus felt a surge of real anger now, because how *dare* she treat him as an inferior, how *dare* she speak to him as if he was no more than one of her serfs, a possession, a pawn, a thing.

Dierdriu said, "You cannot have her, you know." Fergus looked up, because for all Dierdriu's hubris, he had not expected her to be so suddenly direct. He drew breath to speak, and Dierdriu said, "Shall I tell you why you cannot?"

"You do not need to," said Fergus, his eyes holding the golden ones. "She is a Princess of Tara." And thought, Let us leave it there, Dierdriu. Let us not say what we both know to be true. Let us pretend that it is only that Grainne is too far above me, and let us continue the pretence, for I do not think I can bear it any other way.

Dierdriu said, "Yes, she is a Princess of Ireland," and looked at him and waited.

"She is of the old pure Wolfline," said Fergus, meeting her eyes. "And that line must never be defiled or sullied."

"Yes," said Dierdriu, and stood up and came over to him. "But there is something else, Fergus." And now her expression was softer, gentler, the yellow glint in her eyes dimmed.

"She is your sister," said Dierdriu.

Fergus heard his own voice break the silence that followed. "I know."

HE HAD KNOWN for longer than he could remember. He could not remember a time when he had not known. Perhaps he had been told when he was first taken to Court. Perhaps he had guessed, without being told. "Remember," said the man who had reared him, "remember that you need bow your head to no one save the High King." And he had looked at Fergus rather sadly when he said this.

"Of course he did," said Dierdriu. "For to him you were a changeling, you were a *malartan*. Grafted-on stock. He reared you, but he could never have understood you."

No one ever has. Fergus did not say it, but he thought that Dierdriu would hear the cry, and he thought, as well, that she would also have experienced the immense lonelinesses, the sudden fierce panics, because it was inevitable that when you were a creature not quite Human, you would instinctively look for your own kind.

And there are no others left of the old enchanted Beastline . . .

Only there had been. There had been Grainne. Was that all it had been? Like recognising like? The call of kinship? Oh, no, my love, for to believe that is to deny anything and everything we were to one another.

Dierdriu was still seated on the High Throne, watching him, and Fergus knew a quick anticipation, and thought, Is she about to tell me the truth about my birth? and was both intrigued and apprehensive, for he had never been told anything of his true parents.

Dierdriu said, "I am not going to tell you that, Fergus,"

and there was a wariness in her tone now, so that Fergus looked up, startled. "It is not a story that bears telling. But you may know that hearts were broken and minds were splintered." She looked at him. "If the truth had ever become known, Tara would have fallen."

The old, old curse revived, and the Bright Palace threatened? The Dark Ireland waking?

"You were taken away," said Dierdriu, "into safety. You were given into the care of people who reared you well."

Made into a changeling. Cast out by my own kind . . . A Wolfchild abandoned, put out to Humans . . . The thought was instantly and fiercely hurtful.

"No," said Dierdriu. "You were put into safety, Fergus. Your safety."

"And Tara's?"

"Oh, yes," she said. "Tara's also. That was of paramount importance. We all knew it. We all knew that Ireland must not fall under the power of the Dark Lords."

So it was the Dark Ireland you feared, madam . . .

"I have always feared the Dark Ireland," said Dierdriu, and her eyes were huge now, and looking on a terrible possibility. "My ancestors—yes, Fergus, your ancestors also—waged endless battles to keep the Bright Palace and to beat back the necromancers and the dark sorcerers from that other Ireland. And if the truth of your conception had been discovered—"

"Why will you not tell me?"

"It would do no good," said Dierdriu again. "And once you knew, you would wish you did not."

"But we are—Grainne and I—we are full brother and sister?"

"Yes." The light had shifted in the Sun Chamber now, and Fergus saw that Dierdriu's eyes were bright with unshed tears. "Oh, yes, my dear, you are full siblings." And then, reaching out to touch his arm, "I would that it were otherwise, Fergus."

Fergus did not speak. He thought he need not have asked

the question, and he wished he had not asked it. For while I did not know, there was still some hope. Because half kin might have been acceptable . . .

Pain sliced through him, and a terrible cold desolation. Then I must let you go, my love, and after all there is nothing anywhere ever, and there is no one in the entire world . . .

Dierdriu said gently, "Had you been half siblings, something might have been permitted. As it was, there was nothing anyone could do."

"Full brother and sister."

"You are twins," said Dierdriu, "born within the hour. You were born here in the Sun Chamber, Fergus." She stood up and began to pace the floor. "Twins," said Dierdriu, "one of Nature's cruellest twists, Fergus." She stood framed in the great crystal window, her eyes on the plains and the rolling fields and the forests below Tara. "What was done was done for Ireland," said Dierdriu. "You must believe that."

Fergus said in a clear, hard voice, "Why am I not in Grainne's place? Why is she the Crown Princess, while I am only her Captain?"

Dierdriu paused and then turned to look at him. "Yes," she said at last. "Of course you would wonder about that." And came again to seat herself on the High Throne. "You are a Prince of Tara, Fergus. It is your inheritance and your birthright, and although we may appear to have taken that from you, we have not really done so." She frowned, and Fergus waited. "On the night you were born," said Dierdriu, "the Wolves were restless in the forests, and there was the sound, very faintly, of the *sidh* singing at Tara's gates." She glanced at him. "The *sidh* have not been seen in Ireland since my own father's day, but they are still here, Fergus. The most purely magical creatures in all Ireland. No one has ever looked on them and lived to tell of it, for they are greedy for the souls of Humans. But when a High King or Queen is born, they have always come up to Tara's gates, and sung him—or her—into the world. And although it is almost certain death to look on them, Fergus, I stole out of the Palace that night, and I saw the green and blue smoke that indicates their presence, and I saw, just for a moment, the Elven King, Aillen mac Midha, seated cross-legged on the ground. I heard the cold faery music." She paused again, her eyes faraway now. "The music of the *sidh* is the most remarkable thing you would ever hear," said Dierdriu. "Cold and inhuman and filled with their strange faery enchantment. It is said that there is a spell within the music, and that they always spin it for the true heir, and that it protects that heir throughout his life.

"But they have long since vanished from Ireland, Fergus, and it may be that I will be the last Queen to have seen them and heard them. There is a legend that says they will return when the Lost Prince of Tara appears, and that it is he alone whom they will serve. But," said Dierdriu, "that is only one of many legends, and people have always talked of a great and mighty ruler who will appear from the ranks of the ordinary people and lead Ireland to greatness."

The Lost Prince ... Ireland's once and future King ...

"I wept on the night the *sidh* were last seen at Tara," said Dierdriu, "for I knew that they could only sing for one of you, and that there could only be one ruler. I knew that these might well be the *sidh*'s last days, and I knew as well that I must find the courage and the strength to send one of you away."

Fergus said, "But why? I don't understand any of this," and Dierdriu closed her eyes and leaned back, so that Fergus suddenly thought, After all, she is no longer young. No longer the wild young Wolfqueen who rode into battle with the armies of all Ireland at her back, and who took and discarded lovers at will. She is no longer young, thought Fergus, and pity stirred in him, and with it a thread of forgiveness. When he said, "Tell me," his voice was very much gentler than it had yet been.

Dierdriu sat up a little straighter. "What I am about to tell you is known to only a handful of people," she said.

"Certainly it is not known outside of the Bright Palace, and equally certainly it is not known outside of the innermost Council Chambers. It is something that is passed on down the generations, from each High King or Queen to the direct heir." She paused, and appeared to select her next words carefully. "As a Prince of Tara, you are, after all, entitled to be told, but as a Prince of Tara, you must promise, solemnly and absolutely, that you will never, no matter the circumstances, reveal what I am about to tell you."

"I do promise," said Fergus, and Dierdriu looked at him very intently.

"Yes," she said at last. "Yes, you mean it." And then, leaning closer to him, "I should know if you did not mean it," she said. "You understand that?"

"Yes," said Fergus. "We are of the same line you and I, ma'am, and although I have not the ancient Samhailt, I understand it. You may trust me."

Dierdriu said, "You know the ancient curse laid on Tara at the beginning of her history?" and looked at him and waited, and Fergus said, half to himself, " 'If Tara should ever belong to a pure-bred Human, then it will fall into ruin, and the Bright Palace will be no more . . .' "

" '. . . and all Ireland will seethe with evil, and the skies will darken, and the rivers will run with blood.' Yes," said Dierdriu, "of course you know. All Ireland knows.

"But what you do not know, what very few people know, is that there is more.

"When the first High Queen cheated the curse by creating the Enchantment of the Bloodline," said Dierdriu, "the sorceress is said to have turned back and made a curious prophecy." Her eyes were slitted in the gathering dusk, but her voice was clear. " 'You may think to deflect the curse,' said the sorceress, 'and for a while you will do so, for your sorcerers are powerful, and the Enchantment they have woven will endure. Half-Humans will rule Ireland for many centuries. But one day your line will divide, and it is then that the magical Beastblood will fade, and you will find you can no longer strengthen it by lying with the creatures of the forest. *It is then that Tara will belong to the Humans.*'

" 'The Line will divide,' " said Dierdriu, looking at Fergus. "Divide. The sorceress could see into the future, and she could see how her curse might again fall on us."

Fergus said, "The Line will divide . . . ?" and looked at Dierdriu, not understanding, and Dierdriu said, "*Twins*, Fergus. If ever twins are born into the Royal House, then the Enchantment of the Beastline will lose its potency, and the curse will revive. Enchantments can die, Fergus, but curses can not. They can only be set aside for a time.

"Eighteen or so years ago, my dear, you and Grainne were born in this room in the Sun Chamber of Tara. *Twins*. And from that day, the ancient curse has been waking.

"We did everything we could," said Dierdriu, pacing the room again. "We summoned the sorcerers, and we sat long nights in Council, for we knew that we dare not wait until it was time for the Ritual of the Beastline to take place; we had to know long before that if the birth of twins into the Royal House had truly damaged the Enchantment.

"And we did know," said Dierdriu, her face haggard and old now. "The sorcerers knew at once. I do not understand the finer points of sorcery," said the Wolfqueen, and a brief, suddenly youthful grin lifted her lips, "but I know a little. They permitted me to go down into Tara's Sorcery Chambers for this. I was there when they took the Enchantment of the Beastline and laid it across the Silver Loom, and I was there as it fell to shreds in their hands. Have you ever seen a dead enchantment, Fergus? No, of course you have not. It is the most painful thing in the world. It was dead, shrivelled, blown to dust, exactly as the sorceress had said it would be, centuries earlier. The ancient curse was reviving . . .

"And so we separated you," said Dierdriu, and now there was an immense sadness in her eyes. "We decided that you must be brought up apart from one another. The sorcerers believed that that would weaken the strong kinship that would exist between you." And then, seeing his expression, "Oh, my dearest boy, forgive me—"

"It does not matter. Go on," said Fergus. And then, as something else occurred to him, "Was that, then, the only time that twins had ever been born to the Wolfline?"

"No," said Dierdriu, but now she spoke so softly that Fergus had to move closer to hear her. "No. Once before, twins were born."

"What happened?"

"They were separated, but they were separated so fully and so completely, and so soon after their birth, that the threat withdrew."

"How—"

"The Time Travellers took one of them," said Dierdriu, and it seemed to Fergus that an old, never-quite-healed agony was in her voice now. "They took the boy-child, and no one in Ireland ever knew what happened to him." And then, with an abrupt gesture, "But it was a very long time ago, and I do not know the details, for I was never told. And all who knew are dead now." Again the shadow was in her eyes, and Fergus, who would have wished to know more of this, felt her retreat a little from him.

But he only said quietly, "Go on."

"The Panel of Judges was summoned, to decide which of you had the stronger vein of wolfblood," said Dierdriu. "That was believed important, for with the Enchantment useless, we knew that we had to keep the Wolfline alive for as long as we could. We had to give the sorcerers time to find the Enchantment or weave a new one. The adjudging of the beastblood is something else I do not fully understand," said Dierdriu, "but it is a little to do with the eyes, and a little to do with the movements . . . And with other things I have never meddled in."

Fergus said, "And so I was sent away and Grainne was permitted to remain at Tara."

"Yes." Dierdriu's eyes fixed on him. "Yes, we sent you away, Fergus, but I know now that we did not send you far enough." She reached for his hand. "Forgive me for that. But you were of my blood, and I had already lost so much—"

"Yes?" Fergus held his breath; he thought, *Now* will she tell me of my parents?

But Dierdriu only said, "And so you went away, and Grainne stayed, and when you came back to Tara, first as a soldier in the *Fiana* and then as its head, I could not bear to send you away again, Fergus." And then, softly, "And indeed, the damage was done by that time. Why should you not take a high place in the home of your ancestors?"

"Why not indeed?" said Fergus lightly.

Dierdriu looked at him very directly. "When we sent you away, Fergus, you were a babe, no more than a few days old."

"Yes?"

"The secret was kept in the way most secrets are kept, which is to say that although the truth did not get out, *something* got out. Something that became woven into the legend and the myth of the day," said Dierdriu.

She looked at him again, the golden wolfeyes hard and unblinking, and Fergus, staring, said, "The Lost Prince—"

"Yes. Your banishment from Tara began the legend, Fergus. *You* were Tara's Lost Prince."

TARA'S LOST PRINCE. The abandoned Wolfchild sent away, made an outcast, given into the care of the Humans.

Fergus, lying sleepless and alone in the Prison of Hostages, could still feel the pain and the bewilderment, and the terrible knowledge that he, who loved Ireland beyond measure, had been a part of her doom.

Because I was born twin to Grainne . . . because the Royal Line must never divide . . .

Even so, thought Fergus, staring up at the light, even so, there is something Dierdriu did not tell me.

My parents. She did not tell me that.

It was something that had puzzled him during all his years at Court, and it was something that had stayed with him. Who had they been, those poor tragic people who had brought forth the twins who were to fulfil the sorceress's prophecy? How had they felt? How did it feel to know that you were the instrument and the cause of something so enormously and comprehensively dreadful?

Had it been Dierdriu's son? Or a daughter? Strange, thought Fergus, turning restlessly and trying to escape the light, strange that throughout all Court history and throughout all Court gossip (and gossip at Tara had ever been lively), that no one has ever referred to Dierdriu's child, to the heir to Tara who disappeared. No one has ever spoken of the child who must have been born to Dierdriu, and who had given birth to himself and Grainne.

Why not? thought Fergus. And then— She called me the Lost Prince, but supposing there is another Lost Prince?

CHAPTER TEN

GRAINNE EXPLORED THE Grail Castle tirelessly. She could feel the enchantments of the ancient legend-haunted stronghold lying on the air everywhere, but she thought, Even so, I believe this is not a place of sadness.

"You will never quite discover all of the castle," said Raynor. "For it keeps its secrets."

"Secrets?" She thought he looked at her rather searchingly, and she held her breath, for surely there would be strange untold stories about this place, and surely he would know of them? But he only said, "It was raised from the rock by the first High Kings, and it is filled with rather strange magic. It does not obey the same laws as other dwellings."

Grainne, feeling the castle's subtle spells close about her, wanted to know everything; she wanted to find out all there was to find out about this dark fortress. At times she stole out from her bedchamber after nightfall, and stood listening to the night rustlings and the soft settling of the old timbers. Sometimes there were footsteps: not frightening, certainly not threatening, but purposeful and efficient, as if the owner was going quietly and efficiently about some routine task.

Sometimes she lay awake, feeling the castle sleeping all about her, hearing the little sighing sounds as beams settled into place, or the wind as it soughed beneath the eaves, or moaned in and out of battlements and turrets.

At such times, she heard the footsteps, and at such times, she half sat up, and listened. More than once she moved to go in pursuit, but she never quite did.

But she thought that if only she knew the right words,

or if only she had the power, she could summon the enchantments, and lay bare the secrets and understand this place. *There are immense and terrible secrets here,* she thought.

As Tara's Crown Princess and then as its High Queen, she knew something of the castle's history. She knew about Cormac of the Wolves, her great-grandfather, who had been exiled here for five years, and she knew about the others as well: Niall of the Nine Hostages, caught and chained and kept prisoner with nine faithful Lords until he broke out and regained the Throne. Nuadu Airgetlam, Nuadu of the Silver Arm, who had lost his left arm in a battle and been driven from the Bright Palace by the fearsome Gruagach. But Nuadu had returned; he had been made whole by the Court Sorcerer, and he, also, had regained his Throne.

Grainne thought it was strange that she had never before realised how many Kings of Ireland had been exiled and had later returned. Shall I return? Or shall I go down in history as the High Queen who lost Tara for always? She could not let it happen. She would rally the creatures of this castle, and the Cruithin, and drive out Medoc and beat back the Dark Ireland. And Grainne smiled briefly, because it was certainly possible that these thoughts were flowing outwards and being absorbed by the ancient stones. Perhaps she, also, was leaving a few secrets and a few memories behind.

And the castle was not entirely made up of sadness and shadows. There were sudden patches of light that you came out on to when you least expected it. You might walk down some sombre corridors and gaze upon dim, seldom-used halls, and you might run your hand across the scarred surfaces of the old walls, and then, without the least warning, you would find yourself in a sun-drenched quadrangle, or a courtyard where gentians grew or mountain ash flared. You came across patches of happiness here, just as you came across patches of colour.

When Grainne said rather diffidently to Raynor, "People have been happy here, I think," he said at once, "Yes, there is happiness here." And then, with one of his sudden, gentle smiles, "But it is necessary to look quite deeply for it, Your Majesty. And it is necessary for us to hide it as well."

"More secrets?" said Grainne, willing him to unfold. But he only said, "Where people perceive happiness, ma'am, they will ask questions," and he retreated again behind a courteous mask.

"You hide so much here," said Grainne.

"Because it is necessary. Because we do not wish the world to look upon us." He regarded her. "The Cruithin have a little of the old magic," he said, "and the castle itself has its own." He looked at her with his piercing stare, and Grainne, who had begun to understand a little of the castle's strangeness, said tentatively, "The happiness within is not apparent from without."

"It is not intended to be," said Raynor. "The castle wishes to keep its secrets. The Cruithin have"—a pause—"the Cruithin have harnessed some of its darkness," said Raynor. "And they have thrown it outwards."

"It is very forbidding on approach."

"Yes," said Raynor softly. "Oh, yes, it is very forbidding on approach." And, looking at her, "That is the inner darkness turned outwards. You understand why."

The castle was forbidding and *dark* on approach because its occupants wished to keep intruders out. This was interesting and a new idea, and Grainne would have liked to know more. But Raynor only said, quite politely, "There are many such castles in Ireland, ma'am. There are many enchantments which have been woven into dwellings and which need only to be harnessed. It is only that people have lost the secret."

People have lost the secret . . . But it must be found, thought Grainne. Somehow I must find it again . . .

Raynor and his people had made Grainne and the others very welcome. There had been no ceremony about any of it, for ceremony of any kind seemed to be something that they did not embrace. But there was an acceptance, and a you-are-one-of-us that Grainne found restful.

The Beastline were interested in all she could tell them

of Tara and of the exiled Court. They listened and asked a great many questions, but Grainne thought the questions were those of curious children, mentally exploring a fabled land . . . We shall never go there, we shall never *dare* to go there, but all the same, we like to hear of it. We like to think about the might-have-beens. And Grainne, who had her own might-have-beens, understood, and tried to make her stories of the Bright Palace interesting and amusing, and tried to minimise the rigours and the heartaches of exile on Innisfree.

And if she told them of her world, they, in turn, made her free in theirs. They each had their appointed tasks, and their place in the running of the castle, and Grainne, unused to being included in such ordinary daily tasks, felt it enfold her gently and naturally.

Rinnal, the fox man, showed her the garden where they grew their own vegetables and fruit. "For," he said, "everything we eat we must provide for ourselves. Over there is our herb garden, and here are some fruit trees, from which we are cultivating a new strain. We think they will be ready next year, and we are looking forward to tasting the fruit."

Two of the younger ones rather shyly explained about the workings of the creamery. "Butter and cheese," they said, and Grainne was pleased that she understood the machinery, and even managed to churn quite an acceptable pat of butter, which the two Beastline creatures at once stamped with a wooden mould on which was carved, in reverse, the outline of a castle.

Bec, the girl with a badger's furry snout and soft dark eyes, showed her the great sculleries where they all took turns to prepare the food. "All of us, even Raynor," she said, and smiled. "Although he is not the best of our cooks, ma'am. But sometimes he prepares a dish of what we call Cais Breac—that is lake fish cooked in wine, with our own herb cheese. Quite delicious. We eat that when there is something to celebrate."

"Raynor is your leader?" asked Grainne.

"In as much as we acknowledge a leader," said Bec, regarding Grainne thoughtfully. "He is the strongest, you see," she said. "I do not mean physically, although he *is* strong physically."

"Mentally," said Grainne, half to herself, and at once Bec said, "*Yes*. Yes, you do understand. I thought you would." And Grainne was struck all over again by the complete lack of subservience of these creatures.

"When we falter," said Bec, peering into a huge simmering cauldron of something that smelled savoury and good, "it is always Raynor who helps us. It is to him we go when we need support. Sometimes, you see, it is difficult for us."

Grainne said slowly, "It is to be expected that you would despair at times," and Bec responded at once, "Oh no. Never that," and Grainne looked at her, startled.

"To despair is our most grievous fault," said Bec. "Only think, ma'am, of the true meaning of despair. The giving up of all hope. An abandoning of hope that there is something—anything—better. To truly despair is one of the most terrible things in the world," she said severely, and Grainne, listening, thought, Well, yes, of course. How very strange that I should never have seen that.

"We are the failed spells, ma'am, we must live here in secret, guarded by the Cruithin and also by the castle's own strange protections. And although there are times when we falter—*black* times," said Bec, her eyes huge and sad, "we strive never to fall victim to despair." She gave Grainne a sudden, very sweet smile, and Grainne felt all over again the integrity and the tranquillity of these strange beings.

Fintan and Cermait Honeymouth, along with Tybion the Tusk, were establishing cautious friendships with the Cruithin. "Although," said Fintan, "to get to know them you have to find them, of course."

"They're around," said Fintan firmly. "They come and go a bit silently, of course, but that's not to say they're furtive."

"They're hospitable," said Cermait, who, along with Fintan, had spent several very convivial evenings in the low-ceilinged, apple-scented room. "And my word, their stories! My word!"

Fintan said it was not the stories but the poteen, and it was only three nights since Cermait had had to be carried to bed.

"No, I was not," said Cermait.

"Three of us carried you, and I was one of the three, and I had to tip a jug of water over you next morning to wake you."

Cermait said, rather huffily, that it was a well-known fact that even an acorn-full of poteen sent you fast asleep, and Fintan gave vent to a derisive hoot.

"You snored *all night*," he said with relish, and Cermait got up and removed himself from this low vulgar company, because you could not stay in a room with people who told the High Queen that you snored. He said, with great politeness, that he would be in the buttery, always supposing anyone wanted to know, and Tybion the Tusk got up and helped him open the door, just to be friendly.

"He looked so upset," he said.

"I was upset at being kept awake by people snoring," said Fintan, but after a moment he got up and went off to the buttery himself, "because we need to know if the parsley butter is ready," he said rather defiantly. "There's baked lake fish for supper, so I hear, and some nice parsley butter will go very well with it. Bec's baked soda bread as well. I'll just go along and find out."

As THE DAYS slid by, the Cruithin became a little less elusive, and Grainne waited, because she knew that to befriend them, to lead them back into Ireland, would be the greatest service she could render her people.

When at last they began to come out to her in the sun-drenched quadrangle on the castle's south side, where she liked to sit, she was patient and cautious. It was a bit like sitting very quietly in a forest and waiting for a rare and timid wild animal to come out. But when they began to steal away from their tasks to sit beside her and smoke their pipes, Grainne felt more honoured than at any time since she had occupied Ireland's Throne.

The Cruithin were interesting and learned. They talked to her about her ancestors, and about the Bright Palace, which they called *Teamhair* in their soft voices, and they told her about the battles and the people who had made Ireland magical and marvellous and richer in folklore than any country could ever be.

Grainne listened, absorbed and serious, and in her mind she began to see the old Ireland, the Ireland of the Lost Enchantments, very clearly. She could see the Beastline overlords who had sat with the Wolfkings at Tara; proud and noble and dignified, and just very slightly cruel, but charming and strong as well, and utterly loyal to the High King. She could see them standing on the ridge of hill that rose up behind Tara's eastern boundaries, sending out the strong magic of the Samhailt to their creatures, so that the woods and the streams and the hillsides thrummed and quivered with the Mindsong.

"And every wild creature, and every forest animal had to obey," said the Cruithin, their eyes bright. "They had to come streaming out of the forests and down to the Bright Palace, in answer to the summons of their Lords . . ."

When the Cruithin said, "The Enchantment is lost to us, ma'am," Grainne turned to them, her eyes brilliant, and said, "But we shall find it again," and saw them nod and smile, and felt suddenly and deeply happy.

Even so, there was a dreadful sense of loss in hearing these stories of her ancestors; there was an ache and a feeling of bereavement. Ireland has had so much, she thought; there has been so much magic and so much strength, and now all of it has gone. Hadn't it? Can I truly bring it back? thought Grainne, watching the Cruithin disperse to their work again, leaning forward and hugging her knees. Am I being artless when I say that? Am I deceiving myself and deceiving us all? Why should I be the one?

She thought it would not be possible to talk about this to anyone—my burden and I must bear it, she had believed—but she found herself discussing it easily and naturally and very trustingly with Raynor.

"There is such a sense of loss," she said, looking at him to be sure he understood this. "Ireland has lost so much."

"But you are restoring it," said Raynor softly. "You are bringing the magic back," and looked at her and waited, and Grainne said in a whisper, "Am I?"

"Oh, yes, my dear." And there was such a caress in his voice that Grainne felt her heart lurch. "The Cruithin will follow you, ma'am," he said.

"And you? You and the others? Would you follow me also?"

She felt his retreat at once, and saw the shuttered look come down over his face. "I would that it were possible," he said.

"Could it not be?" Grainne felt her heart thudding with such a fierceness that she could almost imagine he would hear it. But he only said, very softly, "For you I would ride into hell. I would endure fire and flood and the agonies of the world. But I cannot face the world that you have left, ma'am. Do not ask it of me."

"I do ask it," said Grainne, standing very still. "Very soon now, I *will* ask it."

"Look at me," he said in a low, anguished voice. "Look at what I am. Deformed. Distorted. A sorcerer's error. A failed spell! If you have any pity, Grainne, do not ask it of me."

Delight ran all over her at his use of her name, and she wanted to reach up and take his face between her hands and say, "You are beautiful and strong and gentle. *Please* do not hide from me."

She fell into the way of sitting with him at supper, liking the custom that the Beastline creatures had of making each evening a little ceremony in its own right.

"We come to the supper table," explained Bec, "rested

and relaxed and ready to engage one another in conversation. Perhaps there have been odd, amusing little things that have happened during our day's work, and we share these. Perhaps one of us is tired or discouraged. Then we all try to lift him out of discouragement."

The nightly supper table was pleasant and restful. It was a focus in the day; a point to look forward to, to work towards. As Bec said, you found yourself encountering something amusing or interesting during your day which you stored up to tell. You knew that the others would be doing the same.

But it was Raynor who told her things about the castle she did not know; how it had been built for the first High Queen of all, and how the ancient pure magic had been woven into its walls. Grainne, listening, watching, saw how his eyes darkened when he became absorbed in something, and how the planes of his face shifted so that at times the eagle-blood was more strongly marked than others . . . how the caplike golden hair shone beneath the light from the wall sconces . . . What would it feel like beneath her touch . . . ? Shall I ever dare to find out?

"The castle will always withhold something," he said.

"That was the first High Queen's instruction when it was being raised from the rock. A place of immense secrecy. A place which could keep within its walls those things which must not be known. She knew," said Raynor thoughtfully, "that long-ago Queen, that there would be times in Ireland's history when things would need to be hidden."

"We have many stories of that first High Queen," said Grainne, cupping the wine chalice between her hands, her expression intent. "How she fought and intrigued and made Ireland great. How she bargained with the sorcerers to build the Bright Palace for her. How she was so beautiful that everyone in Ireland loved her. Men would travel hundreds of miles just to catch a glimpse of her."

Raynor said softly, "But you are so beautiful that men would die for you," and Grainne looked up, startled, because the words had been so soft that she could not be sure she had heard them correctly, yet she knew she had. Her heart began to thud erratically, and she felt as if a great weight was pressing down on her making it difficult to breathe.

Raynor stayed where he was, his eyes on her, and Grainne felt a surge of the utmost exhilaration. I am not mistaken! He wants me! And waited.

But he only said, "I am privileged to serve you, ma'am," and turned away, and Grainne thought, Oh, *damn*! Can he not tell! What must I do? He is the most remarkable looking creature I have ever seen, and I believe I could love him very much, and I believe that with him I could forget Fergus.

FORGET FERGUS. THE thought still brought a pain: for how could I ever truly forget you, my love?

Lying wakeful in her bedchamber that night, Grainne knew that she would never truly forget Fergus.

But since I can never have Fergus, not ever, why should I not have Raynor? There is no disloyalty. Why should I not?

Raynor. The unknown, eagle creature, created out of sorcery, but a creature of such strange, inverted beauty, and such strength. A creature who had never seen a world outside this castle. Grainne had sometimes wanted to renounce Tara, she had sometimes wanted to forsake the Throne and flee to obscurity, but this was a creature who had renounced the world without even knowing it.

And who had still achieved peace of mind.

She would never forsake Tara, of course, just as she would never forget Fergus. But—I believe I could learn to live with the memories, she thought. I could live *comfortably* with the knowledge of those nights with Fergus that should never have happened. I could live in peace with the might-have-beens as well; the elfin-faced, slant-eyed boy who never existed . . . Ireland's Prince . . .

She had hated Dierdriu on the terrible day that Dierdriu had told her that she and Fergus were to be parted. She had bowed her head and accepted Dierdriu's words, for she had known, at once, the truth of what Dierdriu said.

Your brother. He is your brother, Dierdriu had said, her face expressionless, but her eyes compassionate. And therefore he is forbidden to you by every rule, natural or man-made.

Grainne had not questioned the truth or the logic, or even the history that must lie behind this. She had known, instantly and completely, that Dierdriu spoke the truth.

For there was that closeness, that oneness, that immense and remarkable understanding between us ... Was that all it was, my love? Only the call of the blood? Only the instinct of the wolves, our ancestors, recognising a member of the same pack? It does not matter, she had thought, numbly, for whatever it was and whatever it has been, it was forbidden for all time.

Forbidden for all time. If I waited for a hundred years, if I devoted my life to fasting and asceticism and scholarship as the Druids do, still it would make no difference. I can never have him, nor he me.

There had been black bitterness, and there had been a great aching void for longer than she cared to remember now. There had been anger as well at the cruel jest of fate that had brought her into love with her own brother.

She had not shown any of it, she thought. She had smiled and raised rather amused brows at the stories that tumbled in then of Fergus's progress. *An experience of women that would extend over many nations* ... Yes, the words fitted by then, no matter who had written or said them. She had even managed to shrug and say that, after all, the Fiana's Head must be a person of some charm. And she had accepted what had to be accepted, and she and Fergus had parted. *Except that we were never completely apart, my love, for you were always beside me, and you were always there, and I think that without you there, there were times when I should certainly have been crushed by the weight of a Crown I did not really want.*

She had of course questioned the decision that had left

her heiress to Tara, while Fergus, so indisputably a leader, so plainly possessing the natural authority Grainne believed she lacked, was relegated to the command of the *Fiana*.

"A high position," Dierdriu had said.

"But he is a Prince of Ireland!" Grainne had cried. "Why is he not here at Tara!"

Dierdriu had looked at her for a long moment. Then, "My child, you will one day know," she had said. "For now you must bear the loss."

Grainne had nodded, and she had done as she was told, but deep within her had been a spurt of anger, for when had Dierdriu ever borne loss, when had Dierdriu ever lost a lover?

Lying wakeful in her bedchamber, with the Grail Castle silent all about her now, Grainne remembered vividly her emotions all those years ago. Dierdriu had never lost a lover, for Dierdriu had been reckless and abandoned, and had had any man she had ever wanted.

And then Grainne sat up in the bed, and thought, In my position now, what would Dierdriu have done?

And felt the beginnings of a smile curve her lips.

WHAT WOULD DIERDRIU have done?

The Grail Castle was not entirely in darkness when Grainne slipped out of her room and closed the door carefully, but there was not very much light. Was there enough to see her way? There would have to be, because it would be quite difficult to make her way to Raynor's room burdened with flaming torches. Also, it would attract attention. Grainne did not mind about attracting attention, but it would be better not to.

And again there was the quiver of amusement, because had Dierdriu ever been discreet when she went to a lover's bed? Dierdriu, thought her granddaughter, had probably gone noisily and wantonly along brightly lit corridors, brandishing torches, attended by half the Court, very likely conducting a few odds and ends of State business along the way.

None of it would have done for the Grail Castle and the gentle remote creature to whose bed Grainne was going.

The castle was faintly lit by the soft light of the moon, and Grainne, pausing to look down over the courtyard through a small side window, saw how the countryside was bathed in radiance. And smiled, because there was a radiance within her. *For surely he will not reject me* . . . Would he? But if I do not go to him, he will never come to me, said her mind.

She supposed she ought to feel apprehensive, but she felt only deep delight, and it seemed the most natural thing in the world to be making her way through the moonlight to Raynor.

The most natural thing in the world . . . and had we but world enough and time, my love . . . Yes, the echoes were still all about her, and there was a comfort in them, for she felt that she was not alone.

Only that I cannot tell if the echoes are from the past or the future, or some other world altogether.

His room was in the oldest part of the castle, along a narrow galleried landing, with thick dark hangings that stirred faintly as she passed. And although it was no moment to stop and remember those night footsteps that passed her door so regularly, Grainne did remember them. Part of the castle's secrets? Perhaps. Perhaps I shall find out what they mean, thought Grainne, moving on.

The door to Raynor's room was down a flight of steps and through a narrow archway. Someone had thrust a burning torch into an old iron wall bracket, and there was a warm soft light and the faint scent of fragrant wood burning. Pearwood was it?

Grainne stood very still and knew she was going forward into something that might well be a delight, but that might also be a torment. He may reject me. He may take me tonight and then reject me tomorrow. Which would be worse?

But the decision is made, she thought. I think the decision was made long ago. I cannot go back now. And she descended the stairs and, tapping lightly on the door, turned the handle and went in.

There was firelight in the room, a soft gentle radiance that warmed the old stone walls and sent huge, fantastical shadows dancing across the ceiling. There was the impression of light and space, and of great tranquillity. Even so, Grainne, standing in the doorway, absorbing it all, felt beneath the tranquillity an aching solitude, and thought, Yes, he has been quite unbearably lonely here. And knew that the remoteness and the gentle strength had been hard won.

And then a log broke in the hearth, sending sparks cascading, and the shadows leapt, and Grainne remembered all of the old stories, and could almost have believed that the ancient Ireland had awoken at last; that goblins and satyrs and cloven-hoofed, pointed-eared creatures were prancing in the room with them.

And then she looked back at the bed and saw the naked longing in his eyes, and something that was better than desire and that was more enduring than passion broke within her, and she moved forward, and said, "Oh, my dear love—"

Raynor held out his arms and Grainne went straight into them.

HE HAD NO defences and no armour. He had wanted her almost from the first moment, and he had loved her for nearly as long.

They had been desires to be quenched, as he had quenched other desires over the years. He believed himself a near-monster, a deformity, a half-Human creature born of a sorcerer's mismanaged spell-weaving. "But I have feelings and longings," he might have said. "I have a Human side."

It was a part of his creed never to give way to these emotions. He believed that the creatures inside the Grail Castle must not breed, for it was not to be thought of that the nightmare perpetuated by the sorcerers should be passed on. Flawed stock could not be allowed to spawn. He had not laid such an imposition on the others, nor would he have tried to do so, for, he would have said, who am I, knowing so little of the world, to make laws and rules for my fellow creatures? But he knew that the other Beastline creatures looked to him for guidance, and he had accepted the leadership they imposed on him, for he knew that there must always be those who govern and those who serve. Bec had said to Grainne that when they faltered or fell prey to despair, it was Raynor who helped them. "But," she might have added, "we do not know who it is who helps Raynor, for he does not come to us."

He did not go to anyone. He fought his own despairs and his own bitterness, and he had believed that he had built up an inner tranquillity and a strength, so that he was armoured against the lure of any woman.

But when Grainne came to the castle, he knew himself lost, and he knew that the carapace so diligently acquired over the years was melting. The Wolfqueen was waking in him longings and emotions that he had striven to bury. When Grainne slipped silently into his room, desire blazed up so uncontrollably that the banked-down emotions of a lifetime were swept aside, and he knew he would take her fiercely and violently. He would try not to hurt her, but the minute she touched him, the minute he felt her skin against his body . . .

She slid the thin silk robe from her shoulders and stood naked before the fire, looking at him, and he saw the humility and the fear in her eyes, and felt something fierce and triumphant uncoil.

For I am on equal terms with someone for the first time in my life. I have been sought by this remarkable beautiful creature who is offering herself to me . . .

He moved cautiously now, unused to the preludes, unsure of what she would expect. He stood for a moment longer, looking at her, unable to speak, seeing that she was so beautiful it was hurtful to him, thinking that in other circumstances he would be unmanned by such beauty, except that he was not unmanned, that was the very last thing . . .

And then, *Perhaps after all I am not such a deformed thing*, he thought, and a sweet heady joy began to pulse through him.

When he lowered Grainne on to the pile of thick fur rugs before the fire, he was trembling, but when he stood up and began to unfasten his own clothes, he did so with a calm sureness and a gentle authority.

GRAINNE HAD KNOWN that when it finally came to it, she would be afraid—*For I have never known anyone other than Fergus, and with Fergus it was so natural and so sweet*—but she had not expected this sudden rush of tenderness. She had gone to his room ready to play the wanton, certainly believing she would have to seduce him into her arms, and there had been an undercurrent of panic at this.

But the desire and the longing in his eyes had given her strength, and he had moved to her at once, so that she had known, once and for all, that there could never be anything strained or awkward between them.

He had watched her cast aside her thin robe, and he had smiled with such infinite love and such intimacy that pain had twisted through her from breast to womb. He had thrown aside his own robe then, and had stood for a moment looking down at her, the firelight playing over his body, and Grainne had felt her senses tumble, for surely, oh, surely there had never been anything so beautiful and so strong . . . *He is half-eagle, and I have never seen such an exquisite thing* . . . His skin had the golden sheen of an eagle's plumage . . . skin but not quite skin— Oh, yes! thought Grainne, drowning in delight now. When he turned to look at her, the firelight cast shadows across his body, so that she saw his arms not as arms, but as wings . . . *and they will enfold me so strongly and so sweetly that I shall never want to be free* . . . His legs were supple and strongly muscled, and Grainne half closed her eyes, and let her mind race forward, and anticipated the feel of his thighs against her . . . There was a tangle of dark golden hair; it was not rough and harsh but silken, as if the true eagleblood might be centred between his legs . . .

When he touches me, I shall certainly be helpless . . . But I
believe I shall be his, completely and for ever then . . .

WHEN SHE TOUCHES me, I shall be hers for all time, and when
she touches me, I shall be so hungry for her, that I may
hurt her.

The thought was hardly to be borne. Raynor paused,
looking down into the half-closed eyes, and saw Grainne
smile, and saw, as well, that despite her apparent tranquillity,
she had been nervous, and that it had not been easy for her
to come to his room. He thought she would certainly have
had other lovers, for he knew a little of the way of the Court,
and he pushed the thought away. *For she is certainly mine
now, and surely in a way she has never been any other man's . . .*
Even so, he thought that never before had she been the
hunter, and as the thought was framed, Grainne said softly,
"You are right. It was not easy," and Raynor smiled at her
and said very gently, "The Samhailt?"

"I barely possess it," said Grainne, unable to take her
eyes from him. "Although it is my heritage, I barely possess
it. It is only that—"

"It is that we are closely linked, you and I, my love."

My love . . . Natural and right and entirely familiar. I
should be feeling disloyal to Fergus, I should certainly be
wondering if what I am doing is right, and if I am going to
be hurt. She did not wonder if it was right, and she knew
there was no hurt ahead for her. *Not this time.* And oh, Fergus, my dear, lost love, am I doing you so much harm? Was
not the harm already between us, before we had loved and
before we lost, and perhaps before we were born?

She knelt before the fire, facing Raynor now, leaning her
head back as he began to explore her body, feeling his hands,
tentatively at first and then growing more assured, sliding
over her shoulders and her breasts . . . His hands were not
quite skin and not quite plumage . . . Silken and smooth and
so deeply loving that the pain was there again . . .

Only that this one will never hurt you . . .

This one. This strange, remote, eagle creature, whose body was bathed in incandescence from the fire, except that it was not quite the fire; whose eyes were dark with passion, and whose arms, strong and safe, were enveloping her, and laying her down on the thick fur rugs before the fire . . .

There was the pure and unalloyed joy of reaching down to cup his passion between her hands, and of feeling a tremor go through him . . . Fires banked down so strongly for so long . . . He is on fire with hunger, thought Grainne, her senses spinning. He is on fire, and I believe we shall both drown in the heat, and I believe neither of us would care if we did . . .

And then Raynor entered her with a strong swift move-ment, and the fires engulfed them both.

GRAINNE LAY IN Raynor's arms before the fire, warm and drowsy, and more deeply happy than she could ever remem-ber being.

She thought she could so easily stay here, learning the ways of Raynor's people, working with them. Perhaps teach-ing them a little of her own world. Oh, yes, I could do that, thought Grainne, sleepless and still half drowning in the warmth and the sweetness.

I could be happy here, in this great, shadowy, secret-laden place, where there are unexpected patches of happiness, and where memories sometimes echo back, and where you can feel the history of the years swirl about you. You would never quite know what you might find here; you would certainly find un-expected flights of stairs which might lead anywhere at all, and you would surely sometimes come upon doorways you had not known existed. You would continually find gateways, thought Grainne, falling a little more deeply into sleep. Yes, there were gateways here in the castle, where midnight foot-steps trod purposefully down the halls . . .

Footsteps.

The sleep vanished, and she was fully awake at once.

Footsteps. Going silently and steadily through the castle,

somewhere quite near by. Grainne raised herself cautiously on one elbow, trying not to wake Raynor, and looked towards the door. Yes, the footsteps were the ones she heard every night in her own part of the castle. She hesitated, and looked down at Raynor, and saw that he was watching her, and saw, as well, that he understood.

Grainne said, "The footsteps—I have heard them before . . ." and Raynor said, "Yes. Yes, it is time you knew." And reaching for his clothes, he pulled her to her feet, and said, "Come with me."

IF IT HAD been possible for the old castle to grow darker, Grainne thought it would have done so in the hour that followed.

She lost all sense of direction, and, "I never knew quite where Raynor took me," she said afterwards.

As they moved through the halls and the corridors, she felt as never before the layers upon layers of history. She thought she could almost see the memories and she could certainly hear the echoes. Happiness and despair and hope and fear. Plots and counter-plots and escapes and incarcerations. Torments and delights and pain-filled nights and promise-filled dawns.

Cormac of the Wolves, sitting out the long years of his exile; Niall and the Nine Lords chained and starving in the dungeons. Nuadu of the Silver Arm, submitting to the sorcerers so that he might be made whole again. And what of myself? thought Grainne. Am I also leaving a mark here? In time to come, will someone else walk these halls and remember the Wolfqueen who lived here for a time, but who brought the Cruithin out of hiding, and drove Medoc from the Bright Palace? Yes. And she smiled at Raynor and saw him smile back, and felt renewed, and understood how it was that Bec and the others came to Raynor for help.

Raynor said softly, "There is pain ahead for you," and Grainne said, "Yes. I understand."

"Would you wish not to go on?"

"No. I must see whatever there is to see." She thought she knew about pain anyway, because there had been pain in losing Fergus, there had been nights and days and weeks of aching torment.

Raynor said gently, "There are different levels of pain, Grainne," and Grainne looked startled, because he had heard her thoughts.

"I think you are acquiring the Samhailt, Raynor," she said, and saw sudden delight flare in his eyes.

But, "It is just that we are in sympathy," he said. To himself he thought, Supposing she is right! Supposing that after all the sorcerers did not fail? Supposing that I could stand on the hills surrounding this castle and send out the Samhailt, the ancient and precious gift bestowed on the Noble Houses of Ireland? Supposing I could call up the eagles? And then, *What has she awoken?* he thought, and in spite of his deep love for her and his longing to protect her, he knew a tremor of fear. This, after all, was the Wolfqueen, the last of a lineage so old that its beginnings were wreathed in legend and lore and magic. He knew that Grainne was gentle and strong and sensitive; he knew this as if it was something he had been born knowing; even so, he found himself remembering that the Wolfline were said to have old enchantments in their blood, and that the old enchantments were tinged with the dark sinister magic of the first sorcerers, and that the descendants of those long-ago Wolfkings could still spin their own bewitchments and weave their own spells. And, *Is this what you have done, Lady?* he thought. *Have you summoned the ancient golden strength, to bind me to you once and for all time?* He thought he would not care if she had in truth done so, although he knew it to have been unnecessary. But as he walked at her side through the dark halls of the Grail Castle, he remembered, and wished not to remember, that she might well have within her the strange power that could awaken all manner of sleeping bewitchments and lost enchantments. And the things that lie hidden in this castle? Oh, yes, certainly those, thought Raynor, putting out a hand to guide Grainne down a flight of stairs.

Grainne, going cautiously through the castle, thought that this was certainly not a journey she could have made alone.

Alone through the silent halls, where midnight's arch stretches far above us ... I am hearing the echoes again, thought Grainne, staring about her, her eyes huge and dilated.

And the footsteps? Were the footsteps also all about them?

This is like the centre of a dead world's soul, thought Grainne. I think I am beginning to be very much afraid of what Raynor is taking me to.

The old stone walls closed about her, so that at times it seemed to be suffocatingly hot, and she found herself putting up a hand to her throat. There was despair here now—and it is the real and truly terrible emotion, thought Grainne. It was like falling into a black well, where you knew there would never be light, or it was like being cast adrift on a night ocean when you knew no ships would ever pass.

Alone forever, and with no hope, no joy, no warmth ...

I do not think I can bear this, thought Grainne, but even as the thought was framed, she knew that for *someone* it had had to be borne, there had been no escaping it, this bottomless dark pit, this vast endless night sea ...

Raynor said very softly, "Down here," and Grainne hesitated, and then thought, *Yes, but why is he whispering? What does he fear to disturb?*

The steps led downwards, there were crumbling stone walls, so that they had to clutch at narrow ropes sunk into the wall at intervals. The steps were worn away at the centre, and Grainne wondered if it was from the footsteps which passed this way every night, or whether it was simply from age.

"A little of both," said Raynor, and frowned briefly, for

he was hearing her thoughts more clearly now. The Samhailt wakening? The Wolfqueen acting as some kind of lodestar? Is she affecting the castle? he thought. And then—and this was more sinister by far—or is the castle affecting her?

And then Grainne said, "It feels as if we are going down into some terrible prison," and Raynor said, "Yes, it is a prison. It has been used as a prison many times. I do not know how many. But it has a dark and ancient history."

He led her along a cold flagged corridor now, where the walls gleamed faintly with phosphorescence, and where, although wall sconces flared bravely, the light was greenish and lack-lustre, so that it was rather like walking under water.

Raynor came to a stop outside a thick, low door set into the wall, and stood for a moment looking at it, as if summoning up some inner resolve. Grainne saw that there was a small oblong grille set high up. To see in? Or to see out?

At length Raynor said, very softly, "Before we go farther, you must give me your promise that whatever happens inside here, whatever is said, you will not leave my side. You must not, under any circumstances at all, progress more than several paces into the room." The sudden intimate smile lifted his lips. "Should I ask your pardon, Wolfqueen, for appearing to issue orders to you?"

"No," said Grainne in a whisper. "Oh, no, never that."

"Then, I will not," said Raynor. "You will do as I ask?"

"Yes."

The brief smile glinted again. "Unquestioning obedience," he said. "I am fortunate."

And reached for a heavy key and turned the lock. The door swung open.

The room beyond the heavy iron-studded door was larger than Grainne had expected. There was light of a kind, but it was the thin unreal light of the moon, and Grainne, standing still, adjusting her eyes to the room, saw that there were windows high up, and that moonlight, tinged with green from the forest, poured in from outside. There was the sound of the forest trees rustling. Or was it just the trees? Trees did not make that dry, brittle sound, as if old, dead bones were being rubbed together. Trees did not whisper and murmur and chuckle with an evil malevolence . . .

There is something in here that is barely human.

The room looked as if it might be quite comfortable. There were chairs, a table, a deep settle. Through an alcove was a narrow bed. But there were strong iron bars at the windows, and there was the dry, sticklike sound of bones; there was the mindless chuckling again . . .

The room should have been entirely normal. There were normal things in it; there were chairs and a table, on the table was a water jug, a bowl of food of some kind, fruit. The jug and the bowl were chained to the table.

Advancing stealthily into the room, Grainne felt the hairs prickle on the back of her neck. As she moved, the *something*, the creature that chuckled and rubbed its dry-bony hands together, moved with her, as if copying. Was it? Was it only her imagination? Two steps farther in, and the creature moved two steps as well. Grainne stopped, and the creature stopped with her. Three steps now. A slithering of chains, a horrid steel-on-stone sound, and three steps to match.

Grainne stood very still, although she did not close her eyes, for to do so in here, with a creature, a *something* that was watching from the shadowy corners and grinning and copying her every move, was not to be thought of. But she half closed her eyes, and she put her head back very slightly, and felt the shadows stir and felt the *something* wait, and felt the wrongness and the lack of humanity that pervaded the room sweep over her. Like water flooding over your head. Like steam coming at you from a cooking pot over a camp fire. Like a sudden scent, borne on the wind.

A scent. And then she knew, with the extra sense that her ancestors, the wolves, had possessed, she knew suddenly what the *wrongness* and the dry evil intelligence meant.

Madness. There is sheer blazing madness in here. *And we are locked in with it . . .*

Grainne gasped and put out a hand to Raynor. They were not locked in with it, of course they were not. But just for a moment she had felt the weight of emptiness, she had felt how it must be to be shut away down here, bereft of even human companionship, away from the light, losing count of the days. Chained and caged.

Aye, cabbin'd, cribb'd, confin'd . . .

The echoes swirled and eddied all about them, but whether from the future or the past, Grainne was never able to tell. Anger rose up in her for whatever poor pitiful creature was shut away down here, and her eyes blazed yellow-gold in the duskiness, so that Raynor, watching her, thought, Yes, that is the wolflight. That is the power and the light and the strength of Tara's wolves! And felt again the primitive thrill. Grainne was only faintly aware of Raynor at her side now. Her eyes were searching the corners, scanning the farthest recesses of the dungeon that someone had tried to make into the semblance of a comfortable apartment. The unseen creature was still, and Grainne had the sensation of being watched, inspected, assessed. The chains slithered again, and there was a scuttling movement in the shadows, and Grainne turned to see what crouched in the corner.

Her first feeling was of relief. Not Human! After all it is not Human! Some poor animal, some poor travesty that has been imprisoned for its own safety and the safety of others. Some living breathing *thing* that has succumbed to insanity, or been born that way, and which the Beastline and the Cruithin have taken care of. Not Human.

She moved nearer, heedless of Raynor's warning hand on her arm, not exactly pushing him from her, but summoning, without realising, the authority and the remoteness that had come down to her; certainly assuming the unconscious imperiousness that she had never known shone from her, and that was shining from her now in the dim, moonlit cell. Raynor, more closely attuned to her now than he would have believed possible, felt the strength and the sudden arrogance and the automatic shouldering of a burden, and knew that it was this quality, this mastery, that set her so much apart.

The creature in the far corner was watching Grainne's approach from sly, slit-like eyes. As Grainne drew closer, a dry hand, the back covered with teethmarks as if it had been gnawed, came up and, with an abrupt gesture, pushed back the mat of hair that half covered the face.

Horror coursed through Grainne, so that for a moment the stone room tilted all about her.

Human, fettered and chained, with a mat of coarse brown hair, with sly, utterly mad eyes, but *Human*. This is unbearable.

The creature was dressed plainly and simply. Some kind of loose gown, thought Grainne. But nearly in rags. Torn and stained and ripped. Here and there clawed. Anger flared, for surely they could have dressed the poor thing better.

The bright brown eyes were intent on Grainne now and, without warning, a new alertness came over the figure. It had been half sitting in the corner; now it seemed to crouch, as if ready to spring forward. Its chains slithered across the stone floor again, and there was a breathspace when Grainne thought it cowered.

Raynor made a warning movement, but the creature was before him, and in the uncertain light they could see the gleam of moonlight on bare sinewy thighs, which quivered with strength and intent to spring . . .

As Grainne stood, unable to move, bars of moonlight fell across the creature's face, and the planes of its features, the angle of its bones, seemed to melt and dissolve into one another. The eyes narrowed even more and became inverted and reddish; the mouth thinned and slavered; there was the white gleam of teeth, pointed and dripping with saliva . . .

And then it sprang, the dreadful face a mask of blazing fury, the eyes fiery with hatred. The mouth was a mouth no longer, but a muzzle, a pointed snarling maw with snapping teeth that would certainly rend Human flesh to shreds, with a lolling red tongue that would snake out and lick the blood and the marrow . . .

Grainne fell back as the creature lunged, and there was a furious yelp followed by a long-drawn-out howl as the iron chains held and jerked the creature back. But the nails that were nearly but not quite claws had reached Grainne, and a burning, lacerating pain sliced through her shoulder. She staggered and half fell and, as Raynor caught her, the wolf creature gave a howl of triumph and fell back on its haunches, making a scuttling, circling movement as a cat will make a nest for itself before sleeping. A cat. Or a dog or a fox.

Or a wolf . . .

Grainne, sick and dizzy from the pain in her shoulder, said, in a voice she did not recognise as her own, "Who is she?"

Raynor's hand closed about hers. Then he said, very gently indeed, "Her name is Maeve. She is the only daughter of Dierdriu, and the rightful High Queen of Ireland."

And as Grainne stared at him, horror and comprehension dawning in her eyes, he said in a voice of extreme tenderness, "And she is your mother, Grainne.

"But she has been caged inside the Grail Castle for the last twenty years."

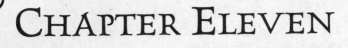

CHAPTER ELEVEN

RAYNOR'S ROOM WAS a refuge and a haven. Grainne sat huddled before the fire, her torn shoulder bathed and dressed, her arms wrapped about her, shivering. Raynor had tipped a basket of logs on to the fire, and warmth and light were washing over the room. But—shall I ever be warm again? thought Grainne. Shall I ever be able to shut out the sight and the sound?

Raynor had fetched wine from a corner cupboard, and was heating it with a thin iron rod which had been resting in the fire's embers. Grainne took the hot fragrant wine gratefully, and cupped her hands about the goblet for warmth. When she said, "Tell me. Tell me everything," she saw his eyes soften and knew that he would surely tell her all there was to know.

"It is not my story," said Raynor, speaking slowly now, "and although I know it, the Cruithin will know the whole."

Yes, the Cruithin would certainly know. Loyal to the death, hiding the shameful secrets of Ireland's Royal House.

"Your mother was born to Dierdriu," said Raynor, "in the days when Ireland's Golden Age was at its height. It was a marvellous time, I think. Tara was the finest, the most glittering Court in the western world. Your great-grandfather, Cormac, had made it so, and Dierdriu, his daughter, continued the tradition. People travelled from remote lands just to be a part of it, for no one was ever turned from the door. Your great-grandfather was the most remarkable High King Ireland has ever known, Grainne; he liked to listen to the talk of people from other cultures, and he liked to learn about other lands." He smiled at her. "In a way, he is still with us," said Raynor, "for Ireland has never forgotten him, and never will."

"True immortality," said Grainne in a whisper.

"Yes."

"Go on."

"Dierdriu was betrothed to a northern Chieftain," said Raynor. "There was no mystery about it, but there was no particular distinction, either. It was as suitable a match as any could be for Ireland's heiress." He smiled briefly. "And they say that everyone knew that Dierdriu would never be faithful to one man. I think no one expected her to be. Also, the Beastline Enchantment was still so strong that it was not judged necessary for the Ritual to be invoked and the ceremonial mating with the Wolves to take place. Perhaps it was not thought important who Dierdriu married."

Grainne said, "It is very carefully and very strictly planned, that Ritual."

"The marriage took place, and a child was born," said Raynor. "They called her Maeve, for a long-ago lady of the north. Shortly afterwards, the Chieftain was killed in a battle, and although there was a time of mourning, it was probably not very great. The marriage had been a business arrangement, nothing more."

Grainne said, "Yes. I understand."

"The little girl grew up at Tara," said Raynor. "She was pretty and loved, and she was biddable and sweet-natured. If she had not quite the fire and the golden glow of her ancestors, nobody remarked it. They would certainly have noticed it, but there are other qualities useful to a sovereign. It was thought that with strong, carefully chosen ministers, she would do well enough when the time came." He paused, and sipped his wine, staring into the fire's depths.

"In time, the pretty, biddable girl began to be sought in marriage. She was fifteen, sixteen. She was a prize to be won. She might have had anyone she chose," said Raynor, and a shadow seemed to fall across his face. "She might have married any of the Chieftains or the Lords who came to Tara, or the foreign Princes, for all knew that Ireland went with her.

"But she disliked them. She was not perhaps very courageous, which was unexpected in one of her ancestry. She was nervous of all men, and preferred to be with the women of the Court. Everyone said it would pass, and everyone still smiled tolerantly on the pretty, amenable child.

"It did not pass. She began to hide away when State banquets were in progress. She ran away from feasts and ceremonies. People began to worry. How could one so shy and so timid rule Ireland after Dierdriu was gone?

"And then one night," said Raynor, his eyes unreadable now, "one night there was a great banquet for Samain, and that was the night that Medoc first came to Tara.

"No one knew him," said Raynor, "no one recognised him, and for that the gate-keepers and the sentries must take great blame. They should have penetrated his disguise and they should have alerted the Royal guards and the *Fiana* and every sorcerer in the Palace so that he could be driven out.

"But Medoc is clever, Grainne. He is called, and with reason, the dark, cruel, beautiful one. He knows exactly how to present himself in the light best calculated to deceive. And it is true that no one ever expected him to walk openly and directly up to Tara and request admittance at the Western Gate.

"But that is what he did, and since he was garbed as a traveller, in a plain dark cloak with a pack on his back, no one thought very much about it. Cormac's hospitality was famous, and no one was ever turned away.

"Medoc was not turned away," said Raynor, sipping the wine, his expression absorbed. "He was asked in with his companion."

Grainne looked up. "His companion? But in all of the legends, Medoc travels alone."

Raynor said, "He had with him a young boy, little more than a child, it seemed. A child with huge dark hungry eyes, and ragged black hair. And a sack on his back."

Silence. And then Grainne said, "The Lad of the Skins."

"Yes. The Lad is one of Medoc's most devoted servants."

"Two of Ireland's greatest enemies . . ."

"Yes. They were invited in, and given a place at the Samain feastings, and they took part in the revelries and the banquets. It is said that they were friendly and ready to be pleased by everything. Medoc talked interestingly and learnedly, and finally, little by little, the entire Sun Chamber fell silent and sat listening to him. He held them in thrall." Raynor paused. "He has many gifts, Medoc, and he has at his beck a wardrobe of enchantments. For this time, he was a charming, rather scholarly traveller. Not young. A pilgrim. The Lad was his attendant—perhaps his son. He fooled them all. And no one was expecting him."

No one had been expecting him . . .

"The Samain revelries were reaching their height," said Raynor, his voice faraway now. "The feasting would go on for seven days. All the banqueting tables had been placed carefully, with full consideration to the dangers that abound on Samain. But," he said, looking at her, "you would know far more of that."

"Samain is the one night of the year when the Bright Palace is vulnerable. It is the night when demons walk and when every evil in the world is abroad. Also," said Grainne, "there is a belief that at Samain the *sidh* sometimes return. They vanished from Ireland during my great-grandfather's time, but on the night of Samain, the gateways between their world and ours open of their own accord, and they come back. They are the most purely magical beings ever known, the *sidh*, and they covet the bodies of Humans. Their king is Aillen mac Midha, and in the past he would sit at the foot of the Palace ramparts, slender, and blue-green, and with the chill faery blood of all the *sidh* in his veins. If his creatures capture a Human, they will steal one of the Human's senses— his sight, hearing, sense of smell, sense of touch, taste. There are terrible stories of how men have had their eyes torn from their sockets, or their tongue ripped from the roots by the *sidh*. And although they have not been seen in Ireland for many years, sometimes they are heard. But despite their greed," said Grainne seriously, "they have always been loyal to the Wolfline. It is said that when a High King or Queen is born, if the child is Ireland's true heir, they will sing him into the world and they will weave a spell of protectiveness."

She stared into the depths of the fire, and Raynor said, "Tell me of Samain. Make me see it," and Grainne turned back.

"They light the Druidical Fires. That is a ceremony in itself. There is a procession to the Plain of the Fál, to the great bonfire, and there is a chant in the Ancient Lost Language. No one understands that now, but we still use it. And there are banquets and rituals and revelries." She put out a hand to him. "And one day you will see it all, and one day you will share it with me," said Grainne.

"Perhaps."

"Oh, yes. But tell me of Samain when Medoc came to Tara."

"The feastings had drawn to a close," said Raynor. "And the Court was about to assemble for the procession to the Plain. It was then that Medoc acted. They say he walked to the centre of the Sun Chamber, and that as he did so, the disguise fell from him, and everyone saw him for what he really was. The dark, evil, beautiful one. The most powerful Lord of the Dark Ireland. He stood at the centre of the Sun Chamber, and a terrible hush fell.

"Dierdriu was on her feet, summoning the *Fiana* and the Palace guard, but although they came running, it was already too late. Medoc had begun to spin the *Draoicht Suan*, the ancient and powerful Enchantment of Slumber. It spun and shivered on the air, and the threads and the filaments began to descend on the Court, covering them with the strong powerful magic. They were helpless, and Medoc had them at his mercy.

"He stood watching them," said Raynor, "and it was as if he was searching for something. At last his gaze came to rest on Maeve, and his eyes widened, and a smile curved his lips. The Princess was powerless; when he beckoned to her, she went to him like a lamb." Raynor's hand came out to Grainne. "She would not have been able to resist him," he said. "For he is dark and beautiful and possessed of all the attractions when he wishes . . .

"He swirled his black necromancer's cloak about her, and he carried her from the Sun Chamber and out through the great doors, and out into the night and none could stop him. He carried her out of the Manor of Tara, and across the Plain of the Fál, and through the Forest of Darkness. There is a folklore that is closely guarded amongst the villages on the edge of the Forest," said Raynor. "A handed-down tale of how a vast yawning chasm opened once in the sky over the Forest of Darkness; of how the people in that part of Ireland saw a glimpse of the true world of the Dark Ireland: the fiery furnaces where the manacles and the chains of evil are forged; the towering Black Looms of the necromancers; dark evil citadels and huge screeching night-crows and ravens; the silhouettes of wraiths and banshees and hags. For a few terrible moments they saw it all, and cowered, covering their eyes. And then there was a screech of triumph as the doors closed and the dreadful mirror-world claimed their Dark Lord and his victim.

"The Court was left trapped in the *Draoicht Suan*," said Raynor, staring into the depths of the fire, his eyes lit not from without but from within. "Dierdriu and the courtiers slept all of the time the Princess was held captive inside the Dark Ireland. No one could dissolve the *Draoicht Suan*. Medoc had spun it truly and well, and they remained as Medoc and the Lad had left them, seated at the banqueting hall, apparently dead.

"Tara's doors were closed," said Raynor, "and somehow the secret was kept. The sorcerers worked long and hard to break the Enchantment but they could not, and the Sun Chamber became a grim and sinister place, where the High Queen and the Court slept a timeless sleep. Great brier hedges grew up around the Palace, and for many months Ireland had no ruler."

"Who ruled?" asked Grainne.

"Those who had not been in the banqueting hall banded together and created an Emergency Council."

"Did the people not know?"

"Tara has always been remote," said Raynor without expression, and at once Grainne thought, And that is not a good thing! Those who govern should be close to those they rule.

"After many months had passed," said Raynor, "they say that the chasm was wrenched open from within, and the gaping hole appeared in the sky over the Forest of Darkness. The villagers close to it believed that the Dark Ireland was about to ride into the world, but only Medoc rode out, astride a coal-black horse, with Maeve thrown across the saddle before him. He rode leisurely through the Forest, and across the Plain of the Fál, and finally along the avenue of trees that leads to Tara. He carried her into the Sun Chamber, and stood eyeing the sleeping Court with amusement. They say," said Raynor thoughtfully, "that Medoc, of all the necromancers, has a sense of humour. And he found amusement in the slumbering Court. As he watched them, he released the spell, and they began to rouse, and when at last he turned to Dierdriu, she was awake and listening to him.

" 'Madam,' said Medoc, 'you see that I have returned what I took. She is yours for as long as you care to keep her. But Tara is mine, and will soon be mine completely. One day, quite soon I shall ride back into your Palace, and I shall reign in your place.'

"He vanished then," said Raynor, "and with his going, the last vestiges of the *Draoicht Suan* vanished. And although there are even today people who know what happened, you will find no one who will speak of it. There are many secrets your House has kept, Grainne."

Many secrets ... Myself and Fergus, thought Grainne. Yes, for sure that was one of the closest secrets of all.

"What happened to—my mother?" she said at last.

Raynor stared into the fire for a long while. At last, he said, "That is something no one can be entirely sure of. But she had lived inside the Dark Realm for many months, she had been forced to see the terrible creatures that hold sway there, and she had been at Medoc's mercy for all of that time. And the creatures of the Dark Ireland, Grainne, are soulless and cruel and evil beyond your comprehension. Their powers are subtle and strong, and they have the knowledge to wake in the minds of their victims that which would be better left unwoken." He turned from the fire to regard her, and Grainne saw the leaping flames reflected in his eyes, hundreds of pinpoints of light. "Your mother was of the Wolf-line," said Raynor. "She was a direct descendant of the High Kings and Queens who had submitted to the sorcery of the Beastline, and lain with the wolves, and given birth to the Royal House.

"The Dark Ireland had woken the wolf, Grainne. Maeve had become a ravening, mindless wolf . . .

"She was brought to the Grail Castle twenty years ago," continued Raynor. "The Cruithin brought her, and they guard her, and they guard the knowledge of her existence. In as much as is possible, we help them to do that. It is a service we can perform for the Royal House. But it is one of the reasons why the Cruithin disappeared towards the end of Dierdriu's reign." He looked at her. "We know only the barest details of what took place after Medoc brought your mother back from the Dark Realm," said Raynor. "For Tara, like this place, keeps its secrets well. But we know of the birth—*your* birth, Grainne. We know that on the night you were born, the *sidh*'s music was heard." He took her in his arms. "You were born shortly after Maeve was returned," he said. "And therefore you had been conceived behind the closed gates of that dreadful other Ireland.

"And since Maeve was your mother, then, my dearest love, Medoc was your father."

————

MEDOC IS MY father. Mine and Fergus's. Lying sleepless in the firelight, Raynor beside her, Grainne thought perhaps after all she had known. Not the entire truth, never that, but that there was something. A darkness. A fear. Something so terrible that it must remain deeply buried, it must never be allowed to emerge into the light . . .

Medoc is my father. I am the daughter of the darkest necromancer of them all.

It has to be faced, said Grainne to Grainne, staring up at the ceiling where the shadows leapt and danced. It has to be faced, as the knowledge that Fergus was my brother had to be faced. It is one more secret within my family, and it is a secret I shall keep, as I kept the secret of Fergus. I faced that, and I can face this, thought Grainne.

Could it be done? Could she come to terms with the fact that Medoc, the evil, cruel Lord of the Dark Ireland, had sired her and Fergus? Could she come to terms with the knowledge that they had been conceived in that dreadful place? She did not know very much about the Dark Ireland; she thought no one knew very much. But snippets and fragments of legend and lore had filtered in from somewhere. And what had Raynor said? A yawning chasm in the sky, through which people had glimpsed fiery furnaces where the chains of evil were forged . . . the necromancers' Black Looms . . . Grainne had once seen the massive Silver Looms that the sorcerers of Tara spun their enchantments on, and she had been awed and terrified and overwhelmed. There would be dark fortresses in that world as well, and the skies would be forever heavy and lit to a reddish glow with the incantations and the dark sorcery that would rise like a miasma from the dark citadels . . . Grainne blinked and shook her head, because just for a few seconds she had seen with dreadful clarity the Dark Ireland, the Evil Realm, the world of malevolence and malignancy. *And my father is Lord of that Realm . . . my father is Ireland's greatest enemy and he has driven me from my Throne . . .*

A deep, hard anger began to rise then, and, as dawn

streaked the skies to the east of the Grail Castle, Grainne felt the golden strength well up again. The power and the light and the strength of the Wolves of Tara ... The power that was turned inwards in my mother, but that *I* shall turn outwards.

O Medoc, thought Grainne, her eyes brilliant, her mind tumbling with images, every sense alive, O Medoc, you may be powerful and clever and subtle. You may be versed in necromancy, and steeped in alchemy, and schooled in the ancient cruel arts of your realm. *But I am the Wolfqueen, Medoc. I have within me the Enchantment of the Beastline that was created at the beginning of Tara's history. I am the descendant of Cormac and Dierdriu, and Niall of the Nine Hostages, and I can beat you, Medoc, I can ride against you, and I can defeat you. I am going to send you back to the Dark Realm of that other Ireland, and we will seal up the Gateways so that you and your creatures and your Lords of Evil will never be a threat to us again.*

And Ireland will be truly safe at last.

THEY STOOD TOGETHER on the hillside that rose up behind the castle.

"The Purple Hour," said Raynor softly, and Grainne smiled, and thought that after all the old legends and the old myths had been right. Twilight, the Purple Hour, when magic was abroad and when spells awoke and enchantments stirred. If you listened very carefully and if you looked very closely, you could see it and you could hear it and you could feel it. Shadows and mists and approaching night, and fingers of deep purple stealing across the forest.

They were all there with her. At her back stood the Cruithin, alert and bright-eyed, ready for whatever might be asked of them. Loyal to the last drop of blood. Close by stood Fintan and Cermait Honeymouth and Tybion the Tusk, and Grainne looked at them and knew a deep and abiding affection for them.

The people of the Beastline were ranged directly ahead,

facing her, as she had asked, and they were watching her with animal stillness. Raynor was a little apart, his eyes unreadable and such an intense concentration about him that Grainne knew he was hearing her thoughts.

He knows what I am about to attempt.

The golden strength was coursing through her, and with it an immense and unstoppable confidence. I know I am right. I know that deep within these creatures, these poor abandoned creatures, are the seeds of the Lost Enchantment, the thin, almost-dead bewitchment spun by the first sorcerers. I know that it is there, and if only, if only I can choose the right words, and if only I can tap the exact right source of power, then I shall see it ignite and flare into life.

There was no thought of failure in her mind, and there was no trace of doubt. These are the Royal lines of Ireland, and I am about to release the bewitchment, and I shall take them out of here, and together we will rout Medoc.

But when at last she spoke, she did so simply and directly, for although the moment was solemn, and although it was probably historic as well, these were not creatures who would react favourably to grandiloquence. Their lives had been plain and unadorned, and it was in such language that Grainne would address them. She glanced across to Raynor again, and saw him bow his head in brief acknowledgement, and she smiled inwardly, for it was Raynor who had given her the clue, the idea, the knowledge of how to approach his people.

"Many years ago," said Grainne, looking at them all very directly, "Ireland's rightful Queen was taken and held captive within the realms of the Dark Ireland. We know nothing of her months there, and we only know that when she returned it was with the dark inner side of her nature woken, so that she must be kept chained and guarded."

A pause. No one spoke, but Grainne could see the listening alertness in them all.

"When Maeve was taken," said Grainne, and those nearest noted that she did not falter over the name, "when Maeve was taken, the huge and fearsome Gateway to the Dark Ireland opened for a time. There are people living today who will tell you how, for a brief, terrible space, they looked straight into that world. How they glimpsed the Dark Lords who hold sway there, how they saw that the skies were dull and clotted with evil magic and black bewitchments. How they saw wraiths and hags and harpies, and the shadows of nightmares and the shapes of ancient and forbidden sorcery." Again the pause. "And now Medoc, the terrible Overlord of that Realm, sits in Tara," said Grainne. "With him are the Twelve Lords of Evil—each one the embodiment of the world's great wickednesses. You know their names," said Grainne, and a shiver went through the Beastline creatures and the Cruithin, for everyone knew the litany: Decadence, Hatred, Vice, Corruption, Jealousy . . .

"Medoc and the Twelve Lords are gathering strength," said Grainne. "Already they have in thrall the villages and the farms that surround Tara. Already they have forced those people to work for them. And it is a terrible thing," said Grainne, "to be forced to toil for a necromancer." She looked at them again, and felt the intense concentration, and thought, and then was not sure, that something else had stirred. A knowledge deep in their eyes? Oh, please let it be.

"Medoc has already summoned the beast Conablaiche and the Lad of the Skins," said Grainne. "They walk in the world today. We believe that now he will prepare Ireland for the rebirth of the monster-god Crom Croich." She paused, and saw the shiver go through them again. Yes, they knew these names; even isolated out here, they knew of Crom Croich.

"It must not happen," said Grainne more quietly, and several of her listeners saw the golden light beginning to glow in her eyes. "We must drive out Medoc, we must send him back to the Dark Ireland, and we must seal up the terrible Gateway that he opened before the creatures and the monsters of that Realm flood through it.

"You must help me to do it," said Grainne, very gently.

"You must ride out with me, leave the Grail Castle, and come with me to Tara." She drew a deep breath, and felt, as if it was a tangible thing now, the intensity of their thoughts. They do not understand, and yet they are beginning to understand. She stood for a moment looking at them, and saw how their heads were tilted in the listening attitudes of forest creatures, how their ears were pricked, and how their eyes were bright and intelligent. Behind them, in the forest, a tiny wind began to whisper, and a faint awareness stirred the air. Delight flooded her in a great wave, and— Oh, yes, I am right! cried her mind. In a stronger voice, she said, "I ask you to do this, because I have the right to ask it. Because of what you are." Another pause. Was the forest wind becoming stronger? "You are the Ancient Bloodline of Ireland," said Grainne. "You are the Noble Royal Lines, the Enchanted Creatures created by the sorcerers at the beginning of Tara's history. You have the power over the beasts." She looked at each of them, her eyes steady and brilliant, the wind scurrying across the forest now, nearly with them. "I cannot do it without you," said Grainne. "I cannot drive out Medoc without the Royal Houses who have been lost, but now are found." The wind had reached them, and it was lifting her hair. She raised her arms. "Send out the Mindsong," cried Grainne. "Call up the creatures whose blood you possess. Together we will form the finest army that Ireland has ever known." The wind was whipping about them now, billowing cloaks out and ruffling the hair and the fur of the Beast-line. Behind them, deep within the forest, a low humming had begun.

"Do it!" cried Grainne, above the wind and the rhythmic sound. "Call up the beasts!" And stood waiting, and saw puzzlement touch them, and knew a moment of pure panic. I have miscalculated. I have lost them. But she stayed where she was, not moving, and the wind dimmed to a steady moan, and the sense of anticipation increased. Grainne thought, Now it is up to them. I do not think I can do any more. It must come from them. Have they understood? Have I reached them? Have I awoken the deep and ancient Beastline Enchantment?

It was Bec who spoke first, puzzlement in her dark eyes, but something new in her voice—assurance was it? "But, ma'am—Your Majesty—we cannot do it. We have no power."

Rinnal said, "We are the failed ones, Your Majesty. The travesties. Look at us."

"I look at you," said Grainne softly, "and I do not see travesties. I see a new interpretation of the Royal Houses. A rebirth of the Noble Lost Lines of Ireland. I see the Enchantment of the Beastline again."

From where he stood, a little removed from the others, Raynor said, half to himself, "A palimpsest."

"Yes," said Grainne. "Oh, yes. A palimpsest. New writing on an old manuscript."

Bec said, rather uncertainly, "But we are not the Ancient Nobility, ma'am. We are not the True Line."

Grainne looked at them all with love and delight, and with an immense tenderness, and said, "Are you so sure?"

THE PURPLE HOUR had deepened to its utmost now, and the shadows were heavy with magic and heady with mystery.

And in the depths of the forest, the humming is still strong, and the wind is still swirling all about us, and something is stirring, something that is so strong and so purely magical that no one has ever been able to resist it . . .

The Lost Enchantment waking. Oh, please, thought Grainne, please let it be that, for I have come so far to find it. And anything will be worthwhile—the loss of Tara, the loss of Fergus—it will have been worthwhile if only I have woken the Enchantment of the Beastline. And, said a tiny treacherous voice, the loss of Raynor? Could you count that worthwhile as well? Oh, no, not that. And then—but if I must, then I must, she thought. Only—not that.

The Beastline were standing close together, silhouetted against the sky. And slowly, slowly, so gradually that it was barely perceptible, the watchers became aware of a change.

At first Grainne thought it was that power was stealing over them, and then she thought that it was not power but strength, only that did not seem quite right either. And then she knew, quite suddenly, that it was neither of these things. It was confidence, and it was awareness, and it was the dawning of knowledge. They were beginning to believe ...

We are the True Ancient Nobility of Ireland ...

Yes! cried Grainne silently. Yes! You are the Enchanted Ones, the Royal Houses reborn, and you have within you the power and the strength and the light, just as I have!

The wind was moaning more strongly now, and there was a sense of something powerful and irresistible drawing nearer.

The Mindsong.

The humming increased and became a chant: low, steady, throbbing. The forest seemed to become alive, and the wind swept across the surface of the trees, as if a giant hand had reached down to caress it.

A great exultant joy was sweeping through Grainne. I was right! These *are* the creatures of the True Line! The Enchantment was not lost! The sorcerers succeeded, and the Beastline still lives!

"The spells succeeded," whispered Grainne, tears streaming down her cheeks and, as she turned towards the forest, the ancient magical Samhailt thrummed all about them, and the skies began to darken with Eagles and Hawks and White Swans, and the hillside became alive with Foxes and Badgers and Hounds and Deer and Gazelle, and Hares and Chariot Horses and Stags.

All rushing down the hillside to obey the Samhailt.

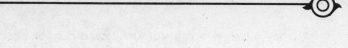

CHAPTER TWELVE

TALIESIN WAS NOT consciously aware of the moment when Fael-Inis's Chariot was pulled out of Calatin's forest and out of Ireland. He thought that at one minute they were still there, in the rose and gold dawn with Calatin and Fribble waving farewell, and the next minute the forest and the house was disappearing as if it was being sucked backwards away from them. And then he thought that of course it was not the house that was disappearing, it was himself and Fael-Inis.

Into the endless Time Fire and into the white heat of the Corridors of Time, where the centuries merge and where all the worlds that have ever been, and all the worlds that are still to come, meet and fuse and become one with the Time Light . . .

All about them were the thin pure flames stretching out endlessly and rising steeply on each side of the Chariot, as if they were travelling at immense speed through a great roaring tunnel. Fael-Inis was standing at the Chariot's head, and his eyes were the exact colour of the fire, and Taliesin had the impression that they were the consistency of the fire as well. His hair fell about his narrow skull in a shining cap of molten gold, and his skin was becoming suffused with the light. He is bathing in the flames, luxuriating in them, thought Taliesin.

Fael-Inis half turned at last, and the three-cornered smile lifted his lips. But he only said, "I *have* bathed in the Endless fire, Mortal, not once but many times." And then the smile widened and became mischievous, and he said, "But enjoy the journey while you can, for the return may be very different."

And there are only seven days ...

Taliesin felt the cool, silky enchantment spun by Calatin brush his body, and experienced a tremor of panic. Seven days, and then the spell would be useless. He would be trapped in the Future, unable to return. He would be there, at the mercy of the terrible days when the Apocalypse unleashed its fury into the world, and burned the earth, and almost destroyed mankind. Fergus and the others had talked blithely about enlisting the help of the machines and the inventions of the Future, and of chaining the Apocalypse and bringing it back to destroy Medoc and the Twelve Dark Lords. They had discussed how they would somehow enlist the help of the people of the Future, "For," Fergus had said, his eyes bright, "if we can capture the Apocalypse and bring it back with us, then surely we are saving the world of the Future from Devastation." But Fergus was lost to them—perhaps for ever—and Taliesin, left to continue Fergus's quest, thought, Yes, but *how* do we go about capturing the Apocalypse? What had Fergus in mind? And remembered how Fergus had been a great soldier, and a practised warrior, the *Fiana*'s great leader. And I am but a dealer in gold and silver and the greedy dreams of men ...

Standing in the rushing Time Chariot, the centuries tumbling past them, Taliesin thought, What if we fail? What if the Apocalypse destroys us before we get to it? He glanced to where Fael-Inis was standing, his head thrown back, the flames caressing his face, and felt better. *I* might fail, thought Taliesin. But this one never will ...

Fael-Inis said softly, "Do not worry, Taliesin. We shall challenge this unknown world, and tumble it about, and if we are very fortunate, we may be able to halt the Four Heralds of the Apocalypse and gain the help we need for the beleaguered High Queen." The smile he flung at Taliesin was straight and unwavering. "And you will find," said Fael-Inis, "that the people of the Future are not, after all, so very

different." And then, "But you know that," he said suddenly. "You understand that men and worlds and ages are
not so different."

"Yes."

"Yes." Fael-Inis was letting the silken reins of the Chariot pour through his hands like water, and Taliesin watched,
fascinated. "You have read deeply, Mortal, and you have
studied the religions of the world. You have tried to acquire
a little knowledge."

"In an attempt to escape boredom—"

"Yes, you would say that." The narrow eyes were unfathomable. "But all the same, you have gained knowledge
and a deeper understanding of Men than most." A brief grin.
"You have not always liked that understanding, and that is
one reason why you have frequently been at odds with your
people."

"A rebel," said Taliesin, just very slightly diffident about
using this term to this creature who was the greatest rebel
the world had ever known.

"We are of the same pattern, you and I," said Fael-Inis.

"Yes?"

"Rebels," he said, and grinned. "But let us turn our attention to this cold, soulless world we are going to, my
friend. You will dislike it, I think. You will find it cold and
bleak and austere. You have a little of the Samhailt, of course,
and you will feel all of these things with ease."

"Yes."

"You have never understood about the Samhailt."

"No."

Taliesin waited, but Fael-Inis only said, "It does not always go where you would expect, the Samhailt. And it is
not a comfortable thing to possess."

"No."

It was not comfortable now. The cascading fire and the
dazzling lights poured about them, but Taliesin could feel
that they were nearing the end of this fantastical journey; he
thought that the salamanders were not moving so vigorously

now, and he thought he could feel the echoes and the emotions of the world they were going into; he could tell that ahead of them was a coldness and such a lack of sharing and friendship that it would be like going down into a deep, dank well.

We are going into a cold and bleak world, and yet for all that, it is the world of our descendants, he thought. And wondered whether, deep down, for all the tremendous anticipation, he was more fearful than he had let anyone see. And then he thought, The Chariot! What will happen to the Chariot!

"The Chariot will come and go as I wish it," said Fael-Inis calmly, apparently picking this up easily. "It will not disappear, but it will acquire protective coloration. I shall summon it if we need it, Mortal. You can be sure of that."

It gave Taliesin an unexpected sense of security to know that the Chariot would be at hand, that it would materialise at Fael-Inis's summoning.

"And it will never appear quite the same to any two people," said Fael-Inis. The grin slid out again. "It would be interesting to know how the people of this world see it," he said.

"Will they see it?"

"Probably not. I think we do not want to draw more attention to ourselves than necessary." He was holding the reins more loosely now, and Taliesin had the impression that the fiery walls and the pouring flames were not rushing past them quite so quickly. It was very nearly possible to pick out chinks in the flames, to catch glimpses of worlds beyond the fires . . . What must it be like to be able to go forward and through Time at will . . . ?

"Extraordinarily tedious in the end," said Fael-Inis, and sent Taliesin the winged smile again.

"Have you been into this world before?" said Taliesin, and Fael-Inis turned the remote stare on him.

"I am in all the centuries and all the ages," he said.

"Sometimes I have a different name, but I am always to be found."

"I see," said Taliesin, who did not see at all, and Fael-Inis laughed, and as he did so the cascading fire seemed to ripple down over him.

"I know a little of this world," he said. "And I know a little of its people."

"Yes?" Taliesin withdrew his gaze from the chinks in the fire and the tantalising glimpses of the worlds that existed beyond them. It was extremely important to know as much as possible about the world they were going into.

"They are a cold people, but also they are frightened," said Fael-Inis. "But it has taken them many generations to reach this state." He paused, and a frown touched his brow. "They reached a crossroads many times," he said, "times in their history when they could have altered course, when they might have taken different roads. There could so easily have been a happier fate for them. But they are not entirely to blame, for no world is ever entirely to blame for what befalls it. They had greedy leaders and they had governments who were short-sighted to the needs of the people, and who were, as well, corrupt within themselves."

"Kings and Queens?" asked Taliesin, and Fael-Inis said, "Not for a very long time. While they had them, they might have been saved, for they had a respect for their Royal lines.

"But there were, as there have always been, usurpers; bands of people who thought that Kings had no place in the world any longer. And so all the Royal Houses of the world disappeared. Not all at once, but gradually. They were assassinated, or they were deposed, or they simply died out. And then people lost respect, they lost the ability to submit to the rule of others who were wiser and better fitted to rule. The people cannot really rule the people," said Fael-Inis. "Not completely. There must always be leaders and there must always be those who are led. The world—*this* world— lost sight of that."

Taliesin was framing a question, when the huge glittering wheels of the Chariot jolted, and the salamanders threw back their heads and the fire rippled and the flames melted and parted, cleanly and easily. Straight ahead of them they saw roads and highways covered with some hard, solid, almost shiny substance, and towering buildings, and everywhere cold brilliant lights against a night sky.

The flames dissolved, and the Chariot melted, and together they fell into the noise and the lights and the cold hardness of the Far Future.

IT WAS LIKE nothing Taliesin had ever seen or imagined or dreamed. It was bleak and ugly and hard. Hard. That was the word that was foremost in his mind as he stood with Fael-Inis. Hard. Everywhere was coated with the grey or black substance of the roads; the buildings were huge, they were square or oblong, and they had harsh corners and uncompromising windows and doors. There was no softness, there was none of the mellowed feeling that Taliesin was accustomed to. He thought that there was certainly a sense of age and of an accumulation of civilisations, but it was the age and it was the accumulation of all of the unspiritual things. Greed and the acquisition of power. The intemperance of a civilisation that for centuries has been allowed to have all it wants.

Fael-Inis said softly, "You feel it, don't you?"

"Yes."

"I thought you would," he said.

Taliesin, still staring about him, said, "But where are the people?" And then, in horror, "Have we after all come to the time after the Apocalypse? Are they all lying dead somewhere?"

"Oh, no," said Fael-Inis. "Oh, no, for once the Apocalypse has walked the earth, these buildings and these cities will all be reduced to smouldering rubble."

"How terrible," said Taliesin dryly, and Fael-Inis smiled.

"I am glad that you retain your sense of irony," he said. "I have lately feared you were losing it."

"I may lose everything I possess and be bereft in a friendless world, but I should still retain a sense of irony," said Taliesin at once, and Fael-Inis grinned.

"The people are all here," he said. "Look." And drawing Taliesin to the side of the road, he pointed to where lights burned in windows, and to where, stretching out below them, there were hundreds of solitary lights, strung out like glowworms. "Each light signifies that a person is there," said Fael-Inis. "But they are locked away until morning." The golden eyes were thoughtful. "They are a very frightened people," he said softly.

"Of—Plague?" said Taliesin, remembering that the first Herald was already here, that Plague in the guise of the Conablaiche was stalking this strange, cold, unwelcoming world.

"Perhaps. Come, shall we walk along here?"

Taliesin found himself glancing back to see if there was any sign of the Chariot, but although he thought there was a sudden thickening of the shadows a little to the left, he could not be sure.

"It *has* become one with the shadows," said Fael-Inis. "But it will be there for us when we wish it."

"To escape with?"

"I hope we shall not need it for that," said Fael-Inis, and led the way along the narrow road hedged with tall buildings on each side. Taliesin thought they were rather grim, rather forbidding structures, and then he thought they were not forbidding but sad. A solitary light glowed from each one, an oblong of bright yellow light.

"Occupancy?" said Taliesin, stopping before one.

"Yes."

"They do not venture out into the streets? Because of the Plague? Or for some other reason?"

"They are afraid of the Plague," said Fael-Inis thoughtfully. "I think we can be sure about that. And they are a dying world." He looked at Taliesin. "You are not seeing the wild, noisy, sexual world that has lived in the Time Travellers' memories," he said. "You are looking on the last days of a world, Taliesin."

"The Apocalypse?"

Fael-Inis sent him one of his enigmatic stares, but he only said, "The Apocalypse will merely administer the final blow. The world is burnt out already."

And the people of this dying, burnt-out world remain inside their houses, thought Taliesin. They shut themselves away, they are locked away until morning.

They came out into a kind of square, with tall houses on every side of them. Taliesin thought there might once have been a square of grass at the centre, with trees and flowers, but the grass had long since died. And then he turned at a touch from Fael-Inis, and saw, directly ahead of them, a garishly lit sign that glittered just above the houses, and that blazoned a message in strange, unfathomable symbols.

At his side, Fael-Inis said, very softly, "So they *do* call it Plague, after all," and stood looking at the cold bluish symbols with his eyes unreadable.

Taliesin said, "Is it—" And Fael-Inis at once turned, and said, "Forgive me, Mortal. I am blessed with the gift of tongues." And he directed his golden stare on Taliesin, so that Taliesin felt a shower of cascading lights, needle-fine and silvery, pouring through his mind. The unfamiliar outlines of the strange austere houses blurred for a moment, and then came back into focus, and he thought it was not his imagination that they seemed sharper now, more definitely limned against the night sky. And then he turned to look at the cold blue lights of the lettering and drew his breath in sharply.

"The Gift of Tongues," said Fael-Inis lightly, his eyes on Taliesin. "All right, Mortal?"

"Yes," said Taliesin softly. "Oh, yes."

"I do not bestow it lightly, you understand," said Fael-Inis, rather mockingly. "But since we are to reside in this remarkable cold world, perhaps you should be given just a little help."

"Thank you," said Taliesin, matching the other's tone, and Fael-Inis grinned, and Taliesin turned back to the shrieking message that towered in letters ten feet high and that shimmered with cold light.

PLAGUE! AS THE SPREAD OF THE DISEASE CONTINUES, THE DRAKON HAS ISSUED THE FOLLOWING DECREES:

1) NO PERSON OR PERSONS TO ENTER INTO SEXUAL CONGRESS WITH ANOTHER WITHOUT THE PROPER SUPERVISION.

2) SEXUAL CONGRESS WITHOUT PROPER SUPERVISION IS PUNISHABLE BY DEATH.

3) THE BIRTH OF CHILDREN IS RESTRICTED TO ONE CHILD PER FEMALE AND IS ONLY PERMISSIBLE ON PRODUCTION OF A BILL OF FULL AND CLEAN HEALTH. BIRTHS OUTSIDE THE LAW WILL BE TERMINATED.

4) ALL FEMALES WILL BE STERILISED AFTER THE BIRTH OF A CHILD.

5) SEXUAL CONGRESS BETWEEN-PEOPLE OF THE SAME SEX IS PUNISHABLE BY CASTRATION.

6) THE PRACTICE OF PROCURATION OF SEXUAL PARTNERS IS PUNISHABLE BY DEATH.

7) THE CURFEW IS NOW IN FORCE FROM THE NINETEENTH HOUR OF EVERY DAY. PERSONS FOUND ABROAD AFTER THAT HOUR WILL BE INCARCERATED IN THE CUIRIM.

And then, in larger, even more brightly lit letters:

ISOLATION IS HEALTH.
CELIBACY IS FREEDOM.
THE WAY TO SALVATION IS TO LIVE ALONE.

And again:

ALL PERSONS ARE TO SPEND THEIR DAYS
WORKING FOR THE COMMON GOOD.
ALL PERSONS ARE TO SPEND THEIR NIGHTS
ALONE.
By Order of the Drakon.

And beneath that, in smaller, but no less brightly lit words:

THE DRAKON'S LAW IS ABSOLUTE.
THE DRAKON SEES ALL.

And a signature they could not read.

TALIESIN'S FIRST REACTION was one of utter disbelief. He thought, But surely this Drakon, whoever or whatever it is, cannot force people to stay inside their homes like this! And then he looked again at the deserted streets, and at the shuttered buildings with the solitary lights, and he saw this brave new world not as the glittering place of the legends, but as sad and forlorn and frightened.

"They are very frightened," said Fael-Inis.

"Of the Drakon, or of something else?" said Taliesin.

"That is perceptive," said Fael-Inis thoughtfully. "Yes, I believe there is something other than the Plague that stalks this world." He stood very still, and Taliesin thought that a frown touched his brow. And then his mood changed again, and he swung round and regarded Taliesin with all the mischief and all the rebelliousness that had shone from him in Calatin's house. "Shall we wake them?" said the rebel angel softly. "Shall we send out the Ancient Beckoning that once spun and shivered at heaven's gateway? That was exiled by the gods because it was so beautiful and so irresistible that Men wept and offered their souls to the Light-Bringer if only they could be allowed to listen to it?" His eyes glinted in the dark square, and Taliesin thought, *He still calls him the Light-Bringer* . . .

"Shall I play the Ancient Spell of Allure and bring the people of this cold dying world out into the streets, Mortal?" said Fael-Inis, and now there was no doubt about it; the reckless wild look was shining from his eyes.

Taliesin said cautiously, "We had thought—Fergus and I—that we would try to enlist the aid of some of them—" and Fael-Inis laughed.

"You are becoming too careful, my friend. Listen, and I will call up the Allure, and if one—if only *one* creature from this bleak and terrible city hears it and responds, then it will suffice. Yes?"

Taliesin said slowly, "Why only one?" And then, catching a little of the other's mood, "Why not all of them?" he said.

Fael-Inis laughed. "Let us see who we can bewitch," he said. And without waiting for Taliesin's response, he seated himself cross-legged on a low stone wall, and let his eyes roam over the buildings and the lights. Taliesin remained silent, and at last Fael-Inis's eyes came to rest on a three-storeyed house, with porticoes and white stonework, at the far side of the square. His eyes grew remote and inward-looking.

"In there," he said, "in that building, is someone who is so strongly at odds with this world that she will hear the Beckoning easily. She understands just a very little about the old magic and about ancient enchantments. She does not quite believe in them, but she would like to believe." He sent Taliesin the slanting smile, and lifted the silver pipes to his lips. "She will come running when I call to her," said the rebel angel, and as he lifted the pipes, an aureole of light began to glow around him.

Music floated across the square.

It was all still there within the music. Everything Taliesin remembered, everything he had heard and felt and dreamed in Calatin's house. Magic and enchantment; the

strong gentle Beckoning that said, Follow me, for I am beauty
and light and power. Come with me to the ends of the earth,
follow me to heaven or to hell, but never once take your
eyes from me. Let the music soak into your soul, and let
yourself become one with the light and with the beauty, for
there can be no salvation without beauty, and there can be
no true happiness without complete submission.

Taliesin was half aware of Fael-Inis's eyes, golden and
slanting, and he was half aware that Fael-Inis was concentrating all his energies and all his powers on the three-
storeyed white house. He thought that something stirred
inside the house; a response, an answer, a creature drawn by
the music and puzzled and dazzled and bewildered, but ready
to obey the music's spell.

But he was caught by the music's enchantment all over
again, and his mind was awash with the joy of it. For a
second he saw splinters of light pierce the dark square, as if
Fael-Inis was sprinkling the music all around them, and as if
it was taking on the substance of thin, sweet light. He
thought that surely the people of this strange, sad world could
not possibly resist.

And then a door at the centre of the white building
opened, and a girl came running towards them.

TALIESIN'S FIRST REACTION was one of the most complete
astonishment. "For," he was to say, "I had seen many types
of women and many different races. And while I had known
that our descendants would be different from us, I had not
thought they would be different in quite this way."

She was rather small and slender, and although there was
a fragility about her, Taliesin had the impression that it was
deceptive. He thought she had an inner strength, and he
thought she would be very determined indeed in a fight. She
would fight like a cat, thought Taliesin, and then, because
the simile seemed suddenly to fit, he went on thinking of
her as cat-like.

Her hair was copper-coloured and glossy and, rather

astonishingly in a female, it was cut short, so that it fell in a
silky mass of curls level with her jaw. Taliesin found this
unusual and rather attractive. But to one accustomed to the
honey-mixed-with-cream skinned ladies of his own world, it
was her complexion that was the strangest part of all. She
was light clear golden brown, a warm honey-without-the-
cream colour. Pale autumn leaves, thought Taliesin, fascinated. The colour of soft doe-skin. Almost as if the copper
colour of her hair had run into her skin.

Her eyes were wide apart and grey, and thickly fringed
with black lashes, and her nose was short and straight. The
upper lip of her mouth curved slightly, and Taliesin thought
it was this which gave her a faintly feline look.

He thought she was dressed very oddly indeed—"ways
of dress change drastically over the ages," said Fael-Inis,
amused—but he thought she was interesting and unusual. He
found it unexpectedly difficult to reconcile the pretty girl
with the cold, greedy, unsharing world they were in, and
then he remembered how Fael-Inis had said that to find a
response to the music, they must find someone strongly at
odds with this cold world. And the girl had certainly responded . . . He looked at her and waited, and thought that
of all the extraordinary things that had happened so far, this
was possibly the most extraordinary of them all.

"Oh!" said the girl rather breathlessly, coming to an
abrupt stop and staring at them. "Oh! Was it you who made
the music—but I never expected anyone to be out here after
Curfew—and it is *so* late, and I daresay the Drakon will be
prowling—" She stopped and glanced over her shoulder.

"If you *are* from the Drakon," said the girl rather defiantly, "you may as well take me to the Cuirim at once. Only
I do not see how *anyone* could be expected to resist the music, for it was *so* beautiful." Again she stopped suddenly, and
Taliesin found himself intrigued by the light, clipped tones,
and by the way her words seemed to tumble along of their
own accord. When she said, "*so* beautiful," her voice was
serious and intense, but when she said, "I do not see how

anyone could resist," there had been a careless, do-with-me-what-you-will manner.

Fael-Inis said, "You are quite mistaken. We are not from the Drakon or even remotely connected with it," and Taliesin heard that Fael-Inis had with ease adapted his manner to their surroundings.

As you must do, if we are to escape here unchallenged.

"We are merely travellers," said Taliesin, and at once the copper-haired girl said, "Oh, tourists! Yes, we get a lot of those, and if they are caught out after Curfew they *always* say it is later in their own city, which is entirely ridiculous because Curfew is the same everywhere. It does not do them any good, of course, because once you are caught, the Drakon is quite merciless." She looked at them rather defiantly, and Taliesin thought that after all she was not really beautiful, she was actually very nearly plain. It was only that there was something that made you like looking at her, and want to go on looking.

Fael-Inis said, "You are abroad late yourself," and at once a hunted look came into her eyes.

"It was only that the music . . . *So* difficult to resist just seeing where it came from . . . It was a good reason for being out after Curfew, but of course I would say that, wouldn't I? Are you quite sure you are nothing to do with the Drakon?"

"Quite sure."

"No, of course you are not," said the girl. "Now that I look at you properly, I can see you are not. You can nearly always tell a Drakon spy anyway. It's the eyes. Cold and hard. Of course, they have to enforce the law if we are to survive, everyone understands that. But they are very harsh. Did you ever read about the old wars at all? The Second War of the World? Doesn't that sound dramatic? I always loved hearing about it. They call it Middle History now, although it's nearer than that, isn't it? Quite recent if you think about it. But when you see Drakon people, you can't help remembering the stories about the German Secret Service, can you?

Gestapo, that's what they called them. Terrible. I always thought that what happened to Germany later—I mean *much* later, at the start of the next millennium—was a sort of judgement. I'm talking too much. If you are from the Drakon I expect you'll carry me off at once."

Fael-Inis said, "We have already told you that you may trust us," and Taliesin said, "And since it is so late, perhaps we should walk along with you." He thought, but did not say, that any young lady abroad so late must surely be dreadfully vulnerable to all manner of unknown dangers. And then, because it was what would have been offered in his own world, he said, "We can see you safely to your home."

The copper-haired girl turned such a sharp look of surprise on him that Taliesin blinked.

"But you know that such a thing is forbidden!" she said. " 'Days to be spent working for the common good, nights to be spent alone.' It's incredibly dreary, but ever since they found the Domesday Clock, they knew they had to try *something* if the world was to be saved—" She came to one of her sudden stops again and looked at them searchingly. "What are you?" she said. "Where are you from?"

"A world outside of this," said Fael-Inis gently, and unexpectedly the girl laughed.

"Oh, no, I *cannot* believe . . . All of the ancient legends? All of the old tales? H. G. Wells and John Wyndham and those really peculiar theories in the twentieth century? Of course, they did not know any better, and they *did* have the beginnings of knowledge . . . And the books are fascinating to read. What used to be called 'classics,' whatever that may mean. But another world . . . Are you sure this is not a joke? Or a trap? But you are *not* from the Drakon, I do know that. And then there was the music . . . Goodness, this is remarkably difficult, but remarkably interesting. I think it is the most interesting thing that has ever happened to me. But if we stay here much longer we shall certainly be caught, because the Drakon's people patrol the streets every half hour . . . Although we should hear them coming, shouldn't we?" She paused and glanced about her. "But even without the Drakon's patrols," said the girl with a different kind of fear, "even without that, there is the Claw." She looked at them, her eyes wide. "I think I am more afraid of the Claw than of the Drakon," she said. And then, in a completely different tone, "You do know that the Claw is supposed to be here?" said the girl.

The square where they were sitting seemed suddenly to have grown darker, and Taliesin thought that a listening quality had crept into the shadowy corners. He glanced over his shoulder, because just for a moment he had thought that something was moving in the deep shadows. Was it? Were those eyes he could see watching them, or only pinpoints of light, some kind of overspill from this world's strange power?

The Claw.

"Of course," said the girl, "I know we all overreact a bit when it comes to the Claw, but the last bulletin did say that the Claw was thought to be in this city, and the Drakon bulletins are hardly ever wrong."

Taliesin thought, She is telling us the truth. She is telling us about something—an animal?—that is loose in this world. The Claw ... Aloud, he said, "You know, it seems very unsafe for us to be sitting out here like this." *In the dark, exposed to the prying eyes of whatever lurks in the shadows ...*

"Yes, but it is *different*," said the girl. "And it is *forbidden* as well." She grinned, and it was a gamine grin, and Taliesin saw that after all the beauty was there, only that it was a vagrant beauty, so that you saw it long after it had gone, like seeing the sun imprinted on your vision if you stared at it for too long. "Forbidden things nearly always turn out to be the most exciting," said the girl. "And the evenings are so unbearably long. Mustn't it have been grand to be able to go where you liked, as they did in the old days? And doesn't everywhere look different at night? It smells different as well."

Fael-Inis, who was watching her rather thoughtfully, said,

"Will you tell us your name?" and the girl spread her hands, as if to say, Oh, why not?

"I'm Annabel O'Connor," she said. "And I live in that white house over there, and when I came running out to find the music, I knew perfectly well that I was probably running into a *questionable* situation. You might be procurers," she said suddenly. "I haven't the least idea of what you are, really."

Taliesin looked up at the garishly lit sign. "Procuration—forbidden on pain of death."

"Yes, but of course it goes on," said Annabel. "And most of us have been sought by the procurers at one time or another. It isn't any particular compliment. I once thought of letting myself be taken by them," she added. "Just to find out what happened at the other end. Only then I didn't. But we have a saying, that if you do not succumb to the Disease, then you will be procured; and if you are not procured, you will be taken up by the Drakon for infringement of the laws. And if that does not happen, then the Claw will probably get you.

"And really," said Annabel, "when you consider that the Domesday Clock has been proven right beyond all question, and that the world is certainly going to end before our eyes, what does any of it *matter*?"

WHEN YOU HAVE grown up knowing that the world will almost surely end before you die, you become philosophical about it for most of the time. Annabel thought that for quite long stretches she was as philosophical as anyone she knew. It was only now and then (like when she had come running helter-skelter from the house into the night streets—absolutely forbidden!) that she forgot to be philosophical and rebelled.

It was actually very dangerous to rebel against anything. Nobody wanted to incur the Drakon's displeasure and risk being castrated or put to death, or even being thrown inside the Cuirim to be forgotten about. Everybody knew someone who had been thrown inside the Cuirim, but nobody Annabel had ever met knew of anyone who ever came out again.

Knowing about the world ending gave you a remarkable perspective on things. It made you want to throw all caution (and probably sanity) to the winds, and try all the things you had secretly always longed to try. But since the Drakon nearly always caught you out, it was probably better not to try any of them, and, in any case, there was nobody to try them with, because everybody was terrified of the Drakon. Annabel was not especially terrified of the Drakon, but if the world was truly going to end, she would stand a better chance of surviving out in the streets, rather than inside one of the Drakon's dungeons. And although it was certainly extremely reckless to be out in the streets like this—well, it was probably very nearly suicidal—the men were rather intriguing and it would be interesting to know more about them, because they were not like anyone Annabel had ever met.

"Tell me who you really are," she said, as they crossed the square to her house. Should she invite them in? This would be reckless in the extreme, but surely no one would know? And although it was (wasn't it) too far-fetched for words to truly believe they were from another world, certainly they were different from anyone in Annabel's world, and this was something that ought to be explored.

The dark-haired one said, "We are travellers," and looked at her rather intently, but the other, the one who had made the music, said softly, "We have told you that we are from other worlds, Mortal," and somehow, when he said this, and looked at her with his slanting, fiery eyes, it was suddenly very nearly believable that they were truly from other worlds. It was suddenly perfectly possible that there were other worlds.

But Annabel hesitated in the tiny square of garden which would once have been green and flowery and now was dried up and barren. She was as sure as she could be that the two were not from the Drakon, and she was sure, as well, that even if they did not come from other worlds, they were not entirely of this world. And the thought of other worlds, other cultures, was so fascinating that it would be worth risking being out after Curfew, and it would probably almost be worth inviting them into her apartment and chance a Drakon patrol knocking on the door to see if there were unauthorised guests. It had never happened to Annabel, but everyone knew that it did happen.

And so Annabel opened the door that led directly into the tiny hall, and said to the two men, "Will you come in?" And hoped against hope that she would not end up regretting it.

Once inside, it felt remarkably normal and safe. Fael-Inis and Taliesin did not feel in the least like strangers. Annabel had asked their names carefully, and repeated them, because they were rather unusual names, and they had shaken hands, which was what people had once done before the Drakon had frowned on needless touching of people, because of the Disease, but which seemed to be the right thing to do.

They were both interested in the apartment, and they were quite complimentary about it. It was very ordinary, of course, and there was only one large room, which was all you could have these days. But the tiny kitchen was screened by a bead curtain, and Annabel had tried to furnish every-where with pretty things, even the things which had to be functional, because if you had to obey a Curfew and lock yourself inside your home from the nineteenth hour every night, you might as well be comfortable. Fael-Inis seated himself in one of the chairs and looked perfectly at home, but Taliesin prowled about, studying the pictures that An-nabel had found somewhere or other of old restaurants and theatres, and had framed and hung on the walls. She liked looking at them, and thinking about how people had once been able to go out to such places, six and eight and ten, all together, to watch plays being performed, and take meals, and drink wine. You could not get wine any longer, because it had been found to be a breeding ground for the Disease, and also because the Drakon did not really like people to drink wine. It freed too many inhibitions, said the Drakon sternly, and they all knew what the freeing of inhibitions led to.

It would have been nice to have offered wine now, as people had done in the old days. Annabel knew how you did it; you said, "A glass of wine?" and you lifted the bottle invitingly in one hand, while you twirled a corkscrew in the other. Annabel had never possessed a corkscrew because there was nothing to uncork any more, and even if she had, she would not have known how to use it, never mind twirl it.

She looked at them rather uncertainly, and then said, "Would you like coffee?" and then had to explain, because neither of them seemed to have heard of coffee before.

"But it is very good," said Fael-Inis, sipping the hot fragrant brew that Annabel had served in thick pottery mugs which had swirly tabby-cat patterns on the side, and which kept the coffee nice and hot. She was pleased that there had been fresh milk, which you could not always get now, because of people being worried about cows getting the taint of the Disease, and also because of transport becoming difficult.

Taliesin said, "Is this what you drink here?" and Annabel said, "Yes, when we can," and Taliesin said, "My poor dear child," and then laughed and drank the coffee and said it was delicious.

"And although it has not the perfumes of Tarshish and Tyre, nor the splendours of the Eastern World, it is a heartening beverage. Do you live here alone?"

"Well, yes," said Annabel, surprised.

"Of course," said Fael-Inis, and looked at Taliesin as if secretly amused. Taliesin smiled unexpectedly, and Annabel saw with surprise that he had a sudden sweet smile. She had thought him a rather stern sort of person, but quite suddenly he did not seem in the least stern. She began to hope he would smile again.

"The Drakon is very strict, you see," said Annabel, because neither of her guests appeared to know about the Drakon, which might have to be explained to them.

Fael-Inis said, "You fear the Drakon because it is harsh and powerful, but you particularly fear it because it is faceless," and Annabel looked at him with astonishment, because no one had ever heard her thoughts in quite that way. She looked at him and thought how very curious this was. Like that old book—what was it called?—where things had got curiouser and curiouser. The little girl who fell down a rabbit hole into another world. Only it was these two who had fallen into her world. I don't believe that any of this is happening, thought Annabel. Aloud, she said, "So you do *know* about the Drakon?" And tried to think where in the world the Drakon would not hold sway, and then remembered about them not coming from this world, and wondered after all which of them had fallen down a rabbit hole.

"We know only a very little," said Fael-Inis, and Taliesin, who was watching Annabel, said, "Will you tell us?"

"It is quite difficult to explain," said Annabel slowly, because clearly it was going to be very difficult indeed. How did you explain about the Drakon? You could quote the edicts. The Drakon sees all. You could say that, but even that would not convey the absolute and total control that the Drakon had over everyone.

At last Annabel said, "It's a small governing body," and found that she was choosing her words with care, because they seemed not to have quite the same words and the same meanings as she was accustomed to. "They rule absolutely, and they are very powerful." She paused. "It is whispered that they are corrupt," she said, "because power *is* corruptive, you know."

Fael-Inis said gently, "Unlimited power is apt to corrupt the minds of those who possess it," and Annabel stared, because this was rather an intriguing idea. Fael-Inis said, "A very great statesman said that, a very long time ago."

"How do you—?" said Annabel. "The Institute of Knowledge does not permit access ..."

Fael-Inis smiled the winged smile. "Because I heard it said when it was said," he replied.

"That isn't any kind of answer," said Annabel. And then, half to herself, "Or is it?"

"Does your—Institute of Knowledge not allow people to know of the happenings of the past?" said Taliesin.

"No. It is believed that too much knowledge would cause people to panic."

"But you have knowledge," said Fael-Inis. "You have somehow read a little of the past history of your people."

"Yes, I was employed at the Institute," said Annabel, and saw them look at her, and realised that *employed* was another word that had no meaning to them.

"We—all of us—must devote a—a large section of every day to working for one or another of the Drakon's aims," she said, speaking rather slowly because it was quite difficult to explain about something so ordinary and so usual as working for the Drakon in one guise or another.

"It is one of your laws?" asked Taliesin, and Annabel said, "Yes. Yes, that explains it quite well. And I was lucky to be sent to the Institute of Knowledge because it is considered to be one of the most interesting of all the Institutes."

"They send you?" said Taliesin, leaning forward. "You do not have any choice?"

"No, of course not," said Annabel, staring at him in surprise.

"Forgive me. Go on. What had you to do at the Institute?"

"I wasn't *important*," said Annabel earnestly. "I helped to write letters and keep reports. The Drakon officers who controlled that Institute received information from other Drakon officers, and it had to be decided how much of the information could be made known to the people." She put down her coffee mug. "But it was interesting," she said thoughtfully, "because so much history was stored there . . . so much of the past." She looked up at them, hoping she was making this clear.

"You studied the past?" said Taliesin.

"Well," said Annabel, "it was forbidden, really." She

leaned forward, her eyes bright. "But it was *so* fascinating. All the reports and the records going back and back to the times when people could behave as they wanted to behave, and when they had machines to do the work for them and when there were governments one to each country. And you could buy all the things you wanted, there was money for everyone, and you could work at pretty much whatever you wanted to work at." She looked at them, remembering how she had stolen down to the cellars that lay beneath the Institute of Knowledge; how she had managed to operate the old machines of the previous century, how she had seen fragments and snippets of history unfold as she sat watching, enthralled.

"I had to be so careful," said Annabel, not seeing the other two now, staring ahead of her. "For one thing, power is so very sparse. There is barely enough for any of us. There was barely enough to work the machines."

"But—you did it?" Taliesin was leaning forward, his eyes intent. "Was it a very dangerous thing for you to do?"

"Yes," said Annabel, turning to look at him. "Yes, for if they had caught me, I should have been taken to the Cuirim at once." The grin touched her face. "I think the danger was part of it," she said. "At any minute, I could have been caught."

"But you were not?"

"No. I saw so many things that the Drakon has tried to keep from us."

"How? I mean, how did you see it?" Taliesin's mind went over diaries, chronicles, perhaps paintings which might illustrate events. But Annabel said, "Well, everything is stored, of course. And you call up whichever bit you want."

"How?"

"You press buttons," said Annabel, and looked at Taliesin, and then laughed. "But the power is so thin that everything on the screens was fuzzy and jerky—" She stopped. "I think you have not the least idea of what I mean," she said, and laughed again, and Taliesin smiled, because her laughter was warm and abrupt, rather like a sudden shower of warm rain. "This is more ridiculous than ever," said Annabel, pouring more coffee from the jug. "I cannot grasp the idea of a world that has not . . . Are you *sure* you are not a new kind of trap from the Drakon?"

Fael-Inis said, very gently, "Remain very still, Mortal," and as Annabel looked up, his eyes grew fiery and inward-looking, and Annabel's own eyes widened, and she said, in a gasp, "Oh! A million needles of light. And gold and silver. And—oh yes! Oh, how completely lovely!"

Taliesin started to say "What—" but Annabel was staring entranced at Fael-Inis, her hands clasped, her eyes shining.

"The most beautiful place I have ever seen," she said. "And the people—there was something different about them—as if they possessed other powers, or as if—I do not believe this—but as if they were not entirely Human." She turned to Taliesin. "Is *that* your world?"

Fael-Inis's eyes lost the other-world radiance. "That is Tara, Mortal," he said. "The Bright Palace. That is the world we are trying to save, and that is the world to which we must eventually return."

"I don't understand any of this," said Annabel.

"You do not need to."

"Is there—" Annabel stopped. "Is there a way I could—"

"Enter our world?"

"Yes."

"Perhaps," said Fael-Inis, but Taliesin saw that the remote look had returned, and he remembered that Calatin's spell would protect only him, and that there were only seven days . . .

He pushed the thought away and said, "Tell us of this world instead. The Drakon—the Disease—"

Annabel turned back to him, and paused, because it would be very nearly impossible to describe to someone from that misty turquoise world, whose people would surely not understand about wars and international quarrels and power-hungry men, exactly what had gone wrong in Annabel's own world. But because they were both waiting, she took a deep breath and did her best.

"Nobody quite knows when it began," she said. "Not *really*. And at this distance, it is difficult to know the sequence of events." She looked at them, her expression serious.

Fael-Inis said gently, "And perhaps because you had that access to the chronicles of your people, you have a better understanding," and Annabel turned to him eagerly.

"Yes! Yes, because you see, it all seems to have been mixed up together. The wars and the dreadful weapons that people were creating, and the freedom men and women had together." She looked at them both, hoping they would understand. "I think," said Annabel, slowly, "that it truly began in the twentieth century," and paused, because for some reason it had always been very real and very near to her, that strange, hectic, brilliant time. "It is not so far back that we do not have the echoes still," she explained. "Although for all that, it is history, of course. People still say, 'Ah, the twentieth century,' you know, and they always look dreadfully wistful. I think it must have been the most marvellous time to have lived," said Annabel.

"That is how long ago?" said Taliesin, trying to establish some kind of time-scale.

But Annabel only said rather vaguely, "Well, about two hundred years," and Taliesin said, "Oh. Oh, I see." And waited for her to go on, because she had a remarkable way of bringing the strange lost centuries of this world alive.

"We think it was towards the very end of that century that the Disease truly began," said Annabel. "Or perhaps at the beginning of the next." She glanced rather uncertainly at the two men. "You see, there had been freedom, that is, sexual freedom for everyone," she said. "And from that, the Disease was somehow born. A terrible thing. People died in thousands, and it was so contagious that at its height they say people were afraid even to touch one another. We are still a little afraid now," said Annabel, and remembered how these two had taken her hand, and how she had felt as if it was something she ought not to do.

"Go on."

"Babies were born with the Disease," said Annabel. "Poor, pitiful little creatures, already dying. It was hereditary, and it was so fierce. They say that people found to be tainted with it were isolated from those free of it. They were shut away in hospitals, all together, with food and drink passed to them through iron grilles."

Taliesin said softly, "How unbearably sad," and Annabel looked at him gratefully, because she had always known this part of the Disease to be sad. To be shut away, confined, never let to see your family or friends, imprisoned with people who were dying as surely and as irrevocably as you were yourself. For there had been no cure . . .

"I think it was the only way," she said. And then, using a word unfamiliar to the other two, "Medication was given, of course. And there would have been comfort of a kind . . . They called it a Plague," said Annabel, and looked up as Taliesin made an abrupt movement with one hand, and then was still. "But they were shut away together until they died."

Fael-Inis said, half to himself, *"O, the pity of it, yet the pity of it."*

"And so then," said Annabel, "the Drakon came into being. It was a harsh and an unyielding force, but it was needed. *Something* was needed. By its severity, it managed to impose some kind of order."

" 'And out of chaos there came order,' " said Fael-Inis, and Annabel at once said, "Yes! Yes, you understand." And smiled at them both, because in some incomprehensible way, they both seemed to understand.

Fael-Inis said, "You must forgive our curiosity, Mortal. We mean no discourtesy. But perhaps we can help your world—"

"Can you?"

"I don't know," said Fael-Inis. "But we need to know

as much as we can about your people. Tell us of the
Drakon."

"The Drakon became a kind of figurehead for the people," said Annabel. "There were meetings and public assem-
blies, and everyone went. In times of trouble, people look to
strength."

There had been meetings and rallying marches. People
flocked to hear the words of the Drakon. It was said that
when the Drakon spoke from a public place, or at a rally,
the streets were deserted, for everyone drew so much hope
and such strength from the speeches. The words and the
edicts and the rallying calls became famous. They echoed
down succeeding generations.

"We shall fight this together, and we shall beat back the
Plague and the sickness that has come upon us . . . Mankind
is not so puny that it need submit to any kind of threat,"
they had said. "The fight will be harsh, and many will perish,
but the sacred flame that makes us better than animals can
not be allowed to die."

The sacred flame of mankind . . . "People liked that,"
said Annabel. "It—touched something in everyone." She
smiled. "And then, of course, there was the most famous of
them all. I do not know where it came from, only that it
was not the Drakon's own creation. I think someone once
wrote the words, and someone remembered them." She
paused, and Taliesin said, "Yes?"

Annabel said softly, " 'This is the way the world ends . . .
Not with a bang but a whimper.' " She looked at them, her
eyes dark with emotion. "Because the world was dying," she
said. "Inch by inch, painfully and slowly and unwillingly.
But it was dying."

"With a whimper, not with a bang . . ."

"Yes." Annabel sat looking down at her folded hands.
"Everyone knew it was happening."

"What happened?"

"The governments did all they could. The Drakon did
more," said Annabel, and looked at them. "I do not like the

Drakon," she said. "I think no one likes it. But in those days, with the Disease at its height, it saved the world. It said the world should not die, not like this, with a whimper. If it had to die one day, then let it be with a final extravagant gesture; a last burst of energy and power that would echo throughout the ages."

"The Drakon did not stamp the Disease out altogether," said Annabel quietly. "But somehow it halted it. By care and strict supervision, and by the dreadful harsh laws."

"People submitted to the laws?" said Taliesin, and Fael-Inis at once said, "Oh, yes. Oh, yes, I think they would have submitted." And then, to Annabel, "For when you are faced with the world dying, you are prepared to do anything."

"They did it gladly," whispered Annabel. "People embraced the new laws; they curbed their sexual appetites. The Disease was somehow halted."

Taliesin said, "But the Drakon had gained control by then," and Annabel said at once, "Yes! Yes, that was exactly how it happened!"

"A totalitarian state," said Fael-Inis, using a word unfamiliar to Taliesin.

Annabel smiled. "That is a word our ancestors used," she said. "It is something they believed they had stamped out."

"Government of the people by the people for the people?"

"Yes, but it did not work," said Annabel. "Because there were always those who must have greater power."

"And where power corrupts, great power corrupts to a greater degree . . .

"A very perceptive writer," said Fael-Inis.

Taliesin, who had been drinking a second mugful of coffee and finding it rather better the second time around, said, "I do not think I am following all of this."

"No, for the concept of such a world is alien to you," said Fael-Inis, and Taliesin said, with his old mockery, "Dear me, you are becoming adept at this strange language." And sent Annabel another of his grins.

Fael-Inis regarded Taliesin thoughtfully, but he only said, "It is a courteous custom to try to use the manners of the people whose world you are visiting."

"I am rebuked," said Taliesin at once. "Visit your wrath on me, and I will be humble."

"*Will* you?" said Annabel.

"No, of course I will not."

"I didn't think so."

Fael-Inis was still seated entirely at ease on the soft-cushioned shape which Annabel had called a sofa. "Comfortable," he had said. "You may have a harsh and bleak new world, Mortal, but you still have some softness left in it."

Annabel had been secretly rather pleased, because the sofa had been a shocking extravagance, and she had had to save her Pledges for six months, and then had had to wait another three before it could be brought to her apartment. But it had been such a truly beautiful colour—flame-orange-red—and it looked so marvellous against the whitewashed walls with the shelves for her books, and she had never really regretted it. And it was so good to hear someone admire it and to see someone enjoy sitting on it. She was just relaxing a little, and thinking that after all this queer adventure was not turning out to be nearly as disruptive as it might have done, when Fael-Inis said without warning, "And now, Annabel, tell us of the Domesday Clock."

Annabel had, in fact, forgotten that she had mentioned this earlier on. She thought it just went to show that it was very easy for your tongue to run away with you when you were interested in something. She had been so interested in these two, and in the music Fael-Inis had played, and in the intriguing air of other-worlds that had hung about them, that she had forgotten about guarding everything she said. It just went to show.

"I can't tell you about it," she said, and knew of course that she would tell them, because clearly you could tell them anything. "It's meant to be a secret," said Annabel, in the sort of voice that had already admitted that it was a ridiculous thing to try to keep secret.

Taliesin said, "But you know of it."

"Because my work has been in the Institute of Knowledge."

"Because you stole down to the cellars and read about things you were not supposed to," said Taliesin, and grinned.

"I'd have been a very good spy," said Annabel thoughtfully. "I didn't get caught, you know. They didn't even suspect. And it was all so *very* interesting."

"Tell us," said Fael-Inis, and as Annabel looked at him, his eyes grew iridescent again. *You can tell me anything, Mortal . . .* Annabel stared at him, and thought all over again how extremely odd this all was. It was curiouser and curiouser.

But she found herself drawing closer to them; she refilled the coffee mugs and rearranged herself on the hearth, because for some reason hearths were good places to be when there was a story to be told, and she thought that the art of story-telling must be being lost, slowly and surely, because people did not forgather in houses around hearths any more. And it would be a shame, thought Annabel hazily, to lose the art of story-telling, especially when so much else had already been lost. It was important to preserve mankind's heritage, to hand on something to the generations that would survive the last days of civilisation. You had to believe that some people would survive, because if you lost your belief in continuity, you lost everything.

Annabel was no longer aware of Fael-Inis's eyes growing brighter and becoming larger, but when he said again, "Tell me of the Domesday Clock, Mortal," Annabel at once began to speak.

And after all, it was quite easy to explain about the great clock that had been set up long ago, sometime in the twentieth century, somewhere deep in the heart of what people had called a neutral country. It had been in the days when mankind was beginning to experiment with the terrible weapons that their scientists and their learned men had forged, and it was in the years when people had become fascinated by the harnessing of the truly great and awesome forces that could be unleashed.

"To begin with," said Annabel, "they looked on it as a tremendous challenge, as something marvellous. That comes down very clearly indeed. They even joked about it. They called it a race, quite openly. The Arms Race."

" 'Arms'?" said Taliesin.

"The weapons," said Annabel. "The monsters that they themselves had created." And she looked at them, to be sure they understood how truly mighty and extensive the weapons had been.

Taliesin, whose mind had been running on the armoury of his own world, said, "But—could not the weapons be taken and locked somewhere in safety? And guarded?" and Annabel, understanding that the blue and green forests that Fael-Inis had conjured up in her mind could not comprehend the forces created by her ancestors, said, "Oh, no. They were so vast, so far-reaching ..." And seeing that he still did not understand, said, "The people of the day used to boast that they could blow up the world twenty times over," and saw Taliesin's eyes narrow in shocked comprehension. "And other countries had to match them," said Annabel, "and not only match them, but go beyond them, and say, 'Ah, but *we* can blow it up thirty times over.' "

"How terrible. And how futile."

"Well," said Annabel, who had often considered this, "the awful thing is that, if you think about it, it is understandable. It made them feel safe, you see. If your neighbour has a large stick with which he might attack you, or if he has a gun or a rifle or a bomb which he might use against you, you could only feel safe if you had a stick, a gun, a rifle, a bomb as well. And you would want it a bit bigger, just to be sure. If I was threatened," said Annabel firmly, "I should want to be sure I could fight back. I was never in a war," she said, "because we don't have wars any longer," and Taliesin smiled at the sudden wistful note. "But if I was," said Annabel, "I'd be sure that my weapons were better than the other side."

"An admirable philosophy," said Fael-Inis gravely.

"We're not supposed to approve of war any longer," said Annabel. "The Drakon thinks it incites people to all manner of wickedness." The grin flared briefly. "I wouldn't mind a war," said Annabel. "I'd fight if somebody threatened my home or my country."

"That is what wars should be about," agreed Fael-Inis.

"That's what I think. But you see, they became frightened," said Annabel, going back to her curled-up position on the hearthrug. "They became afraid of the—the monsters they had created. And although some people tried to pretend that the monsters did not exist, they all knew that they were there for always. You can't uncreate a thing simply by pretending it hasn't happened. The weapons had happened.

"It was about that time that a small group of people formed themselves into a kind of International League. I don't know the details," said Annabel, "and I don't think anyone else does now. They might have been businessmen or bankers or churchmen. Yes, they might certainly have been churchmen, because people still followed the Church then."

Taliesin started to ask what churchmen and churches were, but was silenced by a quick glance from Fael-Inis.

"They wanted, you see, to measure how close the world was to a war where these terrible weapons would be used," explained Annabel. "They thought the war would probably never happen, but they couldn't be sure that it never would. Perhaps there were statesmen in with them as well. And they all thought they ought to calculate the imminence of this final last war. Some people thought it was a senseless exercise, of course, but—"

"But," said Taliesin softly, "if you are about to blow up

mankind and bring about the end of civilisation, perhaps it is as well to be a little prepared." He studied her. "Were those weapons, those monsters, truly so powerful?"

"Oh, yes," said Annabel. "Oh, yes, they were every bit as powerful.

"They agreed, this group of people, that they would try to be continually aware of the squabbles between countries, and of the incidents and the crises, and all the things that might spark off a war. Because wars," said Annabel severely, looking absurdly young as she said it, "can be started from the tiniest of incidents."

"Such as necromancers becoming greedy," murmured Fael-Inis. "Go on, Annabel."

"They wanted to set up some kind of device, designed to show how severe the danger was. How close. It would have to be simple and direct, but it would have to have impact.

"They came up with the idea of a Clock," she said, and then stopped, as Taliesin made a sudden questioning movement. "You do know what a clock is?" said Annabel, half laughing, half exasperated.

"A device for measuring time," said Fael-Inis with exquisite courtesy. "My dear, you should ignore our poor friend, for I fear he has lived a very sheltered life."

Annabel said, "But I cannot begin to understand—" And stopped and laughed the warm, abrupt laughter again.

Taliesin said, "Time has always been measured in some form or other. I do not see—"

"But," said Fael-Inis, turning to him, "in this world, Mortal, the people are ruled by it. Yes?" This to Annabel, who nodded. "Here," said Fael-Inis, "it is necessary to have a very exact idea of time, you see."

"While I was working for the Institute of Knowledge," said Annabel, who had been searching her mind for a way to explain, "it was necessary for me to—to be at my desk at the ninth hour exactly."

"Exactly?"

"A bell would ring," said Annabel. "And if I was not seated at my desk, ready to work when that bell rang, I was severely disciplined, and perhaps I lost a little of the money due to me that day."

"How truly terrible."

"Also," said Annabel, with relish, "I could not leave until another bell rang at the eighteenth hour."

"My poor child," said Taliesin, and Annabel laughed again.

"It does not seem so if you have known nothing else."

"That is why," said Fael-Inis, taking up the explanation, "they have what are called *clocks*, machines which give the exact hour of the day, and the precise minute."

"And that is why," said Annabel, "the notion of a Clock was attractive to those people who wanted to know how close the world was to its final holocaust."

"They were measuring the world's life by hours and minutes," said Taliesin, still not fully understanding, but grasping the concept now.

"Yes. I believe that the Clock itself was sited somewhere in the north of Europe," said Annabel, her eyes faraway now. "Sweden or Switzerland perhaps, although I am not sure. And they met once a year, to move the hands of the Clock forwards or backwards, depending on the events of that year. Depending on the quarrels between nations, and the disagreements between governments. Midnight was what they called the Doom Hour." She glanced at Taliesin. "You—you do have midnight in your world?"

Taliesin said, "Yes, we have what we call the deep midnight, which the sorcerers believe to be a deeply magical time."

"Well," said Annabel, who would have liked to hear more of this, but thought she had better continue, "they called midnight the Doom Hour. If ever it was felt necessary to move the Clock's hands towards midnight, then it would mean that the holocaust was almost upon them. The terrible war that would end the world would have become inevitable." She paused again, and Taliesin said, "Yes?"

"They met for many years," said Annabel. "They did not meet in any particular secrecy, but they didn't make a great display about it, either. They moved the Clock's hands accordingly, and although it was frequently close to midnight—sometimes it was within ten minutes of it—somehow it never quite reached midnight." She looked up. "I think they would have been quite honest about it," said Annabel. "I do not think they would have deluded themselves. That was not their aim.

"And so the Clock never reached midnight."

She stopped speaking, and Fael-Inis said, "But now?"

"The Clock disappeared," said Annabel, "nobody knows quite when, for who does know the precise moment a thing disappears? You only know that you go to look for it, and it is no longer there. The Clock vanished, and no one knew when."

It had not seemed to matter. Annabel, stealing down to the badly lit vaults beneath the Institute of Knowledge, had read the reports and seen the records. Nobody thought that the world was in danger by that time. People had become used to the idea of those terrible weapons forged nearly a century earlier. They had grown complacent. The holocaust would not happen. There was more tolerance in the world. People were learning to respect one another. Nobody wanted to blow up the world any more. It had been a good time to live.

"It was a good time to live," said Annabel. "Countries who had been in a perpetual state of half-war were talking to one another. Richer countries were trying to help poorer ones. The disappearance of what some people had called the Peace Clock, and the dispersing of the small group who had controlled it, was a small matter."

Fael-Inis, his eyes on her, said, "What happened next?"

"It is difficult to know the sequence," said Annabel, as

she had said earlier. "But the time was already beginning to run out for us. There was already concern about the world's resources—food and power and water. There were droughts, dreadful arid months when the rainfall was so low that the great reservoirs began to dry up. Then there were famines—not just one, but many, all following one on top of another. People died by the thousands. And then there was the Disease, which the people of the time called Plague. It became rife and then virulent. Food supplies were dwindling. The rain forests were dying. And the water and the fuel were slowly running out." She looked at them both. "It did not happen quickly, of course," she said. "Not nearly as quickly as I am making it sound. It took years, decades. But it was happening . . ."

The world dying, not with a bang but a whimper . . .

Taliesin said, "But the world still lives. Annabel, the world is surviving."

"No. The world is dying." Annabel looked at him. "It is doubtful if there are many more months left to us."

"You cannot know that."

"I do know it. We all know it. The knowledge is not supposed to be out, but it is. It has leaked, little by little. Even the Drakon knows it can no longer hide the truth. Everyone knows that the world will soon end, although whether it will be with a whimper or a bang, we cannot tell." She turned to look at them very directly. "Some years ago, the Clock was found," said Annabel. "Deep in Ireland's eastern mountains. Miners or pot-holers or explorers found it. It was there. And they found that all through its lost years, it had been moving. Living. *Ticking*. The hands had been moving by themselves. *Forwards*. All of the years when we had believed ourselves to be moving away from the disaster, away from the great, all-destroying war, we were moving towards it," said Annabel, her eyes huge and dark. "The Clock had taken on some kind of life. It had lain there quietly in its mountain hall, and the hands had been creeping slowly forward. Nearer and nearer to midnight. The Doom Hour.

"They have tried to destroy it, but they have failed. And now there is a kind of superstition about it. They dare not attempt its destruction again.

"But they watch it ceaselessly. There are permanent vigils now, through every hour of every day, for they dare not miss the slightest movement now. The Drakon has sent in its own people to mount watch and to record every quiver of movement it makes.

"But it is moving forward all the time," said Annabel. "It is very slow but it is unmistakable. The hands show one minute to midnight now. And when they touch midnight, the world will end. We have come to believe it. We all of us believe it.

"We are a doomed race and a dying world, and there is nothing anyone can do to save us."

To TALIESIN it seemed as if the three of them were entirely alone at the centre of a doomed and lost world. Annabel had brewed up a fresh pot of coffee in the bright, clean little room which she called a kitchen; they were warm and safe and closed in with food and drink and fire and companionship.

But outside is the darkness, and the howling confusion, and outside are the raging winds, and the endless night that is to come . . .

The words formed themselves in Taliesin's mind, and with them came a vision so horrific and so dreadfully vivid that his senses reeled. He glanced to where Fael-Inis sat motionless, but Fael-Inis only blinked expressionlessly like a cat.

The darkness and the howling confusion and the endless night . . . It is approaching, thought Taliesin. Inch by inch, the world is ending. The Domesday Clock is ticking closer to midnight, and somewhere beyond Human vision, the Four Horsemen are waiting to lead the Apocalypse into the world.

And then: I wonder how it will happen? he thought, and as he framed the thought, Annabel, who had been pouring the coffee, said, "We do not know how it will happen yet," and Taliesin jumped, because it was somehow unexpected to find a trace of the Samhailt here.

"But there will be theories as to what will happen?" said Fael-Inis.

Annabel said thoughtfully, "It is a quite strongly held belief that there are a number of countries in the world which still secretly maintain the weapons. Countries that were once shut off from the rest of the world, and sealed away from it. There was a phrase they used," said Annabel, "the Iron Curtain. Part of the world was shut off behind an Iron Curtain, and for many years no one knew what went on in those countries. Our ancestors worked to lift that Curtain," said Annabel, back in the past again, her eyes remote. "They worked very hard to lift the barriers that had been raised. They opened the Brandenburg Gate and they ripped down the Iron Curtain. That is quite old history, of course, but it must have been such a wonderful time to have lived through.

"But the barriers are back; the Iron Curtain of our ancestors has descended in a different place. We hear whispers of faceless leaders who are banding together to overthrow the larger countries. They would be ruthless, those leaders, and if they have the weaponry of the twentieth and the twenty-first centuries, then we are certainly doomed. They will use them against us unless we submit to their demands."

"You would not submit?" said Taliesin, knowing the answer.

"Of course not," said Annabel, and grinned at him. "We used to have an expression, in one of the really *old* wars: 'Death or glory.' They say the men used it going into battle against the enemy, although," said Annabel thoughtfully, "I am not sure at this distance quite *which* enemy, because there have been several, you understand. But it's rather a good expression, isn't it?"

"A battle-cry," said Fael-Inis solemnly. "Yes, it is a very good one."

"Well, anyway, we should fight those greedy, selfish leaders," said Annabel, her eyes bright. "Of course we should."

"Death or glory," said Taliesin.

"Well, yes."

Fael-Inis was still seated quietly on the flame-orange sofa, but the other two suddenly turned to him, and Annabel thought, How remarkable he is. It is as if he has suddenly pulled on an invisible string, and we have both been compelled or commanded to attend to him.

Fael-Inis said, "The Domesday Clock—"

"Yes?"

"Where is it now?"

Annabel studied him before replying. Then she said softly, "It is set deep in the heart of the mountains, in a remote part of Ireland. I do not know the true name of the place, but they say they were once called the Fire Mountains."

Fael-Inis made an abrupt movement forwards, and the dying firelight caught his eyes so that they glowed. Almost to himself, he said, "So they still exist, in this brave new world, do they . . . ?" And then, as the other two looked, "No matter," he said.

"They had to find somewhere very safe for the Clock," said Annabel, because he seemed to be waiting for her to continue. "Somewhere where it could not be tampered with." She looked at them both to be sure they understood this, because it had been very important that people should not tamper with the Clock. "It is deep within the Fire Mountains," said Annabel, "and it is guarded day and night." She frowned, because there had been curious and rather sinister tales of the Clock's guardians. Creatures not quite Human, summoned from out of the past . . . No one had believed this, but there had been an odd and inexplicable note of authenticity about the tale. The Three Guardians, the three terrible Powers from a long-dead world, guarding the Cavern of the Domesday Clock . . .

"They say," said Annabel, "that the Clock is set high on a shelf of rock, narrow but regular. What our ancestors would have called an altar." She glanced at them, but this word seemed familiar to them. "It is lit by burning torches, set high up in the inside of the mountain," said Annabel, "and the torches are never allowed to go out." She paused again, for there had been no reason to ensure that the Clock was always lit, only that no one had been able to bear the thought of the Clock ticking away the world's last days by darkness. "The torches are kept burning," said Annabel. "They are lit and replenished every four hours."

"Firelight?" said Taliesin, for crude firelight did not somehow accord with the legends that had come back of this marvellous age.

"It is the only source of light that we can trust now," said Annabel.

"And so the Domesday Clock is set on its altar," said Fael-Inis softly, "and it is deep within the Fire Mountains which once I knew as well, Mortal, as you know this room where you live." He looked at them, his face alight. "Our task is clear, you know."

"Is it?" said Taliesin, and Annabel started to say, "But what *is* your task?" and found she could not quite frame the question after all.

Fael-Inis stood up and looked down at them both. "We must travel to the Fire Mountains," he said. "We must somehow penetrate to the torchlit Cavern of the Clock.

"And once we are there, we shall stop the hands from reaching midnight.

"We shall save the world."

CHAPTER THIRTEEN

TALIESIN STOOD IN the bright room that Annabel had called a kitchen, and watched her moving about, placing the mugs from which they had drunk coffee in a round bowl made of some hard shiny substance; reaching into cupboards for food and bags.

"Shall you really accompany us?"

Annabel turned round and looked at him and, without warning, the sudden wide grin flashed. "Death or glory, remember?" And then, more seriously, "Are you *truly* going to save the world?"

"I don't know," said Taliesin, who did not.

"You couldn't expect me not to be in on the saving of the world," said Annabel. "I couldn't not want to be."

"It will be very dangerous," said Taliesin, leaning against the doorframe and watching her.

"I know," said Annabel, and grinned the gamine grin again.

"Dangers and darknesses and raging seas," murmured Taliesin. "All the sweet risk of all the perils ever known to ... What is that?"

"Chocolate," said Annabel, wrapping squares of a dark, rich-looking food. "A great rarity now. But very sustaining. And I thought we would take fruit and these biscuits. And the milk. Milk," said Annabel severely, "*fresh* milk is unbelievably difficult to obtain now." She packed it all away carefully, and then stood looking at Taliesin rather shyly. "I do *not* understand any of it," said Annabel. "I don't really believe that any of it is happening. Or if it is, then perhaps it is happening to somebody else, and perhaps I have got into somebody else's dream. Are you a dream?"

"Are you?" said Taliesin very softly, and looked at her, and saw how her hair shone like copper, and wanted to pull her into his arms, and hold her hard against him, and take her back to the untidy house in the Street of Money-Lenders, and watch her curl up by the fire, and see her hair turn to a blaze of colour. It would not do, of course: she was from a different world, and it was impossible that their two worlds could ever mingle ... *And we are spirits of a different sort*, he thought, and knew that this was not so, for they were of the same mould. Remarkable and incredible, and above all ironic that he should penetrate Time and enter a doomed world, and find the one woman above all ...

He thought that she was looking at him and he thought, as well, that she was probably guessing or hearing his thoughts. And because this was not to be borne—for I must leave her here to face whatever terrible Fate awaits this world—he hunched a shoulder and said, "You are very trusting, Annabel," and at once thought, And *now* I have used her name, and it sounded exactly like a caress ...

But if Annabel had heard the caress, she gave no sign of it. She said, quite seriously, "I *do* trust you. Both of you."

"Why? Your world is so harsh—so much has happened to make you suspicious and wary."

Annabel said, "I think it is a little that I have always *hoped*." She looked at him to see if he was understanding, and then went on, "I should like to be able to believe in so much. So much that has been written and imagined and handed down."

"And always," said Taliesin slowly, "always you have woken up."

" '*Awoke and found me here upon the cold hillside ...*' Yes," said Annabel. And remembered, but did not say, how she had read the poets and the dreamers, and gone willingly into dreams, but how the dreams had always dissolved. There had been many cold dawns, many awakenings to cold hill-

sides, many lonely dissolvings of dreams, because no matter
how much you wished and pretended, still the reality was
the Drakon's grim world, where food was running out, and
a Clock deep within the Fire Mountains was ticking away
mankind's last hours. And then, because it would not do to
admit to all of this, Annabel said rather flippantly, "What
should I wear for the journey? What is correct when you are
going to save the world?" And then, in a different voice,
"How shall we get there?"

THE SOFT SWEET beckoning music of the pipes spun and shivered and beckoned in the quiet square, and Annabel stood
very still and felt the music wrap her about, and could not
speak for the sheer delight of it. It was like something you
could reach out and take between your hands, and treasure
and store away, so that you could unwrap it later and savour
its beauty . . .

The Time Chariot came smoothly and easily, materialising from the shadows outside the square, sending shafts of
pure colour into the night. The salamanders bowed their
heads submissively, and tossed their manes, and blurred into
colour and fire and light, and then back into solid shapes,
and then into whirling flame again, so that you could not be
quite sure from one minute to the next if they were really
there.

"They are there," said Fael-Inis. "They bathe in the Fire
Rivers beneath the Mountains of the Morning, and they can
harness all of the world's power and all of the world's
strength and light." He turned to look at Annabel, who was
standing in the spilled light from the Chariot, entranced and
enchanted. Taliesin looked at her, and remembered how she
had talked about always wanting to believe, and how he had
seen the hope in her eyes . . . *Surely there are dreams somewhere*, her eyes had said. *Surely this cold bleak world is not all
there is?* He watched her, and saw the delight dawn in her
expression, and knew that she was seeing the dreams come
tumbling into her world at last. When she reached out a

hesitant hand to touch the Chariot, he saw how the light and
the fire spilled across her skin, and he remembered Calatin's
spell, and made an abrupt movement. But, "All is well," said
Fael-Inis softly. "For we do not travel across Time, yet. The
fires will be cool enough for you both."

Taliesin thought, We do not travel across Time, yet. But
before much longer we shall have to do so. Seven days, and
then Calatin's enchantment will be useless. And even then,
it will serve to protect only one . . . I *cannot* leave her behind! thought Taliesin in silent anguish. And then, Could I
stay here with her? And felt again the desolation and the
despair of the world they had thought would be so filled with
marvels, and knew a great and aching agony. He looked at
her and thought, *She is not for me, nor I for her*, and felt a
strange haunting echo, as if the pain was not being felt for
the first time.

Fael-Inis had moved to the Chariot, and was standing, lit
by the flames, his hands outstretched to them. "Come with
me," he said, and now it was not the quiet, thoughtful phi-
losopher who had sat in the small apartment and drunk coffee and listened to the story of the ending of the world; now
it was the rebel angel again, the creature who had defied the
gods and turned his back on the war in heaven. Annabel
gasped, and put her hand out to Taliesin, and felt herself to
be falling headlong into the world of make-believe where
almost anything could happen, and where chimerical creations lived and walked, and where there were no cold hillsides and no lonely dawn awakenings . . . There was surely
no magic left in the world, and yet there was magic unfolding
before her eyes. *I still do not believe any of this . . . I am Lewis
Carroll's Alice, and I do not believe . . . But we are going to
save the world, and it will be the most exciting thing anyone
has ever done anywhere ever* . . . I ought to be wary, said Annabel to Annabel. I ought to be questioning everything and
distrusting it all. I certainly ought not to be feeling exhilarated and I *definitely* ought not to be looking forward to it.
Death or glory . . . I wonder if they really did say that, or

if it is just something somebody made up. What I really ought to do is turn my back on this weird machine and these two people who are probably adventurers of some kind, and go back into the safety of my own apartment. That's what I ought to do, said the voice of the sane and practical Annabel.

And—how boring! said the reckless Annabel, the one who believed in dreams and enchantments, and who had known all along that there were other worlds, only that you sometimes had to look very hard to find them. How dull and boring! If I do not do this, I shall certainly spend the rest of my life regretting it!

And then Fael-Inis took their hands and drew them forward into the Time Chariot.

WHEN YOU HAVE always lived in a world where the only way to get anywhere is by walking, to skim the earth's surface with a speed so breathtaking that you feel as if you might fall over the edge of the world is probably the most overwhelming experience you will ever know. Annabel, clutching the sides of the Chariot, her hair flying in the soft, warm wind, tried to catch her breath, and then abandoned the attempt. Clearly if you were going to travel like this, you would not be able to breathe, and that was that. She thought she might very likely die from delight, and not being able to breathe, but she thought that to die like this, with delight soaring and exhilaration cascading, would be the most exciting thing ever. When Fael-Inis said, in a voice that Annabel thought of as pouring flame, "Hold on, Mortals!" there was just enough breath left to call back a reassurance, and then the salamanders were streaming effortlessly ahead of them, and below them were the sleeping meadows and farms and towns.

Annabel, clinging to the Chariot, thought hazily that the people of the last century must have felt a little of this when they travelled in the machines that took them everywhere. She had always liked the stories of the machines that moved across the earth's surface, although the Drakon said, austerely, that they had been noisy and dangerous.

The machines had long since gone, of course. The great Oil Wars a hundred years earlier had meant that there was no longer the means to power the machines. The drying up of the Oil Fields had rendered the machines useless. Expeditions had been sent out to find more of the same substances, and research laboratories had been set up, but by that time the power supplies of the world had been dwindling, and there had not been the means.

The machines were still talked about. People could remember hearing grandparents tell about them; how you simply pressed buttons and turned wheels, and how you took yourself anywhere and everywhere. But there had been too many of them in the end, said the Drakon. The highroads had become choked; the people had been ill from the fumes and the gases that the machines used up. There was not enough space any longer.

Annabel would have enjoyed the machines and she was enjoying the Time Chariot. She did not fully understand about it: "And I do not want to," she said, and Taliesin understood this, because when you are faced with something enchanting and magical, you do not always want to know how it works. When you watch an entertainment, you do not want to be reminded that the players have painted faces and that their swords are card and their jewels paste. You certainly do not want to think about the flimsy structures that appear to be castles and mist-wreathed isles, but are really only plaster and timber with men behind them creating an illusion. You want only to believe in the illusion.

And so Taliesin, who had watched the plays and the make-believe of his world, and Annabel, who had only read about them, were easily able to accept the Time Chariot and enter wholly into its enchantment, and find it all entirely believable. Taliesin thought that perhaps Fael-Inis was no more than an illusionist, but if that was so, then he was an illusionist of truly remarkable powers; Annabel, who had been searching for illusions and magic all her life, did not even stop to question it.

"I was enthralled then and for ever," she was to say. "I had fallen completely under the spell of this golden-eyed being, and I do not think I really wanted to be released."

THE ROAD TO the Fire Mountains was dark, but there was a soft spill of light from somewhere.

"Starlight," said Fael-Inis. "A sad light."

Annabel, child of a city, had never experienced such darkness. "There were always lights and there were always other people," she said. "And the patrols were always marching, carrying their lanterns." And then, "Will the patrols be out here?"

"I think so," said Fael-Inis. "Yes, I think they will." And gestured below them. "There are houses," he said. "There are farms and cottages. Yes, the Drakon will be watchful."

Because the Drakon sees all, and because it must *appear* to see all . . . that is the Drakon's strength.

Annabel thought that this dark sombre countryside was like another world. On each side, rearing up steeply, were the rough cliff faces. "The sides of the mountains," said Fael-Inis. "The beginning of the Fire Country."

Ahead of them lay the Fire Mountains themselves, purple-misted and dark and remote. Here and there were vivid threads of colour; orange and scarlet, like tiny far-off rivers of living fire pouring down the mountainside. But they vanished as you looked at them; they were like skeins of silk that caught the light and then disappeared. It was difficult to know if you had really seen them at all.

"You *are* seeing them," said Fael-Inis. "They are the fires that burn deep below the mountains. Sometimes curls of fire escape and that is what you are seeing. There are rivers of fire and lakes of burning flames, all beneath the mountains."

Annabel said, "Were they not once called the Mountains of Mourne?" and Fael-Inis said, "Yes. That is a corruption of an even older name, though. They were once known as the Mountains of the Morning, because of the light that sometimes shone from them. But it was not the light of the morning," said Fael-Inis. "It was the fire that burns in the underground halls and in the deep caverns. It is the light and the fire of an old, old power and an old, old force that was ancient before even the world was spawned." He was looking at the mountains now, his eyes bright. "But I am from the beginning of Time, Child, and you are from the other end of it. At the beginning these were called, and truly, the Fire Mountains and now, nearing the end, they are again called so." He smiled, as the Time Chariot drew to a halt. "Shall we go on? The road is narrow, but if we stay close, we do not need to walk singly."

And to do so might lose us sight of one another ... Nobody said the words, but Taliesin and Annabel thought that nobody needed to, because everyone knew. Annabel was trying not to remember the whispered tales of a terrible entity that the Drakon had called up to guard the Domesday Clock. The Guardians ... Of course it would not be true. Taliesin was remembering that the Conablaiche had walked here, and might still do so. And Annabel had said something about a terrible creature, the Claw, of whom all went in fear.

And then Fael-Inis stopped abruptly and tilted his head, and said, "Listen," and Taliesin and Annabel stopped, and Taliesin said, "I can't hear ..." and then stared and felt fear clutch his heart, for he had heard it as well now.

Hoofbeats. Somewhere quite near, but somewhere over their heads. The sound of horses being ridden hard across unseen plains and unseen skies.

"Is it—someone following us?" said Annabel uncertainly.

"It is the Four Horsemen," said Fael-Inis and, glancing at Annabel, said softly, "The Heralds of the end of your world." And then, as Annabel stared at him, her eyes huge, her face white and pinched, he said, very gently, "They are in your myths, Mortal," and Annabel said in a whisper, "Yes. Yes, of course. The Four Horsemen. Plague, Famine, War, and Death. I had not realised . . . Then there is truly no escape. Only I had not thought it would be like this . . ." And stopped again, and thought that however she had visualised the end, she had not visualised it like this: unseen creatures riding into the world. It was suddenly very easy to imagine the Horsemen—and yes, they *were* in all the legends!— riding hard across the skies, seeking a way into the world . . .

Fael-Inis said, "They have tried to enter the world for countless ages, but always they have been unsuccessful."

"Will they—find a way in now?"

"I have no way of knowing that." He stood, looking up to the night sky, where great dark clouds scudded. "I hear them," he said, half to himself. "I hear their hoofs pawing the ground, and their spurs clicking. They are searching for a chink between their world and this."

"How long have we?" said Taliesin.

"I cannot tell. They are impatient and they are hungry. Their manes are being tossed by the evil winds of the Dark Ireland, and they are hungry for the world," said Fael-Inis, and Annabel shivered, because surely if the world was to end, it should not be like this, helpless before some terrible entity that nobody could fight; it should be in a firework display of explosions and huge glorious battles, where people could ride helter-skelter into the fray. Death or glory . . . Had that ever really been said?

They moved on, more cautiously now, continually glancing back over their shoulders, trying as well to keep an eye on what might lie ahead.

"The Guardians," said Annabel, her eyes fearful. "Terrible creatures called up by the Drakon. I never believed, not really. Only out here, I am not so sure."

Fael-Inis turned to look at her, and after a moment said softly, "So your world makes use of those creatures, does it? How remarkable that I should come across them here."

"Nobody believes in them," said Annabel, "not really."

"I believe," said Fael-Inis. "Just because you have never seen a thing, does not mean it does not exist."

Annabel said, "The Guardians—"

"Tell us," said Taliesin.

"The brotherhood of sorcerers," said Fael-Inis, the far-away expression still in his voice. "Necromancers, and evil enchantresses who will guard any object and kill and maim and devour to preserve that object. They are greedy and merciless and venal." He looked to where the mountains lay ahead of them. "Beneath those mountains," he said, "are the eternal fires, and the burning rivers, and the homes of the salamanders. It is not strange, Annabel, that your world should have been able to summon the Guardians to keep watch over the Domesday Clock. Your world has almost lost the art of magic, but out here, in these mountains, the magic is still here. Can you not feel it?" he said, looking at her, and Annabel, staring at him, said softly, "Yes. Oh, yes."

"If the Drakon called to the Guardians," said Fael-Inis thoughtfully, "*really* called to them, they would certainly have answered."

"Shall we meet them?"

"Yes," said Fael-Inis. "Yes, I think we shall meet them." And glanced at Taliesin. "Afraid, my friend?"

"Helpless with terror," said Taliesin promptly. "Because if you are to offer me up to be a sorceress's sacrifice, I will tell you that there are infinitely preferable fates—" And then stopped and said, "Listen," and turned to stare back down the narrow road with the high rocky mountains on all sides, which made it impossible for anything to hide, but which also made it impossible to hide from anything.

Annabel said, "What is it?" and then heard it as well.

Marching. Steel-tipped boots coming closer. The Drakon's patrol coming up the narrow mountain road after them.

THE PATROLS HAD always sounded like this; Annabel had grown very used to them. There had been a word once—*military*. The patrols were military. They marched exactly in step, and you could hear their boots ringing out in the quiet night. They had cold greedy eyes and they did not hesitate to knock on doors where they thought there might be a law being transgressed. Annabel knew people who had hidden in wardrobes and cellars or who had stood outside on narrow window-ledges to escape. No one ever did escape, of course. The Drakon saw all.

There was nowhere to run to here, and yet they must certainly not be found and caught by the patrol. It was after Curfew—it was very nearly time for the Curfew to be lifted, in fact, and Annabel was out alone with two strange men. She would be taken up at once and thrown into the Cuirim, and there would be an end.

Except that it could not be allowed to happen.

Fael-Inis grasped Annabel's right hand at exactly the same moment that Taliesin took the left. "Run!" he cried. "Forward! Now!" And seemed to spring forward, taking them with him.

The patrol heard them at once, of course; it quickened its speed, and there was the sound of orders being rapped out. "Faster! There are people ahead of us!" And there was suddenly a sense of urgency, because they must not be found, they must not be thrown into the Cuirim.

Annabel was hardly looking where they were going, she was conscious only of Fael-Inis pulling her forward, and of her hand strongly in Taliesin's, and of the night wind stirring her hair. She thought she could not run very much faster, and she certainly could not run very much farther, because her lungs were beginning to rasp and there was a tight pain across her chest, and after all perhaps it would be better simply to give in and she might as well be inside the Cuirim as anywhere else if the world were to end . . .

And then Fael-Inis halted and seemed to sniff the air, and turned sharply into what looked like solid rock, and pulled them through into a narrow jutting entrance. The soft starlight was abruptly shut off, and they were inside the mountain.

They stood for a moment, huddled close together, trying to adjust to the darkness, trying to gauge their surroundings.

Only Fael-Inis seemed at ease, but then, thought Annabel, he can probably see in the dark anyway. He is a creature of fire and light and speed, and I can not think of any danger he could not overcome. And then, because it was distinctly comforting to remember about fiery chariots that would probably ride full tilt at enemies and destroy them in a single glorious swoop, and about golden-eyed immortal beings who somehow crossed Time to save dying worlds, she held on to this rather firmly. If you had to be hiding inside an old dark mountain, it was a very good thought indeed to be able to hold on to.

The darkness smelt warm and dry and very old. Annabel, still managing to conjure up visions of arrows of fire and rebellious and unbeatable angels, thought this was a very old place indeed. It had seen the world born, and it had seen it wax and wane and transform, and quite soon now it would see it die. Annabel shivered, and Taliesin put an arm about her, and there was a sudden surprised delight, because his arm was strong and firm and warm, and the dark old mountain did not seem quite so menacing.

The patrol was nearly level with the narrow opening, and Fael-Inis, in a thread of a whisper, said, "Keep very still. Do not move or speak."

Annabel found herself counting the footsteps. Ten more, and they will be exactly level with us; if they go on for another ten, they will have missed us. And, What a marvellous thing it will be to have evaded them! she thought. She stayed very still, her heart pounding, and presently her eyes began to adjust to the dimness, so that she could see that they were in a kind of narrow cave that might lead somewhere deep into the mountain, or that might not lead anywhere at all. It was probably all wrong to hope it did lead somewhere, and that they would be able to find out where. Perhaps they would have to move further back, and then they would find out.

She wished that her heart was not beating so furiously because the others must hear it, and if they could hear it, perhaps the patrol might hear it as well. They would hear, and they would listen, and then they would be able to track it to its source, like that really old story—Edgar Allan somebody, was it?—where the still-beating heart of the murdered man had lain beneath the murderer's floorboards, beating so insistently that it had betrayed the murderer. I have a telltale heart, thought Annabel. They will hear, and they will find us, and we shall all be thrown into the Cuirim, and the Clock will go on to midnight, and the world will end, and it will all be my fault for having a heart that beat too loudly.

The patrol was level with the jutting rock now, and the men were swishing angrily at the grass. They know we are here, thought Annabel, and pressed closer to Taliesin. We are hunted animals; rabbits or hares or foxes. We are being hunted in the way that people used to hunt foxes many years ago, and kill them. She shrank back into the solid wall of the mountain, and tried not to notice the old, old smell of the mountain, and tried, as well, not to think about the weight of mountain that must be directly above them. All that solid rearing mountain, directly over their heads, pressing down . . .

It was then that they became aware of something moving at the far end of the cave.

Fael-Inis heard it first; he touched Taliesin's hands, and Taliesin, whose eyes had been constantly raking the darkness, felt his senses at once spring to attention.

Something inside the mountain. Something coming stealthily closer. Something creeping and ancient and evil.

Something with claws and teeth and a great grinning, dripping muzzle . . .

Taliesin pushed Annabel back into the solid rock wall, shielding her with his body. Annabel, who was very frightened indeed of whatever it was that was creeping through the mountain towards them, gasped and, incredibly, experienced a sudden jolt of the purest pleasure. There was a breathspace of time when she did not think, I am inside a dark old mountain with what may be a ravening monster

creeping up on us, but—This is the first time I have felt a
man's body like this . . . And was conscious of hard mascu-
line strength and the feeling of warm breath on her cheek,
and clean hair touching her face . . . And firm thighs, and a
core of hard warmth between them . . .

Taliesin felt, for a brief dizzying moment, Annabel's instinctive response, and delight and desire spiralled upwards.
And then the dark old mountain and the creeping danger
closed about him again, and he half turned his head to rake
the shadows, trying to sense how close to them the shuffling,
clawing creature was. He could hear it quite plainly now,
and he thought he could smell it as well. A dry, old, stale
odour that was coming closer all the time.

Was it the Conablaiche? If so, thought Taliesin, it will
be greedy for our living hearts; it will tear them out and take
them for Crom Croich . . . We shall be offered up on silver
platters, and then all will be lost, and Annabel will certainly
never see Ireland, and I shall lose her, and Medoc will have
won . . .

Annabel, her face half buried in Taliesin's shoulder, was
aware of a great listening. Whatever was out there in the dark
underside of the mountain—could it be the Claw?—was sniffing the air, trying to decide where its prey was hiding. In
just another minute it would know, it would smell them out,
and it would come loping across the hard rock floor, and it
would pluck them from this frail concealment, and spit them
on the end of its talons, and it would tear them open . . .

There was a growing feeling of immense evil now, and
of something greedy and implacable approaching.

And then moonlight pierced the cave, so that they saw
the terrible black shadow fall across the rock floor. The
stench of decaying flesh was all about them, and they knew
that the Conablaiche, the Claw, the ancient, evil Servant of
the Dark Ireland, stood in the cave with them.

It could not see them. All three knew it at once. It stood
for a moment, its eyes swivelling, turning this way and that,
searching the dark corners.

There is a tasty morsel somewhere here. I can smell it. There is a toothsome morsel for my Master in this cave . . . juicy gobbets of flesh, and warm, still-beating hearts that I shall offer up on a silver platter, dripping and steaming . . . Come out from your hiding place, Humans, so that I may flay you and snap your ribcages and tear your hearts from their moorings . . .

The moonlight lay across the floor, and they could see the creature in full, terrible detail; they could see that it was composed of every nightmare and every grisly story ever told or imagined or feared.

Huge. Towering. Ten feet high at least. There was a head with a narrow bony skull and a great curving beak. A vulture's head! thought Taliesin, unable to look away. A great vulture's head, with protruding, fish-like eyes that could swivel on stalks and peer into the darkest recesses of men's minds and souls. A hard, bony body, not quite skeletal, but not fleshy either. Rudimentary organs, not quite formed, clung to the hard discoloured bones. Taliesin thought, Yes, it is not quite Human, but it has Human appetites. He saw with revulsion that the creature possessed crudely formed genitals: penis and scrotum sack beneath, and thought again that it might have Human appetites, and tightened his hold on Annabel.

Annabel was managing not to scream, because if they made the slightest sound, the Claw would be upon them, it would reach out and spit them on its talons and tear them apart. The best thing, the *sanest* thing, would be to run back to the road, through the narrow opening, and out into the starlit night. That was what they ought to be doing.

But the patrol was at the opening to the cave. All the time the Conablaiche had been creeping towards them, the patrol had been marching along the road, swishing angrily at the rowan trees, alert to fleeing rebellious people who were at odds with the Drakon. As the three travellers stood motionless, caught between the two enemies, they saw the thin light that had been filtering in suddenly blotted out as the patrolmen discovered the narrow opening and pushed their

way into the mountain. The great echoing cavern was filled
with the loud voices of the Drakon men, and with the stamping of their boots on the rock floor. Both Annabel and Taliesin saw the shadow of the Conablaiche dart across the cave,
and slither behind a crusted formation of stone at the far
end. Taliesin, his every sense straining, caught the faint echo
of the horrid bubbling chuckle he had heard in Calatin's
house, and he knew that the creature would lie in wait for
the patrolmen, and that as soon as they were all safely inside
the mountain, it would rear up from its shadowy corner
and fall on them. And when that happens, there will be no
escape ... He looked to where Fael-Inis was standing, as
still as if he was also made of stone, and he saw a look of
furious concentration in Fael-Inis's eyes. Could Fael-Inis
somehow save them? thought Taliesin, and at once the response bounded back.

*There are spells I can summon, but we are in the world of
Humans, Taliesin, and we must try to escape by Human means ...*

Annabel, listening, caught this as well, and felt a terrible
coldness. Were they, after all, to die like this, in the dark old
mountain? And as the thought took shape, another followed
it, like a sprinkling of light.

*We shall still use the fire and the light and the sunbursts,
Annabel ... Be sure of it ...*

Annabel was instantly comforted, and thought, Well, yes,
of course we will.

The Drakon patrol had spotted them. Annabel, who
knew the whispers that Drakon people could sniff out rebels
as if an extra sense had been bestowed, waited with a sense
of inevitability for them to pounce. And although they would
fight of course (Annabel thought she could inflict quite a
good deal of damage by kicking hard at the men's groins and
perhaps by jabbing at their eyes), they could certainly not
fight the creature that was hiding at the far end of the cave. And
they were trapped between the Drakon men and the Claw.

The patrol was surrounding them; the tallest of the men,

who seemed to be the leader, and who had the cold, hard eyes of all Drakon servants, stood regarding them, his hands on his hips. Taliesin, who had released Annabel but still held her arm, returned the man's appraisal, and Annabel, glancing at him, saw with delight that he was as unruffled as a cat. Confidence surged back, because of course they would outwit these cold-eyed humourless men, and of course they would somehow escape the Claw.

Taliesin said urbanely, "Good evening. You are travelling in strange paths, sir," and the Drakon patrolman stared at him, as if he found him rather odd.

At Taliesin's side, Fael-Inis said, "Have you also lost your way in these dark roads?" and both Annabel and Taliesin heard that he had quenched his usual silken, warm timbre. He did not sound entirely Human, because he was not entirely Human, but, thought Annabel, he sounded *nearly* Human.

The patrolman said, "We're on lawful Drakon business."

"Which," said another at his side, "is the taking up of people who break Curfew and *pry*." He looked to his leader, who nodded slowly, and then inspected Annabel, as if he found her of interest.

"Dear me," he said, "here's a pretty bit. I could get a thousand crumens for you in the Procuration Hall."

Taliesin said at once, "Her price is very much higher than that, my friend," and the patrolman looked at Taliesin coldly.

"You know the rules," he said.

"I know the laws," said Taliesin, who did not know them at all, but remembered procuration was forbidden on pain of death.

The patrolman made a contemptuous sound, and spat derisively on the ground. "Put that one up on the Procuration Floor, and she'd only reach Level Two. Is she broken?"

Fael-Inis made a quick movement and then was still, as if he was saying, I leave this to you, Human.

Taliesin looked the man up and down, and there was a glint in his eyes. "If anyone is to put her up on the Procuration Floor," he said, "I shall do it. This one is mine."

"Ho," said the patrolman, "a rival. Friend, do you not know the punishment for procuration?"

"Yes," said Taliesin steadily. "Do you?"

The patrolman laughed. "I am in a privileged position," he said. "*You* procure for the masses. *I* procure for the Drakon inner body." He rubbed a thumb and forefinger suggestively. "A rich calling," he said. "And the Drakon is used to having the best. You wouldn't believe the opportunities I have to acquire the *choicest* little bits for them. And they would pay me well for this one."

Taliesin said courteously, "I see you are a man of some acumen, sir. But I, in my own circles, am very highly regarded." He narrowed his eyes thoughtfully. "I think if we put it to the test, we should find that I am your superior," he said, "and that being so, you had really do better to leave her to me. Otherwise, you may find you are in a very embarrassing position, sir."

The man laughed. "One of the Drakon's inner circle, are you?" he said. "In that case, you will know very well that procurers do pretty much as they like. And I have the fancy to put this one up for bidding."

Annabel said coldly, "I have not the least intention of being put up for bidding by anyone. But if I *was* put up," she said, "then I should reach at least *Level Four*." She glared at him, and the man laughed and said, "Come here," and made a sudden grabbing movement.

Annabel was wrenched from Taliesin's grasp and sent sprawling on the cave floor. Taliesin moved at once, but the patrolmen were before him, slamming him back against the side of the mountain. Fael-Inis stayed where he was, but Annabel, her senses still spinning, saw light kindling in his eyes.

"Strip her," said the patrolman, and now his eyes were no longer cold, but hot and greedy. "We'll see if you'd reach Level Four." He nodded to two of the waiting men, who moved at once, pinioning Annabel's arms behind her, standing her up between them. Taliesin fought against the two patrolmen who still imprisoned him, but their arms were like steel bands and he could not move. "Strong," said the one on his right, grinning and exposing a row of broken and discoloured teeth. "Practice against those who break the Drakon's laws," said the other, who had a brutish face and short, bristly hair.

The leader was undressing Annabel now, discarding the dark trousers and boots and the thick woollen cloak she had donned for the journey. "Nice," he said, and now a clotted note had crept into his voice. "Certainly I could get a thousand crumens." His eyes flickered over her. "Let's see what's under the shirt," he said in a thick voice. Annabel drew back and braced the muscles of one leg to kick him, and at once the two patrolmen lunged downwards and held both her ankles.

"A *very* well-known ploy," said the leader, grinning at her. "What a little cat you are." He closed in on her, and slid his hands beneath the thin cotton shirt, and the fact that he did not remove the shirt gave his actions a repulsive intimacy. Annabel closed her eyes and felt horror run over her. He had red meaty hands, and the nails were dirty, and he was beginning to breathe hoarsely. His breath blew in her face, and it was dry and unfresh, and all the while his hands were exploring her body, stroking her skin . . . I could be a piece of merchandise, a side of beef that people used to prod before they bought it in the days when you could still buy beef, thought Annabel wildly. I can't think what to do, except that there must be *something* . . . One of the patrolmen was still holding her ankles, one in each hand, and the other had her wrists tight in an iron grip. If he gets any closer, I could bite him, thought Annabel hopefully. I could bite him very hard. This is so unbelievably horrible that I don't think it is really happening. She could see Taliesin struggling, and she could see Fael-Inis motionless in the shadows. Taliesin was powerless for the minute, but Fael-Inis would certainly do something to rescue her—what had he said? *Spells I can summon.* And then she thought that he would expect her to fight for herself first.

The patrolman withdrew his hands, and said to the one who had her ankles, "Hold her legs apart," and as he did so, Annabel saw with a shudder of revulsion his left hand creep between his own legs, and make a sudden involuntary rubbing motion with the flat of his hand.

And then the other one was jerking her feet apart, which made her feel quite unbearably vulnerable, and the patrolman was advancing again, his eyes glittering, a sly intimate grin on his face. "Just to see how much you are *really* worth, my dear," he said. "Just to see if you have kept the laws."

Annabel said, "I don't—" and gasped as he slid his right hand inside her shirt again, between her legs. There was a moment of the purest loathing, and she felt the thick dry hand on her thighs, and then there was a sudden jab, and the man's finger was pushing upwards, exploring, probing . . . Annabel closed her eyes and remembered about death or glory, and about fiery-eyed angels who would come blazing to the rescue if you really needed it, and tried to think that surely this was nothing so very terrible compared with what might be ahead. If the men who held her would just relax their grip, she would certainly bite this revolting creature, even if she could not kick him.

He withdrew his hand at last, and stood looking at her, and Annabel, who was feeling a bit sick, but who would have been torn apart by wild horses before she would have let anyone know, tried not to notice that his other hand was still on his groin, caressing the hard ridge that had risen there.

"So," said the man softly, "so you are a true obedient child of the Drakon. Untouched. And my masters are partial to that." In the far corner, Taliesin struggled, and was again thrown back against the mountain wall by his two captors.

"It would be a pity," said the leader, his eyes still on Annabel, "a very great pity not to—make use of this one before we put her up for procuration." He glanced at Taliesin, and the greedy I-am-superior smile slid over his face again. "One of the *benefits* of the job," he said. "As you will know."

"I never lie with my own merchandise," said Taliesin, sounding bored, and the patrolman said at once, "Are you sexually warped, perhaps, friend?"

"Not to the extent that you and your patrol are," said Taliesin coolly.

The man looked at Taliesin. "That was unwise," he said. "We are not always particular about whether we relieve ourselves on men or women." He turned back to Annabel, and began to unfasten his trousers, and the patrolman who was holding Annabel's ankles chuckled slyly and said, "Share it out a bit, won't you?" and the leader said sharply, "Wait your turn," and opened his trousers fully, and let Annabel see the rearing stalk of flesh.

Taliesin, who was still casting about in his mind for a way to outwit these men, said with a coldness he was far from feeling, "If you have her, she'll be worth far less at procuration," and the patrol leader turned to look at him with sudden surprise.

"Of course I am not going to have her," he snapped, in a voice that said, Where-have-you-been-living-you-fool? "You know the dangers of sexual congress." He regarded Taliesin scornfully. "I served four years in a Plague Hospital," he said. "*And* I helped draw up the latest regulations." He stood looking at Taliesin. "For all they'll have you believe they've stamped it out, it's still rampant," he said. "This one *felt* unbroken, but for all I know she's rotten with the Disease." The sly grin touched his lips again. "But we all know the ways round it," he said. And then, to one of the waiting patrol, "Put in the mouth clamp," he said. "And then lie her flat."

The mouth clamp was a tiny steel-springed contraption, a miniature dual-levered cantilever that would support something, or perhaps hold open something that would otherwise have closed tightly. Taliesin saw its use at once, and horror ran over him in a cold wave. The two men wrenched Annabel's mouth open, and thrust the clamp inside, adjusting it so that she was unable to close her lips.

"All the better to bite you with," said the patrolman, grinning horridly. "Only now you won't be able to, will you?"

Annabel, half choking, gasped and reminded herself about not letting them see she was frightened, and remembered about Fael-Inis and the glinting anger and about Taliesin and about death or glory.

The clamp was attached to threaded screws that set the clamp to the exact degree the men wanted.

"Not too wide," said the patrol leader, standing over her, caressing himself obscenely. "Not too wide. I want to *feel* this one's lips." Annabel could barely breathe, and she could certainly not scream, and even if she could have screamed, there was nothing to scream *to*, because Taliesin was in the hands of the patrol, and Fael-Inis would only call up a spell if they could not escape by Human means . . .

Then a low bubbling chuckle filled the cave, and from its corner the Conablaiche reared up, casting its monstrous shadow across the floor. There was a snapping sound, a grisly, bone-on-teeth sound, and it loped across the floor, making massive swiping gestures with its great gristly arms, sending several of the patrolmen staggering back.

The Conablaiche had fallen on the leader; it seemed to spear him on the end of its talons, and it held him aloft as if inspecting him. *Yes, yes, a tasty morsel indeed . . .* The fish-like eyes swivelled and bulged with horrid appetite.

Taliesin, released by the two who had been holding him, bounded forward and snatched Annabel up, freeing her mouth from the thing they had called the clamp, holding her hard against him.

The patrolman was screaming, dreadful, trapped-hare screams, his arms and legs flailing, and the Conablaiche grinned, its fleshless lips widening, its breath fetid in the airless cave; it brought up its other arm and, deliberately and slowly, gouged the man's now-flaccid penis from his body.

Blood and urine spurted out, and Annabel saw with a shudder of horror that they sprayed the creature's face, and that the creature protruded a great, pendulous, leathery flap of tongue, and licked its bloodied jowls with relish.

Fael-Inis reached for Taliesin and Annabel, and drew them gently into the shadows, and Annabel, who was still feeling sick, thought, But where are we going?

The Conablaiche was bringing its talons up again in a great curving arc, and the three travellers stood for a moment longer, watching the man's ribcage torn open. Blood covered the rock floor now, and the other patrolmen were falling and slipping as they scrambled for the narrow opening. Annabel thought they would not get very far, for certainly the terrible creature would be upon them. And even as the thought took shape, she saw the sinewy arm reach out and knock two more of the men to the floor.

To be dealt with presently, my dears ... The grisly bone-on-teeth sound snapped out again, and the Conablaiche threw back its head and gave a neighing roar of triumph.

The patrolman's heart was exposed now, embedded in flesh and muscle, and the Conablaiche inserted a pointed claw and, with a smooth, scything motion, began to cut around the raw beating heart. The screaming of the patrolman was growing fainter, but blood still pumped steadily from his mutilated body, and the three travellers could see that he still lived.

"Of course he still lives," said Fael-Inis very softly. "Does not the Conablaiche take the *living* hearts for its Master?"

The Conablaiche gave its neigh of triumph again, and held aloft the dripping, steaming gobbet of flesh that was a Human heart.

As he did so, Fael-Inis stepped farther back into the shadows, drawing Annabel and Taliesin with him.

CHAPTER FOURTEEN

LUGH OF THE Longhand thought he was doing rather well. He was not the man to be intimidated by dark nights and rustling creatures in the forest; he was certainly not the man to be intimidated by the towering bulk of Tara itself. Hadn't he been to Tara more times than he could count, and wasn't he entirely accustomed to the splendour and the beauty? Truth to tell, splendour and beauty, although all very well in their way, had never affected Lugh all that much. And Tara did not change.

It did not change and yet it had changed completely. Lugh stole through to the Western Gate and stood for a moment looking up at the Palace.

Tara did not change and yet it had changed completely. As Lugh slipped through the Western Gate—and it was strange that there were no sentries to challenge him—he felt a blackness and a great heavy curtain fall about his mind.

Darkness. Medoc's darkness. It was a bit discomfiting to see Tara, the Bright Palace, like this. Lugh had known, of course, that Medoc had drawn a cloud of darkness over Tara, because Medoc was a dark necromancer, he was a Lord of the Dark Ireland, and it was only to be expected that he would create his own surroundings. Lugh quite saw that. Even so, it was unsettling to see the Bright Palace in shadow. Lugh found himself remembering all the nasty stories about Ireland's enemies. And then there were all those beliefs about the *sidh*, the cold, inhuman faery folk who came up to the ramparts of Tara, led by the Elven King, Aillen mac Midha. The *sidh* were supposed to have a strange loyalty to the High Kings, but Lugh would not trust one of the *sidh* from here to that tree trunk, even if he had ever seen one, which he had not.

It was really quite startling to see Tara like this. Tara ought to blaze with light and glitter with brilliance. Lugh had been accustomed to seeing it as a beacon and a lodestar. Now it was quenched and quiet. In the great Sun Chamber, where once the Wolfkings had held their dazzling Courts, a powerful necromancer dwelled, and the galleries that had sparkled with music and feasting were thick with evil enchantments. Lugh could feel it all round him. And really, really, if you were logical (which Lugh naturally was), hadn't you to admit to a sneaking admiration for the man who had somehow doused the light? Lugh was not, of course, going to support Medoc—dear goodness, of course he was not!—but you had to give credit where it was due. Medoc had taken Tara with consummate ease, and, more to the point, he had kept it.

Lugh was creeping through the galleries now, through the small antechambers with the mystical patterns etched in gold on the floors. He knew these for minor spells created by the Palace sorcerers for the Wolfkings; the sorcerers did not easily give away their secrets, but Cormac of the Wolves had persuaded them on several occasions, and one or two very inferior enchantments had been written down and then etched in gold on the floors. Lugh had always thought this rather pretentious, though he had never said so. But now, studying the etched symbols and patterns, the thought just occurred to him that hadn't the Wolfkings been rather ridiculous at times? Couldn't you argue that Medoc was a far better, far stronger ruler?

And in any case, the Wolfkings' day was over.

At this point in his thoughts, Lugh stopped short and frowned, because wasn't that a terrible traitorous thought to have, and the Longhands the champions and the paladins of the Wolfline as far back as Niall of the Nine Hostages and Nuadu Airgetlam?

But the closer he got to the Sun Chamber, the more he

went on thinking it, and the more he thought it, the more sensible it seemed.

You could not really guard against your own thoughts. They slid into your mind from somewhere, and then there they were. Once you had thought something, you could not unthink it. And Medoc had taken Tara and Medoc had kept Tara, and Medoc was certainly the strongest sorcerer anyone had ever known.

This was all extremely traitorous, of course, but it was also rather a fascinating notion. Lugh, walking cautiously now, began to seriously consider whether he oughtn't to give Medoc a fair hearing.

And he could feel Medoc's presence very strongly now. A dark swirling force at the centre of the Palace; a whirling power that would embrace a man's soul and smother his mind. A force that would certainly wrap itself about Ireland and mould Ireland. Yes, this needed thinking about very carefully.

Directly ahead of him was the Sun Chamber, the heart and the core of Tara. It was said to be the most beautiful place in the entire western world, although Lugh usually suffered a sick headache if he had to be in it for too long, and had to make an excuse to leave.

The double doors of the Sun Chamber were closed, and as Lugh made his way across the marble floors, he caught the faintest sound of movement from within. He stopped outside the doors and hesitated. It would probably be quite a good idea to go inside the Sun Chamber, because it might tell him a bit about Medoc. They needed to know all they could about Medoc.

But Lugh was becoming more and more fascinated by the creature that was Medoc; he wanted to know more about him, and if Medoc turned out to be what he, Lugh, suspected, then the idea of changing allegiances would certainly be looked at. Probably Medoc would be very glad to have a fine warrior such as Lugh in his ranks. Probably he would grant Lugh one or two honours, which Lugh would refuse with a becoming display of modesty, although he would not refuse too firmly, because that would be rude. The Longhands were many things, but rude was not one of them.

It would be extremely gratifying if Medoc granted him some kind of high place in his service, because didn't all the stories about Medoc say that he looked after his own? That would show Fergus and Fintan and Cermait and those silly Tusks!

Still, it was necessary to be careful, because although this was Tara, the Shining Citadel, the seat of every High King of Ireland, it was also the lair of the darkest and most powerful necromancer ever to come out of the Dark Ireland. Lugh knew about necromancers; they were greedy and hungry and eternally on the watch for the glittering kingdoms of Humans. Hundreds of years might pass quite peacefully, and they would leave the Humans alone, and they would dwell inside the Dark Ireland, which was their domain. And then, without warning, they would find a gateway between the two worlds, and they would summon their terrible servants, and there would be wars and battles, and sometimes they would gain control of Tara, and sometimes they would be beaten back.

Lugh knew all of the stories. He knew about the terrible creatures of the Dark Ireland, and about the evil necromancers who dwelled there in dark towers and grim citadels. He knew very well that Medoc was Overlord of many of these beings, and probably he could summon them all and overrun Ireland if he cared to.

He knew, as well, about the Guardians, the rather dreadful band of evil, greedy necromancers, who would guard anything in the world, so long as someone would pay them enough. He wondered, briefly, whether Medoc might have called up the Guardians to watch over Tara, and he remembered some of the stories whispered about them. He remembered that there were three who were female but not Human, and who nearly always worked together, and who were the most fearsome of all . . .

Spectre, who was grey and wraithlike, and who was composed of nightwinds and freezing winter dawns and howling blizzards . . . And Reflection, who many years ago had stolen the legendary Cloak of Nightmares from the Wolfkings, and now used it for her own nefarious ends. The last of the three was the Sensleibhe, who was the most fearsome of them all. The Sensleibhe it was who lured children into her warm, firelit room and then wove them into cloth made of Human skin and Human nails and Human hair . . .

And then Lugh decided that these were such terrible thoughts to have when you were creeping through a dark and apparently deserted Palace that he would put them from him. Anyway, people did not believe in that sort of thing now.

He stood rather indecisively outside the Sun Chamber, because although he was becoming rather interested in the idea of confronting Medoc, it was quite likely that the Twelve Dark Lords would be in the Sun Chamber, and this was a very good reason for hesitating. Lugh did not know very much about the Twelve Lords. They were said to sup with Medoc every night, and to assist him in his sorcery and his rituals. They were each named for some aspect of evil; Corruption and Depravity and Lust and Perversion were but four—Lugh did not know them all and he did not want to know them. He was not overly particular about Depravity, except if you were involved in a war where there was generally pillaging and raping, and which you had to join in with, because people thought you were odd if you did not. But he would certainly go inside the Sun Chamber. He would go in at any minute. He was braver than most men, and he was not afraid of the Dark Lords. He was definitely not afraid of Medoc, because you were not afraid of someone for whom you were going to do a favour.

He would spin a tale for the camp when he got back, which they would all swallow without any difficulty. He would not tell them how he had bearded Medoc in his lair (which in fact he had still to do), but he would say that he had surveyed the lie of the land, and assessed the number of sentries and guards. This would be considered very useful.

He was just sketching out a bit of a tale which the soldiers would like to hear, when there was a definite sound from inside the Sun Chamber. Lugh stood very still and tried not to make any sound at all, and tried not to breathe, because his heart was thumping erratically and making him puff a bit.

The massive doors, carved with the wolf emblem, swung slowly open, and dark blue light, tinged with crimson, poured out into the dark hall where Lugh stood.

A soft and rather beautiful voice from inside the Chamber said, "Come inside, Human."

Of their own volition, Lugh's feet took him forward.

Lugh was already more than halfway to accepting Medoc by this time, of course; he had already argued it out with himself, and he had already convinced himself that it would be to his advantage to give his allegiance to Medoc. This was not changing sides, simply being practical. The Longhands knew how to be practical.

The Sun Chamber was in shadow; it was no longer the blaze of light and colour it had once been, although there was light of a kind; there was a rather warm, rather reddish firelight, and there were curious shadows. Lugh glanced at the shadows and then away, because he had the unpleasant impression of solid figures within the shadows. The Dark Lords . . . ?

The long banqueting table, which could seat a hundred and fifty people with ease, was laid for some kind of feast. The rich spicy scents of roasting meats and of warm, fragrant wine reached Lugh, who remembered, rather unexpectedly, that he was hungry. But he stood uncertainly in the doorway, wishing that the doors were not quite so wide and not quite so high, because to be sure it made a Man feel a bit puny to be framed like this in such a massive opening, and the last thing you wanted in this kind of situation was to feel puny.

As he moved forward, he saw that tall carved chairs were ranged about the banqueting table, and he counted them. Twelve. One for each of the Dark Lords. And one at the head of the table facing the door. Thirteen in all.

Twelve Dark Lords and the one who ruled them: Medoc.

The firelight washed over him, making him a creature of dark shadows and red flickering light, so that for a moment Lugh could not be sure if anyone sat there or not. And then he moved a little nearer, and he saw that a figure did sit there, and that it was watching him, wholly at ease, the fingers of one hand curled about the stem of a wine chalice.

Medoc. The Dark Necromancer. The cruel, beautiful, evil one who had driven out the Wolfline.

(And, let facts be faced, had kept out the Wolfline.)

He was rather smaller than Lugh had expected, and with every step closer, Lugh thought he was very ordinary indeed. His hair was dark and his face was lean and even slightly austere. You had the feeling that he might enjoy good music and wine and the learned, rather-dry tomes of the Druids and the Alchemists.

Lugh began to feel considerably better. This was quite definitely a person he could handle. He could handle most people, of course, but he would admit to having been the smallest bit nervous about meeting Medoc.

Medoc had risen and come forward. It was gratifying to discover that he was not quite so tall as Lugh. It was even more gratifying to discover that Medoc, for all his sinister reputation, was not in the least bit alarming. You could not be afraid of a man six inches shorter than you were, and who seemed to possess the gentle, unworldly features of a scholar. Lugh squared his shoulders and began to feel in command of the situation. It would be nice to think that he might go down in history as the one who had bearded Medoc in his lair. And then he wished he had not used the word *lair*, because it conjured up rather unpleasant visions of dark firelit caves with reddish glows and eerie shadows that danced across the ceiling, and might have been any-thing at all.

A bit like the Sun Chamber now ...

Medoc spoke then, and his voice was soft and gentle and soothing. He said, "You are most welcome, Sir of the Long-hand," and Lugh was at once pleased. He eyed Medoc and said he took that very kindly, because he had heard that strangers were no longer welcome inside Tara.

Medoc looked sad. He said, "Yes, I am afraid that amongst your people I have an unfortunate name. It is a great sadness to me. And things are not always what they seem. Will you be seated? And will you perhaps take wine with me?" The slender white hands reached for chalice and flagon, and Lugh watched as the wine was poured. "This wine is not to everyone's taste," said Medoc, and his dark eyes flick-ered to Lugh and then back again and, just for a second, Lugh had the uncomfortable impression that something that was neither gentle nor scholarly showed in their depths. "It is not to everyone's taste," said Medoc. "But I think you may have a more discerning palate than most." He handed Lugh the chalice. "It is not a wine that everyone could appreciate," said Medoc, and sat back and smiled.

And if it was appreciation of wine they were talking of, Lugh was your man. The Longhands had very delicate pal-ates, which was not something widely known. Of course, you blunted these things a bit by living close to soldiers. You had to join in and drink the most remarkable liquids, just to be one with your men.

Lugh did not, in fact, care for the wine overmuch, but it would not do to say this. Medoc had spotted him as a man of delicate palate, and it would be rude to dispel this image. He sipped cautiously at the wine, and found himself liking it better on closer acquaintance. He did not think he had ever tasted anything quite like it.

"No, it is a very rare vintage," said Medoc. "But I thought *you* would enjoy it." He smiled, and Lugh smiled

back, and relaxed a bit, because none of this was turning out
to be nearly as frightening as he had expected. He sat back
in his chair—very comfortable, these carved chairs—and took
a look about him.

The Sun Chamber looked very nearly cosy. "Firelight,"
said Medoc in his soft voice. "Restful. I find it relaxing just
to sit by a fire at the day's end and think, and perhaps read
a little, and ponder."

Whatever images Lugh might have conjured up of Medoc
inside Tara, they had certainly not included one of Medoc
sitting pondering by the fire. He felt even safer, because you
could not be the least bit afraid of a man who admitted to
pondering.

"There is," said Medoc thoughtfully, "so much in the
world that is not restful now, would you agree?"

Lugh said that was very true indeed, and would there be
a drain more of the wine.

"Yes, it is a wine which improves on closer acquaintance," said Medoc, and Lugh jumped, because this was what
he had been thinking. He held out his chalice and watched
the wine flow into it. Medoc's hands were swift and sure;
they were the sort of hands you found yourself liking to
watch. They were not, Lugh thought hazily, very manly
hands. They were nearly feminine really, white and soft.
There was a dark red ring on one finger, the like of which
Lugh had never seen before, but which seemed to catch the
firelight and glint. It made you blink a bit to begin with, but
then after you had looked at it for a while, you found it was
not at all dazzling. It was quite difficult to look away from
the dark red ring, which was not anything that Lugh would
have worn, but which looked quite at home on a slender
white hand that belonged to a wicked, powerful necromancer.

"I am not in the least bit wicked," said Medoc softly,
and Lugh thought again that he really had a very attractive
voice. "As for necromancy"—there was a shrug, a gesture of

self-deprecation—"I have dipped a little into the annals of these things," said Medoc, "as who has not?"

"Indeed yes," said Lugh, who had never come within a mile of necromancy, and would not have recognised an annal on it to save his life. It occurred to him that Medoc's voice had grown momentarily stronger, almost as if he might be pulling down some kind of power. But this was patently absurd, and Lugh sank back into the warmth of the room and the drowsiness of the wine, and allowed himself to listen to the soft beautiful voice. It was a voice you could go on listening to. There was even a thread of authority in it now. Lugh knew about authority. It was not something you could teach people to have. You either possessed it or you did not.

Medoc possessed a remarkable degree of authority. He was smiling at Lugh and the great, dark red ring (would it be a ruby?) was catching and holding the light, so that Lugh could almost imagine there were fires within the ring, and that goblins with red eyes and pitchforks danced there, and that horned creatures waited there and that cave mouths yawned and . . . *O be wary, Mortal, be wary of the vast caverns of hell* . . .

Lugh blinked and the ruby glowed steadily and quietly and innocently. A trick of the light, nothing more.

"A trick of the light," said Medoc. "But that has shown me you are a man of some perception, Sir Longhand."

Lugh nodded, pleased. He did not trouble to correct Medoc over the question of title because clearly this was only a matter of time. He said that perception was the thing these days.

"Oh, perception has won many a war," said Medoc, who seemed to be wholly in sympathy with Lugh's ideas. "Battles are not always won by plundering and pillaging and raping."

They were not, this was very true, and as far as Lugh was concerned, you could keep pillaging and raping any day of the week. Plundering was different, because you acquired things by it.

"But it is all so barbaric," said Medoc, and Lugh, lulled by the fire and the wine, drowsy from Medoc's enchantment, nodded and went on nodding, because it was difficult to stop once you had started. He wondered would there be any more wine, and he wondered as well whether Medoc was going to offer him a bite of supper. It was not that he was greedy, but only that Cathbad kept them on astonishingly short rations. Lugh would enjoy a good plateful of roast boar, perhaps with some wings of pheasant as a side dish, and maybe a few honey cakes to round it all off.

The food was before him almost before he had framed the thought; succulent roast boar, exactly as he liked it, with the centre a little pink and the edges moist and brown. Pheasant wings stewed gently in mulled wine—a great delicacy. And honey cakes fresh from the ovens, the tops breaking open to spill out the warm fragrant honey beneath. The wine goblet, filled to the brim, was at his elbow.

Medoc said softly, "Eat and drink, my friend, for 'Do what you like' is the only creed worth anything."

Lugh found this eminently sensible. It was shocking, when you thought about it, how in all of the stories told about Medoc, no one had ever said that he was sensible and courteous. People did not set much store by courtesy these days, but Lugh had been properly brought up and he knew what was what. Courtesy and good manners, and consideration for others, there was the thing. Plain old-fashioned politeness. Medoc was a gentleman.

"I am what I am," said Medoc. "And I think we understand one another, you and I."

Lugh said they did, indeed they did.

"And now that we have arrived at such a good understanding," said Medoc, "I wonder if I may impose on your good nature." He looked at Lugh, and Lugh found himself nodding all over again.

"Excellent," said Medoc, and Lugh beamed, because Medoc was the sort of person you would like to find thought well of you. "And of course," said Medoc in a soft purring voice, "of course, I am exceedingly generous to those who serve me. You have perhaps heard that? It is true. I will give much to those who swear allegiance, and who perform the tasks I set them.

"I will give you many things and many honours if you will undertake this task, Sir Longhand," said Medoc, and Lugh, caught all over again by the silken note in Medoc's voice, certainly held by the steady red glow of Medoc's slanting eyes, said slowly, "I will do anything you ask."

Medoc sat back in his chair and regarded Lugh. "The task is difficult and delicate," he said, and a disinterested observer might almost have thought there was amusement in his voice now. "Discretion and imagination is called for. It is not everyone who could do this," said Medoc, "but I have formed a very high opinion of your intelligence, Sir Longhand. I believe that you may be the one man in Ireland that I could . . ."

"Yes?" said Lugh.

"That I could trust," said Medoc, and smiled and raised the hand that wore the great heavy ring, and once again the depths glowed with life. Lugh thought it was perfectly possible to imagine you were seeing pictures in the ring again. And the layers of colour were all there. Red on red on red . . .

And all the fires of hell reflected in between . . . all the torments of the burning dungeons . . . leaping, devouring flames . . . Look deep into the furnaces and be lost once and for ever, Mortal soul . . . look down into the boiling lakes and the beds of raging fire to the ovens tended by harpy-footed furies . . . look into the sins and the passions and the secret shameful desires of the world and be forever damned, Human soul . . . follow the ways of the Dark Lords . . . the only creed is "Do what you will" . . . Follow me, Human soul, and come down into the brimstone pit . . .

Lugh blinked and the ruby dimmed and the fiery caverns shimmered and dissolved, and he was back in the Sun Chamber that was a Sun Chamber no longer, but a dark mysterious lair with a slender, dark-visaged gentleman who had given him excellent wine and a very good supper.

He raised his eyes and looked directly at Medoc and said, "I will do whatever you wish," and with the words the last traces of allegiance to the Wolfkings fell from Lugh of the Longhand, and he was Medoc's body and soul.

Which was exactly what Medoc had wanted.

"Lies have been told of me through all eternity," said Medoc, his eyes unwavering, and Lugh nodded solemnly. He thought he would perform this task for Medoc, whatever it turned out to be, and he would be very pleased to do it. The thought of the Twelve Dark Lords weighed a bit heavily on him, but he would not let this sway him. He would certainly not let the thought of Dorrainge and Fergus and the rest sway him either. Medoc would control the Twelve Lords, and Lugh would control Dorrainge and the others. It went without saying.

"The Dark Lords need not concern you," said Medoc. "They are useful at times." He smiled and Lugh smiled back. "One makes use of the instruments that come to one's hand," he said, and Lugh saw the sense of this at once.

Medoc said, "Ireland is threatened. It is threatened by a terrible menace." He looked at Lugh, and Lugh nodded once again, because he knew all about terrible menaces and dreadful threats. Wasn't Ireland always falling victim to one or the other? To be fair, they had all of them believed that Medoc himself was a terrible menace, if he was not a dreadful threat. One was as bad as the other. But Lugh could see that Medoc was neither. He sat up a bit straighter and waited to hear about the terrible menace. Or dreadful threat. Whichever it turned out to be.

Medoc leaned forward so that the firelight washed over his face and threw a strange, rather eerie mask across the upper part of his features. "As you will know, Sir Longhand," he said, "the Wolfline of Ireland is nearly extinct."

Yes, Lugh knew this, everyone knew this, and it had

been a source of some worry. He watched Medoc rather anxiously.

Medoc leaned back again and regarded Lugh. At last, he said, "Have you ever heard of the legend of the Lost Prince?"

For a very long time, neither of them spoke further. A silence of such brooding quality settled on the firelit chamber, that Lugh thought you could almost have reached out and touched it.

The Lost Prince ... The legendary child who would appear and who would finally defeat the Dark Ireland ... Tara's once and future King ...

Medoc said, "Yes, it is a seductive notion, of course. An attractive myth. And you will find the belief in many countries and in many creeds. People—uneducated people—like to have these foolish dreams and these absurd hopes."

Lugh said he quite saw that and wouldn't a sensible man dismiss it for the superstition it was.

"Unfortunately," said Medoc silkily, "in this case, it is more than superstition." The dark eyes glowed. "A few years ago," said Medoc, "a child was born with the ancient and mystical wolfblood running strongly in its veins. A Wolfprince ..."

Lugh did not speak, and presently Medoc said, "Great mystery surrounded the birth of this child. It was born in the most extreme secrecy ever to attend on the birth of any Prince of Ireland. It was taken by night and given into the care of an obscure family. But for all this anonymity, it is a Prince of the Old Nobility; the *sidh* stole up to the Gates of Tara and sang it into the world, as they have always done for the Wolfprinces." Anger twisted the patrician features briefly, and Lugh flinched.

"It is said that the Elven King, Aillen mac Midha, foresaw such danger for the Prince that he attended its birth," said Medoc. "And wove about it such a strong magic that it was believed the child would be forever safe.

"I learned of the creature's birth by means which do not

concern you," said Medoc, and Lugh at once thought, Sorcery? Did he use sorcery! and Medoc smiled, and said, "Of course I used sorcery. Am I not a member of the Ancient Academy of Sorcerers? Do I not hold the right to wear the Dark Star of Necromancy, and do I not know of every spell spun and every enchantment woven in Ireland?" He seemed almost to sink into a reverie for a moment, and Lugh looked up.

Medoc said, very softly, as if he had forgotten Lugh's existence, "And have I not drawn about the Tyrian sorcerers the Cloak of Failure, so that their absurd, pitiful attempts to re-create the Royal Beastline should never succeed?" His eyes gleamed redly, and Lugh felt an uncomfortable prickling on the back of his neck.

And then Medoc looked up, and smiled, and said, "Of course I use sorcery," and Lugh saw that perhaps after all it would have been a reasonable thing to have done.

"The child must not be allowed to live," said Medoc, looking at Lugh very intently. "The Wolfline is tainted, and it must die out." Lugh, unable to look away from Medoc's unwavering stare, said, "Yes, it must die out."

Medoc leaned back, and appeared to relax very slightly. "For the Wolfline to disappear," he said, "this child, this so-called Lost Prince, must therefore be destroyed." He looked at Lugh and waited, and after a while, Lugh said slowly, "Yes. He must be destroyed."

"He is no true Prince," said Medoc. "He is an imposter."

Lugh nodded.

"An imposter," said Medoc again. "A fake. A cheat." The slanting eyes were still fixed on Lugh, and to Lugh's drugged mind it seemed that they grew larger. "But he is being reared in secrecy, and one day in the future he will rise up and challenge me." He leaned forward, his eyes gleaming redly. "I have Tara," he said. "And I will keep Tara. But to rule, I must have absolute power. There can be no pretenders, no Wolfprinces, no *legends* growing up in secrecy who might raise an army against me. You understand all this?"

"Yes," said Lugh.

"The Prince must be sought out and killed," said Medoc.

"He must be killed," nodded Lugh.

"Destroyed completely."

"Destroyed completely," said Lugh.

"And you will destroy him."

"Yes. Yes, I will do that," said Lugh. And then, with a sudden frown, "But if he is so protected—if there is such secrecy . . ."

Medoc sat back in his chair, the fingers of one hand curled about the stem of his wine chalice. He said, "The child's whereabouts are known to me. He is in a village called Folaim, which, in the old, pure Gael, means a place of concealment. It was not difficult to discover him." He smiled, and turned the ruby ring on his hand, so that the strange red lights began to glow again.

"They will guard the creature as well as they can," said Medoc, and Lugh remembered about the Guardians, about the Spectre and Reflection, and the terrible Sensleibhe, and hoped he was not going to encounter any of them.

"The Guardians serve another at present," said Medoc, and, as Lugh looked up, he smiled. "Had you forgotten that I possess the ability to hear you, Sir Longhand?"

Lugh said, rather hesitantly, "The Samhailt," and Medoc made a quick, contemptuous gesture with one hand.

"A milk and water enchantment, bestowed only on weaklings. There are stronger powers than the Samhailt. It was the Amaranth line who spun the Samhailt enchantment, and presented it to the Beastline of Ireland," said Medoc. "But they forgot that there are others of an even older line, a line far stronger and darker than the Amaranthine. While the Amaranths were perfecting the Samhailt, *I* was spinning a far stronger, far more incisive enchantment. There is no code of honour binding the enchantment that permits *me* to hear your thoughts," said Medoc scornfully. "I can hear whatever I care to." He sipped the wine in his glass.

"The Guardians *have* served me," he said, after a moment, "but they were called from the Dark Ireland to be of use to a world not yet born, and they are still serving that Master."

He looked at Lugh, and Lugh vaguely remembered about Fergus and the journey to the Far Future, and wondered if Fergus would encounter the Guardians, and whether Medoc would know about it.

Medoc said softly, "The Guardians travelled into the Future only because I permitted it." The thin, cruel smile touched his face. "Have you forgotten, Sir Longhand, that I rule in the Dark Domain also? And that every creature who dwells there must answer to me?" He studied Lugh again, and appeared satisfied. "The Wolfchild is hardly guarded at all," he said. "They believe that the enchantment spun by the Elven King at the creature's birth is sufficient." His eyes glinted redly. "And so you must go to the place called Folaim," he said. "You must seek out the Lost Prince, and you must kill him."

"How will I know him?"

"He possesses the wolfblood. You will know."

"But if I do not?"

"Then," said Medoc, "you must kill them all. You must slaughter every first-born boy in Folaim under the age of seven years. And if you are still unsure, then you must slaughter every Manchild under the age of seven years in Ireland." He gave Lugh the narrow gleaming stare again. "We shall revive the cult of Crom Croich to do it," he said.

Lugh said, as if from a great distance, "There is one thing I do not understand."

"Well?"

Summoning his resources, and certainly summoning his courage, Lugh said, "This child. This Wolfprince—"

"Yes?"

"Who were its parents?"

Medoc smiled the cruel, thin smile again. "Oh, Sir Longhand," he said softly, "can you not guess? Were you not at Court seven years ago when the Bright Palace rocked with the whispers of the great and terrible scandal? Do you not remember the stories that were told behind closed doors, and the speculations that took place behind hands? Were you not yourself instrumental in bringing to light a shocking truth?" said Medoc.

"Seven years ago, the creature you know as the Wolf-queen loved and lay with her Captain of the *Fiana*. And as a result bore him, in great secrecy, a son.

"It is that child who is Ireland's Lost Prince. It is that child who must be found and slain."

CHAPTER FIFTEEN

For a very long time, Fergus had been aware of a change inside the Prison of Hostages. He thought that you could argue that where there is no substance, there cannot be change; where there is nothing but the endless pure light, a man cannot be aware of things altering.

But the light that streamed constantly in and threw bars of white brilliance across the floor had changed subtly. Once, he caught the faintest shadow of movement, as if someone (something?) had darted down a long winding corridor outside the cell-like structure where he lay. Now and then he caught sounds, movements, scufflings, whisperings. Creatures outside of his barred stone room.

He was not afraid; he was curious, and he was certainly roused. He thought he would welcome anyone and anything who would end the solitude and the silence.

As time went on the whisperings grew stronger and, now, the shadow that had darted across the light reflected on the stone floor took on a little more shape. Fergus began to be aware of creatures, beings, *Humans*, struggling to reach him. After a time, he began to be aware of a pattern, and he found this extremely comforting. There was an immense security about structure. The days and nights inside the Prison were shapeless, and time had become a solid shining thing to him; *a noiseless, all-embracing ocean, the shadow on the dial, the striking of the clock, the running of the sand* . . . Fergus pulled his thoughts up sharply, because for some reason the images had become abruptly disturbing. The shadow on the dial . . . why should he suddenly see Time as a huge clock, with the hands creeping slowly nearer to death?

The whisperings were closer. Fergus tried very hard not to delude himself about it, but he knew, quite surely, that they were nearer. Stronger. Something was waking in here. *There are other living creatures here.*

He had always believed he could not be alone. The Lad of the Skins was a greedy harvester, there must certainly be other prisoners. But to Fergus, shut in the stone cell, light streaming endlessly in, it had seemed impossible that he would ever reach them. The stone cell was rudimentary, but it was a cell; the window had bars, and so did the door. There was nothing to stop him from walking out of the cell, and yet when he tried, there was nowhere to walk to. Great endless walls reared up before him; infinite skies stretched in all directions.

It was a hard punishment, but Fergus, alone and bereft, thought, I have deserved it. If I had never lain with Grainne, if I had never taken her sweetness and her innocence, *knowing* how forbidden it was, perhaps none of this would have happened. Perhaps she would still be safely inside Tara, and Medoc would never have been able to ride out from the Dark Ireland.

A hard punishment even so, he thought, weary beyond bearing, heartsick beyond endurance for the world he had lost.

Yes, but there are others here with you . . .

The whisperings were stronger now, and now there were soft light footsteps. There was a hesitancy and a simplicity in the whisperings that to begin with he could not understand. Simplicity, thought Fergus, considering this. Something childlike about them.

Childlike.

Childlike.

Comprehension flooded Fergus's mind in great blinding waves, and with it came an immense pity.

Children. The ritual slaughter of the previous century. The slaying of the first-born of every family in the land. Sacrifice to the monster-god Crom Croich. He reached down into memory for everything he had ever heard, and remembered the dreadful stories; the engravings made of the bloodbaths of the day. The torchlit meetings on the Plain of the Fál, for the high priests of Crom Croich's cult had known the power of darkness in their grisly rituals, and they had known, as well, that to carry out the slaughters in the shadow of the Stone of Fál would add immense power to their offerings to the god.

Fergus had seen engravings of the butchered children, their tiny, mutilated bodies strewn about; the flickering torch flames of Crom Croich's priests. The implacable figure of Crom Croich itself, reborn into the world by a dreadful travesty of Human birth; called into being by dark sorcery. The Conablaiche had been present as well, on the fringes, grinning, its talons curved. The Lad of the Skins had squatted close by, the Knife of Light ready in his hand . . .

Those slain children were here with him. They were inside the Prison, thrown there by the Lad after their hearts had been offered to Crom Croich, and after their souls had been taken by the glittering ice-cold Knife of Light.

The murdered children were all here.

Of course, thought Fergus. Of course. And with understanding, he felt the first hesitant communion . . .

Help us . . .

Fergus sat up and felt his mind reach out to them.

Help us, Fergus, for we are fighting our way back to the world . . .

It had been Fergus's own great-grandfather, Cormac, who had led the violent battles that had finally ended the terrible cult. Cormac had hurled himself and his armies into battle, driving back the dreadful religion, executing the high priests who had led it, forbidding the practice then or at any other time in Ireland. Cormac had gone riding furiously and fiercely into battle whenever and wherever there was need.

As I should have done! cried Fergus silently. As I should have done against Medoc! *But I did. I did!*

And you were defeated.

Cormac had led the Crusade Wars as well, those brave, pitiful attempts to rescue the soulless children from the Prison. "For," he had said, "it is a terrible thing to lose a child." He had consulted the sorcerers and the Druids, and he had, so went the legend, promised half a King's ransom in gold to the sorcerers if they could help.

None of it had been any use. "There is nothing we can do," said the sorcerers sadly. "There is no liberation from the Prison of Hostages. Once the Doors of the Sky have closed, there is no road back to the world of Men."

"None that we have been able to find, anyway," amended one of them.

"They will be safe," said the sorcerers, kindly. "They will not suffer, for there is no pain inside the Prison of Hostages."

There was no physical pain, but there was the endless pain of loneliness and of shapeless, formless, aimless years that stretched out before you like that shining, noiseless ocean, like the shadow on the dial, the striking of the Clock, the running out of the sands . . .

Help us, Fergus . . .

Fergus was listening with every fibre of his mind now. They were here with him, the lost children, the slaughtered boys. They had somehow broken through the timelessness and the endless silence, and they were begging for his help.

For we shall storm our way through the Doors of the Sky and down, down into the world again . . .

Anticipation raced through Fergus. I must help them, I must not lose them . . . back to the world . . . He tried to put from him the thought that by leading the children out, then he also would return.

He opened his mind to its fullest extent, and at once there was a flood of such scalding emotions that his senses reeled, and for a while he could not separate the layers.

But there was bitterness, that he did identify. There was

a great sad bitterness: *we have been deprived of our childhood, Fergus. We have been snatched from the world before we had time to know it . . . Of course we are bitter . . .*

They were bitter, but they were unbeaten. They were ready to somehow re-enter the world. Somehow they would do it . . .

Only we need you to lead us, Fergus—oh, help us, for it has been so very long . . .

Fergus said, and did not notice that the communion was no longer wordless, "Tell me why, after all these years? Why, when you have been here for so long, are you now able to make the attempt to break out?"

There was a moment, as if the children were considering him. But at last, "We are being called back," said one of them—Fergus thought that perhaps it would be the eldest. Some kind of leader.

"We are being called back," said the boy.

"We hear the cries for help from the world," said another.

"Children who are threatened by the same cult that took our souls," said a third.

Fergus said slowly, "The same cult—"

The first child said, "Crom Croich. They are reviving the slaughter of the first-born."

FERGUS WAS NEVER afterwards able to tell when the boys ceased to be soft blurred forms and gentle wordless voices; he knew that there was a moment when they were not there, and then there was a moment when they were there with him, but he could not have told how it happened.

The boys were pale and huge-eyed, and there was no mark on them of the terrible injuries that must have been inflicted in Crom Croich's name. Fergus looked at them for a long time, and remembered how the Conablaiche had stalked the land, gathering up living, beating hearts for its Master, and how the Lad of the Skins had followed, taking the souls . . .

"Will you help us?" said the boy who seemed to be a little older than the others; Fergus saw that he had a tumble of dark hair, and a rather reckless, rather attractive gleam in his eyes. Yes, unquestionably their leader. "You see," said the boy, whose name was Conn, "we believe that we are being given the chance to break the bonds of this place and return to the world to fight the Conablaiche." He stopped, and Fergus saw the younger ones shiver at the name. "But we have no knowledge of fighting," said Conn. "And we have no longer any knowledge of the world that exists beyond this place."

Fergus said, "This place . . ." And then, on a stronger note, "Can it be broken from? Is it possible?"

"We have learned a very little," said Conn, "for we are here as victims, and not as a punishment." He looked at Fergus as he said this, and Fergus did not speak.

"There are only three ways to break the bonds of the Prison of Hostages," said Conn slowly. "And even after the bonds have been broken, there is the journey back to the world. We believe that to be a terrible journey."

"Dangerous," put in another boy, a little younger than Conn, but with the same lively dark eyes. Fergus thought they might be brothers, and then remembered that Crom Croich had taken only the first-born of each family. Cousins, perhaps?

Aloud, he said, "Yes? Tell me."

"The first is by a soul being offered in exchange. That is fairly widely known."

"Yes?" Fergus remembered how they had done this for Calatin. It seemed as if it had been in another life. "Go on."

"A second way to break the bonds is to be called back," said Conn. "By someone who is in immense danger—"

"That is what we think is happening to us," said the second boy. "The children who are in danger from the Conablaiche and Crom Croich, just as we were . . ."

They both stopped, and Fergus, listening intently, watching them, said, "And then there is a third way?"

Conn said carefully, "We have also learned that this is a place of—of punishment. Atonement. Because we were here as victims, we believe we have been allowed a little more freedom." He glanced at the stone walls and at the continual white light that streamed into the cell. "We have explored this place," he said, his eyes suddenly distant. "We have found out that there are many levels and many roads that lead into it." He looked back at Fergus. "And only three roads that lead out of it," he said, and now Fergus saw that there was pity in his eyes.

"The third way out?" he said. "Will you tell me?"

"Fergus, it will not be easy."

"Tell me," said Fergus again, and Conn seemed to hesitate, glancing at the others.

At length, he said, "Deep within the Prison is a place called the Stone Hall of Judgement. Within it sit the Judges. We do not understand what they are, for we have never dared to enter the Stone Hall. We know that they are not Human. But we believe that a soulless Human who approaches them will be judged according to his sins, and a punishment pronounced. If he is able to bear the punishment, then it is possible for him to return to the world." Another pause. "If you brave the Stone Hall, and suffer the punishment, then you are shown the way back to the world."

"But even then, it is a terrible and a dangerous road," said Fergus, half to himself. And then, looking back at the boys, "You could take me to this place?"

"Oh, yes," said Conn.

"And the punishment?"

·   "Punishments are made to suit the sin," said Conn. "That we do know."

The immutable law. The ancient rule that punishments were weighed; that penance was meted out in exact accordance with the sin. If you sow thorns, you should not expect to harvest roses. What we drink is what we have brewed earlier. Yes. Not to be argued against, any of it. Fergus thought, But have I not suffered enough already? Surely I have made reparation? I have endured the solitude and the silence. Surely I can now be counted absolved?

He knew that it was not enough. He had sinned, he had inflicted terrible grievous hurt on Grainne. Against these lost children, these forgotten, soulless creatures, he had not been punished at all. These little ones had not sinned. They had been torn from the world, they had been mutilated and ripped open, and their hearts had been offered up to a monster-god.

"What else must I do?" said Fergus at last. "What must I do?" And thought that there was nothing he would not do to escape the Prison of Hostages, and there was nothing he would not do to help these children back to the world.

"First we must take you to the Stone Hall of Judgement. You will have to enter it alone, and you will have to face the Four Judges. It is frightening, that," said Conn thoughtfully. "And we do not think there is any appeal against the Judges' sentence." He looked at Fergus, and sudden compassion showed in his face.

"Yes?" said Fergus.

Conn said gently, "Fergus, the punishment must suit the sin."

And Fergus stared at him, and knew that his sin had been of the flesh, and a dreadful fear flooded his mind.

The sin of the flesh. And the penance must be in accordance with the sin.

For an incalculable time he stared at the boys, unable to speak, certainly unable to think properly.

The sin of the flesh. "Oh, no," whispered Fergus.

"It is the only way," said Conn. "It is the only way to break the bonds and make reparation and lead us back to save the children from Crom Croich."

"Why me!" cried Fergus in agony, and at once knew the answer.

Because you are what you are. Because you are a Prince of Ireland. You are one of the last of the Ancient Bloodline. You are a descendant of the great Cormac, and of Dierdriu, and of Niall of the Nine Hostages. No one has a stronger duty.

And then, most terrible of all—because you lay with your sister, and thus you drew down upon Tara the curse uttered at the very beginning.

All Ireland will seethe with evil and the skies will darken and the rivers will run with blood . . .

"Can I be held responsible for what I am?" said Fergus.

"We are all of us responsible for what we are," said Conn quietly, and Fergus thought, Yes, they have a right to say that.

"And you are a Prince of Tara."

And if I had not loved Grainne, perhaps none of it would have happened. Perhaps the curse would have been deflected yet again, and Tara would have been safe for a little longer, and life, in the end, would have gone on very much as before.

If you pour the wine you must expect to drink it . . .

Fergus bowed his head submissively and held out his hands and the boys clustered about him.

HE WAS AWARE that they were taking him through the vast echoing emptinesses of the great Prison; through high-ceilinged rooms, beneath vaulted chambers of blue and gold and ivory; along dim galleries and crimson panelled halls and through chambers that looked as if they had been hewn from solid gold, and on through rooms where the walls were encrusted with precious gems.

"But they are *living* gems," said one of the children in a soft, awed voice.

Living rubies and emeralds, and great gushing waterfalls of diamonds, and clusters of garnets and gentle opals . . .

There were rooms of marble and porphyry and topaz, and Fergus, his eyes dazzled, his senses swimming, thought, The Gates of Paradise studded with chalcedony and jasper, inlaid with firestones and cedarwood, rimmed with turquoise and moonstones . . .

Conn murmured some of the names as they went. "Although we do not know many," he said.

There was the Land of Ever-Living and the Plain of Two Mists. "To be avoided," said Conn with a sideways glance, and Fergus nodded and tried not to think of where they might be going and of what lay ahead. He thought he ought to be interested in all he was seeing; he thought that if things had been different, he would have been interested and fascinated and unable to think of anything other than the great glittering halls and the achingly beautiful places. Certainly he ought to be storing everything up.

He could not do it. The images, the unfolding splendours, each room more mystical and more brilliant than the last, were too much and too many. Aloud he said, "Have you tried to break out before?" and Conn regarded him with the grave stare that was friendly and becoming familiar.

"Of course we have," he said, and Fergus nodded, because of course they would have tried. "We believe that there are doorways back to the world of Men," said Conn. "Although we have never been able to find one. But we believe that a door is being opened. Opened for us now."

"Because the cult of Crom Croich is being revived?"

"Yes," said Conn. "Because the children must be saved." He looked about him. "But we would not have waited for that," he said. "We would have gone through any of the doorways back to the world."

"Sometimes," said the boy whom Fergus thought must be Conn's cousin, "sometimes we have felt very close to those doorways. We have heard voices calling to us. There were attempts to bring us out. But you would know that."

"The Crusades of Cormac's reign," said Fergus. "Yes, of course."

"And sometimes," said the boy whose name was Niall, "we have thought we could hear the *sidh* trying to lure us out with their music."

"I liked the music," said the smallest boy of all, wistfully. "I'd have liked to follow that."

"We would have done anything," said Conn. "We would have gone through any of the doorways back to the world. We would have gone across the Plain of Two Mists or the Lake of Darkness."

"We would have crossed the River of Souls," said another of the children, and a shiver of fear went through them all, and there was a sudden silence.

Fergus said, "The River of Souls?"

"Dark," said one of them.

"Endless," said another.

"It is the River of the Dead," said Conn. "It flows nine times round the Prison of Hostages."

"There's a Ferryman," put in the youngest, Michael, rather unhappily.

"A fisher of souls and hearts," said Niall.

"Once he has you, you are lost for all time," said another boy.

Fergus said, "But surely . . ." and paused. "But surely, we are already soulless?" he said.

"Our souls are in pawn," said Conn very quietly, as if he feared to be overheard.

"We are hostages," said Niall.

"That is why it is still possible for us to break the bonds," said Conn.

Fergus said slowly, "And the Ferryman lies in wait for souls?"

"He will take you across the River of the Dead," said Conn, "but he may also decide to drag you down into the endless darkness. We do not know who it is he serves, but we know that he serves the Dark Ireland."

"The darkness of that river," said Niall, "would be a far worse thing than the ceaseless light in here."

"But we would risk it," said Conn.

"We would risk anything to break the bonds," said another boy.

"There is nothing we would not risk."

They were moving on now, and Fergus had the impression that they were reaching the heart of the Prison.

The names tumbled about them, beautiful and incomprehensible and mysterious. The Hall of the Golden Pillars, the Star of the Poets, the Vale of Dawnlight . . . And others. Beautiful, meaningless names for beautiful, awesome places.

"We know only a very very little," said Conn, giving Fergus his straight stare. "In this house are many mansions, you see," he said, and Fergus nodded, because there was something familiar about the words, and there was something reassuring about them as well. "In this house are many mansions . . ." He grasped the words, because there was a comfort about them. *Many mansions . . .* I think it will be all right, he said, testing his responses silently. I think I can do it. Can I? Yes, for anything else is unthinkable.

And I cannot fail the boys.

He tried to ask Conn and Niall about the rooms and the empty galleries, but their answers were vague.

"Truly we know so little," said Conn. "And we do not really understand any of it."

The Stone Hall of Judgement, where the Four Judges will pronounce sentence in exact accordance with the sin . . .

"It is for you to enter the Stone Hall," said Conn. "And wait for the Four Judges to speak to you. They will pronounce a punishment," said Conn, "and you must endure that punishment before you can be free."

The punishment for the sin of the flesh . . .

"Then we will be free, we believe," said Niall. "We can leave the Prison, and enter the domain of the Ferryman and cross the River of Souls. Only that way can we hope to escape."

HE KNEW THE place at once, of course. He thought he had been there in dreams and nightmares, and he thought that this must be one of the most secret places of Men's souls.

The Stone Hall of Judgment.

The children were huddled together, their faces white, their eyes luminous with sympathy.

"We cannot come in with you," said Conn, "for each must face it alone. But we shall keep you in our thoughts."

"We shall not let you go," said Niall seriously.

"I shall think extra hard," said Michael earnestly and, despite himself, Fergus smiled.

The threshold to the Stone Hall of Judgment was high and wide and stretched far away. There was a warmth and a soft drowsy scent, and Fergus could feel hidden hands pulling him in.

Come inside, Mortal, for this is the place to which all Men must finally come . . . there is no escape . . .

And then the huge wide doorway vanished, and Fergus was alone in the Stone Hall.

The room was a little like a temple, although it was not like any temple Fergus had ever seen. It was narrow and there were rows of benchlike seats, intricately carved and laid with soft cushions. Fergus, rather intrigued, not yet afraid, slid quietly into the nearest one and sat waiting. He thought that this was some kind of anteroom, and he thought that presently he would be shown what he had to do next.

The walls were embellished with delicately carved screens made of some kind of fragrant wood. Between the screens, the walls were painted with scenes showing screaming Human souls being dragged beneath dark waters . . . The Ferryman! thought Fergus. Shall I see him? And felt his mind flinch from the idea.

Directly ahead of him, facing the rows of seats, was some kind of altar, long and low and covered with heavy linen. A low light burned in an elaborate lamp, and there was the scent of something heavy and exotic and unfamiliar. Fergus, who had talked with the Druids and the Travellers, sought for and found the word *"incense."*

Incense burning in an anteroom . . . Warm scents drifting across the Hall of Judgment, where all men must come to hear their sins read out.

Fergus thought, I am in the Stone Hall, and presently, quite soon, I shall be judged.

Behind the altar, huge and impassive, were four immense, carved figures. They were ancient and rock-like and awesome, and Fergus recognised them: the Four Stone Judges. They would judge you on your life; on all the things you had done and all the things you had left undone; and your kindnesses and your unkindnesses; and on your honesty and integrity, and selfishness and generosity, and tolerance and impatience, and on every action you had ever performed during your life. Nothing would be missed, nothing would be skimmed over. Everything would be inspected and weighed and given its due. The carved faces were enigmatic; there was a flat, stern, eastern look to the features. They sat, half set into the walls of the Hall, their hands placed palms downwards on their knees.

They would wake very soon, thought Fergus, unable to look away. Their blank eyes would open and they would see him, and then the final judging would begin. There would be no concealing and no pretending.

The Stone Hall was not especially hot, but Fergus felt a great stifling heat pressing down on him, so that it was difficult to breathe. Dark red mists swam before his eyes, and he had the impression that something ancient and strong was materialising in the Hall.

In another minute, in just another few seconds, it will be here in all its awful glory, and it will see into my heart, and it will know everything, and I shall be judged.

And then the Stone Judges will awake and the sentence will be pronounced . . .

The ancient force was forming; the walls were pressing in, and there was a thickening in the air, so that Fergus could feel his heartbeat getting slower and heavier, and his mind becoming sluggish, and the blood congealing in his veins.

The Final Judging . . . The nearest of the great carved figures opened its stone eyes and looked directly at him, and as he did so, the other three awoke and looked to where Fergus sat.

The ancient force began to take substance and, as it did so, Fergus saw the first of the Judges open its mouth to speak, and heard, quite distinctly, a great cavernous echoing voice pronounce the terrible punishment:

Castration.

Chapter Sixteen

Fergus lay on the cool marble floor of the Stone Hall of Judgment, the boys all about him.

Conn's voice, quite close, said, "It is over, Fergus. The Judges sleep again," and Fergus blinked and looked about him and sat up. And after all, the Stone Hall was only a long, narrow, rather bare room. There was no carved screen, no terrible paintings of dying struggling souls being pulled below the waters by the Ferryman, no altar or incense. And the massive stone figures had gone.

Fergus said carefully, "You heard the Stone Judges?" and the boys nodded.

"You knew that the punishment would fit the sin."

"Yes."

Fergus said, "One of you must do it to me." And looked straight at Conn.

Conn had turned very pale, but his eyes held Fergus's. "I cannot."

"Yes."

"Fergus, don't make me!" It was a cry of anguish this time. "You will feel it—your body will feel everything—" He stopped, and Fergus said softly, "I know." And remembered how Fribble had explained that the bodies of those whose souls were stolen by the Lad of the Skins could still feel pain. The Eternal Sleep, he had called it. The Living Death. "You must do it," said Fergus, and now it was the old Fergus, the head of the High Queen's *Fiana*, the famous Captain. Conn heard the new note of authority, and looked at him.

"You must do it," said Fergus, very gently, "so that I can break the bonds of this Prison and lead you back into the world. So that the children in the Ireland of now can be safe from Crom Croich." He held the boy's stare unwaveringly, and at last Conn said, "Yes. Yes, of course."

Fergus drew a deep breath, and thought: And although you do not know it, you must do it to save Ireland. For thus mutilated and thus deprived of manhood, desire will die and I shall be able at last to stop loving and wanting and aching for my own sister. The tie that binds us, this dreadful forbidden love I have for her, will dissolve, and then perhaps the old, old curse will weaken and the Ancient Bloodline can once again rule from Tara.

Because you may as well face it, Fergus said to himself, you may as well face it squarely and for all time. There has never been a day or an hour, nor yet a minute, when you have not wanted her, and when she has not been in your thoughts and in your heart. There has never been a time when you would not have welcomed her back into your arms and when you would not have taken again what she gave on those dew-spattered mornings, on those drowsy afternoons in the woods surrounding Tara. She was stronger than you, and when told the truth she turned desire aside, but you did not. There has never been a day when you have not hoped. Now the hoping will die as well.

And what of her? What of Grainne? Would she, also, be set free? Was she even now perhaps free? Perhaps with someone else? I should want her to be happy, thought Fergus, his mind in turmoil. Of course I should. I cannot be so cruel, so selfish, as to want her to live with only the memories. And then a brief smile curved his lips, because the memories would always be there; they would always share what had been between them, and she would not forget. There would always be that for them.

But like this, surely desire would die for her as well? Wouldn't it? I no longer know! cried Fergus in silent agony. I can no longer understand any of it! Only I believe that this is the only way to kill the desire and the love and the sin!

When Fergus sat up and looked at Conn and the others,

there was a different light in his eyes, and there was a determination in his expression.

"Do it now," he said.

"Just the three of us," said Conn. "You and I and Niall."

"Yes," said Fergus. "Yes, all right."

Afterwards he thought—when he could think clearly
again—that he had been grateful to Conn for that. Just Conn,
this strange, grave child who had so rapidly become close,
and just Niall who was Conn's cousin. Just the two of them
and Fergus and the vast echoing Prison walls.

The children would be near. "And our thoughts will be
with you," said one of them, and Fergus remembered that
they had said this to him before. Rather like a ritual. He
found it immensely comforting, and then he was struck again
by their strange, grave, unchildlike mien. But he thought
they had had too long to learn patience and tolerance and
gravity, they had had so many years and so many decades in
here to learn to be unchildlike. Even so, he was glad that it
would be only Conn and Niall who would witness the pain
and the humiliation.

Conn said, "But there is no humiliation. In some lands
it is considered an honour. A distinction."

"There will be a little pain," said Niall. "But we shall
be very quick." But Fergus thought Niall's face was rather
white.

"It will be as difficult for us," said Conn, but his face
was set.

"Will you do it—quickly?"

"Yes," said Conn.

"And," said Fergus, beginning to feel sick, "and you
have a knife?"

"Yes." There was the splinter-light of something catching the glare of the Prison's brightness.

"Very sharp," said Conn gently, and Fergus had time to
see that the knife, like everything else about this place, was
unusual and elaborate.

"Where did you—"

"It was on the altar," said Conn. "Waiting." And Fergus nodded and did not ask again, because there was too much that was incomprehensible about this place. He saw that the instrument in Conn's hands was a kind of hinged clamp with strange symbols etched on it. There was an elliptical opening, there was a section that had serrated teeth . . .

I don't think I can bear it, thought Fergus, but in the next minute he knew that it must be borne.

Conn said, "We are going to tie you down."

"Yes." He had expected this. He thought he would struggle and try to break free, because it would be against Human nature not to. And to try to escape halfway through would be unthinkable. He began to hope very strenuously that Conn would be quick, and he began to hope as well that he would lose consciousness almost immediately. He heard Conn say something to Niall in a low voice, and he heard Niall say, "Very sharp indeed." The splinter of brightness flashed again.

Then Conn said, "Spread the sawdust on the floor.

"And then hold his legs apart."

Fergus had not thought he would feel so vulnerable lying like this; he had been prepared for the fear and the flinching away from pain and mutilation, but he had not been prepared for the helplessness, the knowledge that the most intimate part of him was at the mercy of a boy with a knife. He tried to think: But it is Conn, and I believe that I could trust Conn with anything and everything.

He trusted Conn, but Conn was about to do this dreadful thing to him. And then he met Conn's eyes and he caught the thought that flickered in the air between them: *Fergus, there is no other way,* and he remembered the pronouncement of the Stone Judges. *For you have brewed the wine and now you must drink it.*

If Conn caught Fergus's thoughts, he gave no indication. He said, "Sign to me when you are ready," and Fergus was grateful for this, because he could at least feel in control, he could perhaps summon up every shred of courage and fortitude.

Grainne, thought Fergus, oh, my dear hopeless love, this is for you and this is for Tara, and for Ireland, and for all those children who will be offered to Crom Croich. It is for the hurt I dealt you and for those forbidden, achingly sweet afternoons and those gentle dawns . . . And it is for the child I should have given you, the dark Wolfprince I should have given Tara and now never will . . . Only a travesty left now, my love. Only a half-man, a gelding, no longer able to pass on the thin frayed Royal blood . . . Although, thought Fergus bitterly, perhaps if the gods are unkind, I *have* passed it on; perhaps, after all, I have helped to create a monster-creature, a nightmare Wolfcreature, born out of a sorcerer's greed and sired by means of a Tyrian money-lender's wine . . . Perhaps, after all, I have left Ireland an heir, thought Fergus, and the thought was a bitter one.

Conn was waiting, his eyes patient and filled with compassion. Fergus, looking up at him, knew that very soon he must signal to Conn, that the blade must come slicing down, but that first he must somehow find a great surging wave of resolution and defiance that would carry him through the pain.

And then, because the memory of the effectiveness of the Ice Cauldron in Calatin's house slid into his mind, he began to imagine the resolve and the bravery as a great cresting wave, a rearing wall of armour that would shield him from the worst of it; a huge, fast-moving, sweeping current of self-defence, a rampart that would cushion the worst of the pain; a bastion, a bulwark.

And if I can only build that crest to its highest possible peak, and if I can then sign to Conn, I believe I shall come through this more cleanly and more easily than I deserve . . . He began to see it, quite clearly now, a huge grey-green wall of water, rushing in on him, the tips white-flecked already, foaming and swirling and ready to rise up . . . The water was like glass, like silk, it would provide cover, lee, shield . . .

Up and up, clear glass-green, glittering, catching the light, beginning to curl at the top, beginning to be foamy and creamy, beginning to reach its zenith . . .

In another minute, thought Fergus, feeling strength pour into him, in another minute, I shall bear it, I shall nod to Conn . . .

The wave was sweeping in on him faster now, it was rearing back slightly, it would surround him, it would be a cushion and a bastion . . .

"Now!" cried Fergus, and Conn brought the razor edge sweeping downwards.

Pain exploded in Fergus's body, irradiating outwards; so fierce, so intimate, so utterly and comprehensively agonizing, that the wave he had so carefully constructed in his mind closed over his head in a suffocating blackness. He was drowning in the pain, he was unable to breathe, because the pain was choking him, his lower body was a raw open wound, and his life blood was leeching from him, and there had never been such pain anywhere in the world. The waters closed about him and he sank into the merciful pain-free depths . . .

. . . to wake again to pain, dulled, but still terrible, and to Conn and Niall bending over him, their eyes wide and fearful, their hands gentle.

Conn was saying, "It's all right. Fergus, it is *over*."

And Fergus heard himself murmur, "Yes, over once and for all . . . and she is gone from me now for all time . . . she is safe and I am safe . . ."

There was an interlude, a between-time, which he was later to look on as a time when he was neither quite in the world nor yet quite out of it. He thought that the children came and went, solemn, dark-eyed faces watching him, their eyes filled with sympathy and trust. "For," thought Fergus, restless against the vice of the pain between his legs, "for they are waiting for me to lead them out of this place and back into the world to defeat Crom Croich's grisly cult."

Conn and Niall were with him almost continuously. "I

do not think you ever left me," Fergus said afterwards to Conn.

"I did not," said Conn.

He had thought that this would be the worst part of all; the memory of what had been done, the realisation that never again would he make love to a woman; never again would he feel the slow, sweet stirrings of desire, the excitement of pursuing a lady of the Court. But all through it, like a dim silver thread, was the thought of Grainne and the knowledge that at least he had killed that sweet, illicit feeling.

For her as well? Please let it be for her as well, thought Fergus.

CHAPTER
SEVENTEEN

LUGH OF THE Longhand had explained his new plan very clearly and very simply, and in an altogether friendly fashion. He had not dissimulated in the least bit, but still it had been odd how he had found it difficult to look directly at the wolf-emblem pennants which always flew from the camp's entrance. He would not trouble about this, because he knew now that the Wolfline was nearly extinct, and it was dying. You threw in your allegiance with those who were in the ascendant. Medoc was in the ascendant. Lugh could be sure about this.

He had been very much shocked to learn that the Queen (he still thought of her by that title) had borne a child in secret, and allowed the child to be taken away and raised in secrecy: Folaim, the place of concealment. Lugh remembered very well indeed the rumours and the gossip, and he was rather pleased to think he had been instrumental in bringing the thing to an end. Just a word or two in the right quarters, that was all he had done at the time. And he had been saddened and hurt when Dierdriu, instead of calling him to thank him, and perhaps bestowing an honour of some kind on him (the Order of Nuadu Airgetlam, which was a silver wolfhead, would have been nice), had actually treated him rather coldly.

Medoc's story about the child, the Wolfprince, fitted exactly. Lugh remembered how Grainne had gone on a tour of the Western Isles, and how she had been away for several months. Lugh thought it was deceitful and sly of Grainne, and wondered that she had been able to command such allegiance from the people. Cormac and Dierdriu had been no better, of course. What was in the meat came out in the gravy, and Grainne was really no better than her forebears.

He called the armies together and mapped out the new plan. He only spoke for quite a short time, telling how they would all march on to the little township called Folaim, there to raise further men for the battle. He managed to smudge over the reason for choosing this really rather obscure place quite well, so that it was irritating of Dorrainge, who always made things difficult, to ask awkward questions like: But *why* are we leaving Tara? And: What is so special about Folaim? Or even: But didn't we come to Tara to spy on Medoc?

Lugh did not answer any of these questions directly, because for one thing he did not know how to. Medoc had not told him how he should deal with such a curt approach, and for another thing he was not going to have Druids telling him what to do. He adopted a rather vague manner and said it was all part of a new strategy and it would be a better tactic.

"Why?" said Dorrainge, and Lugh sighed at such bluntness. He said that it was a very good plan, and they would all of them do what they were told, and that the army in general, and Lugh in particular, did not have to be answerable to Druids. He raised his voice towards the end, so that several people who had been nodding off woke up with a start, and four soldiers who had been engaging in a little dilettante dice-throwing at the back, scooped up the dice at once, because a quarrel between Longhand the Lily-Livered and Fatchops Dorrainge would be much more interesting than a furtive game of dice.

Lugh was not going to quarrel. He was not even going to quarrel with Dorrainge, even though he was being given provocation. He made a short speech (only a few well-thought-out words it was) about Duty and Loyalty and Obedience. He would certainly have gone on to talk about Fidelity as well, if he had not been distracted by Cathbad, who was tiptoeing stealthily out, one finger to his lips to indicate that he had no intention of making any noise, but unfortunately tripping over the feet of several people who were sitting on the ground, so that there was a good deal of tutting and shushing, and Cathbad was told he ought to be less clumsy, and Lugh lost the thread of his speech, and had to go back to the beginning which, as Dorrainge pointed out, was exactly what they did not want.

The men were interested in the new plan. They nodded and said wouldn't it be fine to be on the march again. Several of them looked rather unhappily to the dark, saucer-shaped valley where Tara lay, and which was now a blur of shadow. A fine thing to be getting away for the moment, said the men. There was nothing but gloom and black sorcery down there, and if they could break Medoc's nasty Enchantment by rounding up a few hill farmers and one or two shepherds and woodcutters it would be grand. Didn't it just about break your heart to be so close to the Bright Palace and see it shrouded in darkness, only that you couldn't see it at all, and wasn't that the point. They became quite emotional, and somebody went round with the mulled wine which Cathbad had put out, and there was much drinking of damnation to the Twelve Dark Lords, and death and destruction to Medoc and the Conablaiche, and long life and health to the Wolfqueen.

"There'll be a few sore heads in the morning I shouldn't wonder," observed Cathbad, "I'll just gather a few pansies for a brew, or should it be elfwort? Let me see now . . ."

Lugh was glad that it had been so easy to persuade the men to march to Folaim. Of course they would agree to do whatever he told them. That was the sign of a good leader.

It was to be hoped that he would recognise the Wolfprince when he found it. This would make the task a whole lot easier, because no one wanted to go about slaughtering children wholesale. Lugh would look very hard for the signs of the wolfstrain, and since he was a person of some perspicacity, he would probably spot the creature without any trouble. He kept the image of the High Kings firmly in the forefront of his mind; let him once find a child who had the distinctive slant and golden glow to its eyes, the dark glossy hair that resembled an animal's pelt, the three-cornered features that could look at once austere and sly, and he would know. Here is the Lost Prince!

But he had forgotten the really irritating habit that the reckless womanising Cormac had had of seducing anyone and everyone, and he had reckoned without the fact that Cormac (and one or two others of the Wolfline) had been indiscriminate, not to say incontinent, in the spreading of their seed.

When Lugh said crossly that there were bastards everywhere, he was misunderstood. Dorrainge frowned, and Cathbad sucked in his teeth and said, "Oh, dear me, *what* an expression, and me with my sheltered upbringing," and Lugh had to explain.

Dorrainge said, "Oh. Yes I see. Yes, Cormac was a great one for that sort of thing, they say," and Cathbad, who loved gossip, was so entranced by this that he forgot to look where he was going, and tripped over his robes, and tumbled headlong into a thicket hedge, and had to be hauled out by several of the soldiers.

"And I *was* pricked," said Cathbad breathlessly, dusting himself down, and hunched a shoulder and giggled when the soldiers guffawed and said, Yes, more times than he can count, and Lugh had to call them to order, because you could not have this sort of ribaldry among the men. You did not know where it might lead to.

They travelled a good deal by night—"Inconspicuous," said Lugh, and they covered a good deal of ground that way. "No distractions," said Lugh, pleased, although one or two of the soldiers muttered that a bit of a distraction was a good thing sometimes, and got you through a boring march.

Lugh could not have told when he first became aware that they were no longer alone; when they ceased to be the High Queen's army and a brace of Druids and became something a bit different.

He thought it was when they were about two days'

march from Folaim, just as they stopped for a break and a midday meal.

"It's called Black Pig's Dyke, this," said Cathbad, who liked to know all the names, and who had read the maps earlier, and had, in fact, dropped Lugh's best map into a large puddle. "We'll have a plateful of stew each," said Cathbad, beaming.

Folaim was not a very long way ahead of them now, which was why it was odd of Lugh to keep glancing over his shoulder. He thought that it was as they were crossing a narrow river that he began to feel uneasy. A kind of prickling on the back of his neck. He half turned several times, thinking he would see one of the men, or possibly Dorrainge, standing watching him. But there was no one, although Lugh retained the strong feeling that there had been someone; that just before he had turned, the watcher had disappeared.

This was ridiculous, because you did not see things that were not there. But the feeling persisted, and Lugh began to have the impression that the night was going to be altogether too dark and the air altogether too quiet, and the forest through which they were now marching altogether too lonely.

He began to feel very strongly indeed that there was something with them. Something that was creeping through the dark old forest, and something that could see them without them seeing it.

A shadow. Yes, now that Lugh came to concentrate, there was a shadow. An insubstantial form that rode alongside them and kept pace with them. Something that hovered at Lugh's side, grinning and waiting. Lugh frowned, because this was something he had not reckoned on, and he did not care for silent nearly invisible things that rode with you and watched you and vanished when you tried to pin them with your eyes. He frowned and tried to think what the thing might be.

And then, as they rounded a curve in the forest path,

and saw Folaim ahead of them in a little hollow by itself, the shadow coalesced for a minute, and Lugh saw the shape quite clearly, and cold fear gripped his vitals.

Small. Light. Frail. A creature that would presently cry in the night and beg for a share of the food and a place by the camp fire. Something that would certainly be there when Lugh sought out the Wolfprince. Something that would certainly exult and gloat at the killing of the Royal child.

Medoc had sent the Lad of the Skins after them.

CHAPTER EIGHTEEN

WHEN GRAINNE SAID to Raynor, "Come with me to Tara. Help me to drive out Medoc," she knew and Raynor knew that she was really saying: Return to the world with me. Let me give to you those things which have been denied you. She did not say this, because she knew that the knowledge was still too new for them. They had accepted that they were the Enchanted Beastline of Ireland, but they did not yet quite believe it.

"We dare not," said Bec, but her eyes were shining.

Raynor listened to Grainne and watched her face, as if he wanted to absorb her and know her so well that he would never forget her. When she said again, "Come with me to Tara," he turned on her a look of such fierce love and such blazing intensity that she felt her heart stop and then resume a painful beating. He cupped her face between his hands in the gesture she was coming to know, the gesture that said, "You are mine and nothing and no one shall take you from me." And then he said aloud, "Yes. All right." As simply and as directly as that.

It was important to remember that bringing these creatures out of the Grail Castle was only one part of the plan to defeat Medoc, and it was very important indeed not to lose sight of the fact that the Beastline would form only a small fighting detachment. Grainne thought she had not lost sight of any of this; there was, in her mind, the strong wonderful image of the Beastline and their creatures swooping down on Tara, with the ancient banners of their Houses streaming behind them in the wind—Banners that were so

304

nearly lost to Ireland, she thought—but even as she was seeing this image, she still knew that it was the army, the *Fiana*, who would lead the charge against Medoc and the Twelve Lords.

And Fergus? Yes, Fergus must certainly be there, for it was not to be borne that they should regain Tara and Fergus not to be there with them. Grainne could still think, *you are still here with me, my love*; she could still pause in the day's events and send out a thought, a message, an outpouring of strength to Fergus, who might be anywhere at all now, and who might be dead. *Only if you were dead, my dear lost love, I think I should know it.* She thought Fergus was safe somewhere, and she thought he would succeed, because failure was not something she would ever associate with him.

But when Raynor cupped her face between his hands and said, "You are mine," and when he smiled the winged smile that was his strange inheritance and said, "Did you think I would let you go away from me?" Grainne felt delight pour over her in great, brilliant waves.

And the others would come with them; they would leave this dark ancient fortress, which might hold patches of sunlight and happiness, but which also held the miasma of centuries of despair and fear and madness.

When Rinnal said doubtfully, "We do not form a very large army, Your Majesty," Grainne smiled at him and said, "But you will be the quintessence of it all, Rinnal. You and Bec, and your people. The Badgers and the Hares and the Chariot Horses and the Swans."

"And we shall see Tara at last," said Rinnal.

"Oh, yes," said Grainne softly. "Oh, yes, you will see Tara." *For it is your inheritance as much as it is mine.* And Fergus? said her mind, without warning. Isn't it as much Fergus's as well? I don't know, said Grainne silently. I can not tell any longer. Only that I must do all I can to drive out Medoc. It does not matter after that who rules.

Fintan and Cermait and Tybion the Tusk had been commissioned to marshal everyone into a proper fighting force. They had been charmed to be thus employed, although, as Fintan said, the task was not without its difficulties.

"It isn't the people of the Beastline themselves," said Fintan. "They're the easiest creatures in the world."

Cermait and Tybion had tried to count up how many they had. "Six Royal Houses," said Tybion, but Cermait said there were the lesser Houses as well. "People like Bec and Rinnal, and Diarmuid and the Forest Dogs," he said. "And if you allow ten animals per person, well, say a round dozen, that's—dear me, it's rather a lot." He counted up on the fingers of both hands worriedly.

"It's too many by far," said Fintan crossly.

"It's too many *different* species by far," said Cermait, who had lost count and had to start again, and had already reached three different answers.

"It will be all right," said Tybion, and Cermait at once wanted to know how Tybion could possibly think this, what with the Foxes falling out with the Forest Dogs, and the Badgers snuffling and getting under people's feet, and the Hares leaping on to the table just as you were about to sit down to your supper.

Tybion said, mildly, that he thought everyone was getting on very amicably, all things considered, and Cermait said he would not call it amity precisely, not when the Foxes had spent that very morning chasing the Hares, and not when the Dogs had spent the afternoon barking at the Badgers who had decided to dig up the Grail Castle's west lawn.

"It works," said Tybion firmly.

"The stables are overcrowded with the Chariot Horses."

"But nobody seems to mind."

"I'm worried about the White Swans and the Eagles," said Fintan, who was not going to be left out of such a promisingly gloomy discussion. "Mark my words, there'll be trouble there once we set out. I told Her Majesty so," said Fintan, who had not done any such thing, but thought it sounded well. "There'll be trouble before we've done, I said. Of course

Raynor might be able to control the Eagles," said Fintan doubtfully. "You never know."

"It's a grand strong army," said Tybion contentedly.

Tybion was utterly and completely happy. He was enchanted to be here, to be in the High Queen's service, to be helping his beautiful shining lady. He liked the Beastline creatures, and he thought they were courteous and noble and interesting, and that there was a fascinating air of great tragedy about them. Tybion, who had lived what he considered to be an ordinary sort of life, was intrigued by the tragedy and the drama of the Beastline creatures who had spent their lives shut away from the world and were now going to emerge into it. He was wide-eyed with delight, and he thought, as he went about the Castle, that to be sure this was the stuff that dreams were made on. He went about in a happy glow.

Grainne had talked to him, quite privately, and Tybion had stored this away to be relived later. She had said that she believed Tybion was going to be of great importance in the battle ahead of them, in the great fight to destroy Medoc and regain Tara, and Tybion, unable to take his eyes from her, had asked was there really going to be a battle, and Grainne had laughed and said, Oh, yes, for sure there was going to be a battle, and they would be sending Medoc and the Twelve Lords to the rightabout, and wasn't that what all this was about anyway?

"And you are being such a help to me," said Grainne, and Tybion mumbled and blushed and wondered should he kneel down to kiss her hand, but thought better of it, because she was not the sort of person whose hand you knelt down to kiss, unless it might be a State occasion, which this was not. You could easily visualise yourself dying for her, but somehow you could not imagine kneeling before her.

"That's because she's the People's Queen," said Cermait when Tybion tried to explain it later.

"She has what they call the common touch," said Fintan, and then, because he liked Tybion, said quickly, "I didn't mean *you* were common, my boy," and Tybion nodded solemnly and understood, but thought that put next to Grainne they were all of them common really. Tybion knew quite well that he was not noble; none of the Tusks were, because none of them had the tiniest drop of noble blood, and they would not have known what to do with it if they had, so there was no use pretending otherwise. He went away to polish up the picture of dying for Grainne on the battlefield and wondered would a dying speech be considered presumptuous, because he did not want people to think him an upstart, and Fintan, a practical soul, went off to the kitchens, because they could not march against Medoc on empty stomachs.

"They all did so well," said Grainne to Raynor. "They sorted the animals into separate sections, and kept the Foxes away from the Hares and the Dogs away from the Swans, and they even stopped the Badgers from tunnelling underneath the castle's western foundations," she said, smiling. "And they drew up a grand list of provisions." She smiled again and Raynor smiled back.

He was unafraid of facing the outside world, although he knew it would not be easy. I have never known any other life, he thought. But he did not say this; already his mind was leaping ahead, and his thoughts centred on Medoc, the dark, cruel necromancer who had fathered Grainne and Fergus and taken Tara from them. He wanted to confront Medoc, to see him cringe and cower, and was rather appalled at the thought. "For," he said, "I have always been a creature of peace."

But he knew it was the strong enchanted eagleblood waking in him, and he knew he would never forget the moment when he had stood on the hillside behind the castle and sent out the call to the Eagles. He would never forget how he had felt when they had obeyed his call, golden and soaring and cruelly beautiful, their wings beating on the night air, the skies black with their numbers. He had felt it then, the legendary Enchantment streaming into him . . . The power and the light and the strength . . .

He knew that he must ride out with Grainne against Medoc; he must certainly lead the Eagles, those strong-winged creatures who would obey him, so that they might restore the light to Tara.

Tara, the Bright Palace . . . I shall see it at last, he thought, and felt a surging of his spirits, and a sense of homecoming. For it is my heritage as much as anyone's, he thought.

He ached to be at Grainne's side when they rode down into the valley that sheltered the glittering Palace; his whole body and his heart and his mind were already there, riding full pelt down the hillside, scattering the adversary, making the final triumphal march back to the Bright Palace.

Shall I in truth be there? He could see it very clearly, but he did not allow himself to see it for too long. For she is not for me nor I for her. Even though she has given me back my pride, and even though she has made it possible for me to break the chains of my own exile, still I do not see how we can be together. He thought he would have to let her go in the end, his lovely golden lady. He would return to the Grail Castle, but he would never for an hour forget her. No matter my heritage, I am not of her world, he thought.

But he would see Tara in all its blaze of splendour—oh, yes, let me see it, just once!—and then he would forswear the Wolfqueen. She is not for me nor I for her.

Even so, he thought, lying wakeful in the drowsy firelight, even so, I believe I can give her back her kingdom.

AND SO THIS is it, thought Grainne, seated on her horse, a little apart from the others, waiting for the moment when the great portcullis of the Castle would be raised, and the drawbridge lowered, and waiting for the moment when they would ride out across the ravine and down into the world. This is it, the moment you have dreamed about and longed for and yearned towards. Make the most of it, she said to herself, for it is certain that you will never, not if you live for seven lifetimes, know another moment to equal this one.

And all the power and the light and the strength is within me now, and the lost people of Ireland are all with me, and I am leading them back to Tara, and I am leading them out of their long and terrible exile . . .

The Purple Hour was falling, gently, softly, and the air was thick with magic. And let me always keep this moment, thought Grainne, standing quietly while the bustle of departure went on all about her, and the horses stamped their hoofs and tossed their manes, and people ran and hurried and came and went, and the animals tumbled and growled and went pattering and yelping and sniffing and fluttering everywhere. Let me always keep this, just like this, and let me be able to tuck it away somewhere safe in a tiny corner of my heart, and cover it with layer upon layer of happiness and memory and enchantment, so that one day, somewhere far in the future, I shall be able to unwrap it and look at it and feel then, as fiercely as I feel now, the love and the soaring delight, and the pure and undiluted happiness. Let me never forget the delight and the love and the loyalty that I am feeling now.

The portcullis was rising, and the horses were banding together, "For," said Raynor, "when we ride out, we must ride in proper order." There was a whirring and a screeching of disused machinery as the immense drawbridge was lowered, and the purple twilight, the enchanted bewitching blue and green mist, poured into the old dark Grail Castle.

Dust motes swirled and danced and the soft gentle light touched the waiting faces, and showed the happiness and the trust and the delight in every face. And I will not cry, said Grainne silently, although the tears were already gathering in her eyes. I will not cry, because this is it, this is the moment I have wanted and waited for ever since I can remember . . . The exiled High Queen leading the lost people of Ireland back to their own land.

They fell into line behind her now, obediently and naturally and quietly, but for all their tranquillity, there was a feeling of singing on the air, and there was a sense of the most tremendous anticipation.

They are all with me, thought Grainne, waiting for the moment when the portcullis would reach its zenith and the drawbridge would be fully extended for them to ride over. They are all with me. The creatures of the Lost Enchantment. The Noble Houses of Ireland. And the Cruithin, dear and loyal and staunch and as elusive as the flickering lights over the Fire Mountains. And she turned to look at these small dark people with their sly charm and their soft courtesy and their air of belonging to no one. The first Gaels, the one true Irish race, who had more right than anyone to inhabit Ireland, but who would never enforce that right, and who probably did not care about it overmuch anyway, for it has been said, and truly, that the genuine Irish do not care for land and possessions. "Clutter," they say, for they like to travel light. The Cruithin travelled light, but they were travelling with Grainne now, and Grainne knew that whatever else she had done for Ireland, she had never done anything so truly good as bringing back the first true Irish people.

The portcullis was raised now—Midnight's Arch—how could I ever have been afraid of this place? I am leading my people back and together we will defeat the adversary, and Tara will burn more brightly than ever it has burned before.

And then they were through the soaring stone arches and under the portcullis and they were riding down the drawbridge and the night air was cool and sweet against their faces, and Grainne felt, amidst the woodbine and the night-scented flowers, something deeper. Something ancient and warm and good. Something that she hardly dared believe in, and yet something that she knew was there, as real and as tangible as her own skin. Something that was stirring out of a long, long sleep, and that was lifting its head at last. The Old Ireland . . . The enchanted western isle of legend.

As they rode across the ravine and down on to the forest

road, Grainne felt the air heavy with enchantment and heady with bewitchment, and felt, as well, that it was wrapping itself about her, like a soft gentle rainfall, like a cobweb cascade.

She thought, I dare not believe it, but I think I do believe it. I cannot see any of it, but all the same, I think it is there. The lost enchantments waking . . .

It ought to have been frightening to feel the ancient magic waking; certainly it ought to have been awesome. Grainne thought she ought to be frightened, for they were journeying by night, and the road was lonely. And for all their bravery, they were a small enough company. And all the time, all the time, she was aware of the strong, sweet awareness all about them. Every blade of silvered grass, every leaf, every moon-washed stretch of road, was alive and quivering with delight.

Because the Wolfqueen was returning . . .

Oh, yes, let it be that, thought Grainne, in silent appeal. Let it be because I have somehow found the lost Beastline and the Cruithin, and because we are going back to Tara. And please let us regain Tara, said her mind. For if Tara is beyond recall, then there is nothing left anywhere for me . . .

But here, now, with Raynor and the others with her, she thought she could believe that anything was possible. She felt the most remarkable sense of kin with the forest and with the night rustlings, and with the heavy enchanted night. She thought that for all she could not see the creatures of legend, they were there all the same. They were watching and nodding and smiling . . .

The naiads and dryads . . . Furry, cloven-footed beings with three-cornered faces and pointed ears . . . Water nymphs and gentle forest folk who understood the old pure magic that had been handed down before Time began, when men spoke to each other not in words, but in the unalloyed thoughtforms from which the Samhailt had been forged by the House of Amaranth . . .

THE SKY WAS lightening in the east, sending shafts of gold and rose to strike Fael-Inis's Fire Mountains, and they were rounding the curve in the forest road, and Fintan was thinking wasn't it just time to make camp and cook up a bite of breakfast. And then—no one quite knew when it began or where it came from—but everyone suddenly became aware that there was something moving closer; there was a great rush of anticipation, a feeling that something marvellous was about to happen; there was a sound on the air as if someone was drawing a finger round and round an immense glass bowl. A thrumming. A beating of cobweb wings on the air. A flurrying of something that might have been smoke and that might have been fire, but that could quite easily have been only the morning mist, but that everyone knew was not.

With the gentle rushing came the music, soft and cold and haunting, and Grainne felt her heart begin to beat faster, and she put up a hand to halt the others. There was the sensation of something singing just out of earshot, and of something unbearably beautiful moving just out of sight, and then—

"Oh!" said Grainne softly, and reined in her horse, and felt the others fall into silent place behind her.

Blue and green smudges of smoke. Wisps and curls of ice fire, blue on green on blue again; half seen and then gone, dissolving into the uncertain light, melting into the forest and then appearing again. Shapes and half-shapes; things you could not be entirely sure you were seeing, but creatures you knew were there, if only you had the extra sight, and if only you had the extra comprehension.

The *sidh*. The most purely magical beings in all Ireland. Cold and eerily beautiful, with not a single drop of Human blood in them. Ireland's faery folk, soulless and chill, and greedy for the souls of Men, but, for all that, loyal to the Royal House.

The creatures on whom no Man dared look for too long

lest his eyes burn out, and with whom no Man dared commune for too long, lest his senses be stolen away, and his soul be dragged down into the endless caves under the sea.

They sang for me, thought Grainne, her mind bemused with delight, her pulses racing a little with fear, for she knew, as everyone knew, the dangers of looking on the *sidh* and talking with them. They could steal away your sight, they could tear out your tongue, destroy your mind . . .

But they have come again to us, thought Grainne, moving forward at last. They have sought us out, and I believe they are friendly for the moment, and I believe we can trust them.

And because it would have been the utmost discourtesy to have ignored them, she went forward alone, and dismounted, and stood in the clearing and waited.

They are very close, thought Grainne. There is green and blue everywhere, but it is vanishing into the forest, before the *sidh* materialise. They are nearly forming, but they are not quite forming. I can hear them and I can sense them and I can feel them. I cannot see them properly, and I do not think I want to. Except . . .

And then he was there. The slender unearthly High King of the *sidh* who could clothe himself in the semblance of Human form, but who could never, not for an instant, be mistaken for a true Human. Cold and beautiful and filled with the uncanny music of his kind.

Aillen mac Midha. The *sidh*'s Elven King. Remote and aloof, watching them unblinkingly with great dark eyes, inspecting them with the curiosity of one species for another.

The High King of Ireland's ancient magical people sat cross-legged on a grassy bank, waiting with exquisite, impersonal courtesy for them to approach him.

We may all be deaf, blind, speechless, witless before the end of an hour, thought Grainne; still, there is nothing to do but go forward.

Even so, it was several minutes before she could speak. And then he spoke first. "You called to me, Your Majesty," he said. "I am here." And a shiver went through the Beastline and the Cruithin, for his voice was in some way silver, and in some way transient, so that the words took faint shape and lay on the air for a while—thin, pale, shimmering forms. Fintan, who was the oldest of them all, drew in a deep breath of delight, for he knew that they were seeing something which was rarely granted to their world: the Samhailt made visible . . .

Tybion was thinking that the Elven King was the coldest being he had ever encountered. He remembered that the *sidh* dwelled in the rocks and in the seas, and that their homes were the caves beneath the ocean, where there was only cold green waterlight that rippled for ever on the cave walls, and where the floors were sprinkled with the bone dust of the *sidh*'s victims. There was no escape from the water caves, not unless you forfeited one of your five senses . . .

Aillen mac Midha said again, "You summoned me, Your Majesty. And since I am constrained by the ties that bind your House to mine, I have come." And appeared to wait, and Grainne knew that here was one of those awkward occasions when the right words and the right ceremonies were absolutely obligatory, only that no one was ever quite sure what the right words and the right ceremonies were, because there was never any precedent for this kind of meeting.

But she moved to him at once and said, "I am grateful to you for coming, Your Majesty," and Fintan and Cermait exchanged smiles, because wasn't it as natural as breathing to the Wolfqueen to find the exact right words, and to show the exact correct degree of courtesy.

Grainne said carefully, "I have long wished to see you, Your Highness," and Aillen mac Midha smiled slightly as if he had expected this, and nodded as if he found it natural.

"We have never been far from you," he said. "In the first days of Tara, our Houses were inextricably bound. I am forsworn to serve you by the codes of that first Enchantment." The strange inhuman smile slid out again, and Grainne remembered that, after all, this was the creature who held sway over the cruel merciless *sidh*, and ruled over the sinister water caves, and regarded the world of Humans as a hunting ground.

He heard her thoughts without difficulty; he said, "We *do* regard Humans as our prey, but for the moment, we are bound with you against the Darkness," and Grainne thought, Of course! They are creatures of light, the *sidh*, and of course they will be against anything that has quenched Tara's brilliance! And thought that this was the nearest he would come to an outright declaration.

But he surprised her again: he said, "We are loyal to the True Line, ma'am," and looked at her, and somehow managed to convey amusement, as if he might be saying, You see? I am giving you the courtesy title of Royalty, although we both know that my House is immeasurably older than yours. And Grainne, who could never remember to be haughty about the Wolfline, no matter how proud she was of it, nodded, and thought that this was very likely the most remarkable conversation she would ever have with anyone, and that it was probably the most remarkable conversation anyone in the world could have.

Aillen mac Midha leaned forward and Grainne saw that his eyes were the colour of the sea on a summer afternoon. "You have brought back Ireland's lost people," he said. "You have discovered the ancient Lost Enchantment. For that alone, my people would serve you."

"Then your people will ride with us against Medoc and the Dark Lords?" said Grainne, and now her voice held a note of authority, so that several people looked up startled, and Tybion the Tusk was so proud of her that he wanted to run up and down the nearest mountain and shout to every living creature and draw every living soul's attention to her.

The Elven King was still studying Grainne. "We have been with you all along," he said. "For we are charged to spin the spell of protection about all who are born to the High Throne of Ireland. The first High Queen of all bargained with her own sorcerers to secure the spell, and although we fought to keep it, in the end we yielded."

From his place, Fintan said very softly, "The Battle of the Dawn Enchantment," and Aillen mac Midha turned his great, soulless eyes on Fintan.

"Yes," he said. "Yes, it was the Battle of the Dawn Enchantment, for the spell we can weave into our music was the first spell of them all. It was born when Tara was raised from the rock, and we have guarded it jealously." He looked back at Grainne. "But we yielded it to our long-ago ancestress, ma'am," he said, "and we have held by the bargain that was struck with her. When you came into the world, along with your ill-starred brother, we poured our enchanted music into Ireland for you. You do not know it, but that music has protected you many times now." He looked at her very directly, and Grainne held his look, and knew that he saw and understood far more than anyone had ever done. And then, without warning, he lifted one slender arm, and seemed to sprinkle something she could not quite see in the direction of the others. Grainne half turned her head, and glimpsed a thin shower of blue-green droplets, cascades of muted light, falling on the waiting Beastline and the Cruithin, and Fintan and Cermait and Tybion. She thought they blinked and Tybion put up a hand as if to ward something off, and Raynor seemed to move back as if a blow had been aimed at him.

Grainne said, "What—"

"The *Draoicht Suan*," said Aillen. "The gentle Enchantment of Slumber. They will sleep while we talk."

"Why have you done it?" Grainne was still looking to where the others were standing or sitting as they had fallen, the thin gleaming threads of the Enchantment all about them.

"They will take no harm." He looked at her. "But there are things you do not yet wish them to know." He stopped, and Grainne said nothing. "The boy is safe," said the Elven King, and Grainne felt the colour rush to her cheeks, and such a powerful wave of emotion engulfed her that she could only gasp.

"We have protected him," said Aillen mac Midha. "For he is Ireland's Prince, for all that you gave him up, Your Majesty. He has had our protection since we sang him into the world at his birth."

"I had no choice," said Grainne, but through her words there was a sudden singing in her heart, and a sudden soaring joy, because he was not dead, the boy was not dead, Fergus's son was alive and living, and perhaps one day she would find him . . . "I had no choice," she said again, but for a moment her vision had blurred, and she was back in that terrible night when they had taken the child, and her heart and her womb had ached, and mingled in with it had been the yearning for Fergus, her brother, whom she could never have . . . And, oh yes, the *sidh* had been there, she had heard their music, pouring into the chill night, and she had known that the child was in truth Ireland's heir, for the *sidh* only sang for the Wolfline.

The Lost Prince, the once and future King who would drive back the Dark Ireland for ever . . . Grainne stood very still and looked at the slender unearthly creature before her, and knew that he understood it all. He understood about the days when she had loved Fergus, and when she had learned the truth from Dierdriu, and lost Fergus for all time. He knew about the days and the nights and the weeks when she had ached and hurt and been more alone than she could have imagined possible; when she had had to see Fergus and the Court ladies, and when she had had to smile and seem not to mind, because she was Tara's heiress, she was the Crown Princess, and even if Fergus had not been her brother, they would never have let her have him . . .

The Elven King said, "Better by far to have lost your love in that way than to have lost him to another. You never lost his love." The huge eyes were steady. "But you knew that."

"Yes," said Grainne in a whisper. "Yes, I knew."

They looked at one another, and then the Elven King smiled and it was a smile so blindingly beautiful that Grainne blinked. "The boy is safe," he said, and already his form was blurring. "You will find him when the time is right for you to do so." And then, in a fading voice, "And we shall be with you when you ride on Medoc," he said. "I promise you that."

There was a sudden swift movement, a smudge of blue-green, the beating of iridescent wings on the edge of the forest, and Grainne heard Fintan behind her say, "Dear me, did we drop off for a few minutes? I hope I haven't missed anything."

THE *SIDH* WERE with them on their march to Folaim, which was to be their first overnight camp.

"Folaim," Aillen mac Midha had said, and there had been something unfathomable in his eyes. "A strange choice."

Grainne thought it was not really a strange choice, because Folaim was directly on their route to the valley where Tara lay. They had plotted the journey while they were still at the Grail Castle, and the Cruithin had helped. In fact, Grainne thought, now she came to think back, the Cruithin had been quite firm about Folaim being their first camp.

"A good place," they had said in their soft, courteous voices. "Your Majesty will do well to be there." And they had looked at her with their heads on one side, and they had smiled and nodded, but they had not said quite why Folaim ought to be their camp stop.

The *sidh* stayed with them. As Tybion said, you could not but be aware of them. They were in the air and in the night scents and they were occasionally to be glimpsed when the light changed.

"I *know* they are there," said Fintan crossly.

"We can't see them, of course," said Tybion.

"We don't want to see them," said Fintan, who would not have trusted a *sidh* from here to that tree and did not mind saying so. You had to be extremely wary of the *sidh*, said Fintan. Didn't they all know the stories of how the *sidh* would snatch a man's virility right from between his legs if the mood took them.

"But," said Tybion, who was finding all of this so marvellous that he could scarcely restrain himself, "but isn't it the most wonderful thing in the world that they've come to be with us?"

As to that, Fintan was as pleased as the next man. Of course he was. It was only that they must be wary, he said. To be sure, it was great altogether. And if the *sidh* were going to be with them in the battle, then they could be very hopeful indeed, said Fintan. But they would have to be careful, that was all, he said, and went off with Rinnal to discuss what they ought to do about supper that night, because you did not quite know what constituted good manners on these occasions, and nobody seemed to know if Aillen mac Midha should be asked to supper or not.

"But the *sidh* don't eat ordinary food," said Cermait, and Rinnal grinned and said, "I heard they ate the hearts and souls of Humans," and then looked horrified, because of the Conablaiche and the Lad of the Skins and Crom Croich.

"But he's right," said Fintan to Cermait. "They don't eat ordinary food."

"Then it's as well you didn't ask him to eat rabbit stew with us."

"He would probably have eaten our souls," said Fintan, and was put into such good humour at having imparted this macabre note to the proceedings that he went off quite happily to see could he coax a second helping of stew from Bec, whose turn it was to cook.

It was easy and pleasant and unexpectedly natural to sit with the others, about the fire that Rinnal had made, eating Bec's rabbit stew which turned out to be excellent. Grainne felt such a sense of contentment and kinship that she thought she would like the supper and the quiet talk afterwards to go on for ever.

The stew went round very well and there were wild

mushrooms in it and wood sorrel and sharp clean hazelnuts. "Everything I could find," said Bec, delighted at the others' enjoyment.

"It's very good indeed," said Fintan, eating his portion industriously.

"And there wouldn't have been anything like enough for Aillen mac Midha and the *sidh*," said Cermait. "Especially when people have three helpings."

"I didn't," said Fintan.

"I counted," said Cermait.

The stew in fact had gone round very well and there had been large helpings for everyone. "Even allowing for people who are greedy," said Cermait.

"Well, we didn't want any waste," said Fintan. "It attracts predators if you leave wasted food in the forest. Anyone knows that."

When the supper had been cleared away and the Cruithin had asked permission to light their pipes (which they were scrupulous about doing no matter the occasion), the *sidh* returned to the edge of the camp. Fintan said they came too close, but Cermait said that Fintan would have to put up with it. Several people said that it was rather restful to see the *sidh* drifting across the clearing and getting mixed in with the smoke from the Cruithin's clay pipes.

"And it is more than restful to hear the music," said Raynor, delighted. "I never thought to hear such music."

The music began slowly and gradually; one minute it was not there, and the next minute it was entirely there, so that you thought it had probably been there for quite a long while. It was not that it crept up on you, it was more that it was such a part of the forest and the twilight and the fire, that you did not immediately realise it was all about you.

It was almost as if it was music you could not quite hear. And then it was all about the camp, it was pouring into the centre, a great blue and green fountain, an icy waterfall of beauty and enchantment and old, old magic. Grainne thought afterwards that it was as if they had been fed a sleep drug, as if their eyelids had been streaked with the juice of poppies, with mandragora, the drowsy sleep drug, with the golden heavy honeydew of slumber . . .

The music poured into the clearing like a crystal river and, one by one, Grainne and the others slept, and in sleeping dreamed sweetly and well.

Aillen mac Midha stayed where he was on the edge of the clearing, because to have approached too closely would have been dangerous for the Humans. He could see, as Grainne had seen earlier, the gossamer threads of the ancient *Draoicht Suan*, the Enchantment of Slumber which his people had woven, and he could see, as well, within the threads, the other Enchantment, the spell that had been woven at the very beginning for the protection of Tara's Royal Wolfline. It was a slender, rather fragile spell, and it had not always kept the High Kings and Queens entirely safe. But the *sidh* had been charged to protect and weave it for every Prince of Tara ever born, and it had been woven at Grainne's birth, and again for the child whose birth had been so closely guarded that very few people in Ireland knew of it. But Aillen mac Midha knew, because it was not possible for a Wolfprince to be born without him sensing it.

The spell woven at Grainne's birth should have kept her safe from Medoc and the Dark Ireland, but Medoc was the most powerful necromancer ever known, and his sorcery had torn through the gentle, pure bewitchment.

The *sidh* would help Grainne and her people in the battle against Medoc; they would do all they could to protect her, but Aillen mac Midha did not know whether it would be sufficient to save her from what lay ahead.

LUGH OF THE LONGHAND, rounding the curve in the forest, came upon the sleeping High Queen and her small retinue, and thought it was just as he might have expected. You could not trust anyone to do anything these days. Here was Lugh, marching the army strongly and firmly through the forest on the way to Folaim, keeping a weather eye open for any enterprising enemies that might lurk, and what should they come upon but the Queen, Tara's High Queen, lying peacefully asleep with every person who should have been keeping watch asleep as well. Anyone might have crept up and committed all manner of crimes, well, hadn't Lugh himself been able to march right up to the clearing, and no one springing out to challenge him! It was an outrage and a disgrace if it was not a downright scandal, and Lugh did not know when he had been so shocked. He did not scruple to say so.

"I don't know when I have been so shocked," he said, tucking his chins in sadly. "I am saddened," he added, and then, on an inspiration, "*I* should not have allowed the High Queen to be so vulnerable," he said, and shook his head in deep sorrow, which Cathbad said was so false it did not bear thinking about.

"I'm afraid he's very false indeed," said Cathbad to Dorrainge, who was marshalling the men, even though this was not, properly speaking, Dorrainge's job. "I thought it days ago, and now I see it's right," said Cathbad, and Dorrainge, who had thought the same but was not going to admit it, and certainly not to Cathbad who was a shocking gossip, asked had Cathbad not better things to be doing than passing judgments on Her Majesty's soldiery.

"He's as false as a silk pig," said Cathbad, getting his pots and pans together and paying no attention to the people who said he was getting in the way, and wouldn't he help to knock in a tent peg or two, and hadn't they all enough to do without tripping over fat Druids who got in people's way everywhere? Cathbad paid this no heed, because he had a soul above tent pegs, and said he had *far* too much to be doing as it was. "Goodness me," he said, "I've the supper to be seeing to, and where should we be if the men were not fed? In a great deal of trouble, that's where we'd be," said Cathbad, and took himself off to ponder over the evening's repast, and wondered should he attempt a few nice little curd puffs, or would that be a touch too dainty?

Lugh had made a great deal of noise in setting up camp,

partly to discourage the shadow that had followed them, and partly to wake the Queen's people. He did not like the shadow, and while he was not especially worried about the Lad of the Skins himself, it was as well to remember he was out there.

The sleepers were lying all anyhow in the bracken, and Lugh stamped about the clearing loudly, because you could not set up camp with people asleep all over the forest floor, and you certainly could not do so when one of them was the High Queen. It was one thing to throw in your lot with Medoc (not that Lugh had done that precisely), but it was another to show discourtesy to the High Queen. Lugh would not have dreamed of committing a discourteous act if you had paid him, or not unless you had paid him a very great deal.

The sleepers were not pleased to see Lugh and the men.

"Because," said Fintan, "if there's one thing you wouldn't want to see when you wake, it's Lugh Longhand. My word, he doesn't improve with absence, does he?"

Tybion the Tusk could not understand why they had all fallen asleep in the first place, but Cermait said solemnly that it had been the *Draoicht Suan*. "That's what it'll have been," he said owlishly. "The *Draoicht Suan*."

"Rubbish," said Fintan.

"No, it isn't. If that wasn't the *Draoicht Suan*," said Cermait, "you may call me a goatbeard and have done."

"I shouldn't dream of being so rude," said Fintan, and went off to help Cathbad, who was quite flustered at having so many extra people to feed, and had abandoned the idea of curd puffs, and was contemplating a dish of mumbled rabbit, which nobody had ever heard of.

"Rich," said Cathbad worriedly, and shook his head over the necessity for procuring pimpernel or toadflax which, as everyone knew, greatly improved the flavour of mumbled rabbit.

Grainne had welcomed Lugh, but she was not as pleased to see him as it seemed. She asked about the plan of spying on Tara, and Lugh said, "Well, there was nothing to spy on, Your Majesty." He bowed. "There was nothing to see, and nothing to be found about the guards or the sentries."

"I see," said Grainne thoughtfully.

"In fact," said Lugh, "Tara was undefended." And he looked at her with an odd, sly glint, which Grainne found worrying, because Lugh was a great many irritating things, but sly had not, so far, been one of them.

But Lugh did not seem to be concealing anything, and Grainne could not think what there was for him to conceal.

"And," she said later to Raynor, "if Tara is undefended, then why do we need the army and your people at all?"

"Tara is not undefended," said Raynor.

"Can you know that?"

"Medoc is far cleverer than that," said Raynor, and frowned and then said, "How far do you trust Lugh?"

"I don't—" Grainne stopped and looked at him. "Do you think Lugh is a traitor?"

"I think," said Raynor, "that all Men have a vulnerable point, and that Medoc is very clever. That is all." He regarded her, and Grainne thought, Yes, of course he is right. I am far too trusting. And remembered that Medoc was certainly clever, and that he was subtle and cunning, and had the forces of the Dark Ireland at his beck.

She had made Raynor and the Beastline known to Lugh and the army with deliberate ceremony, because it was important that the Beastline were welcomed properly and given homage.

The men had seemed to accept them. They were wary but they were polite. It was almost as if they were saying, Well, we always knew that the old Enchantment had not really died. They welcomed the extra strength to the army, and said to be sure the more people you had on your side, the more chance you had of winning. They wanted to know about the Grail Castle, and they listened to the stories with interest, and made room for Raynor's people, and seemed altogether amiably disposed.

After supper, which was not mumbled rabbit in the end, but braised hare and pickled herrings, they eyed the animals a bit doubtfully, and said it would be grand to have them along, and it was to be hoped they could be kept under control.

"Raynor and the others control them," said Tybion, and Fintan said this was very likely true, but it was disconcerting to march along with a crowd of Eagles and Swans and Badgers and the like, all padding and fluttering and scurrying and barking at your back.

"And I don't trust the Eagles," said Fintan with deep suspicion.

Cermait started to say that the Eagles were loyal, and Fintan said, "It isn't their loyalty I'm worried about, it's their temper." Cermait laughed and told Fintan not to be ridiculous and to pass round the mulled wine. The soldiers, who had listened to this babble with enjoyment, said you never could trust an Eagle in peace-time, although they were great to have on your side in a battle, and wanted to know would the animals be sleeping separately from the Humans, because you heard some odd tales these days.

"*Quite* separate," said Dorrainge firmly, who had heard some of the tales himself, and was not going to have any of *that* kind of thing going on.

LUGH WAS PLANNING the morrow's movements. To a disinterested observer, it would probably have seemed that he was resting quietly on his pallet, and to an uncharitably minded person, it might even have appeared that he was avoiding helping with the work. In fact he was thinking very hard, and this was something you had to do in absolute quiet and absolute privacy. It was better if you could lie on your back as well.

He was deciding what they would do when they reached Folaim tomorrow. He thought it might be time to select an ally as well. Allies were good things to have, provided you chose them carefully. He dismissed any of the Beastline at once, because he had not, truth to tell, been very impressed by them. In fact he was inclined to think that Her Majesty had fallen in with a very doubtful set of creatures, and he hoped there would not be sorrow ahead because of it. And he dismissed Fintan and Cermait, and Tybion the Tusk, almost without thinking about them, because those three were really quite absurdly loyal to the Queen. Well, so was Lugh loyal to the Queen, only Fintan and the other two took it to a silly degree.

That left the Druids. Lugh considered the idea of Dorrainge and Cathbad very carefully, because Druids were people of importance, and anything they supported would be accepted.

On balance, Lugh was inclined to favour Dorrainge as his ally. Dorrainge was a bit suspicious by nature, but if he could somehow be brought on to Lugh's side without knowing it, it would be a very good thing indeed.

It should be Dorrainge. Lugh had considered Cathbad only briefly before dismissing him, because Cathbad, whilst an excellent person in his way, was also a terrible old gossip, and if there was one thing you could not be having in a confidential ally, it was a gossip.

So Lugh would somehow quell Dorrainge's suspicions and he would take him into his confidence, well it would not be entirely his confidence, because Dorrainge would not like the idea of carrying out a task for Medoc, even though it was for the good of Ireland. The thing would have to be wrapped up a bit.

Lugh linked his arms behind his head and frowned and disregarded the rest of the camp who were being very busy and extremely noisy and clattering pots and knocking in tent pegs and swilling mulled wine.

And then he had it. And really, it was quite brilliant, although no more brilliant than you would have expected from a Longhand. But it was so brilliant and so simple that it was a pity Lugh could not show everyone how very brilliant it was.

In exactly one week it would be Samain. The third of the four nights in the year when every evil force was abroad in the world, and when gateways were said to be ajar between all the worlds. Lugh did not believe any of this, but there was no denying that a good many people did.

The Druids believed. It was many years since they had been able to celebrate Samain properly; it was certainly a very long time since they had offered up a Human sacrifice as their predecessors had done. The Queen's great-grandfather, Cormac, had outlawed the practice, and the Druids had bowed their heads in obedience to his law. Gradually the old ways had died out, and Lugh thought it was probably fifty years since the Druidical fires had been lit for Samain or Beltane.

They would revive it. They would revive the ritual fire of Samain in Folaim, and they would invite everyone in the village to join in. And the children would surely come, for children loved a bonfire and a celebration.

And once the children were there, he, Lugh, would be able to spot the Wolfchild with ease.

GRAINNE THOUGHT THE sly glint was still in Lugh's eye when he approached her with his idea of reviving the ancient Samain celebration, and a warning note sounded somewhere on the edge of her mind.

"But it would be a very fine thing," said Dorrainge, who had been primed by Lugh earlier, and could not see any reason why they should not celebrate Samain properly, and who thought that it was rather kind of Lugh to be going to so much trouble.

"Would it?" said Grainne, frowning. "I am not sure—"

"Of course," said Lugh loudly, "it is *quite* unnecessary for Human sacrifice to form part of the rituals." He bowed as he said this, and Grainne said very sharply indeed, "I hope it *is*, Lugh," and Lugh looked deeply hurt, and said that Human sacrifice had not been practised in Ireland since he did not know when.

"The very idea," he said, shocked. "But it would be a wonderful thing if the Druids could be permitted to revive the old pure magic of Samain. It would be a wonderful thing for Your Majesty to be the one to revive it all."

Grainne looked at him rather coldly, and Raynor said gently, "But surely—Samain is one of the four nights in the year when evil is abroad. Some of the rituals are known to lure the evil ones closer."

"But," said Lugh, "surely the gentler bewitchments, the kindly spells . . ." He said this very respectfully, so that it was really rather rude of Fintan to remind everyone that the gentler bewitchments and the kindly spells had once upon a time stretched to including Human sacrifice on a bonfire.

"Human sacrifice has long since been seen for the empty mockery it is," said Dorrainge, who was not going to let their plan be upset by Fintan, who, after all, was nobody at all.

Grainne said wistfully, "I confess I should like to see some of the old rituals. And if there is to be a feast for the people of Folaim—"

"A very fine feast," said Lugh, who had already planned this with Cathbad.

"A feast," said Dorrainge, "and a properly laid bonfire, with the correct woods gathered at the correct times. Wild agaric and dry oak. That," said Dorrainge, "makes the new fire—needfire it is called."

Raynor said softly, "The wildfire of Samain," and Dorrainge said, "Well, yes," and thought it was all very well for Her Majesty to be consorting with these people, and to be sure the Eagles were an old and honourable House, and some kind of alliance would certainly be entirely in order, but it was to be hoped that people who had held authority at Court would still be allowed to do so. He eyed Raynor suspiciously, and Raynor smiled blandly at him.

"Wildfire," said Dorrainge, as if he had been about to say this, and Raynor said, "Quite," and Dorrainge reminded himself that he was Second Druid after all, and a person of some importance.

Grainne said, "It would be a wonderful thing for the Beastline to be part of the full Samain celebration. It would be a welcome for them." And paused, and frowned again, because Lugh still had the sly look in his eyes, and now there was a sudden fat complacent air to him, as if he might have achieved something he had been trying to achieve. But surely there could be nothing wrong about celebrating Samain in the old way, with a feast, and the people of Folaim invited?

And so Grainne quenched the misgivings, and smiled at Dorrainge and said, "Yes. Let us do it."

From the forest, the Lad of the Skins watched, unblinking as a cat.

Chapter Nineteen

As THEY WENT deeper into the mountain, Annabel could still hear the drumming of the hoofbeats somewhere over their heads.

"The Four Horsemen," said Fael-Inis, standing still and listening intently. "The Heralds. But I think they are not yet inside the mountain with us."

"Are they following us?" asked Annabel, who thought they would have enough to contend with without meeting the Horsemen.

Fael-Inis said slowly, "They are following me." He looked at them. "We have brushed before, the Horsemen and I," he said. "They serve one against whom I have fought before."

"The Apocalypse?" said Taliesin.

"It had a different name then," said Fael-Inis, and now it was the remote creature who had walked in other worlds and consorted with different beings. Neither Taliesin nor Annabel spoke and, after a moment, Fael-Inis seemed to give himself a shake. "Now," he said, "it is the Apocalypse we must outwit."

"Yes," said Annabel, and thought that on balance she would prefer the Conablaiche again.

Fael-Inis said, "Listen for the hoofbeats constantly. Gauge their distance. Only by doing that can we know how near they are. You understand?"

Taliesin said, "And the Conablaiche . . . ?"

"For the moment it has gone," said Fael-Inis, and smiled at them. "We shall hear that one approach," he said. "We shall smell it and sense it, and perhaps we shall again outrun it." He led them deeper along the tunnel. "Come now, both of you."

Annabel had expected to find the inside of the mountain dark and stuffy. She had thought it would smell of mould, and that there would be pale wriggling earth creatures. It had been one thing to visualise charging down a hillside, perhaps riding a horse (which she had never actually done), sweeping to victory, but it was another thing altogether to walk along in the dark like this, trying to penetrate the gloom.

The mountain was not especially dark. There were great echoing caverns, and huge crypts and rock tunnels; there were labyrinths and narrow passages, and once or twice they had to bend low to avoid hitting their heads on overhanging rocks. But there was a constant bluish light, and there was immense space, and it was very easy indeed to see their way.

Annabel, walking cautiously between Taliesin and Fael-Inis, began to find it exhilarating, and began to think ahead to what they were going to find.

The torchlit Cavern of the Domesday Clock . . .

They were going to save the world.

This was such a tremendously uplifting idea that Annabel began almost to enjoy the entire peculiar journey. She certainly began to find the mountain fascinating.

But the hoofbeats were still over their heads, and the memory of the Conablaiche was still very fresh, and Annabel shuddered, and tried not to think too much about either of these things, and was very glad that Taliesin and Fael-Inis were there. And then she remembered that if it had not been for Taliesin and Fael-Inis, she would not have made this journey anyway, and saw the absurdity.

It was warm inside the mountain, and although there was a feeling of great space, there was also a tremendous oppressiveness. Their footsteps echoed and the smallest whisper bounced off the walls and reverberated all about them, and all the time there was the knowledge of the hundreds of tons of rock directly over their heads. Annabel found it terrifying and awe-inspiring, and hoped they would not miss anything unexpected, and hoped they would not miss their footing anywhere either, because there were narrow rock bridges over which they had to pass, and there were underground rivers which flowed silently and rather horridly beneath their feet. If you fell into one of the rivers, you would be swept away before you could be saved. You would be taken away, down to the mountain's bowels, and you would never survive, and it would be the nastiest death ... There was something particularly frightening about the thought of the black sluggish rivers and the still lakes where strange creatures might lurk. There was something very sinister about great volumes of stagnant water. You never knew what might lie below the surface.

It was not as dark as they had feared. "Starlight," said Fael-Inis. "It is spilling in through the chinks in the mountain."

The starlight was soft but rather eerie. It disturbed the shadows and showed you things you did not want to see, and that you were probably better not knowing about. Annabel had been treading carefully, because there might be all manner of things on the floor, and she thought she would not look down, because she had the really dreadful suspicion that they were walking on small bones. The bones were very small indeed, and there was a dreadful *dryness* about them, a twig-like feeling, as if the bones had shrivelled where they lay for a very long time.

Marrowless bones ... sharp hollow bones, sucked dry by the creatures who prowl these dark mountain halls ...

Stop it! said Annabel to herself, very fiercely.

It would be much more sensible to think about what they were doing, and about what might be ahead. Annabel concentrated hard on this, and tried not to think about the Guardians who might be lying in wait somewhere, and tried as well to listen for the hoofbeats, which might mean the Horsemen were close behind them.

Fael-Inis said, "They are not so very close yet," and Annabel jumped, because for the minute she had forgotten Fael-

Inis's disconcerting habit of hearing people's thoughts. She said, "What will they do if they catch us?" and Fael-Inis said at once, "They will try to kill us."

"Oh."

"They are sworn to bring their Master, the Apocalypse, into the world," said Fael-Inis. "They will certainly destroy anything that threatens to prevent that." He looked at them. "We have to outrun the Horsemen, Mortals, and also we have to outwit any more Drakon patrols." His eyes glowed unexpectedly. "And then," he said softly, "we have to face the Guardians," and the other two saw mischievous delight in his eyes, and shared a thought: He is looking forward to facing the Guardians! Taliesin, who had been concentrating on thinking what they would do if they met any more patrols, stopped and looked round.

"Do the Guardians exist?" he said. "Or are they only creations of a disordered mind?" The old mocking grin slid out. "Are they perhaps simply visions, filled with sound and fury, signifying nothing?" said Taliesin.

Fael-Inis looked at Annabel, as if he might be saying, After all, my dear, this is your world. I know about the Guardians, but you tell us. Aloud, he said, "Shall we rest? The Horsemen are still quite distant. And we have a way to go yet."

"How do you know that?" said Annabel.

"You know it also, Mortal," said Fael-Inis, studying her. "You have perceptions that are more finely honed than most of your race," he said, and Annabel felt pleased, because Fael-Inis would have met with a great many different people and creatures, and would not make this sort of comment lightly. It was an odd sort of compliment, but it was rather nice. She sat on the floor, because there was no where else to sit, and leaned back against the rockface, and looked at him expectantly.

Taliesin, who had been unpacking their small store of food, said, "Tell us about the Guardians, Annabel," and Annabel frowned, and tried to gather up all the tag ends and the snippets of legend, and the untidy fragments of myth, and roll them into some kind of sensible whole. She accepted a wedge of bread and cheese from Taliesin, and said carefully, "A little is known about the Guardians, but it is not very much. Some of it is probably myth, and some is certainly conjecture, and most people do not believe any of it really." And stopped, and took a mouthful of bread and cheese, and wondered whether people really did not believe, or whether they only pretended.

Fael-Inis said, "In all myths there is always a grain of truth. That is how myths are built." He looked at them steadily. "Perhaps I am nothing more than a myth," said the rebel angel softly. "But, as you see, I am here. I have an existence and a reality. We are making this strange perilous journey together."

Annabel said, "Yes. I see." And wondered if she did. She regarded the remains of the bread and cheese, and accepted the apple that Taliesin handed out, and wished she could put off telling the little she knew a bit longer.

"My people do not believe very much in legends," she said at last. "Although I think they once did. Once legends and myths and folklore were a delight to them."

"To you also," said Taliesin, watching her, and seeing how her face had grown rather wistful.

"Yes," said Annabel, looking at him, and seeing that he understood, and experiencing the sudden jolt of delight again, because she had thought that there would never be anyone who *did* understand. "But it was all a long time ago," she said, pulling her mind back to the matter in hand. "And there have been so many other things . . . Enchantments have been crowded out," said Annabel apologetically.

"But something lingered?" said Taliesin, thinking he could watch her face for ever, and thinking that he had never seen eyes change colour in quite this way.

"Yes. Fragments of myth. Queer stories. Memories.

Whispered beliefs, handed down through families. I suppose," said Annabel thoughtfully, "that is how the real stuff of legends is made and preserved."

"Of course," said Fael-Inis. "If you had not believed in me—even a little—do you think I could be here?"

"I—am not sure," said Annabel, and he laughed.

"No matter. Go on."

"In the main," said Annabel, "we are a practical race, you see. Our lives are built around possessions and machines, and the struggle to find new inventions and new power and different sources of energy and force. I suppose it is all necessary," said Annabel, "because once you have had these things, and are in danger of losing them, you do not give them up easily." She looked at the other two. "It is all very boring," she said, and the sudden smile flashed.

"The legend of the Fire Mountains is a very old one," said Annabel, returning to her story. "There are labyrinths and underground rivers here. In the past, people used to journey here, to try and reach the mountain's heart. Many people made the attempt," said Annabel, her eyes huge and faraway, "but I do not think that any single person ever returned. It was thought that they lost themselves for ever in the dark, or were killed by creatures that dwelled here."

"That will not happen to us," said Fael-Inis, and Annabel felt safe again.

"The labyrinths stretch for many miles," she said. "One of the stories tells of how if you go deep enough and far enough, you will come to the great and terrible River of Souls. Once there, you will have to face the Ferryman, who is ever on the look-out for Human souls." Annabel looked at them. "No one really believes that," she said.

"Nevertheless," said Fael-Inis, "the River exists."

"Within these mountains?"

"Yes. There are doorways between this world and other worlds," said Fael-Inis. "And there are many worlds, and there will be many worlds yet. The worlds rarely converge, for to do so would mean confusion and chaos, and those are things reserved for the ending of worlds." He looked at them both. "But there are gateways," he said. "Tears in the Curtain of Time, through which people sometimes struggle, or fall, or slip. Sometimes it is deliberate and sometimes it is not."

Annabel said carefully, "Is that how you come to be here?" and Fael-Inis turned his golden stare on her.

"There are places in the Curtain of Time where the fabric is thin," he said, and it seemed to the other two that he was speaking with extreme care. "And therefore there are places where it is possible to go through from one world to another." He glanced at Taliesin. "But your world knows of the Time Travellers."

"Yes." But Taliesin was thinking: Places where the fabric is thin, and where it is possible to go through . . . And knew that Fael-Inis was remembering Calatin's spell, and how it would endure only for seven days, and how, after that, there would be no protection for him from the Time Fire. And how there was no spell at all for Annabel.

"The River of Souls is a chink in Time," said Fael-Inis. "It is one of the oldest gateways." He frowned. "But to venture into it is to pass into the Ferryman's domain, and that is the most dangerous journey that ever Man can take." The smile glinted. "You can believe it or not, just as you like. But there are images, engravings on the walls of caves, of foolhardy Humans who embark on the River in frail crafts, and whose souls are dragged, screaming and in agony, into the deep, dark waters by the Ferryman." He looked at them very intently, and Taliesin thought, He is trying to tell us that we may have to take that way back to the world we have come from.

"It is as well," said Fael-Inis gently, "to know the dangers we may have to face."

"Yes," said Annabel, and wondered whether she was understanding any of this. Might it be possible to get into their world from this one through the River of Souls? Annabel, who had never quite lost the images conveyed to her by Fael-

Inis of a misty blue and green world peopled with creatures of myth and legend, thought it would certainly be worth facing the Ferryman. Wouldn't it? *And I should be in Taliesin's world,* said her mind with delight. But they were waiting for her to tell what she knew about the Fire Mountains and the Cavern of the Domesday Clock, and so she reseated herself on the jutting ledge of rock, and tried to remember everything she knew.

"It is not so very much," she said. "And it is only because my work was with the Institute of Knowledge. I had access to things which most people did not have," she said, and grinned, and knew they were both understanding about how she had peeped into forbidden chronicles, and read secret files, and seen carefully guarded information.

"The Cavern was carefully chosen," said Annabel, after a moment. "That is very clear. They considered many other places before deciding on these mountains. It was thought of vital importance to keep the Clock from prying eyes, you see. And perhaps," she said, considering, "it was also thought better for people not to be reminded of the Clock's existence. It was certainly thought better for it to be hidden, so that people could not see the hands moving steadily towards midnight, and could not hear the relentless ticking away of the world's last days. That would have caused immense distress, you see," said Annabel. "They would have started to count. And although the Drakon is arbitrary and tyrannical," said Annabel seriously, "I do think that for this once, it was right."

Taliesin nodded. You could not have half the world's population counting the hours left to them. You could not risk the panic and the distress and the breakdown of civilised life.

"The Cavern is believed to be at the very heart of this mountain," said Annabel. "And it can only be approached by a series of three outer Caverns." She paused. "We believe that the Drakon people have another means of entry," she said, "but the only known way is through the three outer caves. Each cave has its own door, massive and solid and immovable, and hewn from hundreds of tons of solid rock. In each door is a giant lock, and to each lock is a key. And in each of the outer Caverns," said Annabel, "one of the Guardians waits." She looked at Fael-Inis. "I do not know so very much about them," she said, "and what I do is all a mixture of conjecture and gossip." She waited, for surely Fael-Inis would know of the Guardians. If, said Annabel, to herself, they truly exist.

"They do exist," said Fael-Inis, and his expression was serious. "They are a trio of three sorceresses, and they will guard anything anywhere in the world so long as they are paid enough." A brief smile touched his lips. "They are the most venal of all the enchantresses," he said. "They are extremely mercenary."

Annabel started to say something and then stopped, and Fael-Inis looked at her.

Annabel said, "It is only—at some time in my people's history, there were soldiers of fortune who would work and fight for any master. They called them mercenaries."

"Yes," said Fael-Inis thoughtfully, "that describes these three. They are certainly sorceresses of fortune. They are not necessarily bad, but they will turn their powers in whichever direction seems most profitable to them." He paused. "Medoc has used them many times," he said.

"Are they Human?" asked Annabel, and thought it an indication of how absorbed she was becoming in this strange adventure that she could pose a question like this so entirely naturally.

"No sorcerer, no enchanter, is ever wholly Human," said Fael-Inis, and Annabel shivered, because while it had been all very well to read and dream about half-Human creatures in the world she had left, and about creatures who were not Human at all, down here, in the dark old mountain, it was rather different. "Each must have a vein of the ancient magical Amaranth blood," said Fael-Inis. "But over the ages, for many of them, that blood has been mingled with that of the Dark Ireland, and become tainted." He glanced at Annabel, and the mischief lit his eyes. "The females of the Amaranth line are frequently at the mercy of their emotions," he said. "They are seductresses, but they were not always good judges of their lovers." He regarded her and appeared to wait, and Annabel said, rather vehemently, "I don't see that it is only females who misjudge—" And stopped, and saw the amusement in his expression, and grinned a bit sheepishly.

"*Humans,*" said Fael-Inis, his tone serious, his eyes brimful of laughter, "are *much* better at choosing partners. And of the three we are about to meet, there is one who—" He stopped, and shook his head. "But you must see it for yourself," he said.

Taliesin said cautiously, "You know these three we are about to meet?"

"Yes, I know them. I have faced them, and so far I have always been the victor," said Fael-Inis. "When the First Battle of all raged, some of the lesser servants of the Light-Bringer summoned them. They did not add greatly to the Light-Bringer's armies," he said thoughtfully, "but still, they are a force to be treated with care."

He leaned back against the rockface. "The first one we shall meet is Uathach, sometimes called Spectre," he said. "She is the lesser of the three, but she is still a force to be counted. She is wraithlike and grey, and she is sometimes known as Hunger and Thirst, for she will fasten onto your flesh and drink your blood, and then toss the dried-out bones into the mountain chasms far below. She has many names— Sigh, Sough, Storm, Winter-Night, Wail, Groan. She is also sometimes known as Despair, for that," said Fael-Inis, "is the coldest and the deadliest of all Human emotions. We shall have to enter her cave first," said Fael-Inis, "and to do so will be to encounter all the terrors of a howling storm on the darkest night of winter.

"The second of the Guardians is Aife, which means Reflection," said Fael-Inis, and unexpectedly, a mischievous smile touched his lips. "She is very well known to me, that one," he said. "She wears a Cloak of Nightmares which she once stole from a High Queen of Ireland, and it is that which gives her her strongest weapon."

Annabel asked how a Cloak of Nightmares worked, and Fael-Inis said, "Once, the Cloak of Nightmares was Ireland's greatest treasure. It was woven by the Sorcerers of Tara—that is, the *good* sorcerers," he said, "for the first High Queen of all."

Taliesin said softly, "The Human Queen," and Fael-Inis sent him a sharp look, and then said, "I see you know the history of the land of your adoption, my friend.

"But yes, she was the only Human ever to rule Ireland, and it was for her that the Sorcerers wove the Enchanted Nightcloak. It is said that its power fades unless a pure-bred Human wears it," he said.

"Then—"

"Reflection is partly Human," said Fael-Inis, and it seemed to the other two that he frowned slightly. "It is something she is a little ashamed of, that vein of Human blood, but it would certainly have enabled her to wear the Nightcloak of the High Queen to some effect."

"Will it endanger us?" asked Taliesin.

"I cannot say. The Nightcloak has disappeared several times in Ireland's history, and it has been used for good and also for great evil. For the moment, it is in the hands of Reflection, who will certainly use it as much as she can to outwit us." He looked at them. "With the Cloak's help, Reflection can summon up the nightmares of those who challenge her," he said. "She can make those nightmares live. The nightmares will not hurt us," said Fael-Inis seriously, "but the danger will be in telling the nightmares from the reality. And she can sometimes be very subtle," he said, but the grin was still there, and Taliesin and Annabel both received the feeling that Fael-Inis knew Reflection very well indeed, and in fact rather liked her. "You will have to trust me absolutely when we are in Aife's cave," said Fael-Inis.

"And you will have to keep it firmly in your mind that the creatures and the torments she may summon are nothing other than your own nightmares. Also, we must on no account become separated, for, in that way, we can perhaps help one another. She is only Second Guardian and not Third, although she would dearly like to be Third, of course."

"And the Third Guardian?" said Taliesin, and at once Fael-Inis's eyes grew serious. He fell silent, and at length Annabel said cautiously, "It is said—in my world—that it is the Third Guardian who is the most terrible of the three."

"Yes," said Fael-Inis. "Yes, she is very powerful indeed. She has rarely fought on the side of what we would call justice, for she prefers to deal with the creatures of the Dark Ireland. She is a very powerful adversary, that one."

"They call her the Sensleibhe," said Annabel, "and although I have not much Gaelic, I think that means—"

"The Old Woman of the Mountains," said Fael-Inis. "She is a very much more serious foe than the other two, that one, for it is said that she is ageless and deathless, and she is cunning and greedy and clever."

"Our stories say very little about her," said Annabel, "only her name. But I believe she is the most feared."

"Oh, yes," said Fael-Inis. "Oh, yes, she is by far the worst. She it is who controls the trio, and she it is who decides which tasks they will agree to." He studied them. "We shall defeat Spectre if we are strong," he said, "and we shall defeat Reflection if we are clever. But the Sensleibhe has never yet been defeated."

Taliesin said, "But—"

"Of course," said Fael-Inis, "she has never yet been challenged by me." And the mocking smile lifted his face and his eyes flared with the old mischief, and Taliesin and Annabel felt a little cheered.

"We should go on," said Fael-Inis, standing up. "The Horsemen are nearer than they were." He held out a hand to each of them. "We have no time to lose," he said.

But his eyes were bright, and the smile was the one that said, Let us challenge these ridiculous creatures and show them up for what they are! Let us march openly into this strange secret land and tumble it about!

"Let us go straight into the Three Caverns and save the world," said Fael-Inis.

IT SEEMED TO Taliesin that the further they went, the clearer the light became. And there seemed to be an easier way now through the passageways and across the stone bridges. At times they had to bend down to pass beneath low-roofed caves, and sometimes they had to crawl on all fours.

"Undignified," said Taliesin with a lift of one eyebrow. "That I should live to see a Tyrian brought so low!"

"If you will just duck your head," said Annabel practically, "it is possible that you will avoid being knocked senseless by that overhang of rock."

"My senses are as unravished as the quiet waters of the ... You are quite right," said Taliesin. "There was an overhang of rock." And grinned, and said, "I wonder have you noticed how there is always a way through somehow? They say that the road to hell is as easy. Shall we ever find that out or shall we perish down here among the— Is that water I hear?"

"Yes," said Annabel, stopping to listen.

"The River of Souls?"

"No," said Fael-Inis. "You will know when we reach that."

There were great silver-blue chambers with soaring pillars of some kind of stone, and crystal caves where the steady drip of water had formed into stalactites and stalagmites of such breathtaking size and of such uncanny beauty that Annabel gasped.

Once they passed under a natural arch of stone which seemed to be made up of leering faces.

"But it is only the rock formation again," said Taliesin. And then, in a different voice, "Or is it?"

Fael-Inis said, "Not altogether," and they both turned to look at him. "We are entering Spectre's domain," he said, very softly.

"And the Horsemen are nearer?" asked Taliesin.

"Inside the mountain?" asked Annabel.

"Yes," said Fael-Inis.

THEY WERE ALMOST running now, headlong down the tunnel in front of them, and all about them were strange scuttling sounds, as if tiny ratlike creatures ran with them. "But we have not seen anything yet," said Annabel, who did not want to see anything at all.

Taliesin caught, more than once, the red gleam of eyes from the shadows, and he thought that they were in truth being watched now.

The path led down, a steady decline. "Towards the mountain's heart," said Fael-Inis, leading the way.

"And from every world there is a path to the fires below," murmured Taliesin. "We shall go down and down until we reach the everlasting Gates that lead to . . . I suppose this is the way?"

"Can you see another?"

"No. Onwards then. Down, down into the bowels of hell and say I sent thee thither. Into the marble heart of the mountain and into the vasty deep of a strange and secret country. I have never visited it before, and yet I am as certain of the spot as if a chart had been bestowed—I am talking nonsense, you understand, but it is better than listening to the crawling rodents, and it is infinitely better than counting the hoofbeats. I suppose the Guardians will know of our approach?"

The Keeper of the First Cavern. Uathach. Spectre, who is also Hunger and Thirst and the howling night winds . . .

The passage was winding downwards more sharply now in a steady slope, and they were surrounded on all sides by the mountain. Annabel thought it was getting colder, and then was not sure if that was right. The light was still with

them, only it was a colder light, a light without colour ...
it was the sort of light you might see if you woke up in
the hour before a winter dawn and peered through your
window.

*Because I am winter night and I am freezing dawn, and I
am gale and blizzard ...*

And then they rounded a sharp curve in the passage and
there ahead of them lay, "The first of the Caverns," said
Fael-Inis.

In front of them was a massive door hewn into the rock,
and a great iron lock.

And a figure guarding it ...

THERE WAS NO need for Fael-Inis to send out his silent command: *"Caution!"*

Taliesin and Annabel had slowed their footsteps almost
to a stop, and were moving very stealthily indeed.

"We are walking on eggshells," said Taliesin in a whisper
to Annabel. "We are walking on spun glass, on paper-thin
ice. One false step and we may all be plunged into eternal
darkness."

*For this is Uathach, the creature who is Hunger and Thirst,
and who is the dark howling winds of the night ...*

Spectre did not move as they drew near. She stood
watching them from a ledge of rock a little to the left of the
door, a creature of grey shadows and icicle fingers and sharp
pointed nose. Annabel sought for, and found, the word *ravaged.* Uathach was ravaged by her own hungers and her own
thirsts, and by the cold and the storm. And then, But surely
we can find a weakness in her, she thought.

They could see the door quite clearly; a massive outline
carved into the mountain, the outline traced by a thin line
of light, as if once through it you would find yourself in a
brightly lit place. And if only we can get through it, thought
Annabel. Oh, if only we can. Never mind the other two
Guardians yet, let us first defeat this one.

When Spectre finally spoke, Annabel felt her skin prickle,

for she had not expected quite such a cold voice, and she had not expected such desolation. Spectre's voice was the voice of the endless winter night; it was hoar frost and shivering dawn, and shoreless seas, and lowering clouds. It was tears and it was the eaves dripping with night's rain in a cold, lonely house. Stop it! thought Annabel sharply.

"You have come far, travellers," said Spectre, and Annabel gasped, because somehow she had not expected such ordinary speech. "You have come far," said the figure in front of them, and waited and did not move.

Fael-Inis said, in a voice from which all expression had vanished, "We seek the adventure of the mountain Cavern, Lady," and Spectre laughed. Without warning, the quest seemed an impossible quest, and the mountain seemed to darken and close round them.

And that is what Spectre wants! came the thought.

"We seek entry into the inmost Cavern, Lady," said Fael-Inis.

"Many seek it, Mortal, but few gain it. None return to the outside world to tell of it."

Taliesin was wondering how Fael-Inis liked being called "Mortal" and Annabel was thinking that Spectre was not quite what she had been imagining, when Fael-Inis laughed, and leapt on to the narrow rock ledge beside Spectre's thin form.

"Let us have done with pretence," he said. "You know me for what I am, Madam, as I know you. You are Hunger and Thirst and the long desolate nights of winter. I am what you know me to be." Light streamed from him, and Annabel thought, I believe that the thing he hates above all others is pretence and hypocrisy.

Spectre regarded Fael-Inis. "We have met," she said, and Fael-Inis laughed again.

"Yes, we have met, Lady, although I did not know if you would remember."

"I was there," said Spectre softly. "Do you not recall that I was there, Fael-Inis? The First Great Battle of the

World? The Battle that is carved into the history of mankind
for ever more. You misjudge me when you say I do not
remember that."

"Your part was a lesser part."

"But you played no part at all," said Spectre, and seemed
suddenly to grow in stature and tower above them, her
shadow sending fantastic shapes dancing and flickering on the
cavern walls. She leaned closer. "But I was there, Fael-Inis. I
saw the heavens weeping in torment, and I saw the great
armies of Lucifer the Light-Bringer storm heaven's gates. I
felt the dreadful agony of the skies bleeding, and the anguish
of Man being cast out of that which should have been his,
and which he must for evermore travail and suffer to regain."
She studied Fael-Inis; the other two might not have been
there. From the corner of her eyes, Annabel saw Taliesin
begin to inch closer. "I saw all of it," said Spectre, and it
seemed to Annabel that Fael-Inis moved a little, so that Spectre was turned away from Taliesin's wary progress.

Fael-Inis said, "It was a worthless battle, that. It was
doomed. The Light-Bringer should have known he would
never succeed."

Spectre said, "It is the one thing I remember, Fael-Inis.
That you played no part in it. You walked away from it, but
before you did, you stood watching for a long, long while."
Her eyes were fixed on him, and Annabel held her breath.
"Have you really forgotten?" said Spectre softly.

"Let us say that I have." The golden eyes were glowing,
and Annabel thought that Fael-Inis was calling down some
kind of power to keep Spectre's attention. "Remind me,"
said Fael-Inis coaxingly.

"You would take no part," said Spectre. "When the
Light-Bringer was mustering his armies, when the rest of us
were banding together, to follow one side or another, you
stood back and declined every offer made to you.

"And at the end, when Lucifer's creatures were pouring
down on heaven's armies, when the skies were stained red
with the pity and the pain of it, you simply stood back and

watched, and there was mockery and disdain in your face. You stood bathed in the red light of the battle, and you would take no part, even though your participation might have swayed the fight one way or another."

"But the fight still goes on," said Fael-Inis. "It always will."

"You were arrogant and defiant," said Spectre. "You were the creature of music and fire and speed, who declared for neither side, and who elected to walk out alone into the cold world of Men." She was standing very close to him, and Annabel saw that Taliesin had nearly reached her side.

"Did you fear Lucifer?" said Spectre. "Or was it the One against whom Lucifer fought? I have often wondered that. I have carried that image of you with me for so long now; proud, haughty, choosing the cold alien world of the Humans when you might have had so much. You might have turned the tide of the battle, had you wished. But you knew that, of course."

"Of course," said Fael-Inis silkily.

"Do you know what is said of you now, Fael-Inis?" said Spectre. "That it was cowardice that drove you from the battle. That it was lack of courage and lack of strength that sent you down into the world of Men. Does that hurt, Fael-Inis?"

"Not the very least bit," said Fael-Inis, and smiled.

"And so, rebel angel, you would walk into the Cavern of the Domesday Clock, would you?"

"I would."

"You know that to do so, you must win the key of each of the doors from each of the Guardians?"

"I know."

"Are we really to do battle this time, you and I?" said Spectre, and Fael-Inis laughed again.

"I do not fear you," he said, "even though I know all your names. I know that you are Hunger and Thirst and Nightwind and Storm and Tempest."

"And Despair," said Spectre. "The greatest threat of

them all. You know as well as I that when a Human succumbs to Despair, then he is truly lost, once and for all. To despair," said Spectre, "to abandon all hope of everything." The thin grey smile touched her lips. "Let me show you," said Spectre. "Let me show you true Despair, Mortal. Let me show you your poor doomed world. Do you really think you can enter the torchlit cavern and halt the Domesday Clock? Poor futile creatures! You will never do it! Even now, the Horsemen are hard on your heels, they are making their way through the mountain tunnels and the caverns, and very soon they will be upon you. But before they are, let me show you what is ahead.

"Your world is hurtling to destruction. Soon it will be a dead world, a cold empty thing, rolling silently through the wastes of the night. Your race is nearly ended, and all your history and all your struggles and your fine achievements and your vanities will be for naught. See, I will show you what is ahead." And she stepped back and raised her hands, and at once a terrible moaning wind whipped round the cave, so that Annabel gasped and put up her hands. Taliesin pulled her into the shelter of the rockface, and they stood, clinging together, trying to shield themselves from the force.

"See!" cried Spectre, her hands flung outwards, the thin grey cloak swirling about her, her hair writhing about her head as if it was alive. "See the ending of your world!"

And there before them, was the terrible final upheaval. The world dying; sheets of fire, great torrents of rain, boiling seas. People—thousands of them—running frenziedly, screaming, clutching, holding their hands upwards imploringly . . . And then there were empty plains, cities reduced to rubble, smoking ruins. Here and there was a movement; skeletal hands reaching out, the scuttling of rats beneath the rags of the dead and dying. Men fighting one another, wild-eyed, for a mouthful of bread or a sip of water . . .

Everything gone, everything dead, mankind shrivelled and all of the world's achievements, all of the world's careful work, burned up and blown away in the charred ruins of a dead world . . .

Annabel gasped and thrust her fist into her mouth to stop herself crying out, because although she had known—they had all known—what it would be like at the end, still they had tried to pretend it would never happen.

"And there!" cried Spectre, turning again. "There is the creature you have so long awaited!"

An immense shadow fell over the cave, and a great darkness descended. Annabel felt Taliesin's hands close warmly about hers, and drew in a great shuddering breath, because there was something worse, Spectre was summoning up something so vast and so terrible that even though none of it was real, it could not possibly be real, there was the feeling of something unstoppable and immense, something that would gobble up the world and spit it out, something that would tear mankind into fragments and toss the pieces into the dark, swirling universe . . .

Taliesin said in a voice from which the breath had been almost driven out, "The Apocalypse . . ."

There was the image of a clear horizon now, of cliffs and a swirling, boiling sea. And then gradually, little by little, the colour of the sky changed, it became suffused with red, as if a great furnace was bellowing out heat. The clear skies began to heave and pant; threads of fire trickled and seeped out . . . Annabel thought in horror: the skies are bleeding, and then there was a great wrenching, and a tearing sound, and blood and gore spewed forth from the skies, and the skies themselves parted, and there, standing looking at them, was the Beast, the Apocalypse, the Armageddon; a hundred feet high, grinning and slavering, red-eyed with greed, spiny-backed and gristly-jointed, cloven-footed and horned and insatiable, triumph and bloodlust and demonic strength pouring from it . . . Ready to eat the world . . .

And then just as Annabel was thinking she could not bear it any longer, and that the Creature would reach for them at any minute, Fael-Inis shot from his ledge, a pouring arrow of light, and fell on Spectre, knocking her to the ground. Spectre let out a screech of fury, and at once the terrible visions vanished, and there were only the two of them, rolling over and over on the cave floor, fighting for possession of the great silver key,

Taliesin had left Annabel's side, and was standing ready to pounce, but the two combatants moved so swiftly that he could not judge his moment.

And then Fael-Inis suddenly sprang away and lifted his hand with the key gleaming in it, and Taliesin grabbed Annabel and the three of them fell against the locked door.

Fael-Inis thrust the key home, and as they fell through the door, they each heard the hoofbeats thudding down the mountain tunnel behind them.

CHAPTER
TWENTY

ANNABEL OPENED HER eyes and thought that this was the worst yet. Of all the strange, frightening, unexpected things that had happened so far, this was the strangest and the most frightening and certainly the most unexpected.

She had seen, quite clearly, the door of the cavern swing open. "Then has Fael-Inis somehow got the key?" she had wanted to say, only there had been no time. The hoofbeats had been thundering down the corridor, and Annabel thought that Taliesin had cried out that the Horsemen were almost upon them, and Fael-Inis had sprung on Spectre, an arrow of light, fire, and speed all blended together, and Taliesin had been half pulling, half dragging Annabel towards the Cavern door, and the last thing she had seen was Spectre going down beneath Fael-Inis's assault, a whirling, biting, clawing creature, shrieking her rage, calling up tempest and flood and fire . . .

Riding the whirlwind and directing the storm . . . Yes!

There had been an instant confused impression of the most tremendous tempest; of boiling seas and walls of fire, and of massing purple clouds . . . *And of scolding winds that will rive the knotty oaks and tempest dropping fire, and the groans of roaring wind and rain* . . . *the last agonies of a dying world struggling for life* . . .

There had been fear and panic and a driving urgency. Run, run, for the Horsemen are almost here; the Heralds who will precede the coming of the Apocalypse are hard on our heels, they are within the mountain, they are riding full tilt down the caves and through the tunnels, they are fording the rivers and, in another minute, in just another minute, they will be upon us, and they have sworn to destroy us, and if that is allowed to happen, all will be lost and we shall be lost and the world will burn . . .

And then the great door had swung open and Annabel had tumbled through.

It was darker than she would have believed possible. It was so dark that she could not see even the outline of her hand when she held it up before her face.

This is absolutely ridiculous, said Annabel, and discovered that she had said this aloud, and that her voice had echoed rather horridly all about her as if she was quite alone. This was absurd, because they had all fallen through the locked door, and at any minute she would find Taliesin and Fael-Inis.

The Horsemen had been quite close. Annabel had heard them, distinctly, thudding down the tunnels in pursuit. She stood very still and listened hard, but there was no longer any sound of them. This did not mean they could be forgotten, of course. But for the moment there were other things to be thought of. Finding the other two. Trying to make some kind of light. Finding the way to the Second Cavern.

This was more cheering than she had expected, because it was a plan, and a plan would be a good thing to have. It would be something to follow and something to hold on to. It may not be a very good plan, thought Annabel, but it *is* a plan. It was unthinkable that she should stay here like this, waiting for something to happen. The only way that something would happen was if she made it happen.

It was important not to panic. She could feel her way along the tunnel; she could go hand over hand like this, and sooner or later she would be certain to get *somewhere*. She would not have to mind about the dark, and she would not have to think about the weight of the mountain above her. I'll do it somehow, thought Annabel, beginning the cautious journey. Somehow I'll find my way to where there is more light, and then I shall have achieved something, and then I'll think what I ought to do next.

There were scuttling noises in the dark; tiny, clawing, scurrying rodent noises. They would have been very nasty in any circumstances, but down here, half buried in the mountain, and in the pitch dark, they were more revolting than anything Annabel had ever imagined. Something brushed against her foot and slid away into the darkness, and Annabel drew back sharply. But the something was still there; it was soft and cold and sinuous, and—I hope it isn't a rat or a snake, thought Annabel. I think I can cope really quite well so long as there aren't rats or snakes.

She thought there was a sliver of light somewhere ahead of her now. It seemed to be spilling out from a distant source—the Second Cavern?—and it ought to be possible to reach it quite easily. She would go in the direction of the light, and she would not listen to the slithering sounds and the pattering of claw-like feet, and the occasional swishing of thin rat tails all round her.

She began to feel her way warily forward. It would be particularly horrid to tread on one of the pattering, scuttering creatures, but, thought Annabel, if it is them or me, then it will have to be them. Sorry, rats, or whatever you are, but it's every Man for himself down here. And then, because this was quite a lively thought to have had, she said it aloud, rather defiantly.

The thin light was nearer, and Annabel inched forward, treading carefully, feeling her way across the uneven rock floor. If you fell over here, the rats would be on you at once.

She thought she was standing on a narrow ridge of rock, and there was the impression of space beneath her. An underground river? But there was no feeling of water, no rising coldness. Probably it was just another strangely proportioned cavern. Even so, it was important not to miss her footing.

And then the light flickered suddenly, and the cave was illuminated quite clearly, and Annabel very nearly screamed, because she was standing on a precarious rock bridge, no more than a foot in width.

There was no river below. Directly below the bridge was a large dry pit, and the pit was filled with writhing snakes.

For a very long time, Annabel did not move at all. The light had died again, and the cave was as dark as it had been before. But that one brief flare had been sufficient to show the snake nest very clearly indeed. It had shown the narrow rock where she stood, and it had shown that the bridge was very flimsy and very smooth, and that it would be very easy to miss your footing and fall off.

Into the snake pit.

Annabel began to feel her way across the bridge. She thought it would be safer to go on all fours; there would be less chance of losing her balance that way, and she lowered herself cautiously and began to crawl. The brief moment of light had shown a solid wide ledge at the far end, and the light itself had to be coming from somewhere. Even if it was only another cave, it was somewhere else to go. *If I can get across the bridge and on to the ledge, I shall be all right. If I can crawl quietly and slowly like this, I shall be safe. I shall get to the Second Cavern, and the others will be there, and I shan't mind very much about meeting the Second Guardian—Aife, was it? Reflection. Reflection, who guards the Second Cavern, and wears a Cloak of Nightmares stolen from a High Queen of Ireland . . .*

A Cloak of Nightmares.

Annabel stopped and held on to the ridge of rock, and sat very still. A Cloak of Nightmares. And Fael-Inis had said something—what had it been?—about illusions and monsters, and about being able to separate reality from enchantment.

I don't believe in you, said Annabel silently to the writhing squirming nest of snakes below her. And then, because this did not seem to work very well, she repeated it aloud. Her voice bounced hollowly off the sides of the mountain.

"I don't believe in you!" cried Annabel, and this time

she heard the uncoiling snakes, and felt the dry heat rising. She thought there was the ghost of a malicious chuckle from somewhere, and the light flickered again.

Snakes were not cold and slimy as most people imagined. They were warm and dry. They coiled themselves about you and their forked tongues flickered at you and their lidless eyes watched you. There had been an expression: laidly worm, which meant loathsome snake. Annabel had read it somewhere in one of the books you were not supposed to read. Now she wished that she had not.

The snakes did not exist. She was not really alone in this dark mountain. It was a trick, an enchantment, a spell conjured up by Reflection from the Cloak of Nightmares. It was a test, to see what she would do.

Nothing in her life so far had really prepared Annabel to crawl, completely alone, across a narrow ridge of rock in pitch dark with a writhing, squirming nest of snakes directly below her. She thought it might have been easier if someone had been with her, and then she drew in a deep breath, because there was no one with her, and she could not stay here clinging to the rock like this. She would go on towards the light. Probably it was another trick, and there would be another horrid nightmare waiting for her there as well, but that would have to be faced. One thing at a time.

The light seemed to be a very long way off. If she was halfway across, she ought to be nearer to it. The narrow bridge ought not to be stretching out and on, so that it began to seem as if it was longer now than it had been when she began. And then, quite unexpectedly, this was heartening, because this was something that happened in nightmares and if this was in truth a nightmare, the snakes could not really hurt her. Even if she fell into the midst of them (which she was not going to do) nothing so very terrible could happen. Annabel took another deep breath and continued her stealthy journey.

The coiling and the hissing of the snakes was becoming frenzied. They know I am here, thought Annabel. They know that I am trying to crawl away in the dark, in secret, and they are excited. They are waiting for me to slip and fall into the centre of them. If that happens, I shall probably be smothered before they can bite me. No, I shan't, because I shall wake up. I must remember that this isn't happening, thought Annabel. Snakes do not live inside mountains, not artificially like this, and none of it is happening, and very soon now I shall wake up.

But the thought of being smothered by coiling, writhing snakes was so utterly repulsive that for a moment she could hardly breathe, let alone move. And then, because the idea of slipping, of missing a foothold or a handhold, was so awful, she began to miss her footing, and she began to find the bridge slippery, as if a thin film of something oily was covering it.

"But this is becoming childish," said Annabel out loud. And then, rather crossly, "I don't know who you think you are, Aife or Reflection, or whatever your name is, but I don't think much of your spells. I think they are *obvious*," said Annabel very loudly indeed.

If it had not been so dark, it might have been easier, but on the other hand, if it had been lighter, she would have been able to see the snakes. Perhaps it was better not to see them. In any case, she would be bound to wake up at any minute.

The brief light had shown the snakes to be not very far below the bridge. They might not wait very much longer for her to miss her footing. They might even be able to uncoil and slide on to the bridge anyway. But this was so terrible a thought as to be nearly unbearable. "I wish," said Annabel aloud again to the listening darkness, "that you had sent me a proper battle, Reflection. I could have coped with that. I might even have *enjoyed* it," said Annabel challengingly, and waited hopefully, in case the challenge was taken up.

No. Nothing altered in the least. Clearly this was the nightmare, and clearly she had to find a way out of it somehow. And at any minute she would lose the precarious hold

she had on the bridge, and she would fall ... With that
thought the bridge shivered and moved beneath her, and her
hand closed about nothing, and her left foot skidded on a
patch of grease, and she fell ...

... right into Taliesin's arms.

She was lying in a perfectly ordinary cave, with the bluish light they had become used to, and Fael-Inis was watching
them, and there was suddenly something normal and familiar
and comforting about everything, and after all she had been
right, there were no snakes, and no narrow bridges that went
on for ever.

And Taliesin was holding her hard against him, and there
was an expression in his eyes that made her feel warm and
safe and as if she could fight this battle single-handed ...

And then Fael-Inis said, "We are in the domain of Reflection, Annabel."

"The Cloak of Nightmares."

"Yes." He regarded her. "Was it so very terrible, child?"

"Well," said Annabel, "it was very real for a time." And
looked round cautiously.

"Yes, she has her tricks, Reflection," said Fael-Inis. "But
she is sometimes rather childish." He moved away from
them, apparently examining the cave walls now, and Annabel looked up at Taliesin and grinned.

"All right?"

"All right," said Annabel. And then, curiously, "What
were you doing while I was fighting snakes and rats?"

"Praying," said Taliesin softly, his eyes tender.

"Really?"

He smiled down at her, and traced the outline of her
features with a finger. "Listen, my love," he said softly, "I
would sooner lose you to a—what was it?—oh, yes, a snake
pit, than see you at the hands of the Drakon patrol, as we
did earlier on. But in reality," he said, a suddenly serious
note in his voice, "in reality, I could not bear to lose you at
all." His hands caressed the tumble of coppery hair. "I should
like to lock you away from every bad thing in the world,

Annabel. So that nothing harmful or hurtful would ever come near you. So that you would be forever safe."

Forever safe . . .

"Oh!" said Annabel, and smiled.

"You would hate it," said Taliesin calmly.

"Would I?"

"Yes. No cages, ever," said Taliesin, and Annabel saw again the misty turquoise world and knew that there would be no cages there at all. "But," said Taliesin, tightening his hold about her, "I should like to put you in my house, and see you curled up on the hearthrug, in the room where I work, and I should like to sit opposite you at the end of every day, and share with you everything that has happened during that day—all the little absurdities and all the comical events, and the sadnesses and the happinesses which make up life. I would put you in my house, but you would be forever free."

Forever safe . . . forever free . . . Annabel, who did not dare believe that life would possibly be so full of delight, dredged up a token protest.

"What about this question of the different worlds?" Because it would be so easy—oh, yes, it would be the easiest thing ever to yield to Taliesin, and to go with him to his house (what would it be like?) and share the happinesses and the sadnesses and the absurdities of life . . .

I think I had better fight against this, thought Annabel, holding on to sanity. I think I had better remember that things like this don't happen any longer. Sharing, and wine, and being loved . . . Being *free* . . .

And so although she was hating saying it, she said, "What about the different worlds?" And stared at him hopefully, and waited for him to find a way out for them.

Taliesin, understanding at once why she was arguing against him, his mood soaring into pure and untrammelled joy, said, "O my love, have you not yet learned that the world is only a glass that shines. An icicle dome, Annabel, through which the players strut . . . a ladder to go up and down, a perpetual see-saw, a towering wall through which we have to find our own chinks of escape . . ." He stopped and looked at her, and Annabel said, "Do you *always* talk so extravagantly?"

"Nearly always. It is a very good disguise," said Taliesin. And then, more seriously, "I will take you back if I have to traffic with every Lord of the Dark Ireland, Annabel."

"But," said Fael-Inis softly, from behind them, "*'we travel not for trafficking alone, or for lust of knowing what should be known . . .'* Do you truly intend to take a golden road, Taliesin, and find yourself beyond the last blue mountain, or across the angry sea?" He stood looking down at them, and Taliesin grinned and said, "There will be a way back," and Fael-Inis said, "Perhaps. If so, we will find it. In the meantime—"

"In the meantime," said Taliesin, standing up and pulling Annabel to her feet, "there is a Second Cavern and the Second Guardian. Reflection."

"Yes." Fael-Inis studied Annabel. "It was a childish ploy of Reflection's, that one."

"I did see it for what it was," said Annabel.

"Of course. And, as I have said, Reflection *is* sometimes rather childish. She intrigued and plotted for years to get the Nightcloak, and now that she has it, she finds that she is not sufficiently Human to use it to its full extent." He regarded Annabel thoughtfully. "If Reflection had been a pure-bred Human," he said, "I think the snake nest would have been very much worse and the escape very much harder. She makes frivolous use of the Cloak now that she has it, but then she is a frivolous creature." The mischievous light flared in his eyes. "But you shall judge for yourselves. Are you ready to go on now? For we are at the entrance to the next Cavern. And I daresay we are being watched and listened to," he added.

"Well, of course you are being watched, my dears," said an amused, rather husky voice from the darkness. "Do, for goodness' sake come in, for if I do not have someone to talk to, I shall scream with boredom!"

Fael-Inis lifted an amused eyebrow. "Well," he said, holding out his hand to them. "Shall we go in?"

AIFE, SOMETIMES CALLED Reflection, was waiting for them. She came forward at once, a thin ravaged creature with a curtain of black hair and huge eyes with painted-on eyelashes. She wore—Annabel blinked—a clinging silk flame-red gown, with a velvet cloak thrown rather negligently across her shoulders. But there was a smile of welcome on her face, and her hands were outstretched to them.

"And, my dear," she said to Annabel, "you must *please* forgive that bit of fun just now. A snake nest, wasn't it. *Too* horrid for you. That wretched Cloak." She looked at Fael-Inis. "So," said Aife softly, "Fael-Inis. The rebel angel. Dear boy, imagine us meeting again."

"Imagine it," said Fael-Inis.

"After all these years," said Aife.

"After all these years," agreed Fael-Inis blandly.

"Did you know I would be here?"

"Wild horses would not have kept me from this Cavern once I knew you to be its Guardian, Lady."

Aife shrieked with glee. "You see!" she said to Annabel. "*Perfect* courtesy. So refreshing. But then he was always the politest of all the . . . I suppose you are staying, are you? Well, you must certainly come into my little abode. *Too* tiny for words, but there it is. And then we had better discuss getting you through the doorway, for I expect that is why you are here, is it? Yes, I thought it would be." There was a whisper of silk, a flutter of hands, and Annabel and Taliesin found themselves somehow led through into a small, rather richly furnished chamber.

"Oh, it is *too* cramped for anything," said Aife. "*Not* what I am used to, of course, and if I had only *known* . . . If I had harboured the *smallest* suspicion about the living conditions down here, I should *never* have agreed to come in on this one."

"I daresay," said Fael-Inis, "that you had no choice," and Taliesin and Annabel were instantly conscious of his ability to adapt to any situation. There was a lightness in his manner now; he was mischievously flirting with Reflection.

"No choice!" shrieked Aife. "My dears, I was practically *dragged* here protesting! I was virtually *coerced* into it. The only thing they did not threaten me with was blackmail, and I daresay they would have done that if they could have found something sufficiently discreditable about me. My life is an open book," said Aife, gazing at Fael-Inis limpidly.

"So I believe."

"Oh, well, of course," said Aife, "if it had not been for my debts, I should *never* have agreed." She regarded them with her head on one side, and Annabel found herself thinking that Aife was really rather attractive. "*Hopelessly* insolvent," said Aife, and spread her hands. "But what would you do? One must live, you know, and eat, and entertain a guest now and then, and have the odd rag to one's back. And take a lover or two ..." Her eyes slid to Fael-Inis. "I do not always admit to it," said Aife confidentially, "but amongst people such as ourselves—and I can see that *you* are a man of the world, sir," she said to Taliesin suddenly, and inspected him with interest. "*Very* intriguing," said Aife, and Taliesin grinned. "Well, anyway, they were becoming so expensive, the young men," said Aife. "They must be having chariots and golden pomegranates, and they must be haring off to rescue maidens from dark towers and slay dragons, and really, I am the most *generous* of souls. But these things cost money. People simply do not realise." She gestured them to be seated, and arranged herself gracefully on a silk couch, plumping up several cushions. *Cushions?* thought Annabel wildly. Down *here?*

"I like to be comfortable," explained Reflection. "And since I am bonded here for—oh, let us not count it up or I shall become *so* depressed, and there is no use in being de-

pressed when there is no one to be depressed *at*. Sir, you
seem like a gentleman of some discernment, I wonder will
you pour us all a glass of wine. Yes, it is in the cupboard
there—a *very* good brew," she said to the other two. "I have
never bought the inferior stuff, not even in my really *bad*
times. People are far too quick to spot these things, and the
next thing would have been that they would have been
spreading it about that I was on my *beam ends* and threatened
with a debtors' prison! And once *that* got about," said Aife,
"I should have been ruined, I promise you. I should certainly
have been hounded out of the Inner Circle of the Sybilline
Ladies. They are *rather* severe about debt, you know," she
said as she daintily rearranged her draperies.

Taliesin, who had poured the wine, brought it to them
and said, "Madam, I believe you are a lady after my own
heart," and Aife sat up and patted her hair, and looked at
Taliesin with renewed interest, and Taliesin winked at Annabel, and handed the tray with the wine chalices to Aife.

"And no doubt, madam, you will not baulk at observing
the ancient custom of my people, which is to taste each chalice before offering it to your guests."

Aife laughed, and said at once, "Oh, it is not poisoned.
That is not *at all* my style. Fael-Inis will tell you that."

Fael-Inis, sipping the wine with apparent enjoyment, said
tranquilly, "Aife has not, so far as I know, poisoned anyone yet."

Aife leaned forward. "Enchantments and nightmares,"
she said firmly. "That is what I go in for. I keep to my own
line; it is *far* better. When they offered me this post, I accepted *only* on condition that I should be allowed to do the
thing in my own way. Nightmares and the odd bewitchment, I said. Take it or leave it, I said. They took it, of
course, well, they had no choice, because I put it to you
whether anyone would *choose* to be buried alive in this place
for several centuries—dear me, now I have said it—*several
centuries*, and it has the most *enervating* ring, no matter how
quickly you say it." She leaned forward, and Annabel, fas-

cinated, leaned forward as well. "Five hundred years," said
Aife in a confidential whisper. "But not a *minute* longer.
And really, that is quite short as these guarding positions
go." She reclined again amongst her cushions, and regarded
them over the rim of her wine chalice. "Still, I escaped my
creditors, which is something to be *very* thankful for, although when you consider the screaming boredom down
here—well, I wonder sometimes whether there would not
have been *more* life inside a debtors' prison. If it were not
for the *shame*," said Reflection. "And my family would *never*
live it down."

The wine was very good indeed, or Annabel thought it
was, because she had never drunk any before. It tasted of
something faintly fruity and of something very mellow and
soft, and there was a warming feel to it. Taliesin had lifted
his glass to Aife, and said quite solemnly, "Madam, as I
thought, you and I have tastes in common, and were you
not an enchantress, and I a poor Tyrian money lender, and
a Human at that—"

"Well," said Aife, sitting up and eyeing Taliesin all over
again, "as to that, I cannot see that there would be any problem, sir, because I *do* have quite a lot of Human blood, you
know, although my mother would never openly admit to it.
A little peccadillo two generations back. My great-grandfather
and a serving girl—"

Taliesin said solemnly, "It happens to the best," and Aife
leaned forward, and said, "It was possessing Human blood
that gave me the idea of acquiring the Nightcloak in the first
place, you know."

"Really?"

"Yes. Although I have to say," said Aife, disconsolately,
"that it has *not* been quite the success I hoped."

"It is a Human's weapon," said Fael-Inis. "Although I
suppose in your rush to steal it, you forgot about that."

"No, I did not," said Aife crossly, and Annabel, watching and listening, thought, So! We have established that she
is indeed partly Human, just as Fael-Inis said. She will have

Human weaknesses, thought Annabel hopefully. But she found herself rather liking the amiable Aife, and she found herself hoping that there was not going to be some kind of messy fight where Aife might get hurt.

"I suppose," said Aife presently, "that you have encountered Spectre? Yes, I thought you must have done."

"A few winds and tempests, and a storm or so," said Fael-Inis, regarding Aife with amusement.

"Oh, dear me, the poor soul, is she *still* using those?" said Aife, sitting up, her eyes bright. "Oh, she will have to widen her repertoire if ever she is to get on. Winds and tempests—so *old-fashioned*! And really, the sort of thing that *anyone* can do—yes, it is the easiest thing in the world, I could whip up a bit of a whirlwind myself if I put my mind to it. Oh, she will never get anywhere, that Spectre. I told her so—it was at a necromancers' dinner—I remember I wore silver grey and I had a new cloak with sections of a cut rainbow woven into it—*ruinously* expensive—but it created *such* a stir, and I believe I took six lovers that night—it might have been more—but there were certainly six *good* ones. One of them went on to capture the Golden Horn, and I remember that there were some *very* prurient jokes made about it at the time.

"But I told Spectre straight: My dear, I said, if you are to make anything of yourself as an enchantress, you will have to branch out a bit. I even offered to give her a few lessons, but she thought she knew it all. People usually do think so. And so there she is, the First Guardian and no prospect of advancement *at all*, although if we are to be candid, I am only the Second, although *only* for five hundred years. Not an hour longer!

"However," said Aife, "we had better talk about you. Dear me, I did not expect to meet *you* again, Fael-Inis. Are you still racketing about the world in your Time Chariot? Of course you are. My dear," this to Annabel, "my dear, *do* make him tell you the story of how he got that. It is a *very* good tale. Of course, we have known each other for a *very* long time. I shall not say just how long. But it is a good many centuries now. Do you remember the Battle of the Goddess Danaan, Fael-Inis?"

"We were on different sides," said Fael-Inis.

"We always were," said Aife disconsolately. "And then there was the War between the Children of Lîr. Do you remember that one? Wasn't it that night I tried to lure you to bed?"

"I believe there were several such nights when you tried to do that," said Fael-Inis with perfect courtesy, and Aife sighed.

"He would never be lured," she said to Taliesin and Annabel. "My dears, I even took *wagers* that I would get him, but I never did. *So* devastating to my ego, because I have always been considered to be irresistible. They called me that once, you know. Aife the Irresistible. I don't know that I cared for it overmuch. Rather common-sounding." She looked at Fael-Inis again and sighed. "Really, dear boy, it was such a pity," she said. "And so ungenerous of you, because I should have dined out on it for centuries. Ladies' Nights, the Inner Circle of the Sybillines—oh, I should have been asked everywhere, because *everyone* is fascinated by him, and my stock would have risen sky high, my dears. And they all know," said Aife confidingly, "everyone knows that I *always* kiss and tell. Well, it's all part of the fun."

She looked at Fael-Inis expectantly, and Fael-Inis smiled slightly and sketched a bow and said, "Your gain was my loss, Reflection," and Aife sighed.

"You see? Immaculately polite, but *elusive*. Nothing you can ever quite get hold of. I should have washed my hands of him centuries ago."

Fael-Inis said, "It is your habit of flinging your lovers into the river the next morning, or dismembering them and feeding them to jackals and hyenas that is so off-putting, Reflection, my dear," and Aife shrieked with mirth again.

"Oh my dear," she said. "Do they still say *that* of me!

How perfectly ridiculous! And you know as well as I do that it was just a piece of spiteful gossip. You cannot trust *anyone* these days! However," said Aife, "we are straying from the point, and the point now is what we are going to do with you all. Are you sure you want to get into the Cavern of the Clock?

"Well, it is *quite* your affair.

"And there is the ridiculous business of the locked door and the key. The idea is that you are supposed to try to get the key from me and I am supposed to resist. It hasn't changed at all, I suppose? No, I didn't think it had, although they do change it from time to time. And," she said in an aside to Annabel, "they *never* tell me. Still, it makes no difference to me, because as far as I am concerned, you are *welcome* to the Cavern of the Clock. My dears, the *noise*! Positively deafening! Tick-ticking until you could scream. And absurd little men in black scurrying all over the place. I have nothing to do with any of it," said Aife. "I made that clear at the beginning. A bit of spell weaving and a few nightmares and that is *all*. Don't expect me to go into that place, I said, and do you know, they never have. *Cold* people. No charm," said Aife severely. "Still, I have to obey their rules, because that is what I am here for. And we all get checked on now and then—oh, yes, *quite* businesslike. A kind of annual audit they call it, and my dears the things they do if you do not play the game—I could make your *hair* curl, really I could. Still," said Aife, and stood up and quite suddenly seemed very much taller, "still, we may as well get on with it."

Fael-Inis had risen almost at the same instant, and to Annabel it seemed as if he too had grown in stature, so that he now matched Reflection in height.

They eyed one another. "I suppose," said Aife softly, "that you want me to give you the key, do you?"

"Yes," said Fael-Inis softly, and held out his hand.

There was a moment of rather unexpected silence. Then

Aife said crossly, "Don't be silly, Fael-Inis. You know the rules. We have to do battle," and Fael-Inis smiled, and leaned forward to touch Aife's hand.

At once there was a crackle of light, and Aife's form changed into a menacing towering figure, easily twelve feet high, brandishing a staff of pure light, her visage threatening.

Fael-Inis matched her without a second's hesitation, hurling a shaft of fire across the cave, so that Annabel blinked and found the dazzle stayed in her vision for some time afterwards.

Aife resumed her normal appearance, and glared at Fael-Inis. "That was unfair," she said. "If you knew how I schemed and searched, and worked—yes, I even *worked* to get that staff of light, and then you disintegrate it with positively no effort *at all* with one of your flaming torches. Oh, it is too bad of you, it is really!" she said, and turned about and sat down, frowning at him.

Fael-Inis said softly, "But you could acquire a flaming torch, Reflection. One of the easiest—"

"Well, it is not," said Aife crossly. "If I was not partly Human . . . You have no *idea* the obstacles I encounter."

"Yes, you are a mongrel."

"But with the best of both sides," said Aife. "And of course, it is having Human blood that has enabled me to wear the Cloak of Nightmares."

"It suits you," said Fael-Inis, still in the same soft tone, and at once Aife said, "Oh, this old thing. My dear, it is the *veriest rag*!" But she looked at him expectantly.

Fael-Inis said, "I will barter with you for the key, Aife."

"Will you?" A sudden speculative and acquisitive gleam lit her eyes. "What will you offer me?"

Fael-Inis grinned. "I can offer many things," he said, "but to begin with, we will say a torch of fire."

"Really? Such as the one you used just now?"

"Such as that."

"Well, that will do for a start," said Aife. "What else?"

"Shall we say immunity from the Time Fire?"

"Now that," said Aife thoughtfully, "would be *very* useful indeed. Can you really do that?"

"Since you are only partially Human, I can."

"Yes, I will accept that as well," said Aife, and looked at him and waited, and then, as he did not speak, "Dear me," she said, "nothing else, Fael-Inis?"

Fael-Inis moved forward without warning then, and took her hands in his. "Come now, Reflection," he said, and there was a coaxing note in his voice, "come now, my dear, we know one another very well. We are old enemies."

"I would have preferred that we were old lovers," said Aife.

"That too could be arranged," said Fael-Inis, and there was another sudden silence. "Well?" he said at last, and his voice was so low and so intimate that Taliesin and Annabel had to strain to hear it.

"After all these centuries," said Aife thoughtfully. "Dear me, this is all very unexpected." She eyed him. "You will expect me to give you the key?"

"Oh, yes."

"Well," said Aife thoughtfully, "it is against all the rules, of course. But I suppose I could say I was *forced*."

"You could do that."

"And—I can still have the torch of fire and the immunity from the Time Fire?"

"Assuredly."

"You won't change your mind?"

"Did you ever know me to break a promise?"

"It seems a reasonable agreement," said Aife cautiously. "Although you do know that I can give you no help against the Third Guardian." She looked at them. "Make no mistake," said Aife, "the Sensleibhe is quite as terrible and quite as cunning and certainly as evil as the legends tell. You will do well to beware of her."

"The bargain," said Fael-Inis softly.

Aife hunched one shoulder and said rather pettishly, "Oh, very well. But I do think it is the unfairest bargain ever struck. And I should have *much* preferred to have got you by my own wiles."

"No one need ever know," said Fael-Inis, and his voice was positively purring now.

"That is true," said Aife, brightening, and looked at him again. "And it has been a *very* long time since we met, you and I." She stood up and led the way through a small gap in the wall into an adjoining room, through which Annabel glimpsed a silken bed with canopies and rich hangings, and a general air of extreme luxury.

Fael-Inis turned to follow her, and then paused in the doorway and looked at Annabel and Taliesin.

"The things I do for Ireland," said the rebel angel, grinning from ear to ear and following his lady into the bed-chamber.

Annabel's ancestors, at some time in their history, had been very particular about what they had called etiquette, which, as far as Annabel had been able to make out, was simply common politeness and the correct behaviour in a given situation. But they had taken it all very seriously; they had written books about it, which you had to consult so that you knew what to do and what to say, and how to reply to invitations, and how to accept a proposal of marriage, and the proper knives and forks to use when you went out. Some of it had been informative, and some of it had been bewildering, and nearly all of it had been amusing. Annabel had read quite a lot of books secretly, when the Drakon patrols could be trusted not to be prowling.

None of the books of etiquette told you how you ought to behave in a situation like this.

Taliesin was no help at all. He seated himself on Aife's silk couch, poured himself another chalice of wine, leaned back with his feet crossed, and prepared to wait for Fael-Inis.

"I suppose," said Annabel at last, "that he *will* get the key?"

"Oh, I should think so," said Taliesin, his eyes brimful of mirth. He got up and refilled his glass.

"And, Aife *will* let us through into the next Cavern," said Annabel.

"She will," said Taliesin, and grinned and set down his wine. And then, "Come here," he said in quite a different voice.

"Now?" said Annabel uncertainly.

"Yes."

THIS, THEN, WAS a foretaste of that forbidden thing; the act that the Drakon had tried to outlaw, and had hedged about with so many restrictions and so many rules that most people had forgotten that there was supposed to be joy in it.

Annabel had not expected to experience quite such a soaring delight and she had certainly not expected to feel such an incredulous joy. When Taliesin lifted his lips from hers, she clung to him because the Cavern, Aife's silk-hung chamber, was whirling about her head, and there had surely never been anything like this, there had surely never been a feeling in the world to equal this, not anywhere, ever.

Taliesin was smiling down at her, and Annabel smiled back, rather shyly, and began to hope very strenuously that he would kiss her again.

"Of course I will," said Taliesin, and bent his head.

Presently, Annabel recovered herself sufficiently to say, "Is that one of the forbidden things?"

"Not in my world," said Taliesin, and pulled her to him again, and said, "There is far better ahead of us yet, my love," and Annabel stared at him and felt dizzy again, because when Taliesin said "my love" like that, in such a soft caressing voice, that such things were forbidden mattered not a jot, because Taliesin would somehow find a way to take her with him into his own world, and she would sit on the hearthrug in his house, and they would share the absurdities and the sadnesses and the happinesses . . . Like this, with his arms about her, with the sudden press of his body against her, so that she could feel the surge of passion rising in him—Oh, yes, lovely! cried Annabel silently—it was possible to believe it would happen.

Taliesin thought, Yes, I could take her now, here, in this dark old mountain, with half a dozen dangers all around us! Shall I? And he remembered the restrictions and the prohibitions of her world, and took a deep breath and put her gently from him. No. It must wait a while yet, it must wait until they had traversed the dangers and overcome them, until they were far from the memory of the advances of the dreadful lusting men of the Drakon, and until they were back in Ireland, the Ireland of the Wolfkings, with the Darkness of Medoc and his creatures sealed in their own terrible domain again.

And then, my love, we will count the world—all the worlds—well lost, and you will be in my house, and I shall never let you go . . .

He smiled at her, and thought she understood, and thought there was all the time in the world to begin loving her, and then thought, I hope there *is.*

Fael-Inis emerged at last, and Annabel, who had been thinking this might be rather awkward, found that it was perfectly easy to greet him with composure. It was even possible to listen quite sensibly to his plan for the next section of the journey.

"The key?" said Taliesin at last. "Did you get the key?"

Fael-Inis grinned and produced the key from behind his back.

THE THIRD CAVERN. The last of the caves guarding the Domesday Clock. The last Guardian.

As they walked through the tunnels, Annabel found that she was beginning to feel much more courageous. Because they had defeated two of the Guardians already?

Taliesin, who had been listening for the Horsemen, was feeling intensely alive and alert. He thought that this quest would have been remarkable under any circumstances, but that it was very remarkable indeed with Annabel at his side. He knew he would not let her go back to that dreadful bleak world, and then he remembered that if they failed in this quest, there might no longer be a world for any of them to go back to.

After a time, Annabel said, "The Horsemen are not quite so close to us now, don't you think?"

"They are following us, but at a distance," said Fael-Inis, and Taliesin, who had also felt this, nodded.

"Will they try to prevent us from entering the torchlit Cavern?" he asked.

Fael-Inis said slowly, "I think they will try to stop us from destroying the Clock. But also, they must first get past the Guardians, of course." He glanced at them. "That is one of the purposes of the Guardians," he said. "To stop *all* comers from getting to the Clock." He grinned. "That would be a battle worth watching," he said, and Annabel stared, because he spoke as lightly and as amusedly as if a battle between the Four legendary Heralds of the ending of the world, and three evil sorceresses, was quite a trivial affair.

Taliesin said, "If the Horsemen *do* reach the cavern," and stopped and then went on. "If they reach it," he said, "surely they will try to speed the Clock's progress to midnight."

"Oh, yes."

"Because," said Taliesin, still pursuing this thought and not liking it overmuch, "because once the Clock's hands reach midnight, then—"

"Then," said Fael-Inis, "the Apocalypse will ride into the world."

"Will we see it?"

Fael-Inis did not immediately reply. "You saw a vision of it in Spectre's cave," he said, and Annabel shivered. "You should pray to every god you have ever held dear that you will not see it in truth," he said seriously.

There was a moment of complete silence. Somewhere

close by, Annabel could hear the melancholy dripping of water from the cave roofs. A dreadful coldness closed about her heart, and for a really terrible second, she wished she had not come, that she had stayed behind in the safety and the familiarity of her tiny house where, even if there were dangers, one knew what the dangers were, and providing you obeyed the Drakon, you would be let alone.

And then Taliesin said, mockingly, "Dear me, then we shall have to be *very* careful," and Annabel felt safe and back in her skin, and knew that it was entirely right that they should be doing this.

"But of course we shall be successful," said Taliesin. "I have no intention of being associated with anything doomed to ignominious failure."

There was a rather desolate air about their path now. The cave roofs were low so that they had to bend their heads, and the ground was becoming uneven and ridged, and the cave walls were pitted with something unidentifiable. Once Fael-Inis stopped, and a gleam of light fell across a section of wall.

"You see?" he said softly, and reached out a hand to trace the faint lines of carved figures.

Taliesin moved closer and stood for a moment, studying them. "What are they?"

"A record of the First Battle," said Fael-Inis, and in the dim cave his voice was low. "The Light-Bringer storming heaven's gates. Man being cast naked and defenceless into the world below. The final great victory." He turned to look at them. "Did I not tell you that these mountains were the oldest thing on earth."

"Who made the pictures?" asked Annabel quietly.

"I did," said Fael-Inis, and quite suddenly he was no longer the rather amusing companion and the strong ally who had fought with them against Spectre and Reflection, or the reckless creature who had summoned the salamanders and taken them across the world in the Time Chariot. He was a creature of fire and light and speed, who had consorted with angels and gods and devils, and who had possessed the immense courage and the breathtaking defiance needed to turn his back on heaven, to walk away from the great immortal battle that had never ceased to echo down the centuries, and whose outcome had been to lock Man out of Paradise.

"He is what he is," thought Annabel, aware that the words came not from within but from without.

Taliesin, standing on the other side, knew that they had been afforded a fleeting glimpse of the creature who existed beneath the brilliant, mischievous exterior. He is many things, this one, thought Taliesin. He is transcendent, and he is probably immortal, and if he is not quite divine, he is certainly more than Human. He is mystical and celestial and spiritual in a way I do not think we can comprehend. You could know him for a thousand years and not know him at all, or you could know him for an hour and discover everything. But he is elusive and wild, and he will never be captured. He will be no Man's and he will certainly never be any woman's.

Be glad that I am yours, if only for a time, came the swift response and Taliesin smiled and thought it was perhaps not arrogant of him to hope that he had known Fael-Inis as well as anyone might.

The images on the cave wall were intriguing. "And rather frightening," said Annabel, tracing them with a finger. "There is fire and blood and agony in them."

"Yes, there was all of that, Mortal. There will be all of that again," said Fael-Inis, watching her. And then, with one of his sudden switches of mood, "Shall we go on?" he said.

It was an eerie and uncomfortable sensation to walk like this through the dim mountain, knowing that following them were the Four ancient Heralds, the four terrible figures of myth and legend, the Horsemen who had ridden into the world and who would shortly try to fling open the world's Gates and let the Apocalypse in.

The light seemed to be getting dimmer, and the tunnels

were certainly becoming narrower and more difficult to walk through. Several times they encountered piles of rubble where the roof had fallen in, and each time they had to stop and clear a way through.

After some little time—Annabel could not be sure how long, because time seemed out of kilter down here—the light began to change and grow cold and greenish, and ripple against the cave walls. Fael-Inis stopped and lifted his head and appeared to listen very intently.

"The Horsemen getting nearer?" said Taliesin. And then, "No. Something else."

Fael-Inis gestured to the cave walls. "Waterlight," he said. "A darkness. A lapping of water." He turned to face them and took their hands in his. "We are very close to the River of Souls," he said. "We are very near to one of the foremost dangers of the world."

"Can we avoid it?" asked Annabel, who did not like water very much, and who particularly did not like dark ancient rivers that flowed silently and sinisterly and were presided over by nameless evils.

"The River of Souls flows between all the worlds," said Fael-Inis. "It is dark and never-ending and runs nine times around the world. The Ferryman is unceasing in his vigil for souls." He looked at Annabel. "I cannot tell if we shall be able to avoid it," he said.

"Will we see it?"

"You may not do so. You will hear it. You will hear, as well, the echo, for it is said that all the world can be spanned by the River of Souls, and it is said as well that to stand at the mouth of the River is to stand at the epicentre of Time." The golden eyes flickered. "It may be that we shall be called upon to listen to the agonies of the drowning souls," said Fael-Inis, "or that we shall be forced to witness the dying struggles of the worlds that have been before this one."

Annabel said cautiously, "Have worlds died before?"

"Assuredly. And will do so again." Fael-Inis regarded

her. "Nothing is constant, Mortal. Even worlds sometimes die."

With a whimper or with a bang . . .

Taliesin said, "Have you encountered the Ferryman?"

"He has many guises and we are old enemies," said Fael-Inis, but the other two thought that there was a wariness in his voice.

They had rounded a sharp curve in the tunnel, and Annabel had noticed and wondered whether she should comment on the trickles of water seeping through the walls. There was a dank damp feel to the air; a coldness that made you want to turn up your collar and stamp your feet and that seeped into your lungs and made you cough and think of clammy autumn nights when fog clung everywhere and you could not see anything properly.

Taliesin had just started to say, "It is getting very dark," when Fael-Inis put up his hand and halted them.

In the dimness they stared at one another.

Annabel said, "I don't—" and Taliesin said, "Hush. Listen."

And then they all heard it quite clearly.

The ticking of a clock.

CHAPTER TWENTY-ONE

THE LOST BOYS had helped Fergus far more than he would have believed possible. When he first emerged from the terrible agony and the anguish, they were at his side, silent and attentive but with him. He thought that they were determined that he should return to the world and he thought, as well, that without their gentle insistence that he lead them out of the Prison of Hostages, he would have been lost indeed.

But after the first terrible days when he was wracked with pain, and when he could hear nothing and feel nothing beyond the wrenching agony between his legs, they began to talk to him about the world outside the Prison. They drew him away from the pain, they talked to him about the Ireland they had known a century before Fergus was born; of the dreadful days when the cult of Crom Croich had held the land in a merciless grip, and how the legendary Wolfking Cormac had ridden out to destroy the high priests of the cult.

"Remarkable," they said, their eyes bright with a kind of amused veneration, "a marvellous King."

"He would have saved us if he could," said one of them.

"He saved the ones after us, though," said another.

"I saw him once," said Michael. "In a procession. I liked him. I cheered a lot, and people threw flowers."

"But," said Niall, "Fergus will save us, now."

"Fergus will take us back to the world," said another, and they all looked at Fergus with such trust that a different, gentler pain twisted his heart. How can I fail them? he thought.

He would not fail them, and when at last he walked with them, back through the great echoing halls and the golden galleries, and the vaulted chambers of blue and ivory, he did so with a feeling of immense inner peace, so that he thought, Yes, I believe I have traversed the eye of the storm, and found the still, calm centre . . . I think I can return, thought Fergus. I think it will be all right. On through the crimson panelled halls, and through the glittering chambers, and back through the strangely named places . . . Here was the Land of Ever-Living . . . the marble and porphyry . . . the Lake of Darkness . . . *And in my house are many mansions* . . .

As the great Doors of the Sky yielded of their own accord, he felt a tremendous uplifting and a great surge of power. We can do it! We are succeeding! We are going through the Doors of the Sky, through that massive Gateway from which it is said no Human has ever escaped. We are breaking the bonds and going out of the Prison of Hostages, and down into the world. I think it is going to be all right.

The Doors were fully open now; they were standing wide, and Fergus and the children moved as one. Each of them had the sudden feeling that there would be only this one chance, and there would be only a very brief space of time when the Doors would let them through.

There was a shaft of pure light as the Doors caught the rays of the sun, and there was a moment when the Doors were outlined quite clearly against a gold and rose dawn. The Gates of Golden Light, studded with chalcedony and jasper . . .

They did not look back. "We do not dare to," said Fergus, but each of them sensed that the Prison had receded into the mists. "We cannot go back," said Fergus, looking at the boys. "And so we shall go forward. See, there is a path. Leading downwards," said Fergus, who had not had any idea of what they would find. "But I think we are still very high up."

It was cold and sharp, with the bright dry coldness that catches in your throat and makes your eyes prickle with tears, but that also makes you want to take great lungfuls of the clean pure air, and that fills you up with soaring energy.

As they went, Fergus noticed that the children were becoming more solid, their cheeks were filling out and their eyes were shining. Several times they reached out to touch the trees and the bushes growing at the side of the path; as the path wound downwards, one or two of them gathered in handfuls of berries and ate them.

They drank from the clear, cold mountain streams, and they ate the berries; twice they managed to catch a small shoal of fish from the stream, and grilled them on a fire with pointed sticks.

"Marvellous," said Niall, licking his fingers which had become burnt in the grilling process. "I'd forgotten about eating and drinking."

"I hadn't," said Michael. "I missed being hungry."

The crags and the canyons were smoothing out now, and the path was becoming less difficult.

"We are nearing the world," said Conn, and Fergus saw that the boys looked deeply happy. He thought, but did not say, *And to become a part of the world of Men once more, we have first to cross the bridge that exists between all the worlds. The River of Souls, guarded by the Ferryman* . . .

Fergus thought they would surely see the River very soon, and they would surely know it when they did see it. But although he scanned the horizon, and although he watched for any sign of water or lake, there was nothing.

They seemed to have been walking for a very long time when the mountains finally flattened and receded, and the way ahead became dryer and rather barren.

"A plain," said Conn, rather uncertainly. "At least it will be easier to walk across."

"Baked rock," said Niall, a bit dubiously. "Fergus, do you suppose we can cross that?"

Fergus was eyeing the flat, barren, desert waste with misgiving, but when Niall asked if they could cross it, he at once said calmly, "Yes, of course," and smiled at them. "I have crossed far worse than that," he said, and the boys looked at him uncertainly.

"There are *things*," said Michael. "Scuttly things. With slithery tails and scaly skins. I can see them."

"Lizards," said Fergus. "Interesting creatures, lizards. Gentle."

"Nasty," said Michael.

"No," said Fergus, and bent down so that he was on a level with them. "We have to cross this desert," he said. "There is no other way forward. And I promise you it can be done. We can do it. I have led the men of the *Fiana* across dreadful desolate plains, and we have always reached our destination."

But it was more difficult than he had imagined, and it was far worse than he had feared. There was a dry heat in the air now, and the stench of death. Several times they came upon bones, bleached by the sun.

"Small animals," said Fergus calmly.

The boys were remarkable. Fergus looked at them and felt his heart contract, because they were brave and determined and they were so trusting that he could hardly bear it. He saw that they were becoming tired and frightened and hungry, and he knew that after their years inside the Prison they would be confused and bewildered. They ought to have been led gently back into the world by stages. Instead, they were being forced to march across a baking desert.

Fergus put his fears aside. He made them rest every few miles, and he taught them the marching songs of the *Fiana*. He said there was nothing so heartening as a good song to march to. "And then," he said, "you will all of you teach the rest of us a song. Will you?" And saw interest brighten in their eyes.

They liked the songs, and they liked knowing that they would presently be called on to teach their own songs. "For," said Niall seriously, "although we have been together for a very long time, we are most of us from different parts of Ireland and from different times."

Conn said it was altogether great to learn songs from other times and other villages and towns.

"We could tell stories as well," said one of them hopefully, and Fergus smiled, and was grateful as he had never thought to be grateful for the Irish delight in story-telling, and the Irish gift for recounting a tale.

When the sudden desert night fell, Fergus set them to keep watch, turn and turn about. "There is not very much danger," he said, "but there may be the odd prowling creature. If we had the means to make a fire we would do so, but there is nothing we can do. And so each of you must take turns at watching."

Niall said, "I think there is a way to make a fire without sticks—something about striking two sharp stones together. And catching the sun's rays."

"Could we try tomorrow?" asked one of the boys.

"Of course we will try," said Fergus, and smiled, and remembered that by tomorrow they would all be hungry and thirsty, and that they would have to start searching for raw lizards' eggs to eat.

When the sun rose the following morning, the boys were hot and dusty and their eyes were red.

"But we are still here," said Conn, and Niall said wistfully, "Yes, but we're all awfully hungry."

"I wouldn't mind missing being hungry now," said Michael.

Fergus said, and tried to keep his voice light, "Well, there is food of a kind in the desert, but it is not very palatable. But it will sustain us for the moment." And managed to make a very light-hearted matter of searching for lizards' eggs and of cracking the tough thick shells, and dribbling the glutinous liquid on to the sizzling rocks.

"Better with a little fresh milk and some butter," said Niall, eating his with a struggle.

"Better with newly baked bread," said one of the others, and another said, "Oh, yes! I remember newly baked bread."

"I remember fruit and honey and cream from the churn."

"And rabbit stew and baked carp."

"Jugged hare."

"Roast chestnuts and apple dumplings," said Michael firmly. "That's the *very* best."

But they ate the eggs courageously, and gathered a few berries from the sparse desert bushes, and Fergus showed them how to suck the sap to gain moisture.

Conn was just saying that they ought to be getting on again, when Fergus looked up and caught a sound from above.

The beating of wings on the air.

Michael, who had heard it as well, started to say, "What—" and then they all saw the vultures gathering above them.

Fergus did not stop to think, and he certainly did not stop to reason. "If I had," he was to say, "I might have remembered that vultures rarely attack until after death. We would have been safe from them for a time."

But the time might not have been so very long. They were tired and hungry, and there was very little prospect of food. There was even less of water.

Fergus flung down the handful of berries, and grasped the arms of the nearest boys.

"Run!" he shouted, and began pulling them with him, looking back over his shoulder, seeing the vultures swooping and darting, knowing that they had sensed that their prey was already weakened. They would come swooping down, and their great wings would beat on the air, and they would fly at their victims' eyes, rending flesh, tearing muscle . . . Fergus ran, pulling the boys with him, knowing there was nowhere to run to, but running all the same, because surely anything was better than to suffer the talons and the claws and beaks, anything would be better than being ripped open and eaten as you died, bleeding and mutilated on the baking rock.

Conn, who was managing to urge the smaller boys on, gasped out, "But where—" and Fergus gestured and yelled, "On! Keep running! There will be somewhere."

And then Niall said, "There's a kind of cave just ahead." And Fergus saw the gaping hole under the overhang of rock.

Sanctuary.

The space beneath the rock was larger than it looked. It was very nearly a cave, and it seemed to stretch back farther than was possible.

But they all squeezed through; they had all somehow scrambled into the opening, leaving the vultures cawing angrily and beating the air with their wings, and emitting horrid little snapping sounds with their beaks. As Fergus pulled the boys to the back of the cave, they could see the vultures clawing at the opening, pushing their beaks in to peer through the gloom.

"Will they get in?" asked Niall, and Fergus said, "No. No, there is not room. But just to be sure, we will try to fill up the opening with rocks."

The boys began to pile up stones and rocks, shutting out the light.

"It's made it awfully dark," said one of them.

"But it's better than letting those creatures get us."

"They won't be able to get through the rocks, will they? Fergus, will they?"

"No," said Fergus. "We are safe for the moment. Is everyone all right?"

"I scraped my shoulder diving in," said Niall. "But I went head first. Did you hurt yourself?"

"I grazed my arm."

"I went in on my bottom," said Michael. "So I 'spect my bottom's a bit bruised."

Niall, who had been crawling to the cave's rear, said, "Fergus, this is a very *deep* cave."

"It doesn't smell very nice," said Michael.

"But we are safe and dry here," said Fergus, and tried to shut out the knowledge that they could not stay here for very long, because there would probably not be very much air, and before long they would have to go out into the desert again and the vultures would probably be there waiting.

And then Niall, who was still at the back, said, "Fergus—all of you—come here. I think there is a kind of tunnel." And Fergus moved across and Niall pointed, and without warning Fergus found himself slithering down a steep slope, unable to stop himself, sliding at a terrific speed, going helter-skelter downwards with rocks and stones and rubble bouncing and flying, grasping at the ground, but still slithering and falling.

Above him, he heard shouts, and then he heard cries of alarm, and dirt and stones cascaded into his face as he tried to look up. He knew that the boys were following, and soon, at any minute, they would all hit the bottom of the chimney or the shaft, or whatever it was they had fallen into.

And then, quite suddenly, the sliding stopped, and they were on level ground, and although it was dark, it was not pitch dark, and they could see one another.

Fergus, dazed and with all the breath knocked from him, got cautiously to his feet and looked round. They were all together in a dark, high-ceilinged tunnel which stretched ahead of them and wound round to the left.

Fergus turned back to the boys. "Everyone here? Did we all come down the shaft? We'd better have a roll call, I think. Stand still, everyone. Now then. Names and degree of injuries!"

But although there were scraped knees and grazed hands, and although Michael seemed to have lost his shoes ("I'll have to walk in my socks, won't I?"), no one was seriously hurt.

"Bruises and grazes only," said Fergus. "Very good. It could have been much worse."

"Where are we?" said one of them.

"Have we got to go into the tunnel?" said another. "It's a bit dark, isn't it?"

"It's like a nose," said Michael. "It's like a nasty dark

nostril in a giant's nose." He sat down and turned his socks over at the tops. "I didn't think we'd have to go crawling into a giant's nose," he said, and Fergus grinned.

"I haven't the least idea of what it is or where it will lead to," he said, "but we are somewhere other than the plain, and that is something to be *very* thankful for." And still he could not repress a feeling of triumph, because they had escaped from the eternal light of the Prison of Hostages.

The tunnel seemed to take them deep into the earth's core, and Fergus, sorting the boys into single file, thought, Well, I suppose this is all right. Will it take us to the River of Souls? But he could no longer plan that far ahead. And yet, thought Fergus, I believe we *are* closer to the world now . . .

The tunnel was narrow and the floor was ridged and uneven, and here and there slippery and gleaming faintly with phosphorescence. The boys were quiet, flinching from the weird carvings on the sides of the tunnel—"Faces," said Michael in rather a small voice—and Fergus heard his own voice saying calmly, "No. Only an odd formation of the rock."

But all the time he was remembering the Ferryman, and he was remembering how the Ferryman might be lying in wait for them. Supposing he was leading the boys into danger? But I can no longer judge, thought Fergus, going on down the tunnel.

They advanced slowly, silently, because there was something eerie and sinister about the light now.

"Waterlight," said Conn, and Fergus nodded, and felt his heart bound, because surely if there was waterlight, they must be nearing the River of Souls.

There was the sound of water dripping steadily now, somewhere quite near. Fergus, helping Michael over an uneven piece of the tunnel floor, had the impression of tiny web-footed creatures quite near to them.

And then Niall said softly, "I smell water." And as he

spoke, the tunnel widened without warning, and the light changed, and Fergus heard the boys gasp.

Directly ahead of them, stretching as far as they could see, was an endless expanse of dark shiny water, with tiny glinting red lights in it.

The River of Souls.

FOR A LONG time they stood transfixed, watching the dark silky River of Souls, remembering all of the tales and all of the myths: Human souls dragged down and held beneath the surface; the Ferryman sculling the dark tunnels in his craft, leaping on his victims, wrapping his long scaly arms about their necks from behind, pulling them down, down into the dark cold depths . . .

The water barely moved, but they knew that it did move. A myriad of lights danced and glinted and tiny waves lapped gently against the River banks. Fergus saw the boys move back from it at once, and he thought that although the water seemed harmless, it was not harmless at all. It would reach for you, it would pull you out into the centre of the River, and you would never be able to get back . . .

Conn said softly, "The lights are the trapped souls that the Ferryman has captured. They are held beneath the River's surface, as firmly and as endlessly as we were held inside the Prison of Hostages. They are in pawn to the Dark Master," and several of the boys shivered.

Fergus, staring at the River, said, "Does the Ferryman serve Crom Croich?" and at once there was a disturbance in the water, a ruffling of the silky skin, a deepening in the red glow of the tiny lights that were Human souls caught and caged by the Ferryman.

"Hush," said Conn. "Yes, we believe that the Ferryman *does* serve that one. As do all creatures from the Dark Ireland."

"Can't we do anything to rescue them?" said Fergus, unable to take his eyes from the moving lights in the water.

Human souls, living, breathing, *aware* Human souls, trapped and caught and held . . . "Can't we help them?" he said.

"No one has ever found a way to help them," said Conn. "Just as no one has ever found a way out of the Prison of Hostages."

To Fergus, the soft sinister River and the hundreds of tiny winking lights was the most pitiful sight he had ever seen.

"But there are prisons for souls everywhere in the world," said Conn, as if he thought Fergus would know this.

"I can hear them," said Fergus suddenly, and Conn said, "But you couldn't possibly—" He went quiet and looked at Fergus.

"I can hear something," said Fergus. And then, "Or is it just the water lapping against the bank?"

Conn started to say that it was just the water, and then stopped, because quite suddenly, the sound was not in the least bit like water lapping, it was like something very different indeed.

Like something creeping down the dark tunnel towards them?

Niall said in a whisper, "You know, there *is* something," and Michael said in a trembly kind of voice, "And the shadows are different."

"How different? Michael, they're only our shadows," said Conn. And then, "Or are they?"

Michael shuddered and rubbed his eyes, and Fergus remembered that Michael was very young indeed.

One of the boys said in a whisper, "Fergus, I can hear it as well now," and Fergus saw that they could all hear it, and that they were all frightened of it. He looked quickly about him. The great dark River stretched endlessly before them, but to their left the mountain tunnel snaked away a little. Was there a way out there? But we have to cross the River! thought Fergus wildly. To return to the world, we have to cross it! And then he saw that the River wound its way into the tunnel as well, a small tributary, and he thought that at least it would take them away from whatever was coming steadily towards them in the dark, and at least they would be going somewhere, and to go somewhere was surely better than standing here, irresolute, at the mercy of whatever was creeping down the tunnel.

He marshalled the boys quickly into single file again, for the tunnel was extremely narrow. And to fall into the River would mean the end of everything. Or would it? I can't decide, thought Fergus. I don't know if we are meant to plunge into it, or what we are meant to do. But I think we have to keep moving, and I think we have to move away from the creeping stealthy thing that I can hear.

The sounds were closer to them now, and Fergus tilted his head and listened, trying to identify the sounds. It was certainly not something walking, nor was it anything crawling. Something familiar, but something alien. Something that made you see the rhythmic dip of slender wooden paddles, and that made you see the tendrils of slimy weed that you dredged up as you went; the feeling of skimming over water quickly and effortlessly . . . And then he knew what it was.

Oars. The scull of oars coming down the River tunnels towards them.

Something was rowing a boat along the dark underground caverns and something was beginning to cast a huge shadow on the cave walls, and that something would very shortly be in the cavern with them . . .

"Quickly," said Fergus. "Along here! All hold hands. And on no account slip . . ." Because to do so will mean that you will be dragged down into the glinting lights, and you will become another light, and you will be soulless once more, and you will be beyond the reach of any help . . .

And then, as they moved into the tunnel, the waterlight rippling all about them, the green shadows everywhere, they heard, quite clearly, the steady scull of oars.

The Ferryman was coming towards them.

———

THERE WAS A terrible, never-to-be-forgotten moment, when they first saw his shadow on the cave wall, and when they heard the soft splashing of the oars. The River seemed to heave, and there was a soft sighing sound, as if all the captured souls could hear and see and were afraid. The shadow loomed closer, and as they stared they saw a shape, hooded and cloaked, huge and thin and towering and hungry, standing in some kind of small craft, propelling it across the dark waters ... The Ferryman, travelling through the shadowy underworld of his domain, searching for Human souls to drag beneath the River ...

Fergus drew in a deep breath, and said in a low urgent voice, "Quickly! There is no time to be lost! We must run!" And then they were all running, down into the warren of caves and passages, away from the approaching creature that rowed swiftly and silently on the terrible River of Souls, away into the safe, stifling darkness.

Fergus said, "Keep to the shoreline! We must not lose the River's path! And we must not be separated for an instant! Link hands now!" And he half pulled, half forced them along, hearing the pounding of their feet on the hard rocky shore of the River, unable to tell whether the pounding was, after all, his own heartbeat.

They could see the way better than he had expected. Light shimmered and cascaded on the waters and the tunnels were becoming wider. But Fergus thought they might easily wander like this for ever, tired and hungry and lost, playing a grisly game of hide and seek with the Ferryman, who would certainly know they were here, and who would almost as surely set traps and lie in wait, and suddenly appear, barring their way, gathering them into his net, pulling them down beneath the waters ...

Half-formed ideas of constructing some kind of raft raced through his mind, because he knew that to re-enter the world they must cross the River, but he could see no means of doing it; there was no driftwood to be seen and no rope and, in any case, there were too many of them. They must somehow outrun the Ferryman and find a safe place to ford the River.

They were still running, hands linked, the older ones helping the smaller; Fergus thought they had left the Ferryman behind now, but they dared not stop to see. They must go on, until they could come to other caves, until they could come to daylight and to the outside world. Once Conn gasped out, "I believe we are inside a mountain," and once Michael squeaked because his stockinged feet had trodden on a sharp stone, but the children were silent, round-eyed with fear, ready to obey Fergus unquestioningly.

Niall, whose ears were sharp, stopped at the intersection of two tunnels and said, "Listen."

"Oars? The Ferryman?"

"No," said Niall, puzzled. "No, I think we have left him behind."

"What is it, then?" said Fergus. "Niall, what can you hear?"

"It sounds like the ticking of a clock," said Niall, and they all stopped and listened, and Fergus thought that Niall was right; the sound was exactly like a clock ticking.

"But probably it is just water dripping somewhere," he said, but he lingered, because just for a second, there had been the sure impression of an immense clock, ticking slowly and inexorably closer to midnight, showing Time running out, like grains of sand trickling away through someone's hands . . .

And although they had grown accustomed to the River sounds now, they were beginning to hear other noises; muffled and distant, but occasionally recognisable. Snatches of music. Fragments of roaring sounds, the clanking of some kind of machinery.

Fergus stopped and tilted his head, and remembered that the River of Souls was the bridge between all the worlds, and thought, Are we hearing other worlds now? Are we hearing the past and the future and all the unborn worlds and all the worlds born and died and forgotten?

Grating sounds, the harsh blaring of some kind of instrument. A feeling of smoke and dirt and heat and of impatience to be moving. Fergus found this curious, and he half closed his eyes, to listen more intently and, for a breathspace, for the span of a heartbeat, there was an image of metal oblongs that could travel at immense speed, and of people—hundreds of people—inside them, somehow propelling the oblongs along a great highroad. Towering buildings and brilliant lights, and the smell of grease and smoke, and the drone and the whirr of grating metal. And then the image was gone, and the sounds melted, and there was nothing but the soft waterlight, and there was no image other than the shadow of the Ferryman silently stalking them along the darkling waters.

And then Conn said, "There's a light ahead," and Fergus froze and motioned the children into the lee of the rock.

The faint warm light came bobbing into view, silhouetting three shapes, and Fergus felt his heart bound in his breast.

Directly ahead of them were Fael-Inis and Taliesin, and between them was a small slender girl with copper-red hair.

FERGUS RAN TO them at once and he embraced Taliesin and felt tears streaming down his face, and knew he was being absurd, and thought he was probably being emotional, and could not help it and did not care.

Taliesen said, "Dear me, such emotion. Fergus, I am overwhelmed." But his voice was not entirely steady, and he gripped Fergus's hands with fingers that were glad and clutching. His eyes were over-bright, and Fergus found himself unable to speak.

Fael-Inis said, half to himself, "Out of the land of the sky and out of the House of Bondage," and Fergus turned to him at last, and held out his hands, and Fael-Inis took them, and Fergus felt a warm glow and the sensation of silk being drawn gently across his mind, soothing out pain.

"We welcome you back, Fergus," said Fael-Inis, and now

there was affection in his voice, and Fergus felt a lump in his throat and the tears begin again, and was furious, and then did not care.

Taliesin, using the exchange of courtesies between Fergus and Annabel as a shield against the flood of emotion that had swept over him on seeing Fergus, knew at once that something terrible and irrevocable and unbearably sad had happened to Fergus inside the Prison of Hostages. He watched as Fergus took Annabel's hands, and saw the shadows in Fergus's eyes, and thought, Whatever has happened to him in that place—and perhaps one day he will talk about it—it has changed him completely and for good. He is still the great leader and the soldier, thought Taliesin, but some quality that was there before has been stolen. The scholar is still there, thought Taliesin, but I believe that the poet has gone.

Fergus, greeting Annabel, hearing the hasty introduction, saw at once that here was no moderate, agreeable formalist, but a lady who had certainly questioned the shibboleths and the standards of whatever world she had come from. And even like this, even in the rush of finding Taliesin and Fael-Inis, even with the creeping danger following them along the River tunnel, he recognised that there was intelligence and perception in her eyes, and defiance in the tilt of her head. But he grinned to himself, and he wondered what Fael-Inis thought of her, and thought as well that Taliesin might well find that he had a wildcat by the tail. And foresaw a few battles ahead for these two, and was pleased for Taliesin, who certainly would not have wanted his lady to be otherwise.

Annabel took the hand that Fergus held out, and thought, Well, so here is another of the people from Taliesin's world! And saw, as Taliesin had seen, the warrior and the scholar, and guessed that there had once been a lover and a poet, but that these last two had somehow vanished for good. But she felt at once the air of authority that Fergus carried without realising he carried it, and trusted him even before she saw that Taliesin trusted him, and began to feel even more hopeful about their chances of defeating the Horsemen and the Apocalypse.

Fael-Inis was looking at the boys, who had stood rather silently on the edge of it all, not liking to intrude. And then Conn stepped forward rather hesitantly, and smiled cautiously at Fael-Inis, and a curious gentleness stole over Fael-Inis's face. "The little lost ones," he said softly. "The murdered innocents. Fergus, you have brought them out." And then, without warning, he turned and raised his hand. A great silence fell, and Taliesin and Fergus half turned because they both heard the same thing.

"Yes," said Fael-Inis, "yes, you hear it, Mortals. The Horsemen are coming nearer.

"And the Clock is ticking faster."

NONE OF THE others could afterwards quite explain what happened next.

Fael-Inis raised his right hand and described an arc through the air. As he did so, a line of pure golden light followed his hand. Sparks soared, and then the radiance seemed to descend on the children, like stardust, like sprinklings of tiny slivers of fire, or like . . . Yes, thought Taliesin, like the Time Fire. He is bestowing on them the Time Fire.

The power and the light and the speed . . .

The boys did not immediately react, but Fergus saw an odd look come over them, and he thought it was as if something deep and mystical had been wakened in them so that they could not for the moment focus on anything. Annabel, who had been watching closely, thought it was as if an inner fire had been lit, or as if they had been shown something marvellous and given some undreamed-of power.

Fael-Inis stood for a moment looking at the boys, seeing, thought Annabel, the flaring up of the strange power he had given them. And then he said softly, "We are going to save the world, children." And held out his hands, and light streamed outwards from him. "Come," he said. "Come with me now, for the minutes are dying. Come, children, for the

Horsemen are almost upon us." He turned, and seemed to shimmer and blur. Annabel rubbed her eyes and wondered if he was still there, only she knew he was, because the light was pouring ahead of them, down the darkest of the tunnels. He was an arrow of pure light and speed, beautiful and exotic and unstoppable.

The children were with him, they were easily keeping pace, and there was the same brilliance about them, so that they were all bathed in luminescence. Gold light flew from their heels, sending cascades of fire across the dark River to their right. Taliesin and Fergus and Annabel, linking hands, running to keep up, shared a thought: Now we are truly seeing the real creature, the angel of fire and speed who rides the world and travels in and out of Time at will, and whom no Mortal can touch.

They could hear the Horsemen thudding after them now; Fergus hesitated, and turned to look back, and Taliesin pulled him on.

"The Horsemen—the Heralds! Fergus, we dare not let them catch us—" he shouted, and Fergus, his mind whirling and his senses swimming, understood that the Four Horsemen were riding into the world, ready to unleash the Beast Apocalypse.

Their leg muscles were protesting and their eyes were blinded with the effort of following the brilliant light. But Fael-Inis was darting ahead with the children, pouring out seamless fountains of radiance, like wildfire on Samain, like a blazing forest fire, like a beacon, like the northern lights on a clear night sky . . .

Fantastical shadows leaped and danced and gibbered from the dark corners, but Fael-Inis and the boys seemed tireless. And somehow, thought Annabel, somehow we are keeping up. Somehow we are getting closer to the Clock.

Fergus, at the rear, could feel the Horsemen on their heels, and he knew that the immense threat Fael-Inis had intended to turn back was nearly upon them. The ground was shuddering beneath the pounding hoofs, and he could smell the warm, dry, stable smell. He glanced back over his shoulder, and caught a darting shadow. But if only they could get through the tunnels, if only they could reach a place of sanctuary. If only they could outrun the Ferryman and defeat the Horsemen . . . And I was so nearly too late, he thought. If we had not broken out of the Prison when we did, if I had not submitted to the punishment pronounced by the Stone Judges, perhaps we should not have been here, and perhaps the Horsemen would already have let in the Apocalypse . . .

Annabel, running with the others, was listening hard for the Clock, trying to assess how close they were, for it was the Clock they were trying to reach, and it was the steady, inexorable ticking they must somehow halt. Midnight, and it must be so close now, because the Horsemen were already here, they were in the mountain and perhaps the Apocalypse was waiting to walk into the world . . .

And then, without warning, they half fell, half skidded, gasping and helpless, into a kind of intersection of all the tunnels; a great echoing cavern where several tunnels ended. Directly ahead of them was a massive door, hewn into the mountain, and from behind the door came the sound that Annabel had been straining to hear ever since they plunged into the tunnels: the steady ticking of the Clock.

Barring the door was the Third Guardian, and standing next to the Third Guardian was the hooded form of the Ferryman.

THERE WAS NO escape. There was no point in turning back and running away, because the tall shape of the Ferryman would have caught them in an instant. Annabel, struggling to get her breath back, her lungs raw with the frantic exodus along the tunnels, thought that even the boys, still luminous from Fael-Inis's fire, were exhausted. They were trapped, and in front of them were the two ancient evil creatures called the Sensleibhe and the Ferryman, and behind them in the dark tunnels were the Four Horsemen. She glanced at the boys, and saw that the odd, other-world quality was still clinging to them, that there seemed to be an inner strength, and the light and the fire of some unknown power. I am still not sure if any of this is happening, thought Annabel, but at least I am on the right side in the battle. At least I am fighting on the side of the just. And then she remembered all of the wars, just and unjust, righteous and dishonourable, that had been fought, and how often the unjust and the dishonourable had triumphed. But this was not a thought to be dwelled on, and so she turned back to the cave and to what was going to happen next.

None of them could see the Third Guardian very well— "Too much shadow," muttered Fergus—and as they waited for their eyes to adjust to the gloom, they heard her speak. An old voice, a comfortable voice. Annabel, astonished, thought it was the sort of voice you could associate with security and safety. The sort of voice that would have belonged to nannies and children's nurses in the old books. It was a voice that would bustle you in out of the rain, and make you get into a hot bath *immediately*. Annabel, who had been so fascinated by the world's history that she had read as much about it as she could lay her hands on, thought it was precisely the sort of voice you would like to run to if you had hurt your knee or been bested in a fight, or broken your heart. And then she thought, But surely it is not a voice you would expect to hear down here, guarding the torchlit cavern?

"Dearie me," said the voice, "Oh, dearie me, here's a fuss and a bother. Here's a to-do. My goodness gracious me, look at you all, drenched to the skin and liable to catch a death I shouldn't wonder. And the little ones! A mug of my special cocoa, that's what *you* need, my dears, and a nice warm by my fire. Come along in now, do." Button bright eyes regarded them from the darkness, and a door seemed to open, and there was the comforting crackle of starch and the warm, dry scent of clean linen, and of washing airing before a fire with a brass guard that would catch the firelight and glow, and where you might be allowed to roast chestnuts and toast muffins.

"There's freshly baked gingerbread," said the voice, curiously—sinisterly?—in line with Annabel's thoughts. "And I dare say that if we are *very* good, there might be scones and strawberry jam as well. So come along in, my lambkins, and be safe. A nasty night to be out in the rain and the dark and the cold. Come along in to the fire, and the warmth, and come along in to where it is safe."

Fael-Inis turned as if to speak, but Annabel saw that Conn and Niall and Michael and all the boys were moving forward in the direction of the voice, their eyes bright.

"That's the way," said the voice with plump satisfaction, "all of you safely inside. What a lot of precious lambkins. Scones and jam for all and warm gingerbread, and you shall tell me about your adventures."

The boys moved as one, and there was a chuckle and a movement from the shadows, and Annabel thought that something dark and formless moved. But then there was the gleam of an apron, and a whirr of sound that might have been anything at all. Spinning? Was it something being spun?

"All inside," said the voice, and Annabel received the impression of somebody—something?—standing with arms folded, nodding placidly, and counting the children as they went. There was the scent of baking and of log fires and warm rooms, and there was the sound of a kettle singing on the hob. And then, before they knew it, the door had closed, and the children had gone, and the shadowy figure turned to Fael-Inis.

"All inside," said the voice, and now it was treacly and purring, it was a gloating, chuckling voice. "And now," it said, "and now, my dears, for the rest of you."

The Sensleibhe. The Old Woman of the Mountains. Plump and cosy-cheeked and white-aproned. Fat and comfortable and safe and wide-lapped. You might run to her with your problems. You would surely trust her. If it had not been for her eyes . . .

Fergus, who was nearest, saw that the Sensleibhe's eyes were dark and unblinking. They were animal eyes; dark, staring eyes that would reflect not the smallest sliver of light. He saw, as well, that her hands were predatory, with long thick nails, curved like claws.

Taliesin, standing nearby, thought, Well, I suppose she *can* be defeated. Can she? I suppose Fael-Inis will find a way. And we have to try. We have to get to the Clock.

Annabel was very frightened but she was also very angry. She thought that to have come this far, to have avoided the Drakon's patrol and to have outwitted the first Two Guardians, and run willy-nilly from the Ferryman, and then to be barred from their goal by this ridiculous old woman, was beyond bearing. She would have flung herself forward had not Taliesin's hand restrained her.

Fael-Inis had been watching not the dark squat figure of the Sensleibhe, but the thin hooded form just behind her. The Ferryman. The creature had not moved and it had not spoken, but Fael-Inis knew, as the Mortals could not, that it was this adversary they must be most wary of. It was this one who would take what the Sensleibhe left—the gleanings and the pickings. But he remained silent and he watched to see what these two would do.

The Old Woman said comfortably, "Dearie me, I can see you've been told some nasty tales about me! Bless and save us all, who'd have thought anyone could believe an old woman should be a danger to such grand strong gentlemen and such a pretty little lady! Why, if it wasn't for Mr. Ferryman, I'd have long since been pushed out into the world, and a nasty cold place *that* can be! Why, Mr. Ferryman's been a good friend to me." She came nearer to them, and Fergus saw that he had not been wrong; the creature's eyes were cunning and sly and darting.

The Sensleibhe was inspecting them now, walking round them, eyeing Taliesin and Fergus, patting Annabel's cheek. Annabel drew back and scowled, and the Old Woman of the Mountains laughed.

"Dearie me, temper, temper. I should know what to do with you, madam, if you were in my charge. My word, there'd be early bed and no supper for a week for you!" She stood looking at Annabel, and Annabel stared back, because she would not let this creature intimidate her. The Old Woman grinned rather horribly, and moved back to the shadows. As she did so, there was a rather horrid sound of claws ringing out on the rock floor of the cavern. Taliesin and Fergus exchanged a thought: *Is this* the movement to spring? But the silent cloaked figure of the Ferryman moved, and they both stopped, because they knew they would not be permitted to get within two feet of the Old Woman. Fergus thought, He will be upon us and he will tear out our hearts and offer our souls to Crom Croich. And wondered how he knew this so surely. Taliesin, at his side, picked it up at once, and knew Fergus was right.

The Old Woman was seated in the shadows again, and Annabel saw with disbelief that in front of her was a spinning wheel, low and dark and ancient. As they watched, the Old Woman drew the wheel a little nearer and ran her hands lovingly over the machinery.

"It doesn't do to be idle," she said. "And with the morning, there'll be plenty to spin. Well, this *is* a good catch for me, don't you agree, Mr. Ferryman?" And then, as the dark figure did not move, she said, "He doesn't say very much, that one, my dears. But he's a good friend. A good friend and a bad enemy . . . He's been good to me."

Fael-Inis said courteously, "What do you intend to do with the children?" and the Sensleibhe turned to regard him.

"Dearie me, so it's you. Eh, I never thought to meet *you* again this side of eternity." The bright, dark eyes studied him and Annabel thought there was perhaps a gleam of uncertainty now, and hoped that this was not wishful thinking.

"And yet, as you see, I am here," said Fael-Inis, and Taliesin knew at once that Fael-Inis was quenching his fire and his radiance. His voice was colourless, his words devoid of expression. "Tell us what you intend," said Fael-Inis, and the Sensleibhe chuckled and Annabel shivered, because it was a gravelly, liquid sort of chuckle that made you think of horrid, bubbling, greasy liquids, and of things with repulsive names such as mucus and catarrh.

Fael-Inis moved nearer, and the others thought that a faint flicker of light came from him now. "Tell me," he said softly, and the Sensleibhe laughed again, so that Annabel shuddered.

"All the better to help my spinning, my dear," she said, and now there was a dark, leery sort of sound. "For, oh, what rosy cheeks, and oh, what plump limbs and pretty silken hair they have. All the better to help my spinning, Mr. Rebel Angel." She hummed and rocked and the wheel whirred, and Annabel had the feeling that there was something rather grisly about the spinning. And remembered, and wished not to remember, the old, old fairy stories which people had once thought suitable for children, where old women rocked and grinned by firelight, and invited you in to warm cosy parlours where kettles sang on the hearth and gingerbread was baking; where suddenly the firelight burned up a little more brightly and showed you not a comfortable old woman in a frilled cap and button boots, but something very nasty indeed; something that had a grinning maw and wide predatory teeth, and something that was not covered with skin like a human, but with bristly hair, and that had claws and talons. Annabel gulped and took a deep breath.

When the Old Woman of the Mountains said again, "All the better to help my spinning, my dears," Annabel found herself moving forward, and the Old Woman grinned and nodded. There was something unexpectedly soothing about the whirr of the spinning wheel, and there was something compulsive about it as well, so that you had to see what she was spinning, if only for a brief moment.

"See now," said the Old Woman, reaching out a hand. "See what I do, down here, while I wait for the little children to come to me. Dearie me, they all come to me in the end.

Mr. Ferryman goes on the hunt, and they all come here. They curl up by the firelight and they fall asleep, the precious little ones, their cheeks rosy, their eyes heavy with drowsiness. Oh, there's no need of the *Draoicht Suan* down here. All fall asleep when I start my spinning. You see how pretty it is? Come now and take a better look. The gentlemen as well. Eh, gentlemen don't like such things, I know that. But you come now and take a look. No cause for fear. It's only the children I take, you see."

Annabel, drawn forward against her will, unable to resist, felt herself coming slowly into the faint spill of light from beyond the mountain door. The Sensleibhe sat in the patch of light now, her spinning wheel humming. It was rather soothing. Soporific, that was the word. It was soporific. The Old Woman of the Mountains spun and hummed and spun and beckoned, and Annabel could see now that from the end of the wheel, a thin glistening thread was forming. A thin glistening thread, studded here and there with chippings of something sharp, with fragments of something you ought to be able to identify, and surely would if only the light was a little stronger. Skeins and strands and tufts, wet glistening threads, all woven into rope-like fibre that would presently be made into garments . . .

Annabel gasped and backed away from the spinning wheel, for the sharp hard pieces were slivers of human nails, and the wet glistening strands were Human skin and Human flesh, stained with blood, and the dark coarse strands were Human hair.

Human victims, butchered and spun into thread to be woven into cloth for the Old Woman of the Mountains to wear.

The children were to be crushed and ground up and minced and spun into thread. This was what the Sensleibhe wanted them for. This was why she had trapped them.

And then, as they stood transfixed, there was a dreadful harsh clacking noise that made you think of nails clicking against cold stone, and of the beaks of vultures and predators opening and shutting hungrily.

The Ferryman moved into the light and, as he did so, he reached up to push the deep hood back from his head. The cloak fell aside.

It was the Conablaiche itself.

CHAPTER
TWENTY-TWO

AND SO, THOUGHT Annabel, and so at last we have to face failure. We are trapped down here, with hundreds of tons of mountain rock above us, and with rock doors sealed against us. We are at the mercy of the Old Woman of the Mountains and of the creature that my people call the Claw and, somewhere quite close by, the Domesday Clock is ticking the world's life away and it seems there is nothing any of us can do.

The Claw, the Conablaiche, the Ferryman, who prowled the dark waters of the tunnels and hungered for the hearts and the souls of Humans. The terrible ancient creature who owed allegiance to Crom Croich.

Fael-Inis moved first; Annabel thought that he sent a shower of radiance cascading across the floor, and she drew a breath of relief, for surely if anyone could defeat these two, then Fael-Inis could. There was a blur of light and fire, and she saw him launch himself at the Conablaiche, a straight arrow of brilliance that exploded in the dim cavern and dazzled them, illuminating the Conablaiche to dreadful clarity, so that they saw again the snapping vulture head, the protruding, fish-like eyes that swivelled and searched. They shrank from the torso that had sketchy Human organs but was not Human in the least, the rudimentary liver and lungs and ribcage, all blotched and smeared and made hideous by the shreds of Human flesh from its victims, and the hard, bony spine discoloured by Human blood. The Conablaiche was walking the world, seeking out victims for its Master, leaving their souls for the Lad of the Skins, leaving their

butchered carcasses for the Old Woman of the Mountains to
spin into thread . . .

The creature gave its clacking laugh, and watched them:
Here are some fine juicy morsels for my Master . . .

And then it swept Fael-Inis aside with one great movement of its arm. Annabel thought that he fell and lay without moving, and then was not sure, because it was
unthinkable that Fael-Inis should be defeated so easily.

Taliesin and Fergus moved as one. They were across the
cavern and upon the Conablaiche, and for a second Annabel
thought they would succeed, for the creature was brought to
the ground, and they all went down in a horrid whirling
jumble of Human arms and beast bones and fists that punched
and tried to restrain, and grisly talons that scraped and
clawed.

The Conablaiche flung both men back against the mountain, and gave its cruel laugh again. Annabel, backed against
the far side, looked frantically for some kind of weapon,
because perhaps if she could lunge for the creature's eyes it
would give them all a chance. It would be the horridest thing
she had ever had to do, to put out a living creature's eyes,
but it would disable the Conablaiche, and it would give them
all a fighting chance.

Fergus and Taliesin were lying where they had been
thrown; they were gasping and helpless, but they were alive. If
they could be given just a very few minutes to recover, they
would certainly try to overpower the Conablaiche again.

The creature was advancing on Annabel now, Taliesin
and Fergus momentarily forgotten, watching her unblinkingly, a look of pure, gloating evil in its lidless eyes. It gave
a neighing chuckle, and reached down between its legs to
where a rudimentary penis hung, and began to rub itself suggestively. The raw stalk of flesh swelled and reared, jutting
out from beneath the discoloured bones. Annabel, her eyes
distended, stared down at it, and frantic thoughts of scrabbling on the ground for sharp stones which would cut it off

tumbled through her mind. Would it be better to cut it off,
or would it be better to attack its eyes? I shall have to do
one or the other, thought Annabel, half kneeling on the floor,
her hands searching furiously for sharp stones. Anything—a
piece of stick . . . Was that something? Yes! Her hand closed
about it.

The Conablaiche stood over her for a moment, its tal-
oned, skeletal hand still between its legs, thrusting out at her
in a travesty of the gesture made by the Drakon patrolman.
Annabel managed to dredge up the slenderest thread of
amusement: Well, and I have been offered two of these things
since I have been here! She had to bite down the bubble of
mirth, because clearly this was what had once been called
hysteria, and she could not waste energy in being hysterical.

The Conablaiche reached down for her, and Annabel
reached up, the sharp stick firmly in her hand. There was a
really terrible moment when she thought she was not going
to be able to do it; the creature's stench was in her nostrils,
and it was a stench of old blood and rotting meat; its bones
were stained with the fluid of its victims, and there had never
been anything so repulsive in the world ever before . . .

Annabel drew back her arm, and jabbed frantically, frenziedly, and with a violence she had not suspected she possessed, at the huge, lidless eye. There was a sudden, soft,
squelching sound, and, what was much worse than the sound,
there was a soft, squelching *feel*. Annabel felt the stick sink
into the jelly-like matter of the Conablaiche's eye, and touch
something hard and bony behind it. There was a dreadful
sensation of having pushed into decaying fruit, and there was
a sudden stench of pus and rotting fluids.

The creature backed away at once, with a dreadful high-
pitched screech that reverberated round the cave. Blood and
thick white fluid gushed from its eye, and Annabel, shuddering, but still holding the stick, shot back, because the smeary
liquid was spurting from the creature's eye socket, and it was
one thing to puncture an eye, but it was quite another to

have the eye fluid spew out all over you. She crawled across to where Taliesin and Fergus were struggling to their feet.

The Conablaiche was staggering about the cave, its clawed hands clutching its gaping eye-socket. A horrid wetness oozed out and trickled between its talons, and it bellowed in agony. Annabel, glancing frantically over her shoulder, shook Taliesin, and reached to take Fergus's hands, because it was not to be thought of that she should be here on her own, with the Conablaiche screeching in agony . . . And at any minute it would turn back and it would vent its fury on her, and this time she might not be able to get to its other eye . . .

Taliesin groaned, and seemed to half revive, but Fergus still lay supine, and Annabel, her heart racing, sent up a prayer that he was not dead.

And then, as she clutched at Taliesin's hands—because he *must* wake up, they both must wake up!—she heard another sound, beyond the Conablaiche's raw screaming, and beyond the inexorable ticking of the Clock.

The marching of a second Drakon patrol.

THE PATROLMEN FELL on them with such swift and cold efficiency that Annabel had just time to think, So much better organised down here! and to wonder whether, the closer you got to the Cavern of the Clock, the more efficient the Drakon became. They overpowered her easily, and although they glanced warily at the shape of the Conablaiche, they did not seem particularly surprised by it.

Two of the men took the unconscious Fergus, and a third half carried Taliesin. Two more picked Annabel up bodily, and the three of them were carried, silently and swiftly, into the dark tunnel.

As they moved away, Annabel heard the thick, treacly chuckling of the Old Woman of the Mountains, and the whirr of her terrible spinning wheel.

It is not easy to think clearly when you are being carried

through a dark tunnel, alongside lapping water, to an almost-certain death. Annabel was by now very frightened, but she thought they could still fight.

She was dizzy from the suddenness of the Drakon's attack, but as the patrolmen waded into the River, Annabel glimpsed lights ahead and heard the clank of machinery, and heard Human voices.

The lights were not the warm, familiar half lights that Annabel had known for most of her life. They were brilliant and rather cold, as if nobody cared any more about dwindling supplies. Because they knew that time was now so short that there was power and to spare for what was left to them?

The patrolmen bent low to pass under a narrow arch of rock, and then flung the three of them down on the floor. Annabel heard Taliesin groan, and knew that at least he lived. She felt ridiculous tears of gratitude prick her eyes and reached up to dash them away angrily.

They were in a vast mountain hall, lit to cold brightness by the power supplies that the rest of the world had been forbidden. Annabel, unused to such brilliance, blinked and waited for her eyes to adjust.

There seemed to be dark-clad men everywhere, coming and going, severe and absorbed. Annabel knew them at once for Drakon patrols. Directly ahead was a long, low table with several men seated behind it, and Annabel stared at them and knew that they had been brought into the presence of the powerful, all-seeing men who controlled the world. This was the Drakon, and these were the men who had written the stringent laws which people called Draconian, and who sent out the patrols and incarcerated people who broke them inside the Cuirim. These are the people who are the laws, thought Annabel. The Drakon sees all and the Drakon's law is absolute.

The man in the centre was watching her, and Annabel shivered, because he had the coldest eyes and the most humourless features she had ever seen. He was tall and thin and the bones of his face stood out, and his eyes were the colour of a bleak November sky when it is going to snow and blizzard, and when he spoke, his voice was like being caught out in a snowstorm.

"Come here."

Annabel went at once, because despite the coldness and despite the humourless eyes and mouth, the man possessed unquestionable authority. You might dislike him very much; you might fear him to an extreme degree, but it would not occur to you to disobey him.

She stood in front of the table and looked at the men and thought, So these are the real Drakon. I am face to face with the people who manipulate the world and who cause us all to be shut away from one another, and who make the laws and send out the patrols. She put up her chin a little and looked down her nose, which was something courageous people in old books had always done. It did not make her feel any braver, but it probably made her look fairly brave, which was better than nothing. And, because attack was supposed to be the best form of defence, she said, quite clearly, "My friends are injured. That creature you employ has injured them. I should be glad if you would have their wounds attended to." And was pleased that at least she sounded unafraid.

"If they are injured," said the cold-eyed man, "it is their own fault. The Claw is allowed to roam the mountain at will for the express purpose of catching trespassers and those who stray into places not meant for them to know about. You have been very foolish, Miss O'Connor. You and your friends will be thrown into a cell."

"And later?"

The man studied her. "There will not be any 'later,'" he said. "You are inside the Cuirim. The headquarters of the Drakon. Looked at from one viewpoint, you have done very well. You have tricked two of the Guardians and nearly reached the torchlit Cavern of the Clock. That is something very few people achieve." He made a brief dismissive gesture with one hand. "The Guardians are unpleasant creatures," he said. "But they serve us well enough."

"You make use of strange servants," said Annabel.

"We make use of whatever comes to hand," said the man. "The people who discovered the Domesday Clock also discovered that these mountains house stranger things than man has dreamed of for some time." He leaned forward. "Our ancestors believed in gods and devils and dreams and nightmares, Miss O'Connor," he said. "We do not. But I will admit to you that down here, buried in these mountains away from the world, we have come to believe in creatures and forces and powers that we would once have dismissed as primitive superstition. Twentieth-century credulity, Miss O'Connor . . . Perhaps earlier, for the later years of that century were quite realistic."

"Still," said Annabel, "the creatures exist. They are here inside the mountain. I have met them."

"And defeated them, it seems." Again he studied her. "That is to your credit," he said.

"You serve an ancient and hungry god," said Annabel scornfully.

"Superstition again, Miss O'Connor."

"You are trafficking with the devil," said Annabel.

The man laughed. "Your expressions smack strongly of medieval naïveté, my dear. I begin to think we should have kept a closer eye on you. You know the penalty for reading forbidden books and for studying the ways of our ancestors . . . ? Yes, I thought you did. You are too inquisitive, Miss O'Connor. Your inquisitiveness has brought you to a place not meant for you to see."

"Why not?" said Annabel defiantly.

"Because the world is dying," said the man. "We do not want people to know. You are not without intelligence, you must know what is happening. Worlds do sometimes die."

With a whimper or a bang, and after all what does it matter in the end . . . ?

"But until the very last hours," said the man, "it has been necessary to preserve some kind of balance. To safeguard people from this terrible knowledge." He leaned forward. "You are not without imagination either," he said. "You must be able to visualise what would happen if men and women were told or found out how close we are to the end: rioting and looting; despair and drunkenness and hysteria; mass suicides. Isn't it safer, isn't it *kinder* to leave them in ignorance for as long as possible?" He sat back. "Admit it," he said softly. "Admit that we are right."

Annabel said nothing.

"Do you suppose," said the man after a moment, "that it has been easy for us down here? Knowing, counting, measuring the time left? Seeing time run out, and unable to do anything." His eyes were distant and suddenly they were not cold any longer. "The worst part," he said, "oh, by far the worst part, is not knowing where the end will come from, or how it will happen."

Annabel said rather hesitantly, "The faceless statesmen. The secret countries. The weapons of the twentieth century—"

"Yes," said the man. "That is the likeliest. Some kind of demand, some kind of threat. Do what we ask, or we will unleash all our power on you. And the world retaliating. Yes, that is the likeliest way. But we do not *know*!" he said, bringing his clenched fist down on the table. "We know that it will happen, for the Clock is approaching Doom Hour, and we have come to believe the Clock. But not knowing— I think that has been the worst part. You have no idea," he said softly, "of how great the burden is."

After a moment, Annabel said, "You are the head."

"Yes." He looked at her. "I *am* the Drakon," he said, and smiled suddenly. "An ordinary businessman with grey hair. That is what you are thinking." The smile vanished as if a slate had been wiped clean, and the cold cruelty was back. "You understand that we can not possibly let you and your friends go, of course. We shall put you in one of the cells."

He regarded her. "I am afraid you will not come out again. The end is not so very far distant now, you see."

"You are very calm," said Annabel.

"I have lived with the knowledge for a long time, my dear."

"But surely—" Annabel stopped, and then went on. "Surely something will survive?" Because it was unbearable beyond words to imagine everything dead or dying, to think that Man would no longer walk the earth . . .

"We believe," said the Drakon, "that Man *will* survive," and Annabel looked up, because she had not expected him to sense her thoughts so very exactly. "Man will survive," he said, half to himself now, "but it will be in a different form, perhaps. He is an adaptable creature, Man, after all. And perhaps after the fires have cooled and the Disease has dispersed, he will emerge, a little changed, a little different. But still in the world." He stood up. "I am a realist, Miss O'Connor. I make use of whatever instruments come to hand. The Claw and the Three Guardians will continue to work and to serve me." He stood up and nodded to two of the men. "Take them to one of the cells," he said. "And give the Claw its reward." And then, turning back to Annabel, "In any case," he said, "your incarceration is of little account now."

Annabel stared at him, her heart thudding painfully. "Midnight," she said softly. "The Doom Hour."

"Yes, midnight. If the secret countries unleash the forces that our ancestors were so proud of, then the world will burn, and this entire mountain may be rent asunder."

Annabel said softly, " 'And Four Horsemen shall come into the world to announce the Beast Apocalypse . . . they shall stalk the earth and lay it waste in their several ways, and after their coming, the skies shall darken and the seas shall boil and the world shall burn for fifty days and fifty nights . . .' " She stopped and looked at him and thought that a gleam of approval showed in the cold, grey eyes.

But, "An even older superstition, Miss O'Connor. But in the main, you are right," was all he said.

"We are close to the end?"

"Yes. I do not think there is anything that can save us." He looked at her. "The Clock stands at exactly five minutes to midnight," he said.

TALIESIN AND FERGUS came back to full consciousness slowly and painfully. Fergus started to say, "What happened—" and then stopped, because he remembered all too clearly what had happened. They had been defeated by the Conablaiche and by the Sensleibhe, and they had been thrown into the Drakon's prison.

And the Clock was still ticking . . .

Taliesin, who had put one arm about Annabel's shoulders, said, "Fergus, my dear, I beg you will not make use of such obvious questions. Or do you really not know what has happened? Would you like me to enumerate our various disasters in detail?"

"Thank you, no," said Fergus. "I remember everything. I wish I did not." And then, "Is either of us injured very much?" he said.

"We have suffered the slings and arrows of outrageous fortune, but I believe that in the main we have whole skins. I daresay that our wits are a bit astray, but I daresay they always were. And probably we shall be able to think of a way out," said Taliesin, and Fergus wondered if anything discomposed Taliesin.

"Very little, my friend," said Taliesin.

Fergus looked round. They were lying in a stone cell, barely six feet square. Three of the walls were solid rock and the fourth made up of thick iron bars. There was a faint spill of light from the tunnel outside. It was sufficient to show them that the cell was as solid and as secure as it was possible for it to be.

Taliesin said, " 'Iron bars do not a prison make.' Or do they? I suppose we *shall* find a way out, shall we?"

"I hope so," said Fergus. "I don't think we have very much time."

"Very little," said Taliesin, and looked at the other two and thought, Oh, my dears, if only you knew that it no longer matters. We are trapped in this cell, but also we are trapped in this world now. Calatin's spell was to last for seven days, and seven days will soon have come and gone: we have no way of returning to our own world.

Fergus was inspecting the cell carefully. "For," he said, "every prison has its chink."

"The floors and the walls and the roof are of solid rock," said Taliesin. And then, "Fergus, we have to get to the children."

"I know," said Fergus, not turning round.

"We have to get to the Clock," said Taliesin, half to himself.

"Could we somehow dig our way out?" said Annabel, trying the floor with her feet. "No, it's solid. And there's nothing to dig with."

"We could bribe the guards if we had anything to bribe them with," said Fergus thoughtfully. "Annabel, are the members of the Drakon bribable?"

"I suppose they would be," said Annabel.

Taliesin, from the shadows, said, "Every man has his price. Are there any other prisoners down here?"

"There must be," said Annabel. "This is the Cuirim. No one ever comes out."

"I wonder," said Taliesin thoughtfully, "what Fael-Inis would do in this situation?"

"Blast the lock with a bolt of light," said Fergus at once.

"Lure the guards with his silver pipes," said Annabel. And then, because the thought of losing Fael-Inis was unbearable, she said, "I daresay he will help us in any case." And so strong, so violent was the hope, that she turned to look down the dark tunnel, half expecting to see him appear.

Taliesin said, "We could lure the guards ourselves. By calling them. And then we could spring on them."

"Yes, for they must have keys." Fergus turned back, his eyes alight. "Yes, listen, if we could—" He looked at the other two, horror dawning in his eyes. "It's too late," he said. "Annabel, Taliesin, we are too late. *Listen.*" And stared at them, and saw his own horror reflected in their faces, and knew that they had heard it as well.

Hoofbeats coming down the mountain tunnel towards them.

The Four Horsemen . . .

CONN AND NIALL, with Michael and the others close by, woke from a deep, warm sleep, peopled with soft, happy dreams, and with the memories of the world they had been driven from. They were nearly back there now. Fergus would take them back, and the others would be there as well: Taliesin and Annabel and the strange, golden creature called Fael-Inis who had drawn them with him through the dark tunnels, so that there had been no time for fear, only a marvellous exhilaration, and a feeling that anything was possible and everything was within their grasp.

Michael, who had woken up first, sat up and looked round, because it had all been a bit muddled last night, and a person liked to know where he was.

The room was quite small and it was lit by a fire, which was very nice. Michael had always had a fire in his bedroom. It made you feel extra safe, and you could lie and watch the leaping flames make pictures on the walls and the ceiling.

He had done that on the night the creature came. He could remember it very clearly indeed. There had been rain outside; fierce, lashing rain that hurled itself against the windows and made you feel glad that you were lying inside warm and snug and safe with a fire. He had listened to it that night, but mixed in with the rain had been something else. Something outside. He had lain for a long time listening to it, but he had not called out, because the something might have heard him. He had known it was there, though. It had peered in through the chink in the curtain, and it had tried the locks. It had sniffed at the door—Michael had heard it—and he knew that it had claws and nails and teeth, and that it was trying to get in so that it could get to him while he lay in bed. He had pretended it was not there, because that was always a good thing to do if you woke up in the middle of the night and thought there was a something trying to get in. You pulled the covers tight over your head, and you shut out the frightened-ness, and quite often, well very nearly always, the next thing you knew it was morning and the sun was shining, and you were being called to hurry to breakfast, and everything was all right again.

But the covers had not helped that night, because the something that prowled and sniffed and peered had got in, and had come creeping across the bedroom. Michael had kept his eyes squeezed tight shut, as tight as they would go, but he had known quite definitely that the something was in the room, and he had not dared to move in case the something pounced on him, and it had all been quite dreadfully scary, and he would not remember any of it.

He certainly would not remember it now, not when Conn and Niall and the others were here with him, not when somebody was rocking slowly and comfortably by the fire . . .

It would have been better if the somebody had not cast quite such a huge shadow on the walls. There was nothing wrong with the shadow, not really, only that it made you think that people were not always what they seemed to be. Sometimes they turned their heads to look at you, so that you saw that they had slit eyes and grinning lips and a muzzle, a great, wide, dripping maw that would open wide to devour you. *All the better to spin with, my dears . . . my dears . . . my dears . . .*

That was what she had said last night, "Come inside, my dears," and in they had gone. And then the door had clanged to, and they had been in here with her, and there had been firelight and the rocking of a chair and a spinning wheel and, quite suddenly, it was all too scary for words.

In a minute, Michael would open his eyes. It would be

a good thing to do, really, because he would see Conn and Niall and the others. You would not be afraid of anything in the world with those. Conn could do absolutely anything and Niall could do very nearly anything.

He opened his eyes a chink. Yes, there was firelight. And an old woman—he remembered now—who was doing something with a spinning wheel. Michael's grandmother had had a spinning wheel, because they had kept sheep, and there had always been nice fluffy wool for jerkins and mittens and leggings. Michael had been allowed to help spin the sheepwool into the thin, strong wool strands, and it had been interesting. He would quite like to see the spinning now. The lady was nodding and smiling and beckoning, and she was quite old, she was nearly as old as his grandmother had been, which was extremely old, and so there was nothing to be afraid of. It was silly to feel the creeping fear that made you remember about *somethings* that prowled and sniffed and got in to your bedroom when you were asleep. He would go and see the spinning and perhaps he would be allowed to help.

The lady seemed to know his name. "Michael," she said, in a rather thick, slurry sort of voice. "Michael. How nice."

People could not help their voices. This lady could not help having a slimy purr. She probably could not help having black glittering eyes either. She reached out and stroked his arm, and he flinched, because she did not have an arm like most people, but a kind of tentacle thing with hard stringy muscles, covered with bristly black hairs, with the hands curving into talons.

Michael tried to back away, but the Sensleibhe had him in her cruel grasp. "Come a little closer, my dear," she said in the horrid, slurry, blurred voice that made you think of grease and thick bubbling mucus. "Come a little closer and see the spinning."

Michael, who did not want to see the spinning at all now, and who was hoping rather desperately that the others would wake up and see what was happening, felt himself pulled nearer and nearer to the whirring wheel, and closer and closer to the treadle that went in and out and that jabbed and stabbed and began to look nastier the nearer you got to it.

"You see?" said the Sensleibhe. "You see, Michael, all the things I use for spinning. Little boys are especially good." And she reached out her other hand and stroked him again. "Come a little closer," said the Sensleibhe, and gave the horrid chuckling again. Michael twisted out of her grasp and shot back across the room and collided with Conn.

The Sensleibhe advanced on them. Her hands were reaching out and her eyes were greedy. She was grinning, and she was no longer an old lady like Michael's grandmother, but a hungry ravening thing with a dripping maw that would gobble you up in minutes, with a muzzle and teeth and fangs ... you would be minced and chopped, and she would pull you into the spinning wheel, and you would be turned into thread, all studded with your nails and bits of your hair and shreds of your skin ...

"Come nearer, my dears," said the Old Woman of the Mountains. "All the better to spin with ... Little boys for the spinning wheel ... Come a little nearer."

The boys were all wide-awake now, huddled in the corner, staring at the dreadful creature that was creeping towards them across the firelit room.

"We'll fight you," said Niall loudly, and the Sensleibhe laughed.

"Such precious poppets," she said. "Fight? Dearie me, you won't fight me, my lambkins. Not a bit of a fight will you put up, or I shall have to fetch Mr. Ferryman to you. He's waiting, you know. Did you know that? He's just outside the door now. Shall we let him in? He's standing just outside the door in the dark, very quietly listening and waiting. Shall we open the door and see him standing there in his long dark cloak and with his face covered by the hood?

"And you all know what Mr. Ferryman does, don't you? You've all met him, haven't you? You know how he creeps into children's bedrooms and steals across the floor while they're asleep, and gobbles them up. You've all met him, my lambkins, haven't you? Shall we let him in now?" And she began to move to the door.

Michael thought afterwards that it was Conn who shouted, "No!" but he was never sure. He thought he might have shouted it himself. He thought they might all have shouted.

The Sensleibhe had moved with incredible swiftness to the door; she could not really be old at all, because old people did not move like that, they did not scuttle. The Sensleibhe scuttled. Michael reached for Conn's hand, because Conn was a good sort of person to hold on to if something nasty was going to happen.

All the better to spin with . . . skin and teeth and nails and hair . . . all made into thread . . .

And then something very strange happened. It was so strange and so unexpected that none of them could ever quite explain it, and certainly none of them could ever describe it.

The Old Woman of the Mountains had reached the door, and she was grinning and nodding and reaching for the door handle. In another minute, the door would be opened, and there he would be, the dreadful creature they all remembered, the monstrous *something* that had crept into their houses while they slept and crawled up the stairs to their warm safe bedrooms and found its way into their beds . . .

The door was opening, and Michael had drawn breath to yell, when they all saw it.

Lights, and people running, and confusion. Dark-clad men hurrying about and shouting. And a sound so immense and so steady that for a moment no one knew what it was. Pounding. Drumming. Getting nearer.

And then they saw them. Sweeping through the dark shadow tunnels of the mountain halls towards them were four great creatures of such size and such strength and such dark and terrible beauty, that the boys gasped and cowered back. Horses, but horses such as no one had ever seen in the world. Great gleaming stallions, Barbary steeds, somehow made of shadows and of long endless nights and of eternal black seas. Their flanks were shining ebony and their saddles were crimson leather, and their eyes were like glowing coals, fiery and inhuman.

Michael gasped and felt Conn's hand tighten about his. One of the boys said in a whisper, "What are they?"

"I don't know," said Conn, his eyes never leaving the leaping, pawing creatures. "But *she's* afraid of them."

The horses were coming down the tunnel now, rearing and stampeding. "And they are being ridden," said Niall, whose parents had kept and trained horses for the Court. "They are being ridden harder than any horse I ever saw ridden."

The horses seemed to burn with a kind of dark radiance, so that although you could see the radiance all about them, you could only see them as black shapes, at the centre of the unearthly light. They had neither form nor substance, and yet they were real and terrifying, and although you were afraid to look at them, you could not take your eyes from them.

They could make out the shapes of the riders more clearly now; they could see billowing cloaks and the glint of black armour. The riders wore visors, each one pulled down so that their faces were invisible.

"Faceless riders," breathed Conn.

There was a sense of timelessness about the riders, and a feeling that no matter how long you looked on them, you would never see them properly.

The horses were coming nearer now, and the boys could make out the fiery breath and see the gleam of spurs and rein and bit. "And although we were frightened," Niall was to say, "we could not move. We could not take our eyes away."

The Four Horsemen entering the ancient mountain, riding down into the depths of the mountain halls, where the Domesday Clock was ticking to the end of the world . . .

And then one of them said, "Look! The Old Woman! She is terrified!" And somehow, the terror of the Sensleibhe gave them all fresh courage, for the Old Woman of the

Mountains was backing up against the walls, staring in dread at the Horsemen, her eyes bolting from her head.

And then there was a tremendous wind, and a great rushing sound, and the riders were standing up in the stirrups, driving their steeds on, and the boys could see them with blinding clarity, and the light was glowing and they were dark and terrible and unearthly and filled with immense power.

And then, quite suddenly, they were past the door, they were disappearing along the dark tunnel, and the radiance was dimming, and the sound of the hoofbeats was dying, and the Sensleibhe was no longer a threat.

Conn turned to look at the others, his eyes shining, "Now," he said, "out and after them! Ready?" And stood looking at them with such delight and such strength that they began to cheer, a bit raggedly at first, and then with more assurance.

"After them!" cried Conn, and the boys poured out of the cave and out into the mountain.

To TALIESIN AND Fergus and Annabel, the approach of the Four Horsemen was the worst nightmare they had ever experienced. They stood close together, grasping the iron bars at the front of the cell, straining to see through the shadows, hearing Drakon men running and shouting, feeling the panic well up from the heart of the mountain. Fergus, accustomed to action, found himself wanting to tear the iron bars aside and go bounding out into the mountain, attacking the Drakon patrols, forcing a way into the torchlit Cavern of the Clock. Taliesin, quieter, far more detached than the volatile Fergus, remained very still and felt the terror and the chaos soak into his mind, and thought, After all, is this truly the end? Are we about to witness the world dying? Ought I to feel privileged to be here?

Annabel was the least frightened of them all. She thought it was because she had lived with the knowledge for so long, and she thought that when you have dreaded and feared a thing, you find that when it is at last upon you, it is not so terrible as you had thought. She found that she was clinging to the thought of Fael-Inis somewhere inside the mountain, and she found herself watching for the wisp of light and the faint shimmer of fire that would herald his approach. For he cannot have abandoned us! thought Annabel, standing between Fergus and Taliesin. And he cannot be dead, for surely he is nearly immortal!

At her side, Taliesin said softly, "He will not abandon us."

"Then where is he?"

"Perhaps he is—injured," said Taliesin, but Annabel knew he had been about to say, perhaps he is dead.

The hoofbeats were thundering closer now, and the three travellers knew that before many minutes had passed, they would be witnessing the dreaded coming of the Heralds, the emissaries who had been prophesied and foretold by generations, and who would precede the coming of the Beast Apocalypse into the world. Plague, Famine, War, Death . . .

The Horsemen came sweeping by and there was fire and darkness and flying flames and great splintering forks of lightning. Iron-sinew'd and satin-skinned, fierce as fire, violent and cruel and relentless they were. Pegasus ridden by Bellerophon, ridden by Jehu: marvellous and terrible and as unstoppable as the angels.

Tongues of fire and flame shot from the horses' hoofs, and the three travellers moved back at once. The tunnel was bathed in brilliance, and the sound of the hoofs and the ringing of the spurs and the bridles was deafening. The Four Horsemen of the Apocalypse rushing down on mankind . . .

Smoke belched out into the tunnel, and the sparks lit dozens of small crackling fires that ran along the ground and burned.

"Shall we burn!" cried Fergus, his eyes brilliant, his hair tumbling over his forehead. "Is this to be the end?"

They were half blinded by the smoke, and their eyes were stinging from the flames, but they could see the Horsemen turning the corner. "They are going away from us!" shouted Annabel through the tumult. "Down the tunnels!"

"They are going to the Clock Cavern!" cried Taliesin. "Fergus, we must somehow stop them—" And then jumped back as flames licked the ground beneath the bars at the front of the cell.

As the Horsemen rode hard round the curve, disappearing into the darkness, a spark from one of their hoofs flew out to hit the door. The lock gave and the door fell open.

Annabel and the two men looked at one another . . . "After them!" cried Fergus. "I do not think we have very much time left!"

No one stopped them as they ran gasping and frantic in the direction of the black Horsemen.

"Follow the sounds," cried Taliesin. "The Clock—can you hear it?"

"Yes," said Fergus. "Yes, it is quite close."

"Don't lose it," gasped Taliesin. "There is so much noise, but we dare not lose the sound."

The noise was deafening. Drakon men were milling about everywhere and there was the thick smell of smoke and the acrid tang of the flames from the Horsemen.

"The patrols and the guards are panicking," said Annabel. "They are afraid of the Horsemen."

"Because of the Horsemen they are hardly noticing us," said Fergus. "We might walk unchallenged anywhere we like."

They hesitated only once, at the intersection of three tunnels. Then, "This way," said Taliesin, and Fergus nodded. They were not only hearing the Clock now, they could feel it. Taliesin, leading the way, Annabel between the two of them, thought it was like a great beating heart, like the fluttering of a giant pulse. And we dare not let it stop. Tick, tick, tick . . . If it stopped, they would know they had failed. If it stopped, the Horsemen would have reached the Cavern and the world would end. Taliesin found himself praying to all the gods he had ever heard of that the ticking would not stop. A heartbeat, a pulse, a pendulum . . . While it ticks and flutters and swings, we still live, there is still hope. Tick, tick, tick . . .

Fergus was racing along the tunnels, and he, as well as Taliesin, was feeling the Clock's heartbeats. If it stopped, they were all dead. If it stopped, the Horsemen had triumphed and the Beast Apocalypse would walk into the world . . . Shall we actually see it? wondered Fergus, and remembered how he had once thought they would chain the Apocalypse and take it back to Tara to defeat Medoc. But Medoc was in another world and in another time, and it might be that they would never be able to return to it . . . Then this will be our world, thought Fergus, appalled. This dreadful, bleak, cheerless place will be our world . . . And if we cannot reach the torchlit Cavern in time, there will be no world for any of us. Is it still ticking? Yes, I can still hear it.

Drakon men were everywhere in the tunnels now, scurrying in every direction, confused and panic-stricken, shouting to one another, trying to avoid the licking flames that had sprung up in the wake of the Horsemen. Several of them were stamping at the flames, and several were dashing buckets of water on to the ground in an endeavour to stop the path of the fire.

Taliesin and Fergus and Annabel were scarcely aware of running now, but the tunnels were rushing past them, and they could hear the Clock's heartbeats getting nearer. Once Annabel thought they were in the river tunnel again, because water lapped about their feet and washed over their ankles. And then they turned another curve, and Taliesin pulled them into a left-hand fork, and the River of Souls, if it had been, was behind them again.

They must be very close to the Clock now. Annabel thought that it was almost becoming a part of them. Tick, tick . . . Please let it go on, prayed Annabel silently. We are so near, we are nearly there. Only a very little longer. And the Horsemen have not yet reached the Cavern; I can still hear them. If only we can get there in time . . .

And then Taliesin gave a shout, and Fergus said, "There it is!"

Directly ahead of them, through a wide arch of rock, lit by burning torches that were never allowed to go out, was the cavern of the Domesday Clock.

"Unguarded!" cried Fergus, moving forward. "Quickly!" And then—"Can you see the Clock?" he shouted, and Taliesin, who was standing framed in the archway, shading his eyes with one hand, said softly, "Yes, I can see it.

"And it stands at exactly one minute to midnight."

BUT THE CLOCK was still ticking. It was ticking swiftly and surely, and the hands were moving slowly, inexorably, but it was still ticking. And we are ahead of the Horsemen, thought Annabel. Somehow we have beaten them. If only we can do it, if only we can climb up to it . . .

The Cavern was smaller than they had expected. There was a high vaulted ceiling, and there were arches and niches in the rockface. Taliesin glanced at them, and thought they were probably natural rock formations. Shadows stirred above them, and several times they caught the soft beating of wings. But no one came to challenge them, and nothing came creeping out of the shadows, and as they stood there, it seemed to each of them as if a tremendous hush had descended.

Wall brackets were all round the Cavern, and burning torches were thrust into each one, lighting the Cavern to eerie life. There was the pungent scent of wood burning, and there was a feeling not only of extreme age, but also of great silence and of great peace, as if this was the heart and the core and the centre of the world.

Taliesin, absorbing it all, thought that after all, when you are at the heart, you do not need to be other than silent. Outside the Cavern was roaring confusion; they could hear running footsteps and shouts; great boulders were beginning to fall from the tunnel roofs, and the fires kindled by the Horsemen were roaring through the mountain.

But we have come to the epicentre, thought Taliesin. We are at the eye of the storm and here all is tranquillity.

And then, because he had seen temples and places of worship to various gods, he was strongly aware of a feeling of silent homage. They have looked on the Clock as a kind of god, he thought. A deity. A creature to whom they must pay homage.

The Clock was directly ahead of them, set high on a ledge of rock. The mountain walls gleamed with a faint blue phosphorescence, and on each side of the Clock, candles burned. An altar . . . A place of homage . . . Sacrifice.

The Domesday Clock: the dreadful sinister instrument that had lain for centuries inside the dark mountain, untended, forgotten, and yet continuing to tick. Measuring out the world's last years, until mankind would die and the world would end, either with a whimper or a bang, it did not really matter . . . Ticking in the dark by itself, unaided.

Small wonder, thought Taliesin, that the people who had found it had set it on a high altar and lit candles and burned scented logs before it. And then, because he had been trying to visualise the kind of device this strange austere world might have made to measure their time so precisely and so soul-chillingly, he studied the great machine with close attention.

The Clock was bigger than any of them had expected, although Annabel thought they had not really known what to expect. It was massive and oval-shaped, and it gleamed palely, so that it was difficult not to think of it as alive.

The hands were dark and ornate; the figures stood out elaborately against the pale background. Annabel thought they had once been called Roman figures, but could not be sure. And round the face, carved and etched and coloured in sombre greys and blacks, were four figures.

Four figures . . . An hour ago, we should not have recognised them, thought Taliesin. Now they are burned into our memories for ever.

Plague, Famine, War, and Death . . . And they are here in the mountain with us . . . They are raging through the mountain halls, and very soon, at any minute, they will come surging through the tunnels, and they will be in the cavern with us, and when that happens, the hands will touch midnight, and the ticking will stop.

There were thirty seconds to go.

Fergus was already climbing up the steep wall of the cavern, finding footholds where footholds did not exist, reaching for tiny jutting sections of rock, pulling himself up and up, hand over hand, scrabbling for purchase, slipping back sometimes, but going onwards. Taliesin was behind him, slower, but following in Fergus's path, reaching for crevices in the rock, dislodging flurries of boulders and stones, sending them cascading downwards.

They had to turn the hands back as far as they could.

Annabel, knowing there was nothing she could do, certainly knowing she could not reach the altar ahead of them, stayed where she was, her nails digging into the palms of her hands, her eyes never leaving the Clock. It was dreadful to have to stand here like this, unable to help, hearing every tiny sound in the cavern. There were scufflings and rustlings in the Cavern now; where once it had been silent and somehow watchful, now it seemed as if it was coming alive. Several times, Annabel turned her head because, just for a moment, it had seemed as if there was a movement in one of the low narrow tunnels leading out of the Cavern.

Twenty-five seconds . . .

The Horsemen were over their heads now, thundering closer with every second. Annabel was vaguely aware of forked light illuminating the tunnel they had just come through. At any minute . . .

Eighteen seconds . . .

Fergus was inching higher, and Taliesin was on his heels. There were several feet to go before he gained the ledge. Surely they must get there in time, it was not bearable that they should reach the Clock and then fail.

Is it worse to see it happen? wondered Annabel. Is it going to be worse to know the exact second when the hands reach midnight? Would it have been better to stay in the cell and not know? Of course not!

Tick, tick . . . Thirteen seconds. I can't bear it, thought Annabel. I shall turn away and close my eyes. But she did bear it and she did not turn away. She kept her eyes unwaveringly on the Clock.

Fergus and Taliesin were nearly there. They were on the altar at the left-hand side. They would have to crawl along the ledge—Annabel could see how perilously narrow it was. There were more of the narrow tunnels leading away from the ledge. Perhaps that was the way the Drakon people entered the Cavern. If they had been able to find the way through the labyrinth of caves, they would have reached the Clock much quicker.

Ten seconds . . .

They would not do it. Annabel could see very clearly and very coldly and very surely that they would not do it. If they could have gone faster, if the ledge had been wider and safer, so that they could run . . . If they could have found another way to the Cavern, through one of the tunnels that opened directly onto the ledge . . . And if the Clock had not been so vast . . .

Eight seconds.

And then from one of the narrow tunnels light streamed outwards and there was a flare of movement. Annabel stared, not daring to believe, not daring to hope . . . In a cascade of pure golden light he was there, and Annabel gasped, and Fergus and Taliesin turned.

He was filled with light and fire, and he was in front of the Clock now, a little to the left of it, and light was pouring from him, and his eyes were glowing with all the radiance he had possessed since before the First Great Battle, with all the power that he could harness; and he was blindingly beautiful and he was invincible, and he would save the world and turn back the Horsemen . . .

The being of fire and light. The rebel angel who would defy the world and challenge the gods and win. Oh, yes, he will win! cried Annabel in silent joy, He will win. For if anyone can save the world, he can.

Six seconds.

Taliesin and Fergus stayed where they were, their eyes on the slender figure by the Clock, their hearts pounding.

Five seconds . . .

Light poured from Fael-Inis now, and he drew himself up to his fullest height, and turned to the Clock.

Four seconds . . .

A bolt of pure light shot from his pointing hand, swift and sure, and hurtled towards the Clock's face. The cave rocked with the impact, and showers of sparks fell from the roof.

Three seconds.

The watchers were as still as stones. The light exploded against the Clock face, sizzling and smouldering. Cascades of iridescence showered everywhere. The minute hand hesitated.

There was another tick.

Two seconds.

Annabel could hear the Horsemen, she could smell the hot fiery breath of the rushing horses . . . Has he done it? Has it been strong enough . . . ? A bolt of pure light . . . Oh, please, *please* let it have been strong enough, let him have succeeded, for to fail like this would be unbearable, we shall not be able to bear it, it will be the worst agony ever, anywhere . . .

Light, pure and coruscating, split the Cavern, and there was a great thunderclap somewhere above their heads, and a sheet of flame reared up in the Cavern. The floor rocked beneath their feet, and chasms began to open everywhere. Jagged lightning tore across the Cavern and speared the altar. The Domesday Clock began to teeter on its narrow ledge, and fireballs of red and orange poured in from the roof. The mountain began to split and great fissures opened up. Annabel saw Taliesin and Fergus lose their precarious hold on the narrow ledge and fall, clutching each other, down the steep side of the rockface.

Annabel thought she was shouting, "The Clock! Has it been turned back? Oh dear God, has it turned back?" but her voice was drowned in the tumult of rocks falling and the mountain splitting, and the screaming of people, and the running of feet and the crackling flames.

There was one final blinding sheet of light that illuminated the Cavern to painful brilliance, and Annabel and the two men saw with sudden delight Conn and Niall and Michael and the boys come hurtling through the archway, their faces white and smeared with dirt, but their eyes brilliant and alive. Fergus shouted something, and the children went to him in a single movement.

And then the intense vivid light flamed again, and they turned to see Fael-Inis for the last time, outlined clearly above them on the high ledge where the Clock had lain, silhouetted against the dark background of the mountain, his arms outstretched, his head thrown back, fire and light and radiance pouring over him and through him, the flames and the heat and the wild blazing fire engulfing him. And despite the danger, despite the fact that the mountain was tumbling about them, and that everywhere was in flames, and that they might all be about to die, still the three travellers stood still, the children clustered about them, looking at him, seeing him for what he was . . . the angel of fire and light and speed . . . the proud, arrogant, lonely rebel destined to walk the earth for ever . . .

There was a wrenching pain and the faint, far-off rushing of chariot wheels, and a whirling, dizzying sensation, and the heat and the smoke seemed to blur and merge, and Annabel closed her eyes against it, because she could not bear it any longer, it was not to be borne . . .

An immense stillness descended on them, and Annabel opened her eyes and sat up.

Fergus's voice said in a strange, distant expression, "Tara."

Tara. The Bright Palace. It lay across the valley from them.

CHAPTER TWENTY-THREE

THE COURT HAD made camp in the folds of hillside overlooking the little township of Folaim.

"And a very good camp it is," said Fintan, pleased. "Very comfortable. Not that you'd have expected it, what with people and animals all together, but it's working very nicely. I said it would," said Fintan, who had not said any such thing.

Smoke rose from the Cruithin's fires: "They keep themselves *to* themselves," observed Cathbad; close by, the army had settled itself into groups of threes and fours. Occasionally a snatch of song could be heard; now and then there was a burst of laughter.

"Rude jokes, I daresay," said Fintan, trying to listen.

Cathbad scurried about with his pots. He was in a great state over the forthcoming banquet. "Because," he said seriously to Grainne, "it has to be *right*, Your Majesty. There's no sense in having a banquet if you don't have it *right*. Dear me, what a flurry I shall be in, shan't I? I wonder now, could we manage a few sod eggs—well, that's begging your pardon, ma'am, for appearing to sound *vulgar*, but it's what they're called. What you do is you boil the eggs first—some people call it seething them, but I don't," said Cathbad. "And then you make a nice little sauce, and if Tybion the Tusk has taken my seething pot to catch trout *again*, I shall be very angry.

"And then," said Cathbad, "I'll make a marigold tart—well, several tarts, really, because one is *never* enough. And wild duck," said Cathbad, with solemnity. "My word, there's nothing to equal a few wild ducks on Samain. Properly stuffed, of course, that goes without saying. I'd better lay a few traps. My word, I *am* going to be busy."

Fintan was heard to tell Cermait Honeymouth that they would all of them be as overfed as pigs. They would certainly be too full to indulge in any of the traditional Samain activities.

"You never do anyway," said Cermait. "Were you thinking of leaping through the bonfire this year? The last time you tried that you got singed in the—"

"No, I did not," said Fintan loudly, because several of the younger soldiers were listening and it would not do for people to know.

"You couldn't sit down for a week," said Cermait with relish.

Rinnal and Bec, and several others of the Beastline, had gone into the forest to gather the wood for the fire.

"Rowan and dry oak," said Tybion, who was going with them. "And agaric from the birches, to make the needfire. It has to be *right*," said Tybion, unconsciously echoing Cathbad, who was by this time contemplating borage stuffing for the ducks, which he had not yet thought how to catch, and a first course of bean soup.

"We all like that," he said, beaming.

"I don't," said Fintan.

"It's warming," said Cathbad.

"It's purgative," said Fintan crossly, and went off to supervise the gathering of the wood, because you could not trust the youngsters to know the proper rituals.

Lugh and Dorrainge had removed themselves from the main body of the camp, so that they could hold a serious and responsible discussion about the exact nature of the celebrations.

They were getting on rather well; Dorrainge was beginning to think that he had misjudged Lugh, who had even broached the question of some kind of sacrifice on the bonfire, which Dorrainge rather supported. He said there was nothing like a sacrifice on a Samain bonfire.

"I rather thought a small pig," said Lugh, and Dorrainge tucked his chins portentously into his neck, and said, A pig, very possibly. Yes, a pig might serve the purpose nicely. It was necessary, he explained, to appease the forces of evil that stalked the world on Samain. That was why a sacrifice was a good idea.

"On Samain the barriers are lowered," he explained. "The boundaries that exist between all the worlds are swept aside. The dead may walk, and the Dark Ireland will certainly be very close to us." He looked at Lugh severely. "Also," said Dorrainge, "the *sidh* mounds are flung wide open."

Lugh said that this was very true indeed, hadn't he always heard it to be the case, but felt it necessary to point out that they already had the *sidh* with them, or almost with them, and had they settled about the pig?

"I cannot see that it would hurt," said Dorrainge, stroking his chin and being careful not to say that he was rather fond of roast pig. If you were contemplating a Samain sacrifice, you should not let your judgement be swayed by the thought of eating it afterwards. It would be very indelicate.

"We could eat the pig afterwards," said Lugh, and Dorrainge remembered that the Longhands were all famed for their lack of delicacy. He said that it would have to be thought over, but that a sacrifice was certainly worth considering, and passed on to the idea of a few virgins to leap ceremoniously through the bonfire. He hoped that nobody would suggest reviving the Sacred Chant, because he could not remember it. If people knew that the Second Druid of all Ireland did not know the Sacred Chant, they would all start wanting Fribble back and telling each other that Fribble would have known the Sacred Chant backwards—which would have been disastrous of course: to recite the Sacred Chant backwards was simply asking for trouble.

Lugh said that they ought to have the Sacred Chant, pretending not to notice that Dorrainge groaned, and said it would all be altogether grand, and had they established about the sacrificing of the pig yet?

"We'll do it," said Dorrainge, who thought you might as well be hanged for a Sacred Chant as for a sacrificial pig, and went off to see about the laying of traps, thus sending Cathbad into a whole new flurry.

Lugh thought he was doing really rather well. He had set up the Samain celebrations, very nearly single-handed, because you could not count Dorrainge, who was now mumbling to himself and making hasty jottings of unpronounceable phrases, and you could not count Fintan or Cermait or Tybion the Tusk, and you certainly could not count Cathbad.

But a good leader knew about delegation, and Lugh was once again going to make use of Tybion. He called him aside, and told Tybion to go on down to the village and invite every single living soul to come up to the bonfire that night, and—Tybion must mind this carefully—to be sure to bring along the children, because it was what Her Majesty wanted, said Lugh, and Tybion, charmed to be of service to his lady in this small way, promised not to miss a single household in Folaim.

Which was precisely what Lugh wanted. It had been a brilliant idea to send out for the children. Even so, Lugh was not comfortable about what he had to do. It was one thing to agree to kill a child when you were in Medoc's firelit lair, with Medoc's powerful personality exerting its influence. It was another thing altogether to contemplate it on a cold hillside with half of Her Majesty's Court, the army, and the Bloodline, to say nothing of the entire Cruithin contingent. Lugh had even lost some sleep worrying, which was unusual, because as a rule he was a very sound sleeper. It came of a clean conscience, and a tranquil mind.

There was nothing clean or tranquil about pussyfooting around in the dark with the bonfire yards away, trying to see was the Lost Prince, the prophesied Wolfchild, skulking somewhere. Lugh supposed the Lad of the Skins would be around to make sure it was done, but this did not help very much.

The child should be easy to recognise, which was the one straightforward thing about it all. A Wolfchild amidst Humans ... Yes, it would be easy to spot.

And once he had found it, he would have to kill it.

GRAINNE WAS VERY nearly completely happy. She thought she had never known quite such deep contentment, and such well-being.

It was not enough, of course. She had woken the Old Ireland, she had found the Cruithin and the *sidh*; best of all, she had brought back the Bloodline.

And there was Raynor. Remarkably, incredibly, she had Raynor. Enough happiness there for several lifetimes.

But it would not be enough, not until a Wolfprince again sat in the Sun Chamber, not until a direct descendant of the great Cormac and of Niall of the Nine Hostages again held Tara.

Not until Fergus returned.

The thoughts of Fergus were still a bruise on her heart; an ache that had not yet quite left her. The knowledge that he might be dead, that he might be lost to her forever, somewhere in a distant and alien Future, was scarcely bearable. Was he safe? She thought he was, for, thought Grainne, how could he not be safe, and I not know? It seemed a long time ago now, those far-off nights and those misty mornings. I know it happened, thought Grainne, drowsy in the afternoon sun, watching the Court and the army prepare for the evening's celebrations; I know it happened, and I know it happened to me. But I think that I am seeing it from a distance, *through a glass darkly, behind a veil* ...

But I should surely know if Fergus was dead. And then— But should I know if Fergus's son was also dead? she thought.

The Lost Prince. Ireland's heir. *I* was the one who lost him, thought Grainne, staring ahead of her. I denied him his birthright. I denied him Tara. For that alone I should be made to live in unhappiness for all my days. For I shut Ireland's true Prince out from his kingdom, and I do not believe he will ever be able to return.

THE PURPLE HOUR was approaching when the soldiers set up a circle of burning torches, stout ash sticks thrust into the ground, which they had ignited so that the scene was lit to weird life.

Grainne, seated at the head of the table with Raynor at her side, smiled to see the men so pleased, and remembered all of the Samains she had seen celebrated at Tara, and all the ritual processions to the Plain of the Fál, and the kindling of the Druidical Fires. Shall I ever see Samain celebrated at Tara again? Please, yes.

Cathbad had decorated the table with trailing ivy garlands and was presiding over platters of wild duck, "Nicely stuffed," he said, and dressed pheasant, and an array of sweetmeats. There were steaming cauldrons of soup ("I shan't have any of that," said Fintan) and mead, and mulled wine which Tybion and Rinnal had brewed over the Cruithin's fires. The Cruithin, interested and bright-eyed, had contributed some kind of drink made from apples and honey and, as Cermait said, it would have skinned the soles of your feet if you fell into a vat of it.

The villagers of Folaim stood a little apart, shy, but pleased to be included in the modest celebrations, certainly delighted to be presented to the High Queen.

"Loyal," said Tybion the Tusk, who had gone faithfully and doggedly through the village, and had rounded up every single person. "They'd follow you into hell and beyond, ma'am."

"It was thoughtful of you to bring them up," said Grainne, and smiled, and Tybion frowned and started to say that he thought it had been Grainne's request, but then was distracted by Cathbad, who had tipped up the soup and was running about in a panic, trying to mop it all up.

The villagers thought it was a fine old sight to see on a

Samain, and compared it all favourably with their own celebrations. To be sure, they always celebrated Samain properly and respectfully, they assured Dorrainge and Lugh.
Didn't they have their own fire every single year, and didn't
they all sit down to the finest banquet ever seen in Ireland?
Let one of the dark forces try to get through tonight! cried
the people of Folaim, and wouldn't it find itself frizzled up
on the instant!

They bowed awkwardly to Grainne, because they were
farmers and landowners and woodcutters in the main, and
bowing to the High Queen of Ireland was not a thing you
allowed for when you were tilling land or chopping trees or
gathering fruit. But they knew what was what, said the villagers happily, and swept clumsy bows, and said they were
delighted to be here, and shuffled the village reprobate into
line, because hadn't Seamus the Ancient a terrible old habit
of saying the wrong thing, and it the High Queen! The children stood rather silently, round-eyed and awe-stricken, staring at the mounds of food, and Cathbad, who was rather
fond of children, at once rounded them up and shepherded
them to his array of spun sugar confections and crystallised
fruits.

And then the soldiers stepped forward to fire the bonfire
in several places, and the flames leapt into the sky, red and
orange and scented with the agaric and the dry oak.

Grainne, watching, sipping the wine that Tybion, faithful as ever, had poured for her, frowned, and Raynor at once
said, "There is something wrong?"

Grainne said slowly, and very quietly, "I think we are
being watched."

Raynor did not speak for a moment, and then he said
softly, "Yes."

"There is something watching from the shadows. I *feel*
it watching us," said Grainne.

"It is not," said Raynor, "necessarily evil," and Grainne
turned to look at him.

"On the night of Samain," she said, "every evil force in

the world is abroad. That is why these rituals take place. They are barriers," said Grainne, her face serious. "Barriers to replace the natural ones that are lowered on Samain."

"Between this world and the Dark Ireland," said Raynor. "Yes. We too know of this. On Samain the Gateways between the worlds are wide open, and it is possible to pass from one world to another with ease."

Grainne said, "That is why the rituals must be so exact. The procession to the Plain of the Fál. And the Sacred Chant . . . I do not pretend to understand that. I think no one has understood it for hundreds of years, for it was old when the world was young. But it is a strong magic, the Sacred Chant, and if it is to form part of the ceremony, it has to be exactly right. If the Chant were to be repeated wrongly, if it were to be inverted or in some way changed . . ."

"But if it was done in ignorance—?"

"I do not think it would matter," said Grainne. "The gateways will already be opening. The creatures of the Dark Ireland will be waiting and watching their chance."

And out there in the forest, something is watching us, I can feel it watching us . . .

She smiled at him. "But we should not spoil your first proper Samain with that. On Samain there are always strange forces abroad. I have felt them before."

"At Tara?"

"Yes. And in other places." She paused, and Raynor saw her eyes darken.

"Tell me," said Raynor, and Grainne, looking at him again, saw the yearning in his eyes, and knew that he was saying, Make me see it all. For I can still not believe that I shall see it.

"You *will* see it," said Grainne, and smiled at him. "You will see *Gaillimh* which is on the far western coast, and where, when the sun sets, it turns the sky to a sheet of flame. That is one of the most beautiful places in the world. And you will see *Cnoc Aine* where there are the burial mounds of the *sidh*—that is strange and disturbing and filled with faint music, and not entirely in the world of Men at all. And there are the Northern Isles, which are beautiful and friendly but tragic—"

"Tragic?" said Raynor, hearing her voice change.

"I found them so," said Grainne, and Raynor saw and felt the shutters come down over her eyes and over her mind, and knew that there were still things about her he did not know or understand. But one day she will tell me, he thought. I must believe that one day she will trust me sufficiently to tell me everything.

He would not yet say it. He thought she was his more completely and more gladly than he had ever believed any creature could be. But she is not quite yet entirely mine, he thought. There is still a small part, a corner, that she is keeping from me. And then: But why should she not? he thought. Why should any one creature expect to know and own and understand the whole of another? And he lifted her hand to his lips, for this touching, this gentle communication of one person with another, was something still new and remarkable for him, and to sit like this, with a banquet laid out before him, and with the unthinking instinctive homage of the people to Grainne, was something he had still to come to terms with.

The feast was getting well under way. Lugh sat at the foot of the table rather solemnly; Fintan said he had deliberately manoeuvred himself into this position to appear important, but Cermait said this was unkind, because Lugh could not be important if he stood on his head.

The soldiers were quaffing the apple brew in alarmingly large draughts, and several of them had begun an impromptu rendering of "A Nice Little Bit of Comfort for the Maid of Bunclody," which should not be allowed with children present.

"Although they won't understand the half of it," said Cermait, who had been joining in a bit furtively, but who had forgotten the last verse.

The soldiers accepted the ban amiably enough, and commenced instead a spirited rendering of "When Rafferty Raffled his Pig," which, as Fintan said, was a sight worse in the end.

"I've never heard it," said Tybion hopefully.

"No, and you don't want to," said Fintan, who liked Tybion, but who did not approve of bawdy songs on Samain.

Dorrainge had begun the Sacred Chant at last. "Good," said Fintan, settling down and looking to see where his tankard of apple brew had gone. "A good bit of solid tradition's what's needed now. This'll quiet them down," he said to Cermait, who was sharing the half of a wild duck with Rinnal. "My word, it's grand to hear the Old Ritual again," he said, who would not have known a syllable of the Ritual if it had leaped from the ground and struck him, but who liked to preserve the legend that he knew a bit about everything.

"Dorrainge's being very self-important about it," said Cermait, through a mouthful of duck leg. "I wonder should we help him."

"You don't know the Sacred Chant," said Fintan dismissively.

"Neither does Dorrainge, from the sound of it," said Cermait.

"Well," said Fintan, worried, "it's to be hoped he *does* know it, because if he's going to get it wrong, he might as well not say it at all. In fact," said Fintan, "he'd be as well *not* to say it, because it might call up all kinds of things."

"What sort of things?"

"Well," said Fintan, "I don't think we ought to put names to them." And he glanced furtively over his shoulder to the shadows, because you never quite knew what might be abroad on Samain.

"Still, it's a grand tradition," said Cermait.

"It's a forgotten tradition," said Fintan. "I hope there isn't trouble ahead."

"Rubbish," said Cermait, and took himself off to Cathbad's corner of the feastings to see was the roast pig cooked yet, and went off to fetch a sharp pointed stick to test it, because roast pig had to be thoroughly cooked if they were not all to be taken with unmentionable ills half the night.

Dorrainge was standing before the fire, his hands outstretched, his head flung back.

"He's making the most of it," muttered Fintan, but was not paid any attention.

Lugh Longhand was only half listening to Dorrainge, although he did notice that Dorrainge appeared to be stumbling once or twice, and it did just cross his mind that it was to be hoped that Dorrainge, the fat fool, did not mix the Ritual up or make a fool of himself. Lugh was feeling personally responsible for the entire course of the evening, and it would not do for Her Majesty and half the Court to see that things went wrong. Perhaps Dorrainge would recover himself. Perhaps—although this was not very likely—he had taken a drop more than was good for him of the Cruithin's apple drink. A number of people had certainly done that, thought Lugh disapprovingly.

The shadows were closing in on them. It would only be night falling, of course, but Lugh found the shadows disturbing. He knew that the Lad of the Skins was somewhere out there; he thought that the Conablaiche might be watching as well. He looked to where Dorrainge was still holding everyone's attention, and he thought, As well now as at any other time, and slipped from his seat. No one would see him go and he would not be so very long.

The children were grouped together, seated cross-legged on the grass, their small faces intent, their expressions serious. They had been given small portions of supper, which they had eaten with industrious pleasure, and they had been given a tiny sip of mead each, diluted with spring water. They were rather well behaved, the children of Folaim; they had not interrupted their elders, or run about screaming and fighting; they had not had fights with pieces of bread or flipped damson stones at one another, or made fun of Cathbad, or fallen into the cider cauldron.

Lugh moved cautiously round the outside of the circle of people, every one of whom was watching the bonfire, some of whom were trying to hear Dorrainge's Ritual Chant. The soldiers had, as Fintan had feared, begun a rival chant to the tune of "When Rafferty Raffled his Pig," but no one was paying very much attention to this, and it would probably trail off into silence before the really rude verses were reached.

The children were quite near to the fire. The red glow was casting shadows on their faces and turning their hair to crimson. It was strange, now that Lugh came to think about it, how many people in Ireland had really dark hair with red lights in it. Chestnut, or the colour of beech trees in autumn. Sometimes travellers came to Tara; great fair-haired, fair-skinned, deep-chested people who had sailed the northern seas to find the glittering Palace, and who had flashing blue eyes and hair the colour of a sunrise. Lugh dared say that was all very well, but he preferred the Irish. Dark, slight, pale-skinned, fine-boned people. There was breeding in the Irish. You could always tell.

The children of Folaim were small and slender, and they were nearly all dark-haired. Lugh stood where he was, more or less completely hidden by the shadows of the trees behind him, studying the small faces intently. Surely, surely, these were nothing other than the sons and daughters of good honest farmers and woodcutters and cottagers. Weren't they?

And surely, it was among precisely these sort of ordinary people that the Queen's friends would have hidden the pretender?

Folaim, meaning, in old Gael, a place of concealment . . .

Surely Medoc had not been wrong?

At the very back of his mind, Lugh knew that Medoc had not been wrong. He knew that the creature, the Lost Prince, the Wolfchild, was here. He remembered tales of hunters, and of how, nearing their quarry, they began to smell it and sense it and know it to be within their reach. He thought that there was no logical reason to know that the Prince was here, but for all that, he did know it was here.

He was still scanning the circle of faces, examining, discarding, sure he would recognise the child when he saw it.

Smooth-skinned faces, the unmarked faces of extreme youth. Smiling faces, untidy ones . . . a gap-toothed boy giggling with his sister, two tough-looking imps who would certainly be applying for entrance to the *Fiana* when they were older . . .

The Ritual Chant was soaring into the night sky, and Dorrainge was flushed with the effort of sustaining it. Lugh was fairly sure that Dorrainge had missed large chunks out. He supposed it would not matter in the end, and it had to be remembered that Dorrainge was not used to chanting the entire Ritual by himself. It seemed to have grown considerably darker since he had begun, and it was certainly a good deal colder, but that would just be the winter night. It was nearly always cold on Samain.

On the far side of the bonfire, the Cruithin were listening to the Chant. Lugh noticed with disapproval that several of them had lit their pipes, which was surely extremely discourteous to the Ancient Chant. He was rather surprised, because hadn't the Cruithin always been spoken of as courteous and reverential to all of Ireland's rituals? But he could see, quite clearly, wisps and curls of red heat rising; there was an odd heavy feel to the air as well now, which probably meant that the Cruithin were smoking something particularly unpleasant in their clay pipes. Lugh would have to have a word.

Dorrainge was definitely stumbling over the Chant now, and Lugh could see one or two people frowning. It just showed that you could not really trust anybody, not even Druids, these days. Probably Dorrainge was distracted by the thick crimson smoke from the pipes, and by the strange scent. If you happened to be fanciful, you could almost imagine that you were smelling fiery furnaces and burning coals, and that there were slanting red eyes peering at you from the depths of the dying bonfire . . .

This was nonsense, of course. Lugh would not give such whimsical absurdities any attention. He would concentrate on searching the children, because that was what he was here for.

The children were rather attractive creatures. Was that just Folaim or something more? Had the strange, beautiful Wolfchild, the Prince of Tara, been hidden where it would be least noticeable? Lugh carried on looking.

Small, dark-haired little things they were: a blue-eyed art-less charmer of six or seven summers who would certainly wreak havoc in male breasts in ten years' time; a chubby little roly-poly, eating plums with delight and listening to the soldiers; a snub-nosed freckled little soul who looked as if she might break into giggles at the smallest opportunity; a slant-eyed child with tip-tilted cheekbones and hair that grew close to his skull like an animal's pelt . . .

Lugh stopped and fixed his eyes intently on the boy, and something incredulous and fearful sprang to attention in his mind.

Golden eyes. *Wolf*eyes, narrow and watchful: the eyes of the High Queen. Dark glossy hair and slanting cheekbones; ears set just that fraction too high to be wholly Human, and that were just that little bit pointed . . .

Lugh stood very still and thought, I have found him!

The Lost Prince . . .

Had he? Had he in truth so easily and so quickly found the Wolfchild, the misbegotten Prince, born in secret to the High Queen? The creature about whom myth and legend had somehow grown up, just as myth and legend had always grown up about the Wolfline.

Was this the one who would topple Medoc and bring down darkness and destruction? The child whom Lugh had promised to kill?

He stood there and drank in the child's every feature and every movement, and knew that this was indeed the one.

There was the unconscious grace that was wolfish, and there was the slenderness and the elfin-look; the three-cornered features of the ancient Wolfline of Ireland. Lugh stood and looked and could scarcely believe his eyes.

But yes, this was the one. This was the one with the ancient mystical wolfblood. This was the one who was a direct descendant of Cormac, of the wild Dierdriu. This was the real thing; the strength and the power and the might.

Could he be killed? Could Lugh do it? Could he stalk the creature through the dark night and scoop it up and sink a knife into its heart? Could I? murmured Lugh, and as he framed the question, there was a slight movement beside him, and he turned his head.

Standing beside him, thin, white-cheeked, ragged and hungry-eyed, was a shape that made Lugh shudder.

But he knew that if he, Lugh, could not bring himself to kill the Wolfchild, the Lad of the Skins certainly would.

THE COURT AND the soldiers and the Beastline were not quite sure when the Sacred Chant became blurred and clotted and somehow mingled with the heavy, crimson-tinted sky, and with the burning scents, as if the doors to an immense furnace had suddenly begun to open.

Grainne, listening intently to Dorrainge, had known with a deep inner knowledge which had nothing to do with conscious learning but that was pure race-memory, that the Chant was *wrong*. It was inverted, displaced; Dorrainge was altering its structure, so that the ancient ritual was no longer perfectly balanced.

He has upset the pattern and he has disturbed the delicate interleaving of the enchantments that create the barriers and keep at bay the Dark Ireland . . .

She could feel Raynor's sudden alertness, and there was a moment to be grateful for it—he understands!—and she was trying to think what should be done.

For if the barriers are in truth destroyed, and if the gateways are beginning to open, then we are in the most terrible danger . . .

Grainne thought that she had half risen, although she did not remember pushing aside the chairs, and she certainly felt Raynor with her. The skies were filling up with the malevolent red light, they were becoming lakes of crimson, seas of living boiling colour . . .

The Doors to the Dark Ireland unfolding . . .

Dorrainge had fallen back, his face white, sweat streaming from his brow, a look of horror in his eyes. People were huddling together, pulling shawls and cloaks closely about them for comfort; everyone was staring upwards at the glowing, panting sky.

Grainne felt Raynor's hand close about hers, and then saw him move unhesitatingly into the centre of the people, and lift up a hand to gain their attention. She sensed that he had drawn breath to speak, and she felt, even at several paces, the sudden authority that enveloped him. People turned to him, gratefully, trustfully, because here was someone who would know what was happening. The crimson glow fell directly across him, so that for a moment his hair was no longer a cap of gilt, and his eyes were no longer shining topazes; he was a creature of the skies, strong and warlike. The Noble House of the Eagles reborn . . . *And if Fergus is lost to us, then he could lead the* Fiana *and vanquish Medoc* . . .

The thought came unbidden, but with it came an immense strength.

And then, without warning, crystal clear on the curdled night air, came the sound of the music.

It was like nothing anyone had ever heard. It was cold and terrible, slicing through the malevolent darkness as piercingly as a knife slicing through whey. People shivered and felt for one another's hands, and moved closer together.

Was it the *sidh*? Grainne, still standing where she was, turned to scan the forest, because the music seemed to be coming from the trees. And surely the *sidh* had been with them earlier; mischievously chasing in and out of the feasting, blue and green smudges, never quite materialising, elusive and fey and icily beautiful.

It was not *sidh* music. This was something chill and un-earthly and terrible. It was calling and it was luring, but it was an evil call, and it was a malignant lure.

And then it changed again, and somewhere deep inside it was the sound of crying.

A child crying in the night.

The women of the company leapt up at once, searching the shadows, several of them running across the clearing to where the children sat together, their faces anxious as they looked for their own sons and daughters.

All there. None of the children had slipped away to work some small mischief. Each was accounted for.

Grainne had scarcely noticed the exodus of the women. She had stayed where she was, staring into the forest, listening to the crying, knowing it was something that could not possibly be ignored, because it was desolate and lonely, and it was filled with the cold, dark nights, and it was the most pitiful sound she had ever heard.

Raynor was at her side in a single movement. "Grainne, you must not—"

She thought that Raynor was holding her back, but she could not stay, even for him. It was out there, the child, the poor, lost, pitiful thing, it was somewhere out there in the dark. She tilted her head, trying to hear it again.

Help me . . . I am lost and alone and I am afraid of the dark . . .

The crying was stealing over the listeners now, and Grainne felt her heart flinch with the desolation of it.

I am lost and alone . . . I am shivering and ragged . . .

Oh, Fergus, thought Grainne, pain closing about her, Fergus my dear, lost love, what did I do when I let them take your son? I cannot bear this . . .

A bite of food . . . a warm fire . . . I have been wandering alone in the dark, and I am frightened and I am friendless. Help me . . .

Grainne said very clearly, "This is unbearable. We must find the poor child."

I am shivering and in rags . . . I am so hungry . . .

She began to move towards the sound of the crying, dimly aware that Raynor was restraining her, pushing him away. Raynor, his eyes on her face, only partly understanding, felt a coldness enter his heart. For a moment longer he was able to remain detached, to think, This is something dreadful and evil, and this is an old and a terrible enchantment and we must fight it, and Grainne must be kept safe.

Let me in to your fire and your love . . . I have so little . . . I have never known what it is to be loved . . .

Grainne began to move towards the dark trees now, the memories alive and hurting, memories that were six years old, nearly seven. Memories which ought to have been long since safely buried, a wound which ought to have healed and skinned over but which was as open and as raw as it had been when she had let them take Fergus's child away. Fergus's son. Ireland's Lost Prince . . .

She broke away from Raynor's arms and ran straight into the dark forest towards the crying.

CHAPTER
TWENTY-FOUR

ANNABEL AND TALIESIN, with Fergus and the boys following, began the cautious descent down the hillside. Annabel was bemused and caught in thrall; she had partly understood what had happened, but she had not wholly understood.

"None of us wholly understands," said Taliesin. "But later I shall take you to the Druids, and they will spend hours pondering over it all, and perhaps they will come up with a solution and perhaps they will not." And Annabel stared at him, and felt the joy all over again, and wondered if she dared believe that they had truly left her cold barren world behind and somehow entered this *beautiful*, ancient, magical land.

"Of course," said Taliesin. "Now you are in my world." And smiled.

Fergus had been standing a little apart, looking about him, trying to gauge exactly where they were. "Somewhere overlooking Tara," he said at length. "But I am not sure exactly where." He looked at them. "But there is something different," he said. "Something has happened."

"Yes?"

Fergus said softly, "The Old Ireland has woken at last," and there was such delight and such reverence in his voice that Taliesin and Annabel stared at him. "All of the old lost enchantments," said Fergus. "Can you not feel that they are all about us?"

Taliesin said lightly, "Fergus, my dear, I am only a Tyrian and a money lender at that, and if I deal in dreams and enchantments, then I do not admit to any of it." But although his voice contained all the old mockery and all the old irony, there was something in it that was neither mocking nor ironic. Fergus knew and Annabel knew that Taliesin felt the strange whisperings and the barely seen, only-just-heard stirrings about them.

For the Old Ireland, the Enchanted Island, is awake again . . .

Conn and Niall and Michael and the boys were sitting close together, their faces intent, their expressions deeply happy. They had not said very much, but Annabel had known how they were feeling, because she was feeling the same. A deep, deep happiness; a delight so strong that you dared not speak in case you shattered it, almost a refusal to believe. *Can* this possibly be meant for us? Dare I believe? But when Michael said to her, "Are we home again?" Annabel at once said, "Yes, Michael, home," and Michael smiled and went back to Conn's side, and curled into a tight little ball and sat absolutely still as if he did not even dare to move in case the precious fragile happiness should break.

Taliesin said, "Will you survey the terrain, Captain? For no one else has the least idea of where we are, and as the *Fiana*'s head—or are we lost beyond hope? Tell us, if you please, for if we are to wander in the wilderness like lost souls for a hundred years or more, it will be better to know. I suppose that *is* Tara, is it?"

"Yes," said Fergus softly, looking across the valley again. "That is Tara. The Shining Palace. The bright city. In darkness still, for Medoc still reigns there."

Taliesin said, half to himself, "And the light is no more, and which is most hateful, darkness or light, and which is most blessed, despair or hope? Do we go direct to it, Fergus?"

"Ride on Medoc?" said Fergus.

"I admit it appears to me a foolhardy thing to do, but whither ye go I shall follow, and whither ye lead I shall . . . Would it be better to take this road that appears to go nowhere at all?"

"It's a dark road," said Niall, uncertainly, and several of the boys looked up.

"Oh, radiant dark," said Taliesin, "oh, darkly fostered rays. Darkness of slumber and death, forever sinking and forever mantling the world.

"Fergus, I wish you would stop staring across the valley."

But Fergus did not move. "We cannot yet march on Tara," he said, "but when I do, I shall do so with all the might and all the power and all the glory of Ireland behind me." He turned back to them, his eyes shining. "The Future did not help us," he said, "but I believe that here in this world, we will be able to raise an army so strong that we shall rout the Darkness from Ireland at last." He looked at the boys. "Already we have these," he said, and smiled. "And there will be more who will join us. And when I defeat Medoc," said Fergus, looking at them very straightly, "I shall do so thoroughly and soundly, and with a triumph so great that it will echo down the ages. There must be no question of failure. To ride on Medoc now, just these few of us—"

" 'We few, we happy few, we band of' . . . Yes," said Taliesin thoughtfully. "That would be disastrous. We should be taken and captured at once. Medoc would throw us to the creatures who serve him."

And if that happens, everything we have attempted and everything we have suffered will have been for nothing . . .

"So," said Fergus, "for the moment, Tara must be closed to us." And he turned his back on it with finality.

Taliesin said, "Then shall we take this road that appears to lead nowhere and see if we find ourselves anywhere?" And, half to himself, "Although it is a long, dark, lonely road, and—what have I said?"

"The long, dark, lonely road," said Fergus, staring at Taliesin. *"Of course."*

"Well?"

"The Grail Castle," said Fergus. "This is the long, dark,

lonely road that leads to the Grail Castle." And he looked at them, his eyes shining, "This is the road the Queen took. This is where we must go."

As THEY WALKED cautiously along the wide, curving road, they were aware of the overwhelming darkness again.

"Yes, it is very close to us," said Fergus, and glanced back at Conn and the others. "But it is still sufficiently far for it not to be a danger," he said.

Annabel, who thought it was as if dark heavy mists gathered in waiting on the edges of the road, said, "What is it?"

"The Dark Ireland," said Fergus, and the others noticed that he spoke very quietly as if he feared to be overheard, and that he never ceased to scan the shadows that clustered on the sides of the road. "I believe that the Gateway that exists between our world and the Dark Realm is unfolding. And if that is so—" He stopped, and then went on. "If that is so," said Fergus, "then every evil that ever lived, every force that ever tried to bring down the Wolfkings, will be waiting and watching." He looked at them. "This is Samain," he said. "And it may be that before the night is over, the denizens of that terrible world will have broken through, and will be loose in the true Ireland. If the Gateway is in truth opening, then Medoc will already have called up the Twelve Dark Lords."

Taliesin said, "What of the Conablaiche?"

"It may be here already," said Fergus. "I do not know. But it is possible that it was thrust back into this world with us."

Annabel said carefully, "What *did* happen in the mountain?" and Conn added eagerly, "Yes, what did happen, Fergus?"

"Tell us," said several of the others, and Fergus said, "But I don't know what happened. I don't think we shall ever know."

"Did the Clock stop or did we stop it?" said Annabel, and saw again the figure of Fael-Inis, lit to brilliant life, hurling a bolt of pure radiance at the Clockface. "Were we in time to turn the hands back?" she said.

"I don't know that either," said Fergus. "There was a dreadful crash—some kind of explosion. If it was the Apocalypse in truth, perhaps it was that which jolted us back here."

Taliesin said thoughtfully, "The Clock had reached the very last second before midnight."

"Yes," Fergus frowned, "but surely if the terrible devastation prophesied *had* taken place, then Annabel's people would have had some warning. Wouldn't they?"

"I don't know," said Annabel. "But I do wonder if the Apocalypse did come. Or whether I shall ever know if it did."

Fergus sat down on the side of the road and leaned back against a tree trunk, and the others sat with him. Behind them was Tara, still shrouded in dark mists and the evil miasma of Medoc and the Twelve Lords. Ahead of them would be the legendary Grail Castle, and Fergus, who knew all of the stories, thought they would be fortunate indeed to reach it in safety. But for the moment, he looked at them all and said, "Do you truly want to know what happened? Annabel, do you really want to know if your world ended, if it burned and if the Four Horsemen rode across the earth and let in the Beast? If cities were razed and if mankind was annihilated?" He smiled at her very gently. "You see, we have heard the stories of what happened," said Fergus. "We have had Time Travellers here. People who lived in the days after the Apocalypse is said to have walked. People to whom the Apocalypse is a terrible folk legend. A myth. They know it happened, but they do not know how or when or why. Only that some terrible and overwhelming catastrophe came to the world, and that mankind was nearly destroyed."

Taliesin said, "The legends that the Time Travellers bring are fearsome . . . How the world burned, and how the seas were great boiling masses; how the skies rained fire and molten lead. How there were poisonous substances in the air, so terrible that to breathe was to burn up inside."

Fergus said softly, "And even when the fires cooled and the world was a charred, smoking ruin, even then, the horrors did not end. People lived for years in the ruins and the rubble of the destroyed cities and towns, eking out some kind of existence, trying to preserve the flame of humanity ... Stealing food and looting it, searching for water."

Eating the rats before the rats ate them ... Fergus did not say it, but it was the picture that had always haunted him from the stories about Annabel's world.

"That is so dreadful," she said. "Did we stop it after all? Was it possible that we did? For if people who lived after it happened brought back the legends—" She stopped and frowned. "I do not understand," said Annabel. "If there are records that it happened, that dreadful final holocaust, how could we even begin to hope that we stopped it."

"Can you unmake history?" said Fergus softly. "That is the question we had to ask before we travelled to your world, Annabel. And the answer is that none of us knows. The Druids would tell you that Time is continuous, that it is relative, and that if you know how to do it, you can slip back and forth through Time. But none of us has the understanding to grapple with its concept. Perhaps when Taliesin takes you to meet the Druids, they may have a part of the answer. They will certainly want to know you and to hear about your world."

"My world was sparse," said Annabel. "Barren and sad. Dying. I daresay it is very disloyal of me, but I am thankful to have left it." She looked at them. "It will be easy for me to forget it," she said.

"Nevertheless, you will find that it holds great interest for everyone here," said Fergus. "You will be asked about it." He smiled. "We shall not let you forget it so easily," he said. And then, standing up, "Are we all sufficiently rested? Shall we go on?"

As they moved on down the road, Taliesin thought that Fergus was once more in truth the leader of the High Queen's *Fiana*. He had donned, without thinking about it, the authority and the imperiousness of one who has been used to command. Taliesin, watching Fergus, thought that there was something in him that would always take charge of any situation. Was it simply the quality of leadership? Or was it something more? Curious and rather fascinated, he fell into step with Fergus and, at last, noticing that Annabel and the boys were a few steps behind, said, "Fergus, what did they do to you in that place?"

Fergus was startled; he thought, Is it apparent? Will people know? And felt again the sick agony and the swift black torment that had descended as Conn brought the knife down between his legs . . .

Castrated . . . rendered impotent, made emasculate. Even now, even with every ounce of fortitude summoned, the mental anguish was very nearly more than he could bear. How shall I support it! he thought, and knew that it had to be supported. For it was the only way. Only by submitting to the Stone Judges could I have broken the bonds of the Prison and brought the boys back to the world, and only that way could I have returned to drive Medoc from Tara and restore the light to the Bright Palace.

Yes, and only by doing so could I quench at last the sweet forbidden ache for my sister . . .

He had determined that no one should know; that he would become an illusionist, that he would wear false colours to the world, and that the world should never guess what had been done to him.

But he looked at Taliesin very steadily, and said, "It is nothing I did not deserve." He smiled, and saw Taliesin's concern, and felt his sympathy. "One day I shall tell you," said Fergus. "But for now it is too new. Too raw. Perhaps one day quite soon I shall be glad it happened."

Taliesin said lightly, "I am yours to command, Captain.

When you speak, I shall listen." And then, "Tell me, have we far to go to the Grail Castle?"

ANNABEL HAD SPOKEN truthfully when she had said she was thankful to have left her world behind. She had been instantly and completely enchanted by this strange unknown land where blue and green mists shrouded the forests, and where bewitchments stirred in the air, and where there were magic castles and dark sorcerers and High Kings and Queens who were not entirely Human. She had been rather intrigued by the stories of Grainne, and she had certainly been fascinated by the legend of the Lost Enchantment of the Beastline, and the curse placed on Tara at the beginning.

"Tara can never belong to the Humans," Fergus had said in one of their brief rest-stops on the road to the castle. "For that to happen, for a pure-bred Human to occupy the Sun Chamber, would mean that Ireland would fall and Tara would crumble."

And all Ireland will seethe with evil and the skies will darken and the rivers will run with blood ... And if the line should ever divide, then the curse will fall upon Tara ... if twins should ever be born into the Royal House ...

To Annabel, child of the stark barren Future, Fergus's stories were the stuff that dreams were made on, they were food and drink and sustenance. She drank everything in, and thought that despite the sinister dangers of this strange, enchanted land, she had never been so completely and utterly happy in her life.

She thought they might not get to the Grail Castle at all; she remembered all of the old forbidden fairy stories of her world that told of strange dark castles which disappeared when you got to them, and that housed secrets and spells and prisoners, and that were guarded by brier hedges and thickets which you had to hack your way through. I am living in a fairytale, thought Annabel, and smiled, because the thought was quite the most absurd she had ever had, but it was perfectly true all the same.

When Taliesin said, "Perhaps the Grail Castle does not exist, other than in the minds of people who imagined it," Annabel looked at him gratefully and knew what he meant.

"It does exist," said Fergus. And stopped and pointed directly ahead of them. "See?" he said. "It is waiting for us."

Directly ahead of them was the towering, forbidding bulk of the Grail Castle, rearing against the night sky. And deep within the dark fastness of the halls, a single light was burning.

THEY CONCENTRATED ON the light. "A good light," said Fergus, and hoped he sounded more confident than he felt.

"A light to brighten the world," agreed Taliesin with the utmost courtesy, and Fergus grinned and thought that this journey would have been dull indeed without Taliesin.

"I am friendship itself," said Taliesin smoothly. "Do we have to cross that narrow bridge to get to the drawbridge?"

"I wouldn't like to be up here on my own," said Niall.

"It's a bit dark," said Michael's voice rather quaveringly. "Is anyone at home?"

"I think it's deserted," said Fergus. "There isn't a light after all."

"Did we imagine the light?"

"Probably."

Fergus was eyeing the castle with a mixture of misgiving and fascination. His ancestors had called this place Scáthach, the Castle of Shadow, and it had long been used as a place of exile. Fergus knew the castle's history very well, and now, staring up at it, the dark clouds massing at its rear, he found himself remembering every sad dark story that had ever been told or sung or remembered about Scáthach: Niall of the Nine Hostages, lying chained and desperate with the nine faithful lords; Nuadu Airgetlam of the Silver Arm, forced by the sorcerers to submit to a terrible punishment. And Fergus's own great-grandfather, the famous wild Cormac, imprisoned by an enchantment, abandoned by his own kind, but served by the loyal Cruithin out here until he was rescued by a Human.

Still, thought Fergus, standing very still and surveying the grim bulk ahead of them, still, people have penetrated to the castle and lived, and people have been exiled here and returned. He thought that Grainne would surely have got this far, for the road had been easier and smoother than he had expected. But he thought she was no longer here; the Grail Castle seemed deserted. There were no lights now—*Did* we imagine that flare? wondered Fergus—and there were no sounds carrying across the dark; no cheerful clatter of crockery from the nearby sculleries, no jingling of harnesses from the stables.

There had only been that solitary light burning . . . or had it?

Slowly and cautiously, they began to walk across the narrow bridge.

"Don't look down," said Conn.

"Why not?"

"It's a long way if you fall. It's a moat," said Conn, "only there's no water left in it any more."

"We ought to be roped together like people climbing a mountain," said Michael from the rear. "Then if one of you falls, you pull everybody else with you."

"That's not the idea."

"I've seen it happen," said Michael firmly. "You all go slithering and bumping together until you reach the bottom."

"Well, we don't want that to happen here," said Niall. "So if you do fall, we shan't come slithering and bumping after you and you'll be left behind."

"I'd climb back up," said Michael.

The courtyard was deserted, and the walls of the castle towered above them.

Shut in on all sides, thought Fergus, shivering, and turning up the collar of his cloak.

The windows were in darkness; they were slitted windows, and they were suddenly a bit sly. You felt as if eyes might be watching you, as if somewhere behind the walls there might be watchers. Fergus thought he caught a flicker of movement behind one of the windows, as if someone had dodged back into the shadows.

They crossed the courtyard warily, peering into the stables and the outbuildings, pushing open doors.

"Nowhere is locked," said Niall, and Fergus said softly, "Oh, no. No, Scáthach was never a prison of locks and keys."

"What then?"

"It's a place of exile," said Fergus. "But the locks are not locks of iron and the bolts are not bolts of steel." He looked at Taliesin and Annabel. "To be imprisoned here is to be placed under the restraint of a spell," he said.

"How do people break such a spell?" asked Annabel, and, despite the danger, and despite the great dark castle, was rather pleased to find that she could bring this out as if it was the most natural thing in the world to enquire about the efficacy of spells.

"Spells can be broken," said Fergus, "but it is difficult." He looked up at the walls. "Cormac of the Wolves was rescued from his imprisonment by a pure-bred Human," said Fergus. "For the spell placed on him had allowed for that." He looked at her and said very softly, "The spell that broke Cormac's exile began something like this: *'Open locks, to the Human's hand ...'*" He smiled, and just for a second Annabel shivered, because there had been something very faintly not quite Human about him.

But she said, "Oh. Yes, I see," and wondered whether she did.

The massive studded doors were half open and rays of the blue-tinted twilight lay across the floor. Dust motes danced in and out of the shadows, and they stood for a moment looking through the open door, each of them thinking, Is this right? Dare we enter? And—Should it be so easy? thought Fergus. Annabel, standing between the two men, felt as if it was a massive dark cloud, the immense loneliness and the fears and the strange mixture of sadness and surprised happiness that permeated the castle. She thought that this was a place where people had endured great torment and great isolation, but that it was also a place where people had found a strange content. Surprised by joy, thought Annabel, who had read the forbidden works of the almost-forgotten nineteenth century, and the almost-lost poets of earlier centuries than that even. She stood in the dark, gloomy, old Castle of Shadow, and thought that Wordsworth and Byron and John Donne would certainly have known about dark shadow castles where single lights burned, and where mists swirled and moods and emotions eddied.

They were standing in the great sunken hall, and the boys were moving cautiously about, fascinated and wary, examining the deep stone hearth—"Big enough to roast an ox," said Conn—and tracing the wolf emblems that were carved into the stone. Fergus stood very still at the exact centre of the hall and felt, without warning, a deep sense of belonging. He thought, So after all, this is my family's oldest, most myth-laden stronghold. This is the enchanted Castle of the Wolves, the legendary Grail Castle, the Fortress of Shadow, Scáthach, the ancient moated keep that has lived in people's memories. And he felt his blood stir, and felt, as well, a deep aching sadness, because the magical mystical heritage which had come down to him would end with him. I am a Prince of Tara, he thought, but I can never be acknowledged and I can never acknowledge it. Would the line end with him? He thought it would not, for Grainne would marry and have children. The knowledge hurt, but not as much as it would have done before Fergus's ordeal in the Prison of Hostages. Even so, I should have liked a son, he thought, and the pain twisted again, and the dark memory of the Prison of Hostages rushed in. He stood very still and fought it down, and knew there would be many days and certainly many nights when he would have to fight this black and bitter despair. Yes, I would have liked a son, thought Fergus.

The boys had been opening doors, forgetting their fears in the castle's calm, exploring the rooms and the passages

that led off the central sunken hall, and Niall and Michael
had discovered a huge, stone-flagged scullery.

"With food," said Michael hopefully. "Quite a lot of
food, actually," and Fergus laughed, and was back in the
present again, where there were dark castles to be explored,
and enemies to be routed and enchantments to be beaten
back, and supper to be cooked and eaten.

The scullery was bright and warm and somehow safe.
Bunches of herbs hung from the beams and there were
strings of onions and wild garlic, and there were rows of
gleaming copper pans on the huge oak dresser. Annabel,
peering into cupboards, thought there was surely a great
reassurance in the mingled food scents: fresh parsley and
chopped onions and newly baked bread and stored apples.
The way to store apples properly was to make sure that no
one apple ever touched another, otherwise you got bruised
skins. But apples had been a great luxury in Annabel's
world. "Eggs!" said one of the boys, opening a cupboard.
"A huge dish of them!"

"We'll cook them," said Annabel at once, and hoped she
could remember how you made things like omelettes and
how you scrambled eggs.

Conn and Niall laid a fire of twigs in the range in the
corner, and Annabel cooked the eggs carefully, adding a dash
of milk and butter, and heaping everyone's plate with great
fluffy spoonfuls of them.

"A feast," said Taliesin.

Fergus had found bread, which they sliced and spread
thickly with butter, and there was half a ham in one of the
cupboards, and some dishes of potted meat. Michael brought
out the apples. "And I polished them shiny," he said. "You
should always do that with apples."

There were flagons of cool sharp cider. It was the
grandest meal they had had: "Ever since I can remember,"
said Conn.

They ate and drank hugely, and forgot about the brooding old castle and managed to forget about the single flaring light they had seen on their approach. Fergus knew that quite soon they would have to leave the security of the scullery and find out if that light had been real; Taliesin, his every sense alert, was thinking that even though no one had yet come out to challenge them, the castle would certainly not be empty. Empty places had a different feel, and the Grail Castle had not felt empty. Somewhere inside the grim old fortress were people, creatures ... But I cannot tell how many or what their attitude to us might be, he thought. Annabel, drowsily content, was thinking that it must be almost midnight, and wondering whether the thought of a clock ticking its way to midnight would ever cease to make her shiver, when Taliesin suddenly said, "Listen," and everyone looked up.

Taliesin looked upwards, his eyes narrowed. And then they all heard it.

Footsteps overhead.

That single flaring light had not been an imagined light. There was someone in the castle with them.

Someone in the castle. Someone inside the great, dark fastness, walking stealthily and carefully. In the dim, dark rooms, perhaps at the end of long echoing galleries, or in the turrets that would be approached by means of narrow winding stairs ... somewhere out there, someone was waiting for them. Listening. Perhaps watching them.

Taliesin and Annabel shared a thought: But what kind of creature would not have come out to see who we are and what we want and what we are doing? What kind of creature would have listened to us raiding the sculleries and cooking a meal and drinking cider, and not challenged us?

What kind of creature had its lair at the centre of this dark enchanted castle?

Fergus was on his feet, looking at the boys, and the boys were standing up as well, their eyes bright, their faces expectant. Taliesin, detached as always, thought, They would follow him into hell and back, I believe.

Conn said, "Is it an enemy, Fergus?" and Fergus said, "I don't know," and grinned.

"Is it the first of the battles?" said Niall.

"It might be. Afraid?" asked Fergus, still grinning.

"Terrified," said Niall, and grinned back. "Who's going to lead the way?"

"I could lead the way," said Michael from the other end of the table. "I wouldn't mind."

Fergus said softly, "At least let us explore a little," and the boys grinned delightedly, and Michael beamed and was so pleased that he tipped his chair over backwards and had to be picked up off the floor and dusted down.

Fergus was standing in the sunken hall, seeing how the castle was not, even now, entirely in darkness. There was a soft reddish glow from somewhere, and there was still the dusky blue twilight spilling in through the slitted windows on each side of the huge studded door. Where the two lights merged, there was a soft purple hue. Behind him, the scullery was a square of bright warm light and life; there was something comforting about that.

But they must leave the light and they must go into the darkness of the castle to find the creature who lived there, and who had lit that single candle and who walked furtively about at midnight . . .

When Taliesin said softly, "Shall we explore the entire castle, Fergus?" Fergus said, without taking his eyes from the dark stair at the far end of the hall, "No. Oh, no, we shall never do that."

"No?"

"It keeps its secrets," said Fergus. "The legend tells that you might live here for fifty years and never know it all. There will always be an unexpected flight of stairs that you come upon that you have never seen before, or a doorway you have never noticed. There will always be a few places that the castle will never yield to you. And then, just as you have stopped trying to uncover the secrets, the castle will let you in to one of them. But you will never know it all."

Annabel said, "Shall we then perhaps not be able to find the—the person we heard earlier?" And could not decide if this was a good thing or not.

"I don't know," said Fergus, grinning. "Let us see."

A MIDNIGHT PROWL through the enchanted castle. I don't really believe any of this, thought Annabel, who was in fact believing in it all more fully and more intensely than she had ever believed in anything in her entire life.

We are creeping through an old, old castle, wreathed about in myth and legend, soaked with the history and the lore of Ireland's great Heroes and Princes and Warriors. Every tale ever told about this ancient misty world has, at some part, a tale about this place. What had Fergus said as they sat over supper? Every exiled High King of Tara. Every rebel Prince and every outcast and every vagabond King. Ishmael and Hermit and Anchorite: lone wolves, every one . . . Yes! thought Annabel, feeling the memories come tumbling into her mind, seeing the images clearly and plainly, not knowing, but half guessing, that this was a place where the echoes of the past and the future lingered.

But I don't really believe it, thought Annabel, following Fergus and the boys up the dark silent stair. Of course, I don't really believe it. I expect I shall wake up quite soon.

But she did not wake up and she did not really expect to. I don't want to wake up, thought Annabel. To wake up now would be dreadful. I wonder what we are going to find?

Fergus was leading the way, and Taliesin, falling a little behind, thought it was as if Fergus knew exactly where they were going—some kind of extra sense at work again? And then, as they rounded a corner, and the moonlight slid across the floor, Taliesin saw Fergus tilt his head and listen, and he noticed for the first time the slant of Fergus's cheekbones, and the way his hair grew flat on his skull, and the narrow flaring eyes.

Taliesin stood very still and stared and thought, After all, Fergus is a Prince of the Royal House. Small wonder that

Fergus possessed that complex mixture of authority and courtesy; that he could be imperious and impatient, but he could also be warm and loyal and mischievous. No wonder he knows the way, thought Taliesin, watching Fergus lead them through the empty, shadowed galleries and down twisting stone steps and along moonwashed corridors. He has never been here before—I *know* he has not—but it is his family's heritage, this place, and the knowledge is bred in him. I wonder where he is taking us.

Fergus was not conscious of following a definite path, but he found himself moving surely and swiftly through the castle; unhesitatingly choosing left or right as the choice arose, opening doors and descending stairs. The castle was silent now; there were no footsteps, but each of them knew that the owner of the footsteps was still here.

Taliesin had time to hope they were not walking into a trap, and Annabel had glanced to see that the boys were all still with them, when Fergus stopped abruptly, and they saw that they were standing at the head of a narrow stairway that went downwards, with the steps worn away at the centre, as if generations upon generations had trodden down them. There was a thin rope linked into the stone wall.

Fergus stopped, staring down the stairway, and Taliesin, who was still watching him closely, thought, Yes, he can see in the dark. And felt a strange shiver, for there was something uncanny about a being not entirely Human, a being that was partly wolf.

They could feel the oppressiveness of the castle over their heads, and they could feel as well the despair and the fear that hung here. Annabel thought, Something dreadful has taken place in this part of the castle, and several of the smaller boys shivered and looked uncertain.

Then Fergus said, "There's someone coming," and a bobbing light appeared, coming slowly up the stone stairs.

It was the worst moment yet. Annabel was frightened, but she was also intrigued. She thought she could not have moved if she had wanted to.

The footsteps were light and quick; they were quite ordinary footsteps. They certainly did not seem to be the footsteps of some ancient sinister being who lurked in deep dungeons. They were normal footsteps, thought Annabel. They belonged to someone who was performing an ordinary, everyday task, and not troubling to be particularly quiet or furtive.

The light was bobbing as if it was a lantern which somebody was carrying. It was just a bit lower than it would have been if an ordinary-sized man had been carrying it. And then it rounded the corner, and a small dark person stood looking at them, and Fergus and Taliesin both saw that it was a Cruithin, and knew a sudden, swift delight, for the Cruithin had been gone from Ireland for so long. So, thought Fergus, with deep contentment, so they are still here, are they? And moved forward at once.

The Cruithin, who had stopped when he saw them, said, rather warily, "I suppose you've come to take the prisoner, have you?" And then moved nearer, his eyes on Fergus. Taliesin saw a look in which disbelief and purest joy both warred for mastery, and thought, He is seeing something that he finds so wonderful that he scarcely dare believe it. And looked back at Fergus and waited.

The Cruithin said in a voice of delighted reverence, "Sire. Forgive me."

And fell to his knees.

This place had awoken the wolfblood in Fergus; Taliesin and Annabel found it fascinating.

The outlawed Wolfprince ... Tara's heir ...

"No," said Fergus, as they sat once more round the long scrubbed table in the scullery, the Cruithin, whose name was Mongan, seated with them. "No, I was never Tara's heir." He looked at them, and Taliesin saw the sadness in his face. "I was never Tara's heir," said Fergus again, "and I shall never be its High King." He looked round the table and saw them all listening intently. I have to say it some time, thought Fergus, and drew a deep breath. "To rule Ireland is my sister's right," he said, and in the same moment felt the sudden lifting of an immense and terrible weight. *I believe I am free. I believe I am beyond the storm, through the tempest.* My sister. I can say it without pain now.

Mongan said, "Begging your pardon, Sire, and if it isn't speaking out of turn, which I hope you know I'd never do—"

"Yes?"

"Your sister, that is, Her Majesty the Princess," said Mongan, and stopped again, and looked at Fergus.

"Well?"

"She is not the Queen," said Mongan. "She is not Ireland's High Queen."

"I don't—"

"The High Queen is here," said Mongan. "She has been here for the last twenty years." He looked at Fergus directly. "Your mother is here, Sire," he said.

MY MOTHER. FERGUS stood in the larger-than-expected stone room, and felt, as Grainne had felt, the pity and the waste and the dreadful bitterness of it. This creature, this poor pitiable creature to be High Queen of Ireland, to be the one with the right to occupy the Ancient High Throne, to rule from the glittering Sun Chamber.

He had left the others outside, for he had known, quite surely, that this was something he must face alone.

"You should be careful, Sire," said Mongan. "She—the lady is subject to sudden changes of mood."

But Fergus had stepped quietly across the threshold, and stood absorbing the emotions that lay on the air.

She saw him before he saw her. She was silent and still in a deep shadowed corner of the far room, her eyes hard and unblinking through the tangle of hair. As Fergus searched the shadows with his eyes, her hands curled into a predator's gesture, and the slight movement caused the chains to slither on the stone floor.

Fergus turned at once, saw her, and felt the horror rise up in his throat. Worse than I had believed possible. A thou-

sand times worse than I could have imagined. And then: She
is a wolf, he thought with dread. She is a ravening, slavering
thing of the Dark Ireland. I can *smell* that she is, he thought,
and as the thought formed, he saw the red glint and caught
the white gleam of teeth already salivating with hunger. But
he moved closer, seeing that she was chained, thinking that
he would be able to judge the length of the chains, and move
back if she sprang forward.

And then, without the least warning, she spoke.

"I shall not spring at you."

The voice, the inflection, the timbre, was dreadfully and
shockingly Grainne's, and Fergus stood, unable to speak. And
then, with a mental effort that came from outside himself,
he said softly, "Why will you not?"

The thin lips drew back in a brief smile. "I shall save
you," said Ireland's true Queen.

"For what?" The hairs were lifting on the back of Fergus's neck; he could feel the coalescing of the air and he knew
it for the gathering madness of the creature before him.

"The lady is subject to sudden changes of mood," Mongan
had said, eyeing Fergus uneasily.

"I shall save you for my Master," she said, and grinned
and licked her lips suddenly with a long red tongue.

Staying where he was, Fergus said, "Tell me your name,"
and waited, and saw the characteristic narrowing of the eyes
again, the sudden tilt of the head. Oh, yes, she is so nearly a
wolf that there is hardly any Human feeling in her.

"In that Realm where I am the chosen one of the Dark
Lord," she said, "and where I reign each night, I am called
Damnaithe."

She paused and regarded Fergus, and Fergus said softly,
"*Damnaithe*. The damned one."

"You have the Gaelic, then."

"A very little."

"But in *your* world," she said with sudden contempt, "I
was once known as Maeve."

Fergus studied her. "You do not care for what you call *my* world."

Damnaithe said, "Once someone has entered the Realm of the Dark Lord, and been made free of it, your world is narrow and colourless and vapid."

Fergus lowered himself cautiously to the floor, and sat looking at her. After a moment, he said, "You have been there often? To the Realm of the Dark Lord?"

Her head came up at that, and something triumphant gleamed in the hard, inhuman eyes. "I was taken there twenty years ago," she said. "The Gateway was opened and I was taken by *him*."

Fergus said carefully, "But since then . . ." and saw the terrible smile slide out again.

"I am taken there by *him*," said Damnaithe softly. "He comes for me and takes me from this place of nothingness. Every night, after they have left me alone, he enters by the secret Gateway, and carries me with him to his Dark Domain."

Fergus had just time to think, Of course she is mad beyond recall, but even so, she is convinced that she speaks truly, when Damnaithe turned her head and lifted one arm and pointed.

"You see?" she said, her eyes gleaming in the light from the wall torches. "He is approaching."

As Fergus followed her pointing hand, the darkness became tinged with crimson, and the oblong shadow of a huge door fell across the cell. Malevolent red light poured in, and as the shadow door began slowly to open, Fergus became aware of a dark figure, clad in a swirling black cloak, watching them.

Medoc.

THE INSIDE OF the stone cell was glowing with the crimson light, and Medoc was framed in the great doorway. Fergus had time to think, the Door to the Dark Ireland! And it is opening! And then Medoc had moved out of the framing doorway and the red light beyond it, and was in the cell with them.

He strode to where Damnaithe was stretching out her arms eagerly, his cloak billowing out behind him, and scooped her up, running his hands down over her body. Fergus, unable to look away, had the brief impression that it was as if Medoc was renewing some spell spun a long time ago. For the space of a heartbeat, he glimpsed a thin, sticky, silver web curling about Damnaithe's ravaged body, and then he saw her arch her back and shiver with sensuous delight, and a look of slavish adoration come into her face. Her eyes slid round to where Fergus was still half crouched on the stone floor.

"Did you think me mad?" said Damnaithe, her voice blurred with exultant lust now. "They all think me mad, you know." She moved away from the dark-clad creature. "I was never mad," said Damnaithe softly. And then, turning back, "And if I was, then I was glad to be so," she said.

Medoc had not spoken, and he had barely moved, but Fergus felt as if it was a tangible thing, the power and the authority and the—yes, and the beauty!—that flowed outwards from him. He ignored Damnaithe now, his eyes were on Fergus, and Fergus felt Medoc draw the thoughts from his mind as easily as if he had reached out a hand and plucked them. Medoc smiled; he said softly, "Yes, Fergus, I am the dark, cruel, beautiful one. The legends and the tales do not lie." And smiled. "Have I not bequeathed a little of that to you, my son?" he said, and Fergus, his senses reeling, his mind plunged into a turmoil of half memories and half suspicions, stared, and then said, in a whisper, *"You?"*

"I, Fergus." He moved gracefully across the room, and Damnaithe's eyes followed him jealously. "I fathered you, you and your ill-starred sister," he said. "Did you never guess that? Did you never suspect that you were conceived in my Dark Palace, in the necromancer's lair." He stopped, and Damnaithe said, in a gloating whisper, "The Dark Palace . . ."

"I seeded this creature there," said Medoc, his eyes like

burning coals now. "*I* caused this creature to spawn you and your sister, Fergus, *there* in that other Ireland you tried so long to fight." He studied him. "You half guessed many times," said Medoc. "So many times, when there was a dark sensuous pull at your soul, or when you were aware of the beckoning of all of the shadow beings, and all of the evil undersides of men's natures. So many times you were aware of the darkness within you." He moved closer.

"Did you think, Fergus," said Medoc softly, "did you really think, when the Tyrians took you into their Sorcery Chambers, that it was *your* desires that made you such a willing lover for the she-wolf?" He smiled, and Fergus blinked, because it was a smile of such cold evil, and yet a smile of such infinite beauty.

"That was my bequest to you, Fergus," said Medoc. "It was my darkness and my legacy to you." He studied Fergus. "And that being so," said Medoc gently, "what a very great pity that the sorcerers' work was to no avail."

Fergus said, carefully, "It failed?"

"Oh, yes," said Medoc, and smiled the catsmile again. "My son, you did not think I should allow a vagabond group of Eastern money lenders to re-create Ireland's strongest and most magical enchantment? How innocent you are, Fergus. I have long since drawn the Cloak of Failure about their absurd attempts."

"I failed," said Fergus, half to himself. "They trusted me and I trusted them, and still between us, we failed."

And so after all, I shall never give Ireland an heir . . .

"My powers are more widely reaching than you ever knew," said Medoc. "And in the end, you will have to admit it, you know." He paused, and then said in his beautiful silken voice, "But you are a Prince of the Dark Ireland, Fergus, just as much as you are a Prince of this colourless world. You should not forget that."

"And yet," said Fergus coldly, "it seems that for all you call it colourless, you still covet our world, Medoc."

"I covet it all," said Medoc and Fergus caught the sudden

greed in his voice. "And I will have it all, my dear. You will see that. I, and this creature whom your Cruithin servants believe mad, but who is not mad in the least."

Damnaithe was at Medoc's side now, her chains just barely stretching from the iron rings that embedded them into the wall. "I played the part well, Medoc," she said softly. "No one ever guessed," and Medoc turned to smile the cold dazzling smile and said, in a voice that poured over the cell like liquid silver, "You have served me satisfactorily, my dear," and Fergus saw Damnaithe shiver again with catlike pleasure.

"Are you ready to come with me to Tara, Damnaithe?" he said. "Tara, the Bright Palace that once was yours, and will be so again. For the Last Battle of all?"

"Ready," breathed Damnaithe, and her voice was filled with such extreme servility that Fergus, who had been disliking her immensely, felt a sudden pity. To be held in such thrall to this evil enchanter . . .

"She would not have it otherwise," said Medoc at once, his eyes on Fergus. "For she has dwelled in the Mansions of the Dark Ireland, and she has walked in the enchanted nightfields, and she has supped at the cauldron of necromancy." He turned to smile at Damnaithe. "And now she is ready to reign over your world and to turn Tara into the Court of Demons and of Endless Darkness," he said. "I have tutored her for many years, and now she is ready." Again the smile. "When Dierdriu had your mother brought here, she believed that she was hiding her from me," said Medoc. "She believed that the Cruithin would keep her safe." This time the smile was the smile of a cat playing with its prey. "And although the Cruithin tended her, and fed her and looked after her, they never guessed that I could still reach her." He looked at Damnaithe. "Once she had dwelled in my Realm," he said, "once I had taught her the ways of that world, and made known to her the Twelve Lords who serve me, she could never have lived fully in your world again."

"Lust," said Damnaithe, smiling at him with dreadful

appetite. "Perversion. Jealousy. Depravity. Are they with us yet, Master?"

"They are waiting for us at Tara," said Medoc, and Fergus knew that they both spoke of the Twelve Lords of Darkness.

"You will meet them, Fergus," said Medoc, and the red light that surrounded him dimmed a little. He stepped back and, as he did so, he held out his hands to Damnaithe. "Your new kingdom is waiting, my dear," he said, and now his voice was so filled with a caress, it was so deliberately seductive, that Fergus blinked beneath its dark allure. He shook his head to clear it, because just for a fleeting instant he, too, had felt the pull of the enchanted nightfields and the dark mansions of Medoc's Realm . . .

Medoc knew at once. He turned back to Fergus and smiled deliberately and with full understanding. "You would be welcome in my world, my son," he said softly, "and far more than I have ever been welcome in yours."

Fergus said loudly, "You will not succeed, Medoc."

"We shall see. My lady and I will certainly vanquish the army your sister has raised."

"My—" Fergus stopped, but a sudden hope had welled up within him. So Grainne had been here, she was still fighting. She was still *safe*.

"She has woken the Beastline," said Medoc. "She has unlocked the ancient Enchantment you had believed lost."

Fergus said slowly, "So she has broken your Cloak of Failure, has she, Medoc?" and saw the narrow dark eyes show red sparks of fury.

But Medoc only said, "She has called up the beasts of the forests and the fields, and she believes herself ready to ride against me." He held Damnaithe against him, and Damnaithe writhed in ecstasy, her head thrown back. "Grainne will not succeed," said Medoc. "I am the ruler of the Dark Ireland, the Ancient and Powerful Realm, and my powers are far greater than any of you has ever imagined. My armies will beat yours and my sorcery will swallow you whole. Tara will never be yours, Fergus. I shall fling wide the Doors that have for so long been closed between our two worlds, and my creatures will pour into Ireland and devour it." He was moving back, and Fergus, knowing that he was about to retreat into his Dark Realm, taking Damnaithe with him, tensed his muscles ready to spring on Medoc and disable him.

At once Medoc held up his left hand, and Fergus was caught and held, so that he was unable to move.

"Do not be absurd, Fergus," said Medoc. "You would like to slay me. But I am protected; I am a sorcerer, with the blood of the first Amaranths, and you would not get near enough to inflict even a scratch. Do you truly suppose I should venture even this far without first ensuring my safety?" He smiled, and held up his other hand, and at once a shower of something that was not quite fluid but not quite solid poured across the cell, crimson and gold and with the colours flowing in and out of one another. "I have an armour against this world," said Medoc and, turning his back on Fergus, he snapped with ease the chains that had held Damnaithe. For a moment the two of them stood limned against the evil red light, framed in the half-open doorway. Fergus, still trapped in the spell that Medoc had thrown out, strained his eyes, and caught fleeting glimpses of dark towers and barren landscapes, of brooding turrets and lonely mountains. The Dark Ireland . . .

"We shall defeat you, Medoc," he said softly. "Be sure that we shall defeat you."

"You cannot." The eyes were mocking now. "Your puny armies and your pitiful half-beasts can never defeat the might of my creatures.

"But it will be interesting to watch you try," said Medoc, and then a soft mocking laugh echoed round the cell, and there was the sound of an immense door clanging shut.

Fergus was alone in the dungeon.

Chapter Twenty-five

Grainne had not been aware of moving. One minute she had been standing close to the bonfire—they had all been standing close to it—and she had been listening and searching the shadows that lay thickly beneath the trees, because it was from somewhere out there that the crying of the child came. And although she had not been aware of moving, it had suddenly seemed that she had been running headlong into the dark forest, straight to the crying. She had picked up the poor, thin, ragged little thing that lay under the trees, and she had comforted it and soothed it, thinking that there could be no more desolate sound and there could be no sadder sight. She had carried it carefully back to the warmth and the light, telling it how it should have warm milk to drink and a plateful of good food, assuring it of affection and welcome, stroking the dark hair from its forehead and smiling down into the huge eyes that stared up at her.

The revellers had fallen silent; they were standing watching, dark silhouettes against the leaping flames. The scent of roasted meats was still on the air, and the sharp tang of the mulled wine that the soldiers had brewed. The Beastline were close by. Grainne looked up briefly to see Raynor's eyes on her, golden and watchful, and she thought he started to say something, but she could not be sure.

And all the while, deep within her, she knew that it was not the poor pitiful creature she was comforting, but the child born six years ago. *Fergus's son and mine ... Ireland's Lost Prince.* And I have never ceased to ache for him, thought Grainne; there has never been a day nor yet an hour when I have not thought of the boy and wondered how he had grown up and tried to imagine how he would look . . . I have never been able to shut out the thought of Fergus's son and mine somewhere out there in the dark night . . . I could never be sure that he was properly looked after, that he was loved and protected and fed and kept warm and safe. Unbearable to think of a child, made of such love, being itself unloved.

She had been told that his foster-parents had been carefully chosen, that the boy would grow up well cared for, surrounded by love and comfort. But I could never believe it, thought Grainne, staring down at the huge hungry eyes of the child she held. I have never been able to bear the sound of a child crying. I could never bear to hear the tales of the Lost Children, sacrificed to Crom Croich in Cormac's time.

She carried the shivering child to the fire, and laid it down, and turned to cut meat and bread into cubes, and poured wine and water. In a minute the child would sit up, it would stop shivering and lap the wine and water, it would reach hungrily for the plateful of food . . .

"Please won't you eat a little?" said Grainne, bending down and proffering the food. As she did so, the flames of the bonfire leapt into the night sky, and the hungry-eyed child sprang to its feet and stood grinning and leering, and a shudder of horror went through the watchers.

The Lad of the Skins stood very still, the fire burning up behind him; then he raised both his hands and threw his head back, and, as he did so, the skies behind him seemed to split and tear. Evil-smelling smoke belched forth, and as the split widened, tearing open the night sky, beyond it the watchers saw the grinning, leering, demon-faces of the terrible denizens of the Dark Ireland.

Raynor, who had crossed the clearing in a single step, and was at Grainne's side, holding her hard against him, cried, "The Gateway! The Gateway to the Dark Domain is opening!" and people began to scream and turn to run towards the safe shadows of the forest.

The Gateway yawned wider, and Grainne, transfixed,

unable to move, stood staring into the terrible other Ireland, the Domain of the Necromancers, where Medoc ruled.

There was a sudden stirring deep within that other world, a sudden swirling of the smoke and a screech of triumph and homage from the creatures of the Dark Ireland. Out of the gaping chasm that had rent the skies above Folaim appeared a dark-visaged figure.

Medoc, with Damnaithe at his side, walked into the clearing and stood in the midst of the watchers. A sudden silence fell, and Medoc smiled and, lifting his hand, beckoned to Grainne.

As he did so, a thin sticky web, a snail's trail of slimy, evil Enchantment, fell across the watchers.

There was a moment when Grainne was able to think, The *Draoicht Suan*! And there was another moment when she knew, quite surely, that this was not the *Draoicht Suan*, the legendary gentle Enchantment of Slumber, but something different, something far more insidious and evil.

Medoc said softly, "They will wake when I wish it," and he smiled at her, and Grainne blinked, for it was a smile of such evil beauty, and of such cold cruelty, that her senses swam.

"So, my dear," said Medoc softly, "at last I find you. At last we meet. Ireland's Crown Princess." He gestured to the waiting figure at his side. "You have met," he said, rather dismissively, and Grainne stared, and Damnaithe laughed.

"The child appears witless," she said, and there was a rather horrid purring note to her voice. "She will do very well as a plaything for your Lords, Master. And then the Lad will have his way with her." She looked to where the Lad of the Skins was standing watching, panting slightly, his eyes on Grainne. "You have done well," said Damnaithe. "Our Master will reward you." And made an unexpectedly regal gesture of dismissal.

Medoc was still watching Grainne, and there was something behind his eyes which Grainne could not fathom.

At last, he said, "You have tried to impede me at every

turn. You have tried to come between me and that which I am sworn to possess."

"Yes?" said Grainne, putting up her chin.

"Tara," said Medoc, and now there was a sensuous and a *savouring* note to his voice. "I am sworn to possess Tara, Grainne. But you knew that."

"You already have Tara."

"Not completely. Not until I have removed the accursed Wolfline from Ireland." He stood very still, regarding her. "You could never have defeated me," he said. "You woke the Lost Enchantment of the Beastline, and you called up the *sidh*. But I am the most powerful necromancer of them all, Grainne. I ride at the head of the Dark Armies, and I command the Twelve Lords, and the Dark Ireland is only waiting for me to open up the Gates, and then it will flood in." He smiled. "I can summon the Guardians and the Conablaiche," said Medoc. He moved nearer, and Grainne stayed where she was. "And before many more hours have passed," said Medoc, "Ireland will see once again the birth of Crom Croich into the world. Crom Croich, who eats the living hearts of its victims, and to whom all Ireland shall swear allegiance." He was standing before her now, and Grainne was dimly aware of Damnaithe close behind him.

"A sacrifice," said Damnaithe gloatingly, and Grainne looked at her, and felt a terrible cold chill close about her heart. My mother, and she would give me to Medoc.

Medoc said, "Yes, a sacrifice. For my Master is greedy, and also he is particular." He smiled. "What better offering can I make to him than the Crown Princess of Tara," said Medoc. "You will be the worthiest sacrifice I shall ever make, my dear."

"My armies will never let it happen," said Grainne, and Medoc laughed, his red-flecked eyes gleaming.

"Where are your armies, Wolfqueen?" he said. "Where is your beloved Fergus, your brother, and where are your Beastline Lords?" He made a swift gesture to where Raynor and the others stood motionless, caught in the tendrils of the malignant spell. "Where are your faithful staunch Cruithin and the warriors of your people?" said Medoc mockingly. "And where, my dear daughter, are the brilliant magical *sidh*? Where is Aillen mac Midha who cast an Enchantment when you were born, and whose *sidh*folk are allowed to serve and protect the Wolfline? They are helpless," said Medoc. "They are caught in the lightest and easiest of spells and they cannot even break free."

"The *Draoicht Suan*?" said Grainne, knowing that it was not.

"The *Draoicht Suan* is a pale spell," said Medoc.

"Insipid," said Damnaithe, and laughed and tossed her tangled mane of hair. "Send them a nightmare, Master," she said, pressing against him again. "Send them the harpies and the Furies. Send them the flesh-eaters of the Ebony Mountains and the blood-drinking trolls of the Red Caves, and the demons of the furnaces." She slid to the ground, rubbing her face against his hips, and laughed again, a horrid, bubbling, curdled laugh, and Medoc bent down and removed her twining arms from his body quite gently, and put her from him. Against her will, Grainne remembered that Medoc, of all the necromancers, had ever been spoken of as a gentleman.

"The stories do not lie," said Medoc, and Grainne knew that he had heard this with ease.

"What are you going to do with me?" she said.

Medoc looked at her for a long moment, his eyes thoughtful. And then, "We are going back to Tara," he said.

THERE WAS NO point in struggling or trying to run away. Grainne knew there had never been any point. Medoc would fling an enchantment to bring her down within seconds. In any case, the landscape for miles around was still lit to weird, unnatural life by the boiling red skies of the Dark Ireland, and there was no hope of concealment. There was no use in calling for help either, for no help could possibly come. Grainne cast a desperate look to Raynor, and saw that he, that all of them, were held fast in the spell, the travesty of the *Draoicht Suan*. They were blind and deaf, and there was no help to be had.

"How long will they be like that?"

"Until I decide to let them go," said Medoc.

"They will find a way to break the spell."

"No."

"They will march on Tara," said Grainne defiantly.

"They will not get within yards of it." He regarded her almost with affection. "My poor child, do you not understand even yet? I have called up the Guardians, I have summoned Spectre and Reflection and the Sensleibhe, and no living creature has ever defeated those three." Medoc glanced to where the Lad of the Skins stood, grinning. "The Guardians will protect Tara," said Medoc carelessly. "Your armies will not get past them." He stopped and seemed to study Grainne very intently. "There is one more thing," he said, and now his voice was a caress.

"Well?"

"Six years ago," said Medoc, "you gave birth to a child, Grainne." Again the smile, terrible and inhuman and beautiful. "It was fathered on you by your brother, and therefore it inherited the wolfblood from you both." He studied her. "The child was taken from you," he said. "It was then that the legend of the Lost Prince arose. Your people believe in it, Grainne."

"Yes."

"They believe that one day the child will rise up and drive out my armies."

"Yes," said Grainne softly, watching him.

Medoc's beautiful lips thinned. "I have spent years searching for that child," said Medoc. "I have expended more time and energy than you could possibly imagine, and I have used every dark Beckoning I could find to draw the child to me." He glanced to the shadows, where the armies and the Beastline and the people of Folaim were still sleeping.

Grainne said, hardly daring to breathe, "You feared it? You feared the Prince?"

"Let us say I knew it to be a danger," said Medoc. "A threat. A Royal Wolfchild. I preferred it to die. When I finally rule completely, and when Crom Croich holds sway in Ireland, there must be no pretenders, you see. No Wolfprinces to grow up in secret and amass armies to ride on me. Your son is a threat, Grainne."

"They sent him away," said Grainne, half to herself. "I never knew where."

"But I know," said Medoc. "I knew of his birth, for there have always been those who would work for me, and I knew the exact moment he was born, Grainne." He leaned closer. "I heard the *sidh* singing him into the world, my dear, just as they had once sung for you."

"Yes," said Grainne, staring ahead of her, and just for a moment she was back in the birth chamber, torn apart with pain, barely able to breathe, her senses blurred and her heart in torment for the child being born, whom she would never be allowed to know. And through it all, she had heard the singing: faint, beautiful, comforting. *For after all, this is a Wolfprince, and after all, we shall spin our Enchantment, just as we spun it for his ancestors ...*

"For several years I lost him," said Medoc. "I lost sight of him, and I lost the knowledge of where he was. But I worked and I paid the sorcerers, and I sent out spies and I laid traps. Finally I found him as, of course, I must have done. I should not have allowed him to escape me, Grainne." He was standing before the fire, at the very centre of the sleeping revellers, lit by the flames. "He was brought to Folaim," said Medoc. "And he is still here. I smell him and I feel him and I know he is here. Your son, Grainne. The child you bore your twin brother in secret. The Lost Prince, the Wolfchild who will one day rise against me."

Grainne said in a whisper, "You cannot know that."

"I do know it. I sent out the fool they call Lugh of the Longhand to kill him for me, but he has proved a squeamish tool, and I do not trust him. The boy is here," said Medoc again, "and I shall have him."

"Here?"

"Yes." His hand came out to her and closed over her arm painfully. "That is why I have come," said Medoc. "I have come to take him back to Tara with you, so that there I may offer you both to my Master, and render your souls to the greatest god Ireland will ever know."

Crom Croich ... the Crown Princess and the Wolfprince both slain and sacrificed ... And then all Ireland will run with blood and the skies will be forever dark ...

Medoc lifted his head and turned to look at the circle of children, and a slow smile touched his lips. He lifted his free hand, and a shower of dark red sparks whipped across the clearing. Grainne received the sudden impression of a rope of fire and, as she formed the thought, the rope snaked about one of the small dark figures on the other side of the fire.

Medoc stayed where he was, his eyes on the small slender shape. And then the child moved into the circle of firelight.

MY SON. MY son and Fergus's. The might-have-been child of fire and light and grace; the slender, slant-eyed boy with wide-apart eyes and mischievous lips; the Royal forbidden Wolf-child with the magical ancient blood of every High King and every High Queen—Cormac, and Niall of the Nine Hostages, Mab the Wanton and Dierdriu the Madcap—every warrior Queen and every hero King ... Patrician and beautiful and wolvish, and just very faintly dangerous, certainly not wholly Human ...

The lost Wolfprince.

He was wide awake; his dark hair was turned almost to crimson by the fireglow, and red pinpoints of light danced in his eyes, giving him the look of a devil or an angel or both. There was the narrow skull, the glossy dark hair like an animal's pelt ... And his eyes! thought Grainne. Once you had looked at his eyes, you could never have mistaken him for a pure-bred Human ...

The ancient Royal Wolfblood, alive and strong and

ready to fight for Ireland . . . Certainly able to call up the Wolves . . .

And then Medoc nodded to the Lad of the Skins, and Damnaithe moved into the light, and they both swooped on the boy, and, as they did so, Medoc turned back to Grainne. There was no time to think properly, and no time to feel joy at the child's closeness. There was no time to be afraid. Medoc had enveloped Grainne in the swirling cloak, and there was a great rearing black stallion waiting, and they were galloping hard across the countryside, and there was no time to think or wonder, or even to breathe, for the countryside was rushing past them, and Medoc's arm was about her as firmly as a band of steel and there was no possible escape.

But despite everything, she felt a soaring delight in the boy's presence—Fergus's son and mine!—and there was an exhilaration in the knowledge of where they were going.

The Crown Princess and the Lost Prince, returning to the Bright Palace . . .

Grainne had known that Tara was soaked in Medoc's darkness and she thought she was prepared for it. But it was still a shock, it was a dreadful sickening jolt, to see it suddenly there ahead of them, in all its dark intensity, shadowy and dense . . .

For Medoc and the Twelve Lords have put out the light . . .

This is the worst yet, thought Grainne. I do not think I can bear this. But then she looked to where the Lad of the Skins and Damnaithe were riding alongside, the child held firmly between them, and knew that there was much worse to come.

The child looked across to Grainne; his hair was whipped into disarray and the night wind had painted fingers of colour on to his high cheekbones. He smiled at her briefly, blindingly, and Grainne felt her heart lurch, because it was Fergus's smile, the boy was Fergus over again, but with the slanting eyes of their great-grandfather Cormac, and the mischievous grin of Dierdriu.

And then they were down the avenue, and the beech trees were on each side, and they were riding hard to the Western Gate where once had flocked the travellers and the scholars and the pilgrims of the world, and the terrible darkness was closing about them.

There was time to see the boy become suddenly intent; to see him become alert and to see his eyes narrow. Grainne thought, He is recognising it. He is coming back to the Palace of his ancestors, and although he does not know, for he cannot know, he senses it.

The portcullis was lifting to admit them, and the drawbridge was lowered, and they were riding hard across the drawbridge, the horses' hoofs ringing out sharply.

And then they were inside, and the portcullis was lowered again, and Grainne and the Lost Prince were shut inside the Dark Palace with Medoc.

And the armies of Ireland and the powerful enchanted Beastline she had striven so hard to waken, and every single person who might have rescued them, were held helpless in sorcery far away in Folaim.

RAYNOR HAD NOT been aware of the exact moment when Medoc had flung the heavy dark Enchantment of Slumber at the revellers; he thought it ought to have been possible to see it and feel it and sense it, but it was not. At one minute they had all been feasting and laughing and drinking the mulled wine and the mead. And then, without warning, there had been the towering figure of the dark cloaked being, and there had been dull red lights all about them, and it was as if a great weight had descended on their eyes, so that it had been impossible to keep them open. There had been a drowsy scent as well; something exotic and languorous, so that you wanted to surrender to it: and you wanted to drown in it, and let it carry you away wherever it wished . . .

The thought that this was the *Draoicht Suan* flashed through Raynor's mind, and then he saw the cruel, dark figure standing in the firelight, and he knew that it was not the gentle, kindly *Draoicht Suan*, but something far deadlier, and something that carried with it a sinister threat.

He had fought the Enchantment, and although he had not quite beaten it, he had not quite succumbed to it either. His limbs had been heavy and tired, and a mist had swum before his eyes, but he had been able to see what happened, and he had heard Medoc's words distantly, as if they came through a long, narrow tunnel.

Medoc was taking Grainne and the Wolfchild to Tara to kill them.

If it had been possible to break the Enchantment and tear Medoc apart, Raynor would have done so and found delight in it. For Ireland? said his mind rather mockingly, and at once was the response: No! For Grainne! He cared about Ireland very much, but he would never care for any living creature as strongly as he cared for Grainne. The knowledge that Medoc had her was anguish and torment, and he fought the dark Enchantment with every ounce of his strength and with every shred of his energy.

If there had been help from outside somewhere, it would have made the task just about possible, but there was no help, because there was nothing and no one who could come to their aid.

And then, on the outer rim of his clouded vision, Raynor saw a wisp of blue-green smoke ...

AILLEN MAC MIDHA did not approach too closely to the Humans, because to have done so would have been dangerous for them. They were vulnerable; they were unable to look upon pure magic and on undiluted enchantments, these Humans. For them to have seen the *sidh*, properly and fully in their cold inhuman beauty, would have burned out their eyes and shrivelled their senses. Aillen mac Midha's people had frequently hunted Humans and stolen their senses; they had done so for countless centuries and they would continue to do so, for only thus could they pour into their music the beautiful aching joy and the strong Beckoning. But the Prin-

cess was in the direst danger, and with her was the Lost
Prince who had been born in secret and raised in concealment. Aillen's people knew of the Wolfprince's birth; they
had sung him into the world and they had spun their enchantments about him.

They had known that this was the one who would finally drive back the Dark Ireland . . . the greatest High King
Ireland would ever know.

Eireann, the One True King . . .

And now the child was in Medoc's power and the Princess was with him.

The Elven King sat for a long while on the grassy tus-
sock, surveying the sleeping armies and the Beastline and the
Cruithin with his narrow glittering turquoise eyes. He did
not move, and to an onlooker it might have seemed that he
was weighing up the two sides of the situation.

The Lost Enchantments and the Lost Prince against the
Dark Ireland.

The *sidh* could dissolve Medoc's Dark Spell of Slumber,
but it would be dangerous for the Humans. It would be dangerous for them because their senses were vulnerable: sight,
hearing, sense of touch, sense of smell, taste, might be burned
out. One of the Princess's people would almost certainly have
to pay the price to the *sidh*.

Eyes, ears, tongue, nose, fingers . . .

The Elven King gave himself a shake and stood up. There
could be no choice. If the Princess and the Wolfprince were
to be saved, Medoc's spell must be lifted.

No matter the cost.

CHAPTER
TWENTY-SIX

GRAINNE WAS LYING chained on the floor of the Sun Chamber, with the darkness of Medoc all about. The Sun Chamber was in the most complete darkness she had ever known; it was a place of near impenetrable shadows and of evil night creatures; of dark sinuous beings who would creep stealthily towards you and of black formless things that would writhe and materialise on the outer limits of your vision.

Directly ahead was the massive crystal window which had been so precisely angled that it caught the first dawnlight every morning and the last starlight every night. Grainne, brought up inside Tara, bred into the tradition of the brilliant glittering Citadel that Tara had been, felt the loss of Tara's brightness like a knife-twist in her heart. This was the Sun Chamber, this was the place her ancestors had called *Medchuarta*, Tara's heart, its core, the dazzling prismatic centre, the Ancient Seat of the High Kings of All Ireland . . . Shrouded in darkness by Medoc's evil.

I am in his power finally and at last, thought Grainne, pulling at the chains that held her wrists and her ankles bound. I am in the power and at the mercy of the strongest, most evil necromancer ever to come from the Dark Ireland. Medoc, the dark, beautiful, evil sorcerer, and the Twelve Lords . . .

She knew a very little about the Twelve Lords; she thought that very few people knew much about them, for there had grown up a belief that even to know or speak their names was to make it easy for them to find their way back to Tara. But Grainne, growing up in the Shining Palace, had

487

listened to the stories and the legends, and she knew more than most about the sinister shadowy Lords, who were said to sit with Medoc in his dark halls, and to assist him in his sorcery. She had heard their names, and she could remember some of them, though not all. There was the Lord of Corruption, and there was the Lord of Depravity, and of Perversion, and the Lord of Vice. Names to frighten children with: Decadence, Degeneracy, Impurity, Greed; the list went on, and they were every one of them names to frighten children with.

Children . . .

He was lying beside her, as tightly chained as she was, but despite this there was an alertness and a watchfulness about him, almost as if he might be curious and intrigued, and certainly as if he was ready to turn any situation to their advantage.

At length, Grainne said softly, "Are you all right?"

"Chained," he said. "But all right. And you?"

"The same."

Grainne said hesitantly, "You must forgive me, but I do not know your name." And waited.

He turned his head to regard her, and a sudden smile touched his eyes. "Erin," he said, and Grainne smiled, because of course they would have called him Erin, *Eireann* meaning "Ireland."

"Erin, do you know where we are?"

"Tara," he said, his eyes glowing. "We are inside the Bright Palace."

"Are you . . . ?" She stopped, because surely it would be wrong to use the word "frightened" to him.

But he put out a hand and said, "You can use the word to me, madam." And smiled, and Grainne felt as if she had been given something precious and rare and more valuable than all the riches of the world, for he had heard her thoughts, and he was surely using the Samhailt, the ancient bequest that was only ever bestowed on the Ancient Royal

House ... "I am only a *very* little frightened," said Erin seriously. "And I know this place—"

"Yes?"

"Perhaps it was a dream." He looked at her, and Grainne knew at once that he was willing her to say that it had not been a dream. For a moment, memory slipped sideways, and she was back in that terrible night when he had been born, and the brilliance of the Sun Chamber had been a sick mockery to her. He had been only a few hours old when he had been taken from her, but, looking at the slanting dark eyes, now she thought, *How far back can memory go?* Can he possibly have retained some scrap of awareness? She said carefully, "It may not have been a dream at all."

The dark eyes narrowed. "You were there," said Erin. And then, in delight, "Yes, I remember. You were there." *You know what happened,* said his expression. *One day you will tell me.*

"Yes," said Grainne gently. "One day I will tell you."

"The Bright Palace," said Erin, as if he liked the sound of the words. "Tara."

"Not so very bright at the moment."

Erin looked at her. "But it will be again," he said. "It will be bright again." And grinned, and quite suddenly Grainne felt an upsurge of confidence, because the Dark Ireland had been defeated before, and the Wolfline had been exiled and returned before ...

And this is Ireland's heir, this is the Lost Prince, the son I bore and thought never to see ...

"Are we going to escape, madam?"

"Yes," said Grainne, her heart beating painfully. "Yes, Erin, I think we are going to escape. We will make a plan and we will be very watchful, and we will escape."

"Are they going to kill us?"

Grainne drew breath to speak, although she had no idea what she was going to say, only that it was immensely important to reassure him, and important not to lie to him.

"I think—" she began, and stopped, and they both looked towards the great double doors of the Sun Chamber.

The doors were opening slowly, and the darkness was altering, it was becoming tinged with crimson. Crimson, the colour of anger and malevolence and vice and sin . . .

Medoc and the Twelve Dark Lords stood framed in the doorway.

Medoc wore the ceremonial robes of the Academy of Sorcerers, and on his left breast shone the Dark Star of Necromancy. Grainne remembered, and wished not to remember, that it was Medoc who had destroyed by sorcery the original priceless Codex of Necromancy, that manuscript of incalculable age revered by every sorcerer in Ireland, and who had tricked the Academy into accepting the corrupt and warped Charter for Enchantry. Medoc it was, as well, who had created the terrible fearsome Order with the insignia of the Dark Star that he now wore on his breast.

He walked forward calmly and quietly, the Lad of the Skins at his heels, and the Twelve Lords fell into line behind him. As they did so, Grainne saw a sliver of moonlight fall across the floor, so that she saw the Dark Lords clearly and terribly.

Clad in unrelieved black, every one. Garbed in the black matte armour that legend ascribed to them; the visors lowered but the eyelets gleaming softly. Grainne, watching from the corner where they lay, had the thought that if you reached up to lift one of the visors, you would find that behind it was nothing. Faceless beings. Each of the Lords carried a black spear, from which flew a black pennant with his insignia: Corruption, Decadence, Greed, Impurity, Lust . . .

Medoc came to the exact centre of the Sun Chamber, and stood looking down at them both. When he spoke, his voice held a deep savouring pleasure.

"The Crown Princess and the Wolfprince," he said. "Ireland's Lost Prince. I bid you welcome to Tara, madam. You will not escape me, for no one has ever escaped me."

"No one has ever escaped you yet," said Erin, and regarded Medoc with his narrow stare. Medoc became very still, and the two of them eyed one another. Then:

"So," said Medoc softly, "so, you have the arrogance and the insolence of your ancestors, do you, Wolfprince?" He moved nearer. "You know who you are, don't you?" said Medoc, and Erin said at once, "Oh, yes, Medoc. I know who I am." And sent Grainne a look that said, *Forgive me. And trust me.*

"I cannot remember when I began to know," said Erin. "I cannot remember when I knew that the dreams were not really dreams at all." He studied Medoc. "I have walked in these halls before," he said, and turned his head to look about him with detached interest. Grainne was struck all over again by his complete absence of fear. *Because he knows we can escape?*

Because it is important that this evil one does not sense our fear . . .

He had not moved, and the chains were still about his ankles and wrists, but Grainne felt his thoughts pierce her mind as clearly and as easily as spring water flowing down a mountain.

Erin said, "Are you going to sacrifice us to Crom Croich, Medoc?"

"I am."

"I thought you would," said Erin. "Will it make you very powerful?"

Medoc laughed, and at his side the Lad chuckled horribly. "Listen, Wolfchild," he said, "I am more powerful than you can possibly imagine."

"Listen, Medoc," said Erin, "you are in the Ancient Royal House of my ancestors, and I am going to drive you out."

For the briefest moment, surprise showed in Medoc's eyes, and then his lips curved, and he bent down so that he was on a level with Erin. "I have flung aside your House," he said. "And I have toppled your accursed line."

"You still consort with a Wolfqueen," said Grainne, who

was drawing more strength than she could have believed possible from Erin. "Where is Damnaithe, Medoc?"

"When I am ready I shall call her," said Medoc. "She will come."

"Poor creature," said Grainne, half to herself.

"She is content with her lot," said Medoc curtly, and turned back to Erin, and Grainne, watching, listening, thought, Medoc is disconcerted by Erin. He is not afraid, but he is surprised. Erin is throwing him off balance. She looked again at this slender remarkable child who could sit chained and bound in the power of the wickedest necromancer in all Ireland, and still manage to throw him off balance. "Damnaithe it will be who will occupy the High Throne," said Medoc.

"But you will rule through her," said Grainne.

"Of course." There was the smile again, thin, cruel, quite beautiful, and utterly evil.

"It will not happen," said Erin. "It is a very great pity for you, Medoc, but it will not happen."

"It will," said Medoc.

"No," said Erin calmly.

"Who will prevent it, Wolfchild?"

"I shall," said Erin. "I know everything about the Wolf-kings, and I know that I am the one who will destroy you." He smiled as he said this, as if he was offering Medoc some kind of present. "But you knew that," said Erin. "You *did* know it, didn't you?" Again the sly, mischievous smile. "I am the One True King," said Erin.

Medoc said, "A pity you will not live long enough to prove that."

"I shall," said Erin calmly. "In me the ancient enchanted wolfblood is stronger than ever it was before. I have the power and the light and the strength, Medoc. I have the Samhailt and I can call up the wolves, and I *will* call them up, Medoc. I am the vanquishing of the old, old curse that you have tried to revive." He smiled. "You have ruled in a sort for some years now, but you will not do so for very much longer." Again the smile—grave, considering: "But I hope you will proceed with your foolish ritual, Medoc, because we will be interested to see it." He glanced at Grainne as if to say, Is that all right? Can we watch? and Grainne, alternately terrified and fascinated, fiercely proud, said gently, "We shall find it intriguing, Medoc." And smiled up at him, and said, "Do please proceed." And thought, Well, at least I am managing to sound as untroubled as Erin. How does he do it?

All a pretence, madam, came the mocking response. *But we have him puzzled.* Aloud, he said, "Go ahead and summon Crom Croich, Medoc," and Grainne, listening very intently, knew at once that Erin had spoken calculatedly and deliberately, so that Medoc would be annoyed.

But if Medoc was annoyed, he gave no sign. He turned on his heel, and nodded to the Lad of the Skins, and at once the Lad sprang up grinning, and followed Medoc to the centre of the Sun Chamber. Grainne noticed that Medoc was standing directly over the ancient symbols etched into the Sun Chamber's floor, whose origins were so old and so wreathed in myth and mist and legend that no one knew what they meant any more.

"I know what they mean, my dear," said Medoc, turning his dark, slanting eyes on to Grainne and smiling the beautiful, cruel smile. "I could tell you how, at the very beginning, when Tara was raised from the rock by the sorcerers, the hags and the harpies and the Furies and the banshees came pouring out of the Dark Ireland; for Tara was then so beautiful and so desirable that every sorcerer and every necromancer and every enchanter sent out bewitchments to capture it.

"But no one ever did, for Tara's own sorcerers were wily and far-seeing, and they sank into Tara a protective spell, and the *sidh*folk came up to Tara's ramparts and poured their music into its halls and into its battlements and into its fabric. Tara is wrapped about with enchantment and spells, my dear, and it is here, in the great Sun Chamber, that the spells are strongest." He gestured to the symbols that caught the light faintly and gave out a bluish glow. "There is immense power here," said Medoc, "and where there is power it can be harnessed. I shall harness it, and I shall use it, and we shall send it outwards and call down the great god-idol of all Ireland."

Crom Croich ...

"Yes, Crom Croich," said Medoc, and smiled. "But you knew that. You will meet him," he said, "and you will honour him and render to him allegiance."

"No," said Erin.

"You will!" said Medoc, and his eyes were shooting sparks of light. "You will, for I shall force you to do it." He regarded them both. "And after you have done so," he said, "I shall *feed* you both to him." He paused, and the Lad of the Skins gave his low, bubbling chuckle. "I shall call up Crom Croich's greatest and most loyal and diligent servant," said Medoc, "and then we will summon the god himself."

Crom Croich, who eats the living hearts of its victims ...

"And then," said Medoc, "when I have appeased the god with the hearts of the Crown Princess and the Wolfprince; when their hearts have been torn from their bodies and their souls taken to the Prison of Hostages, *then* my rule will be absolute. The Conablaiche will once again walk abroad, scouring the countryside for prey; the first-born boys of every family in the land will be taken for sacrifice, and the great religion of Crom Croich will once more hold all Ireland in its grip." He moved from the central carved portion of the Sun Chamber's floor, and came to stand over them again. "Tara is finished, Wolfprince," said Medoc, speaking directly to Erin. "Once Crom Croich is in the world, Tara will fall and its light will be quenched, and the land will seethe with evil and the skies will darken and the rivers will run with blood."

Erin said very softly, "You may have put out the light, Medoc, but you will see that I can restore it."

"We shall see," said Medoc, and turned back to the Dark

Lords and the Lad of the Skins. "Begin the ritual to Crom Croich."

CROM CROICH. THE king-idol of all Ireland. The being of pure gold who demanded the fresh hearts of its victims. The terrible hungry monster-god who had taken scores of children and eaten their hearts, and in whose name the Crusade Wars had been fought several generations earlier. The god to whom every person in Ireland must offer the first-born of every stock: sheep, pigs, cattle, hens . . . boys. Grainne could remember the old stories of how every family in Ireland must send a representative to the gathering called Mag Slecht, where Crom Croich materialised in all his dark glory, and how every person present must bow down to the ground until their foreheads and the soft part of their noses and the caps of their knees and the points of their elbows broke; where it was whispered that three-fourths of the men of Ireland died of these prostrations.

Dreadful and pitiful and more cruel than anything Grainne had ever heard of.

Somehow it had to be stopped. Grainne lay back in the dark Chamber and murmured the words aloud. "It must not happen."

"It will not," said Erin very softly. "You will see."

"What can we do?"

He turned to survey her, and the shadows lay across his face, so that Grainne saw for the first time the wolf's mask, and felt a thrill of delight and fear. The descendant of the Wolves of Tara . . . And then she thought, But so am I, and felt in that moment the strength she had felt on setting out for the Grail Castle.

The power and the light and the strength of the Wolves . . .

"Yes," said Erin, watching her. "Yes, that is how we shall do it, madam." He sat up and glanced to where Medoc and the Dark Lords had disappeared through the great double doors. "They cannot hear us," he said, "but perhaps they can sense what we are saying. You understand that?"

"Yes."

Erin regarded her, his head on one side, and Grainne saw with delight and terror mixed that his ears were pointed.

"One thing can save us," said Erin, and Grainne said, "Yes?" and knew, in the same moment, what he was about to say.

Erin said, very gently, "You had not the power to do it before. Not alone. But together we have power and to spare—" And stopped and looked at her again, with the way she was coming to know of expecting her to understand.

And I do understand, said Grainne silently. I understand and I am afraid and filled with pure delight at the thought.

"Well?" said Erin, waiting.

Grainne said slowly, "We have to call up the Wolves of Tara."

THE CLEARING WHERE the Wolfqueen's armies slept was becoming shrouded in the cold blue and green ice-fire of the *sidh*. Slender formless creatures moved in between the trees and in and out of the rocks and the hills and the grassy forest floor; beckoning arms and cold slanting eyes peered and smiled and, at length, gently and softly, the sticky filaments of evil sleep woven by Medoc began to fall away from the sleepers.

Wake to us, Humans, for we will lead you back to the world of the living, and we will ride with you, wild and fearsome to drive out the Dark Adversary from Tara's Halls. It will be the greatest battle Ireland has ever known, for it will be the only battle when the ancient and magical people of Aillen mac Midha have joined with you ... Together we can defeat the Dark Lords, Humans, only there is a price that you must pay ... We must take one of you and take his senses ... it is the age-old law, and we cannot waken you unless you give one of your number to us ...

And you must waken, Humans, you must open your eyes, and you must surrender to our music, for only thus can you put off the evil slumber spun on Medoc's Dark Looms ... only thus can you find strength to put aside the heavy mandragora sleep of the necromancer. Hear our music, Humans ... let it soak into your skins and let it trickle into the most secret corners of your soul. Hear it and feel it and drink it ... stand still and become one with it ...

And give us one of your number, Humans. Let us take his senses: sight, hearing, smell, taste, touch. For only thus can we spin our music and save you. Whoever looks on us now will become blind, deaf, witless, speechless, for ever ... But it is the price you must pay for our help, Humans ... It is the price that must be paid if Ireland is to be safe ...

The blue and green smoke whirled and towered and, as the music poured into the clearing, Lugh of the Longhand opened his eyes and looked directly at the *sidh*.

A shout of triumph went up, and the *sidh* closed in.

RAYNOR WAS THE first to become fully awake, to blink and look about him and remember what had happened, and push away the clinging remnants of Medoc's nightmares. He thought he recalled trying to fight the dreadful darkness that was shot with crimson and laced with evil, and he certainly recalled struggling, because he had known at once that this was black sorcery, Medoc's ploy to stop them all from following him to Tara. To succumb meant to abandon Grainne utterly and forever to Medoc, and this was something so unendurable that Raynor would have done anything in the world to prevent it; he would have let the *sidh* take him to their underground caves; he would have let them cage his soul in the Prison of Hostages; he would willingly have given his sight, hearing, senses ...

There was a ripple of light and the sensation of gentle, cruel mirth and malice at that, and Raynor knew that the *sidh* were still very close, and that they were hearing very clearly.

Oh, yes, we would have taken you, eagle one, had you been

the first to awake ... we would have taken you gladly, for you have strength and beauty, and we would have enriched our music by taking you ...

Raynor stared round the clearing, trying to make out the blurred moving shapes.

Come with us, eagle one, come with us beneath the ocean where the waterlight moves ceaselessly against the walls of the caves, and where you will walk on the bones of all the Humans we have taken, and where we will steal one of your five senses to pour into our music ... Again the laughter, and Raynor thought, We dare not fully trust these creatures.

Oh, yes, you can trust us, you can be sure of us, for we have taken one of your number, and we are carrying him far far away, over hill and over dale ... we are carrying him beyond the skies and beneath the oceans, and he will never return to the world ...

Raynor said, "Who have you taken? Who is it?" And looked about him, trying to see who was no longer there.

We have taken one who was no friend to the Queen, eagle one ... and now, because of it, we will ride out with you, we will join with you against the Dark Ireland. The Elven King bids us do it, but we do it gladly for the Ancient Royal House ... We are what we are, and our music is made from the emotions and the perceptions of Humans ... We have taken what we want now, but beware of us, eagle one, for we shall return, and we may steal you away that time, for we are greedy and soulless, but our music is the most beautiful sound you will ever hear ...

The laughter filled the clearing again, cold and unearthly, and Raynor closed his mind at once, for he knew as well as anyone the dreadful seductive power of the *sidh*.

Tybion the Tusk had woken at almost the same time as Raynor; he too had heard the chill music, and felt the *sidh*'s lure, and had felt, as if it was a tangible thing, the dark sluggish Enchantment dissolve and slide from him. He thought he was now strong enough and fierce enough to storm Tara's ramparts and pull down the Palace walls brick by brick to rescue Grainne, and he was certainly angry enough to rip

Medoc from gut to groin and spill his innards all over the
Sun Chamber's polished floor. This was a far more blood-
thirsty notion than Tybion had ever entertained or expected
to entertain, and he wondered why it did not horrify him.
But he was not in the least bit horrified; he wanted to be off
at once, ripping Medoc apart and wreaking some extremely
gruesome form of punishment on the Twelve Dark Lords
(disembowelling? boiling alive?), and he could not understand why the others, with the sole exception of Raynor,
were still wandering about rubbing their eyes and being confused. Tybion was not the smallest bit confused; he was wide
awake and brimming over with energy and plans and plots,
and it was very irritating indeed when people such as Fintan
and Cermait Honeymouth and Dorrainge the Druid were
not running and scurrying and shouting for the horses and
sounding the advance. They ought to have sounded the advance long since, said Tybion firmly, and would not listen
when Cathbad tried to explain that Medoc's nasty Enchantment had sat more heavily on some of them than it had on
others. Tybion said that this was utter nonsense and sheer
absurdity, and there was no time to be lost, because if they
were to rescue Her Majesty, they ought to have set out two
hours ago. For good measure, he prodded one or two of the
most recalcitrant souls with the toe of his boot, and became
very nearly angry with Fintan who, said Tybion, ought to
have recognised Medoc's spell the minute Medoc started to
weave it, and warned them all.

"But there's the point," said Fintan, on whom Medoc's
Enchantment had sat rather weightily. "There's the point.
We didn't any of us know until it was too late."

"Utter balderdash," said Tybion, and Fintan, never at
his best when woken from sleep, and certainly not at his best
when woken from a necromancer's sleep, became very tetchy
at this. He said it was all very well for Tybion to be bright-
eyed and bounciful; it was all very well to be all of this at
Tybion's age. Fintan had been those things himself, said Fintan lugubriously, and pretended not to hear when Cermait

remarked, in not quite an undertone, that this was stretching the truth a bit, because Fintan had been born middle-aged. These things were well and good, said Fintan, raising his voice a little, but if you had eaten a smidgen too much of Cathbad's roast pig, and if you had drunk maybe a thimbleful more than you ought of the Cruithin's mead, and on top of that had had a nasty black sorcerer tying you up in knots and nightmares, you were apt to take a bit of time to gather up your wits. They were all of them gathering up their wits, said Fintan, and glared at Cathbad, who said people took longer to do this because their wits were so wildly astray in the first place. They would set off at any minute, said Fintan.

Cermait thought that this was the thing to be doing; they would surely set off pretty soon, he said, because there was no saying what might have happened while they had all been asleep. From which the others gathered that Cermait had no more notion than Cathbad's roast pig of what had gone before, and certainly had not the smallest suspicion that Grainne had been carried off by Medoc for purposes best not thought about.

"I wouldn't trust Medoc," said Cermait sagely. "Not from here to that tree would I trust him."

"He's got the Queen!" said Tybion loudly, and Cermait said if that was so, it was the most terrible thing that had ever befallen Ireland, and he was very sorry, but the entire thing had been a bit hazy, well, if they wanted the truth, it had been very hazy indeed, and if Medoc really did have Her Majesty, oughtn't they all to be doing something about it instead of standing about holding a meeting. They were no better than Lugh Longhand, said Cermait, and he was very surprised indeed, and he was especially surprised at Tybion the Tusk, of whom he would have thought better.

At which Tybion lost his temper in good earnest and said they none of them had any romance in their souls, and that they were no more fitted to be in Her Majesty's service than one of Cathbad's pigs, and took himself off to find the army's musicians, so that the proper advance could be sounded.

Cathbad said, "Oh, dear me, can't you any of you *see* that half of us are still under Medoc's nasty Enchantment," and Fintan sat up and looked more alert than he had done for some time—several people said he looked more alert than he had done for years—and wanted to know the exact form the Enchantment had taken. He accepted a tankard of mulled wine, which Cathbad was distributing on the premise that mulled wine never hurt anyone, and said Tybion was right, they ought certainly to be mustering their forces.

Cathbad, who had now finished giving out the mulled wine, was simmering a cauldron of soup, which he had just boiled up from one or two odds and ends of the Samain feast. You had to be prepared for anything to happen, said Cathbad and although he had not himself been precisely prepared for Medoc, because Medoc was not the sort of person you expected to meet in the ordinary way, it just went to show that you should never relax your guard. Cathbad had not himself been prepared for Medoc to stroll into the middle of the feasting, as cheeky as an intoxicated fieldmouse, and he had not expected to be bewitched either, because it was not something you normally expected.

If anyone wanted to know, Cathbad had found it all a very horrid experience. He had suffered an unspeakably nasty nightmare, in which every creature he had ever cooked had grown legs and wings and teeth and feet, and had come running after him to dismember him and fling him into a stewpot. He felt quite breathless still after running across a dark landscape with pigs and turtles and positively dozens of rabbits in hot pursuit, waving spoons and ladles and carving knives, and shouting things like, "Let's make a Druid pie," and, "Cathbad-stew for supper," and, "I say we fricassee him." It had been quite shudderingly nasty, and Cathbad had been very glad to wake up. He had gone off at once to stir up a pot of soup which would warm everybody, and prepare them for what might be ahead, and he thought he would certainly add the bones of the roast pig and the wild ducks and the rabbits, if only to remind himself that pigs and ducks and rabbits were eaten by people instead of the other way about. He would put in a few spoonfuls of chopped parsley as well, and some onions. Onions made a really good strengthening broth, never mind Lugh complaining that anything with onions in it went right through him. Cathbad would not have cared if the onions ran right through Lugh and out the other side. Now he came to look, Lugh was nowhere to be seen, but this was not something that anyone need trouble about, because they would all have a bit of peace.

Tybion the Tusk was very nearly distracted by this time. He discovered that Raynor had been quietly deploying the Beastline creatures and studying a map showing the quickest route to the Bright Palace. Bec and Rinnal had been putting together foodstuffs, and several of the others had been stamping out the embers of the bonfire and making sure that Cathbad's cooking fire was properly smothered with earth and damp grass.

This was not something that it had occurred to Tybion to do, but he was very pleased to see such evidence of preparation for the march.

"But of course we are going to march on Tara," said Raynor, looking at Tybion in surprise. "Did you think we should not?"

"Oh, no," said Tybion. "It's only that—" He tried to think of something sensible to say, because Raynor had the way of looking at you with his hard golden eyes, so that you felt he saw into your mind.

Raynor said gently, "It is only that the others are not yet properly out of Medoc's spell." And he smiled suddenly, and Tybion smiled back, and felt the smallest bit silly and wished he had not been quite so sharp to Fintan and Cermait Honeymouth. He said, quite humbly, that he would very much like to ride alongside Raynor and the others when they set out, and Raynor said, "We should count that an honour, Tybion." Tybion beamed, and felt that after all they might succeed in getting the Queen out of Medoc's clutches, because Raynor was a person who made you feel confident and sure of yourself, and, thus restored, he took himself off to apologise to Fintan and Cermait, and also to several people whom he had not offended at all, all of whom very politely said not to mention it; they were all of them distracted and in a state of confusion anyway.

Raynor, outwardly calm and composed, was in a far worse agony of mind than any of them knew. He believed that none of the others had guessed at his inner torment, and he thought this was how it must be. A Princess of the Ancient House of Ireland could never join her life with a parvenu of a Beastline, with a nobility created by a band of enterprising sorcerers. He remembered what he had thought on that first night: She is not for me nor I for her. He could still think of it, even while his body was remembering, and even while his heart was torn apart with longing. I shall let her go, thought Raynor. I shall let her go, even though I can hardly bear to think it. And then, without warning, a thought surfaced: At last I shall see Tara, he thought, and with the thought, came a flame of rebellion. But why should I not see it? thought Raynor, his eyes suddenly glowing, his mind lit to new awareness. *Why not?* I have the Enchanted Beastblood, I have the right. Why should I not see the lights blaze, and why should I not see the doors sealed against the Dark Ireland? *Why should I not be at the forefront of the battle to rescue Grainne?*

Fintan and Cermait had woken up properly now, and were rounding up people sternly, and wanting to know why so much time was being wasted when Queens were being held captive by wicked necromancers.

"There's no time to be lost," said Cermait, and Fintan agreed, and looked round for Lugh, who might be a fool, but who was in nominal charge of the army.

"Oh, he's sulking somewhere, I expect," said Cathbad.

"He'll have gone off in a sulk, and very likely we shan't see him this side of the Winter Solstice."

"And very nice too," said Cermait. "It's high time we saw no more of him. And if you want to know what I think," said Cermait, even though most people did not, "it's that Raynor is perfectly capable of leading the charge on Tara, *and* of destroying Medoc! He's got authority," said Cermait firmly, "and that's something people respond to. Mark my words, everyone will follow him without even stopping to think." And he nodded as if agreeing with himself, and glared at anyone who might have considered arguing against him.

No one did argue, because most people were becoming rather impressed by Raynor. As Cathbad said, he did not say very much; he certainly did not put himself forward in any way, "But you can't help but be aware of him," said Cathbad.

"He's very well organised," said Dorrainge unwillingly.

"I'd follow him into hell and back," said Tybion, and was frowned at by Dorrainge, because hell was not a word you should use, even if you believed in it, which Druids did not.

Cathbad said they ought all of them to remember that in the legends the Beastline had been Princes of Ireland. And wouldn't they all of them recall the great Conaire of the Eagles? demanded Cathbad, getting very excited. Conaire, who had ridden alongside Cormac himself in the historic battle against the terrible Erl-King. "I'd follow Raynor anywhere," said Cathbad devoutly, and would not listen when one or two of the soldiers said vulgarly that Cathbad would follow anyone anywhere.

But Cermait was right; the men were responding to Raynor and quite a number of them were heard to remark that breeding showed: hadn't Conaire of the Eagles been some kind of cousin of the Wolfline anyway? Wasn't it time and more that they had a drop of the ancient Enchanted Beastline blood back with them?

"Rubbish and nonsense," said Dorrainge, who liked to

believe that all Men were equal, but he said this quietly, so that not many people heard. And he took himself off to search for Lugh Longhand, because you could not have the nominal head of the Queen's army disappearing just when you were going into an important battle. Dorrainge had not yet settled with himself whether he would ride in the charge, because Druids were supposed to be peace-loving people; still, you could not have Medoc riding off with Ireland's Queen and plotting fresh evil. Lugh would have to be found, said Dorrainge, because didn't they need the head of the *Fiana* to lead them in all this.

"But he isn't the head," said Tybion, overhearing. "Fergus is the head."

And then Cathbad, who had been scuttling about under pretext of gathering up the soup bowls, but who had in reality been eavesdropping on any promising bits of gossip that might be going, turned round and beamed and pointed, and said, "But there *is* Fergus."

And everyone stood up and stopped what they were doing, and looked, and Tybion let out a raucous cheer.

Fergus, Taliesin, and Annabel, and the lost boys from the Prison of Hostages, were walking towards them down the hillside.

LUGH OF THE LONGHAND was confused, which was not a thing that often happened. He had been the first one to wake from Medoc's dark spell, which was no more than you would have expected, and he had seen at once that the clearing was positively awash with the *sidh*. This had been extremely worrying, and Lugh had blinked and rubbed his eyes in the hope that the *sidh* would have vanished when he opened them again.

They did not vanish. They wreathed closer if anything, and Lugh began to have the impression that slender, snake-like blue-green arms were writhing towards him.

Come away with us, warrior of the Fiana . . .

Well, of course, Lugh Longhand was not going to be

taken in by *that*! Dear goodness, didn't everyone in Ireland know the *sidh* for what they were, and wasn't it an ignorant man or a fool who looked on the *sidh*, looked on them fully and properly and saw them in all their unearthly beauty and lost his wits and his senses and his virility, or worse.

If anyone was going to commit the supreme folly of looking a *sidh* in the eye, it was not going to be Lugh of the Longhand.

The trouble was that once you had glanced at them, even by mistake, it was quite difficult to look away. Well, it was impossible actually. And there was a sort of beckoning, a slender, silky, "Come hither" sort of feeling.

Yes, yes, come to us, warrior of the Fiana, *for we are the most beautiful beings in the world, and there are few who have looked on us and lived to tell of it . . .*

And of course, it would be rather nice if it could be a Longhand who became the only Human ever to look on the *sidh* and see their world and live to tell of it. This was a very interesting idea, and Lugh would very much enjoy seeing the legendary water caves, which he would probably be able to escape from with the utmost ease. Also, if there was going to be a march on Tara, it might be tactful if Lugh was out of the way when it happened. This was not cowardice, merely discretion, because it was pretty certain that Medoc would refer to the arrangement he had had with Lugh about the Wolfchild being killed. Actually, it was a foregone conclusion that Medoc would refer to it, and as publicly as possible, because Medoc was a mischief-maker and he would probably enjoy giving Lugh away before the entire Court and half the Druids and the Beastline and the Cruithin. This was something that could not be allowed to happen. Lugh would be better off exploring the *sidh*'s water caves and bringing back a grand tale for the story-tellers. It would be good, as well, to be able to rival the tales of the silly battle that everyone else was going off to wage on Medoc. Lugh would have something different. The story-tellers would very likely thank Lugh for it for generations to come.

He was surprised at how quickly they seemed to reach the *sidh*'s caves, because he had not been aware of travelling anywhere at all. He had, it is true, been conscious of soft silky arms entwining him, and of cool turquoise smoke obscuring his vision, and now and then of narrow glittering eyes watching him, and beckoning him deeper and deeper into the soft, formless lights.

This was ridiculous, of course, because eyes could not beckon in that way.

Oh, yes, they can, warrior of the Fiana. *There are eyes that can beckon, and there are eyes that can eat your soul* ...

Lugh thought they might be in some way travelling under water now, and he remembered that in all of the tales, the *sidh* dwelled beneath the ocean, and lived in the cool green water caves, and sometimes came out and sang their gentle seductive music and lured unsuspecting Humans down into the caves' depths. And then he thought that it was not water they were travelling through but sky; a huge expanding infinity of sky, fold upon fold of it opening up before him.

We are below the oceans and beyond the skies, warrior of the Fiana ... *we are beyond the bounds of infinity and into the starlit worlds that are forbidden to Humans. There are many worlds, and there are many creatures* ... *Man is not the only creature, warrior of the* Fiana. *You shall see our world, and we shall not let you leave it ever again* ...

And then the lights were changing, and Lugh glimpsed the roaring ocean beneath them, and saw the cave openings, and quite suddenly they were there, in the cold green caves, and they were going down and down, and surely they were going to the earth's centre, only that it was so cold, and people had always told how the earth's centre would be hot ...

But the caves were cool and rather clammy and damp feeling. It was not the least bit dangerous, and Lugh was not the smallest bit frightened, but on the contrary, very interested. To be sure, he could have done without the cold, but that had to be expected, because the *sidh* were chill faery beings, they had the cold inhuman blood of the Elven King's people in them, and you had to expect that their dwelling place would be cold. And there was sufficient light to see by; there was a soft green waterlight rippling on the walls.

Lugh was not afraid, dear goodness, of course he was not! He would tell all this as a very good adventure when he got back. Ah, they'd all have to look to him after this. Anyone at all could ride on Tara and drive out Medoc, but no one in the world had been to the *sidh* caves and returned to tell of it.

Even so, the caves were chill and rather eerie. There was the sound of the ocean somewhere over their heads, and there was the sound of singing in the water as well.

The music of the waters, Fiana *warrior . . . we make it and we preserve it, and we pour it back into the world for your people to enjoy. But we have to take from you before we can give, Human, we have to take Human senses to make it . . . Sight, hearing, touch, taste, smell . . . which shall YOU give to us,* Fiana *warrior . . . ?*

The *sidh*'s voices were whispery and really rather nasty. Lugh did not know when he had heard anything quite so nasty, in fact. You could discount pretty much of everything they said, and Lugh would discount it. Even so, you could not discount the fact that the *sidh* were here, in the cold green tunnels, and that they were beckoning and luring, and pulling so that you did not have much choice but to follow them.

And the light was not as good as Lugh had thought. It was rather dim as a matter of fact; a few good stout candles would not have come amiss, or one or two well-placed wall brackets. Lugh would have brought his lantern with him if there had been time. It was a good lantern, fashioned from horn, with a hole cut in it for the lighted candle to shine through. You could not beat a good strong lantern flare in a dim cave. It showed you where you were going. It would have stopped Lugh treading on the small, twig-like objects beneath his feet. This was in fact quite as horrid as the *sidh*'s whispery voices, because every time he moved, the twig-like things crunched, or sometimes they disintegrated, and a tiny cloud of evil-smelling very dry dust stirred.

Bone dust, Fiana warrior . . . the bones of all the Humans who have ventured into our world. With every step you are scattering the bones of your fellow creatures . . .

But we shall gather it all up for our music, Fiana warrior, for there is no part of a Human that we cannot use in our music. Which is it to be for YOU . . . Eyes, ears, tongue, lips, skin . . . ?

This was all becoming very disconcerting. Lugh was not precisely frightened, but he did begin to wonder whether it had been an altogether wise decision to follow the *sidh*. If there had been more light instead of this absurd green dimness, he would have felt considerably better. He would certainly have felt very much braver.

And then, without the least warning, there was light of the most dazzling degree. Lugh moved a bit uncertainly, the *sidh* pushing him forward. He felt his sight blur and his senses swim.

Opening in front of him was a great silver-blue cavern, and directly ahead of him, seated on a massive carved silver throne, watching him from narrow turquoise eyes, was the Elven King.

LUGH KNEW EXACTLY what they were going to do to him now, because you could not live in Ireland without hearing the stories about the *sidh*.

They stole any one of the five senses to weave into the music. It was this, said the stories, that made their music so beautiful and eerie and unearthly. It was this that made it so powerful, so that Humans could not resist it, said people, and told how you should never look on a *sidh*.

And now, here was Lugh, standing in the *sidh*'s water caves, actually in the Elven King's silver cavern, entirely at their mercy. There did not seem to be any escape, although if one was to be found, Lugh would be the man to find it, of course. He wished he was not remembering every grisly tale ever told about these creatures; how they tore out Men's eyes and their tongues; how they took their time in doing it . . .

It flickered across his mind, rather wildly, that this was just the occasion for a bit of a speech, but no words rose to his lips, and then he remembered that he might not have any lips quite soon, and he might not have any tongue either, and he felt so sick that he did not think he could have spoken anyway.

Aillen mac Midha regarded him from his brilliant inhuman eyes, and Lugh shivered, because the creature was cold, so cold that you could freeze to death standing here.

The Elven King smiled, and it was a terrible and beautiful smile, cold and merciless, and yet with some kind of understanding in it. Lugh had the feeling that Aillen mac Midha saw right through to his soul (if you believed in souls, that was), and that he did not much like what he was seeing.

"I do not like it," said the Elven King, and Lugh saw, as they had all seen outside of Folaim, the words take substance and lie on the air, like silver filaments of thread.

"I do not like what I see," said Aillen mac Midha again. "I see that you have been a traitor to your kind, *Fiana* warrior."

Lugh started to say that he had not been any such thing, not a bit of it, and the Elven King raised one slender hand for silence.

"You intrigued with the dark necromancer, Medoc, to kill the Prince," he said, "and therefore you are no friend to the Queen."

Put like that, it sounded really much worse than it had been. Lugh started to explain, because weren't the Longhands faithful and true, every one of them, but Aillen mac Midha forestalled him again.

"We are constantly hunting in your world for victims,"

said the Elven King, "for it is only by luring Humans to our caves, and taking their senses and their souls, that we can survive. A question of practicality, you understand? It is a war that has long since raged, and both sides know the rules."

Never look on the sidh . . .

Aillen mac Midha smiled the eldritch smile as if he had heard Lugh's thoughts with ease.

"We could have taken any one of you from Medoc's Dark Slumber," he said. "And to take at least one was necessary, for if we were to dissolve the evil Enchantment he had spun, there had to be a price."

A price . . . and Lugh would pay it.

"We took *you*," said Aillen mac Midha, "because we knew that you had murder in your heart for the Prince. And we are constrained to protect Ireland's Royal House, *Fiana* warrior. We spun the Enchantment about him when he was born in secrecy to the Queen, and we have watched him and guarded him ever since. Did you really think," said the Elven King, "that we should allow anything to stand in the way of the Prince and his rightful inheritance?"

His rightful inheritance: *Tara*.

"He has yet to fight Medoc," said Aillen mac Midha, "and we can not tell whether he will be victorious, for he is younger than we would have liked, and Medoc and the Twelve Lords are more powerful than they were at his birth." The narrow glittering eyes regarded Lugh with the pitiless stare of a predator. "But, the Prince must be given every opportunity," said Aillen mac Midha. "We have removed his enemies before now, and we are removing you."

And you will lose one of your senses to us, Fiana *warrior, and you will go into our music, and our music will be poured back into the world. True immortality, Human . . . you will not quite die. We shall use every part of you and you will not quite die . . .*

The Elven King remained perfectly motionless, perched on the massive, elaborate silver throne. But his eyes were watchful, and there was a wariness about him.

At length, he said, "You are well come to our world, Human," and paused and smiled. "But you know our laws."

Any one of the five senses . . .

Lugh gulped and found nothing to say, and Aillen mac Midha smiled again and lifted his left hand.

The *sidh* surged forward, avid and writhing.

"One of his senses," said Aillen mac Midha softly. "Which shall it be?"

And then, into the silence that followed, during which Lugh could hear the singing of the ocean above them, and could hear as well the faint, far-off chanting of the *sidh*'s music, the Elven King said very gently, "We will take his sense of *touch*.

"Peel his skin off. Flay him."

Lugh did not escape. Immediately Aillen mac Midha had pronounced sentence, the *sidh* whipped about his arms and his legs, pinioning him so firmly that he could not move, twining their silken arms about him, and then stripping his clothes from him, so that at last he stood naked and trembling before them.

Silvery laughter filled the cavern now.

A poor specimen . . . we should have taken the eagle one, Majesty. This one will not enrich our music . . .

"Nevertheless," said Aillen mac Midha in his silvern voice, "we have him, and he is our prize for dissolving the necromancer's spell. And he is a traitor to his own kind, and for that alone he must die. Do what you will."

The laughter rang out again, and now Lugh could see the *sidh* as clearly as ever a man had seen them; he could see them in their blue and green faery garb; cold and terrible, but so beautiful and so alluring that he knew the sight would stay with him for ever.

For ever is a long time, Human . . . Let us say, throughout Eternity . . .

The twining arms had become sharp and pointed now; hundreds of slender gleaming knives and pins that would slide beneath his skin. He felt the coldness of steel, and knew it could not be steel in fact, and he tried to struggle, but the silken cords held him down. He tried to cry out for help, for surely there would be someone, but the knives and pins were already beginning their work . . .

Pain began to explode all over his body in dozens of different places, and there was the feeling of slivers of light penetrating his skin. He thought they had started with his fingertips, and he experienced the truly sickening pain of having every fingernail bent backwards, far far back until the nail was ripped out, and his fingers were a mass of raw agony.

He dared not look, for he knew he would see his fingers being stripped of their skin, and he could feel the white-hot knives sliding deeper and farther up his hands and then his arms.

He thought he must surely be bleeding in hundreds of places now, but when he caught sight of the floor, there was no blood, only a trickle of colourless fluid, seeping on to the ground beneath him.

The *sidh* were surging closer now, pressing in on him, and he tried to cry out, but the pain was smothering him, and he was drowning in the blue and green smoke and in the glinting eyes of the Elven King.

More, more, Human. Give us your sense of touch . . . You will not need it, we will strengthen our music with it . . .

There was a dreadful thin tearing sound now, and the pain was searing his arms and covering his shoulders and his neck. He dared not look down now because, if he did, he might see raw flesh, muscle, bone . . .

A part of him still unaffected by the pain became aware that the *sidh* were slitting his body now, laughing and swooping down on him, beginning to pull back the skin of his chest.

He was screaming with the torment and the cruelty of it now, for surely, surely, there must be someone who would come to help him; it was not to be thought of that he should die like this, in these terribly lonely caves, at the hands of these cold faery creatures . . .

His entire body was a raw open wound, and he felt a dreadful slithering sound, and he knew that the internal organs held in place by skin were shifting, and that if he moved and if the *sidh* cut any deeper, his insides would slither on to the floor, and when that happened he would be lost and these creatures would devour his soul, and he would be soulless, lost forever.

There was a final wrenching pain, and he shuddered and cried out, and merciful blackness began to descend on him like great smothering folds, and the caves were receding, and the world was spinning, and the pain was fading and soon, soon he would feel them cut his soul free and cast it into the Prison of Hostages . . .

The Elven King sat watching from the carved silver throne, resting his chin on one hand, his eyes thoughtful.

It was some little time before he saw the soul emerge at the hands of the *sidh*, and stand before the silver throne, its head bowed humbly.

Aillen mac Midha said softly, "The soul of a traitor. I think we have no use for it." And then, nodding to the waiting *sidh*, "Cast it into the River of Souls," he said, "there to await rescue or the end of the world."

He stood up and walked slowly to where the wet formless thing that had been Lugh of the Longhand lay.

"A traitor," he said again. "But he has served a purpose for us." And then, giving himself a shake, he turned back to the waiting *sidh*.

"We must return to the world," he said in his silvered voice. "For the Wolfqueen's battle is not yet won.

"And the Lost Prince is still in the most terrible danger."

As FERGUS WALKED slowly and rather unsteadily across the grass, a great wave of delight washed over the watchers. As Bec was to say later, it was a truly remarkable moment.

The Captain of the High Queen's *Fiana*; the warrior and fighter and lover, reputed to have been Her Majesty's lover some years ago, reported as having lain with most of the women at Court, had returned. Amongst the soldiers, there was a great surge of confidence, and a feeling of: *Now* it will be all right. *Now* we shall be able to rout Medoc and restore the Wolfqueen. They began to cheer, and then fell quickly silent again without quite knowing why. Nearby, the Beast-line creatures and the Cruithin stood very still and waited and watched Fergus approach. Dishevelled, exhausted look-ing, he was no different, and yet entirely different. The peo-ple nearest to him, one of whom was Tybion the Tusk, had the impression that although Fergus was back with them, he was not fully back with them. Tybion, who held Fergus in reverence, thought it was as if Fergus had experienced some-thing so vast and so terrible and so truly awesome that he would never quite be able to be fully in the ordinary world again.

Fergus walked alone down the hillside, knowing that Taliesin and Annabel and the boys were deliberately keeping back, and feeling grateful to them for it. They did not fully understand, but they understood enough to know that this rejoining of his people, this reclaiming his army, was some-thing precious and private and solemn. He stood still and felt the night wind lift his hair, and he looked at the waiting armies and the Cruithin, and felt an angry ache rise up within him. For, this is not how I wanted it! he thought. This is not the homecoming I visualised! He had wanted to come riding back in triumph, leading the boys, certainly with Tal-iesin and Annabel close by; riding at the head of them all, ready to topple Medoc, sure of a great victory.

And Grainne. He had always thought, in his visualising, that she would be there, watching, welcoming him back. She would have come running to him, her hands outstretched. Wouldn't she?

She was not here. He knew it before his eyes had taken in the fact that she was not with them, and panic seized him. Had he, after all, endured so much and come so far for it all to be to no avail? Had Medoc taken her?

He stood looking at them all, absorbing the picture they

made—the waiting armies, the creatures of the Beastline. Fergus paused at that, studying them, understanding at a level of his mind that was still detached that the Lost Enchantment was in truth awoken. I shall feel great joy at that some time soon, he thought. But for the moment, he could only think that Grainne was not here.

For a very long time, no one spoke. Fintan and Cermait said afterwards that Fergus had looked deeply happy, and then looked unsure of this, but Tybion the Tusk said quite positively that Fergus had looked unbearably sad. And while no one paid this much heed, because Tybion was always ascribing emotions to people who had probably not experienced any emotion at all, it was generally felt that Fergus had somehow changed.

"Although I could not say in what way," said Fintan.

"He's known trouble," said Cathbad solemnly, shaking his head. "My word, he'll have a few tales to recount. We'll be able to gather round and hear them, I expect. Cinnamon wine and honey biscuits," said Cathbad, nodding, because you could not tell a good tale without some kind of sustenance.

Annabel stayed where she was, at Taliesin's side, and saw Fergus approach the strange beings, and felt the remarkable enchantment of this blue and turquoise twilit land close a little more firmly about her, and felt the bleak stark world of the Drakon move a little farther back from her mind. She thought that very soon this world would cease to be strange and unfamiliar to her; she stood looking at the creatures assembled in the clearing and knew that she would come to know them, every one of them, and that some of them would become close to her.

This is the true Ireland, thought Annabel, a spring of complete contentment welling up inside her. This is the heart and the core, and it is so wonderful and so beautiful and so brimful of elusive enchantments that the air all about us is alive and thrumming. Her eyes went to the Cruithin, silent and alert, their eyes bright, and she saw that these small dark people were surely the ancient fey beings of legend and lore: Human, but possessed of their own gentle woodland magic. Behind the Cruithin were the soldiers, and Annabel's eyes widened because, for all her world's fighting talk, for all its vainglory, and its history of war and battle, she had never come anywhere near to seeing the true trappings of war. *Death or glory* . . . yes, I can believe that people really did say that and think that, thought Annabel.

And then she looked to where the Beastline stood, and her eyes went from Bec, watchful and quiet, to Rinnal, whose head was tilted, and then to the others, the Beastline of the Chariot Horses and the Beavers and the White Swans. And Raynor, a little apart as always, his hair a golden cap, the dying bonfire glinting on his golden skin. She experienced delightful recognition. I have never seen such creatures. I *know* I have never seen them. But I know them from dreams, thought Annabel. From legends and race-memory. I never dared believe they existed, and yet I never ceased to hope that they did exist somewhere.

The remains of Cathbad's fire burned up suddenly, sending a gentle glow on to the night, and sending sweet-scented smoke across the clearing. Fergus walked into the centre of them all and stood looking at them.

And then his eyes went to Raynor.

It was the most extraordinary moment anyone had ever witnessed. The two figures stood very still, looking at one another, and to the watchers it seemed that something very singular and very unusual was passing between them. One or two people felt distinctly uneasy, because didn't they all of them know about Her Majesty and Raynor and the nights inside the Grail Castle, and weren't they all beginning to look on Raynor as Grainne's consort. And very suitable as well, they had all thought. But then after all, this was Fergus, the *Fiana*'s Captain, and if no one had known for sure that there had once been something between Grainne and Fergus, most people had guessed. It was to be hoped that this meeting would not be an awkward one, and it was to be hoped, as well, that nobody lost sight of the fact that whichever of them the Queen finally ended up with, she had still to be rescued from Medoc's hands, and that pretty quickly as well.

Tybion the Tusk had been dashing about trying to marshal everyone into some kind of order, because there was no time to be lost, but even he stopped and stood stockstill and looked at Fergus and Raynor, and was thrilled to the depths of his romantic soul. He would have been hard put to have said which of the two he admired the more, or which of the two he was trying to visualise next to Grainne on Tara's High Throne.

At last, Fergus said, "I give you courteous greeting," and everyone relaxed a little, because this was rather an ancient but very chivalrous salutation.

Raynor, his eyes wary, said, in the same polite tone, "You are well come, Captain, and timely returned," and people began to feel better, because both of them were exchanging ancient and extremely honourable words of greeting.

Fergus glanced at the assembled company, and the waiting soldiers, and a rather bleak smile touched his face. "You appear to be held in some esteem by everyone," he said, and the listeners looked up in alarm, because there was the faintest challenge in Fergus's voice.

Fergus felt the alarm that rippled through them and understood at once. But he stayed where he was, and he watched the golden eyes in front of him, and thought, Yes, the others are waiting to see what will take place here. Because there is something between Grainne and this one? I do not know it, not for sure, thought Fergus, but I can *feel* that there is something. Grainne, my dear lost love, is *this* the one I shall lose you to?

Raynor said with deliberation, "Were you thinking I

have taken your place, Captain? You must surely know that I could never do that." And looked at Fergus with his straight golden stare. "That would be impossible," he said.

"You are generous," said Fergus, and a smile touched his lips.

"I have learned to recognise facts, Captain." There was a sudden unconscious arrogance in Raynor's voice, and Fergus felt the pain twist like a knife-thrust in his heart because, for sure, this was the one who had supplanted him with Grainne. This strange golden creature, neither quite Human nor quite eagle. So this was her choice. This was the one who would rule Ireland at her side. He does not yet know it, thought Fergus, but I know it, and the others know it as well. He has authority and integrity, and that curious blend of gentleness and strength and imperiousness. I have lost Grainne to him, and I think I shall lose Ireland to him as well.

This is going to hurt, thought Fergus. This is going to hurt more than I thought possible. I think I shall bear the pain for a long time to come. And then without warning, he thought, But will I? and a tiny greenshoot of hope uncurled. Am I not already through the whirlwind, and am I not already through the tempest, and have I not already found the eye of the storm? And I always knew that I could never have Ireland, thought Fergus. I always knew that.

The eye of the storm, the centre of the maelstrom . . . I am not quite there yet, thought Fergus, still looking at Raynor. Not quite yet, my dear precious girl.

But I shall let you go, my lady, my love, and I shall pretend, and the world will never know what has happened to me, and I think that in time the pretence will grow into reality.

He moved then, and touched Raynor on the left shoulder, in the customary gesture of friendship and acceptance. He saw Raynor smile, and he saw that there was acknowledgment in the smile, and understanding.

The watchers relaxed, and nodded to one another, and began to feel safe, because Fergus was back with them, the *Fiana*'s head was in their midst again, and he would lead them in the battle against Medoc and the Dark Lords, and surely, surely, with such an army, they could not fail to be victorious?

But would it be in time to save the Queen?

CHAPTER TWENTY-SEVEN

As MOONLIGHT SILVERED the Sun Chamber and lit the scene to eerie life, Grainne and Erin, bound and helpless, watched Medoc return, the Dark Lords and Damnaithe walking in procession behind him. Grainne saw that Medoc's eyes were glowing, and she felt a cold, dark evil emanating from him.

He stood at the exact centre of the Sun Chamber, at the heart of the curious pointed symbols and carvings etched into the floor. In the uncertain light, Grainne thought that she could have believed the floor to be of solid silver, and at once Medoc turned to regard her.

Silver indeed, my dear, for the sorcerers have always known the power of precious metals.

Behind him was the great dais, where once the Ancient Throne of Niall of the Nine Hostages had stood, and where the great Cormac of the Wolves had held court, and where Dierdriu had entertained lovers and diplomats and travellers. Where once Grainne herself had held court for a few short months.

The Dark Star of Necromancy gleamed on Medoc's breast, sending out spears of light, so that he appeared to be at the heart of a gathering darkness, with a nimbus of light all about him. The Lad of the Skins crouched at his feet, neither quite in nor quite out of the silver light, his dark eyes huge and watchful, and Damnaithe stood with her eyes fixed on Medoc.

Medoc threw back his head and held out his hands, palms upwards in the age-old gesture. Grainne, who had seen the sorcerers and occasionally the Druids do this, knew at once that Medoc was drawing down power, that he was harnessing and channelling the force poured into Tara at the very beginning by the first sorcerers, and by the *sidh* who had known that Tara must be protected from the Dark Ireland.

The power would not be the gentle safe pure blue force of the strong and good enchantments, but the terrible force of the necromancer. As they watched, the light surrounding Medoc became darker, shot with crimson, and Grainne felt a chill enter her heart, for this was in truth the dark and cold evil that would summon Crom Croich, and that would eventually destroy Tara once and for ever.

The Lad of the Skins was silent, but the Twelve Lords had moved, and Grainne saw Damnaithe turn to watch them, and clasp her hands tightly together with lascivious anticipation. The Lords took up a stance around the walls, as if they were sentinels surrounding Medoc. And where before there had been emptiness, a void behind the dark visors, now something was stirring ... Damnaithe shivered with pleasure, and began to prowl round the walls, peering into the visors, stroking the dark armour. From where she lay, Grainne could not see directly into the visors, but she knew that behind every one, eyes would be opening.

The Twelve Dark Lords were waking ...

With the thought came the names Grainne had sought to remember earlier and been unable to. Now, staring at the figures, she did remember; she knew every one of them, and their names tumbled into her mind as easily and as clearly as if they had been written on the Sun Chamber's floor.

Debauchery. Lust. Greed. Decadence. Selfishness. Conceit. Perversion. Jealousy. Hatred. Deceit. Vice. Avarice.

All there. All here now inside the dark lair of the necromancer. The Twelve Evils. The Twelve Wickednesses. The sins of Men and the evils personified ...

They were becoming more solid and more alive every minute, and Grainne could feel the evil lying on the air now, tangible and real, clotting the Sun Chamber and curdling the shadows, so that you could easily believe that creatures lurked in every corner, and that eyes peered at you from the darkness.

Damnaithe was still moving round the Sun Chamber, occasionally pausing before one of the Dark Lords, running her hands over the unyielding surface of the armour, shuddering with animal lust. Grainne, watching, saw Damnaithe move now upright and now on all fours, and saw the slavering cruel features of a ravening wolf again.

Yes, she is more wolfish than ever I believed it possible, but it is the evil merciless side of the wolf . . . Grainne glanced to where Erin still sat quietly at her side, and remembered that they too possessed the same strange blood, and for the first time was afraid of her inheritance.

For this mad ravening creature is my mother, and this evil dark lord is my father . . .

She would not remember it. She would see these two for what they were, and she would see Medoc as beautiful but corrupt and steeped in evil and in vice.

If they are evil, then surely we are strong and good . . .

The thought sliced into her mind like a spear of light, and she knew it was Erin, and confidence returned.

And if we can but call up the Wolves of Tara we shall surely be safe . . .

Can we do it? said Grainne silently, and at once came the response, swift and sure, and with a child's conviction, that if you believe strongly enough you can do anything in the world.

Yes! Yes, we can do it!

I do believe, thought Grainne. It is our only chance. And then: But even if we can do it, will it be in time? And will it be enough without the army? For we are still alone here. Raynor and the others are far away on the cold hillside of Folaim, held in Medoc's evil bewitchment. And Fergus is trapped somewhere between this world and that of the Future . . . Grainne spared a thought for Fergus, whom she might never see again, and knew that if he had been able to come to her, he would certainly have done so long since.

There had been no news of his quest, and surely he would have returned if he could. There was a rather terrible pain at the thought that Fergus might be dead, but it was not something she could yet give attention to. There would be time to grieve when Medoc was defeated . . . Only let Fergus be all right, prayed her mind. Let him be all right somewhere, and oh please, *please* let him be able to know Erin.

Erin, the One True Future King . . .

He caught that, of course, and there was a flare of amusement. *Not for a very long time, madam . . . you have many years left . . .*

And despite the danger and despite the nearness of Medoc, Grainne knew a swift sharp delight, because of all the things Erin might have turned out to be, he was turning out to be brave and filled with the reckless charm of his great-great-grandfather. He might be Cormac born again, thought Grainne.

The Sun Chamber was becoming suffused with the heavy reddish light that Medoc was drawing down, and he was bathed in the crimson glow, a slender figure, silhouetted against the coruscating light. Grainne, unable to take her eyes from him now, was conscious of a deep, secret fascination. I am witnessing a necromancer calling up the Dark Ireland. I am seeing things which no High Queen of Tara has ever seen before. *And this is my father . . .*

It was a thought to be shaken off at once, and also to be shaken off was the sudden wish to know more, to explore the strange shadow realm where Medoc ruled . . .

The Dark Lords were with them in reality now. Grainne could feel it, even had Damnaithe not been watching them with a dreadful, frenzied exultation. There was a thickening of the air, a sluggishness in the shadows, and there was the miasma of ancient corruption, and of an old, old evil.

Sinister and quite terrifyingly alluring . . .

Grainne drew in a deep breath. As she did so, Medoc turned to look at her, and a slow smile touched the corners of his mouth. He knows, thought Grainne, staring at him. He knows what I am feeling . . .

And then something light and pure and swift stirred at the corners of her mind, and she knew it again for Erin, Fergus's son, calling to her, sending out to the Samhailt.

The Wolves . . . Help me . . . I cannot do it alone . . .

But will they be strong enough? cried Grainne in silent anguish. *Can they defeat all of this?*

Medoc had stopped chanting now, and was standing motionless. Grainne thought that even so, even silent and unmoving, authority and power still poured outwards from him. She thought that if he beckoned to her now she would not be able to resist. She would walk to stand before him, and she would do his bidding . . .

The nearest of the Twelve Lords moved then; he stepped forward and bowed his head in obeisance.

"You called to me, Master. I am here."

"Speak your name."

"I am Debauchery," said the voice from inside the black armour, and Grainne shuddered, because there was a thick, treacly, *knowing* timbre to it. You felt that the owner of the voice would find nothing too revolting and no action too disgusting.

"I walk the streets by night," said the voice from within the armour. "I take my prey from the young and innocent. I am sexual excess and I am forbidden appetite. There is nothing I will not do to indulge my senses."

"Who is your Master?"

"You are my Master, and I serve Crom Croich," said the Lord.

"It is well," said Medoc. "Take your place." As the Lord of Debauchery stepped back, the next Lord came forward, and again Medoc said, "Speak your name."

"I am Perversion," said the second Lord, and his voice was soft and rather horribly intimate. You could easily imagine lying in bed in the dark and hearing a voice like this whisper dreadful suggestions in your ear. Grainne shuddered, and the Lord of Perversion went on. "I take my prey from the dark and warped side of Men's natures," he said, and now there was a caressing note to his voice, and there was the same *knowing* note as well, as if he, like the Lord of Debauchery, could see into the dark corners of Men's natures, and see their most secret fantasies. "In my sway," said the Lord of Perversion, "men and women perform every obscenity ever imagined. I am responsible for men desiring men and women desiring women. I am responsible for men mating with animals, and for the inflicting of pain for sexual pleasure. The sins committed in my name are many and varied, and my followers are legion."

"Who is your Master?"

"You are my Master," said the Lord of Perversion, "and I serve Crom Croich." And again Medoc said, "It is well. Take your place," and the Lord took the second place next to the Lord of Debauchery. As he did so, Damnaithe, who was crouching on the floor next to the Lord of Debauchery, reared up and embraced him, writhing against the hardness of the carapace, her head thrown back. Grainne stared and felt horrified, but felt, as well, a rather terrible pity, for surely the creature was only like this because of Medoc's enchantments and Medoc's beckoning spells, and because of what she had seen in her sojourn in the Dark Realm.

One by one, the Twelve Lords came forward now, and one by one they answered to Medoc, and gave their names, and swore their allegiance.

Hatred: vicious-sounding and angry, so that Grainne knew that behind the visor would be red glaring eyes and teeth and claws ... Selfishness: cold and hard, so that you knew the Lord would have small narrow eyes and a tight, mean mouth; he would be vain and self-absorbed and self-indulgent.

Decadence came next, weary-sounding, and although his eyes were in shadow, you knew they would be as old as sin, as if they had seen everything there was to see. Grainne found the Lord of Decadence very horrid indeed; he made her think of thin pale-visaged gentlemen who reclined on comfortable chairs and sipped good wine, and watched while nubile young girls were paraded before them. When the Lord of Decadence said, in his bored voice, "Master, my appetites are jaded and surfeited, and it is the task of my followers to explore ways to rouse me," Grainne knew that the image had been a true one. When Decadence took his place, Damnaithe flung herself on the floor in front of him, pulling her ragged skirts up above her waist, caressing herself obscenely with stiff jabbing fingers. Grainne, repulsed but unable to look away, saw the visored head tilt consideringly, and caught the red glint of interest from the half-concealed eyes.

Jealousy was called after Decadence; particularly horrid, with hungry eyes and grasping hands, and a smothering voice. And Deceit: sly and slimy and furtive. He would lure you into giving him your trust, and then betray you and hurt you quite dreadfully.

Avarice and Lust and Conceit came next. Conceit was remote and patronising, and faced with him you would feel every drop of confidence you had ever possessed drain away. He would make you feel small and silly, and he would certainly humiliate you.

To each of them, Medoc said, "It is well. Take your place," and at length the Twelve Lords were ranged around the Sun Chamber, still silent and watchful, but no longer empty suits of armour. Ancient evil emanated from every one of them, and the Sun Chamber glowed with heavy dark enchantments, and old, almost-forgotten sorcery. Grainne, half lying, half sitting in the corner where she and Erin had been flung, thought that it was becoming difficult to breathe.

Medoc held out his hands once more, and the shadows slithered and there was a rather dreadful wet creeping sound, as if something was stirring in the farthest corners, and Grainne, her arms about Erin now, thought that it was easy to imagine that something sinuous and snake-like was forming in the corners and slithering towards them.

And then the shadows solidified, and there was no doubt any longer what Medoc was summoning.

The stench of rotting fish was in their nostrils, and there was a harsh snapping sound, like horn on bone, and there was a grating laugh.

Grainne turned her head slowly, because this was the worst yet, even though she had known there would be no escaping it. If Crom Croich was to be called up, Medoc would certainly need his terrible servant to assist him in the ritual.

As Grainne searched the shadows, there was a movement, lurching, loping. The shadows parted, and the something solidified, and the moonlight shifted, so that they saw it clearly. There was a sly darting movement and the snapping grating laughter came again.

Here I am, Master ... You called to me and I returned from the Far Future, from the Mountain Halls ...

The Conablaiche was in the Sun Chamber with them.

As soon as Grainne saw it, she knew that Medoc was having difficulty in controlling it. And for sure, this was not the furtive hungry creature of darkness; it was not the shadowy legend who prowled the cobbled streets of Ireland's remote villages and hill farms after nightfall to snatch up sleeping children and offer them to Crom Croich. This was no midnight shadow, no creeping furtive servant. This was a monster, rampant and lusting for blood; a dreadful being, a ghoul, a nightmare apparition, raging and greedy and very nearly uncontrollable. It loped across the Sun Chamber, and stood before Medoc, a great hulking shape with shreds of flesh clinging to its skeletal figure, and fragments of skin adhering to its talons. It dripped with the blood and the juices of its victims, and it was hungry and salivating. Grainne saw that it had only one eye; that the other was in some way damaged; it hung from the eye-socket on a dreadful string of raw red muscle, and the creature pawed at this from time to time, as if trying to thrust it back into its terrible skull.

For the space of a heartbeat, Grainne and Erin both thought it would fall on Medoc, and they waited, hardly

daring to breathe. But Medoc went forward at once, walking
in a circle about the creature, intoning a spell, and Grainne
saw the Conablaiche hesitate. It did not flinch, but the single
eye became watchful and, although it made clawing movements with its gristly arms, it did not move nearer.

Medoc stood looking at it for a moment before appearing
satisfied that the creature was penned in the circle he had
made. He returned to the centre of the Sun Chamber, and
light began to glow from the carvings at his feet. He again
threw back his head and stretched out his arms, and crimson-
tinged light streamed from him. There was a deep, far-off
thrumming, and the air shivered. A vast coldness crept over
the Sun Chamber, and Grainne knew at once that it was the
great chill of an enormous approaching evil.

*Heartchill, bonechill, and you will never be warm again.
Crom Croich is drawing near . . .*

Grainne drew Erin closer to her for warmth, even though
she knew that the terrible cold could not be fought.

For Crom Croich was struggling for rebirth into the
world of Men . . .

The Sun Chamber was pulsating with horrid life now;
the crimson light was throbbing rhythmically as if a giant
heart was beating, or as if something great and powerful was
striving for life.

Crom Croich, entering the world of Men again, taking
on the substance of flesh . . .

And then Medoc moved aside, and on the spot where he
had been standing, at the exact point that the sorcerers and
the *sidh* had created the enchantments that were to have held
Tara safe, something was materialising.

At first Grainne thought it was only the gathering of
more shadows, and then she thought it was something a bit
more than that. Medoc began to chant, and the light throbbed
and pulsated faster, and the thing was forming . . .

A wet glistening sack, repulsive and amorphous. A giant
cocoon, shivering with movement from within, pulsating and
twitching, wet and raw and slimed. Not quite flesh and not

quite spirit. It reared up before them, a lumpish column, a giant chrysalis, growing stronger and more incarnate with every minute.

Crom Croich, reborn into the world of Men . . .

Very softly, Erin said, "What is it? What are we witnessing?" and Grainne, unable to look away from the heaving, panting thing before them, said, "The birth of a god."

The thing was nearly twenty feet high now; it was a living pulsing sack that might at any minute burst open and vomit forth the dreadful monster-god.

The cocoon was heaving spasmodically now and the pale sack was beginning to split in places. Rivulets of a thick, not quite colourless fluid oozed out and seeped on to the floor of the Sun Chamber.

The birth of a god . . .

The Twelve Lords had moved silently, and were surrounding the creature now, the dark miasma of their presence hanging on the air. They were chanting the god's name in steady, measured tones.

Crom Croich . . . Crom Croich . . .

The creature was taking a shape now; rudimentary arms were sprouting from the upper portions of the glistening sack, and stump-like legs protruded from the lower. There was a bulge at the highest point that would be a head in minutes, and there were bulbous excrescences that would become eyes . . .

Crom Croich, the word made flesh . . .

The Conablaiche was cawing and scrabbling at the floor with its claws, and eyeing the birthing greedily, and the Lad of the Skins was grinning in his corner, his lips wet and greedy, his teeth gleaming with saliva that ran down his chin. He slewed his eyes round to where Grainne and Erin lay helpless.

Soon to be in my hands . . .

The giant embryo was forming. The rudimentary shoulders and legs were rudimentary no longer. The god was being born before their eyes. Shoulders, arms; thighs and legs and feet. A thick neck. Pendulous features and slit-like eyes. The birth sack was splitting more fully now; there was a wet pulpy noise, a glutinous sucking sound, and from within the birth sack came a stronger and much more definite movement than anything that had gone before. The birthsack was disintegrating; in another minute, Crom Croich would stand before them, newly born, terrible, greedy, demanding sacrifice . . .

As Grainne and Erin half lay, half knelt in their corner, Medoc turned and walked with slow deliberation to the waiting Throne, the famous and symbolic seat of power, the Seat of every High King and Queen of Tara, from the first ruler of all, whom some called the cursed Queen, through the great Niall of the Nine Hostages, and Nuadu Airgetlam of the Silver Arm, down through the reckless charming Cormac, and Dierdriu, until it had come down to Grainne, whom some had called Grainne the Gentle.

And once that was my Throne, and once I held Court here, and now Medoc occupies it, and if I am remembered at all, it will be as the Queen who was defeated by the Dark Ireland, and who was sacrificed to Crom Croich. And I shall die, and Erin will die, and Fergus will never have known him, and Raynor will be for ever alone, and Tara will be lost, and Ireland will be lost, and everything my people have done will all be in vain.

And then, without warning, certainly without understanding, something pierced her mind, and she half turned her head to look at Erin. *Something white and silvery and as pure and as clear as spring water, and as strong and as beautiful as crystal* . . .

Erin's thought-forms came clearly into her mind.
The Wolves . . . you must help me . . .
Grainne felt the silver light flooding her mind, and she half closed her eyes, and wrapped her consciousness all about it and, quite suddenly, she could sense it all, she could see the long slender twining cord that would reach out and circle the wolves, and bring them back to Tara.

The silver cord that never breaks . . .

Strength poured into her, and she knew it for Erin's strength, and then there was a brief flare of awareness, and Grainne thought, I believe it is working! and felt the silver cord thicken, and felt the distant response.

And then Erin said, very softly, "Listen. Do you hear?"

And Grainne looked at him, her eyes shining, because she had heard, and it was the one sound she had never believed she would hear again.

The howling of wolves.

NOBODY IN THE Queen's armies, or in the ranks of the Cruithin or the Beastline, had dared to ask themselves if they would be in time to rescue the Queen, but every single person assembled on the moonlit hills outside Folaim thought it. Medoc had the Queen, he had imprisoned her inside the Bright Palace, and he had surrounded her with his own darkness. It was all very well to tell each other that Medoc was a gentleman, and he would treat Her Majesty with courtesy; you could be courteous and gentlemanly at one and the same moment you were cutting out somebody's heart. Fintan said he could have wished that that particular example had not been used, because it conjured up nightmarish memories of Crom Croich and the Conablaiche, but Cermait said stoutly that this was nonsense; nobody, not even Medoc, would really consider reviving the cult of Crom Croich. But he looked doubtful and he followed it up by saying that they ought to be setting off right away.

Fergus had taken up his old position at the head of the waiting armies, but it was noticed by everyone that Raynor was close at his side. Dorrainge said, in his cold-fish way, that Fergus and Raynor would not get on, because they were no more alike than turnips and threadworms, but everyone knew that, beneath the skin, Fergus and Raynor were of the same mould.

Tybion the Tusk's romantic soul was thrilled to the core by the sight of these two remarkable creatures preparing to rescue the lady they both loved. In fact, what with the battle, and the possibility of dying gloriously for the Queen, Tybion thought that if he could have been sure of Grainne's ultimate safety, he would have been happier than he had ever been in his entire life. But he put these thoughts resolutely aside, because he had been given the command of the Cruithin by Fergus, and this was such an honour that Tybion scarcely knew what to do with himself for delight. He found the Cruithin to be perfectly amiable and entirely obedient, so that it was as well that he did not realise that the Cruithin did not really need leading, and that Fergus was simply making Tybion feel useful. The Cruithin would probably do whatever they wanted to do in the battle, and since whatever they did would probably be of immense help, it was immaterial who led them. It was fortunate that Tybion did not know this.

Fintan and Cermait had decided to ride with the Beastline because, as Fintan said, coming straight from the Grail Castle, they would not be accustomed to battles, and it would be a good idea to guide them. Cermait said this was very true indeed. The Beastline did not need guiding, any more than the Cruithin, but they were all far too polite to say so.

Dorrainge had decided to bring up the rear, since the Druids were peace-loving people, and anyway, Dorrainge himself, as Second Druid, had to be a bit removed from any danger. It was important for the Second Druid not to be killed or injured; it was particularly important for him not to be killed. He did not say this, and he was going to be unobtrusive about keeping to the rear. It was to be hoped that Cathbad did not do something silly and emotional, like flinging himself into the front ranks, because this would draw down unwelcome attention to the Druids, which was not something the Druids would like.

Taliesin and Annabel had stayed a little apart, watching everything, helping Niall and Conn and the boys to sort out horses and arm themselves with swords and bows.

"Marvellous," said Conn, grinning.

"I shall kill a very lot of enemies," said Michael, who had been given a minuscule sword, and who was going to be kept out of the real fighting, but who did not know this.

It had not previously occurred to Annabel that you could truly fight a war by getting on to a horse and brandishing a sword and riding off crying death and destruction to the other side, even though she had read about this in the forbidden books. It would be tactful not to go around telling these people about the way wars were fought in her world, the world of the Drakon, because it would have sounded patronising. Annabel, more used to buttons being pressed, and machines being sent out over enemy territory, and screens and electronic intelligences being consulted for battle plans, was intrigued.

"This is a much more *exciting* way of fighting a war," she said to Taliesin.

"Wars aren't meant to be exciting," said Taliesin. And then, "Or are they? *Mars approaching . . . leaden rain and iron hail . . . into the tumult and the fire and the—* What are you doing?"

"I'm fastening on spurs," said Annabel, sitting on the ground and trying to inspect the soles of her boots. "I borrowed them from one of the soldiers. I expect I shall have to give them back when it's all over, and they're not what I'd call comfortable, but you can't have everything in a battle. But of course, you can't ride into battle without the proper equipment," said Annabel firmly, because it was always as well to be firm about something you cared about, and it was not to be thought of that she should not join in the battle, this immense war charge they were all going to make on Tara, now that she was here.

Taliesin said thoughtfully, "And I daresay that 'a pair of good spurs to a borrowed horse is better than a peck of oats.' Do you know I find it quite remarkable how the echoes reverberate about a battlefield. I know that somebody will some day say that, because I can hear it and I can feel it, and if it has not been said already, and perhaps to better purpose, then certainly it will be said in the future. I should very much prefer you not to take part in this battle, Annabel."

"I know that," said Annabel, who had been expecting this.

Taliesin took both her hands, drew her aside, and looked at her very straightly. "Listen, lady," he said, and Annabel stared at him with delight, because when Taliesin said "lady" in just that voice, it was precious and private and so filled with promise that it was very nearly impossible not to do what he wanted. Only, said Annabel to herself, the trouble is that what he wants is for me to stay safely out here in the forest and miss everything. And I will *not*.

"Listen," said Taliesin, not firmly, but very carefully, "this isn't going to be an affair of glory and excitement and galloping to victory. It isn't an adventure, Annabel." And stopped, and thought how ridiculous this sounded, because surely all war was an adventure of sorts. "People will get killed," he said. "Wounded. Maimed. People will die in agony, or live in agony for hours before they do die." He paused, and his hands tightened about hers. "And we might be defeated," said Taliesin gently.

There was a pause. Annabel said, in rather a small voice, "Might we?"

"Medoc is the strongest necromancer ever to come out of the Dark Ireland," said Taliesin. "And his creatures are fearsome and merciless. Fergus is not invincible."

"Well, I won't stay behind," said Annabel, who had not thought about them losing the battle until this minute, but who would still not have missed any of it for a King's ransom.

"Obstinate child," said Taliesin. "Are we then to ride forward as if the hounds of hell were chasing us, slaying Medoc's dark creatures as we go?"

"I shan't get in the way," said Annabel, who had thought it all out, and was in fact planning to ride at the rear of the Beastline people with Bec. "We thought we'd be all right there," she said. "We don't expect to do any actual *fighting*."

"Of course not."

"But after all, I *did* disable the Conablaiche," said Annabel. "Don't forget that I did that."

"I do not forget," said Taliesin. "It is only that . . ."

"Yes?"

He paused, and then said, very softly, "It is only that if I am to take you back with me to my house in the Street of Money Lenders, and see you curl up by the hearth, and drink wine with you, and talk to you, and find out about you . . ."

"Yes?" said Annabel, scarcely daring to breathe.

Taliesin smiled. "It is that I should like you whole and unmarked," he said. And then, in a different, much more intense voice, "Oh, Annabel," he said softly, "we are going to shut out the clamouring world, and we are going to create our own world."

Our own world . . . Annabel stared at him, and saw, for a heartbeat of time, the images and the visions.

Taliesin said, "Firelit walls and an immense deep reservoir of happiness. Days spent working, nights spent together. Companionship and sharing and laughter and wine and music . . ."

And friends to make and worlds to explore. And Taliesin there . . . And I shall never be lonely again . . .

Annabel did not say any of this, but she reached out to touch his face with one hand, and smiled back at him.

And then Taliesin said, in a different, more practical voice, "I believe that Fergus is ready for the charge."

FERGUS THOUGHT HE was as ready as he would ever be. He felt odd and rather unreal, as if he had not yet completely returned to the world. And cold . . . *I think I shall never be truly warm again,* he thought, and wondered if it was only the lingering coldness of the soulless, or if it was a deeper cold. *I shall never properly love a woman again, ever . . .*

He turned to face the waiting armies, and the Beastline and the lost boys, and for a moment felt that he was seeing them from a great distance, from the far end of a tunnel, from behind glass . . .

Now we see through a glass darkly. But then face to face.

I am seeing them through glass, thought Fergus, still looking at the rows of soldiery, and the colours and the glinting armour and the weapons and the pennants. I am seeing through a glass, but before we reach Tara, I must somehow be face to face with them . . .

This is where I belong, thought Fergus. After all, this is where I belong, and this is what I know. Fighting and making war and winning war. Trying to keep Ireland safe.

Ireland. Oh, yes, thought Fergus, feeling the merest breath of warm air melt the ice about his heart. Yes, after all, it is Ireland that matters.

The memory of the Prison of Hostages, and of the mountain caverns, receded a little. This is the real world, thought Fergus. This is what I understand, and this is where I belong. He saw how they watched him, and how they were waiting for his command, and he saw, as well, as clearly as if it had been drawn out in front of him, the battle plan, and the route they would take, and the way in which they would ride on Tara. He turned his horse about and surveyed them all, and without warning, light kindled in his eyes.

For I am the head of the High Queen's *Fiana*, and I can lead these people to victory, and I can restore the Wolfline to Ireland. He lifted his arm in the gesture that meant *Make ready*! and felt a shiver of anticipation go through the waiting creatures. Fergus, his every sense alive now, saw spears of pure white light pierce the twilit skies, and knew it for the Samhailt, the ancient and most purely magical gift, only ever bestowed on the Royal Houses of Ireland. He looked at Raynor and Rinnal and Bec; at the other creatures of the Beastline, and knew the white light to be of their making; he knew that they were mobilising the beasts; the Eagles and the Foxes and the Hares; the Chariot Horses and the Deer; the Hounds and Gazelle and White Swans and Stags.

Ireland's greatest army of all, the ancient Enchantment rediscovered . . .

And only one thing is needed to complete it, thought Fergus, and as he drew breath to commence the charge on Tara, he heard, faintly and from a great distance, the sound that no one in Ireland had ever thought to hear again.

The howling of Wolves.

Chapter Twenty-eight

The chanting in the Sun Chamber had become a throbbing rhythmic sound that made Grainne's head ache and her senses swim. At the centre of it all, something gold and solid and incredibly powerful was forming, and Grainne and Erin both knew that Crom Croich was very nearly with them.

The Twelve Dark Lords were circled about the almost-born god, and from behind their visors, evil intelligence showed. Decadence, Debauchery, Lust, Perversion, Selfishness ... Grainne could identify them all now; she could recognise the corruption in each figure.

Conceit, Avarice, Hatred ...

Damnaithe was writhing and growling deep in her throat, her eyes glinting redly, her face a snarling mask. Grainne looked at her, and looked away immediately, feeling a deep loathing, and hating herself for feeling it.

There was a final convulsive movement from the thing at the centre of the Sun Chamber; a wet sucking sound, and a moment when Grainne actually felt within her own body a wrench as the creature tore through the birth sack. The now thick and horny surface of the sack split and began to fall from the heaving thing within, and the creature clawed its way out.

The dull, golden skin was smeared and matted with blood and with a thick, glutinous fluid, and the face was clotted with gore. There was a short squat neck and a low brow, and a blunt, tumescent skull. Grainne had seen carvings in old caves of ancient civilisations, and she remembered how those early Humans, said to have evolved from apes, had possessed the same low brow and hulking shape. But in Crom Croich's features, there was a terrible intelligence; the eyes were small and slit-like, but they glowed like rubies catching the light; there were broad flattened nostrils, and beneath them was a wide gaping orifice, a maw, a yawning gullet.

All the better to devour you with, my dear ...

Medoc had moved forward and was standing before the great rearing shape of the god. With not the slightest trace of subservience, he went down on one knee and placed his left hand on his breast. There was a movement from the god; Grainne thought that its hands gestured, and then Medoc stood up again, and turned to where the Conablaiche and the Lad of the Skins were watching. The Twelve Lords fell back, and Medoc stepped over the circle which had imprisoned the Conablaiche.

At once the creature bounded forward, and stood surveying the company, its beak opening and shutting, its talons curving, its remaining eye swivelling and searching.

Medoc turned back to Crom Croich and said, "We are all ready to serve you, Master. We have the sacrifices here," and as he spoke, the Conablaiche snapped its beak with a horrid harsh sound, and its restless claws rang out on the silver floor. At Medoc's heels, the Lad of the Skins gave his low, bubbling chuckle, and scuttled across the floor to where Grainne and Erin half lay against the wall.

The Twelve Lords moved as well, silently and swiftly, Damnaithe in their midst; they suddenly seemed taller, and as they formed a half circle about Grainne and Erin, their shadows fell starkly across the two prisoners.

Medoc stood looking down at them both for a long moment, his lips curved in the beautiful, terrible smile, his eyes shining darkly.

"Kill them," said Damnaithe, and crouched low on the floor, panting slightly. "Kill them, and let the blood flow."

"She is impatient, you see," said Medoc, never taking his eyes from Grainne. "She is impatient to see Crom Croich served. But so am I, my dear," said Medoc in his beautiful caressing voice. "So am I." He stayed where he was, his eyes still on Grainne. "The Crown Princess and the Wolfprince," he said, and there was a lick of pleasure in his voice that made Grainne shudder. "The worthiest sacrifice I could devise for my Master." And then to Damnaithe, "Keep back," he said coldly. "Your worthless hungers will be appeased later." As Damnaithe cringed, Medoc nodded to the nearest of the Lords.

"Make them ready. Prepare the altar. Light the sacrificial fires."

ANNABEL HAD NOT been aware of the moment when the people of Tara began the final great sweeping charge down the hill. She had ridden cautiously, unused to being on horseback, but finding it surprisingly easy.

"The easiest thing there is," said Bec, next to her, and Annabel was grateful for Bec's presence.

Taliesin, a little ahead, turned in the saddle, his eyes narrowing suddenly. "Look ahead, Annabel. You see? The Shining Citadel. The Bright Palace."

And Annabel managed to slow down the horse, and stood with them all looking down into the saucer-shaped valley with the huge sprawling palace.

Tara, the Bright Palace, the brilliant citadel, the radiant lodestar of all Ireland, which drew travellers and pilgrims and scholars and poets to its centre. The Aurora of the Western World, shrouded and smothered in the darkness of the necromancer.

A great silence fell on the watchers, and Fergus, at the head, felt tears prick his eyes, and did not mind whether or not anyone saw them. He remembered how Fael-Inis had looked at him in Calatin's house, and how he had known then that he had failed in allowing Medoc into Tara, and that he had continued to fail for not raising a strong and massive army and attempting to drive Medoc out.

But Medoc was invincible! We all knew that. I had not

the resources then, thought Fergus, and at once came the answer.

It does not matter. You could have tried.

Fergus bowed his head in silent acknowledgement and, as he did so, felt stir within him the fierce resolve and the determination that, even if he lost his life in what lay ahead, he would put rout to Medoc and his evil, and he would restore Tara to the Royal House.

Even if Grainne is dead? said his mind.

Even then.

He turned to rally the people again, for this would be the final great battle charge, and there must be no fumbling and no falling back. They must go down the hillside in a single clean movement, and along the great road that led to the Western Gate; they must fall upon any of Medoc's creatures that might be lying in wait, and they must kill them instantly. Only then could they reach the Sun Chamber, and only then could they rescue Grainne.

He paused, because there was never anything quite like this last on-the-brink moment, the final few seconds before going forward into a battle, and he felt himself filling up with energy and strength and confidence, so that he remembered every battle he had ever fought and every war he had ever won, and he thought, Yes, of course! *This* is where I belong! And he looked to the armies with sudden, all-embracing affection, because these were his people, and they would ride with him, they would fight to restore Ireland, and they would fight to return Grainne to Tara.

He looked to where the Beastline were waiting, the animals in line behind them, and he felt undiluted delight at the sight, because wasn't it decades, wasn't it several generations, since the Enchanted Royal Houses of Ireland had ridden in battle. There was the most tremendous sense of anticipation, and Fergus thought that he could almost imagine that all Ireland was waiting and all Ireland was poised to surge down into the dark, saucer-shaped valley.

And if only Grainne is still safe, then I believe I shall not care about anything else, he thought.

He looked back at the assembled armies; at the Beastline who were serious and intent; at the Cruithin, small and elfin and certainly possessed of the pure gentle magic of their people. The boys were there as well; Conn and Niall and the small Michael, and all the others. All with me, thought Fergus. All certainly ready to follow me. And with the thought came another: But will it be enough? Will there be sufficient of us to drive out Medoc and his evil?

I can't do it! thought Fergus in a sudden agony of doubt. I don't think I can do it! We are not enough! And: I cannot fight Medoc's enchantments with people alone! cried his mind.

But then, over the far horizon, from the west, mingling with the twilight, as elusive as the mist over the Mountains of the Morning, came the swirling, sinuous shapes of blue-green smoke, and at the heart of the soft cool creatures which were nearly but not quite solid was the eldritch figure of the Elven King. Aillen mac Midha, the creature of chill faery blood, the being whose people poured music into the world, and who came up to the ramparts of Tara at the birth of a Wolfprince and sang him into the world, and wove their fragile enchantments to protect him. Music began to fill up the night, and there was a challenge in the music, as if the music-makers were girding themselves for a tremendous battle.

Fergus had just time to think: the *sidh*! Aillen mac Midha and his faery *sidh*folk! Making good their long-ago promise to protect the Royal House of Tara. Riding into the centre of the High Queen's armies. They would not materialise; Fergus knew this quite definitely, for if a Human looked full upon the *sidh*, upon their awful cold beauty, it would burn out his eyes or scorch his flesh or destroy his mind. But he looked with delight at the blue and green radiance, because the *sidh* would have their own enchantments, and only by using forces other than swords and arrows and bows could they hope to defeat Medoc.

From the other horizon, from the eastern hills, came the rushing sound of chariot wheels. Red-gold fire shot into the sky, and Fergus stood transfixed, unable to believe his eyes, because it surely could not be, it surely could not happen twice in so short a space of time . . . he would not come to the world of Men so soon again . . . Over the crest of the hill appeared Fael-Inis, standing at the prow of the Time Chariot.

And streaming in his wake were the Royal Wolves of Tara . . .

ANNABEL WAS BREATHLESS and dizzy and the wind was rushing past her making a whistling sound, so that it was difficult to hear anything, and it was very difficult indeed to feel any sensation other than the speed of the charge, and the urgency that was driving them all. She thought that Taliesin was shouting something, but she could not really hear, and then she thought that someone was blowing a bugle, and this was such a marvellous stirring sound that she would have liked to turn round in the saddle and see where the sound was coming from, but she was swept on by the headlong gallop of the horses. And then she thought that the sound was not from within their own armies at all, but from the spinning maelstrom of light and smoke and colour that was the *sidh*.

The sounds of the beasts were all around; the night sky overhead was filled with the beating of wings, and Annabel, glancing up, saw the soaring golden creatures that were following Raynor, and a little behind them, smaller and darker, Hawks and Night-owls and, in their wake, a blur of white which was the Swans. She could hear the Hounds baying, and the Foxes, and the deep resonant note of the Stags.

And ahead of them all, pouring down the hillside, leading them on, was the immense golden Time Chariot, creating its own radiance, fiery light shooting from its wheels, lighting the hills and the forests and the valleys to golden life.

The salamanders were flowing effortlessly on and on, and they could see Fael-Inis, his wild golden hair whipped by the wind, standing at the prow, urging them on, forcing a path down to the dark valley. Annabel gasped and saw that the Wolves were immediately behind Fael-Inis, keeping up with the Chariot with ease, their eyes gleaming redly, their long lean bodies bounding forward, their fur sleek and dark.

The Wolves of the Royal House of Ireland, converging on Tara, ready to tear apart the adversary who held the Wolfqueen captive . . .

Annabel thought that Taliesin was shouting to her to be careful because they were nearing Tara's outer boundaries, and she thought that close by Conn and Niall were calling to Michael to keep back, and the thought just formed that she ought to try to look after Michael, who was brandishing his sword and shouting, and then they were down the last stretch, and the massive ancient trees that stood sentinel along Tara's great western avenue were all about them, and Tara itself was rushing upon them, dark and massive and shrouded in Medoc's evil, and they were going to do it, they were going to ride straight in through the legendary Western Gate unchallenged, and it was going to be all right . . . One glorious sweep to victory, death or glory, and they would be inside the Palace and they would rescue the Wolfqueen and Ireland would be safe . . . They were going to win . . .

And then the Wolves checked in their headlong flight, and the salamanders reared up so that a fiery glow poured upwards into the dark sky directly over the Palace. Fael-Inis swerved and the Chariot shuddered to a halt, sparks of heat shooting from its wheels.

Directly in front of them, barring their way, were the Three Guardians from the mountain halls. Spectre, Reflection, and the Sensleibhe.

IT SEEMED TO Grainne that the howling of the Wolves had stopped. Fear caught and held her, and she half turned her head towards Erin.

A light shone in his eyes that had not been there before, but he did not speak, and Grainne thought that perhaps after all she had been mistaken. Perhaps she had misheard that dim distant howling, and perhaps it had been too much to hope for. And then the gentle pure light of the Samhailt flowed into her mind again, and with it the strength and the confidence.

It was not too much to hope for and you did not mishear, madam. It is only that the Wolves are not so close as we need them to be .... I do not know if they will reach us in time. And then, with more directness than he had yet shown: *But we dare not give them our attention, lest the necromancer and his servants sense their approach ...*

The Twelve Lords were ranged about the Chamber now, intoning the sacrificial incantation, and four small braziers had been brought forward and placed at each of the four corners of the altar. As they watched, Medoc set fire to the braziers, and a sharp, pungent smoke leapt up.

The monstrous figure of Crom Croich moved at last. It lurched and waddled as if its short stump-like legs were un-used to movement. Slowly, tortuously, it dragged itself to the altar and settled there, crouching and lowering, the blood and gore still smearing its dull gold skin, its tiny red eyes unblinking.

Grainne thought that that movement, that shuffling gait, that slow ponderous walk to the altar, had been as bad as anything that had yet happened, because while the god had been motionless, it had been very nearly possible to think of it as a graven image, a statue, something inanimate. Graven images and statues did not demand sacrifices; they did not watch, slavering, while the hearts of their victims were torn out, and they did not reach down with their great muscular arms to the silver platters held up to them, and scoop up steaming, still-fluttering hearts and convey them to gaping wet maws ...

Crom Croich was seated at the centre of the altar, and Grainne, unable to look away, her heart racing, thought, Am

I to die here butchered by the Conablaiche, sacrificed to the greatest evil Ireland has ever known . . . ? Would the ancient altar witness the ritual deaths of the Crown Princess and the Wolfprince?

Medoc turned to smile at that, and for the first time there was true affection in his eyes. "Very soon now, my daughter," he said, "very soon, you will be given in libation to my Master." As he spoke, the Conablaiche gave its hard cawing sound, and the Lad of the Skins chuckled and began to reach for his knife. Grainne thought, The Knife of Light. Our souls to be hurled into the Prison of Hostages. And then there will truly be no escape, and there will be nothing any more, ever.

Medoc was watching her. "Flesh of my flesh," he said, very softly, "does that hurt, Grainne? Blood of my blood and of my bone. Tainted stock, my dear. You and your son both."

Tainted blood . . . the dark blood of the necromancer . . . This evil beautiful being lay with my mother and rendered her witless and Fergus and I were the results . . . Something dark and serpent-like slithered in Grainne's mind, and she thought, After all, would it not be better to let the Ancient Line die out? After all, is it not better to cut out a canker? Tainted stock. And Erin too. Would Ireland not be the better?

At once there was a fierce response from Erin. *Do not think it! It is what he wants you to think! It is part of his sorcery! There is no taint, madam, save the taint that enters the mind, and there is no shame, save that which enters the heart! The Wolfline must* never *be allowed to die!*

I am sorry, rejoined Grainne, and blinked and shook her head, and felt the dark slimed thoughts dissolve.

Medoc was facing them now, the monstrous rearing figure of Crom Croich directly behind him, its red glistening eyes never leaving them. The Dark Lords were moving in and the incantation was becoming louder and stronger.

Crom Croich . . . the blood . . . the life and the heart and the core . . .

The ritual chant was humming and pulsating in their ears, and the Sun Chamber was becoming heavy and the air was dark and sluggish. Grainne thought it was the miasma of the evil that the Twelve Lords carried with them now.

Decadence and Perversion, Avarice and Debauchery ... all of the sins and all of the frailties and all of the failings ever committed and dreamed of and feared ...

She thought, And the Wolves? Are they nearer? and tried to hear and could not. Had they after all imagined it?

We did not imagine it, came Erin's instant response. *They will not fail us.* But Grainne caught for the first time a note of fear in him, and she remembered that he was only six years old. Six years only, and soon he might be butchered and mutilated on the altar and his soul taken to the Prison of Hostages. He will be the Lost Prince in truth then, thought Grainne, for there is no rescue from the Prison.

Medoc's dark eyes were shining with hard unnatural light and the Dark Lords were still chanting, and she could feel the power irradiating from the altar, dreadful waves of malignity. The Lad of the Skins was scuttling across the floor towards them, and for the first time Grainne saw the lumpish dragging sack he wore on his back.

For the gathering up of souls, Wolfqueen ...

The Conablaiche was at his side, a nightmare shape, grinning and emitting harsh, cawing sounds. The Conablaiche was standing with its legs slightly apart, thrusting itself towards Grainne, grinning and snapping its beak, the fish eye gleaming.

Medoc looked at it and then down to where Grainne lay. "Well, madam," he said softly, "shall I give you to this creature first?" And smiled. "Well, we shall see. It is an impatient creature." He directed one of his dark shining looks at the Conablaiche, and said, "Wait, you."

Erin said very clearly, "If you allow that, Medoc, I shall surely kill you."

Medoc laughed, and it was as clear and untroubled a sound as Grainne had ever heard.

"Threaten away, Wolfprince," he said. "Soon you will be lying on the altar, and soon you will feel the Conablaiche's claws tearing open your chest, and you will feel your lungs and your mouth filling up with blood. It is an honourable death, Wolfprince, although I do not expect you to see it like that."

The Conablaiche was so close that the stench of rotting meat and bad fish was making them feel sick. For a really terrible minute, Grainne thought she would, to her humiliation, be sick and then she took several trembling breaths and felt better.

The wolves? Erin, the Wolves?

Nearer, I think, came the rejoinder. But Grainne thought she could no longer feel the Wolves. Because Medoc's enchantments were so strong now that they were sealing off the Sun Chamber? Yes, perhaps. And then she could not decide if this had been a good thing to think or not.

The fires in the braziers had burned up strongly now, and there was a pungent scent of incense and herbs, which mingled with the stench of the Conablaiche. Mist swirled and the altar was humming with magic, but Grainne knew it was not the strong good magic of the real true Ireland, but the tainted magic, the diseased enchantments and the malevolent bewitchments of the Dark Ireland that Medoc led. She thought, The Sun Chamber, the beautiful, almost-sacred heart of Tara, is tainted and it is thick with malignity, and I am not at all sure that it can ever be pure and beautiful again.

And again the dark insidious thought stirred: Why not, then, let it all go to Medoc?

With the thought came the whisper of sound in her ear.

"Why not indeed, my dear," and she turned sharply, and saw one of the Lords close at her side.

"Why not let it all go to Medoc, Grainne?"

Conceit? Yes, it was the sly insinuating voice that could somehow get inside your head and inside your most private feelings before you realised it. Grainne frowned and tried to close her mind.

"It would be so easy, Grainne," said another of them and, this time, Grainne thought it was Selfishness. *"So easy to give in, and let Medoc take it all. And then you would see our Land, Grainne, and it is far more beautiful than ever you imagined."*

"All of your senses served, my dear ..." whispered Decadence.

"All of your hungers fed," said Greed, and chuckled wetly.

"No restrictions ... do what you wish, my dear," said Hatred, and there was the red flare behind the visor as he moved closer.

"No restrictions, Grainne ..." The whispers were magnified, and the Lords were all about her, pressing closer.

"You would be a Princess of the Dark Ireland, Grainne, for Medoc is your sire, and Damnaithe your dam ... You would rule from the Black Mountains that look across the Lake of Night, and you would be revered by our people, Grainne ..."

Grainne put up her hands to cover her ears in an attempt to shut out the dreadful whisperings.

"You would walk in the Nightfields and you would reign from the Ebony Throne ..." said Avarice. *"And all the dark glistening jewels would be yours."*

"All the beautiful young men of the world would be yours," whispered Decadence.

"To do with as you wished," said Perversion.

Grainne, her hands still covering her ears, said loudly, "No! No, I won't listen! Stop it!" And stared at them, her eyes distended.

There was a contemptuous laugh from Damnaithe's corner. "She is of no interest to us," said Damnaithe. "She is insipid and colourless, and we do not want her. Fling her to the Conablaiche, and then offer her and the child to Crom Croich."

"I would liefer by far be given to Crom Croich than rule in your Realm, madam," said Grainne and Damnaithe laughed again and tossed her head, and turned her back.

"You were offered the choice," she said, sounding bored.

"Better to reign in hell than serve in heaven?" said Grainne. And then to Medoc, "Well, sir?"

"You *are* offered the choice," he said, his eyes watching her.

"There is no choice to make," said Grainne. But she was aware, deep within the innermost recesses of her mind, of a tiny, insidious voice.

You would rule there absolutely . . . all the dark glistening jewels would be yours, and all the beautiful young men would be yours . . .

And you have never seen the Dark Island in all its terrible and fearsome beauty . . .

Grainne said again, more loudly, "There is no choice to make," and then looked at them all steadily, and felt Erin's hand in hers, and knew that he was still listening for the Wolves.

And then she was aware that Medoc was standing over them, and in the crimson pulsing light he seemed to tower to twice his normal height, and he seemed to be wrapped in the dark malevolence of his own evil. There would not be any escape, there could not possibly be, for the altar was glowing and ready, and Crom Croich was rearing above them, and the Conablaiche was moving into his place, with the Lad beside him, and the Lad had drawn the glittering Knife of Light to take their souls when it was all over . . .

Medoc bent down to lift Grainne, and she was aware through her fear that there was an unexpected gentleness about him, and she remembered that in all of the stories Medoc was said to be a gentleman. As he carried her across to lay her on the altar, two of the Dark Lords lifted the struggling Erin and followed.

And then Grainne felt the cold hard stone of the ancient sacrificial altar beneath her, and felt them lay Erin next to her, and saw the monstrous gold shape of the terrible hungry god-idol blot out the light, and knew that they were truly and completely lost.

FERGUS HAD NOT hesitated. The minute he saw the Guardians, he knew that the only way to fight them was to ride straight at them. With the thought came a movement at his side, and he turned to see Raynor with Taliesin bringing their horses alongside. Gratitude flooded Fergus's mind, and he thought, These are the ones I can trust! And felt the fragment of a thought from Taliesin: Never trust a Tyrian, my friend, and remember that I am most regrettably sober today!

Tybion the Tusk was riding hard across to join them, with Fintan and Cermait close behind. All of them to be trusted, all of them ready to follow Fergus into hell and beyond ... And then he thought, And it may be hell we shall see before we are done.

Spectre was already standing a little ahead of the other two, her long pointed fingers outstretched, whiteness riming her silhouette. Instantly a howling icy wind rose and moaned and raged furiously about them, stinging their cheeks and bringing tears to their eyes. Ice formed beneath their feet, and the horses' hoofs slithered and lost their grip. Panic swept through the armies as the horses fought for their footing, and people began to be unseated, and the horses whinnied in terror and reared up. The Beastline animals began to whine and bark, and Spectre laughed and lifted her hand again, and this time lightning split the heavens, and thunder crashed directly overhead. Several nearby trees were struck and fires flared up in half a dozen places.

Annabel flinched and saw Tybion start forward, and, to the left, Conn and Niall and the other boys were fitting arrows to their bows.

"Useless!" cried Spectre, and her shrieking laugh rang out. "Am I not winter night and freezing dawn, and am I not gale and blizzard and tempest? I can make the skies bleed and pant, and I can cause the heavens to rain torment on to your puny armies!" And once more she raised her hand, and to the scattered and tumbled armies it seemed that the night-sky was torn open. There was a brief blinding glimpse of fiery light, as if the door to some immense furnace had been pushed ajar, and then as they flinched, trying to shield their eyes, a torrent of fireballs began to fall, searing the darkness and starting up great columns of fire.

Taliesin caught the end of a thought from Fergus: If we do not stop this, Tara will burn, and then Grainne will truly be lost! and he turned his horse about and tried to pinpoint Spectre's whereabouts, because everywhere was smoke and belching flame now, and everyone was running wildly about, and those few who had been able to remain mounted could hardly see.

He thought that Fael-Inis had not moved; he could see the Time Chariot standing quietly a little way off, and he could see the slender form of Fael-Inis. There was time to think, Is he going to help us? and there was time as well to remember that in all of the stories, Fael-Inis had been the one who had walked away from the battle, "and never declared for either side." Taliesin thought, But I do not believe he will not help us! and then he saw, on the outer edges of vision, the blue and green smoke of the *sidh*, and as he half turned, he saw them pour into the battle, whirling columns of iridescent light.

The *sidh* did not form, but those nearest to them could see faint dim shapes in the coiling smoke. Thin sinuous arms and round, seal-like heads and slender, serpentine bodies. Here and there were long narrow turquoise eyes, greedy and avid . . . Spectre let out a piercing shriek and went down in a whirling mass of glittering wings and swooping mist creatures, and as she did so, it seemed that the raging storm and the terrible icy blizzard lessened.

Spectre seemed in some way to be shrinking; Annabel, who was clinging very hard to the idea of war being glorious and exciting amidst the horror, heard a terrible sucking sound, and remembered that Taliesin had said something about the *sidh* being greedy for the five senses—sight, speech, hearing, taste, touch. And although it would have been very much better not to have heard what the *sidh* were doing to

Spectre, the sound echoed across the battlefield. Annabel tried very hard to remember that Spectre had been cruel, and that she certainly served Medoc, and that she had been trying to prevent them from entering Tara to save the Wolfqueen.

Spectre shrivelled and seemed to dissolve into pools of horrid grey slime on the ground. As the blizzard blew itself out and the fires started by the lightning and the showering torrents of fireballs sank a little lower, Reflection said, "Dear me, how tedious all this is. I suppose it is up to me now." She stepped forward, and pulled the Cloak of Nightmares tightly about her. "Too boring for you all, my dears," said Reflection, gazing at them with her great dark eyes. "And of course, Fael-Inis, the dear creature, would never *dream* that I might enter into battle against him." A brief mischievous look was directed to where Fael-Inis still stood, holding the salamanders in check. "A spectator once more, Fael-Inis?" said Reflection. "I suppose it was not to be thought otherwise." And the Cloak of Nightmares shivered and Reflection became enveloped in pale, translucent light.

Great gaping pits opened up before the army's feet, in which snakes writhed and monsters crawled and gibbered. The landscape shifted and became dark red and menacing— The colour of nightmares, thought Annabel wildly, and strove to remember that they were only nightmares, that nothing that Reflection could conjure up could physically harm them, only their fear. Giants with no faces strode silently over the surrounding hillsides and stood looking down on the armies . . . There were bubbling lakes of slime with grasping, struggling hands coming out of them to drag you down if you went too near; claw-footed harpies who flew through the air and fastened on to you and would gouge out your eyes and squash them to the ground; grinning skeletons, cauldrons of boiling blood, sea monsters and oceans of oily water . . . Annabel, gasping and trying very hard to hold on to her sanity, was suddenly plunged into a swirling underground river. At any minute the dark greasy waters were going to close over her head, and when that happened, there would be no escape, because overhead were hundreds of tons of solid rock . . .

Great lumbering nightmarish machines came crawling out of the forest, massive mincing machines that had cavernous human faces, which would scoop up Human limbs and Human torsos and mince them into blobs and gobbets of raw meat . . .

The army was in chaos now. The horses were stampeding, and most of the men had been unseated. The Beastline creatures were in the midst of their animals, rallying them, sending out furious white sparks of light that were the ancient mystical Samhailt taking shape. Everywhere the creatures were snarling and whining and yelping. Annabel saw Raynor standing at the centre of a whirling golden storm of Eagles, his hands outstretched to them; near to him, Rinnal was half hidden by leaping, snarling Foxes. Fintan and Cermait and the Cruithin were laying about the nightmare creatures, slicing at scaly heads and raining blows on writhing snake-like beings. Cathbad, incredibly, had gone running off to the dreadful lumbering machines, and was scattering stones in their path in an attempt to disable the clanking grinding metal. He was rather green about the gills, but he was shouting at the machines and daring them to come down in the midst of the armies.

Tybion the Tusk had not hesitated. He had seen Conn and Niall and the boys firing arrows at Spectre and Reflection, and he had seen, as well, that Spectre and Reflection had both been able to deflect them. And then he had seen the *sidh*, led by Aillen mac Midha, go streaking down on to Spectre, and he had seen Spectre fall and begin to liquefy, and he had thought, So that takes care of *her*! And had turned to survey the other two Guardians.

He realised at once that Fael-Inis was waiting for them to finish off the two minor creatures, and that when that was done, he would deal with the Sensleibhe for them. Tybion, who had never before seen Fael-Inis, but who knew the stories, found himself understanding exactly what Fael-Inis was doing. It was as if the golden fiery creature was telling them that they must help themselves first before he would help them. They must use their own strengths and their own weapons, and only after that would he come into the fray. All right, thought Tybion, setting his jaw firmly; all right, we shall see. And he looked at Reflection, who was standing wrapped in the Cloak of Nightmares, surveying the tumult she had created. Nasty, thought Tybion. Yes, extremely nasty. I daresay she will send out something perfectly unspeakable and entirely unbearable before I can get near to her. He shuddered and tried not to remember his own nightmares, and tried very hard to visualise the good dreams: the soft rain of a spring morning, and the blazing colours of autumn, and peaceful hillsides and firelight and mulled wine, and revels in the Tusk family, and the music of the *sidh* and the Queen's smile. Oh, yes, that above them all. He could do it. He would ride straight at Reflection and somehow he would kill the creature, and that would leave only the Sensleibhe.

And, thought Tybion, if Fael-Inis does not deal with the Sensleibhe, then I think we might as well hand over Ireland to Medoc anyway! He gathered up the reins and dug his heels into his mount's flanks, and rode straight at the pale glittering figure of Reflection, unsheathing his sword as he did so.

It was more difficult than he had thought it would be. Spectre's tempest had almost died, but it had not quite died, and from the corner of his eyes, Tybion could see the swirling mists of the *sidh* still busy about Spectre's decomposing form. There was still the breath of an icy wind on the night air, and Tybion knew that Spectre was not quite dead. He narrowed his eyes against the cold, because a cold wind was always at its bitterest when you rode straight at it, and concentrated very hard on autumn-lit forests and Grainne's smile.

The wind was still very cold indeed. The thin sheet of ice had almost melted from the ground, but there were still treacherous patches which had not melted at all. Twice his horse skidded and almost fell, but each time Tybion managed to keep it going on. If only he could get near to Reflection, if only he could fight his way through the nightmares and reach her; it was important to remember that the scaly monsters and the slithering snakes and the clutching sinewy hands could not hurt him. Once Reflection was dead, the Cloak of Nightmares would cease to be activated, and the nightmares would all vanish.

He was within yards of Reflection—"Within feet," Fintan was to say afterwards—when Reflection turned and saw him. She seemed to study him thoughtfully, and then there was a vibrant sizzle of light, and a hydra-headed creature, whose head was a writhing mass of snakes with teeth and claws, darted at Tybion. Tybion knew it was only a nightmare, but it was a particularly horrid one; he had often run from the thing in his dreams, and in every dream he had tripped headlong and lain panting, the breath knocked from him, helpless as the creature hovered above him. He glanced at it uneasily and tried to remember about the soft waterfalls and the bonfires in November and dew-drenched dawns.

He swerved instinctively, and as he did so, the creature darted at him again, and a gristly arm shot out. Claws ripped at Tybion's shoulder, and there was a white-hot sizzling. Tybion gasped and clapped a hand over his left breast, because it had felt exactly as if a burning hot wire had pierced right through to his heart. The chaotic scene about him tilted, and when he could see again, he thought that Reflection had called up another of the nightmares, because now he was seeing everything through a dark, wavering, ripply light.

He would not heed it. It would be a flesh wound; the claws of the hydra-headed monster had torn his shoulder, and it was nothing to pay very much attention to. Anyone could be wounded in a battle. He would deal with Reflection, and then he would get it bound up. He took a tighter hold on the sword, which was quite difficult suddenly, because his hands and arms were feeling a bit numb, and his legs were growing heavy. He was not entirely sure that he could feel his legs any longer; he was certainly not sure if he could see where he was going, because of the darkness and the way in which his vision was blurred and wavy.

But Reflection was directly ahead of him now. He could see her pale, nearly pellucid figure, and he could see the Cloak swirling and hissing as if it possessed a life of its own. He remembered that the Cloak of Nightmares had been one of Ireland's most treasured possessions. It had been woven by the sorcerers for the first High Queen of all, and although it had many times been lost to the Royal House, it had always been found again. Tybion, riding straight at Reflection, trying to keep a tight hold on his sword, thought it would be a truly great thing if he could restore the Cloak to the Royal House now.

He was riding hard across the nightmares, and he found he was no longer very much afraid. All about him were boiling cauldrons of blood and lakes of slime and faceless giants and creeping rodents and huge gobbling machines, and his ears were ringing with dreadful clanging sounds: echoing thunderclaps, and giant nails being drawn across tin surfaces, so that every nerve in your body winced and your teeth were all set on edge; but he knew that these were other people's nightmares, and although the snake-headed thing had wounded him, that had been his own nightmare. Other people's nightmares would not harm him. It was important to remember this.

He rode straight at Reflection, lifting his sword high, and then bringing it down in a sweeping arc. Reflection darted out of his reach, but as she did so, the Cloak slipped from her and fell in a soft pool of silk. At once the nightmare creatures vanished.

Tybion thought that Reflection had moved back to where the last and most terrible of the Guardians—the Sensleibhe—still waited, but he could not be sure. He was finding it difficult to stay in the saddle now. He knew he had been wounded, which was a very honourable thing to have happened, only it was beginning to hurt so very much. Someone would attend to the wound quite soon, and then he would be able to join the others, and they would be inside Tara, and he would see the Queen again. It was unthinkable that he should not see her, not when they had all come so far and endured so much. Yes, he must certainly see her again. But it was growing darker by the minute, and he wondered if the dying Spectre had somehow darkened the night air, or if Reflection had hurled a last nightmare before the Cloak slipped from her shoulders. In another minute he would not be able to see anything at all.

The pain in his chest was quite bad now. He was beginning to gasp and struggle for air, because it was actually extremely severe. Something was filling up his mouth; a thick, gluey substance, and there was an iron band round his chest.

And then he was lying on the ground, although he was not sure how this had come about, and his head was in somebody's lap, and he managed a smile, because of course it would be the Queen; this was how he had visualised it, except that he had not thought it would hurt so very much. But it would certainly be Grainne whom he had loved so very much and so very faithfully, and for whom he would happily die. When a voice said urgently, "Tybion," he smiled rather waveringly, and said in a conversational voice, "I always loved you so very much." There was a pause, and then a soft voice—it *had* to be Grainne—said very gently, "And I loved you, Tybion."

This was so marvelous that it was very nearly unbearable. Tybion narrowed his eyes and frowned in an effort of concentration, because everything seemed to be slipping away, and he was finding it hard to remember where he was or what he was supposed to be doing. But Grainne was here with him, she was holding his head in her lap, and there had never been a happiness so great, and he would remember this moment for as long as he lived. When she bent over him, he could smell the clean scent of her hair, and he wondered whether it would be disrespectful to reach up and take her hand. She seemed to understand, and at once her hand closed about his, and the fingers were smooth and supple and reassuring. He tried to say something to her; he thought he was trying to tell her that he wanted her to be happy, because he could not bear to think that she would not be happy, but she seemed to understand again, and although he could not see her, he felt that she was smiling at him, and he smiled back, and held out his hands, and then the darkness closed about him and his head fell back.

Annabel looked up from cradling Tybion's head, and Taliesin saw there were tears streaming down her face. "He's dead. Taliesin, he's dead."

"Yes."

"But he was only—he was so very—"

Taliesin said, "He thought you were the Queen."

"I know."

"Don't think about it," said Taliesin. "There is no time now. Later we will think."

Annabel said, "Yes. Of course." Because there was no time at all, not if they were to vanquish the Sensleibhe and gain entry to Tara, not if Tybion's death was to be worthwhile.

Taliesin said, "There will be time to grieve later," and Annabel looked at him gratefully, because of course there would be time and of course they would all grieve for Tybion. There was still a battle to be won, and there was still the last and most evil of the Guardians to be defeated.

Raynor had led the eagles into the attack on the Sensliebhe, and they were flying at the creature, aiming for her eyes, swooping down in great golden angry arcs of light. Fergus had ridden into the ranks of the soldiers and was gathering them up for a concerted attack on the Sensliebhe. As he turned his horse about, preparatory to leading the charge, he saw the Old Woman of the Mountains rear up and seem to become almost twice her size, and stand surveying them from a ledge of rock, her eyes flaming in her plain round face, her claws glinting in the twilight.

There was the cackling laughter that Fergus remembered from the Mountain Halls, and the light glinted again on curved claws and cruel talons, and caught and held the dark animal eyes.

"Such a lot of pretty dears," shrieked the Sensleibhe. "Dear me, all grist for my spinning. Come along now, my pretty ones, come along, my lambkins, for there's only friendship to be had here. Only friendship. Bless us all, I'm an old woman and I can't hurt a hair of your heads." The chuckle rang out once more. "And all that silken hair," said the Old Woman of the Mountains greedily. "All that pretty soft hair, for the spinning, and all the white tender skin, all for shredding."

Fergus cried, "On and at her!" and stood up in the stirrups and rallied the armies. The soldiers let out a rather ragged cheer, and dug their heels into their mounts' flanks, and Fergus brought his own mount headlong across the terrain, riding straight at the Sensleibhe.

At once she lifted her hand and, as she did so, streams of crimson light shot from her claws, so that Fergus had the impression of riding directly against a stream of magenta fire. He flinched and crouched in the saddle, and the Sensleibhe laughed again and raised the other hand. The fire spat again and Fergus, looking up, saw several of the Eagles fall from the sky, and saw Raynor throw up a hand and half fall from his mount. Bec ran alongside and Fergus saw that Raynor's face had been laid open by the sizzling spears of fire. Blood poured from the wound, and Raynor shook his head impatiently and pressed a cloth to his face before mounting again.

The Sensleibhe was laughing horridly now, sending the crimson flames shooting into the night, surrounding herself with an aureole of angry light, so that none could get near her. Fergus set his teeth and swerved round to lead another charge, because they must destroy this one, there was no question but that they must get past her and gain the Western Gate of the Palace. Reflection did not worry him—bereft of the Nightcloak her powers were greatly lessened—but the Sensleibhe was another thing altogether. Fergus had not thought of what might be happening to Grainne, because he had not dared to think of it, but now, facing the Western Gate directly, he felt such a terrible cold despair clutch his heart that he thought he could have flung the Sensleibhe to the ground and stamped her into a jelly. He took a firmer grip on his sword again and tightened the reins of his horse. One last charge might disconcert the creature. Surely she did not possess inexhaustible powers?

And then a soft voice at his side said, "Captain! To the Time Chariot!" and Fergus turned sharply to see Fael-Inis at his side, perfectly composed, lit to blazing light by the Sensleibhe's fire.

"The Time Chariot!" cried Fael-Inis again, and pulled Fergus with him. "It is our only chance against the creature's fire weapons! Come with me!"

As they ran through the smoke and the heat and the confusion, Fergus shouted, "I thought you were to be only a spectator of this!" and Fael-Inis turned to look at Fergus, his golden eyes glowing.

"I cannot fight your battles, Captain," he said, "you must fight your own battles. But when the adversaries are too great for you, and when the cause is just, then I am permitted—even I am constrained—to step in and do what I can. And the Wolfqueen and the Lost Prince must be rescued."

Fergus started to say, "The Prince . . ." but they were at the huge Chariot now, and the salamanders were pawing the ground, and the Time Chariot was landing. Fergus had just time to think, I suppose this *is* the answer, and then the Chariot quivered and seemed to leap forward, and the radiance burst all about them, and the salamanders shot forward joyously, their fiery breath filling the night sky and spilling on to Tara, so that for a moment it did not seem to lie in such shadow.

Fael-Inis laughed and turned to look back at Fergus from where he stood at the Chariot's prow, and his eyes were so wild and his whole bearing was filled with such recklessness and with such abandonment that Fergus said no more and concentrated on what was ahead.

The Chariot swerved to bring itself into direct line with

the Sensleibhe, and Fergus thought, but could not be sure, that there was music singing on the air now, but it might only have been the rushing of the wind, and then again it might only have been the *sidh*, still busy about the dying Spectre. But, I believe it is Fael-Inis's legendary silver pipes! thought Fergus, and delight exploded within him, for surely, surely there had never been a battle to equal this one, and surely they were going to rescue Grainne and destroy Medoc.

Then Fael-Inis seemed to gather up the salamanders for one last great effort, and the Time Chariot gave a great bound forward, and the lights and the fireglow blurred and they sped down to where the Sensleibhe was standing.

FIRE STREAMED OUTWARDS, and Fergus, at the exact centre of the light, could no longer see anything with any clarity. He was blinded, gasping, dizzy and helpless with the sheer speed of the Time Chariot, and with the brilliant light, and with the fire and the radiance of the salamanders. He could only wait and cling to the Chariot's sides, and trust the insouciant creature whose eyes were glowing with pure mischief, and who might certainly have walked away from the First Battle of the Heavens, but who was most definitely not walking away from this one.

The rebel angel was fighting on the side of the Humans, leading the Wolfqueen's armies against Ireland's enemies, against the terrible Dark Ireland . . .

And then Fael-Inis half turned and shouted, "We are nearly there! Hold tight now!" He grinned. "And be ready to deliver the death blow!" he shouted, and Fergus raised his sword and gripped the hilt with both hands, and fixed his eyes on the Sensleibhe and prayed to whatever gods might be appropriate that he would not miss.

For if you do, Mortal, there will be no second chance . . .

They were almost upon the creature now, and she had wheeled about to face them, crimson light still sparking from her claws. Fergus thought that the pure bright Time Fire was somehow deflecting the crimson sparks, and he certainly thought that the dark angry flames were flying upwards harmlessly and melting into the night sky over the Palace. And then they were near enough to see the Sensleibhe's evil grinning eyes, and Fergus remembered how she had lured Conn and the boys into her room inside the mountain, and he remembered the grisly spinning wheel with the shreds of Human flesh and the parings of Human nails and the skin and the gristle and bone, and fierce anger filled him up. As the Chariot swerved, he leaned forward over the side and drove his sword hard into the Sensleibhe's breast.

There was a piercing shriek and a splitting sound, and the thing that had been the Sensleibhe, the leader of the Guardians, the Old Woman of the Mountains who lured children to a firelit room and killed them and wove them into cloth, seemed to soften and collapse. Reflection, from her place of safety high on a ridge of rock, screamed and drew back, and then Fergus withdrew his sword and thrust it into the Sensleibhe again. There was a dreadful pulpy feeling, as if he had stabbed into soft, rotten fruit. Liquid, mushy, putrescent . . .

The Sensleibhe fell to her knees, and they saw her clawed feet grip the ground in a death agony. Her body began to dry and shrink, and she grew older and older. At last, she was a tiny mummified old woman, wizened and monkey-like, clutching at the air and struggling for breath. And then even that faded, and she was a heap of brown flesh adhering to stick-like bones, and then the bones themselves crumbled into grey dust. The dust stirred and blew away and then there was nothing at all.

Reflection seemed to shimmer and blur, and then they caught the tail-end of silvery robes as she whipped about.

"She is escaping!" cried Fergus, both hands grasping his sword. "Fael-Inis, we cannot let her go!" He turned to where Fael-Inis was reining in the salamanders, and saw the fiery golden eyes grow suddenly gentle.

"Let her go, Fergus," he said. "Without her hell-sisters she is no longer such a very dreadful threat." And then, in a different voice, "Poor Aife," said the rebel angel softly, "she will never achieve true greatness." And then, appearing to give himself a shake, "And you saw how the nightmare creatures vanished the minute the Cloak slid from her." With one hand, he gestured to the scene before them, which was scattered with wounded and dead, but which was now free from the gruesome terrible army of creatures Aife had called up with the Nightcloak's aid.

"Well, Captain?" said Fael-Inis, the delight glowing in his eyes. "Shall we advance to the Bright Palace?"

To ANNABEL, WHAT happened next was the most remarkable thing of all the remarkable things that had yet happened to her in this beautiful but sinister world. Every time something new came along, she had thought, That is the ultimate surprise. That is the pinnacle, the zenith. Nothing can surpass that. And then—sometimes only minutes later—something did surpass it.

But nothing would ever surpass that extraordinary walk through the halls of the Ancient Palace of the High Kings and Queens of Ireland.

Tara, the shining city, the bright citadel . . .

Fael-Inis and Fergus had come back to the waiting armies after the Sensleibhe had been slain. Annabel had found the Sensleibhe's death rather terrible, and she had had to remind herself quite sharply about how Conn and Niall and Michael and the other boys had been lured into that sinister firelit room, so that they could be killed and then woven on the Sensleibhe's grisly spinning wheel.

Fergus had been swift and efficient and quite ruthless in deploying his army. Raynor had been with him, and Raynor had been just as swift and efficient, and although Annabel did not think that Raynor was wholly ruthless, she thought she would not like to make an enemy of him. She was getting to know the Beastline people quite well now—probably there was nothing quite like going through immense danger for bringing you close to somebody—but Raynor was still a rather distant figure. Annabel, studying him, listening to the stories of the Grail Castle and of the strange lost Beastline creatures who had lived there in exile, and of Raynor who had been their leader, found herself regarding him with something akin to reverence. Bec had told her how close Grainne and Raynor had become, and how they were all hoping that Grainne would take Raynor as consort, and Annabel was becoming more and more intrigued by Grainne. She thought that someone who could be loved by Raynor must be extremely special, and she began to hope very strenuously that they would rescue Grainne from Medoc.

Fergus and Raynor had sorted the armies out now, and made sure that the wounded were tended, and that the dead would be taken to be prepared for ceremonial burial after the battle.

At last, the two of them stood looking at one another, and Fergus said with sudden formality, "Will you be at my side when we enter the Sun Chamber?" and Raynor paused for only a breathspace before replying, "It will be my honour, Captain."

Fergus studied him for a moment, and then, "She will wish you to be there," he said, and there was a note of sadness in his voice now, so that those in earshot—which was very nearly everybody—knew that Fergus was deliberately and publicly relinquishing any claim he had ever had to the Queen. Cathbad was quite affected by this, and had to blow his nose rather vigorously, and retired to the rear, where he began to plan the feast to celebrate the Queen's betrothal to Raynor.

"Premature," said Fintan, a realist.

"No, it isn't," said Cathbad, who adored betrothals and weddings and christenings.

"We've got to rescue her first," said Cermait.

"We've got to get past Medoc first," said Fintan. "I suppose we *are* going in, are we? They seem to be taking a terrible long time over it."

But then Fergus leapt on to a sharp outcrop, so that he was able to look down on them all, and smiled, and the wind lifted his hair, and the famous reckless we-shall-win look was back in his eyes, and several people began to feel very much better about what was ahead, and everyone began to think that after all they might defeat Medoc and restore the Wolfqueen to Tara.

Fergus grinned. "Well, my friends! Are we ready?" And then, as a rousing shout of assent came from them, "Then," said Fergus, "let us advance!" And leapt down from the slope and looked at Fael-Inis and grinned as if to say, How was that? and Fael-Inis grinned back and looked rather like a cat, very composed and amused, and moved into place at Fergus's side, with Raynor on his left.

There was still a faint light from the embers of Spectre's fireballs, and by it Annabel could see that despite the bravery, and despite the rallying speeches, both Fergus and Raynor were white and strained. Raynor's face was scarred where the fireball had scorched it, and Fergus was smeared with blood—whether his or other people's, Annabel had no idea. Annabel looked at them both and thought that neither of them could bear to acknowledge that Grainne might be already lost, and then quite suddenly she realised that Fergus and Raynor both knew, with that strange extra sense they possessed, that Grainne still lived.

But Medoc has her, and we dare not lose any more time . . .

They had not, in fact, lost any time at all. They had taken every opportunity and they had not hesitated at all. Even so, Fergus made a careful selection of the ones who would accompany him into the Palace, choosing several lieutenants to bring up the rear, summoning Fintan and Cermait Honeymouth, and beckoning out the Beastline creatures, and Conn and Niall.

Lastly he turned to where the *sidh* waited on the outer rim of the scene, and everyone knew that although Fergus could not compel the *sidh* to accompany them, he would very much like them to do so.

"He does it well," murmured Taliesin at Annabel's side. "Would you say he is almost royal?"

"Yes," breathed Annabel, unable to take her eyes from Fergus. "Yes, I would say it."

"I also," said Taliesin. And then, in a different tone, "Look at the light."

"It's Fael-Inis," said Annabel after a moment. "Or it's the *sidh*."

"It's more than that," said Taliesin.

It was. There was the vivid strong light of the Time Fire, and there was the incandescence that perpetually surrounded Fael-Inis. There was, as well, the cool elvish light of the *sidh*. "A muted light," said Annabel, who found the *sidh* fascinating and terrifying, and who could have listened to their music for ever.

The light was all of this and none of it. From within the dark hidden heart of Tara, from the place that had for so long been caught and held fast in Medoc's evil magic, a faint shimmer of luminous colour was appearing. It was as fragile and as elusive as a will-o'-the-wisp or the flickering lights over the marshes on a winter's night, or a string of glow worms deep in the forest. Faint and fragile and elusive, and so uncertain that you had to look twice and then thrice to be sure you had not imagined it.

But it was there and no one had imagined it, and every person present knew it was there. The light was beginning to burn again in the Bright Palace . . . Cathbad had to blow his nose all over again, and could not even be cheered by the planning of a banquet for tomorrow night, when they would undoubtedly be sitting in the Sun Chamber, celebrating the restoration of the Wolfqueen.

Incredulous joy was showing in every face now and, when Fergus turned to summon them to follow him, they fell into place silently.

Taliesin said softly, "Annabel. Look at the Wolves," and Annabel, who had been a bit fearful of the Wolves (extremely fearful of them, if she was honest), turned to look and saw the most extraordinary change in them. Until now they had been watchful and rather distant from everyone.

Fintan had said that they were loners. "They'll keep their distance," he had said, and Cermait had said he hoped they would keep their distance, because wasn't it a well-known fact that only the Royal Line could control them.

Now, falling into line behind Fergus, the Wolves were obedient and very nearly subservient; their fur was sleek and their eyes were bright with anticipation.

"Interesting that," said Fintan thoughtfully, and studied Fergus rather more intently than he had been used to doing.

Cathbad said it did your heart good to see the Royal Wolves returning to the Palace, and mopped his eyes and said he was *that* overcome. "I shan't ever be the same again," he said, and did not listen when several people said they were very glad to hear it.

They walked in procession along the avenue of trees, and the great Western Gates of the Palace loomed ahead of them, a great frame beneath which they would pass.

"Very historic," said Fintan wisely. "Dear me, these Gates could tell a few tales, well I expect they do tell them, if only we knew how to hear."

"They'll most likely be barred against us, won't they?" said Cermait.

But the Gates stood ajar, and again there was the faintest spill of light from within.

Annabel, at Taliesin's side, somewhere in the middle of the procession, remembered an echo of something from her own world, something from an old war, she thought, fought and won and recovered from two or even three centuries before she had been born.

"And the lights went on again all over the world . . ."

The lights were coming on again inside Tara, and it was remarkable and beautiful and awe-inspiring and terrifying, and if Medoc was possessed of any shred of feeling at all, he must be seeing it and he must know that his reign of shadow was almost over.

Fael-Inis stopped at the exact centre of the Western Gates and, making not the smallest ceremony about it, lifted the silver pipes to his lips. Music streamed out into the night and, as Fael-Inis moved into the shadow cast by the Gates, it seemed to the watchers that the music poured out behind them like a foaming wake in an ocean.

And wherever the music touches, it leaves light, thought Annabel, staring. And even though her own world was growing fainter and dimmer, and even though she did not regret having lost it and never would regret having lost it, still there were the echoes and there were the fragments of memory and drifts of scholarship and literature and learning.

"Through this house give glimmering light" ... *"I with the morning's love have oft made sport"* ... *"Light Ethereal, first of things, quintessence pure"* ...

And then, as if an echo came from both Fergus and Taliesin now, one of the most beautiful and one of the most apposite of them all.

> *"Put out the light and then put out the light.*
> *If I quench thee, thou flaming minister,*
> *I can again thy former light restore."*

Thy former light ... We are restoring the light, thought Annabel, drunk with delight and heady with the beauty and the strength of it all. We are restoring the light to the Bright Palace, and Fael-Inis is sprinkling light everywhere, and the entire Palace is glowing, and soon it will be a beacon of iridescence, and the whole of Ireland will see it, and the whole of Ireland will rejoice.

Thy former light restored ...

To Fergus, it was joy and peace and home-coming all rolled up into one: If I am never happy again, if I can never know another moment of pure happiness, then at least I am knowing it now, he thought. To be here, like this, to be forcing a path through Medoc's darkness, to see the darkness part and give way to golden brilliance, to see the lights burning again in the home of my ancestors ... He thought he would probably never acknowledge his right and his claim to the Ancient Throne: That is for you, my dear lost love, he thought. But he thought people would probably guess if they had not already done so, and he sent a glance to the Wolves, still padding silently behind him.

I have not quite the power and the light and the strength, but they have followed me and they have answered me.

And the light was beginning to glow again. *"Through this house give glimmering light ..."* Fergus, like Annabel, like Taliesin, did not know where the words came from: the past, the future?—but he knew that somewhere, at some time, someone sensitive and gifted and far-seeing had understood about restoring light where there had been darkness, and he knew that someone had visualised with ease a slender radiant creature with molten hair and strange glowing eyes, who was not entirely Human, but not quite divine, who could work pure strong magic and who could dart in and out of a shaft of light, and defy the world and challenge all the creeds and all the religions.

The rebel angel, who walked away from the First Battle, and never declared for either side ... But he has declared for us, thought Fergus. He has fought this battle with us and for us, and I believe that because of him we shall now defeat Medoc and the Twelve Dark Lords.

Through this house ... On and on they went, the music from the silver pipes casting its sprinkling of flame and its pure soft radiance, and Fergus felt Tara, the Shining Palace, the radiant citadel, waking and lightening and singing with joy all about him.

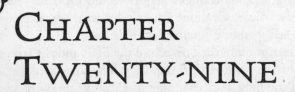

CHAPTER
TWENTY-NINE

DEEP WITHIN THE Sun Chamber, the darkness was heavy and stifling. Grainne could feel the cold stone of the altar beneath her, and she could feel, in more senses than she had ever felt anything in her life, Erin at her side. Medoc stood over them, with the Conablaiche and the Lad of the Skins at his side, and she stared up at them, helpless, knowing that there could be only a few moments left to them.

She did not think there was any escape. That faint far-off howling, even if it had been the Wolves, had been too distant. The Wolves might reach them—the armies might even reach them—but it would be too late. She and Erin would both die, and their souls would be thrown into the Prison of Hostages, and the Wolfline would be dead for ever.

And Ireland would be Medoc's.

She thought that Medoc heard her thoughts very clearly, for a brief, rather gentle smile touched his lips. And then he said, quite softly, "My dear, even now it is not too late." Something tender touched his lips. "You are flesh of my flesh," said Medoc. "You could swear allegiance to me, Grainne." He reached down and took her hand and, as he did so, he sent a sliver of light slicing through the cords that bound her to the altar stone.

"Come," said Medoc. "Come with me and see, Grainne."

He lifted his left arm again, and the Star of Necromancy glinted on his breast, and light poured outwards and Medoc described an oblong on the darkness. At once the oblong took on the outline of an immense Door and, as Grainne caught her breath, the Door opened slowly.

"The Dark Land," said Medoc softly. "The Enchanted Realm of the necromancers and the world of the shadow beings. *My* world, Grainne. The kingdom where I rule absolutely." He moved, and Grainne, helpless, caught in sudden and terrible fascination, moved with him. The Door was opening wider to admit them, and through it she could see the red-lit land, Medoc's land, the Dark Realm, the world that her ancestors had for so long striven to keep out.

And I am entering into it . . .

Dark sinuous arms reached out, and slender hands pulled her in. There was a rushing sensation, the feeling of being sucked into a dark narrow tunnel, there was the sense of entering some lightless place, a world where light would never penetrate, where there would never be fields and sunshine and rain and summer afternoons and spring dawns.

Through the red mists, she could see imp-like creatures, grinning goblin creatures with leering faces and evil eyes. There were writhing shapes, raven-black and smoky, and there was horrid echoing laughter all about her.

The Wolfqueen entering the Dark Realm . . .

Medoc was drawing her farther in now, his hand was holding her hand, and his skin was cool and silky. Ahead of them were fields and lakes of glassy blackness, and beyond that were towering mountains with distant castles, more lonely and more menacing than anything Grainne had ever seen. Paths snaked through the mountains, glowing and sinisterly beckoning, and here and there were clusters of houses, huddled together, and here and there were low-roofed buildings from which came a fiery glow.

Grainne thought, The Sheds of the Dark Looms! and knew that the red glow was the dreadful effluence, the waste matter from the evil bewitchments spun on the necromancers' Looms.

Yes, but to walk here, to rule from the castles in the mountains, to hold sway over the powerful enchanters of this land . . .

There was a dull humming everywhere, and there was a heavy drugged feeling to the air. You could very easily surrender to it, you could easily allow it to over take you. It could be very sweet, this heady, spell-laden world . . .

"You see?" said Medoc softly at her side. "There are enchantments and bewitchments here. There are spells and charms and curses and incantations without end. You could rule here, and you could have all of this, Grainne."

If you will bow your will to mine and relinquish Ireland to me . . .

"No," said Grainne, not daring to look at him. "No."

He turned to face her then and, as she looked, he towered above her, his eyes filled with malevolence, power streaming from him. "I could compel you to do it, Wolfqueen," he said, his voice cold but his aspect forbidding. And then, in a softer, more insidious tone, "*Shall* I compel you, Grainne? Shall I take you to the furnace houses where we burn the flesh and boil the bones of the Humans we draw in through the Doorways? For we have ever used Humans in our work, Grainne. Or shall I show you the Nightfields where we hunt Men and tear the flesh from them for our enchantments? Shall we travel across the Lake of Darkness into the River of Souls, and see below the surface of the water the trapped souls of Humans? And shall I let you see the spinning of the Dark Looms, which would make your famous Silver Looms appear like children's playthings? They would burn out your soul," said Medoc softly. "To look on the Dark Looms calling down the force would burn out your soul. But you could command them, for *I* would give you the power.

"Rule with me," said Medoc, and now he was no longer the menacing necromancer, but the beautiful, dark, slender being, and his voice was caressing and seductive. "Rule with me," he said. "Become one of the dark sorceresses. I could teach you, Grainne. I could spend long evenings and lazy afternoons with you, teaching you." The smile was that of a lover now and, without warning, there was a sudden sexual pull. Medoc reached out and traced the line of her face, and there was a moment when his hands brushed the thin stuff of her gown, and she felt her breasts respond. "Help me to rule both of these lands," said Medoc, "and you will see how great are your rewards."

Grainne drew in a huge breath, and sought and found the clear light cord of the Samhailt. *Erin!* she thought, and the cord strengthened.

Still here, Madam. Do not let him overpower you ...

Grainne looked at Medoc coldly, and said, "Turn your mindless creatures on to me, sir. I do not care for your world," and at once saw icy fury in his eyes.

But he only said, "I wove deep and dark enchantments so that the accursed Wolfline would die. I lured the creature who is your mother to my bed, and ensured that you and your brother would be born." He leaned closer to her. "Twins, Grainne," he said. "I ensured that the creature who calls herself Damnaithe would give birth to twins, in order that the ancient curse would revive, and the Beastline Enchantment would die. I do not intend to have expended those enchantments in vain, my dear. If you will not renounce Tara, then you and the Wolfprince must certainly die." He turned about, the dark cloak swirling angrily, and Grainne felt herself sucked back through the terrible land over which he ruled, across the Nightfields and the Seas of Darkness, back to the Doorway, and back into the Sun Chamber.

She felt herself thrown back on to the altar stone, and she felt Damnaithe's eager hands on her, tying the cords, binding her down again. Frustrated anger welled up in her, for she had been free, for that short time she had been free, and surely she could have found a way to defeat Medoc.

He will be defeated, madam ... the Wolves are nearer; if we can but keep him at bay for a little longer ...

Hope surged up in her, but she quenched it, for Medoc, with his dark powers, would certainly hear her.

Medoc was standing looking at Erin now, his face in shadow. "If you knew," he said softly, "how many years I have spent searching for you. They hid you well, Erin."

"But not well enough," said Erin coolly.

Medoc laughed. "You could never have escaped," he said. "They gave you to the Humans, but you would always have been noticeable." He studied Erin, and Erin stared back. "After all my planning," said Medoc, "still you were born. Still you have survived." He walked round the altar. "You understand, do you, that you must die? That I can risk no pretenders."

"I understand."

Grainne said quickly, "Medoc, if you would release him—allow him to grow up somewhere far from Tara . . ."

"To lead an army against me in ten years' time?" Medoc smiled. "Come, my dear, you have more intelligence than that. You know that this one would never rest until he had tried to regain the Ancient Throne of his ancestors."

"But if he could be made to promise—to renounce his claim . . ."

"I do not need to claim what is mine!" Erin was watching Medoc through narrowed eyes. "For all you have gained Tara by your sorcery, Medoc, you will never really be Ireland's true Ruler. You are a usurper." He smiled. "I think you fear me," said Erin.

"Let us say I prefer to dispose of irritations," said Medoc, and Erin smiled as if he found this understandable.

"While you live, Wolfprince, you will always be a threat," said Medoc, and his eyes went to the monstrous waiting shape of Crom Croich. "And my master is expecting sacrifice tonight," he said. "I have summoned him, and I have brought him into the world of Men, and for that alone I must appease him." As he spoke, Crom Croich's little red eyes glinted greedily, and a smile twisted the thick wet maw.

"The Crown Princess and the Wolfprince are worthy offerings," said Medoc. "My master will grant me so much power for that, and so much strength, that I shall have all I ever wanted."

He stood back and signed to the Conablaiche. "And now," said Medoc, "these creatures are yours, my trusted servant." And then, to the Lad of the Skins, "And they are yours, my devoted follower," he said. "Rip out their hearts so that we may feed them to the Master. Take their souls and carry them to the eternal light of the Prison of Hostages."

The Conablaiche's claws rang out on the silver floor as it came scuttling forward, its beak clacking, and the Lad of the Skins moved as well, a quick darting movement, the Knife of Light gleaming in his hands.

Grainne thought, So after all we are to die at the hands of this dark, beautiful, evil one. After all, Fergus and Raynor and the others have failed, and after all the Wolves will not reach us. She looked up to where Crom Croich was towering above them, its monstrous bulk heaving and panting, the thick lips beginning to stretch.

Tear out their hearts and let me taste them, for I am greedy tonight, and this is the Crown Princess and the Lost Prince . . .

And through the great double doors of the Sun Chamber came streaming the Wolves of Tara, sleek and beautiful and filled with avenging fury, and behind them were Fael-Inis and Fergus, Raynor and Taliesin . . .

THE EVIL CRIMSON light became instantly shot with streaks of pure white brilliance, and Medoc fell back at once, one hand flung up as if the light had seared his eyes. A great roar went up, and the Wolves erupted across the silver floor, their teeth bared and their faces masks of blazing hatred. They fell on the Dark Lords in a snarling, whirling mass of fur and teeth and black armour, and the Dark Lords, taken unaware, reeled back. Fael-Inis shot forward, an arrow of pure light, to where the Lad of the Skins cowered and, as he did so, Fergus, Raynor, and Taliesin, with the Cruithin and the small army at their heels, surged forward. Grainne, helpless, unable to move, felt delight explode in her heart, to be followed by an entirely new fear as Fergus and Raynor, with a single purposeful movement, made for the Conablaiche, their swords glinting angrily in the baleful red light.

The glowing brilliance was shifting and changing, and

the crimson aura of evil was struggling against Fael-Inis's light. The Sun Chamber became a moving whirling tunnel of crimson and silver and white and orange as the two forces fought for mastery. There was the ringing sound of steel against armour, and the Sun Chamber seemed to be filled with the High Queen's avenging armies and with the legendary lost Wolves of Cormac, so that Grainne, fear and delight and confidence and terror all tumbling about together, thought, They are going to do it! I truly believe they are going to succeed! And forgot about the cold hard altar slab and the monstrous towering bulk of the terrible creature that Medoc had summoned, and was certainly not aware of anyone at her side until a soft, rather hesitant voice spoke.

Annabel, whose own world had certainly not prepared her for anything like this, and who was not at all sure how a High Queen ought to be addressed, said rather breathlessly, "Madam—that is—Your Majesty . . ." and Grainne turned her head, and saw Annabel, and smiled with such warmth and such interest that Annabel blinked and understood at once why Fergus and Raynor were both prepared to fight to the death for the Queen and why Tybion had died happy, and why the armies had gone without hesitation into the necromancer's lair to rescue her.

"Could I somehow untie you?" said Annabel, and Grainne said, "Oh, yes, if only you would, and Erin as well," and quite suddenly it was perfectly easy to explain about how they had all stolen along the western avenue, and through the Palace, and how they had been afraid they would not be in time, and about Fael-Inis and the Wolves and the *sidh*. Grainne listened and, once her hands were free, helped Annabel with the chains that bound Erin, and seemed to know about Fael-Inis and all the other things.

"But we knew the Wolves were coming," she said, and her eyes went to the snarling angry Wolves with such delight that Annabel blinked again, and remembered that after all this was the Wolfqueen, and that the blood of the Royal Wolves was in her veins.

"It was only that we were unsure how long they would be and how close they were to us," said Erin gravely, and he and Grainne exchanged a smile, and then turned back to Annabel, and Annabel smiled back and knew that there was no question but that they must win this battle.

"Can we fight?" said Erin, suddenly and disconcertingly a small boy now, his eyes bright as he turned to survey the armies.

"You would be cut to pieces at once," said Grainne. "And so would we. But we will watch our chance and there may be something we can do to help." And then Annabel felt Grainne's hand come down over hers in a painful grip, and Grainne said in a whisper, "The Dark Lords. Look at them." And Annabel, who had actually been trying not to look at them (and who had been trying very hard indeed not to look at the Conablaiche), looked and said, "What is happening to them?"

"They are changing," said Grainne, staring to where the Lords had moved back from the fight. "They are sending forth their dark inner selves."

Debauchery, Decadence, Perversion, Hatred, Avarice . . .

Fergus, with Raynor and Taliesin, had cornered the Conablaiche, and Annabel thought the creature must already have been disabled by Fael-Inis's bolt of light, because it was backing away and very nearly cowering. Its jelly-like eye swivelled and glared and, despite its cringing mien, it was clawing out at them. Annabel saw Fergus bring his sword slicing down on to the creature's gristly jointed arm, and a pale viscous fluid spurted from the gaping wound. There was a stench of rotting meat and old blood and decay, and Annabel shuddered, and held on to her courage, and remembered about it being a battle they must win at all costs, and tried to see what they could do to help.

At her side, Grainne said, "Damnaithe—look!" And they both saw that Damnaithe was creeping alongside the wall of the Sun Chamber on all fours, the Knife of Light held between her teeth, advancing on Fergus from behind. "Come on!" cried Annabel, and they flung themselves on Damnaithe, knocking her to the ground, wresting the knife from her hand, sending it clattering across the silver floor.

Grainne snatched up the cords that had bound her to the altar earlier, and tied Damnaithe's hands and ankles; as she straightened up, Annabel saw that she was very pale. Annabel reached for the Knife of Light and, as her hand closed about it, it shivered and splintered and dissolved into a myriad of tiny glinting sparks that rolled and danced and disappeared.

"Another evil gone!" said Grainne, and looked at Annabel, her eyes golden and shining, and Annabel, caught at once in the exultation, saw all over again why Grainne's people were ready to die for her without hesitation, and began to understand why people had fought for King and Country, and risked their lives, and courted danger and death.

Fael-Inis had surrounded the Lad of the Skins with dazzling glowing light, and the Lad was screaming and putting up his hands, trying to ward off the light and tearing at the air in front of him.

"What is he doing?" cried Annabel, and Grainne said, "He is blinding him with the light. He is sending pure white light straight at his eyes!"

The Lad was still screaming, but the sounds were quieter now. Blood was pouring from his eye sockets and, when at last Fael-Inis withdrew the piercing spears of light, and the Lad turned his face to them, they saw the great gaping holes where his eyes had been.

Annabel said, in a voice from which all expression had been driven, "You are quite right. He has burnt his eyes out."

"It is a fitting punishment," said Grainne, and her voice was so stern that Annabel turned to look in surprise. Grainne said, half to herself, "I wish I could feel pity for the creature, but I cannot. The children whose souls he imprisoned . . ." And Annabel looked at Erin, and understood, and remembered all over again that here were weapons her own world had never dreamed existed, and wondered whether the bombs and explosions that destroyed her world were worse or better.

Taliesin, his dark hair tumbled, his eyes brilliant, was leading the Wolves against the Dark Lords, striking out at them with his sword. Annabel could see that the Lords were changing, and that from within the armour and the dark visors shapes were beginning to emerge. Dreadful nightmarish shapes; things that were not Human and yet which had, rather dreadfully, a vestige of Human appearance. As Taliesin brought his sword glinting down again, one of the Lords—Grainne thought it might have been Deceit—made a sudden vicious clawing movement, and Taliesin staggered back and half fell against the wall on the far side of the Chamber, one hand clutched to his shoulder.

"Injured only," said Grainne, as Annabel gasped and started forward. "Do not move—you will be dead in minutes if you attempt to force a path through the fighting. And look to the Dark Lords!"

Annabel looked and saw the hideous shapes solidifying, and shuddered. "What of Medoc?" she said. "Is he dead? Will he fight?"

"He is over there," said Grainne, who had never lost sight of the dark slender figure of Medoc. "He has the god Crom Croich with him. See?" And pointed through the tumult and the smoke and the heat to where Medoc was standing a little apart from the fighting, in Crom Croich's shadow, his dark cloak wrapped about him. "He will not fight," said Grainne, "for no true necromancer would ever engage in hand-to-hand fighting. But he is calling up the Twelve Evils; those are his weapons, and it is those we have to fear now."

Annabel, curled into the corner with Grainne and Erin, said, "But Medoc is—is he not one of the Lords?"

"Medoc is all of them rolled up into one," said Grainne, her eyes on the twelve creatures. "He is every evil and every sin and every wickedness ever committed or dreamed or thought or planned." And then, half to herself, "And I cannot let him have Ireland," she said and, at her side, Erin, without taking his eyes from the terrible battle, reached for her hand.

He will not have it, madam.

The Twelve Lords had by now distanced themselves from the Queen's people, and they were ranging themselves against the far end of the Chamber, seeming to grow in stature with every second. The black armour was glittering and writhing, as if alive, and although the creatures that emerged could not possibly be Human, Annabel saw again that here and there were Human characteristics.

In another minute, in a few more heartbeats, they would all stand before the Queen's people, in their dark and terrible majesty . . .

Grainne and Annabel were on their feet now, Erin between them. Annabel thought, I am extremely frightened. I am more frightened than I have ever been of anything in my entire life, but I should certainly be much more frightened if it were not for these two. And remembered what Taliesin had told her about the power and the light and the strength of the Wolfline. She glanced at Grainne and Erin, and for a moment she felt it, a golden strength, a soaring stream of pure courage, and thought, Yes, Taliesin was right. And then, on another note, *Taliesin?*

He was lying half slumped against the wall, his sword arm wounded and looking as if it might be broken, but, through the smoke, she saw him smile at her rather mockingly.

Not dead yet by a long way, lady. And she remembered that none of this would have been bearable without Taliesin.

And when this is all over, we will be together, Annabel . . . The thought came as clearly and as strongly as it could possibly be, and Annabel felt a wave of hope, because they would find a way to rout these nightmare creatures, and they would find a way to drive out Medoc and the Dark Lords.

The Dark Lords . . . The small band of men that Fergus and Raynor had believed would be sufficient had been beaten back by the towering raging beings that had now fully emerged from their armour. The Wolves were growling and cringing, their ears flattened, their eyes red and baleful, but even the Wolves would not approach these dark demonic entities that Medoc had called up to defend him.

Great billowing shapes uncoiled, and the Twelve Great Evils were there in the Sun Chamber.

Debauchery, the Overlord of the Twelve, and the least Human of them all. He was a shifting, nearly formless mass of thick oily substance that was not quite smoke and not quite fluid and not quite flesh. There was a dingy muddy taint, and at the centre were a pair of evil glowing eyes, terrible opaque eyes that made you think of old, old gods and of ancient creatures with Human appearance but webbed hands and feet that would peer up at you from the depths of dark underground lakes. He did not speak, although Grainne glimpsed the rudiments of a slash-like mouth, but if he had spoken, the voice that would have issued from the centre of the shifting greasy smoke-fluid would have been thick and clotted and slimy, and if he had taken Human shape, he would have been dark and covered with scales.

Next to Debauchery was Lust: a nasty one this, made up of a fast swirling crimson pillar of smoke that twisted itself into a great thick column of flesh and took on the appearance of a huge erect phallus with a monstrously swollen tip. There were glinting eyes three quarters of the way up the phallus-shape and long bony fingers—dozens of them—that squirmed and that would pry and prod and insinuate themselves into every bodily cavity they could find . . . Grainne and Annabel both gasped and grew back, and Lust gave a low, treacly-sounding chuckle, and the eyes widened and several pairs of hands reached out. Pale thick fluid, giant's semen, oozed from the pulsing tip of the terrible column of flesh.

Next to Lust was Selfishness: an amorphous jelly-like creature, very nearly ovoid with thick, pitted skin, small, mean features and a tight, prim mouth, all crammed into the centre of the ovoid.

Decadence was exactly as Grainne had visualised earlier: a thin-faced, pale gentleman, wearing a dark red velvet jacket, and with cold old eyes that inspected and discarded, and with pale polished skin. His hands were slender and smooth, and much too well kept, and they would curl lovingly about the stem of a wine glass and they would stroke young tender flesh under cover of darkness . . . Grainne disliked Decadence very much.

Hatred was a huge mask of glaring red eyes and teeth and claws; Jealousy—another nasty one, this—was another shifting changing shape, rather snake-like this time, sinuous and insinuating. He was green and the surface of his skin was faintly iridescent with what might have been fishscales. He would be cold-blooded and slimy. He had glaring yellow eyes and you could easily imagine that he would come writhing and squirming out of some dreadful steamy swamp. He would worm his way into your mind and coil his serpentine body about your thoughts, and his forked tongue would flicker and dart and he would whisper poison into your mind.

Greed, who was next, was made up of huge quivering sections of fat and blubber that ran and squelched because there was no skin to contain them. Here and there were patches of grease on the surface, and here and there, deep in the raw fat, were gaping wet mouths that made constant guzzling, sucking, lapping noises . . . *All the better to gobble you up with, my dear* . . .

Annabel, who had been just about able to cope with Decadence and Lust, found herself sickened all over again by Greed.

Deceit was thin and small and rat-like. He had a long slithering rat tail and a sly shifty eye. He was not quite a rodent, but he was not quite a Human. He would scuttle into corners if the light fell on him and vanish into the dusty shadows if you tried to catch him. He would have a beautiful voice, and if you trusted him, he would hurt you quite dreadfully.

Conceit: beautiful and weak-mouthed; Perversion: a sinister figure in a long dark cloak with a deep, wide-brimmed slouch hat hiding his eyes. He would lurk in fog-shrouded streets or in dark forests where he could swirl his black cloak about you and take you to his lair and do things to you that you would probably prefer not to know could be done . . .

Vice and Avarice were twins, joined down the centre of their bodies. Annabel, who remembered about something called Siamese twins, thought they were particularly repulsive. They each had a wide, flat, curving, cruel mouth like a shark, and there were at least eight sets of arms and curved talons. Vice had a long downward-pointing beak like a vulture's, and Avarice had a hard bony skull and a black shiny mandible like a giant beetle . . .

The Twelve Dark Lords were free of their concealing armour, out in the world to batten on their victims and fight for Medoc and Crom Croich . . .

Fergus and Raynor had both been backed against the wall by Decadence and Debauchery, and the twins Vice and Avarice; Greed was waddling towards the Wolves, licking and mumbling and guzzling, a monstrous, nearly liquid mass of wet, slopping blubber. The Wolves whined and cringed, but Grainne and Annabel saw that they did not actually back away. A shiver went through Erin, and Grainne knew that he was pouring every ounce of strength and confidence into them.

Taliesin, whose right arm was useless and hanging at his side, had managed to crawl round the edges of the room; Annabel saw him from the corners of her vision, and at once tried not to look, in case anyone should follow her gaze and see what he was trying to do. He was the farthest away from the Dark Lords, and it was just possible—oh, dear God, yes, it was just possible that he could take at least one of them by surprise. Some kind of diversion, thought Annabel wildly; if only he can create a diversion, then perhaps the Wolves can surge forward again and Fergus and Raynor can lead the men back in, and perhaps we shall be victorious after all.

As Taliesin inched carefully across the floor, Jealousy

undulated and seemed to dissolve slightly; livid green scales shimmered, and a rope-like coil slid out and knocked him to the ground. An evil throaty chuckle rang round the room.

You see what happens to Humans who try to fight us . . .

The Twelve Lords were moving forward now; they were shifting and coalescing, forming and reforming, almost becoming one terrible entity and then separating again. You could not fight them because they were terrible and invincible, and they were not Human. You could not fight creatures like this with Human weapons . . .

Decadence and Perversion moved forward, and reached for Grainne and Annabel, pulling them to the centre of the room; as they did so, Lust swirled forward, the huge penis-shape quivering and throbbing. Annabel gasped and thrust a fist into her mouth, but Grainne stood looking at the rearing form.

"Well, my dears," said Decadence, in his smooth, weary voice. "Shall we feed you both to our brother? Shall we stretch you over the tip of his phallus? Shall we see him enter you and split you apart?"

The rearing shape of Lust chuckled, and clutching hands reached out from the column of hard, throbbing flesh.

"Take them to the Dark Realm and give them to *us* for pleasuring," said Vice, and Avarice said, "We should know how to bend them to our Master's will," and chuckled, and Vice's curving beak snapped with anticipation.

And then, as Annabel and Grainne both felt themselves being pushed closer to the chuckling trunk of flesh, Fael-Inis, who had been standing framed in the huge crystal window, said in what they both afterwards thought of as a voice of fire and light, "Medoc! Look to the skies! Listen to the echoes!"

And everyone in the Sun Chamber heard the same thing, and Taliesin and Annabel both felt fear mixed with a sudden hope, because this had happened before, inside the mountain . . .

On the other side of the Sun Chamber, Fergus turned

his head, and recognised the sound also, and dared not believe that this might be their deliverance.

Hoofbeats approaching them through the dark skies . . .

The Four Horsemen of the Apocalypse . . .

Medoc moved at once. He strode forward and stood at the great window, staring into the skies, his head tilted, his eyes dark and intent. Everyone moved back from his passing.

Fael-Inis moved to his side, and Taliesin who was nearest, and who was to wonder afterwards if the pain of his broken arm had made him see things not really there, thought he had never witnessed anything so clear-cut and so remarkable as these two disparate beings: light and darkness; the rebel angel of fire and light and speed, and the dark, cruel, beautiful necromancer. Both of them framed in the immense, intricate crystal window.

And then Fael-Inis said softly, "*You* called them into being, Medoc. *You* sent them into the Far Future with your creature, the Conablaiche."

Medoc did not reply, and for a moment the silence in the Sun Chamber was absolute.

"But you failed to control them," said Fael-Inis. "And you must know, Medoc, that the ancient immutable law decrees that any creature who summons an entity from outside the world, and then fails to control it, must perforce be at that entity's mercy. They have been baulked of their prey," said Fael-Inis gently and rather pityingly, "and so they are coming to the one who summoned them to take their revenge."

He turned to Fergus, who was listening very intently. "Captain, you went into the Far Future to chain the Apocalypse and bring it back to destroy Medoc," said Fael-Inis, and those closest to him saw that his eyes were shining. "You thought you had failed.

"You did not fail, Fergus. By breaking out of the Prison of Hostages, by leading out the slaughtered children who were Crom Croich's victims in the last century, you forced open a chink between this world and that of the Future. You created a bridge, a nexus, a tear in the fabric of Time, Fergus. It is through that chink that the Four Horsemen are now coming.

"And they are very close now . . . they are nearly upon us . . ."

Fergus could not speak. He stood listening, his eyes never leaving Fael-Inis's beautiful grave face.

Fael-Inis turned to hold out his hands to Annabel and Taliesin, and Annabel, who had been hoping that she could pass unnoticed in this rather awesome company, found herself walking forward, and found her hand taken by Fael-Inis, and thought it was rather like taking the hand of something molten and white-hot, but something that would never burn you.

Fael-Inis said, "In the Mountain Halls of the Drakon—the Far Future's ruler—you escaped the Four Horsemen. You thought you had left them behind. You certainly thought they had been destroyed there.

"They were not destroyed, because they are indestructible. They are timeless and ageless and they will eternally stalk the world, seeking those evil ones who will try to use them. The Four Horsemen—who you also know as the Four Heralds—followed you back. They are riding through the night now, and they are riding through the skies, and if you listen closely, you will hear that they are almost upon us."

Hoofbeats; pounding, galloping hoofbeats, drawing nearer and nearer, growing louder and louder . . .

Fael-Inis had released Annabel's hand, and moved back into the frame of the crystal window again. As he did so, it seemed to the watchers that light began to stream from him; it poured from his fingertips and his head was becoming suffused with an aureole of light. The Sun Chamber began to glow and pulsate with beauty and brilliance and strength, and both Grainne and Fergus gasped, and Grainne felt tears sting her eyes, because they were seeing the Sun Chamber being reborn to all its former beauty. Raynor, who had dreamed of but never thought to see this, stood very still and felt the pure delight of the moment soak into his skin.

Thy former light restore . . .

And then the Sun Chamber was plunged into whirling confusion, and Annabel felt Taliesin pull her aside and there was a great howling wind somewhere, and although her eyes were tight shut, there were great exploding lights everywhere, and there was the almost deafening pounding of the hoofbeats, and the Horsemen were in the Sun Chamber with them.

The Four Horsemen of the Apocalypse . . . the ancient messengers, the Heralds that precede the coming of the Beast.

Annabel opened her eyes and saw, for a never-to-be-forgotten instant, the great rearing figures of the Horsemen, etched in fire and bathed in blood-red light, awesome and fearsome and as old as Time. She saw them sweep Medoc up, and then she saw the monstrous shape of Crom Croich thrown into the air by one of the glinting hoofs, and fall across the leading Rider's saddle. There was a howl of protest and fear from the Dark Lords, and a screech of fury from Damnaithe as she disappeared.

And then the Horsemen were streaming out of the Chamber, into the skies trailing chaos in their wake, into the strange other-world they had been summoned from, and the Dark Lords were dissolving, and Medoc and Crom Croich were gone, and there was a crackle of light across the eastern sky.

Silence, deep and enveloping, fell upon the Bright Palace.

FERGUS OPENED HIS eyes and saw the pale, clear shafts of light spilling in through the crystal window of the Sun Chamber.

"Dawn," said Grainne softly. "The first light." She looked directly at Fergus and smiled, and for the first time since his return, Fergus looked at her properly, and felt delight and tranquillity.

The eye of the storm and the heart of the tempest. I

think it is going to be all right, thought Fergus. My dear lost love, I think it is going to be all right. I shall meet you and love you and there will be no pain, except perhaps . . .

Except perhaps for the son I never gave you. Ireland's heir.

Fergus turned his head, and saw Erin.

CHAPTER THIRTY

No one who had any pretensions to being anyone—which is to say just about everyone—would have dreamed of missing the Ceremony that followed almost immediately on the vanquishing of Medoc and the Dark Lords.

"The Ritual of the Fál," said Dorrainge. "The embracing of the Stone of Fál by the destined Ruler. I suppose Her Majesty knows best," he said disapprovingly. "But if she had asked *my* advice, I should have said, Leave well alone, ma'am. I never did like the Ritual of the Fál," said Dorrainge, and would not listen to the people who asked why not.

"It's because you never know if the Stone is going to answer," said Cathbad, "and of course if *that* happens, you might be left with no King or Queen at all. It's quite difficult," said Cathbad, worried, and Dorrainge, listening furtively to this, began to wonder whether Cathbad was, after all, quite Druidical material, because Druids ought not to gossip.

Most people were rather intrigued and certainly interested in the Ritual, which had not been performed—"Dear me, since Cormac's day," said Fintan. "We shall find it very interesting."

"The Druids won't," said Cermait Honeymouth.

"The Druids don't approve of anything they haven't thought up for themselves," said Fintan.

In fact, the Druids were being very cagey about giving their support to the reviving of the Ritual. "Waiting to see which way the cat jumps," said Fintan vulgarly, and was told to be quiet and pay attention to the ceremony.

"The Druids are more concerned with seeing that Fribble doesn't have too much to drink and disgrace everybody," said Cermait.

Fribble had come back for the Ceremony of the Fál. He had travelled from Calatin's house in Calatin's cart, which he had borrowed, and he had donned his best robes, and had accompanied them all to the Plain of the Fál, paying no attention at all to Dorrainge, who said it was all quite absurd and Fribble ought to have known better.

"At his age," said Dorrainge, rather unwisely, so that several people frowned and told each other that they had never liked Dorrainge, and that in any case, Dorrainge himself was no spring chicken.

Fribble was very interested in the Ceremony of the Fál.

"I'm very interested indeed," he said. "I've come back especially to see it. I've had a very nice time with Calatin; I've learnt a lot of things I didn't know. But if I hadn't come back, the fat fool would have had himself elected as Chief Druid, which would never do. I hear Fergus returned from the Future; well, I thought he would. He'll have a good tale to tell, I shouldn't wonder. And that Tyrian. Is he here? I wouldn't mind seeing him again. He always brings his own wine, you know. You don't mind entertaining somebody who does that, do you?"

"Sir," said Taliesin, at Fribble's side, "allow me to offer you a measure," and Fribble turned round and beamed and said, "Well, just a drain to keep out the cold."

"It is fire and warmth and the very breath of life," agreed Taliesin blandly.

"Here's to it," said Fribble, causing Dorrainge to suck his teeth and remark that he had always said that no good came of consorting with sorcerers, and Fribble had acquired some very indelicate expressions.

"No, I didn't," said Fribble, who could usually be trusted to hear what people did not intend him to hear. "I'm what you call one of Nature's gentlemen. I know how to behave and I've got very good table manners. Speaking of which, I expect we'll all be having a banquet later, will we? You need a banquet after this sort of thing.

"Whose idea was it to hold the Ritual at the Purple Hour, I wonder? Of course, you need all the magic you can get, and the Purple Hour was always believed to be the strongest time for that. I don't know that I believe it. But we'll need a banquet afterwards, although it'll be midnight, if it won't be breakfast-time, by the time we get back to Tara. They tell me Cathbad's roasting a few boar. I thought he would. I daresay it's highly suitable when you think about it.

"Bless my soul, there's Rudraige the Tusk. I'd better go across and have a word. A very bad business that about young Tybion. Don't go away. I shall want to hear about the Future, you know." He beamed at Annabel. "Very interesting," he said. "I didn't know they had people in the Future. Tell the Tyrian to bring you to see me. Don't forget."

"I should like that," said Annabel, who would.

"Bring some wine when you come," said Fribble, and set off across the Plain to where Rudraige was assembling a small party of Tusks who had come to see the Ceremony and pay homage to the Queen. He wanted to be sure not to offend Rudraige, who was Head Tusk and reputed to be rather wealthy.

Fintan was explaining to anyone who would listen (and several people who did not want to listen but could not get away) the exact nature of the Ritual.

"And they do say," he said solemnly, "that when the Stone is embraced by the destined King of Ireland, it shrieks aloud." He nodded as if agreeing with himself, and then glanced furtively over his shoulder, and drew a little nearer, with an air of the utmost secrecy, so that his listeners, hoping he was about to impart some interesting—and with any luck, shocking—nugget of information, did the same, and Cathbad, who had not been one of the company, but who had scented gossip, tip-toed on the outside of the circle, and tripped into a rabbit hole and went headlong in the dust.

"He had to be helped up and dusted down in full view of most of the Court and the entire Beastline," said Dorrainge, displeased, and added that none of it was dignified behaviour for a Druid, and Cathbad's Code of Entry might have to be reviewed at the next Solstice.

"Bother dignity and bother being a Druid," said Cathbad, and went away to consider could they serve whole roast swan at the banquet, or would that be a touch discourteous. In any case, they would none of them be sitting down to the feast much before midnight at this rate, because nobody seemed to know how long the Ritual might be supposed to last, and so far nobody had seen the Queen.

"She'll make a proper entrance when the proper time comes," said Fintan.

The Beastline were deeply interested in the Ritual, and in the Stone of the Fál, and listened to everything that everyone had to say.

"They even listened to Fintan," said Cermait.

"The Stone shrieks aloud, you see," said Fintan, who had lost his original audience when Cathbad fell into the rabbit hole, and was preparing to start all over again with a new one. "When the true King embraces it," he explained.

"Or the true Queen," put in Cermait. "Don't forget that."

"I meant that," said Fintan. "They knew I meant that. You did know, didn't you? Mind you, I don't know that I believe it," said Fintan, who in fact believed devoutly in every sliver of myth and every shred of legend ever related, but who would not have admitted to this even in the face of torture of the most extreme kind. "And of course, we've none of us ever seen it performed," he added for good measure, because it would not have done for people to have thought him credulous.

Taliesin was regarding the great rearing Stone. "I am sceptical about the entire thing," he said. "But then I am a cynic and a rogue, and fit company for no man and certainly fit company for no myth." He looked at the Stone thoughtfully. "I find it difficult to believe in Stones that cry aloud for chosen Kings," he said.

"Or Queens," said Cermait, and was told to hush.

But for all the doubts and for all the scepticism, for Taliesin was not alone, a feeling of anticipation was creeping over the twilit Plain. There was a sense of excitement, a feeling that something marvellous and mystical was about to happen. There was a faint humming on the air, and Bec, lifting her head, said, "The *sidh*. Or is it?" And frowned, because although the sound was a little like the *sidh*'s music, it was mingled in with the expectancy and the anticipation.

"But the *sidh* are certainly here," said Rinnal. "Over there. See?"

"And it is their music," said Bec, with contentment.

The music was all about them now; it was singing on the air, and it was mingling with the soft sweet twilight.

"Like music you can feel," said Conn, who stood with Niall. "Like music you can eat and drink."

"I'd rather eat and drink Cathbad's banquet," said Michael, but he did not say it very loudly, because he was as awed as the rest of the boys.

And then, just as the music and the anticipation and the excitement was reaching an almost unendurable pitch, and just as Annabel was thinking that she could not bear it any longer, Grainne, with Erin at her side, and Fergus and Raynor just behind, came walking slowly up the hill and stood on the far side of the Plain.

A great stillness descended on the waiting Court, because while they had never forgotten, not for a moment, that Grainne was the High Queen, the descendant of the great Rulers of Ireland, most of them had grown used to seeing her as she had been for the past weeks; informal, unceremonious. Dressed in plain dark breeches and leather boots and a cambric shirt, with her hair cut short. They had become accustomed to seeing her move about the camp, eating their ordinary camp suppers, joining in with the bonfire singing, listening when Fintan or Cermait related a tale or two.

Being one of them and being one with them, the soldiers had said, and had liked it. It had meant you had to curb your language a bit, and your drinking as well, but nobody had minded this. Everybody had known what was due to the High Queen. One of the soldiers who liked to think he had a bit of a turn for a good phrase had called her the People's Queen, and this had been taken up.

Now, quite suddenly, she was none of these things. She was no longer the slender gentle creature who had helped them to serve supper, and who had laughed with them when Cathbad had added sugar instead of salt to a hare pie, and she was no longer the unassuming companionable friend who had helped in the plotting against Medoc and in the planning of journeys and in the drawing up of battle strategies.

She wore the ceremonial robes of Tara; the gold and black, silk on velvet, and on her head was the thin gold circlet forged by the *sidh* centuries earlier for the great Niall of the Nine Hostages, and she was the granddaughter of Dierdriu, and the great-granddaughter of Cormac, and she was the descendant of the magical enchanted Wolfline of Ireland.

Every person present knew that the sudden hush and the sudden unspoken homage was due to far more than ceremonial silk and velvet and gold. It was the instinctive recognition of the centuries of seigneurial mastery that ran in her blood. It was breeding, heredity, and it was that remarkable blend of power and charm and cunning that had made the Wolfline great.

The power and the light and the strength of the Wolves . . .

The Wolves were with her, upwards of a dozen of them, walking obediently at her heels, sleek and lean and alert. Several people eyed them uneasily, because didn't Wolves have the terrible way of altering their moods in the blink of a whisker! Nobody wanted to be eaten by the Royal Wolves, never mind it was the grandest thing ever that they'd returned, never mind that it had at one time been the most honourable death that could befall a man.

Taliesin, at Annabel's side, thought, *How* does she control them? What does she do to make them obedient and wise? And, as he watched, he saw the thin pure light in Erin's eyes, and knew that it was not Grainne who was controlling them, but the slight dark child at Grainne's side. Erin . . . Eirann, Ireland's Lost Prince . . .

And then, because it would always be in Taliesin to see the layer just below the surface, as he had seen that the light in the boy's eyes was the silvered light of the Samhailt, he looked at the child again, more deeply. And now he saw the wolfmask that lay across Erin's face, and he saw, as well, that Erin had Fergus's smile and Fergus's way of walking, and thought, So that is it. Is it? Yes, I believe so. How extremely sad, thought Taliesin. How cruel that those two should be siblings. He wondered whether Fergus would ever tell him of what had happened inside the Prison of Hostages, and then he wondered whether Fergus needed to tell him. There was a look of peace in Fergus's eyes, the look of someone who has fought torments and waged struggles, and won.

Erin was as plainly dressed as his ancestor Cormac had always been. No ceremony, thought Taliesin, his eyes never leaving Erin's face. But I believe he does not need any. He never will need any. His presence alone is a ceremony. How very curious, thought Taliesin, and felt Annabel slip her hand into his, and knew that their thoughts were running alongside, and remembered that, quite soon, after the banquet, he would take Annabel back to the tall narrow house in the Street of Money Lenders, and that she would curl up before the fire, and the fire would turn her hair to molten gold, and that he would never let her go . . .

Annabel was more or less aware of Taliesin's thoughts, and she was filled with delight. To stay here, in this magical marvellous world, to be with Taliesin, to become close to these people: Grainne and Fergus and Raynor and the Beastline; Fintan and Cermait, and Fribble and Cathbad and the Druids. They will become close, thought Annabel, and knew it would happen. And then, because there was no room for anything more now, she turned her attention back to the Stone, and saw that it was beginning to glow, and thought that she was mistaken, because it was probably the twilight casting strange shadows, or perhaps even the *sidh*, and saw that it could not be any of these, and shivered with delight.

The Stone waking . . .

THE AIR WAS laden and heavy with enchantment now, and in every face was the utmost joy, because this was it. Wasn't this at last the Old Ireland waking, the Ireland they had yearned for and sought, and tried to awaken; and hadn't the Queen somehow woken it for them? This was the enchanted, mystical Ireland, the world of turquoise twilights and misty dusks, and of half-Men, who sometimes walked on all fours like beasts, and sometimes upright like Men; the land where people could spin magic, and where bewitchments could be had and where spells could be spun . . . This was the fabled land of Cormac of the Wolves and Niall of the Nine Hostages, and Nuadu Airgetlam of the Silver Arm; of Dierdriu and the *sidh* and the first Queen of all who was sometimes called the cursed Queen, and who had raised Tara from the rock by magic and charm and cajolery. All stirring and waking and living, and all there with them.

There was a humming on the air now; something that was not the *sidh*'s music, something that was ancient, and that had been ancient when the world was young, and something that was filled with deep pure magic and with strong bewitchment.

The Stone waking . . .

Erin moved forward then and, as he did so, Grainne fell back, and the humming and the anticipation grew in intensity, and Annabel thought that she could not bear it much longer.

Erin reached out and embraced the Stone with both arms. There was a sound, as if hundreds of great birds were flying past, or as if an immense wind was blowing on the Plains.

Annabel, who had been unable to look away from Erin's

steady approach to the Stone, felt undiluted joy wash over the watchers, and saw in their faces such pure pleasure, and such immense happiness, that for a second there was a sharp loneliness, and a feeling of isolation, because she was not one of them or one with them, and this was something she could not share completely with them. She thought, They are becoming my friends, every one of them, but still, this is something they are born to, it is their heritage, and it is something my world has never known ... We lost the magic and the enchantment, thought Annabel. We lost the heritage we should have had, and inherited only destruction and sickness and a dying world.

And then she looked to where Grainne was standing, and saw Grainne smile at her, and saw that it was a smile that included Annabel in all of this, and that within it was the shared memory of how they had fought Medoc and the Dark Lords, and stood together against the dangers, and delight unfolded within her, because of course she was a part of it, and of course she was sharing it. How marvellous it all is, thought Annabel. And then: And how fortunate I am to be here with them all. She could hear the great Stone beginning to hum now, and there was an uncanny music in the sound, and she knew that she was hearing an old, old enchantment, and she felt the happiness surrounding her, because for sure they were all welcoming Erin, they were acknowledging him as their Prince ...

There was a rushing sound above them, the feeling of something powerful and swift approaching—Immense wheels riding across the sky, thought Annabel, and so strong was the image that she looked up to the skies, and saw that others were doing the same, and strained her eyes to see, because surely, surely he would be with them at such a moment ...

And then he was there, briefly and insubstantially, but he was there, golden and glowing, his eyes slanting, seeming to be on fire ... The rebel angel travelling through the skies ... The Time Chariot hovered for a moment to the east, splendid and unearthly, aflame with the Fire of Fael-

Inis's music and, for a breathspace, they heard again the silvery fragile music of the silver pipes, and felt the pull of Fael-Inis's enchantment.

Come with me, Mortals, and we will challenge the world and tumble it about, and will win, *Mortals, we will* win . . .

And so we did win, thought Annabel, and smiled, and found that tears were streaming down her cheeks, and did not care, and then brushed them away impatiently, because she would not bear it if she did not see everything of the Ceremony.

The Stone was crying now; it was shrieking aloud, and Erin's face was intent and absorbed, as if he might be drawing power out from the Stone.

"Or," thought Annabel, more intrigued than she had ever been in her life, "as if he might be pouring it in."

And she stayed quietly where she was, and looked at the others: at Grainne, whose face was shining with more happiness than Annabel had ever seen in any creature's face ever before; at Raynor, at her side, calm and strong and gentle and wise. At Fergus, who stood a little apart, but with a look in his eyes as he watched Erin that was proud and humble and grateful and filled with the contentment of someone who has fought some strange inner battle, and been victorious.

The Druids were nodding and watching, happy to see such an ancient tradition honoured, and the Cruithin were on the far side, their eyes bright, their heads tilted in the characteristic alertness. The Beastline creatures were nearby, quiet and absorbed in everything.

Last of all, Annabel looked to where Taliesin stood beside her, and the deep joy welled up and threatened to spill over, because surely, oh, surely, this was more than anyone could ever expect to find in a single lifetime.

And then Erin stood back, and turned to look at them all, and his eyes were alight, and his whole being was transformed, and there was a glow about him, and every person present fell to his knees in homage to Ireland's Lost Prince.

IN THE CHRONICLES of Ireland, there is a chapter much read and much related and considerably loved by the Irish. It tells, in the beautiful simple language of the Cruithin, how the gentle and much-loved Grainne, sometimes called Grainne the Gentle and sometimes also called the People's Queen, gave up the Throne in favour of her son, and how she lived to a wise and tranquil old age in the Grail Castle with her beloved Raynor of the Eagles, and of how the castle, in their time, became a place of pilgrimage, and of light and laughter and music and learning, and of how they helped many poor and deprived people in the land.

It tells, as well, of how Fergus, the mighty Captain of the Fiana, stayed at Tara, acting as Regent to the child Erin, schooling him and guiding him and polishing him into the famous and strong High King he was to become. It tells of how Erin's companions were Conn and Niall and Michael and all the lost boys who came out of the terrible Prison of Hostages into the world, and who served Ireland and Erin faithfully and well, and were rewarded with high honours.

But always, always, in the telling of this remarkable and stirring chapter of Ireland's history, the story-tellers will end with the same words:

"And it was only when the Lost Prince came to Tara, that the Enchantments woken by Grainne truly began to live, and it was then that Ireland saw the birth of the Golden Age of Erin."

Erin. Eireann. The Once and Future King.

ABOUT THE AUTHOR

Bridget Wood is the daughter of an Irish actor. After a convent education she worked in newspapers and the legal profession. She was married to a journalist for four years and now lives and writes in Staffordshire.